DUKES OF MADNESS

ROYALS OF FORSYTH U

ANGEL LAWSON
SAMANTHA RUE

NORTH SIDE
COUNTS
KNT
KING: LIONEL LUCIA
CHILDREN: LETICIA (MISSING)
LAVINIA (SOLD)
COUNTS: BRUNO PEREZ, LARS
COUNTESS: SUTTON
PLEDGES: CASH "MONEY" MALLIS (DEALER)
LOCATIONS: THE LUCIA MANSION
WEST END
DUKES
ΔΚΣ
KING: SAUL CARTWRIGHT
DUKES: NICK BRUIN, SY PERILINI,
REMY MADDOX
DUCHESS: LAVINIA LUCIA
PLEDGES: BALLSACK, WEASEL
MANAGER: MAMA B
CUTSLUTS: VERITY, HALEY
ARCHDUKE: MORE LIKE ARCHCUTE
FAMILY:
SARAH (MOM/FORMER DUCHESS)
DAVIS BRUIN (DAD/FORMER DUKE)
MANNY PERILINI (DAD/FORMER DUKE)
TIMOTHY MADDOX (DAD)
LOCATIONS: THE CLOCK TOWER (HOME)
THE GYM (TRAINING/FIGHTS)
THE BUNGALOW (PARENTS' HOUSE)
THE CLIFFS
BARONS
ΒΡΝ
EAST END
PRINCES
ΨΝΖ
KING: ASHBY
FAMILY: FELIX ASHBY
(MURDERED BY NICK)
SOUTH SIDE
LORDS
ΛΔΖ
KING: KILLIAN PAYNE
LORDS: TRISTIAN MERCER, DIMITRI RATHBONE
QUEEN/LADY: STORY AUSTIN
FAMILY: DANIEL PAYNE (DAD/FORMER KING/DEAD AF)
WORKERS: MRS. CRANE (BAMF), AUGUSTINE (MANAGER)
LOCATIONS: THE VELVET HIDEAWAY (BROTHEL)
THE PAYNE MCMANSION
THE CRANE MOTEL (CHEAP BROTHEL)
THE AVENUE (MAIN STREET IN SS)

FOREWORD

Royal Readers,

First off… have you read Dukes of Ruin? The Lords? If not you definitely need to circle back to Dukes of Ruin and I also suggest starting at the beginning with Lords of Pain for the full experience.

Second, as always, friends and family–keep moving. We love your support. We do not love having to make eye contact after reading the darkness and smut in our books and frankly, our hearts. Thanks for everything tho.

If you're like me and you skip ahead, STOP HERE. Don't read this book if you don't enjoy dark, bully romance. Don't. Because you're going to have a problem and that's okay. It's okay not to like dark romance. It's NOT okay to read stuff you don't like and then bash it all over the internet like it's your J.O.B.

Anyway…

Now that it's just us, y'all know we left Lav and her Dukes in a tight spot. This book is going to address many of the open threads from that book and pull on more. It's going to hit on dark themes, emotional and physical. No one in this book is getting out unscathed as we touch trauma, angst and the dark desperation these characters feel in their fictional hearts.

Nick Bruin... well, he needs to atone for his sins and it's not going to be easy.

T/W: non/dubcon, mental health crisis, self-harm, sleep disorders, drug abuse, mentions of past off-screen abuse, violence, murder, gore, OW, gaslighting, captivity, and emotional manipulation.

For the full list of warnings (as well as other Forsyth U extras) please visit our website.

Angel & Sam

1

Sy

It takes me an hour to get back to the tower. I take one left for every two rights, meandering down side streets and grimy alleyways in a slow crawl back to West End. It doesn't look like I'm being followed, but this whole getaway driver thing is more Nick's thing than mine. The whole time, my phone buzzes away like an angry wasp in the center console, stopping only to begin its insistent whirring once again. By the time I get halfway down the Avenue, it's become background static that I can almost ignore.

I shake my head, muttering, "Jesus Christ, Remy." He's such a *picker*. Once something gets in his head, he just... fucking picks at it, over and over, until it drives him and the rest of us up the wall.

Every now and then, I turn to glance at the sad heap currently curled in the back. She's so still that if it weren't for the jerky rise and fall of her ribs, she'd look like a corpse. I guess I always knew

Lionel Lucia was a sick bastard. The Counts have always had sadistic tendencies. What house in this town doesn't?

Still, the children of Kings have always been protected. Privileged. Sacred. It's why the Princes kick them out like machines. Nothing has ever been as precious to Forsyth as its own blood. It's why Nick could waltz right in and get a straight shot to the belfry.

Tainted goods or not, Lavinia Lucia is Royalty.

Wrong. That's how it felt in Lavinia's bedroom, standing over that chest, a wave of realization crashing into me. Before I even opened it, I knew I'd find her inside. I didn't grow up in the Royalty, but I've been touched by it enough that the sight of North Side's heir, stuffed into the confines of an old cedar chest by her own goddamn family, struck me as so *wrong*—so fucking profane—that my stomach still squirms uncomfortably at the thought.

Davis Bruin's decision to abdicate his position, and my mother and father going with him, suddenly makes more sense. The Kings aren't just powerful. They're monsters.

I wait until we're a little closer, the tower looming just to my left, to pick up my phone and finally answer. "What?"

"It's been three fucking hours!" Remy explodes. I can practically hear him pacing over the speaker. "I've had one foot out the door and my finger on this trigger all night."

"Would you chill the fuck out?" I snap, checking my rearview. "We'll be there in five."

"We?" Remy's tight, stunned voice comes through the speaker. "You found her? You got her?"

It wasn't technically the plan. I was just going to scope it out first, try to figure out where Lionel had shunted her off to before calling in for Remy. I could tell him it just seemed easier, in the moment, to get her from Lionel's mansion than to wait until she'd been secured in the Counts' own territory. But it'd be a lie. The truth is, no part of me could have closed her back up in that chest. It would have been the more strategic move. Lionel was only out for a few minutes. I didn't have any lookouts.

But the second she flung herself into my arms, I knew I couldn't do it.

"I've got her." But even as I say the words, I shoot her a dubious look. I'm not sure what Remy's expecting to see when we get up there, but this isn't the Duchess I drove away from several nights ago. "I need you to get some supplies. Remember that weekend after you pledged?"

Remy responds in a confused tone, "When I got shitfaced?"

Shitfaced is a really nice way of putting it. He was so dehydrated that I had to pilfer the gym for something medical grade. "The bags are in with the other things. Just have it ready."

There's a short pause before he asks, "She needs IV fluids? Why?"

"I'm pulling up now," I tell him. "Flip the breaker on the elevator, would you?" I hang up before he can respond. Remy's not the best guy in a crisis, but I've found that giving him clearly defined tasks makes him focused and less prone to catastrophizing. I pull up to the curb and jump out, wrenching open the back door, but all that greets me is Lavinia's motionless figure, curled into the same fetal position I found her in back at her father's house.

I take a deep breath and scrub my fingers through my hair, thinking. She's pale and gaunt-looking, shivering, bruised all over. She's injured, but it's hard to say how badly. I form a mental list of priorities. Dehydration is first. This means I need to get her up that tower before anything else.

I lean in, ducking my head to observe her face. "Can you walk?" When she doesn't answer, I reach out to touch her hip, giving her a gentle shake. "Lavinia. Hey! You have to get out now." I watch as her eyelids flutter, two dazed eyes appearing beneath wet lashes. "Come on, up, up."

She doesn't protest as I coax her into a sitting position. I can only barely stop my nose from wrinkling. If I had to guess from smell alone, Lavinia was in the box the entire four days, and the thought comes to me again. The wrongness. *What the fuck?*

"What time is it?" Her voice is a quiet, painful-sounding croak as she stares out the open door, eyes glazed.

"Almost midnight," I answer, giving her arm a soft tug. "We need to get inside. Someone could be watching." I have no idea how long it will be before someone notices she's gone. An hour? A week? *Jesus.* I shoot a glance down the alley, half expecting to see headlights. This wasn't as clean as I wanted it to be. The initial plan had phases and contingencies, fail safes and back-ups.

This one just has a disoriented girl in my back seat, staring unseeingly into the night.

I snap my fingers in front of her face. "Lavinia!"

This spurs her into a stiff, mechanical sort of motion, her legs awkwardly scooting her battered body toward the open door. I stand back as she emerges on unsteady feet, a hand gripping the door. I know her knees are going to give out before she even takes the first step. I shoot forward, catching her around the middle, and she lets out a soft, pained sound that makes me wince.

"Like this," I say, slinging her arm around my neck. I hold every pound of her frail, trembling weight she'll allow me to, and I'm struck by something foreign and upsetting. I don't quite understand it, but it's what compels me to pull her close, ducking my head to say, "That's good. You've got it. Just step here." Then, quieter, "Good girl." I don't stop to question the impulse, and despite the seemingly patronizing tone, she doesn't so much as shoot me a glare for it.

That's how I know it must be bad.

I get us through the doors, but don't allow myself to feel any relief. I may have made it back in one piece, but eventually, her father is going to notice her missing. "This way," I tell her, guiding her toward the elevator.

She lifts her head, blue hair brushing the too-sharp points of her cheekbones, and then freezes.

Any color that might have returned to her face on the drive here vanishes instantly when she sees the elevator. Something cold and dark slams over expression, and suddenly, I'm looking at the same crushed, desperate girl that had clung to me in her bedroom.

She lurches backward so fast that I almost don't catch her when she stumbles. "No," she groans, long and miserable. "I said I'd be good. You said I was good." I'm expecting the tears this time, but it's still such an alien thing to see her face crumble into a body-wracking sob. It doesn't seem right. For all that I've thought Lavinia weak in body, she's never been weak in spirit. It isn't until now I realize how much I'd come to appreciate that about her. It was such a non-Royal trait.

A *West End* trait.

A Duchess trait.

I'm so caught up in the loss of it that it takes a long moment for me to understand why it's happening.

"*Shit.* Look at me." I grab her face in my hands, forcing her to look at me with those big, terror-filled eyes. "You can't walk up all those stairs. They're too narrow for me to carry you, or I would. This is just to get us to the top. It's not like your father. It's not..."

It's not like Nick, I want to say.

But that'd be admitting I knew about those times my brother had chucked her into the elevator for safekeeping. Whatever fragile trust she's put in me since opening that chest will probably disappear if I tell her that. It's not like I had anything to do with it. Most of the time she's spent under this belfry, she's been more Nick's Duchess than mine. But she's not thinking rationally, and that's made all the more clear when another of those deep, agonizing, body-shaking sobs escapes her throat.

"Don't make me. Please, don't make me." She stares up at me with exhausted eyes. "I can't."

"You can. It's only a couple of minutes." Without thinking, I thumb away a tear, that dull upsetting feeling turning my stomach once again. "I'll be in there with you."

She pulls in a wet, shuddering gasp, eyes so wide and bloodshot that she looks downright unhinged. "I'll die. I'd rather die."

"Hey!" I snap, something hot flaring in my chest as I pull her to her full height. "You see that door you just came in? When a Duke loses a fight, he spends the night somewhere else, because losers aren't allowed to walk through it. To the victor go the spoils, Lavinia. A Duchess is no fucking quitter. Pull yourself together!"

"Make me sleep again," she pleads, breaths coming quicker. She winds a fist into my shirt, voice rushed and insistent. "Do the thing… make me pass out."

I growl in frustration. "Your body is already stressed. Cutting off oxygen to your brain was risky enough the first time. You're going to have to woman the fuck up."

Her face crumbles into a wretched sob, but she just as quickly sucks it back in. It's fascinating to see, like her whole being flinches to hold back the force of it. God, do I know that feeling. I experience it every day, forcing my impulses down beneath the churn of my mental ocean. The terror is still in her eyes, but there's also a hardness that covers it. It isn't real. It's a flimsy performance that's given away by the hitch of her shoulders. But it's enough.

I jab the button to open the doors before that determination can fall away, reaching out one-handed to yank the gate open. Inside, a dim bulb illuminates the space, flickering anemically. I give it a brief, wary glance, because it's almost too small a space for *my* comfort, and I'm not the one who just got out of a cedar chest.

She's going to fucking lose it.

"Close your eyes," I order, pulling her against my chest and thrusting us inside.

I try to make quick work of it—closing the gate, slamming my hand over the button—but she's hyperventilating before the elevator even lurches into motion. Her body trembles like a leaf against mine, and my arms wind around her shoulders instinctively.

"It won't be long," I promise, although I don't know why.

It must be because she's so small, so afraid, so…vulnerable. That must be why I feel the urge to wrap her up and hold her against me. That must be why I feel this sense of responsibility, like I want to protect her all of a sudden. That upsetting feeling in my stomach churns and flips, and I can't put a name to it, but it's some strange mixture of anger and tenderness, and fuck *me.*

Maybe this is what Nick feels.

No wonder he's such a fucking headcase.

Lavinia's hands ball into fists around two palmfuls of my shirt, so tightly that I can feel them shaking against my ribs. I'd know that tremble anywhere. It's the vibration of restraint, pushed to the very edges of someone's capability.

She's gasping, "I can't, I can't, I can't," and every inch of her feels impossibly tense, as if she's been made of stone.

In an effort to keep her focused, I ask, "When did they put you in there?"

Her forehead digs into my sternum as her back jerks with rapid breaths. "Immediately," she says, confirming my fears.

"The whole time?"

A jerky nod.

Fuck.

There's another suspicion niggling at the back of my mind, and as the elevator chugs upward, I allow myself to voice it. "That wasn't the first time, was it?" Her forehead rolls against my chest, and I duck my head, watching her strained face. "How often? Come on, tell me."

The point is to get her to speak—to think. But her answer is so instant that she obviously didn't have to put any thought into it at all.

"All the time," she wheezes, flinching when the elevator shakes. "When I'm bad, he... sometimes once a month. Sometimes every week. Sometimes every day." Her breath speeds, and I realize she's thinking about it, being trapped in that tiny box, unable to move or break free.

It's almost a relief when she goes limp, her body giving out under the stress of it. I still spit a curse as I gather her up against me, that upsetting feeling returning to the pit of my stomach. Suddenly, I regret not choking her out downstairs. If she was just going to pass out anyway, it would have saved her the stress.

I keep my fingers against her jugular as the elevator climbs. Her pulse is strong, but too fast. Her head lolls to the side, still etched with tension even in unconsciousness, and her skin is clammy, cool to the touch. So much of this could've been solved with some intel and a solid plan, and I'm mentally berating all three of us when the elevator finally grinds to a stop.

Remy is waiting so closely that his tattooed fingers are wrenching the gate open before the door even stops sliding. The second he lays eyes on us, he freezes, a divot digging into his brow.

"What happened?" he breathes, shoving the gate the rest of the way open. "What the fuck happened to her?"

I bend down to sweep a wrist beneath her knees, hoisting her into my arms as I burst through.

"Run a bath," I say, brushing past him. "Make it really warm, but not too hot."

"Sy," he says, eyes tracking her limp form. "Tell me what *happened*! She looks fucking dead!"

There's a thread of enraged panic in his voice that brings me up short, and I turn to him. "Listen to me, Remy," I wait until his wild eyes meet mine to say, "She's in shock. She's dehydrated. We need to warm her up and get that IV in her. Got it?"

He's gone before I even finish, dashing into the bathroom. A second later, I hear the gurgling of the bath getting started, so I lay her down on the nearest couch and get to work on her clothes. I work her boots off first, jostling her body as I yank them forcefully free. I'm just tossing the second one aside when Remy returns. The silver locks of his hair are standing in that special level of chaos that tells me he's been pulling on it for the last four hours, but when he shoves it out of his eyes and kneels down on the floor beside her to rip open the packaging on the IV needle, I know his head is where I need it.

"Do you know how to do that?"

His green eyes rise slowly to mine. "Do I know how to use a *needle*?"

"Fair point," I mutter, moving to the head of the couch to slide her shirt up her body, over her head, down her listless arms. "Let's get her bra off before you put that in."

It feels less strange than it should to undress her, Remy pulling her pants and underwear down her thighs as I struggle with the bra. I've got both hands crammed beneath her back, feeling for the clasp, when Remy hovers over her to touch the tattoo beside her hip. I watch his lips move as he counts the points of the star, but he's not looking at it.

He's looking at her. "Vinny," he whispers, brushing her hair aside as he frowns at her slack face. "Hey, wake up. Why isn't she waking up?"

Instead of admitting that I don't know, I finally get the bra free —fucking annoying, overly complicated, bullshit contraptions— and fling it across the room. "Do the IV now."

Remy is on top of it, settling on the floor beside her to open an alcohol soaked wipe. I watch as he takes her hand in his, his inked skin turning to reveal the bruises covering her knuckles, but he doesn't fixate on them like I know damn well he wants to. He rubs the wipe over the vein on the back of her hand, and then gently pinches the needle to position it. This is the thing about Remy. He has the steadiest hands I've ever seen, and when he ducks his head, eyebrows furrowed in concentration, it's with the same laser focus he uses to prick art into someone else's skin.

I'm so fascinated by the sight of him easing the needle beneath her skin that I don't even realize there's someone standing behind me.

"What the fuck?"

A quick glance over my shoulder reveals Nick's slack face. It's probably the most he's said since that night we returned from the cliff. He must have heard the ruckus, because lately, he barely shows his face outside of his bedroom. He's completely stopped going to classes. He won't answer Mom's calls. He only made a perfunctory appearance at Remy's fight on Friday, leaving immediately after to do god knows what. Not that he missed much. The celebration was weirdly solemn and short-lived, and some pledge we call Ballsack straight up asked me where the Duchess was.

Remy doesn't flinch at the sound of Nick's voice. "Get out," he murmurs, pressing down on the plug. I have a piece of tape torn from the roll ready for him and he takes it smoothly, never looking away from the needle as he carefully fixes it to her skin.

The fact Nick is shirtless, clad only in a loose pair of sweatpants, tells me he was probably already in bed. He's standing ramrod straight in his doorway, dark eyes glued to the naked girl currently occupying his couch. His lips form around words that never emerge. Not until he settles on, "What the hell is she doing here?"

I turn away, teeth gnashing against the impulse to shove and hit and hurt. "I went and got her. And good fucking thing, too, because she'd probably be dead otherwise, you fucking idiot."

Remy makes quick work of uncoiling the tubing, and he still has that laser focus, but I can see the storm brewing in his eyes. "What happened?" Remy asks. "What did they do to her?"

They. It takes everything in me not to spin around, to ask Nick what the fuck he was thinking, to tell him that *he's* the one that did this to her, but I just press my fingers to her jugular again, searching for her pulse. "She's been locked inside a wooden chest for four days."

Remy's movements stutter and he looks up at me, brows crushed together. "What? *Why*?"

At this, I can only let out a humorless chuckle. "She said her dad used to do it a lot—as punishment. If I had to guess?" I turn to glare at my brother. "Collecting his daughter from the guy who's been taunting him for months made Lionel a little aggressive."

Nick's normally a little difficult for me to read. I'm not sure when he got so good at hiding his reactions and painting over them with something else, but I know it was sometime around high school coming and going. And the real rub of it? His time in South Side just made him better at it. He left an angry, stone-faced teenager and came back this blank, stoic soldier. It's part of why I might believe him—that he went to South Side to investigate Tate's death—but I still can't trust him. How could I ever trust something that hides from me?

But he's not hiding now.

I watch the force of the realization crash into him like a sledgehammer, and for the first time in years, I think I might finally see my brother. I see the breath punch from his lungs and the color bleed from his face. I see the jolt of self-loathing in his eyes, accompanied by something dark enough to be grief, and I want to say, *yes*. Yes, there's no coming back from this. This isn't some playground squabble. This is something big enough that even the way he's been moping around this tower for the past four days doesn't touch the gravity of it.

I don't have the chance to say anything, though.

Not before Remy slams into him.

I didn't even see him hurtle past me, and from the way Nick's eyes are staring right through Lavinia, neither does he. Nick flies back, slamming into the wall. That dark, mournful look never even leaves his features.

"What gave you the right?" Remy snaps, bearing down on him with another shove. "You think because you're a Bruin you own everything in this fucking tower?"

The third shove, which sends Nick's head banging into the wall, snaps him out of whatever daze that seeing Lavinia had put him in. He jerks forward, shoving Remy back, to snarl, "How the fuck was I supposed to know what he'd do to her?"

Remy's eyes narrow into slits, his toned muscles strained and flexing as he steps up to Nick. "You didn't care. You never care. You do whatever you want and damn the consequences."

The mask falls over Nick's face, carving it into stone. "That's rich coming from you. Exactly how much of that junk have you put up your nose this week?"

I'm off the couch before Remy's punch lands, but not quick enough to stop it. "Hey!" I bark, making a futile grab for his shirt. Nick's responding punch has Remy stumbling to the side, but he rebounds with a hook at Nick's jaw. The sound isn't good, nor is the way Nick crashes into the end table, falling into a tense heap as the lamp flickers and goes dark.

The energy of it is an odd mirror of Remy's fight on Friday, which had been void of his usual flash and showmanship. The fight had been difficult to watch, Remy going hard but a touch too determined. Out of the three of us, Remy's always been the best at taking a loss. The fight isn't about winning to him. It's about the art of it, showing the crowd something beautifully profane. Remy usually has fun in the ring—a demented sort of fun, but fun nonetheless. But there'd been no performance to his relentless jabs and unforgiving hooks, and even after, when he was sitting sweaty and bloody in the locker room, perfectly victorious, he didn't even look happy about it.

He just stared up at me, the cut on his nose bleeding sluggishly, and asked, "Don't you ever get sick of losing people?"

And that's exactly how Remy's looked these past few days. Sick. Ill in the way that makes him too quiet and eerily still. It's the reason I went to North Side tonight, because Remy was right.

I am sick of losing people.

Nick's up in an instant, barreling toward Remy with murderous eyes, and I get this split second awareness that they might actually fucking kill each other. Remy's got that mindless glint of casual destruction in his eyes, and Nick...

Nick is looking at him like Remy might as well as be Lionel.

When it comes to anger, my brother copes in one of two ways: Beat the shit out of the person responsible, or just whoever is closest. It's why I have such a hard time believing him about Tate being murdered. True or not, he needs someone to blame. Someone to hit.

I'll be damned if that's going to be either of us.

I leap between them, meeting Nick just in time to plant my palms on his chest and send him careening back. Nick lands hard on his ass, eyes flashing in rage as he staggers upright. Before he has a chance, I say, "Remy's right. You need to leave."

Nick pushes to his feet. He's over by Lavinia now, towering over her, and he shoots her a glance before swinging his glare back on us. "Fuck that," he says, as if he's someone who has the right to look worried about her. "The only reason she's here is because of me. Both of you would have thrown her back to the wolves if I hadn't—"

"But only one of us actually did," Remy counters.

I'm guessing from the twitch of his muscles that Nick has an opinion on that, but he never voices it.

Because Lavinia begins to stir.

She makes a soft, pained sound, and Nick's gaze whips to her, face going slack again. I can see the exact instance he realizes he's not ready to face her—to look her in the eye and accept the hurt and hatred that would meet him.

He grabs his shoes and keys, and then as my brother is wont to do, he runs away.

The door closes behind him with a decisive *thud*.

2

Lavinia

I COULD BE unconscious for minutes, hours, or even days. Time doesn't matter—not anymore. Everything is a series of 'forevers' now. Forever to drive away from my father's. Forever to get out of the car. Forever to walk through the doors. Forever to withstand the elevator. I begin rousing to the thought that it can't possibly be one life when it feels as though I've lived so many.

"Watch her head," a voice says.

Another replies, "This will wake her up, right?" There's an undercurrent of panic to the voice, and there's something familiar about it. It invokes the memory of air and night, hurt and exposure, a smile as sharp as a knife's blade, and a touch as piercing as a needle.

Remy.

I feel weightless yet unimaginably heavy, as if I'm being cradled by a loud gravity, swaying and lurching. It doesn't take long to realize why. I remember Sy's scent, but I remember Remy's, too. Sharp and masculine, but with an edge of metal. I smell it now, realizing that my nose is an inch from his neck, his strong arms holding me against his chest. The points where our skin touches feels hot enough to singe me, but I'm shivering, and the more I swim back into consciousness, the tighter my jaw gets, teeth beginning to chatter.

"Is it warm enough?" Remy's voice rumbles.

There's an odd rustling sound—water, I realize—and then Sy's voice answers, "Yeah, it's good. Hey, look at me. Head check?"

There's a pause, and then Remy's muttered, "Seven."

Sy responds, "Okay. Go ahead and put her in."

I jolt toward awareness at his words. Put me in? Into the chest? Into the elevator? Where are they going to put me now? I groan, pushing weakly at Remy's arm. Why won't they just leave me be? When is it going to stop?

"She's waking up," Remy says, tightening his grip. There's relief in the rumble beneath my ear. I feel the sway of him walking and I'm powerless to stop the descent when he bends, lowering me, dropping me, putting me *in*.

The panic is short-lived because suddenly, I'm immersed in warmth, my nerves awakening with the pinpricks of heat that level out into the loss of my shivers. When my eyes finally open, it's to the sight of my naked body inside a bathtub, steam rising lazily from the water that covers my chest. There's a hand cradling the back of my head, but when I wrestle my exhausted gaze up to blazing blue eyes, it slides away.

"Sy?" I rasp out.

"There you are," he says, crouched like an awkward, bulging gargoyle beside the tub. He must see the question in my eyes, because he explains, "You passed out on the way up. Don't fiddle with that." He grabs my hand when I try to rub it, turning to show me something taped to my skin. "We've got you on an IV. It's a saline solution. You'll be alright; we're just getting some fluids into you."

Remy is standing beside him, reaching up to hook the IV bag to the rod above the tub, but he doesn't take his eyes off mine. That razor-edged smile quirks his lips. "You've got good veins, Vinny."

Everything feels hazy and... *off*. The more I let my gaze take in the bathroom—the bathroom at the top of the tower, I realize—the more suspicious I get about it. Sy rescued me. He brought me back. He's making me better. Warming me up. Staring at me with those shrewd, worried eyes. And Remy is restless, fussing with the IV tubing. There's a bruise yellowing on his jaw, and a disquiet brewing in his eyes, and none of this makes sense.

None of this adds up.

"Is this real?" I ask him. "Am I... am I really here?"

In my periphery, I can see Sy pull a confused face, but Remy...

Remy lowers to a crouch and holds my stare, the lines of his face solemn and sure. "This is real." But he knows better than anyone that words won't do. When he reaches up to take off his shirt, I find my eyes drawn to the ink there. How many times have I seen those words on his stomach? *Memento Mori*. How many times have my eyes traced the scar below it—the scar I'd made myself, the first night I met him?

But what Remy shows me is the tattoo on his arm.

"Our Lady of Sorrows," he says, taking my hand. "Remember?"

Slowly, I count the points of the swords, my fingertips brushing over the warm skin. *One, two, three, four, five, six, seven*. My hand falls away, heavy but reluctant.

Sy catches it, frowning at my pinky. "I think your finger might be broken."

I look at it dispassionately, the swelling and bruising. "It is." For no reason I can think of, my eyes go to their own hands. Remy's knuckles are red and bruised. Sy's are bearing shallow little cuts all over, some more scabbed than others.

Sy shoots Remy a dark look and gently places my hand on the lip of the tub. Instantly, Remy disappears. "What else? Is anything else broken? Does anything hurt?" Sy asks. The gentleness of his voice fits like a glove that's two sizes too small, as if he's writhing to fit into the mildness of it. Watching Sy make an attempt at compassion is like watching a bear use a pair of tweezers.

"I don't think so," I answer, and it's only now that the awareness of my body hits me. Bare. Exposed. Scrutinized by his blue eyes. I cover my breasts with the arm that isn't hooked to the IV.

Sy clears his throat. "Let's get you cleaned up," he says, shifting toward my head. "Can you dunk your head?"

I feel bizarrely calm, too tired to wonder what's going to come next as I slide myself beneath the water. By the time Remy returns with an ice pack and a small, tattered towel, Sy already has my hair lathered up. It feels a bit like I'm a lost dog being tended to, but unlike before, the thought arrives to me without the sharp edge of acrimony. Sy's fingers roughly massage my scalp and I bring my knees to my chest, hugging them as he aggressively scrubs the last four days away.

I feel hollowed out, too empty to contain a full emotion, but there's a small flip in my chest at the way Remy watches me, his eyes never leaving mine. There's a time I wouldn't have been able to hold that stare. Too intense, too searching, unbearably plunderous. Now, I find myself unable to look away, as if some part of me is clinging to the squirming discomfort of being under his focus. The last time I saw him, he was pushing our mouths together, demanding yet somehow painfully sweet.

Sy says, "Dunk," and I rearrange my limbs, sliding down with muscles that don't feel like my own anymore.

Just as Sy runs a sponge over the ridge of my spine, Remy says, "Let's go."

Sy throws a glance at him. "What? She only has one hand."

Remy grabs Sy's upper arm, coaxing him up. "She's trying to find her body. Let her clean up and we'll come back."

I stare at him, stunned to have this grasping confusion put into words, and then I fumble for the sponge. "I can do it."

Sy gives me a look that's as skeptical as I feel, but levers himself up. My neck cranes as he stretches to his full height, like he's slipping back into his own skin. "Call us when you're..." He makes a vague gesture, waving a hand toward my body, and then turns to lumber out into the living room, Remy following.

They stay close enough that I can hear the soft hush of their voices, the words indistinct, fluttering through the door like thin, tattered threads. Whatever they're saying, there's an urgency to the discussion, Remy's voice more of a hiss than anything.

I wash myself clumsily but violently, scrubbing away the sweat and fear until my skin turns an angry red. Inch by inch, I do just as Remy said. I find my body again. These are my knees, bruised and sore. These are my calves, tired and strained. These are my thighs, soft and weak. None of it feels like mine, but it doesn't feel like anyone else's either. These are limbs, patches of skin, miles of veins and tangles of tendon, ready to be called home for whoever comes to claim them. I conquer them methodically, wiggling my toes to remind my feet whom they belong to, curling my ankles, inflating my lungs, blinking my eyelids. I remember that I'm made up of these mechanical parts, and I set each cog into motion, rusty joints and stilted breaths, until I can call them my own. Unlike the clock above, I refuse to be perpetually broken.

By the time I'm done washing, I can barely sit up straight. The exhaustion captures me, pushing me down. It takes a surge of energy that I'm not sure I possess to call out to Sy.

"I'm done."

The words are thin and weak, but somehow he hears them, striding through the door with a large, fluffy towel in his hand. Remy hangs back as I unplug the drain, struggling to lift myself out of the water. But Sy doesn't make me. He throws the towel over me and effortlessly scoops me up, giving me one adjusting bounce before I settle against his chest. It's undignified, this entire thing one humiliation after the other, but my arms immediately wind around his neck, cheek resting against his shoulder as he brushes past Remy, carrying me.

It isn't until I see the main room, my loft and the clock, the empty couches and vacant chairs, that my muscles seize with an abrupt panic. "Don't," I say, voice cracking miserably. "Don't let him take me back."

"I have this whole problem with the concept of wasted effort," Sy rumbles, ambling toward the door closest to my loft—his bedroom. "No one's taking you back."

A nervous glance over Sy's shoulder reveals that Remy is close behind, carrying the IV bag. "He's not here," he says, hanging close when Sy pauses by the bed. "Nick won't be back. Not for a while." Lower, he adds, "Not if I have anything to say about it." There's a sharp, vengeful glint in his eye as he hooks the bag to the iron bedpost.

The bed looks too good to be real. I remember the last time I was in it. The darkness, the paralysis, the fear, the slow build of pleasure as Sy rutted between my legs, and then the white-hot release of it. I remember it, but it feels like another life to consider this man—the same man who's so carefully lowering me to my feet—is the same one who gasped raggedly into my neck and came undone above me, bruising and selfish.

Sy holds me upright, tucking the towel around me as Remy leaves the room. I'm not sure at first what they're waiting for, my gaze drawn to the neatly made bed.

He tightens his grip on my waist. "Just a little bit longer."

I swing my gaze to his, wondering what the endgame is here. "A little bit longer until what?" I ask, knowing this must be it. The catch. The other shoe dropping. The condition.

But he just gives me a strange look, saying, "Until you can rest."

Remy comes back then, holding an old duffle bag. The flinch that jolts me when he strolls through the door is something I might come to feel embarrassed about later. "Sy rounded up all your stuff before Nick could throw it out," he explains, unzipping the bag and turning it over onto the bed. Out tumbles just about everything I'd spent two weeks amassing here: Five books, six pairs of underwear, two bras, two t-shirts, two strappy tops, three pairs of pants, two pairs of shorts, one sweater, a hairbrush, and a pair of mismatched socks.

Remy gives the bag another shake, but when nothing else emerges, he turns it over, searching the corners of the duffle for something. "That's it?" he says, throwing me an incredulous look. "These are all your clothes?" I blink in response and Remy sighs, picking up one of the more sensible pairs of panties. "We'll deal with that later." He crouches, giving my ankle a tap. "Lift."

I clutch Sy's shoulders as Remy pulls the panties up my legs, his warm knuckles grazing the soft skin of my thighs as he shimmies them upward. I'd welcome the heat of embarrassment, but I'm too tired for even that. He pushes the towel up with it and there's a suspended moment where his fingertips linger over the bruises darkening my legs. He doesn't poke or prod; he simply looks at them, an oddly pensive look capturing his features.

It's short-lived once the towel flutters to the floor, his eyes jerking up to my exposed breasts. But once he stands, he doesn't reach for anything else from the pile. He grabs a sweatshirt hanging on the back of Sy's door, working it gently over my head, feeding the IV bag and tube through the wide sleeve before carefully threading my hand in behind it.

Afterward, Sy gives me to him.

That's precisely what it feels like when he steps away, placing Remy's hands on my waist. "Get her into bed. I'll heat something up." On the way out the door, he mutters, "...going to drag ass at my physics lecture in six hours."

Remy doesn't push me into the bed so much as he tips me toward it. There's a wild energy to him that might make my hair stand on end if my body had the energy to sustain it. As it is, I find it hard to focus on anything but the unending softness of the mattress and the empty doorway.

I can't help the instinct—nearing on premonition—that Nick is going to suddenly walk through it.

"You're not saying much," Remy says, moving my sad pile of clothes aside. "What's with all the burnt umber? Did they scare your voice away?" The words themselves strike me as teasing, but the intensity of his stare imparts them with such a painful earnestness that a lump rises to my throat.

Not knowing how to answer that, I remain silent.

He exhales hard, taking the marker out from behind his ear. "Sy makes me do this thing sometimes. He calls it a head check. Scale of one to ten." He perches on the side of the bed, picking up the hairbrush beside the table. He inspects it before uncapping his marker, pressing the felt to the back of the brush. "Ten is the best you can be. You know what's real, so much that you don't even think to question it, but you also feel it. The realness, I mean. Everything is crisp and clean, like a new sheet of white paper."

The back of the brush is almost completely black now, and he pauses, looking down at his forearm. He traces the scar he'd slashed there that day we were up in the belfry.

"One is the worst you can be. Nothing feels real except for the certainty that nothing *is* real, and that's the dangerous part about it. People like my dad... they think I'm just weak-kneed. But the truth is, I'm never more confident than when I'm at one on a head check. It's because they burrowed in." He presses two fingers to his temple, an angry hurt filling his eyes. "They dug into the fleshy parts and burned away the story, but the sparks can sense the empty places. At least, that's what Sy says." When he finally emerges from his thoughts to look at me, it's with inquisitive eyes. "I know it's not the same with you, but do you think you can—"

"Five." Only a portion of that made any sense, but this answer feels right. "I'm... a five."

I don't see the shadows haunting his expression until they fade away, leaving a peculiar grin. "Ah, five's not so bad. I've had some good times at a five. Stole a car and took it all the way to Northridge, no headlights the whole way."

Remy pushes me up into a sitting position, and I can't find it in me to be suspicious when he slides into the bed behind me, pulling me back into his chest and gathering up my hair.

"I was going to come for you that first day," he says, running the brush through the ends of my hair. His nose is so close to the shell of my ear that I can hear the breath he speaks the words with. "Sy made me wait, though. He said if we did it wrong, they could hurt you. It made sense at the time. Sy isn't like the rest of us. Guy's never had a passing thought in his life. He needs to catch them, wrestle them down, make them say 'uncle'." He puffs a low laugh, his chest expanding against my back. Abruptly, he thrusts the brush in front of me, voice coming out in a muttered rush. "But I wanted to. See?" He only gives me a second to look at the scribble-painted plastic, dried but still giving off a distinct marker-odor, before returning the bristles to my hair.

There's a suspended moment where my eyes fall closed at the rhythm of the bristles, pulling me back—releasing, pulling, releasing—and I don't even try to decipher what that's about. I know the low burn of satisfied comfort in my chest isn't real. This is just so much better than being in the box. But I feel it, all the same, and for a second, I become liquid-lax, melting into the hard, powerful cradle of Remy's body.

And then I feel him.

His cock is hard against the small of my back.

Gradually, my muscles regain their tension, and Remy, intuitive as he is, gives a deep hum.

"It's your skin," he whispers, reaching around me to touch the knees I've drawn to my chest. "I've never seen anyone bruise as pretty as you. Do they hurt?"

I swallow thickly, nodding, but I know now what I need to do. It's almost a relief, knowing the cost. Funny that I used to think myself above it, as if my body were so sacred that it was too much to pay. Now, I easily reach behind myself, grasping the hardness beneath the denim of his jeans.

He releases a quiet breath, grabbing my wrist and prying it away. "It's not like that, Vinny." Gently, he places my hand into my lap, resuming the brush's strokes through my hair. "It's the violet. I like the way it looks, not the way it hurts."

It'd throw me off kilter if I were on it to begin with. As it is, it's easy to sink back into him, taking the reprieve at face value. Maybe there will come a time when I need to repay all this tenderness. When it comes, I resolve to remember the way I'm feeling right now, so grateful to be in a place where warmth and space and softness even exist. It doesn't mean I'll forget that these men are erratic—hot and cold—vicious one minute, sweet the next. It's a constant rollercoaster, and I'm too tired right now to try to do anything but take advantage of the highs and prepare myself for the lows.

The long, gentle brushstrokes and familiar warmth of Remy's body lulls me into a deep, consuming sleep. It's peaceful. Calm. The exact opposite of who I know these men to be: agents of chaos.

I also know better than to think this is going to last.

3

Nick

I DON'T DRIVE AWAY from the tower. The thought of sitting in a car, waiting on traffic lights, trapped in the silence of my own breaths makes my skin feel too tight. Instead, I walk, heading south on the Avenue, fighting off the tug of two equally destructive and kinetic magnets. The one latched to my back threatens to pull me back West, to the Dukes, to family, toward Lavinia.

To the people that hate me.

I left so fast, I didn't even think to put on a shirt, and the October air is getting crisp. Hell, I barely remembered to grab my shoes before rushing down the stairs, the thought of being in that tower one second longer makes my stomach roil. Even though my jaw still smarts from Remy's punch, he wasn't the reason I ran away like a bitch.

It was her. Lavinia. My Little Bird and her broken wings.

The sight of her on that couch, skin sallow, purple and bruised, ribs visible, packed a harder punch than Remy's first ever could. It was the thought of her opening her eyes and looking into mine, because I've spent the last four goddamn days trying to forget them, and fine.

Fine, I'm a pussy.

I don't care who knows it.

My fingers curl tight, emotions rocking through me, wild and furious. When I left her with her father, I knew it was a punishment. I just didn't think...

Yeah, asshole, you didn't want to.

"What was that?" A junkie asks, and I skid to a stop. He's propped up against the chain link fencing rolled over a store window, left eye twitching. "You call me an asshole?"

"Nah," I say, jolting at the realization I'd spoken the words aloud. For a second, my muscles tense and shiver, eager at the prospect of a brawl. But it hadn't helped to throw fists with Remy and I doubt whaling on some tweaker is going to do much, either. "Sorry, man."

I pick up my pace, striding down to the corner, ignoring the pull at my back. Going back will result in another beatdown. I've never seen Remy so livid, so wild, in my life. Not even after Tate. Back then, he was desperate and broken. Tonight, he was like a terror. Another round will come my way if I try to get back in the tower. That much is obvious.

I bite back a scream, slamming my fist into a hard metal street sign.

Slam! Fuck Lucia.

Slam! Fuck Perez.

Slam! Fuck North Side.

Slam! Slam! Slam! Slam! Slam!

I hit, and I hit, and I hit, until the sign is dented and smeared with blood. If my knuckles ache, I don't feel it through the numbness. Only one person deserves a punch. *One*. And I can't very well bash my own fucking teeth in, can I? So I allow the other magnet, the one that's provided me with a sense of purpose for the past two years, to drag me toward it. My other home.

South Side.

The walk is long enough that I'm no longer shaking with rage when I see the neon light of the Hideaway buzzing overhead like a beacon. It's cold, but despite the fact I'm not wearing a shirt, all I feel is hot and impatient. I weave through the cars and walk up to the front door. This place and I go way back—the Velvet Hideaway. I was here when Daniel erected the sign. I was here when we were moving in beds by the dozen, installing the security system, digging the foundation for The Pit. In some ways, this place is more my legacy than the tower in West End ever was.

I spend a second looking up at it, all its windows and empty places. There was a time I'd be buzzing differently at the sight of this house, electrified with the anticipation of going down to the basement. By the time we'd moved Lavinia into this place, Daniel had already laid down the law where I was concerned. No more time alone with her. He said I was getting too interested, too invested.

"Never let your dick write checks your ass can't cash, Bruin."

Daniel was always good at that, making a threat sound like sage advice. It hasn't really hit me until this exact moment, but I possibly —maybe—sort of miss sitting in his office, surrounded by the sharp scent of cigar tobacco and liquor. Daniel was full of himself, but he also wasn't stingy with his praise. A job well done never went over his head. He had a way of making all this feel... right.

Briefly, I wonder what he'd have to say about what I did to Lavinia.

I don't really need to, though.

He'd tell me that's business. I offered her something special and she spat in my face. He'd tell me that's what I get for catching feelings, as if she had the right to them. He'd tell me to pull on my boots and get to work, because there's plenty of pussy out there in the big, bad world, and the finest is located right here.

The bouncer, Frank, stops me before I cross the threshold. He's a massive motherfucker that Killian recruited from the Forsyth football team after blowing out his knee. He casts a wary glance at my face, my bare chest, and then down to the blood dripping off my hand. "Nick," he says, tone even. "You're hurt."

"Ran into a street sign on the way over." I hold up my hands, palms facing out. "I'm not looking for trouble. Just here to let off a little steam."

His eyes tighten. "Augustine isn't going to let you near any of the girls looking like that."

Internally, I bristle at the thought of being turned away. I helped build this fucking place with my own two hands. Some of these girls were sent up from the Avenue based on my own personal fucking recommendation. "You don't need to worry about Auggy, and you sure as hell don't need to worry about me." If he doesn't let me in, where will I go? To my parents? Jesus. Not a chance. I'm all out of homes. "I'll be chill, promise."

He sighs and says, "I'll let you in, but only because you did me a solid during Mardi Gras." He turns and reaches behind him, returning with a black suit jacket in his hands. He throws it at me. "Put that on. You can't go in there without a shirt."

"Thanks, man," I say, shrugging it on, wincing when my busted knuckles drag across the fabric. "Owe you one."

"Yeah, yeah, just clean yourself up before you get any action." He opens the door and gives me a last hard look before letting me pass. "Show your ass and I'm dragging it out of here. Killer doesn't tolerate bullshit."

"Noted." I slip by before he has a change of heart and walk under the crystal chandelier, toward the main room. I still remember how this place used to look like before Daniel gussied it up into Forsyth's best and tackiest whorehouse. His son, Killian, has kept it running, but already I see the difference in how father and son operate their business. It's less of a sleazy lounge and more of a modern playground. On the patio out back is a bar, packed with both men and women who are here more for the atmosphere than the pussy. The Pit I'd put so much of my blood and sweat into is notably dark and vacant since Killian got the keys and his Lady demanded it be shut down. No secret as to why. Story Austin's public show with Rath last year pulled some serious numbers and she's still not over being blackmailed into doing it.

Other than that, everything seems to be business as usual. There are still dozens of girls roaming around the lounge wearing sexy little outfits that leave little to the imagination, but at least the current King's girls look healthy and clean.

My eyes skim past the tits and ass to the familiar door that leads downstairs. Used to be a time that was all I cared about. Getting down to Lavinia, smirking at her petulant little scowls, tossing her something sweet just to see the spark of satisfaction in her eyes. It wasn't the same, though. Back in the early days, all of her frantic energy contained in one shitty motel room, there had been an energy between us. Sure, she still hated me. And yeah, she still kicked me. And it's true that she still tried to run and hit and scream. But—

But what?

There was just this feeling. Like we were all each other had, two prisoners of South Side—a strange, dirty place that both of us were alien to. Back then, the hatred was just part and parcel of it. The contempt, the rivalry between west and north, was a little piece of home for us.

So why does it feel like I lost her the second she crossed that threshold to the basement?

That's where I went last time I was here, pretending I wasn't the one who'd violated her hours earlier. That the ink in her flesh wasn't Remy's skilled work. That my own brother didn't watch, getting hard at the thought of shoving that telephone pole between his legs into her pretty cunt. It was the morning Killian and I made our deal, one that I'd set into motion months before. Ultimately, I had to fight for her, win her against Perez, but that wasn't a hardship. *That* was me marking my territory. Lavinia Lucia was the love of my goddamn life, and I would have done anything for her.

Or so I thought.

Maybe I don't even know what love is. Or maybe I've been saturated with the rot of South Side for so long that nothing comes out and nothing gets in. Or maybe my love is just like the rest of me.

Ruinous.

Mangled.

Selfish.

Fuck if I know. I only know one thing, and it's that rejection isn't a sting. It's a goddamn amputation. 237. Mayhem. I gave her everything in my power to bestow. I showed her my love, and she showed me her hatred. I stole for her, bartered for her, carved her out the best place in the only life I've got, and it didn't even scratch the surface of her skin.

As I take a seat at the bar, I hear her words ringing in my ears. *"I'll never love you! I'd rather die in that fucking elevator than be with you. I'd rather be with Perez!"*

Bitterly, I think, *Called that bitch's bluff*, but the satisfaction that should accompany it was lost days ago to the wetness of her eyes as she got down on her knees and begged.

She *begged* me.

For once, she looked at me and saw someone worth appealing to.

And it was out of desperation.

Nothing more, nothing less.

Without really meaning to, my gaze makes contact with Auggy's down the bar.

"Pretty Nick," she says, eyeing me with a coldness I'm not expecting. "Looks like your day's been as shitty as you are."

In the mirror behind the bar, I get a good look at myself for the first time since leaving the tower. She's not wrong. Even in the shadowy light, the pulpy shiner and split lip Remy got in before Sy broke us up looks like I went three rounds with a cranked-out gorilla and lost.

"Feel like it, too," I admit. "Isn't this where men go to make their shit days better?" I glance back at the room, assessing the merchandise. My eyes linger over a pair of twins sitting by the fireplace. I've seen them around here before, but we've never been formally introduced.

"Sorry, we're all out of shit-day improvement plans." She gives me a small, fake smile. "But I can make it worse if you'd like."

My eyes narrow. Auggy is a tough bitch who's never been anything but civil to me. "What crawled up your ass and died?"

She shrugs, rubbing a glass between a towel. "Maybe I just don't like you anymore."

"I don't need you to like me, I need you to serve me," I toss back, shoulders straightening. "I've still got a shitload of credit in this joint, in case you've forgotten." Daniel only ever let his best men run free on the merchandise, and I was always one of them. Doesn't mean I always took him up on it. I've got enough credit here to fuck my way through the first two floors.

"I haven't forgotten. Around here, we seldom do." She slams the glass down in front of me, never breaking my gaze as she reaches for a bottle of water, uncaps it, and pours it in. "There. Service with a smile. And look at that, it's free."

I hold her stare, unblinking. "I'll take two shots of whiskey and both brunettes." Jerking my chin toward the twins, I send Auggy a dark grin. "Don't fuck with me, Augustine. I know who really runs this joint, and he won't—"

I hear a snort behind me, accompanied by a familiar, rasping cackle. "I doubt you know who runs this joint, shit-for-brains." Mrs. Crane circles around the bar and stands next to Auggy, hunched in that ancient way of hers. Fuck. I'd somehow forgotten that there's someone in between Auggy and Killer when it comes to the operation of this place. She gives me an unimpressed look, from the shiner I'm sporting to my bloody knuckles. "So you and your limp ballsack finally crossed the wrong person, eh?" She flicks the lighter and presses the tip of her cigarette against it, taking a slow drag. "Or that's what I heard."

I narrow my eyes at her, annoyance flickering through me at the way they're both regarding me. Like I'm the trash someone dragged in on the bottom of their designer shoe. "What did you hear?"

Mrs. Crane sniffs. "That you finally got your dick into the Lucia girl and dumped her at her daddy's feet like a used condom."

I press the cold glass to my knuckles, lowering my eyes to hide the flinch. "Who told you that?"

"Sonny, I've got forty-years in this town. There's nothing that happens in any cobwebby corner of it that I don't know about." She clucks her tongue. "It'd be smart of you to start thinking with your brain and not your fists for a while. As you can imagine, our expectations are low."

My fingers tighten around the glass, tearing at the cut on my knuckles. "Maybe I wouldn't have had to if your golden boy, Killian, hadn't given me a raw deal." Lurching forward, I point my finger at her. "She was never the Dukes' to take."

With the speed of a viper, the old woman slaps my finger out of her face and sneers. "Point that finger at me again and the next place you'll find it is sitting next to your prostate."

I stare at her. Delores fucking Crane. Everyone knows she's a true G, and she's never had to say it. She's just got this spirit, this hardness, this *fire*. There's only one other woman I know that could walk through so much hellfire and come out stronger.

Fuck. Fucking fuck!

I swallow the water and slam the glass on the counter. "So, what? You going to deny me service because of some gossip?"

Auggy and Delores share a look, and the older woman shakes her head. "I'm not some low-rent pimp, Pretty Prick. My girls fuck who they want for the price they want." She sweeps a hand out, saying, "Whoever will have you is welcome to whatever disappointment you've got swinging between your legs," and then vanishes behind a door.

"Come on, Auggy." I'm too tired to put on any charm, and it galls me to know what I must look like, a man on the edge of breaking. "I just need a drink and a good fuck. The best way to get over someone is by getting under someone new, right?"

She looks away, face tense. "I told her it'd be good with you. Did you know that?" She nods to the door leading down to the basement. "I stood in that room and told her it wouldn't be so bad. That she should feel lucky to snag the position of Duchess." Jerkily, she retrieves a bottle of whiskey, splashing it sloppily into my empty glass. "You made a goddamn fool out of me, Nick. But I'm about to do you a favor."

I take the glass when she's done, throwing it back and savoring the burn. "Oh yeah? And what's that?"

"Little piece of advice." She swipes the empty glass out of my hand before it even touches the bar. "Learn how to get down on your knees for something other than licking pussy because this is going to take Olympian levels of apology."

"I'm not apologizing to anyone," I say, voice rising. "Not that it's any of your goddamn business, but I didn't do anything wrong! She's the one who rejected me! She was riding on my brother—*in public*—just to provoke me." *I told her that I loved her.* I can't bear to admit it. I sneer, wrenching the bottle of whiskey from her grip, ignoring her flinch. "Why is everyone so surprised it worked? If anything, everyone should thank me. I saved the Counts a trip across town."

"Nick," she says, hand dropping beneath the counter. She keeps a pistol under there. I know. I'm the one who supplied it. "I think you need to go."

But I'm not ready to leave. I came here to fuck this... this sick fucking *feeling* out of my system, and I'm not leaving until that happens. I walk toward the fireplace, making eye contact with one of the twins. Up close, she's pretty enough, *different* enough. Short, dark hair. Small tits. Thick gold chains looped around her neck and wicked, razor-sharp nails studded in jewels. I can do this—her—*them.* I can fuck it away. I can make them scream.

But at my nod, she whispers to her sister, her perfect carbon-copy, before standing up and leading her pointedly away. And just so I can't possibly misunderstand, they get three steps toward the staircase before shooting me matching icy, steel glares.

I snarl, taking a swig from the bottle. "Your tits are too small, anyway."

The next girl I approach is more Auggy's style, sleek and full of presence with her black hair, almond-shaped eyes, and bronze skin. She's draped over a settee, looking bored.

I tip the neck of my bottle toward her. "What about you, beautiful? Got some time for—"

"Nope." She has the guts to look me right in the eye as she says it, which is the only reason I grit my teeth and leave without telling her she's not even that great.

But the third girl I try is just the same, rebuffing me with a tart scoff. "I'm all booked up," she says, inspecting her nails, as she very clearly is doing fuck-all for the foreseeable evening.

I save the fourth girl in the room for last. She's a little too blonde, a little too curvy, a little too shrewd-looking. The moment I approach her, I know it's a mistake, that all of her delicate yet hard features are just going to drive the knife in deeper. And yet...

"What about you?" I move to graze her cheek with my dirty, blood-stained hand, but before I make contact, a massive hand clamps over my shoulder, dragging me back.

"Touch any of these girls without permission, and you'll wish you were back in the fight with whoever gave you that beatdown." Killian looks down at the blonde. "Sorry about that, Candy. He won't bother you anymore. Right, Nick?"

I snatch my shoulder from his grip, jaw tight. "I have credit."

"And nothing to spend it on." I don't miss his balled-up fist, or the gun holster strapped against his side. I briefly wonder if Lavinia would be sad to find out I'd been shot and killed by the Lord King. "Keep your mouth shut and leave, and I'll think about not adding to that nice collection of bruises you've got there."

"I'm not leaving until—"

"Buy a clue, Bruin! None of them are going to fuck you. Not after what you did to your 'Little Bird'." When all I do is stare dumbly at him, he snorts a laugh. "Maybe loyalty isn't something you're familiar with anymore, so let me spell it out for you." Harshly, Killian explains, "Birds of a feather flock together. You fuck with one of them, you fuck with all of them. You're persona non-grata around here. They wouldn't fuck you for all the money in the world, let alone for free."

Pushing forward, I demand, "So make one of them! You're the big bad boss, aren't you? Baby Payne, finally all fitted in his crown." I look him up and down, in his expensive wingback shoes, pressed trousers, and black button-down, sleeves rolled up his forearms to reveal his tattoos. "Your dad—"

"Why are you still speaking? Didn't I just tell you to shut the fuck up?" He reaches out to grasp my arm, dragging me toward the door, and I'm not saying I make it easy, but Jesus. This motherfucker is strong. We're halfway to the door—to Frank, who's waiting on his boss to hand me over. I'm ten feet from being thrown back into the night where I have nowhere to go—no *one* to go home to.

I twist until I'm out of his grip and jump back. "Killian, wait. Seriously, don't throw me out."

He whirls to bear down on me, barking, "You come to my territory, my place of business, my people, and throw around your weight like it means something?" His eyes are fiery and full of threat. I'm not scared of anybody—I lost that instinct a long time ago—but I know a lost cause when I see it. Killer Payne can live up to his name if he's pushed far enough. "Give me one good reason!"

I look over to Auggy and Mrs. Crane, who clearly was the one to tip Killer off. Fucking narc. But that's not what makes my fists curl. It's the Hideaway. South Side. His territory, his business, his people. It's the way Killer fits into it like he's always been here—even though I know he hasn't.

Killian Payne has it all.

And I have nothing.

"If you send me back out there," I tell him, knowing he senses the plea in my stare, "then Killer, I'm not going to come back. Do you get me?"

Someone behind me scoffs, like it's funny to think me never coming back to the Hideaway is any kind of big loss. But Killer doesn't laugh. Some of that steel seeps from his features, the hand on his holster falling away. That's how I know he understands. Right now, I've got a broken heart and nothing to lose.

Someone will die.

Could be Lionel, could be Perez, could be me.

Killian sighs, "You're a walking fucking disaster, Bruin," and waves Frank off. "Come with me."

THE BAG of ice lands on the table with a loud plop right before Killian eases into the creaky leather chair formerly owned by his father. That and the large, framed rendering of South Side's footprint, a blown-up map of each street and building, are the only things that remain from Daniel. If I found myself nostalgic for the atmosphere of his father's company earlier, then I won't find it here.

A photo of Killian and his Lady is on the desk, the two of them dressed nicely, like it was taken at an event. Neither are looking at the camera, their eyes focused on one another. I look away, ignoring the pang in my gut. His framed Forsyth jersey is mounted on the wall. Over on the bookshelf where Daniel kept his prized Cuban cigars, is a football encased in a clear box, signatures scribbled across the smooth rawhide. A cut glass award—*Forsyth Student Athlete of the Year*—sits next to it. I narrow my eyes, and I'm not sure, but it looks like a bit of blood has stained the etching. A row of championship rings, embedded with diamonds and other jewels, is displayed just beneath it. The ring he actually wears is a King's ring, the Lord's skull shiny and gold.

I look down at my own, the brass Bruin already losing its luster.

Yeah, Killian's got it fucking all, hasn't he?

"We've all heard the rumors that you took the Lucia girl back to her father," he says, leaning back and propping his elbow on the arm of the chair. "They were probably spreading word of that the second you turned your back." I open my mouth to speak, but he gives me a hard look and holds up his hand. "I've also become aware that my father withheld some of the information about that..." he grimaces, "transaction. I didn't know about the deadline. I apologize for that."

I raise my eyebrows, wondering if I can speak now. He sighs and waves me on.

"To be fair," I say, "he kept that information from me as well. She didn't even fucking tell me until it was too late to do much about it."

"That's your excuse for kicking her back to that snobby psycho?" Killian looks unimpressed, just as Mrs. Crane had earlier. Clearly, they spend too much time together. "Do you have any idea how weak the Dukes look now?"

"It doesn't matter," I reply, still nursing the bottle of whiskey I'd snagged off Auggy. "She's back now."

Killian freezes, and then sits up. "She's *what*? Since when?"

I shrug. "Since my brother went and stole her back, about... oh, say, three hours ago."

There's a tick in his jaw, nostrils flaring. "Oh, you fucking morons. Are you trying to turn Forsyth into your own militarized dick measuring contest?"

If we're measuring dicks, my brother surely would win.

My cheek lifts in a sneer. "Like you wouldn't do the same for your Lady."

Instantly, he argues, "Perez tried to rape her! You didn't see me gunning anyone down. How fucked are the three of you that I have more restraint? He kidnapped Story!"

I tilt my head. "And what did you do?"

Killian pauses. "Well, I went and got her." I raise a hand, as if to say '*There you go*', but he shakes his head. "No one kidnapped Lavinia. You gave her up. You sold her up the fucking river and then you reneged."

Nothing is as hard to say as this: "Actually, I didn't have anything to do with it." I give him a tight, joyless smile. "It was all my brother and Remy. They wanted her back."

"Jesus Christ, Nick." Killian's shoulders curl, like he's suddenly got the weight of Forsyth on them. And then he strikes out to snatch my bottle of whiskey, taking a long pull. "The deal was that I gave you a shot at getting into the Duke's tower, which would bolster my position with Saul, which would get all of us one step closer to ousting him. But now all you've done is put a target on *your* back." He levels me with a long stare. "What good is it having an inside man if he's dead?"

"I told you back then, and I'll say it again. I don't want his position. I never, not once, wanted a shot at being King." But the words are only half true, and from the way Killian is eyeing me, he knows. I might not want the crown, but it felt good to be back at home. Back with my boys and Mama B at the gym. Back in the ring, fighting for the right reasons. Back in the West End. Back with the stone and the metal of it all. That's what the West End is. It's hard and unyielding and old, made of the sturdy bones of the earth. Everything in South Side is flimsy and disposable. There's nothing here to really lean on.

There may still be some pull for me back to South Side, but it's nothing like the call of West End.

Killian takes another long swig of the whiskey and sets it carefully, thoughtfully, onto the desk. "People like you and me... we don't get a choice about our destiny, Nick. It's in our blood. It's in the soil we walk on, the air we breathe." He shifts, the chair creaking from his weight. "I could've killed you a dozen times over. Do you know that?"

I snort, but deep down, I know it's true. I was a trespasser in his world, only invited in because I was willing to do anything and everything his father asked. I only wanted in to investigate Tate's murder, but he doesn't know that. I lift my chin. "So why didn't you?"

"Thought about it a few times." He admits this openly, unflinchingly. "Not because I felt threatened or anything. My dad's plans for me were set in stone. As you can see," he wryly adds, gesturing to the office. "But sometimes it was like..." He taps the bottle, face pensive. "Sometimes it was like you got the best parts of him. The trust, the praise, the renown. You got all of that, and you never had to deal with the other bullshit. The fights, the way he had to control everything—"

"Him trying to sell your girlfriend." On second thought, "I got that, too."

Killian looks up, scowling. "Maybe I didn't kill you because I saw something familiar in you." He shrugs and spins the bottle, staring into the amber liquid. "A kinship. Not like the one I have with Tristian and Rath. No matter how close we are, they'll never understand what it's like to come from Royal blood." He looks like he may say something more about the two of us, his reason for not taking me out, but he shifts gears. "Tell me about the girl." He points to my face. "The bruises. What brought you crawling back down here tonight looking for pussy and trouble? How bad, exactly, did you fuck up?"

I inhale, trying to push a full breath of air past the rock that's been lodged in my chest since I saw Lavinia on that couch. "I think they really fucked her up, Killer." I swallow down the taste of bile. "Her dad... he hurt her. He's been doing it for years, and the thing is? She pretty much told me. I just didn't listen." All that shit about the elevator. The screams. The paranoia. She laid herself bare, as much as possible, and I fucking walked all over it, too worried about my own dick and my own needs to care. "Or didn't want to listen, I guess." Shrugging, I try to avoid the thought swirling through my mind. Sy said he found her in a chest. I'd bet everything I have—which is exactly fucking nothing—that it's the same one I saw in her room, when I broke in weeks ago. "Sy brought her home. He and Remy are taking care of her now."

He points to my face. "And your face?"

"Remy. He just fucking... unleashed."

His lips quirk. "He has feelings for her?"

"Feelings?" My laugh is half scoffed. "Remy needs things. He needs his special sheets, and fancy paint brushes, and designer fucking shoes. He doesn't get feelings; he gets dependent." I roll my eyes, but a part of me twists at the truth of it because this isn't the first time I've been responsible for ripping one of those dependencies away. Clearing my throat, I shift, uncomfortable at the thought of sharing so much about Remy to an outsider. "Let's just say they weren't exactly happy about me handing her back over to the Counts."

"I bet not." He snorts. "I can't imagine if I unilaterally made a decision like that about our Lady, even back at the beginning. The guys would have slit my throat." He crosses his arms over his chest, the dark twisted ink creeping up his arms. "You may be in line for the throne, Nick, but they're still your equals for now. You don't interfere with a Royal and their woman. Ever. She belongs to them as much as she does to you. You knew the stakes going into this."

"But she—" I start, the tirade building, but the glare he gives me shuts me up.

"This isn't about Lavinia, or your brother and Remy. It's not about Lionel or Perez, or the fact you look like you barely escaped a tornado. It's about you. You're at a turning point, Nick. We all get there. I've been there, and it almost swallowed me whole."

I rub the bridge of my nose, exhaustion sneaking up on me. "The fuck are you on about?"

"It's time for you to decide what kind of man you're going to be," he says, pressing his palms onto the desktop. "Are you the South Side mercenary my dad wanted you to be? Or are you the West End protector your family needs you to be? Because you can't be both." He stands, looming over me, and for a second, I think I see it. The ways we're alike. The kinship.

There for a while, we shared a dad.

We hated him. We learned from him to make being at his side seem worth it, but we looked into the abyss and it looked back, leaving its mark on us just as sure as the ink on our skin. It made us a little bit of what we couldn't stand about the man, and now we have to pick it all apart, find the stuff worth keeping.

I want to ask him, *How do you even fucking begin*?

But he speaks first. "You can't come here looking for an escape every time things get rough, and you can't just throw away your problems. The sooner you figure that out, the sooner you get back on top." The adrenaline has finally worn off and I'm left exhausted and aching all over. He circles the desk. "Come on, let me find you a room and you can sleep it off."

I lift myself up, wobbling and catching myself on the desk. "What if it's too late?" I ask. "What if I fucked this up for good?"

It's the first time I've really considered it. What if I've lost them —and her?

"You're a Duke. Fighting is in your blood." He opens the door and the fast-paced music from the lounge pours in. "The question is, what—or who—are you willing to fight for?"

4

Lavinia

THE SCREAM CATCHES in my throat, my arms and legs cramped and trapped. I'd kick out, but the walls of the chest close in around me, spine contorted and aching. I look for the light that seeps through the slats in the wood, but it's not there. There's nothing but my heartbeat and frantic breaths to count the passage of time. How long have I been in here? Days? Weeks? Maybe I've always been here. Maybe all that I am is contained with this awkward, narrow margin of panic. Maybe I was born here, and I'll die here. Stardust. Isn't that what Remy used to call me?

"Hey, hey, it's okay." The words pierce the surface of the darkness and I cling to them. The deep, smooth timbre of the voice is close enough that I can feel the warmth of it. "You're safe."

Am I?

I think, slowly processing that it's Sy's voice. I begin to remember the last... however many hours it's been since he pulled me from the chest. The drive, the elevator, passing out, the bath, and then falling asleep against Remy's chest. But that doesn't mean I'm safe. Is Sy the kind of person that saves a girl just to break her later?

No, that's his brother.

The weight of his palm settles on the tense curve of my spine. "You're not in the box," he tells me, voice rough with sleep. "You're in the tower. In my bed. It's almost morning."

The shudder of release cascades through my limbs, the paralysis falling off like scales. I remember the last time he found me like this, how he used my prone, frozen body for his pleasure. I'm not getting that vibe from him, though. Maybe, like Remy, all they see is hurt and trauma, not the woman I used to be.

Maybe they don't even want me anymore. The broken toy, used and discarded, only to be fished back out of the trashcan.

Ashes to ashes.

Dust to dust.

The idea is more unsettling than I'd like to admit.

"Lavinia?" he asks, climbing over my body so he can see my face. The lamp is bright on the other side of the room, silhouetting the strong lines of his face. He takes my hand from the pillow, careful with the IV as he turns it, pressing his fingers into the thin skin of my wrist. "Are you feeling sick? Any dizziness? Pain?"

Swallowing, I rasp out, "Where is he?"

There's a beat of silence, his eyes moving back and forth between mine, searching. "Nick? I told you. He's not here. Even if he tried to come back, we wouldn't let him in. Remy's keeping watch."

I shake my head. "No. Not..." My jaw clenches with the unwillingness to say his name. "The kitten, I mean. What did he do with him?" We made a deal. If I wasn't here to care for him, then Nick was supposed to pass the kitten off to Verity or one of the other cutsluts. Someone who'd take care of him, love him.

But Nick breaks promises.

I know that now.

Sy blinks. "The kitten."

"The Archduke," I say, feeling uncontrollable tears welling in my eyes. "He got rid of him, didn't he?"

When Sy answers, "No," it's like a fist clenching around my lungs. "He kept him."

I exhale with my whole body, shivering. "He's still here?"

Sy's eyes narrow. "Yeah, he's probably in Nick's room. That's where he's been staying."

"I need him." Later, I might think to be embarrassed about the way my voice cracks, but for now, I just stare beseechingly into Sy's eyes. "Please?"

He stares at me so long that a bloom of worry builds in my chest, but finally, with a set jaw, he mutters, "Christ. Give me a minute."

He steps out of the room, and I hear the sound of his bare feet on the wooden floor, followed by the click and snap of doors opening and closing. The low rumble of his voice carries back. "...bring her back from the brink of death and all she cares about is that stupid cat." A door slams, and another opens. "Where are you, you fucking—there you are. Stay still." Rustling and cursing follows. "Come here, you little shit!" he says. "Don't you fucking hiss at me!"

He appears a minute later, expression tense, eyes dark, but all I really see is the white ball of fur struggling against his chest. I try to push myself into a sitting position, but my arms feel so weak that they tremble under the weight of my torso. I manage a slight slide up the pillows before Sy unceremoniously dumps the thrashing kitten on my thighs.

"Archie," I cry, gathering his squirming body to my chest. He's stiff at first, but one sniff of my hand and his little tail begins whipping side-to-side. I press my nose to the top of his head, cooing, "Hey, my little fighter. I missed you. Did you miss me?" Sniffling, I give him a furtive onceover, confirming that he's unharmed. He seems bigger—stronger—as if the passage of days has gotten away from me. Time moved and everything grew and changed.

He settles almost instantly, his little motor-purr kicking to life. Archie's eyes are as blue as Sy's, and when he strains up to rub his cheek against my chin, I allow myself a feeble smile.

Sy's at the foot of the bed, glaring down at his knuckles. A bead of blood dribbles down his thumb, and when he looks up, our eyes meet over the distance.

If I had the words, I'd explain that he's more than a kitten. I've spent years in boxes—large and small—and I've never left a hand-print. The Archduke is a shifted destiny. "Thank you," I whisper, cradling Archie closer.

"You won't be thanking me when he gives you some stupid, cat-transmitted disease." Sy gestures to me, my bare legs hidden under his blankets. "Right now, your immune system is probably running off nothing but three sucrose molecules."

I smooth my palm down Archie's fluffy back. "I'll be fine."

Sy's eyes catch on something. The hairbrush, which Remy must have discarded on the bed, hours ago. Sy reaches down to pick it up, eyebrows tugging into a knot. "He painted it black."

"That's okay," I assure. It was in the care package the girls sent to me when I first got here, so it's not like I'm attached to it.

Sy gives me a long look, like I'm missing something obvious. "Solid black means he's sorry about something."

Blinking, I say, "Oh." Either I'm as loopy as Remy or I've spent too much time with him, because it makes perfect sense to me. Why say sorry when you can paint it?

Sy releases a sharp breath, putting the brush on the nightstand. "Well, since we're all awake, we might as well try to get some food into you," he says, grabbing a shirt. He pauses for a beat, mouth tightening. "If that fucker pisses, shits, or pukes in my bed—"

"He won't," I assure him, collapsing against the pillows.

Sy looks aggressively skeptical about this assertion, but leaves the room anyway. Things are a little clearer than they were before, even if they're still fuzzy at the edges. My head feels like it's full of cotton, and my legs—god, my legs ache. Everything hurts, but nothing so much as they do. Any hope of finding a comfortable position is lost the second I try to shift around. My muscles are stiff and sore, and even extending my arms is torture.

Luckily, Archie is a good distraction.

He tramples the blankets around my stomach for a few moments, kneading his little claws into them. He gazes up at me all the while, and I spend a long time wondering what he's thinking. Did he think I abandoned him? Or did he just wait for me, assuming I'd be back? Eventually my thoughts wander to the vacant patch of bed beside me. Mere minutes ago, Sy had been sleeping there. I roll this over in my thoughts, trying to decide how and why that happened. The thought of being in Nick's bed—the possibility of him waltzing in at any moment to find me there, weak and vulnerable, makes my empty stomach churn and roil. But if he's really not here, if his bed is just sitting in there empty, then I would have expected them to put me in it. Tucked away. Unable to bother them.

Why keep me close if they aren't going to use me?

I hear voices out in the main living space, but they're quiet and distant and strangely comforting, and mostly I'm just grateful for it. To not be alone. That sense of comfort is enhanced by Archie's purr, and I know it's silly, but I like to think I can feel the tender places knitting themselves back together.

I almost fall asleep.

It's the sound of approaching footsteps that makes me go rigid, eyes flying toward the door.

A moment later, Remy appears, white hair even more disheveled than usual. He braces a hand on each side of the doorjamb, watching me. "Don't fall asleep," he says, fingertips tapping the wood. "This is Sy's third attempt at giving you this soup. He'll fucking lose it."

My eyebrows furrow. "Third?" I remember the first, but nothing else.

Remy hums. "You almost woke up a couple of hours ago. Tossing and turning, but passed out again." He finally enters the room, only to fall clumsily onto the bed, into Sy's empty space.

"Sun'll be up soon. Things might go cyan." He laces his fingers behind his head, sprawling out, and despite the fact he likely got very little—if any—sleep over the night, he's practically vibrating with energy, foot bouncing. When he turns his head to look at me, his eyes are wide and shining, dilated to a single rim of emerald green. Casually, he says, "I'm going to kiss you."

That's all the warning I get before he pushes his mouth against mine.

As his lips gently brush against my own, I'm so damn thankful that I don't have any strength. If I did, I'd have to make a choice of whether or not to shove him away, and then I'd have to face the possibility that I wouldn't, because Remy has this thing.

This thing where he kisses so sweetly.

He tilts his head, and the kiss is shallow, soft. He never moves to deepen it, to pry my lips apart for his eager tongue. It's a sensual graze of skin against skin, as if he's simply saying hello.

"I wanted to tell you," he says, right into the crease of my mouth. "I finally found the stars."

"For fuck's sake, Remy." Sy's voice jolts through the hush of the moment. "Could you at least wait until she doesn't need an IV to start humping her leg?"

Remy flops to his back, looking unconcerned. "I was just catching her up."

"We need to get something in your stomach," Sy says, balancing a mug and a bottle of water in his hands. "Sit up."

Shakily, I try to push myself into a sitting position, jostling Archie as my body gives a stilted lurch. I don't protest when Remy grabs my shoulders, levering up my torso. When I dig my heels into the mattress, his green eyes catch my pained expression.

"Legs must hurt like a bitch, huh?" Remy doesn't give me a chance to answer, grabbing my waist to wrench me effortlessly up the bed. He props me against the headboard like a ragdoll. "We've got some muscle cream," he says, jumping up and zipping out of the room.

The flicker of irritation that runs through me is sharp, but short-lived. Even in the most ideal of circumstances, there's nothing worse than being helpless. But in circumstances like these?

"Suck it up," Sy says, placing the mug—with the soup, I realize—carefully in my hands. "Literally. If you want your strength back, then you need to eat," he pointedly sets the bottle of water down on the table beside me, "and drink. Get your electrolytes up."

The soup is warm, but not hot, the heat barely seeping into my palms as I lift it to my mouth.

"Easy," Sy says, rocking forward to steady the mug when my wrist trembles.

Archie jumps up and spits at the motion, the white fur on his back and tail bursting into a defensive flare.

Sy snatches his hand back a split second before his paw swipes out. "What the—fuck you! This is *my* bed!"

Archie flattens his ears and hisses so bodily that his fuzz shivers with the intensity.

Sy's eyes go flinty, fists and teeth clenching. "I swear to god, I will punt this motherfucker all the way back to East End."

Frowning, I drag Archie back against my hip. "What did you do to him?"

Sy's eyes bug out. "What did *I* do to *him*?" He holds up his hand, littered with scratches. "He's been terrorizing me since day one. Fucking glorified rodent, running around here like he owns the goddamn place."

"Chill." Remy returns, giving his friend a pat on the shoulder. To me, he says, "He hasn't done anything. Sy's just got this whole aura about him. Controlling as fuck, self-righteous, joyless. In other words, the Archduke can sense he's a gaping asshole." As if to bolster this point, Remy reaches out and gives Archie a scratch beneath his chin with no difficulty whatsoever. "You'll warm up to him."

"The fuck I will," Sy growls.

Remy's eyes roll. "I was talking to the cat. Now, let's see what we're working with." He yanks the covers back, revealing my bare, bruised legs, and then sits down on the bed, facing me. I clutch the mug of soup to my chest, startled, but Remy just soothes me with a hand on my shin, picking up my legs and settling between them, a calf on each knee.

Sy abruptly becomes interested in something on his desk, sitting down in the chair and opening a worn-looking, leather-covered notebook. "*Eat*, Lavinia."

Remy gives me a look. "See?"

Reluctantly, I lift the mug to my lips, finally getting a good taste of the contents. Chicken with noodles, just the right side of salty.

"Like I was saying before," Remy begins, squeezing some menthol-scented cream into his palm. "I figured it out. The stars, remember?" He meets my gaze as his hands begin rubbing the cream into my calves. "I know why I kept seeing you falling."

"Uhhh," is all I have to offer, overwhelmed by both the soup and the sensation of his skilled fingers, kneading gentle circles into my muscles.

"Remy," Sy says, voice soft but firm, even though he doesn't look up, pen moving over the notebook. "Leave it. She's not up for this shit right now."

"It wasn't you I was seeing," Remy continues, ignoring him. He was right before about Sy having an aura. It's dark and unapproachable, a subtle impression of threat. But right now, Remy's aura is so disjointed that I can't focus on anything else. It's frantic and too alert, like a buzzing that never really goes away. "I was remembering your sister."

Sy slams his pen down, and then turns to glare at him. "What did I just fucking say?"

But I'm frozen, the mug suspended in front of my mouth. "You know my sister?"

"Not even remotely," Remy replies, making me wince when his fingers dig into the backs of my knees. "That's the thing. I've never even met her, but she was there."

I lower my mug. "*Where*?"

"At the cliff."

I look at Sy, the confusion making my head spin. "When was this?"

"The night Tate died," Sy explains, running his fingers through his dark, curly mop of hair. The shirt he'd grabbed off the floor earlier clings to his torso, wrinkled and thin, and it strikes me that he looks exhausted. "It was a little over two years ago," he goes on, retrieving his pen only to tap it against the notebook. "Remy seems to think he was there when it happened."

Remy turns to snap, "I fucking was there!" and his next squeeze of my calves is less of a knead and more of a vicious clench, making me cry out. He whirls around, muttering, "Shit," and then, "Sorry, Vinny, sorry." I breathe through the ache, stiff and reluctant when he lifts my ankle to his shoulder, forcing me to stretch it. "I *was* there, though. And so was Leticia. That's why I kept seeing you in the stars. You look so much alike, and it's the only time I've ever seen her—there, at night, on the cliff."

My thoughts come in tumultuous waves, smashing up against my mind in fits and starts. "Two years ago?" I struggle to think, to catch the threads before Remy's fingers make them recede into a pulsing awareness of my aches. "That... would have been around the time she went missing?"

"Exactly." Remy's mouth is pressed into a tight, grim line, but his eyes shine with a disturbing excitement. "So you should tell us about your sister. Why would she have been there? What's she like? Is she into the drug game? Did she roll with the Counts, or—"

"Enough!" Sy stands, giving Remy a stern but fatigued look as he gestures to me. "Jesus, Remy, look at her. She can barely hold her soup up. Let her rest."

I'd wilt under the intensity of Remy's green stare, except I'm already there. Bone-tired. Sore. So fucking lost.

Remy ducks his head, watching as his fingers skate up my thigh. They pause on a bruise and he spends a long moment staring at it. The excitement fades from the sharpness of his features, leaving something shuttered and dark as he gently lowers my feet to the bed. "Later then," he says, standing.

I guess it all makes sense now.

The kindness.

The tenderness.

The aching sweetness of that kiss before.

I'm important now because he thinks I know something.

Sy presses his fingers into his eyes, groaning. "I have to get ready for this lecture."

That's when I notice the faint light of morning glowing through the window over his desk. Has it really only been seven hours since Sy lifted me out of the chest? He nods at me, the faint stubble over his jaw making him look unfairly haggard. "Eat and drink what you can, then get back to sleep. You've still got a few hours left of that IV."

"You're leaving me here?" I ask, almost dropping the mug. "Alone? All day?"

Nick will come back. He'll come back and he'll find me here, and then he'll—

Remy takes the mug out of my hand. "Don't worry, Vinny. I'm staying." There's an odd blankness in his eyes when he reaches out, brushing the point of his tattooed knuckle over the line of my jaw.

Relief at knowing Nick can't get to me, allows me to exhale and sink back under the covers. But I don't close my eyes. Instead, I watch Remy as he leaves. These men have proven they value me. At least on some level. As Duchess or just a toy they don't want anyone else to have? I don't know. Remy turning cold, making me feel unbalanced—guarded—is so familiar that it covers me like a blanket. One I drag over me until I curl into the Archduke's purring body and fall asleep.

~

I DREAM ABOUT LETICIA AGAIN.

I dreamed about her before, too, when I was in the chest, but I never saw her—I only heard her voice. This time it's the opposite. I'm inside the house—my father's house—and I'm looking out the window to where she's swaying on the swing set, the pale light of the moon catching like fire in her golden hair. She's younger here, still sporting the budding curves of late middle school. Her legs kick and bend, and she's sitting perfectly straight, face set into a stony serenity. It's one of the things people like most about my sister. The poise. Tisha never breaks frame. She's exactly what my father only pretends to be, shaped so precisely by his lessons that she grew up into this perfect visage of relentless dollhood. I used to wonder how badly it galled him to watch her. Does my father see her as his masterpiece? Or does the sight of her make him feel inadequate?

I don't know how long I hold onto the dream, but it feels like I watch her on that swing for a very long time. So long, in fact, that she ages right before my eyes, growing from the slender middle schooler to the young woman I remember last seeing two years ago. She grows sharper, more refined, hair longer, and she never looks away from me—not once.

It should be unnerving, but it's not. There's an odd peacefulness about it all, deathly quiet even when the wind blows, whipping her hair around her face.

And then she begins decaying.

Her cheeks go gaunt and gray, eyes milking over. The skin over her knuckles, wrapped around the swing's ropes, splits and curls. Her legs kick and bend, kick and bend, and she deteriorates right before my eyes, her gaze never leaving mine.

A pinch tugs at the back of my hand, stinging, and I lurch away from the window, waking with a full bodied flinch.

Instinctively, I yank my hand back.

"Chill, Vinny." Remy's soft voice cuts through the sleep. I blink and the hard line of his jaw comes into focus. "I'm just taking out the IV. Don't go all green on me."

The sting only lasts a second, and then he swipes something cold, wet, and astringent-smelling over the skin. I'm aware of the rustle of my sheets and the feel of this thumb on my hip, counting stars, even though he told me it's all real. That he saw her.

Leticia.

Still, I need to ask. "Did you really see her?" I whisper.

He looks up from my hip. Remy has fascinating eyes—green, but so bright that they could be yellow in the right light—and I find myself lost in them for a long moment. Until he nods. "I saw her."

The words are quiet but sure, and carry with them one captivating fact.

Maybe Remy isn't so crazy after all. "Do you know what she was doing up there? With Tate?"

The puzzle pieces are too much for me to try to sort and link together. Leticia. Tate. Cliffs. Death. "Nothing makes sense," I mutter, voice thin and wan, and I want to ask to see his Lady of Sorrows—to know this is still real—but I don't.

Warm fingers brush over my forehead. "We'll talk about it later, then. Sleep, Vinny." And then Remy tells me something I'd said to him weeks ago. "It'll be better when you wake up."

But I think of that dream—of watching Leticia on the swing as her skin grows papery thin, cracking and curling, and my hand reaches for him just as he steps away. "Could you… stay?"

He pauses, head tilting. "You want me to lay with you or something?"

Once the thought is put to words, it sounds terrifying. "Could you… read to me? Just for a while. It helps—"

"It helps you know when you're dreaming." He blinks twice, and then starts looking around the room, fingers tapping his thighs. "Right, let's see what we've got." He picks up a thick, heavy book from Sy's desk. It's got colorful adhesive tabs sticking out every which way, and Remy flips to a blue one. "He's been researching whatever they were doing to me at Saint Mary's." Staring at the page, he warns, "This shit's so boring, it'd make paint peel."

"I don't care." I tuck my hand beneath my cheek, watching as he reclines in the empty spot beside me. He shifts around, tucking a sleeping Archie between us. His eyes haven't regained any of that manic wildness from before, but now there's a weight to them, his eyelids heavy as he scans the page.

But when he opens his mouth, it's not to read. "Did Perez fuck you?"

I run my palm down Archie's back and wonder if it'd make a difference. Perez fucking me. Would that make me used goods? "No," I answer.

He swings his gaze to mine, searching. "One of the other Counts? One of your dad's guys?"

"My dad would never let any of them have me. Not until..." I trail off because I suppose it's moot now. Marrying Perez suddenly seems like such an impossibility, and it hits me—really hits me, maybe for the first time—that this is what being a Duchess means. That I'm spoken for. Claimed. Off the table.

Remy cements this with a single question, eyes blazing into mine. "Then whose thumbprints are bruised into your thighs?"

I go still as stone, hand freezing against the curve of Archie's sleeping back. Suddenly, the coldness in his eyes before makes sense. I pull my limbs in tight, as if that could protect me from the memory of Nick moving over me, digging his way inside. Tucking my arms around myself, I just shake my head.

But Remy knows.

I can see it in the way his eyes shutter, face going blank.

He turns back to the book. Clearing his throat, he begins, "Neuropsychiatric stimulation therapies. Principles and practices of electroconvulsive therapy. Part one..."

I don't fall asleep.

I dive into it, rushing for the reprieve.

~

"Son of a—" the curse is a grinding whisper followed by a soft thud. I roll over and see Sy easing between the sheets. His forehead is furrowed, a dark scowl settled on his mouth. Even half asleep, I know that look.

Sy vs. the Archduke.

Our eyes meet in the dark and he freezes. There's a tense beat of silence before he speaks. "I hate your fucking cat." Then, awkwardly, "You need any water? Food?"

The clock across the room says 1:32. No light comes in the small window at the top of the brick wall. He's shirtless and wearing black shorts—just going to bed.

I shake my head, distantly wondering where Remy went. I can still hear his quiet, rough voice in my mind, reciting the words off the pages, but that must have been hours ago.

Sy's lips form a tight line, jaw tensing. At first, I think it's a sign he doesn't believe me about the food, but his eyes dart down to the swell of my breasts and then back up, a motion so quick that it strikes me as involuntary. His pupils swell and contract.

When my stomach twists, it's a dull, lost sensation flickering back to life. As involuntary as his own glance, I look down at his lips. The night of the Baron's equinox party seems like a lifetime ago, but I still remember the way he kissed me, clumsy and desperate and too forceful. That must be why I'm thinking of it now. I never had the chance to process it, to compartmentalize it, to stuff it into the back of my brain as something unimportant—a one-off. How odd to think of those lips as having been on mine, warm and wanting. And now that I'm in his bed, in the dead of night, weak and pliant, he's free to have it again.

A long beat stretches on where the only movement between us is the pulsing muscle in the back of his jaw. Until…

Mew?

Archie breaks the moment, pushing the air back between us. Sy scowls down at the kitten, who's curled against my neck, and without another word, he positions a pillow between our torsos.

He turns the other way, rolling on his side.

It's a respectful gesture that worms inside my brain. Sy's never been *respectful* to me, making it perfectly clear what he thinks women are useful for. I've lost count of the times he's called me a whore and a slut. It dislodges another question that has been worrying me. It's a question I've ignored, but as I stare at the pillow-wall it filters to the surface.

Did Remy tell him what Nick did to me? Does he think I deserved it? It's hard reconciling the two different sides of him. The one that hurts versus the one that heals.

It takes me longer to get back to sleep this time, and I'm not convinced Sy's asleep either. A smoldering heat builds between us, even over the distance. Finally, I hear the steady rhythm of his breathing. I focus on that sound until my brain settles down and once again, I slip away.

"I HAVE A SECRET."

I jolt awake, heart racing, arms searching, looking for her.

Of course, Leticia's not here.

She's not here, but she's in my head, filling it with questions and worries, and I let it drive me upright. Sweat runs down my back, cooling from the touch of air. The sun shining in through the window is bright and warm, with all the luster of a bright autumn morning illuminating every corner of the room. Once my pulse settles, I also process that I'm alone, and I'm okay with it.

I swing my legs over the side, testing the weight of my legs. It's not the first time I've stood or walked. Both Remy and Sy have assisted me on trips to the bathroom, hovering awkwardly outside the door, but they were quick trips with only one destination in mind: to get back to the bed.

Right now, I want nothing more than to leave it.

Using the regained strength in my arms, I push off the mattress and immediately reach for the wall. I stand apprehensively, testing my legs' ability to hold my weight. I steady myself and then take a tentative step, then another, my bare feet silent against the floor.

The bedroom door is already open; a sign the guys are keeping an eye on me. Time has passed in vague increments of light and dark, sleep and wake, and even that seems fuzzy and ill-defined, arriving with no order. How many days has it been? My brain no longer marks time in the passage of days, and it bothers me, not knowing.

I enter the main room, my steps stilted and careful, and pause when I see Remy asleep on the couch. His long legs stretch over the end, bare feet dangling. He has his arms crossed over his chest, like he'd fallen asleep in the middle of some unspeakable brood, enhanced by the faint divot between his eyebrows.

I listen for Sy, for anyone else, and when I'm certain I'm the only one awake, I tiptoe past him and focus on my destination.

Nick's room.

His scent hits me at the threshold and my spine grows rigid. I didn't even know he had a specific scent until it slaps me in the face. It's warm, musky, *male*. The first thing my eyes dart to is the bed. The memory of Nick tying me down, pushing himself inside, comes flooding back.

"You hurt me, I hurt you."

I shake it off like a mist that's threatening to cling to me. I'm not here to relive the past. I'm here to find proof of it.

Instinctively, I know this is where I'll find what I'm looking for. Nick was Daniel Payne's most sterling protégé. He has a way of knowing his enemy's weak spot, and I'd given him that knowledge when I'd asked him to steal it for me.

Taking a deep breath, I step into the impersonal room. Nick never decorated. He didn't hang artwork like Remy or fill a bookshelf like Sy. He only wanted one possession in this room—*me*.

I avoid the bed until I realize there's nowhere left to search, but then it clicks. He'd want it close, a trophy to touch at his every whim. Of course, it'd have to be here, on this bed where he already took so much from me.

I walk over and lift the pillow.

Underneath, next to the long, sharp blade of a knife, is the cigar box, elastic bands still in place.

Slowly, I lower myself to perch on the edge of the mattress, removing the bands one at a time. When they're piled in a stack beside me, I turn the box, and take a deep breath. I feel like Remy, unable to trust my memory anymore. To know what's real or not. I knew my sister had secrets. She loved them. Traded in them. But hearing what Remy said, that she was up on the cliff the night their friend Tate died?

It doesn't fit. Leticia is the perfect daughter, my father's favorite. She did everything right—*better*. Except... she *did* have secrets. Often, she'd sneak out at night, forcing me to cover for her with sharp sneers and whispered threats. I just figured she was hooking up with frat boys at the University—sowing wild oats until our father shackled her to Perez.

In no world did I think hers would cross with West End.

I lift the tiny gold latch and lift up the lid. Inside are Leticia's treasures: A granite rock, a dirty, stained ribbon, a receipt with scribbled numbers on the back. I pick up the bullet, holding it up to the light, like that could solve some incredible enigma.

It doesn't.

I set those all aside, laying them across the top of Nick's mattress, until I get to the photo at the bottom.

Nothing about the picture made sense to me before. Two striped socks in the foreground, a body of water, and trees in the distance. It's an overlook, a cliff. I study the feet, trying to find a clue, something that will tell me why Leticia kept it here, in this box of odds and ends.

In the end, I just feel like a fucking moron, knowing I've missed something so obvious. I blame it on the fact I haven't been able to really inspect the contents of this box. First, I had to hide it from my father, and then I was traded around Forsyth like a wayward pet. But now, I see it, plain as day. It's all in where the toes are, pointed toward one another, pinky toe to pinky toe.

Same socks.

Different girls.

5

Sy

It's been four days, and Lavinia's done nothing but sleep.

She wakes up every now and then to accept the food I bring her, tired eyes shining up at me through bedraggled hair as she tastes the soup. Sometimes, she'll rasp out a low, "Thanks." Sometimes she won't say anything at all, adjusting the kitten to lay at her side as she prepares for the chore of consuming sustenance. That's what it looks like when she eats. Like it's just work. Sometimes I'll sit at my desk, working on a paper or finishing my lab notes, but most of the time I leave her be, always hyper-aware that she's in my bed, waiting for the next time I return.

Either way, it's always quiet. Even the air in the tower around us feels reserved, as if there's a frailty that could be shattered by the smallest sound. The wariness never really leaves her eyes. Every time Remy or I enter the room, she goes stiff, as if she's expecting someone else. Nick, probably.

But he never comes home.

At night, I climb into bed beside her, and I'm not really sure why. The kitten and I always go five full rounds before he lets me settle on the mattress, swiping out with sharp claws as he shrinks into the curve of her sleeping form, like he's her bodyguard or something. I'll stand there and curl my fists, glaring at him until he finally retreats, curling into a tight ball against her neck, and it's stupid. I could sleep on the couch, or even in Nick's bed. It's not like he's using it.

Instead, I slide carefully under the blankets and nurse my stinging, kitten-slashed hands, the darkness amplifying the sounds of Lavinia's slow, measured breaths, and I sleep. I wake up. I go to class. I come home. I do it all over again.

Except this morning, when I wake up to find her tucked up against my side.

She must have rolled over and curled against me at some point. There's a long stretch of time where I just lie there, flat on my back, cataloging the warmth of her skin against mine. Cool hands, hot feet, warm breaths. The realization doesn't hit me so much as it just… arrives.

I've been waiting for this.

No.

I've been *hoping* for this.

The touch of her chin against my shoulder. The warmth of her body against mine. The rhythm of her breaths, so close that I can feel them, fluttering like gossamer. The weight of her next to me. The thrum of someone's life pressed against the thrum of mine.

My dick is harder than steel, but it's not just that. Not just her tits or the way her lips look, plush and parted. It's not even about the way I'm holding myself back from rolling on top of her, thrusting wildly into the soft cradle of her thighs. It's just this. The touch. Not a punch or a shove or some athletically deliberate hold. This is softness and comfort and…

Sweet.

That's when I know, all these nights I've been getting into bed beside her are just like back in the old days when I'd throw myself into a crowded, rowdy party and wait for someone to start some shit. The flash of anticipation, the buzz of energy building, cresting —can't be blamed, didn't start it, not my fault.

I stare at my open laptop across the room, to the big digital clock floating around the screen, and I give myself ten minutes— not a second more or less—to indulge.

Her hair smells different than it used to. I'd washed it with Remy's shampoo before, not even thinking, only now I miss the scent of hers, honey and the faintest hint of flowers. The Archdick has fucked off somewhere, and now it's just her, one of her bruised knees prodding into my thigh. I think about touching the skin there, about moving my fingertips higher, about grabbing her hand and placing it on my bare chest. I think about the texture and the heat, and how if she touched me with even the smallest hint of intent right now, I'd come my fucking brains out.

And then my time is up.

Crawling out of bed is the hardest thing I've had to do all week.

~

"Do you think they were fucking?" Remy asks, passing the blunt.

"Probably." I snort, taking my attention off my journal long enough to inspect the ember of the blunt. "You know Tate's type."

Remy's mouth quirks and it's a perfect mirror to what I'm feeling inside. "She always did love her some premium, high-maintenance pussy."

"And what could be higher maintenance than Leticia Lucia?"

Talking about her like this, thinking of Tate having something good, takes away the sting of her possibly hiding it from us. Still, maybe we're reading it wrong. Last night, when Lavinia gave Remy the picture—likely just to shut him up from the constant barrage of questions regarding Leticia—we knew right off it was Tate. Remy had inked those flowers on her ankle himself. We all know what it looks like. The socks. The feet curling toward one another. Maybe they were fucking.

Maybe.

Forsyth is gray and dreary even at ten in the morning, a mist hanging over the city like a noxious cloud. I add to it, exhaling a heavy stream of smoke into the air. This is only my third time up in the belfry. The first night after moving into the tower, the three of us came up here without even having to discuss it. Only Dukes are allowed in the belfry. There's a very select group of people who have seen Forsyth from this vantage. It's all part of the experience, having an exclusive perspective, and it went without saying that it'd be one of the first things we did. It is an incredible view, but there are at least three buildings in the distance that are as high or higher than our clock tower. It's not the height that makes it unique. It's the fact that we can see all points of Forsyth from here. West, east, north, south. Every King would love to have this, to hover above it all, knowing that everyone is beneath them, small and insignificant. That's why it can only be us, the fists of Forsyth.

We earn our spoils.

"She seems better today, doesn't she?" Remy takes the blunt, pinching it between his fingers before bringing it to his lips.

"So do you," I note, writing that down under today's date.

R: Alert. Active. Appears to be in good spirits. Continuing medication, but with difficulty. Six hours of sleep. Marijuana @ 10am. No other substances.

I thought it'd be stressful coming up here with him, knowing what I know. I think of him standing on that ledge and looking down, and something frantic and painful slams into the pit of my stomach.

I turn to another tab in my journal, jotting it down.

All subjects present with possible PTSD.

Maybe that's it. Remy and his fear of losing hold on what's real. Nick and his twisted idea of justice and fairness. Me and the way I feel strangely responsible for it all. Maybe we're all stuck in some awful loop of grief over Tate, searching for a way to break the chain and only ever strengthening the links.

In any case, I'm surprised to find it's not so bad, sitting here with Remy on what could easily be the edge of the world. I see the appeal, understand why he's been so antsy to get up here all morning.

We need to remember that the world is bigger than us.

"Well, I'm better now," he says, eyes falling closed as he savors the weed. It's been two days since he last snorted that junk Cash Mallis had given him. Four days since I returned from Lionel Lucia's mansion with his daughter in my back seat. Four days since we put her in my bed. Four days since Nick left. "She just seems better, like she has more energy. More cyanine blue than green. Don't you think?" There's a hopefulness in his eyes when they open, and I don't have it in me to extinguish it. "She took a shower by herself this morning."

All of this is written in another tab of my journal for the day.

L: Lethargic but alert. Fatigue. Sufficient appetite. Appears hydrated. More verbal today. Resuming normal hygiene, unaided. Tactile; uncharacteristic but not medically significant.

"Yeah, she looks better." A part of me wonders why he cares. Why, sometimes, he comes into my bedroom at night to check on her. How he gets home from class and makes a beeline for my bed to see whether or not she's awake. It's as if she's his first and last thought of the day, and it's fucking weird. "I've never seen you like this over a girl," I admit, taking the blunt back.

He squints, even though it's too overcast for a ray of sun. "Like what?"

Shrugging, I take a moment to find the right words. "Like... invested. Like you care about her." If it'd been someone like Haley, he wouldn't have pushed and pushed, pestered me until I rescued her. This much, I know.

"She's our Duchess," is his reply, but even though it's said flippantly, like it's the most obvious thing in the world, I can tell there's something lingering beneath the words. "I think I like her."

I stare at him. "And you're working that out *after* making me trespass on enemy territory to snatch her?" Rolling my eyes, I playfully bury my fist into his shoulder. "No shit you like her. I'm just not really sure why."

He slaps my hand away. "Please, like you haven't been dick-brained over her for weeks."

I don't say that I'm still thinking about waking up to her pressed against me a couple hours ago, and I definitely don't say that I'm wishing time would move faster so I can climb back into that bed and maybe have it happen again. "That's different," I argue. "I didn't say she wasn't hot. You don't get attached to pussy for no reason. I know you."

He looks down, forehead wrinkling. "At first, I thought it was just because she made me remember. I didn't even know why yet, but I just knew she was important. And then..." I watch as his eyes go distant, because Remy is like this sometimes—painfully earnest, willing to spill it all out.

It's the best and worst thing about him, the way he wears his heart on his sleeve, like it'd never occur to him such a thing could be a weakness. If he can find it—if he can wade through the chaos of his mind to form a feeling into words—Remy will always speak his truth. It's not always comprehensible or rational, but it'll always be honest. I think that's what enrages me most about whatever that doctor must have done to him. That she had someone so open, so willing to show every morsel of his thoughts, and they just fucking plundered it like savages.

So I wait patiently as he sorts through it, hitting the blunt a couple more times, a glaze settling over his eyes before the spark within them finally catches. "I think she's the first person that ever took care of me."

My jaw drops and I steal the blunt, yanking it away. "Then what the fuck have I been doing?!"

Remy's pursed grin pushes his exhale of smoke into a sideways stream. "Nah, it's not the same. You take care of me because you want to fix me. With you, there's a goal post. But Vinny, just..." He tips his head back, the sun catching his hair. "That day she talked me off the ledge—right over there, actually—she took care of me. She talked to me, patched me up, let me use her skin, and there wasn't any... expectation. Like she didn't need me to be better or fixed. She just needed me to be the best I could, and that was enough." When he finally looks at me, there's a flicker of apology in his eyes. "Tate's the only one who ever treated my bullshit like that."

My stomach sinks. "Remy... she's not Tate. She can never be—"

His eyes flash angrily. "No one knows better than me that we can't replace Tate. You think I want Vinny because she fits in her place? I'm just saying, it's nice not to be someone's project for a change." Lower, he adds, "Plus, she's got my ink now, and that makes her mine. Oldest dibs known to mankind."

I could probably mention that the Lady has his ink, too, as well as half this damn frat and a good portion of his old high school graduating class. Instead, I fight back a scowl. "I don't think of you as a project."

"Sure you do," he insists, giving my journal a pointed look. "But what you don't realize is that you're my project, too. There's a reason I let you henpeck me to death. It makes you feel better. Gives you purpose, keeps you close." He nods, watching the trail of smoke as it marries into the city mist. "One day you're gonna realize it's futile—that you can't fix me, you can't *win*—and it's going to seriously piss you off. But until then, we're good, brother."

I scoff. "I can always win, Remy. *Always*."

He basically ignores this, flicking his hair from his eyes. "Anyway, I don't know why you're giving me the third degree. You're the one who's been doting over her like a flustered nightingale."

"What? You're full of shit." But when I hit the blunt, I hold it in, pinching out a terse, "You were the one brushing her hair."

He laughs, head shaking. "No, it's good. Because you might not be able to win against whatever's wrong with me, but her?" He looks up at me, considering. "If she'll let you—if you really want to

—you could fix her." There's a question there that I'm not exactly ready to answer.

Do I want to fix Lavinia Lucia?

I redirect the conversation the best way I know how. "You should try to smooth things over with Nick."

A dark look passes over his face. "Fuck Nick."

I raise an eyebrow. "I thought you said you were tired of losing people?"

"I am." Despite this—or maybe because of it—Remy's shoulders curve dejectedly. "He's just such a shit sometimes, you know?"

"I know." After a long pause, I add an ominous, "But…"

Remy nods. "He's our shit."

"Right."

For better or worse, Nick is our problem to deal with. We haven't heard from him since he ran out of here, but a call came from South Side a couple days ago letting me know my brother's crashing at the Hideaway, and it fucking gnaws at me.

Nick doesn't belong there. Not in the Hideaway, not on the Avenue, not in the place in the distance where the mist meets the smog, blanketing South Side in a thick barrier of haze. I spent two years pushing the truth of that down, letting him do as he pleased, resisting the urge to march over there and drag him back, and I think I might regret it.

Nick ran away.

But no one came for him.

"We need to go get him," I decide, closing my journal.

Remy leans forward to watch it flutter downward into the fog. "What if he tries to take her back?" Looking at me, I see the frustration in his eyes. "How can we trust him?"

"He won't take her back." I've never been as sure of anything as I am about this. I saw the look on his face when he felt the force of what he'd done. My brother might be impulsive, selfish, and stubborn as hell, but he's not a masochist. He won't hurt her again because he wouldn't be able to take the wound it'd make.

I'm so caught up in this thought, my stoned mind just as hazy as the sky before us, that when my phone buzzes with a notification, I'm strangely certain it must be my brother. As if I could call him home with nothing but a carefully focused thought.

It's not Nick, though.

"Shit!" I fumble for my journal and the bottle of water I'd brought up here with me.

Remy frowns. "What's up?"

"Saul's downstairs," I say, rushing to gather our things.

In an instant, Remy is diving for the hatch, and I know he must be thinking the same thing I am: that Lavinia is down there.

Alone.

Still recovering.

Unprotected.

I haven't been *doting*, but yeah, nursing Lavinia back from the edge of death has been a lot of work. I guess I've known deep down that I have my own trouble to deal with, which is why Saul's appearance at the tower shouldn't be unexpected. Just really fucking inconvenient and ill-timed. She *has* been looking better today, point of fact. She's been more alert, her vitals seem solid, body functions returning to normal. Remy and I had gone up to the belfry for some much needed decompression, and now we're stoned out of our goddamn minds, skidding to a stop at the bottom of the stairs.

Saul has let himself in.

He's standing near the wall of composite photos that line the back wall, eyes flicking over each small circular photo that makes up a membership class. A thick-necked soldier stands by the door, not daring to step fully inside, because we all know he's not Royalty.

I'm acutely aware that I'm wearing nothing but sweats, including shoes. I'm also unarmed.

"Saul," I say, alerting him to my presence. As if he doesn't know.

"Simon," he says, taking one last look at the photos before turning. "It's been a long time since I've been up here." He glances around, eyes sweeping from the clock in the loft, then down to the rooms. He points to my bedroom, his King ring catching light. "That was my room." He grins with calm nostalgia. "We had some good times up here, your parents and I."

I've never spoken to Saul about his time as a Duke with both of my fathers. I definitely have no interest in hearing about my mother's time as Duchess. I know he's not happy there's a real Bruin back in the house. My half-brother is the only real threat to his position.

To Remy I say, "Hey, why don't you go ahead and get the laundry," and I know when he instantly nods that he understands the code.

Dirty laundry.

My brother.

Remy doesn't linger, throwing Saul a nod before grabbing his keys and moving toward the door. I don't miss the quick glance he shoots at my bedroom door, and I'm pretty sure Saul doesn't either.

A dip of Saul's chin and the soldier lets Remy through.

"I'm sure you didn't come down here to reminisce about the good ole days," I say, crossing my arms over my chest and positioning myself between Saul and my bedroom. Lavinia is in there, probably cuddled up with her dick of a kitten, nose buried in my psychology textbooks. That girl will read anything. "I assume you want to talk about the Counts."

"You assume correctly." He unbuttons his suit jacket and sits in the worn leather armchair. His shoes are shined to perfection, his shirt crisp and ironed. Saul Cartwright isn't just a King, he's the athletic director at the University. A legitimate job. Something no other house can claim. To the outside world, he's an established, respected man. But in West End? He's a brutal gun runner and domineering figure, just as ruthless as any of the others. I knew there would be a consequence for retrieving Lavinia, and I knew he would be the one to issue it. "That makes it twice now that one of you has broken into the Lucia mansion. The first time, I managed to smooth it over, but now?" He picks a piece of lint from his shoulder. "Well, obviously it's a step too far."

"She's our Duchess," I remind him. "You saw us win her. She's ours to claim."

He agrees, "She's yours to claim. She's also yours to forfeit, which is what you did."

"It's what *Nick* did," I correct, muscles tensing. "And he had no right. Remy and I were never consulted, and frankly, Lionel knew he was playing a risky game by not disclosing the arrangement made between him and Daniel."

He taps his finger against the arm of the chair, eyes narrowing. "This is a question of property."

"And Lavinia is ours."

Saul looks unimpressed with my quick reply. "So stamp your name on her ass, brand the Bruin into her cunt, fill her scrawny little belly with your cubs. But Lionel Lucia is a King. The importance of his property always supersedes yours. *Always.*" He sticks out two palms, weighing them. "And yet, here you are, continually trespassing on it."

He's got me there, but I don't regret rescuing Lavinia. Not after how I found her. "So what? You want me to grovel to him? Hand over a shipment of weapons? Suck his dick?"

Saul's easy expression turns to stone. "You'll go nowhere near him or his property ever again. Stay away from Lucia. This feud has gone far enough. We need his business, just like he needs ours." He spins the ring on his finger. "This is a fragile ecosystem, Simon, and you two have managed to rock it like an earthquake in the few weeks you've been here." His eyes meet mine. "I had my concerns about having the two of you in the tower at the same time, and so far you haven't proven me wrong. Lucia's calling for assembly, a Duke has gone absent, and for some reason, the Princes are missing a foot soldier. Blood kin, at that." His eyebrow raises in question, but he's not the only one trained in schooling his expression. I'm not saying a fucking word about what happened to Felix that night. "If you two continue on this destructive course, I'll have no choice but to take action."

Two? Not Remy? I can only assume he has an extra layer of protection that comes from having the last name Maddox.

"There won't be any more problems," I say, giving him a firm nod. "I have no further interest in the Counts, now that the Duchess is back home."

Home. Is that what it is for her? After years of living with a sadist, then being confined to shitty motel rooms and South Side's swankiest brothel, I find it hard to imagine this doesn't rank top spot. Then again, maybe a cage is a cage is a cage.

Saul lifts his chin, assessing me. "I wish I could say that your word is enough, Simon, but I have to make an example out of you. You see, things don't look good for us. To the casual observer, it might seem as though I don't have my own goddamn Kingdom in order. What do you think I should do about that?"

Eat shit.

I've always had a civil rapport with Saul, but the truth is, hearing him call West End his Kingdom makes something flare within me. It's not like he earned it. My Pops walked away and let him take it. Nick and I have more of a claim to West End than Saul ever has.

Wisely, I don't say any of this. "I don't know."

"Well, I do." Saul reaches into the interior pocket of his suit jacket and removes a small square of paper. He hands it over and I reluctantly reach out to take it.

8 Huff Street—11pm.

"What's this?" I ask. "A job?"

"A match. Tonight."

I frown at the address. We mostly fight at the gym, on our own turf. Anything outside of that and we lose control of the setting and crowd. It's risky. "But this is outside of Forsyth. I don't fight in open territory."

"Oh, you'll fight," he says, pinning me with a simmering glare. "And what's more, you're going to lose."

It takes a solid thirty-seconds for the words to process. "You want me to throw a fight." My stomach drops like a boulder. "You're going to bet against me."

He gives a slow, cold smirk. "Which is why you're going to lose unexpectedly, *believably*, crushing the hopes and dreams of every sucker who puts money on the easy odds. A windfall of that magnitude just might begin to compensate me for all the trouble you've caused with this Lucia situation." He stands and re-buttons his jacket, nodding at my closed bedroom door. "Oh, and the little Duchess you've got tucked away in your bed? Take her with you. She needs to understand that her father isn't the only King she should fear."

6

Sy

*T*AKE *the exit ramp and stay in the left lane...*

The GPS and the low hum of my Trans-Am are the only sounds as I drive past the boundary of Forsyth proper. It feels wrong going to a fight without Duke backup, let alone one in open territory, but it's nothing compared to the odd, twisted heat I get in my chest when I look over at Lavinia in the passenger seat.

It's too soon for her to be out in public. Although we've pumped her with fluids and as much food as she could handle, she was skinny even before Lionel starved her for four days. Dressed, she looks passable, but even the leggings look baggy on her narrow frame. That doesn't even go into the yellowing bruises hidden beneath the fabric. But her eyes are clear and present as she watches the passing scenery, face relaxed, no signs of the tension I know she must be feeling. Every now and then I see her in my periphery, tucking her hair behind her ears, redirecting the vent's heat, tracing a design into the fog covering her window.

She's been so fucking quiet the last four days, nothing like she used to be. It's odd to think there was a time I would have preferred her like this. Meek and soft and mechanical, the very opposite of disruptive. Now, I find myself wishing she'd snarl some smart-ass remark, show me that some pieces of her still remain and she's still willing to exercise them. At least then I'd know we're making some progress.

Maybe, once Nick comes back.

My knuckles grip the steering wheel and I slam my foot on the gas.

"He got you pretty good," she says, breaking the quiet.

I raise an eyebrow. "Who? Saul?" My jaw clenches at the idea of her thinking he's beat me. "Saul's not better than me." I don't know why, but for some reason, I need her to know that.

"No, the Archduke." She leans over and runs her fingers over the red scratches.

My muscles twitch at the sensation. I feel that same surge of heat that filled me when I woke up to her tucked against me this morning. "Arch*nemesis*. Evil little shit," I mutter. Looks have never been as deceiving as they are when it comes to that two-pound ball of viciousness. "How can something so small and vulnerable make someone bleed so much?"

The comparison with the girl next to me isn't lost.

I do a double-take at the weak smirk she's giving me.

"Is the big bad bear really bested by a kitten?"

"Hardly." My sneer doesn't have half the heat it should. Probably because she's still touching me. I shift, uncomfortable at the show of weakness, and her fingers slide away.

"Did you put ointment on them? You should. Cat scratches can easily get infected."

"It's fine," I say, listening to the GPS as it prompts me to the next turn. It's a dark road, with industrial buildings on both sides, but it's not completely isolated. Dozens of cars line the road. "It's not kitten scratches I'm worried about tonight."

She looks at me, shadows slowly passing over her face as I inch down the narrow road, looking for the right place. "Is this when you tell me what we're about to get into?"

I'd only told her that Saul was sending the two of us on a job. Not the specifics. She'd seemed worried enough about leaving the house—about whether or not I was going to make her get in the elevator again, about who would watch the Archfiend—that I didn't have the heart to tell her what I'd been directed to do.

Or maybe I just didn't have the ability to admit it to myself.

Fight to lose?

It goes against every cell of my being. I've never lost a fight. *Never.* Not even back in high school when fights were little more than ten cocky guys in a parking lot, sparring over something as petty as words. Not even when the stakes are low. Not even when the person I'm fighting is by all accounts bigger and better.

Saul couldn't have given me a harsher punishment than this.

Destination is on your right...

I ease the car to a stop and look up at the warehouse, perched on the shoulder of the narrow road. The thud of music is loud enough to vibrate through the car. There's a faded, rusty sign hanging over the door. Wilcox Enterprises.

"Sy?" Lavinia prompts. "I really need to know if we're about to get chainsaw-massacred in there or something. I love surprises as much as the next girl, but—"

I give her a look. "There is no possible way you like surprises." She holds my eye for a beat, her lips twisted as she tries to decide if she's going to argue that, but her expression is clear. It's time to come clean. "Saul sent me down here to fight." I sigh and lean back against the seat, gazing out at the building crowd. "More importantly, he sent me to lose."

"He wants you to lose?" Her eyebrows knit together, and then part. "Oh, this is your punishment for coming for me."

"That's the gist."

"He's ruining your win record, and your reputation." Listening to her say all the pieces aloud doesn't make me feel better. "And he sent you way out here, away from Forsyth, to make it even more believable. Everyone back home would know it if you threw a match."

I give her a tense, tight smile. "Seems like you're up to speed."

She pulls her knee up to her chest and peers up at the building. "Are you going to do it?"

"Fight?" I give a low, derisive scoff. "Of course. I'm not some little bitch who's scared of taking a few hits. I can handle whatever they throw at me."

"Should I roll down the window?" she asks, leveling me with a long look. "Is your ego going to take up all the air?" And there she is. Lavinia Lucia, the defiant, obstinate, self-destructive daughter of Royalty. Warmth spreads across my chest. It's surprisingly nice to see her back. She rolls her eyes. "We all know you're the biggest and baddest in all the land. But are you actually going to throw it?"

"Lavinia, I'm a soldier. Saul is my general." Shaking my head, I feel the pull of my ego being sucked back inward as I admit, "I didn't earn the position of Duke by not following directions."

She twists a lock of hair around her finger. "You came and got me."

"No one told me not to."

"So if..." Her features darken, and she shakes her head, adding, "Never mind." Her fingers hook in the door handle and pop it open. She steps out and stretches, back arching. I notice the wince, the pain still lingering from her days locked inside that chest. A moment later, she's curled back into herself.

"Look," I tell her, after grabbing my bag from the trunk, "we'll get in and out. Be back home before dawn."

She nods, but I see anxiety lurking in her eyes. The last week—only eight days since the Barons' Equinox party—has been a fucking tornado, and the last thing I want to do is take her somewhere that unravels all the work we've put into making her better. Suddenly this seems so stupid. So wrong. I stop in front of her, clutching the handle of the bag in my grip. "If this is too much for you, say the word and we're out of here. I can take whatever Saul throws at me and leave you out of it."

She tilts her head, searching my eyes. Whatever she finds there, a flash of indignation crosses her features. "Let's get one thing straight, Simon Perilini." She takes a step closer, craning her neck to glare at me. "You might have saved me, but I'm not some wilting Victorian damsel who needs to be babied. I've been through a lot worse than some stupid dick-measuring contest with fists. You didn't treat me like spun-glass before, and you're not about to now."

I raise my finger, twirling it. "Is this enough space for *your* ego?" If the words were meant to have any bite, then the relief I feel at the pure steel in her eyes knocks it away.

"I'm the Duchess," she insists, pulling herself to her full height. "I understand the parts of my position that don't include being a sex doll, so let me back you up, wrap your hands, and clean you up when it's over because *that* is something I'm actually willing to do." With an intensity I wouldn't think her capable of, she adds, "I've got this."

Still, I'm not really satisfied until I see the determination in her features is holding. There's a spark here, an energy returning to her eyes that I don't have it in me to snuff out. "If shit goes sideways, you come back to the car, call Remy, and leave." I reach for her hand, pressing the keys and my phone into her palm. At her decisive nod, I finally give in to the impulse that's been nagging at me since I climbed out of bed this morning. I slip an arm around her shoulders, tucking her against me. "And stay close. You're my ring girl tonight."

We enter through the backdoor, and I don't have to worry about Lavinia getting out of my reach. She sticks to my side like glue, her arm winding around my waist as we stride through the short hallway. Fluorescent lights hang overhead in rusty cages and the room we spill out into reeks of sweat and cheap beer. I check in with the trio of undesirables manning the front table, shouting my name over the loud bass. I'm met with a long, considering onceover from a guy with more facial hair than sapience, but he must be the guy running the match, because he nods me toward the back.

A flurry of chatter follows the two of us as we head to the ring. Lavinia presses closer but doesn't shrink away. Together, we watch as news of my appearance ripples across the crowd. One guy lets out a loud, "Oh, *fuck*, the Dukes are here?" But it's not just about me being a fist of Forsyth. An older man we pass turns to the person at his side and says, "That's Sy, the Perilini kid..."

Suddenly, the crowd is turning, a frantic energy building as they weave through the bodies.

I realize they're rushing the betting table.

"Shit." So does Lavinia. "They know who you are."

I give a tight nod because it's true. A win record like mine makes waves. No doubt this 'windfall' will be more than enough to appease Saul.

"Sy Perilini?" a guy in a tracksuit asks. Gold glints from his teeth, ears, neck and fingers.

"That's me."

"Thought you weren't going to make it," he says, eyes flicking over to Lavinia. I tighten my hold on her. "You're up next. You can wait over there." He jerks his chin toward a low bench behind the ring. The gym back home makes this place look like a rickety, open shack. No locker room. No showers. No privacy.

When the next fight starts, drawing the eyes of the crowd away from us, I make it a point to observe the structure, get a feel for how tightly this thing is organized. Back home, the rules are loose but generally work in our favor. What's a little mayhem among enemies, after all?

This doesn't look much different. Slowly, like a battery being recharged, the crowd, the smell, the sound of skin pounding into skin, energizes me. I drop the bag and unzip it, tossing the tape to Lavinia. She catches it, seeming more alert than she has since I got her back. The smolder of light flickers in the shrewdness of her eyes.

"All good?" I ask her, but I know the answer.

She pulls off a long strip of tape, cutting it with her teeth. "Never better."

It's the first time we've really done this process together. Usually, it's Haley. Maybe Verity. Already I sense that Lavinia's process is different. She's diligent, quick, not lingering over form, only function. Her fingers graze over the cat scratches, soft but firm, sending a wave of heat rushing from my belly down between my legs. My cock kicks back to life, so I guess the four-day reprieve on self-control has expired.

Not now, I beg my body, but I know it's useless.

If she notices, she keeps it to herself, winding the tape around my knuckles, and then securing the end. She's quiet, eyes cast down, fussing with the tape. I reach out and tip her chin upward, and I can tell myself it's just to make sure she's still here—still full of steel and resolve—but it's a lie. My gaze zeroes in on her mouth like a laser, and without really wanting to, I find myself wondering what it'd be like to push my lips against hers. Waking up with her skin pressed to mine this morning has burrowed into my psyche, flooding me with thoughts of flesh and heat.

Slam!

"Fuck," the guy who crashed into us says, giving us a stoner's grin. Beer sloshes all over our feet. "Sorry about that, bro. Look alive!"

The tension snaps and my hands ball into tight fists, the tape cutting off circulation. The stoner cowers, suddenly aware that he tangled with the wrong bear.

"Hey." Firm hands land on my chest. "Save that rage for the ring."

I move my gaze to hers, nostrils flaring. "Right." I jerk my chin at him. "Get the fuck out of here."

He scrambles, leaving the two of us together. The moment is lost—thankfully. Everything about the last week has sent me off kilter. Having Lavinia Lucia as a pet project is one thing. Becoming a slave to the throb in my balls after years of careful self-control is something else.

The fight before ours ends with the clang of the bell.

"Ready?" she asks, grabbing the bag and stuffing the tape inside.

"Are you?" I ask, knowing that this isn't just overwhelming. It's new.

She pauses for a moment, as if she's considering it, and then pushes two of the purple elastic bands off her wrist. Quickly, she separates her hair, taking a bunch on each side, creating two sweet but sexy pigtails. When she's finished, she strips off the oversized hoodie she's been wearing and reveals a black tank top. My eyes go right to her nipples, which harden the instant the cooler air hits her skin. The bruises are distraction enough, but when she pulls her shoulders back and lifts her chin, she owns them, looking every inch the Duchess we've claimed her as.

Without a word, she slips back under my arm, fingers toying with the waist of my sweats. Up ahead, the loser of the prior fight is half-conscious and being carried out of the ring by two of his friends. When I'm given the go ahead by the ref, I climb through the ropes and then bend, gripping her around the waist and hoisting her up.

Across the ring, my opponent enters, ducking through the ropes. His eye is sporting a large, tender-looking bruise, new enough that it's clear he's already had a fight tonight. In one quick survey, I see that he's right-handed but favors his left side. The sole of his shoes are worn at the heel and there's a long scar over his knee. As I catalog his weaknesses, fire builds in my chest. It's the competitive spirit I was born with. It's woven in my skin, spiked in my blood, and Lavinia was right to tell me to save it. Not just my rage, but the cravings festering below my muscles, driving my blood to a fast, hot thrum.

I pull off my shirt, revealing my upper body. The crowd reacts. They should. I'm two hundred and twenty pounds of cut perfection. Hooking my thumbs in my sweats, I drop my sweatpants and a different, softer rumble passes through the crowd. Lavinia's eyes dart down and that familiar shame burns through the tips of my ears, but she doesn't give me time to dwell on it.

"Lean down," she mouths.

My eyebrows furrow.

"For luck, remember?" Her hand flattens on my chest and runs upward, until it's cupped around my neck. When I obey, she curls forward to press a kiss to the pulse point on my neck, lips brushing the overheated skin. The zing of electricity jolts between us, and I touch her jaw, because I'm on the knife's edge of reason here. Fighting, fucking—the two impulses are difficult enough to untangle when her lips *aren't* on me.

She pulls back, sending me a grin that somehow manages to look both sweet and depraved. "Fuck him up."

~

THE CROWD CHEERS, feet stomping, bells ringing. Or maybe that's my ears? Blood drips into my eye, but I can still see my opponent, lying flat on his back, eyes glazed. The final blow was a classic uppercut. He tried to fake me out, mis-stepped and left himself wide open.

Someone grabs my wrist and pulls it into the air, declaring me the victor. "The Fist of Forsyth wins again!"

"You did it!" I hear, and spin. There she is, all compact body and wide, shocked eyes. "Holy shit, you did it."

"I did." There's a moment where the dread hits me, but it abates just as quickly. The truth is that I never even considered throwing the fight. It's not in me. From the first swing, all the answers came to me. It was as if the clouds parted inside my brain, leaving me with the perfect solution, and I knew right then I was going to win. I don't even have the capacity to feel bad about it. Winning is never bad. Winning is what I do. I'm so deep in this primal mindset that a part of me is certain no one could blame me. Not when I hear the spectators chanting my name, someone shoving an envelope of cash in my hands. Not when I shakily pull my sweatshirt over my head, only absentmindedly accepting Lavinia's rush to help.

"Saul's going to shit a brick," she says when we get outside. The night is warm, loud, and too dark to make out much more than the wide, scared set of her eyes. "What if he—"

"He's not going to send you back." High on the victory, this feels like a promise I can keep. I give the envelope a solid tap against my palm. "I'll give him this and Remy can throw in a fat stack. It just occurred to me. If he wants compensation for his troubles, then what's the difference, right? Money's nothing."

The frown doesn't disappear. "Compensation? Sy, look—"

"Relax." I pull her against me, blinking the sweat from my eyelashes, and I don't even try to tamp down my wide, wolfish grin. "To the victor go the spoils."

Her mouth pinches. "Either winning a fight turns you into a cocky optimist, or you're seriously concussed." She leads me to the car, because I'm not concussed, but I'm undeniably a bit wobbly. The other guy definitely got in a few good shots. My ears are still ringing and there's a twinge in my bicep. I don't feel bad, though. I feel like everything is finally slotting together. Lavinia is better. Remy is acting like himself. Nick is going to come back, and we're going to be good. All of us.

I actually feel pretty fucking awesome.

If I'd had my wits about me, and if I hadn't been so goddamn smug, I'd probably hear the crunch of gravel, and if I weren't so distracted by the clean scent wafting off Lavinia's pretty hair, I might see the shadows shifting between the cars. And if I hadn't spent days trying to keep the monster in my pants under control, then maybe—just maybe—I wouldn't react so slowly, just a second too late.

Or that's what I tell myself when the first hit slams across my back.

7

Lavinia

I DON'T SCREAM—NOT soon enough to warn him.

On edge all night, I notice the shifting shadows, the crunch of gravel, the way the air moves strangely, in that certain sort of way that makes someone aware they're not alone. I'll regret it later. I'll look back on the way I just dumbly stand here as the hooded man swings the bat, slamming it right into Sy's spine, and I'll feel like a fucking idiot.

Now, I scream. "Sy!"

Just as Sy swings out to snatch the bat from the other guy, a second man, taller and thicker, darts out from around a truck, grabbing Sy from behind and pinning his arms at his sides. The tall guy holds him there as the other one raises the bat again, and if I have any lofty notions about intervening, they're instantly snatched away.

A third one appears from out of nowhere, shoving me effortlessly to the ground, my chest slamming onto the gravel.

The fall rattles my teeth, but before I can do much more than cry out, the attacker's knee is pressing hard between my shoulder blades. "Get off me!" I snarl, bucking against his weight.

"Relax, sunshine," the man says, leaning into the weight of his knee as he plants a palm on the back of my head, mashing my face into the ground. "This won't take long."

It says something that my surge of blinding panic isn't even about the scuffle happening a few feet from me. It's not the sound of Sy's harsh, pained grunts or bone meeting flesh. It's not about the speed with which it all happens, the flurry of movements, the loud, clipped breaths. It's not even that I see Sy fall, tumbling to the ground like a limp sack of meat—just like Felix had when Nick shot him.

Mostly the panic is about my not being able to move.

The knee in my back presses down, wringing the air from my lungs, and one of the other guys kicks out, planting his boot into Sy's abdomen. I know he's not dead when Sy's hand shoots out to grab the guy's ankle, sweeping him off his feet with a powerful jerk. The hooded one is quick to retaliate, and in the melee of the struggle, I see Sy rising up on his knees, swinging wildly, blindly, *recklessly*. It's nothing like the deliberate strategizing I'd seen in the ring back there. This isn't a man fighting for the win. This is a man fighting for the *kill*, so crazed that when I get a flash of his face, he's got his lips pulled back, teeth bared into an animalistic expression.

Something about it spurs me into motion. I'm not in the chest. I keep telling myself that. These are men, muscle and meat, vulnerable in their own ways, and I'm not Lavinia Lucia. Not here. Not when I'm with Sy.

Right now, I'm the Duchess.

And I brought a weapon.

I wiggle my arm, trapped beneath my body, until I can just get two fingers into my waistband. The fixed-blade knife I swiped from under Nick's pillow is hard and warm from my own body heat, and

I can feel as I inch it free that my weight is holding the leather sheath in place. I rock to the side just as Sy stumbles to his feet, swaying, to slam his head into the hooded man's nose. There's a sharp howl, and then a loud curse, and Sy is dropping to his knees once more, unsteady.

The hooded man is between us—me and Sy—and he has the bat again. He lifts it, planting his feet wide, and I get a good, hard look at his leg. Jeans. White socks. Worn trainers.

Soft spots.

I strike out with lightning speed, and it's hard. They don't tell you that—that stabbing someone actually takes some brute strength—and my muscles have weakened from eight days of lying down, doing nothing. The power with which I bury the blade into his Achilles tendon is driven by little more than optimism and pure spite.

I wrench the knife back, feeling the sickening drag of bone and flesh.

The bat suddenly clatters to the ground.

"Ah! Fuck!"

The hooded man spins and stumbles, reaching for his ankle as he crashes to the ground. It all happens very fast. The guy pressing me into the asphalt spits a curse and dives for the knife, but I stab it upward, plunging it into his forearm, and he jolts back.

As soon as the weight leaves, I scramble forward to Sy's bag, my knees stinging against the pavement. The hooded guy is still howling in pain, blood gushing. I'm not sure where I find the strength or the momentum, but I manage to get the bag unzipped, find the gun he's brought, and roll myself between him and the attackers before the man with the injured forearm even gets to his feet.

I raise the pistol, cocking the hammer.

"Don't!" I warn when one of them reaches for the bat. He freezes, flinching back, and my heels slip against the pavement as I push myself closer to Sy, who's fallen prone to the ground. "I've had a shitty week and will gladly kill every last one of you fuckers."

They must see the truth in my eyes, or recognize me for who I am, a Lucia, because I see the wariness cross their faces.

They retreat slowly, the shorter one who'd held me down fleeing first. Another guy—the one who'd come with the bat—is barely standing on his injured foot, fists curling. "Fuck this bitch," he mutters to the tall one. The words are pushed through gritted teeth. "The message has been sent. Dukes follow their King. *Or else.*"

He hobbles away between the cars, and then the last one follows, not taking his eyes off my gun until he ducks behind an old van.

Still, I wait, gun raised, eyes vigilantly scanning the shadows for any signs of their return. The moment I'm sure they're gone, I whip around to check on Sy. I tuck the gun into my pants before grabbing his face, pulse racing with adrenaline.

"Hey, hey," I rush out, giving his cheek a small pat. "Look at me. You with me?"

He doesn't *look* 'with me'. His eyelids flutter, but he doesn't meet my gaze, rolling slowly to his hands and knees. The movements are stilted and look painful, and he shrugs me off when I try to help him. It takes him three tries to get his feet underneath him, but then he almost tips back over and it doesn't matter that he doesn't want my help. I duck under his arm, winding it around my neck.

"Come on," I coax, turning him toward the car. "We need to get out of here, in case they come back."

Luckily, he drags his feet clumsily along with my steps, and thank god, because there's no fucking way I could carry Sy to the car on my own. Even if I hadn't just spent four days locked in the box, dehydrated, and malnourished, he's just too big. Halfway there, his weight starts to grow heavier, and there's a strange rattle in his exhale that doesn't make me feel good at all.

"Just get to the car," I tell him, bearing as much of his weight as I can. "Then you can rest."

He mumbles something, but all that comes out is a thick stream of blood and saliva. Jesus Christ. Why didn't he throw that fight?

Because you didn't want him to?

Because he's a stubborn Duke who's obsessed with winning?

None of it matters now. He's hurt and barely conscious. As we lurch across the parking lot, his set of keys burns a hole in my pocket. Two weeks ago, I would've taken the opportunity to hop in the car and drive as far as I could away from Forsyth before they tracked me down. But a lot of shit happened in the last two weeks, and this asshole...

He once tried to sell me for a goddamn pocket watch. He's made it very clear that I'm not worth more than the scum on the bottom of his shoe. His hatred isn't like the others'. It was never about me being a daughter of North Side. It was never about my name or my pedigree. It wasn't rivalry that drove him to treat me like that. It was just *him*. Some primal part of Sy just despises me for what I am.

And he saved me.

Sy risked everything to pull me out of that dark, rancid place, and then he spent days making me strong again, and here's the real kicker. He hasn't expected anything in return. He hasn't acted on the hardness in his pants or the tension in his muscles. He's had me near to him, unable to fight back, vulnerable to any manner of vicious words. But nothing.

And now, after all of that, he's paying a price. The reason he's been beaten to a bloody pulp is the consequence of that selflessness, and it isn't fair.

It isn't fucking fair.

"Just a few more steps, big bear, and we'll figure this out." We get to the car, and I prop him against it, ignoring my body's own twinges and aches. I manage to get the door open and together we navigate him inside. He slumps in the seat, one leg hanging out, and I bend down to heave it inside the footwell, cramming him in and slamming the door before he topples out.

I catch my breath, but I don't linger. Pulling out Sy's phone, I tap Remy's number and hope like hell he doesn't have his music blaring. It rings and rings, eventually going to a voicemail recording that informs me, "*This inbox is full.*"

My shoulders fall.

Shit.

I scroll down to the next contact and hover there, my heart rising like a brick into my throat. He'd come if I called him—that much I know. But no matter how long I stand there staring at the name on the screen—*Nicky*—I can't do it. I can't face him. Not yet. Maybe not ever.

There are his mom and dads, and Mama B, but I write them off instantly. I learned long ago not to trust parents. There's Verity, but I don't see her being equipped to deal with this. There are also a slew of nicknames I assume belong to the guys in the frat. But the thought of calling any of the DKS boys right now makes me uneasy, as if I need to shield Sy from being seen like this to his lessers.

I do a quick search for the only person I know who could possibly understand what I've been through, and then I press the phone number in.

The other end picks up and loud music pulses in the background. "Hello?"

I sink back against the car with relief, words surging out of me in a rush. "Where can I hide out for a few days away from the Counts and Dukes?"

"...CAN'T fucking believe I'm doing this," I say, skin crawling as I peer up at the building in front of us. In my periphery, I see Sy's head slump forward, and I whip around to catch him. "Hey!" I snap, shaking his shoulder. "No sleeping."

He rouses and squints at me, then out the window. Sluggishly, he speaks. "Where are we?"

"Somewhere safe—" I grimace at the junkie leaning against the wall, "—ish."

Auggy had answered the phone when I called the Hideaway. She didn't ask any questions when I told her I needed a place to lie low for a few days. Something in her voice told me she knew more about my situation than I anticipated. She just shot me the address and told me someone would meet me there.

I didn't realize the location was the same shitty motel Daniel Payne had me held captive in before locking me in the Hideaway basement. We're deep in Lord territory. Sy would kill me if he was coherent. But I'd asked for a place to hide from both the Dukes and Counts, and this checks all the boxes.

"Goddammit." I never wanted to come back here. If it were up to me, this shithole would have been torched instead of Daniel's sterile, up-town office building. It doesn't seem fair that the Crane Motor Inn is still standing, but then again, nothing is.

Fair, that is.

I climb out of the car, grabbing Sy's bag on the way out, which is when I see the figure coming down the motel stairs. When the silhouette's face hits the streetlight, I freeze, caught halfway between wrenching Sy's door open and juggling his bag.

Moronically, I ask, "She sent *you*?"

"Come on," Story says, jerking her chin toward Sy's hunched over body. "Let's get him inside."

Still, I take a step back, trying to figure out why on earth Auggy would send the Lords' Lady of all people to help me. "Look, I appreciate the gesture and all, but this is the result of some nasty beef and I'm not sure the Lords want to get involved."

She laughs, her dark hair sleek and shiny in the moonlight. "One of your Dukes has been shacked up at the Hideaway for four days. We're already involved." She moves around me to open the passenger-side door. "But that's not why I'm here. Auggy told me you needed help and... well, I wanted to. Help that is." She tucks her hair behind her ear, revealing a black leather cuff with a gold skull. "I owe you one, don't I?"

I raise an eyebrow, trying to figure out how I'd done something to earn favor with another Royal. I don't know much about how the Royal women navigate one another since my mother died when I was young, but I'm well aware they aren't known for comradery and support.

I'm not in the position to quibble.

It's easier for the two of us to get him up the motel stairs than alone, and I'm relieved to see Story already has a key. The room is two floors up. I brace myself for the scent of mildew and must when she opens the door and I'm not disappointed. The room is identical to the one I'd been kept in, although there's no water stain on the ceiling, and the antenna isn't broken on the TV. *Yet.* Probably, no one else would notice the difference between these rooms, but me? I know my old room just as well as my own skin. I know its scars and marks with an intimacy that would drive a weaker person to madness.

I don't give myself time to dwell on the swell of misery that fills me just being here. "Bed," I grunt, ready to off Sy's weight. We drop him on the mattress and it shudders a creak. "Grab that side of him, will you?" Gesturing to his arm, I remove the zip-up he'd put on after the fight. "I need to see how bad the bruising is on his stomach and ribs."

What we reveal is his warm brown skin, mottled with dark blooms already spreading over most of his upper body. Story mutters a low curse when she sees the damage, but I'm not surprised. I saw the blows he took from the bat, the kicks, the absolute beatdown.

"Counts?" she asks, glancing up from a particularly gnarly welt.

My mouth thins. "Saul."

She snaps upright, jaw dropping. "His own King? Seriously?" At my nod, she adds, "Motherfucker."

"That sums it up."

Silently, we get to work, grabbing all the towels in the bathroom and wetting them in the rusty sink. Grabbing the First-Aid kit from his duffle bag, I carefully begin cleaning the crusting blood from his face, doing my best to avoid the clotting splits in his skin. The one on the bridge of his nose is particularly bad, and although it doesn't feel broken, it's definitely going to need a few stitches. Fortunately, when I pull his eyelids back, I don't see any major damage to his eyes—as blue and gorgeous as always—just the swelling beneath them. It makes me hopeful that we can make it out of this without any major damage.

"Are you okay here for a minute?" Story asks after bringing me the rinsed cloth.

I pause to give her a quick once over, wondering if all the blood and gore are too much for her to take. Stupid, though. She's the Queen of South Side. Chances are, she's seen a lot worse. "I've got this," I tell her, making sure she sees the significance in my eyes.

If someone's going to take care of Sy, it's going to be me.

You heal me, I heal you.

"I get it." Story gives me a small smile. "I'll be right back."

The door clicks behind her, and I leave a cool, folded up cloth over the jut of his cheekbone, split from a nasty hit. I pick through the First-Aid kit for the right supplies. Pulling off the adhesive for a butterfly bandage, lining up the pieces, cinching the cut together. His breathing levels off, and he dozes while I work. Somewhere in the middle of this, the adrenaline slowly waning, I pause, fingers skating down his jaw. It occurs to me that I've never taken the time to look at him, always too busy trying to scheme and survive and *avoid* to bother measuring him up as a person—as a *man*. Now, without his hard, angry gaze staring back, it's almost too easy to let my eyes wander.

Even these last few days, while he's been caring for me at the tower, he hasn't slowed. He brings me food, water, books—hell, even Archie, despite Sy hating him. He manages to both keep his distance and hover over me. But now that we're alone, and he's incapacitated, I take a moment to study his body.

His cheekbones are sharp, cut high like his brother's. His eyelashes are long and thick. His lips are dark pink, one side swollen and puffy. I press my fingertips to them, feeling the pulsing heat, and I get lost inside a question that's suddenly crucial.

Why is he so nice to me all of a sudden? Is it because Remy thinks I'm important? Is it because he found me in such a pitiful state that it'd be too easy—no challenge at all—to hurt me more?

I draw away, using my hands to feel his ribs, searching for

cracks or breaks like I'd read in one of the books from the library. I travel down his abdomen, taking time to check every inch, criss-crossing his hip bones, feeling hard muscle, but nothing out of place.

His body really is pristine. I let my palms linger over him, the perfect form of an athlete, toned from years of diligent training, solid and sure. The lower my hands get, the lower my eyes descend, until my gaze becomes glued to the ever-present bulge between his legs, hidden beneath his sweats. I've had that cock in mouth, forcefully driven, in a moment of rage. I've felt it sliding between my ass cheeks inside his parents' basement, rutting against me as I fought through a panic attack. I've even experienced it willingly, grinding against him in a candlelit forest, in a disastrously successful attempt at making his brother jealous.

But I've never just... looked at it. I've never examined this *thing* that causes him such strife. Nick said he's still a virgin, and that explains a lot. A girl would be mad to willingly let him push this monster inside her body. Most guys in Forsyth would use their dicks as a weapon if they were packing this much heat, but strangely, Sy never has. He's taken his pleasure from me, sure. But it's never really been about the hurt of it, the pursuit of possession. He did those things in spite of his size, not because of it. I see that now.

Even covered by his sweats and flaccid, the outline of his dick is obscenely obvious. Thick and settled next to his leg, stretching down his inner thigh. I dart a glance at his face, suddenly nervous that he's seeing me check him out, because he'd get the wrong idea. My curiosity isn't sexual. I don't want to fuck that beast. I just want to know the full extent of it.

Luckily, his eyes are closed, his breathing still even.

I tentatively rest my hand below his hip bone, inching down. Spreading my fingers wide, I graze the outer part of his shaft—

"Okay, babe, talk to you later." The door swings open and Story walks in. I jump back, reaching for his hand and fumbling for the ointment. Wryly, she explains, "Dimitri has an assignment due later this week and he just won't do anything if I'm not standing ove—" She pauses, and I stare back. Her eyes dart between me and Sy. "Everything okay?"

"Yeah, just trying to get this," my cheeks burn as I tear the package open with my teeth, "ointment open." The paper gives and the creamy white gel oozes out. I swipe it across his knuckles, fresh scrapes over the old scratches Archie gave him. Some are from the attack. Others are from the fight before.

She bends and tugs up the leg of her jeans. Before I can figure out what she's doing, she pulls out a gun from her boot. "You got a weapon?" she asks.

I tap my hip, the place where Sy's gun is still tucked against my skin. I don't mention the knife. She's a Lady, after all.

"Good." She checks the chamber of hers and walks over to the window, pushing back the curtain to peer around the iron bars.

"Yeah, that doesn't open," I tell her, eyes narrowed on the gun. Chances are she got it from her Lords, and chances are *they* got it from the Dukes. It doesn't settle the unease in my chest.

"Dimitri sent someone we trust to watch the street." She lifts her chin at someone below. "If Perez or Saul try to make a move, we'll be ready."

I stand, putting some distance between me and Sy, and face Story. "You don't need to stay," I tell her. "I think we'll be okay."

"I'm not leaving until I'm sure none of those assholes followed you." She looks over at Sy, jerking her chin. "And until he's out of the woods."

Carefully, I assess her. "Why are you helping us?"

"He saved you, right? When Pretty Nick sold you out." Her jaw tightens and she looks away. "That's the word on the street anyway. Everyone's saying Sy went in and got you back."

Nodding, I move my gaze to his sleeping form, voice flat. "It's why he got jumped tonight."

Her brown eyes fall on him, and for a moment, it seems as though they hold a hundred questions. She doesn't voice them, her words emerging resolute. "Then he's worth protecting." Her shoulders bounce with a little laugh and she raises her phone, giving it a wave. "So long as I check in. It wasn't easy to convince my guys."

I eye her phone. "They don't have a tracker on you?"

"Oh, they do." She lifts her hair and presses her finger against a spot of skin below her ear. I know the location well. "We fought about it at first, but it makes them feel better—and allows me more freedom."

"You call being tagged like a pet 'freedom'?" I cut my eyes toward Sy. His eyes might still be closed, but I know it's possible he can hear me. I don't care.

"I call that being a King's Queen. It's a position I agreed to." Her mouth sets and she averts her eyes, tucking the phone back into her pocket. "And from what Killian has told me, I now understand that you didn't." She looks at me through her lashes, something resolute settling over her features. "That's the apology I owe you, Lavinia. When I met you at the Baron's party, I was under the impression things were different. I asked for this life, and despite the picture that was painted for me, I realize now that you didn't have that choice."

I shake my head, giving a quiet, bitter laugh. "You don't know the half of it." But her words give me pause. "What picture was painted exactly?"

Sighing, she moves to the chair beside the bed, dropping heavily into it. "Daniel and the Kings were planning to take me—groom me—as their little toy virgin." The grimace on her face is severe. "But I ran away, and when I came back a couple years later," she gestures to me, "there you were. A new 'asset'. And I guess I felt responsible, like—"

"Like I was your replacement."

She nods, suddenly looking very tired. "I felt like you were there because of me." She raises her eyes to mine. "Because I ran away. Because I was a coward." Her fingers fidget with the worn arm of the chair. "I think my Lords just didn't want me to feel like that. So when they told me about you, and the plan to get you out, they pretty obviously... embellished some things."

My eyes narrow. "Like what?"

"Like Nick loving you," she answers bluntly. "Or that he protected you, and wanted to free you, help you, be with you." She lifts a shoulder, shrugging weakly. "They just made it sound so..." Here, her face scrunches guiltily. "Romantic?"

"For someone who wants to believe it," I say, scoffing, "that's a nice story."

"Yea, I'm good at those." Her mouth slants deprecatingly. "And then I heard about the break-in at the Hideaway, and the old Dukes doing those things to you."

It's an effort to keep my scoff silent. I guess she still only knows half of the story if she still doesn't realize it wasn't the old Dukes who broke in.

It was the new Dukes.

Her eyes well with tears that make my stomach squirm uncomfortably. "Killian just made it all sound so perfect—letting Pretty Nick win you. Protect you. I thought we were saving you, Lavinia, but really, we were just handing you to a complete asshole." There's a plea in her gaze that's so earnest, I find myself unable to hold it. "I didn't know. I'm sorry."

I spend a long moment in complete stillness, staring down at Sy. The damage to his body looks brutal, but bruises will fade. Cuts will heal. "That sounds like a nice story," I repeat, raising my gaze to hers. "Are you ready to hear the truth?"

Her face morphs into something calm and determined, and when she leans forward, I think I see it in her eyes. The hardness that makes her a Queen. The steel that gives her courage.

"Tell me."

~

THREE HOURS LATER, there's a knock on the door.

"Sweetheart?" Tristian Mercer enters the shitty motel room looking like a runway model who got lost on the way to a show.

None of us look as incongruous with the surroundings as he

does with his impeccable hair and tidy clothes. His eyes flash in relief when they land on Story, but he watches Sy carefully as he kisses her on the cheek, grazing the cuff on her wrist with his fingertips. When Sy doesn't move, still dead to the world, Tristian's shoulders relax.

He holds up a bag. "A cheeseburger *and* fries," he says, voice dripping with disdain. "But since I was hoping that request might be a hallucination, I added a salad and a kale smoothie."

"Don't worry, Tris, it's not for me." Story grins and hands me the greasy bag. "Lavinia needs some meat on her bones and I don't think greens are going to do the trick. Don't," she warns, thrusting a finger at him, "start."

For the first time in a week, I find the smell of food doesn't turn my stomach upside down. I sit at the crappy, circular table in the corner and immediately dig in, unwrapping the burger and biting into it with a gusto I'm not expecting to feel. Story and I have been talking for hours, and I think she's sensed that the adrenaline crash has been a real bitch. Days of nothing but brothy soup was destined to make me ravenous at some point.

"Yeah, you mentioned that." Tristian reaches into his jacket pocket and pulls out three pill bottles and a fancy glass jar. Turning to me, he sets them down on the table, tapping the top of one of the bottles. "This will help with your immune system and the other one is for muscle repair." He slides over the jar and the third pill bottle. "These are for your boy over there, courtesy of Rath and me."

The pills are painkillers that I know from my experience with the Counts pack a hell of a punch. Reluctantly, I open the jar to find an odd, sticky brown substance inside. The label brightly declares 'natural honey.'

"Manuka honey," he explains, dipping his chin toward the jar. "It's good for wounds. Nature's antibiotic. Just make sure the wounds are dry before putting it on."

I stare at the strange, handsome man who may be the heir to the only fortune comparable to Remy's father. I knew a lot about

Royal men even before I began shacking up with them, and this whole experience of being Duchess has only bolstered what I've always known to be true. With them, nothing is ever free. "You're helping us out? Why?"

He shrugs, but his eyes dart to Story's, and even though he falters, I think I know what he wants to say. Or maybe it's just what I need to hear. Would the Lords do anything for their Lady, even if that means giving asylum, food, and *supplements* to a rival house?

He slides his hand around Story's back and pulls her against his side. "One of Daniel's unexpected legacies was giving us an unprecedented alliance with the Dukes. Two of your men are currently out of commission. It's not good for us if West End is weak. Patch him up and get him back on his feet."

Maybe there's a strategy to this after all.

"Well, thanks for the food," I say with a mouthful of hamburger. "You should probably go before he wakes up. I suspect seeing you here would just undo all the healing."

"You're probably right." He bends down to press a slow kiss to Story's mouth, licking at her lips until she parts them. I chew on my food and watch the way he palms her ass, getting a vivid memory of Nick doing the same as we walked into Friday Night Fury. The kiss goes on and on, and I get the feeling he wants me to watch, so that's what I do. I chew and I watch him devour her much like I'm doing to this delicious hamburger.

Story is the one to push him away, looking dazed and flustered. "Really?" she says, voice dry. "Time and place, Tris."

He licks his lip, sending me a smirk. "Good luck, Duchess. Don't keep my girl tied up too long. Killer's already halfway to busting in here himself."

Story rolls her eyes and shoes him out. Once he leaves and the door is locked, I sigh and broach the conversation I've been avoiding.

"So Nick is at the Hideaway."

Every bit of softness and mirth drops from her expression. "He showed up five days ago looking like he got jumped in a back alley."

There's no mistaking the small smirk on her mouth. "Auggy and Mrs. Crane tried to kick him out, which he didn't handle well. Killian had to intervene."

I think of the yellowing bruise I noticed on Remy's face. I knew something went down while I was out of it, but it must've been worse than I thought if he went running back to South Side.

"Why didn't he just toss his ass out on the street?" Or better, bury a bullet in his head and put us all out of our misery.

"You heard Tris. There's a bigger game at play. Chess pieces are all over the board and they're not ready to make any sacrifices." She sits across from me and stabs her straw on the table, unsheathing the plastic. She spears it into the green smoothie. "Killian is trying to do things differently than his father. It's not easy, and it definitely won't be fast, but he wants to be his own King."

I eat a fry and lick the salt off my fingers. "So I guess it'd be a bad idea if I slit Nick's throat?"

"Probably." She snorts. "If it were one of the others, I'd be the first to hand you a knife." Sighing deeply, she levels me with a significant look. "But Nick is a Bruin, and Forsyth loves its blood legacies."

My eyes tighten. "Not always."

Wincing, she tucks her hands into her lap. "God, I'm sorry. You're right. It must be different for daughters."

I think of my sister, a flash of memory from that dream of her on the swing set, and I want to tell Story that it's not different for all of us. Some daughters get doted on and protected, while others...

But that wouldn't quite be true.

Leticia was groomed to be an heiress, with all the privilege that entailed. But it had pitfalls a son would never have to endure. "Well, Forsyth loves its sexism most of all."

Story nods. "No doubt that taking out a *male* legacy will upset the ecosystem." There's a beat of tense silence where I'm pretty sure my appetite has disappeared, but then Story straightens. "But that doesn't mean you have to forgive him." She sips at her drink, looking suspiciously sunny all of a sudden. "And you certainly don't have to forget."

Sluggishly, I wonder, "What does that mean?"

She shrugs, eyes darting over to where Sy is sleeping. *Hopefully* sleeping. I get the gesture. Talking about Nick like this in front of his brother is dangerous for an outsider. "These aren't functional men we're dealing with, Lavinia. They may be handsome, but they've been trained in a violent, restrictive, misogynistic world. They're raised to be gods and everyone around them is put here to spread their legs or do their bidding." She leans forward, arms crossed on the table. "Except us."

I shake my head. "That may be how it is in the Lords' house, but not with the Dukes. I know for a fact I'm expected to spread my legs."

"I've heard other Royals speak, you know. All that stuff about Royal women needing a firm hand to keep her in line?" She reaches out to tap the gun I put on the table. "They're the ones who need a firm hand. Someone strong—strong enough to take what they dish out and return it threefold. Someone who can take their tantrums and petty outbursts." Smiling, she props her chin on her hand, looking strangely innocent for someone I know for a fact is willing to pull a trigger. "Sometimes that means bowing, but sometimes that means striking back."

I arch an eyebrow skeptically. "You did that?"

"I did some... pretty drastic things." She plays with the straw. "Things that quickly escalated and got bloody, violent. I'm not saying I'm proud, but I also can't regret it. Sure, there were a few fires, but once the dust settled and we all rose from the ashes, there was a new respect there." She carefully regards her smoothie, a pensive line in her brow. "It's their language, Lavinia, and you have to speak it before they can learn yours."

"You're different." I point to the food Tristian Mercer brought over as a pretext to lay eyes on his Lady. "The three of them fucking worship you."

"They really do." Her phone buzzes with a text, as if proving the point. "The difference is that my Lords are pillagers. They steal, claim, and possess. Your Dukes..." She looks over at Sy, still handsome despite the swollen bruises and cuts. "They're fighters. *Protectors.* If you want to survive this, you're going to have to give them a chance to be who they are. Maybe they need to lose before they realize there's something to win." She stands, grabbing her smoothie and her bag.

"You're leaving?" Truthfully, I wasn't comfortable with her being here in the first place, but now I find myself dreading the thought of being alone in this place.

It's 3am.

It's the quietest it gets here.

She gives me an apologetic look and heads to the door. "I've had more than one run-in with Pretty Nick Bruin, and I know he imprinted on you at some point along the way. You have more control in this situation than you realize, but to grasp it, you're going to have to work with them instead of against them."

I stand, tossing my wrapper on the table. "Thanks," I say, cheeks heating awkwardly as I gesture to Sy. "For helping me out, and everything. And tell Auggy and Mrs. Crane, too, would you?"

"I will." She gives me a tight smile and a moment later she's gone, the door locked. This time, though, it's locked from the inside.

I'm not a prisoner.

That idea is probably the hardest to shake.

8

Remy

THE FIRST TIME I came to the Velvet Hideaway was six months ago. I was with Sy. We'd come to speak to Killian Payne about settling our debt for letting Nick off the hook for Daniel's murder. That negotiation would later result in three of Killian's tattoos, a single letter on Tristian Mercer's chest, and the daisy on his Lady's wrist.

Sy felt bad about it at the time. He knows how I am about tattooing people—can't just be anyone or any old design. But the cost seemed worth it. Even if I were doing some shit design on some shit person, it was the price of getting Nick back, which made those tattoos important, sacred in ways the people wearing them couldn't even begin to grasp. It was good enough for me.

The second time I came to the Velvet Hideaway, I was blitzed out of my mind, breaking into the basement to defile their asset.

I didn't like the Hideaway either of those times, and I don't like it now.

Cutting my bike, I narrow my eyes at the building, a coldness settling into my veins. It's a newer construction, all clean lines and fake elegance. Apparently there's a sterility to new buildings that even turning one into a whorehouse can't shake off. It reminds me of my dad's house. His office. His hotels. His investment properties. I grew up in buildings just like this: unfeeling yet somehow still exhaustingly performative. Probably why it took me so long to leave the church, this itching need to stand somewhere that has a history, a soul, a wisdom. My father's the kind of man who'd pay a hundred grand for the first shade of white his eyes landed on. No life, no warmth, no creativity—but hey, if the price tag is high enough, it must be luxurious, right?

I scoff, climbing off my bike.

Walking up the steps, I keep my wits about me, my hand never too far from my gun. I wasn't invited. The septic maw of South Side would welcome anyone into its trap, feeding off desperation, debt, addiction, and sex, but a rival Royal will always be watched. It's hard to walk into this place and not instantly go on the hunt for a new supply of those stimulants Cash loaded me up with before. They'd gotten me through some hard nights and harder days, but it's not safe here.

Even walking through the door makes my skin feel too tight, my nerves coiled for a confrontation. What I get instead is a tall Latina number, slinking through the foyer to greet me. I spend a brief moment fascinated by the way her black dress hangs on her curves, the folds and sways, stark against her tawny skin.

Pausing, she gives me a long onceover before purring, "Well, hello, gorgeous. How can I help you?"

Because I'm a gentleman, I hide my gun. "I'm looking for Augustine."

Her dark eyes twinkle with the smirk curving her mouth. "Sorry, heartbreaker. Augustine's been off the menu for ages. But I can assure you," walking forward, she presses against me, palm on my chest, "there's nothing she has that I don't."

I stare down at her, face blank. "I'm looking for something specific."

She cocks her head, pouting. "Like what?"

"A guy." It's a struggle to keep a straight face at the way her expression falls. "He'd be about my height. Covered in tattoos. Surly and stupidly aggro. Bit of a prick, really. Goes by the name of—"

"Pretty Nick." She steps back, rolling her eyes. But she knows who I am now. I can see it in the way she rights herself, the awareness that I'm not Sy, so I must be the Maddox. It settles eagerly into her aura, turning it an unseemly amber. "You know, if Dukes are going to keep encroaching on Lord territory, one of you could at least do us the courtesy of throwing down some dick. This isn't one of your daddy's hotels."

There it is.

"It's not my dick you want." Pulling out my wallet, I flip through it for three Benjamins, extending the bills with a flick of my fingers.

Her eyes narrow and she reaches out to snatch them away. But then she slides up against me again, fingers dipping into my pocket. "Trust me when I say it is." When she pulls back, the money is gone, tucked away into my pants. "Or at least it *was*."

Brow furrowing, I pull it out, insisting. "Just take it. For your troubles and pointing me in the right direction."

"I earn my money, and I'm damn good at it," she says, face set into a deliberate neutrality. "But if you want to give someone your *charity*, then I'm sure they'll welcome it on the Avenue."

The girl walks away, hips swaying, and I get this glitch in my brain where I think of calling her back. I imagine miles and miles of that smooth, golden skin beneath me, and my pants get a little tight. I haven't had a good fuck in forever. Nothing about this year is turning out how I thought it would. For one, I figured I'd have a Duchess who was ready and willing to get down and dirty. I also thought I'd be rolling in cutslut pussy, because really, has any Duke in the history of Forsyth reserved his cock for anyone?

Because for some reason, I am.

Not only that, but I have been. Since the night Vinny stepped into the tower, my dick's been on lockdown. I told myself it was just because I knew it'd be so fucking good with her. What's the point of filling up on peanuts when you're about to be served a juicy porterhouse?

But that's not really it.

I knew it the minute my ink buried into her flesh, when I marked her. She became mine.

Suddenly, that's the only thing my dick wants—to claim the parts of her I haven't yet. To make it real. To make it final. A marriage of bodies. A declaration of permanence. To bury myself in her pussy and watch as she takes every desperate inch of me. To see the look on her face when I show her what belonging to Remington Maddox means.

Annoying.

That's what it is.

I'm young, hot, and rich as fuck. I could have any pussy in this place, and I could have it every day—morning, noon, and night.

So why the hell am I holding out for hers?

"You should." Nick's voice breaks me from my thoughts. I turn to find him propped against the entrance to the lounge, arms crossed. It's been four days, so his black eye is more of a muddled yellow color, just like my jaw. The muscles below my eyes twitch when I take in the shirt he's wearing—Forsyth University Football.

Killian's.

I snort. "I should *what*?"

He jerks his chin toward the hallway. "Get your dick wet. Take her for a spin."

I scoff, following his gaze. "Nah. See, unlike other people, I have a basic concept of loyalty. But hey, you like her so much, you fuck her."

"Tried." He pushes off, cramming his fists into the pockets of the same sweats he'd run away wearing. "No one here will take me. There's a brothel-wide embargo on my dick." There's a lot I want to say to that. Before I can, he deflates, shaking his head. "Come on, man. Not here."

Coldly, I ask, "Where else?" I know when Nick drops his eyes that he's hearing what I'm putting down. He's not coming back to the tower until we hammer this shit out.

Jaw tensing, he dips his head toward the back of the house. "This way."

I follow him down the hall, past a large room of whores who look bored enough that two Dukes sauntering through their pad draws their full, unadulterated attention.

Nick notices, explaining in a droll voice, "Not much business here in the mornings and afternoons. There's a little spike around lunchtime when the corporate types roll through on their break for quickies. But mostly it stays dead until nightfall."

I don't really give a shit, but I take this in, following him through the house and out the backdoor. Nick leads me to a large, industrial-looking garage in the back. It sticks out like a sore thumb amongst the sleek, soulless wealth of the main building. That's how I know Daniel had it built. Guy never did have an eye for the finer details.

Inside is a cavernous space, empty and full of echoes. Despite the crisp fall weather, the interior is hot, the metal roof drawing in all the heat of the sun. The middle of the room is sunken, cordoned off by railings that surround it.

Inside the sunken part, there's a bed.

"That's the pit," he says. "He'd make us fuck girls in there." Nick's eyes are fixed on the bare bed, shadows filling his eyes, and for a second, that word—'*us*'—makes my eyes narrow. "Killian's shut that shit down." Then he shrugs. "I'm guessing Sy sent you here? To what? Settle things once and for all?" When he turns to look at me, there's an understanding there. I think that might be what pisses me off the most. That Nick knows what he did was wrong. That he looked at the situation, acknowledged how fucked up it was, weighed it in his mind, and somehow justified it enough to do it. It'd be easier if this were all a big misunderstanding, but that's not reality.

When Nick bends down to tighten his shoelaces, I do the same.

It's not really what I want.

What I want is the old Nick. The guy we could count on, no matter what. The guy who once looked my father in the eye and told him to eat shit. The guy who still came to my house afterward, because Nick doesn't get embarrassed. I want the guy who'd braid Tate's hair and then come with me to jump some seniors who were talking shit.

I want my best friend.

But what I get is Daniel's soldier. Over and over. That asshole didn't just get under his skin; his toxicity is pumping in his blood. Crimson and bronze.

Nick stands straight, chin raised, looking down his nose at me like he's got any fucking right. He's got this mask he wears when he's out on a job. Stone cold blankness. He's wearing it now as he stares me straight in the eye, and suddenly, all I can think about is him putting those bruises into Vinny's thighs, fucking her with that goddamn look on his face, like he's above it all. I think of him filling her up before throwing her away, just like he'd done to me and Sy two years ago.

And then I pull my fist back, coldcocking him so hard that my bones rattle, from knuckle to sternum.

The crack to his jaw, the way his head whips around, the stunned grunt he makes... it's all so satisfying that I find myself winding up for another one, fist flexing. He looks at the ground, spitting out a glob of blood, and then turns his gaze back to me.

But he doesn't hit back.

He's still as a statue—frozen—as if he's just waiting for the next blow.

A bitter snort escapes me. "What's wrong, Nicky? Been a traitor for so long, you've forgotten how this goes?" Ever since we were kids, Nick and I have settled our beefs with a solid round or five. Neither of us are much for grudges—that's more Sy's thing—so all we've ever needed was to blow off some steam, land a few jabs, make each other hurt a bit. It's the way we've always squared up.

Nick just raises his arms in invitation. "Take another shot, brother."

My lip curls. "Beating the shit out of someone who won't fight back? Little satisfaction in that." But I do it anyway, my fist tightening, and the second hit, a nasty mollywhop to his temple, actually has him staggering back. "Then again, a little is something."

Nick spends a moment shrugging it off, giving his head a tight shake before regaining his posture, feet spread, chin raised.

My blood boils.

I plant my palms on his shoulders and shove, growling, "Fight back!" Nick takes a step back, planting his feet, but doesn't raise a hand. Eyes flashing, I shove him again, and then again, his solid body being propelled in bursts across the floor of the sweltering building. Sweat drips over one of my eyebrows and I snap, "Fight me, you fucking bitch!"

Nick just locks his jaw, taking my next shove with a bitter grin. "No."

I get in his face, snarling, "Because South Side has turned you into a weak, two-faced coward." Another shove.

Finally, there's a spark in his eyes. It's not much—he's still got that fucking stone mask on—but his muscles tense as he shoves me back. "Because I fucking deserve it! Is that what you want to hear, Remy?"

Violently, I slap his arms away. "Fuck that! We all know you deserve it! What I want to know is why!"

The stone mask shatters, Nick's face contorting into an ugly, vicious desperation. "Because I was fucking killing her!" he explodes, shoving me with a momentum that has me hurtling back. "You think you know? You have no fucking idea. You don't love her!" He bears down on me, fists clenched, face red. "You don't know what it's like to give everything to someone, just to have them throw it back in your face. You don't know what it's like to fight this... this fucking *instinct*, every second of the day, to just take it."

I spring back, pushing him by the throat. "But you did," I snarl, teeth bared. "You took it. I saw the fucking bruises! I know what you did to her!"

I visibly watch his next words rise to the surface, sounding so raw and unhinged that it's as if they're rending their way through his vocal chords. "And I watched a piece of her fucking die while I was doing it!"

I'm not sure I've ever heard Nick scream before. Not like this, not out of anger. He and his brother have control down to an art form. But this? The heaving chest, the bald hysteria in his eyes...

It makes me go utterly still.

Nick stands there for a long second, panting as the fury slowly recedes. What's left afterward is a grim sort of exhaustion. When he slumps to the floor, it carves his shoulders into a tired, dejected line. "It should have been perfect. It should have been—" He drops his forehead to a palm, shaking his head. The rest comes out in a raggedly thin whisper. "She cried."

I close my eyes, drawing in a long, calming breath. "The fuck are you talking about?"

He doesn't look at me when he answers, fixing his gaze to some unidentifiable, distant point. "You know, sometimes girls cry and it's just like... tears and snot, and it's mostly just annoying, but this was..." He wets his lips, face going an ashen gray. "It was like she was dying, Remy. Not in a literal way. In that way where... there's just nothing left inside."

My face twists in confusion. "Because you fucked her?"

He finally lifts his gaze, eyes hooded and blank. "Because I broke her."

I bark a disbelieving laugh. "Well, if you didn't, her father sure fucking did!"

He bursts, "I wasn't thinking about—" but the words clip off with a click of his teeth. "I just knew if I kept her, I'd do it again."

"So she's gotta eat shit because you don't have any fucking self-control?"

"I had two years of self-control!" he snaps, shoulders tensing. "Fuck you, you don't get it."

I scoff. "That's the issue, isn't it? Just like always. You have a problem, you go off and solve it alone. I hate to break it to you, but you're not good at it." Buzzing with frustration, I urge, "So fucking tell me what the problem is for once instead of making it worse."

There's a long beat of silence where I'm convinced this is useless. And then he lets out a slow breath, head hanging. "When I'm with her, it's like... there are things I need. *Need*, not want. And if they don't happen, I go out of my goddamn mind."

I raise an eyebrow. "Things you need?"

Nodding, he explains, "I need to touch her. I need her to look at me. I need to taste her. I need everyone to know she's mine. I need *her* to know she's mine. I need her attention. I need—"

"What you need is massive amounts of therapy. I mean, Jesus Christ, Nicky." I sink my fingers into my hair, tugging at the roots. "I'm not going to pretend I don't want her pretty fucking bad, but she's just a girl."

Nick slides me a look through the corner of his eyes, and yeah. Fair.

She's more than just a girl, and we both know it.

Instead of voicing this, he goes on, "I knew whatever her dad had in store for her was probably messed up." He tips his head up, smiling joylessly. "But more messed up than me?"

I rub my temples against the brewing ache in my head. "Fuck."

He nods. "Pretty much."

The fucked up thing is, I can see it. The path from Point-A to Point-B, carved with the best of the worst intentions. It didn't make any sense to me before, and if I'm being honest, it doesn't really make sense now. It's crazy.

But sometimes, I am, too.

I let out a sigh that might never end, dropping down next to him on the cement floor. "Nick," I start, resting my elbows on my knees. "From what I've heard, Vinny's had a kind of fucked up life."

His eyes narrow. "You can't make me feel any worse than—"

"I'm not saying this to make you feel like shit," I insist. "You and Sy... you've got a really nice family. You've got three nice parents who love you. *Three* of them. You both had a good upbringing. You had counselors and summer camps and awkward parental talks that probably ended with hugs or gift cards or whatever. And you had each other. Yeah, you fight, but you and Sy care about each other. Hell, most of your fights are *because* you give a shit about each other."

He rolls his eyes. "What's your point?"

"My point is that you had the fucking dream, and look how you both turned out. Neurotic, obsessive, impulsive, insecure, basket cases." I turn to him, giving him a long, significant look. "Now imagine if you didn't have any of that." Nick looks away. "Vinny's got issues, bro. She's used to being treated like shit, and she was raised in the Royalty, where people don't give anything away without wanting something in return." Softening a blow has never been something I bother with, but right now, I make an attempt. "I kind of think the harder you want her, the more she's going to turn away. And I don't think she can help it. You're like the person-version of that box her dad had her in. You suffocate her, man."

"So you're saying I should give up." The stone mask returns, but it's not the same. This one isn't carved out of arrogance. It radiates grief. "I should watch her suck your dick and ride my brother and just..." Nick stares out over the sunken part of the building—the pit, he'd called it—and shakes his head. "I don't know how to let her go when she's right in front of me."

"I'm saying you should let her have some fucking room to breathe." I push to my feet, feeling sore and wrung out for someone who didn't even take a hit.

"How?" he asks.

Shrugging, I offer him my hand, watching as he looks up at it. "You could start by saying you're sorry."

He laughs. It's depreciating and lacking in humor but that's how far this has gone. "An apology seems pretty fucking weak, bro. I mean, Hallmark doesn't make a card for shit like this."

"No, they don't, but even you can suck it up and just say the words." But I couldn't. I covered a fucking hairbrush in black marker, and she doesn't even know what it means. Then again, I had a lot less to be sorry for.

He sighs and takes my hand. I heave him off the ground. "You think she'll accept it?"

This time I laugh. "Not a fucking chance."

He grimaces. "Then what's the point?"

I roll my eyes, because god*damn*. "The point is you're a Duke. A Bruin. You belong in the tower and she does too. She's our Duchess. The instant Sy broke into the Count's mansion, that was sealed. For life." His jaw tics. "Yeah, your big brother is the savior now. But that little act? It came with consequences."

For the first time since I got here, his spine straightens. "What consequences?"

"Saul was at the tower when I left. I don't know what he wants, but you and I both know it's going to be painful."

"Shit," he says, and something flickers in Nicky's eyes.

Purpose.

And like that, he's drawn back in.

9

Lavinia

Sy is the worst patient ever.

"Stay still," I snap, hands chasing him as he leans away.

"It smells gross," he snaps back, scowling. His words are still a touch slurred, so his general condition ruins some of the intimidation factor. Here, all battered and bruised, perched on the edge of the bed with his elbows on his knees, head hanging heavily between wide, slumped shoulders, I forget to be afraid of him. Ever since he woke up, five hours ago, he's been moody and sour, but also quiet and sullen. He's obviously nursing a mild concussion, and god knows he has to be lit up with aches and pains, but when he stood up to walk to the bathroom earlier, he didn't so much as wince.

He refuses to take the pain pills.

I dab at the split on his lip gently, coating it with the sticky honey. "You're well enough to travel now," I try, moving to his cheekbone. "We can probably head back to—"

He wrenches his head to the side, glaring at the shabby comforter. "No."

It's been eighteen hours since he was attacked. His cuts are scabbing over. His bruises are darkening. He says there's no blood in his urine, but I don't really believe he'd tell me if there was. I've fed him the half of the burger I didn't eat and sports drink from a pallet he has in the trunk of his car.

But I can't do much here.

Sighing, I lean back on my heels, kneeled on the floor in front of him, to inspect my handiwork. "Sy, look—"

"I can't go into the tower right now," he says, not for the first time.

I throw my hands up. "Why the hell not? Saul's boys won't possibly come for you there. You're protected when you're up there. One way up, one way down." Gesturing to the room around us, I note, "But here, we're sitting ducks." If someone discovered us—my father or Saul—we'd be toast.

He links his fingers together, squeezing his fists, and I watch as the abused skin over his knuckles thins and splits. "The night I brought you back into the tower, what did I fucking say?"

I search through my memories of that night, which are hazy at best, and try to remember. I know I was so terrified of the elevator that I passed out on the way up. But before that, when he was psyching me up, trying to convince me that everything was going to be okay, I told him I'd rather die. And he said...

You see that door you just came in? When a Duke loses a fight, he spends the night somewhere else, because losers aren't allowed to walk through it.

My groan is rough and frustrated. "You can't be serious. This is some stupid Duke ego thing?"

He replies in a gruff, quiet voice. "I lost."

"Jesus, Sy, you were outnumbered three to one." I duck forward to catch his gaze through a swollen eye. "You didn't lose. You were just... overpowered."

He doesn't answer, pitching to the side and dragging his feet up to lay on the bed. He sets his head back on the pillow, tongue darting out to wet his lips. Suddenly, his face contorts, a gagging sound emerging from his throat. "What the fuck? You said that was honey."

I hold up the jar. "Manuka honey. It's not like... regular honey."

He grimaces. "It tastes like shit. Where the hell did you get this?"

I know well enough to brace myself before I say, "Tristian Mercer brought it."

He jolts up, back rigid as he gapes at me. "Are you fucking kidding me? You let a Lord in here? While I was *unconscious*?"

"I needed help and didn't know who to trust. Remy didn't answer his phone, and it's not like I could trust some random DKS guy." I screw the cap back on the honey and set it on the bedside table. "Saul's the one who did this to you, so he was obviously out of the question. Who's left? My father?" I bark a laugh that must sound completely crazed. "So I called the Hideaway. The women there... well, they were my only support when I was locked up. I asked for a favor, and they came through."

He closes his eyes and takes a deep breath. I'm well aware that his frustration isn't just about me calling South Side. It's about how everything in our lives is an utter shit show and he has no control. I get it. I've lived it for years now.

"I've done my best to make us safe here," I tell him. "And I think there are South Side soldiers watching the motel. But..."

But we should go home soon.

I don't speak the thought, letting it linger heavily in the air between us, not just because I know he'd argue. It's the first time I've thought of the tower as home and not felt a sense of defeat.

"Fucking hell." He scrubs his hair. "Now we're going to owe them. Double."

Putting away the bandages, I mutter, "Because Nick's there?"

"Or was," he answers, sounding just as unhappy at the mention of his brother as I feel making it. "Hopefully Remy's got him home by now."

So much for any thought of 'home' bringing me comfort.

"Speaking of, he texted. Remy," I clarify, crossing the room for the phone I left on the rickety table. I carry it back over to him and sit on the edge of the bed. "I replied and told him we were safe, but I didn't take any chances on someone discovering our location."

He opens the messages and taps out a series of words and emojis I can't decipher. A reply comes back almost instantly, similarly unreadable. He tosses it across the bed where it bounces off the yellowing sheets, muttering, "We need to get you a phone."

I blink at him, unable to parse the thought. My own phone? I haven't had anything like that in years. "How long?" I ask, watching him carefully.

His forehead creases. "Until you get a phone?"

"Until we can go back." I roll my eyes. "Another day? Two? What are the rules on this idiotic concept of losers not being able to enter the tower?"

Sy swallows hard at the word. *Loser*. "Three days," he answers, eyes going tight when he shifts.

Sighing, I concede one thing. "You're going to need it to heal up. Get your strength back." The groggy scowl he sends me makes me smile. "Yeah, sounds familiar, right? Time for a little payback."

He gingerly pulls the comforter over his bare chest, already looking half asleep. "If you bring me soup and a kitten, I'm fucking out of here."

Sy isn't the only one who's exhausted, and I watch as he falls into slumber, breath evening out, before I climb beneath the blankets and do the same.

I WAKE up in the silent hours of the morning.

It must be a force of habit. Back when I was being kept here, I'd sleep during the evening. Otherwise, I'd be treated to the girls in the rooms parallel to mine, screaming and moaning as whatever shitty John took his fill of her. But it's always been quiet here after 2am. If I keep my eyes closed and pretend not to smell the musty sheets, I can almost imagine I'm somewhere else.

Except for the fact I'm waking to the sound of Sy's heartbeat beneath my ear.

Sometime in the night, I must have rolled toward him, seeking his warmth, because now I have a leg thrown over his thigh, my hand resting on his bare stomach as I burrow mindlessly into his chest. For such a fit guy, Sy is surprisingly comfortable to sleep against. Not hard, but comfortingly firm and radiating heat.

If he wakes up to this, he's going to be pissed, but I give myself a few moments to dread rolling away, back to the cold vacancy on the other side of the bed.

Then, I rise with his sigh, his chest slowly expanding, and I realize he's awake.

I flinch back, dragging my limbs away and putting some distance between us. "My bad," I croak, unable to make out much more than the outline of his face in the dark. "Not enough pillows in this shithole to construct your usual perimeter."

His quiet, "Whatever," is full of strain.

"Shit." I rub a hand over my face before reaching over to turn on a lamp. "Was I hurting you? Let me check your ribs."

When I try to pull the comforter back, he grips it tight. "It's fine."

"No, it's not." The bruising is horrific and I've been worried this whole time that he broke a rib or punctured something without knowing. "Just let me see."

He gives me a hard stare before letting go of the comforter, pressing his shoulders against the pillow. I don't allow my eyes to linger over his body, instead getting right to the problem area. Gently I touch a particularly dark bruise and he hisses. "Fuck."

"Sorry, sorry!"

He keeps his hands on his lap, on top of the blanket, obscuring his crotch. I take great pains to avoid looking at it and seek a distraction while I check out the other tender spots on his torso. "I've been thinking..."

He sucks in a breath when I press down on his side. "Not until tomorrow night."

I give him an exasperated look. "Not about going back. Remember how we were in the library that day, when Perez cornered me? What you said..."

A line forms above the cut on the bridge of his nose. "Only I'm allowed to upset you?"

"No, Sy." I shoot him a glower. "You told me my punch sucks."

He snorts. "Actually, I believe I said you hit like a girl. A guy would never tuck his thumb."

I might press a little too hard on my next pass, making him wince. "The point is, I'm not good at it. Fighting."

He grunts, swatting my hand away. "Physically, at least."

"And," I go on, satisfied that I didn't harm him with any accidental cuddling, "if the last couple months have taught me anything, it's that I'm woefully unprepared to defend myself." I stare at his mottled flesh, and bitterly add, "From anyone."

There's a long stretch of silence where nothing except his labored breaths are apparent. And then he whispers, "Hey," and tilts his head to force our gazes to meet. "If this is about those guys back there, there's not much I could've taught you to fight them off. I couldn't even fight them off and I've got over a hundred pounds on you."

I swallow the lump that's formed in my throat. "It is about them, but... it's also about Nick, and Perez, and my father's fucking henchmen. It's about Tristian Mercer and being trapped in here alone with you," I gesture to the door, "with nothing but a cheap lock between us and whatever is out there. I don't need to be able to win a fight against them. I just need to be able to get away if I have to."

His expression is hard, cut from stone, and I know I shouldn't have asked him. Remy would have been better, maybe. I should have waited and asked him. But I've never seen Remy fight, and Sy…

He's good.

Really good.

I move to stand, but he grabs my wrist and pulls me back down. "It's *our* job to protect the Duchess. What happened back there wasn't on you. It was on me." His eyes ping back and forth between mine, flashing in a searing anger. "You weren't the one who lost that fight."

"You and I both know I can't always be with you and Remy. I need to be able to do this. I'm so tired, Simon." I reach out and gently touch the butterfly bandage under his eye. It should make him look weak or vulnerable, but it just makes him more intimidating. And, strangely, handsome. "I'm so fucking tired of being held down by the men of Forsyth."

I stand, and this time he lets me, his fingers dragging lazily across my wrist as I walk away. I disappear into the bathroom, closing the door behind me. Ignoring my reflection, I turn the squeaky knobs until the water rushes out, dipping my hands in to splash on my face. Admitting that I need help, to him in particular, cuts to the bone. I've shown a weakness here, one that transcends my inability to fight off three hulking men. The fact that it wasn't enough to get him to agree is just an extra dose of humiliation.

It casts a light on the sad state of my life to say that having a phone would completely change it. Sy will give me one, and he'll protect me, keep me safe. But I'm not stupid. All of those things are contingent. They can be snatched away at his whim. We're on good terms now, but what about when we get back to the tower, where his brother is probably waiting?

I sit on the toilet and drop my hands into my face. It's not like I can hide in here forever, but who knows? Maybe if I wait ten minutes, he'll just fall back asleep, like it never even happened.

That plan is shot to hell. When I walk back out, he hasn't moved. In fact, he's levered himself upright, shoulders propped against the pillows, and appears wide awake.

Fuck.

"I think Tristian may have put some protein bars in the food he left if you want one," I say, heading to the table. I feel his eyes on my back.

"I'm not hungry."

"Oh, okay." The room is suddenly too small for the both of us. This whole situation only works smoothly when one, or both of us, are asleep.

"Lavinia," he says, and then, softer, as if he's testing the shape of it on his tongue, "Vinny."

I look over. "Yeah?"

"I guess... maybe I can teach you some defensive moves." His weary blue eyes sweep over me. "But if you want to be trained, I'm not going to go easy on you. You're going to have to gain some weight, add a little muscle mass and work on your stamina, which we both know is shit."

My heart flutters and I turn to him fully, daring to feel a morsel of optimism. "Yeah, we do."

He looks away, sighing. "But, you're right. You need to be able to defend yourself, as much as you can." Suddenly, his mouth twists into a smirk, a soft laugh bouncing his chest. "You know, for such a tiny chick, you sure do have a lot of enemies."

"Says the guy who just got jumped by one of his." I pick up the protein bar and turn, tossing it to him. He isn't looking, though—not at my head.

His eyes are quite obviously glued to my ass.

The protein bar smacks unceremoniously into his chest, making him flinch. "I said I wasn't hungry," he repeats, setting it aside. "But I've been thinking about something, too. Something you can do for me in return."

My stomach plummets. "What?"

He shifts under the blanket, clearing his throat. "At the Equinox party, you..." His eye twitches. "You made me look good in front of all those people."

My eyebrows shoot upward. "You want me to make you look

like a sex god or something? Like some gratuitous PDA?" When all he does is stare at me, unblinking, the hair on the back of my neck rises. Slowly, I realize, "No. You don't want to look good." That's not Sy at all. He doesn't like winning because of appearances. It's about the show of superior skill. "You want to *be* good."

His cheeks turn pink and he fists the blanket, looking away. "That night, you kind of... coached me."

As far as I can tell, he only has one weakness.

"Sy Perilini has never lost anything. Virginity included."

Nick said that before I climbed into his brother's lap and talked him through an epic dry-hump. *Coached*, as he said.

"You want me to, like, sex-train you?"

He pulls a face. "Don't say it like that. That sounds ridiculous." Not as ridiculous as this genetically superior, well-endowed man, asking me to coach him in sex.

"Sy," I start, wondering how to approach this. We've just gained some sort of tenuous allyship and I find myself really not wanting to ruin it. Nevertheless, "I can't fuck you." When his eyes shutter, I'm quick to explain, "Physically, I'm not sure I could even take it. I've had sex a few times—" Three times: once with a shy, handsome boy I went to high school with, and twice with his shit of a brother. "—but I'm not, like... really experienced."

I run both palms down my hot cheeks, wondering why I'm even saying this. I can't fuck Sy because I don't want to fuck Sy. That should be enough.

At first, I'm sure we're both going to just crawl into two separate holes and die of mortification, but then Sy's gaze jumps to mine. "You've never fucked Remy," he argues. "But you've done enough with him that you know he's..." His lip curls. "Good at it."

Annoyingly, I now find myself thinking about it; what Remy's like in bed. No doubt, being with him is like riding a rollercoaster. I bet Remy stretches before he gets started, really limbers up. I bet he fuels up on something—liquor, stimulants, carb loading. But no, that doesn't sound right, either. I bet with him, it comes out of nowhere, unplanned, impulsive, covered in ink and paint at four in the morning. Either way, I bet a night with him would leave a girl limping down all those tower stairs.

"Well..."

Sy lets out a disgusted sound. "See? You've never even had his dick and you're hot for it."

I shake myself out of it. "What exactly are you looking for then?"

If he wasn't so injured, I'm pretty sure he would transform into the Hulk and smash his way through the paper-thin walls of this motel and run as far away from this discussion as possible. But he's not.

"I'm not stupid. I know I'm not... normal," he says, pushing down the blanket. I've seen his cock. Felt it, tasted it. I know he's not average down there. I look at the hard line of his cock against his leg, noticing that it's bigger now than it has been in days. He's horny. "Bitches—*women*—they all talk about wanting a guy with a huge cock, but the second they see or feel it, they're pounding sand." He lifts his chin. "You did."

He's right. Every time I look at it, I get a funny feeling in my stomach. It's some horrific mixture of desire, curiosity, and bone-chilling fear. "Yeah, well, the first time I saw it, you were attacking me with it. Come to think of it, the second and third times weren't much different."

He huffs but doesn't disagree. "But you don't go around telling everyone about how shitty I am in bed. *They* do." What shocks me is that he's genuinely distressed, running his fingers through his hair. "Normal guys like Remy and Nick... they got to experiment. Fumble around. Train themselves."

"But girls never let you get that far," I say, understanding.

He really gets going now, hands flying in the air. "And it shouldn't fucking matter! I'm the best fighter in Forsyth. I have a nearly perfect GPA. I'm a Duke, for fuck's sake. But all people ever talk about is how bad I am at *this*." He thrusts a finger at his crotch. "And that." He thrusts a finger at *my* crotch.

"So you *do* want to look good," I hedge, perching on the edge of the bed. "You just also want to back it up."

He looks away, still red-faced. "Basically."

Gently, I try, "South Side has a lot of working girls who'd—" At his sharp, incredulous glare, I raise my hands. "...who are all loyal to a rival house. Fine, I get it. So... what? You want to practice on me? Use me like a cum covered pin cushion?"

"Jesus Christ," he mutters. "Why are you always so fucking difficult? I agreed to help you, can't you do the same for me?"

I lean back on the bed and lay a hand on his leg. His breath hitches and I watch the length and width of his cock expand. "Maybe..." I lick my lips, too aware of his eyes darting to the motion. "Maybe we could try some things. Kiss me."

His head snaps back. "What?"

"Kiss me," I repeat. "You're getting hard, Sy. The natural progression of this is that you kiss me. Let's see what we're working with. Seduce me." He groans, head falling back, and my jaw drops in outrage. "What, you can cram your cock into my mouth, but you don't want to *kiss* me?"

He glowers up at the ceiling. "That night of the party, we kissed plenty."

I shrug. "Whatever. Remy kisses me like he's a goddamn soldier going off to war. Forget all this stuff about dicks. When it comes to women, that's what makes him better than you."

The challenge sparks in his eyes and suddenly he's bolting toward me, mashing his mouth against mine.

Jesus, I should have known.

This isn't about sex.

It's about winning.

I grab his jaw to soften it, his lips harsh and too stiff against mine. He adjusts his posture without ever separating our lips, rolling to prop up on an elbow. I can feel the swell of his cut against my kiss, and when we part our lips to deepen it, I can taste a twinge of that honey salve.

Sy kisses awkwardly at first, like he's taking a test or ripping off a Band-Aid, eager to get to the end. I let my hand trail down his neck, landing on his chest, and then I slow it, licking lazy against his warm tongue. Gradually, he sinks into the rhythm, adapting to the plunge and retreat, and it's... good.

It's just as good as it was the night of the party.

Maybe even better, without the weight of everyone's eyes on us. This is completely without artifice, and even when he stumbles, knocking our teeth together, it just enhances it, like I'm seeing a part of Sy that's unbearably private.

The gruff vibration of his groan sends a shockwave down into the pit of my belly, igniting my nerves into a tingling mess.

"Touch me," I say against his lips, coaching him. I feel his arm moving, hear the shuffle of the comforter as it rises, feel the momentum of his swirling tongue kick up a notch, and then...

He grabs my tit.

I pull away, glaring. "Really? Right for the goods?"

His eyes are heavy and glazed, lips wet and red. "What?"

"Have some game, Sy, Jesus." I pull his hand away, pointedly settling it on my hip. "Remember that it's not all about you. You have to be patient."

The muscles beneath my palm flex. "That's hard to do when I'm on a fucking hair trigger all the time."

I don't even need to look down to know he's rock hard. "Isn't that why you guys are supposed to jerk off? To deal with stuff like that?"

He pulls his hand from my hip, flopping back to the mattress. "I try not to do that so much." Back to glaring at the ceiling.

Now, I let myself look, and sure enough, his cock is raging at full staff, thick and obscene beneath his pants. I clear my throat, startled at the sight of it. "Why not? You obviously want it."

He drags his fingers through his hair, tugging hard enough that his knuckles go white. "If I give in, then it'd be all I'll do. It's easier if I just... hold it in. Control it."

God, his head and his body are a mess of mixed up repression and denial. No wonder he's so pissed off all the time.

I reach haltingly for the waistband of his sweats. "Can I... uh, see?" Truthfully, the question is more for myself than him.

"Why?" he asks, watching me warily.

"Just... let me get a lay of the land here."

His jaw tenses, shoulders rigid. It's not just anger, either. The moment my knuckle touches his skin, finger hooked into his waistband, he releases a thinly veiled shudder, eyes slamming closed. Slowly, I lower the elastic, getting a flash of his dark, wiry hair. His hips rise, and I wrench the pants down low, his cock getting caught and then snapping free, landing heavily against his belly.

My cunt clenches just looking at it.

I open my mouth to speak, and he cuts me off. "I swear to god, if some smart ass remark comes out of your mouth, I'm going to fucking lose it."

I roll my eyes. "I was going to say that it's not so bad." Straight up, the thing's a bit of a nightmare, but it's not exactly ugly. It's aesthetically a perfect cock, from the flushed, swollen head to the strong shaft. There aren't any scary curves or bulging places. It's veiny and dark, just like the rest of his skin, and it's fine. There's just *so much of it*. "It's just, uh, a little intimidating. Like the rest of you."

His shoulders unwind, just a notch, and I stare at it, tilting my head to scrutinize it from every angle. It's hard to believe I've had it in my mouth, thrusting against my lips, surging against my tongue.

I lick out now to taste the remnants of Sy's kiss on my lips. "I'm going to touch it."

But he snatches my wrist before I can, blue eyes blazing into mine. "You have no fucking idea how close I am to—" His teeth clench, the knot in the back of his jaw flexing. "If you touch me right now, I won't be able to control it."

I pause. "What, like, you'll come? Well, maybe you should. It can't be healthy to keep yourself all backed up and—"

"That's one way it could go," he cuts me off, eyes smoldering. "The other is that I pin you to this bed and use you like... what did you call it? A cum covered pin cushion?"

I yank my wrist back. "You're saying you can't control yourself when you're horny? That's bullshit."

"I do control myself," he bites out. "I try not to get horny at all. Which, by the way, is really fucking difficult when some girl is traipsing around your living room in spandex every day."

My jaw drops. "That's why you were such an asshole to me before? Because I made your dick hard?" But my own words bring back the memory of Nick's, the day he won me in that fight.

"If he's this bitchy, you must really get his motor revving. He doesn't like being reminded he's not a robot."

And I remember that day at the gym, when he'd forced me to my knees, eyes frantic and pained.

"You did this... You've been doing it for days... Making me feel this... You made it happen... You take it away..."

So that's why he's been so nice to me lately. I guess it's hard to get it up for someone who's so weak and battered that she can't even walk on her own. But I'm looking at it now—his gigantic cock—and it seems to understand that sex is something it wants again.

I blow out a long breath, face feeling hot. "I'm going to touch you," I repeat, ignoring how it makes his cock jump, "and you're going to lay there and do *nothing* until I give you an order." When he parts his mouth to argue, I say, "There's a knife under my pillow. If you try to hold me down or take something that's not on offer, I'm going to cut your fucking balls off."

His jaw clicks shut. There's an inferno raging in his eyes, but he trains them on the ceiling and swallows, his throat jumping with the motion.

I ask, "How long has it been? When was the last time you... you know." He cuts his eyes to mine and then looks away, lightning quick, and I gawk at him. "Not since that night of the party?"

Silence.

I don't go for it directly, threading my fingers down the trail of hair under his belly that I've been eyeing for days. It's as soft as it looks, baby-fine, and his lower belly caves with my touch.

I haven't even touched it yet, but he gives a full body shudder, growling, "Oh, fuck," and slams his eyes closed. I keep mine wide open, watching his cock swell.

My first touch is barely more than a graze of my fingertip along the shaft. The muscles in his thighs lock right before his cock twitches, a long string of precum dribbling down to his hip. There's this sound he makes, deep in his throat, a sort of rumbling whine, and an emptiness in the pit of my stomach flares suddenly to life.

His hips surge up and I take my hand away, chiding, "Be still."

His breaths are loud, hissing through his gnashed teeth. "Don't fucking tease me."

"It's not a tease," I insist, finally wrapping my fingers around the shaft. "It's training."

I watch as his fingers twist into the sheets, but only distantly. Mostly my eyes are trained on the head of his dick, which gives another strained surge of fluid. I've never seen a guy leak like this, and I'm strangely fascinated by it, the way this muscle reacts to the slightest touch. When I give a light, testing squeeze, more of the sticky fluid weeps out.

Sy keens.

My eyes dart to him, but he's digging his head back into the pillow and his eyes are squinched so tightly that the bandage on his cheek is straining.

"Relax, Sy." I give him a slow stroke, watching the resulting tremor run up his limbs. His muscles are coiled so tight that I can see every tendon in his neck. "What are you holding back?"

"Everything," he grunts, stiff as a board. I look back at his dick, at the fluid that's pooled beneath the head, and drag my lip through my teeth. It's funny to think I'd had to threaten him before—that he'd had to warn me he might lose control—because here, holding the heavy weight of him in my hand, I realize it's actually much different.

Right now, I have unutterable power over this man.

"Do you think... could you kiss me? When you're like this?" Instantly, he shakes his head, thrashing tightly from side to side, and I firm up my voice. "Try. Kiss me, Sy."

He lets out a harsh breath that's edged with frustration, and suddenly, he's lurching up onto an elbow, grabbing a thick, painful fistful of my hair, and crushing our mouths together.

The second our tongues meet, he comes, grunting into my mouth.

His cock surges and jerks, and the rest of his body follows it, shuddering as his other hand clamps onto my fist, forcing my fingers tighter. Sy makes a sound like a wounded animal, and then my hand is met with the warm slickness of his release.

"Easy, easy," I say, pitching toward the hand that's currently tearing hair from my scalp.

He doesn't say he's sorry. He just lets go and flops back, and even though I know it's over, his hips are still flexing, cock giving one last gush, adding to the considerable mess on his belly. The back of my neck is damp with sweat. My pulse is pounding in my ears. There's a tingle in my thighs that I know all too well isn't going to go away.

I don't think I've ever been so horny in my goddamn life.

I clear my throat, holding my hand out to the side. "Let's, um, clean up."

Sy doesn't even bother reaching for the tissues on the bedside table, instead fumbling around on the floor for one of the towels I'd used to clean him up before. His face is still red, but his muscles are looser, eyes hooded as he lazily wipes at his stomach and chest. Falteringly, I point to a spot on his collarbone before lifting a corner of the towel to swipe the cum away.

That beast has some wicked momentum.

When I disappear into the bathroom to wash his jizz from my hands, I find that my own face is aflame, and there's a brief, shameful moment where I wish I were back in the tower.

Remy would take one look at me and know.

He would slide up against me. He'd kiss me and stoke the fire between my legs into a raging blaze. He'd make me feel his hands on me, and sure, he'd take. But he'd also bring me pleasure—

whether I wanted it or not—and right now, I really, really fucking do.

The thought is startling and pulls me back from the edge, because I can't be this. I can't be like the Lady, who'd gladly spread for her Lords. The Dukes aren't my boyfriends. They're just the sentries standing between me and Forsyth. And if I need to train Sy to understand what sex is supposed to be, then I'll do it because I know he'll take it seriously, and because it serves a purpose.

But none of this is real.

When I return to the room, Sy has the comforter pulled back up to his chest. The scowl has returned to his face. "You were carrying your bag in your right hand."

I blink at him, pausing in the doorway. "What?"

"After the fight," he says, sliding his eyes to mine. "Lesson one: always leave your dominant hand free."

"Oh." I linger there in the doorway for a moment, trying to get my bearings. I squeeze my thighs together and give him a nod. "Okay, good point. But that's not really the kind of lesson I had in mind."

"Neither is making me nut," he counters. "A stiff breeze could do that."

My eyes narrow. "The orgasm wasn't the lesson, Sy. It was that the more you deny your body's urges, the more they're going to rule you."

"Whatever," he replies, looking away. "I was handling things just fine before you came along."

I correct, "Before *you* came along. I don't know why you act like I'm inflicting myself on you. The three of you were inflicted on me."

His nostrils flare. "You know what I meant."

"Well, excuse me for having the sheer audacity to fucking exist," I snap, every ounce of my libido exiting stage left. There's a long stretch of tense silence before I decide sleep is the only remedy to this. Flinging the comforter back, I move to stuff my pillow between us—absolutely no more cuddling—only to get a good look at what's going on beneath his pants. My jaw drops.

"Seriously?" I screech, flinging a hand toward it. "But you literally *just*—"

The shutters slam over Sy's face, teeth grinding. "I fucking *told you* this is what happens."

"Yeah, because you probably have years of spunk backed up in that thing!" Shaking my head, I crawl into bed, keeping my distance. "You need to do it every day. Isn't your mom a sex therapist or something? You should—"

"Talk to my mother about my dick?" he asks, voice a cold deadpan.

Yikes.

"Maybe not," I sigh, turning off the lamp. Once the room is dark and silent, I find myself thinking about tomorrow. About going home. About seeing Remy. About seeing Nick. I find myself wondering, "Did he tell you what he did?" Instead of an answer, I get the rustle of sheets as Sy turns to look at me. "Nick," I clarify, swallowing thickly. Remy must know by now, but it's been nagging at me. The possibility that everyone does. "Did he tell you that he..."

Another beat of silence, and then, "He what?"

So he doesn't know.

I almost just roll over and go to sleep. The less people who know, the better. "He tied me up," I say instead, speaking more to the dark in front of my eyes than to the man beside me. "Before he took me to my dad—after you dropped me off. He tied me up and he—" I get stuck for a moment on the verbiage, unable to form my lips around the word I want to use.

Sy opts for another. "He fucked you?"

My smile is brittle and empty. "Yeah. If that's what you want to call it."

This time, the quiet around us is filled with dreadful, awful things. Mostly because I know what he's going to say as soon as the sigh falls from his lips.

"Lavinia, he's my brother."

It shouldn't surprise me. Blood is thicker than whatever it is that's bound me and Sy since he came for me that night. If it comes down to a choice between me or Nick, I know who he'll choose.

When I feel his touch on my cheek, I realize it's wet with the trail of a single tear. "I never make promises. You know as well as I do that in our world, a promise is just another word for debt. But I promise you this." His thumb slides away, soft as silk. "I won't let him hurt you again."

Hours later, after Sy has turned away and fallen asleep, I know that it's useless. Sy thinks his urges are his weakness. Remy probably assumes his moments of instability are his weakness. Nick probably thinks *I'm* his weakness.

But I know the truth.

Nothing makes a Royal as weak as their loyalty to the broken machine of Forsyth.

~

WE LEAVE the motel the next night, gathering our shit and locking the door behind us. Things have been quiet and solemn since we woke up this morning, partly because we've been anticipating our return to the tower, and partly because of what happened in bed last night.

Sy is walking a little easier, but he still has a bit of a limp, holding his side gingerly as we cross the lot to his old Trans-Am. When he says, "Lesson two: always check behind the car and clear the back seat before getting in," it's the first mention that's been made of our agreement. I don't tell him that I already learned that lesson, remembering that first time I tried to escape the tower, only to realize halfway into putting the SUV into reverse that Nick was waiting in the backseat, armed and furious.

I'm too nervous about getting back to the tower to do much more than raise my chin in acknowledgement, stuffing our things into the back.

Sy drives, even though the oncoming headlights make him visibly tense up, eyes squinting until they pass. "You can still sleep with me," he says, voice abrupt in the silence of the car. Shifting uneasily, he adds, "I mean... in my bed. Or Remy's, even. If you're scared of Nick."

I give a noncommittal hum, gazing out at the passing scenery.

He lets out a long sigh. "Christ, don't be pissy. He's a Bruin, and you've always known what that means. Nick's a Duke, and you're the Duchess." His fingers tighten on the steering wheel. "We have to find a way to make this work."

"And if we don't?"

He looks over at me, eyes dark. "Then we'll be divided, and Saul and your father will beat us."

Of course, he's right. But he's also fucking crazy if he thinks this can work. Last night, when I confessed everything Nick had done to me, I felt disappointed in his response, and I'm not sure I like it.

I think it hurt.

We arrive on the crest of midnight, the moon hanging high in the sky, and I crane my neck to see it—the moon, and the illuminated windows of the top floor.

"I called ahead," he says, grabbing his bag from the backseat. "They're awake."

When we first step through the doors, I watch as something shivers through Sy.

"Losers aren't allowed to walk through it."

That's another weakness: the inability to take a loss.

When he turns to the stairs, I begin, "Shouldn't you use the—" and he cuts me a look.

"What? Use the elevator? Are you going to get into it with me?" When I shake my head, he says, "Of course you aren't. Are you going to go up this dark, empty stairwell all alone, knowing Nick's here?"

My jaw clenches and I look away. "No."

"That's what I thought." There's a trace of annoyance in his voice when he gestures upward. "So we're walking up together. Let's go."

The climb takes a long time. Sy heaves himself up the stairs more than he walks, pulling himself along the railing with his upper body strength. Halfway to the top, he pauses, panting, and when I duck beneath his arm to take some of the weight, he shoots me a brief, exasperated glance.

And then he begins climbing again.

We walk the rest of the way up like that, my holding some of his weight as he lumbers heavily toward the top. I see the hesitation in his eyes when we reach the party room, as if he's considering just stopping here, claiming one of the couches, and never moving again.

But because he's Sy, he powers on, up the last flight of steps to the main living quarters.

Sy enters first.

I don't even pretend like I'm not using him as a meat shield, hovering directly behind him as he calls out. I doubt I'll ever be ready to see Nick again, but since I don't have the luxury of picking a date, here I am.

Luckily, Remy appears first, coming around from the couch only to go stock-still at the sight of him. "What the *fuck*, Sy?"

"Should see the other guys," Sy mutters, dropping his keys on the table. "Virtually unscathed."

I glare at the back of his head. "Hey!"

He twists to shoot me an irritated look. "Yeah, our girl got in a good shot. I, on the other hand, managed to pummel the business end of a bat with my skull."

After sweeping his eyes over me, Remy walks up to him, eyes tight as he grabs Sy by the chin and turns his head, inspecting the damage on his cheek. The moment stretches on, the air around us growing strangely electrified, and I realize I've never really seen Remy angry before. Peeved, sure. Annoyed. Restless. But the calm depth of darkness in his eyes when he steps back is worse than anger. It's bloodshed, senseless and uncontainable, and when he pulls his gun from his waist, racking the slide, even Sy moves back a step. "We'll retaliate," Remy says.

"Against who? Our own fucking house?" Sy grabs the gun. "Don't chamber a round in the house, idiot."

"You're saying Saul did this?" Remy's fists flex. "Our own King."

Sy clears the loaded round, jaw tight. "Yeah, I recognized two of the guys. Remember Franklin from our freshman year? And that douche, Donaghy?"

"The 'roid head?" All three of our heads swing in the same direction. Nick stands in his doorway, looking casual as you please. "Fucking hate that guy." His chest is bare and he's raising a bottle of water to his lips, staring down the bridge of his nose at me.

Everything comes flooding back in Technicolor, high-definition. Those eyes staring down at me as he forced himself into my body. Those lips unforgiving against mine, even when I was sinking my teeth into them, making him bleed. The metallic flavor of it on my tongue, the way it made him groan in delight.

Mostly I remember the way he looked in the warehouse, handing me over to my father and Perez.

I remember begging.

I remember him walking away.

Grunting, Sy makes his way to the couch. Going from the motel to the car, then up the tower stairs, is the longest he's moved in days. He needs to rest. Still, I find myself straining toward the security of his retreating form.

Remy's eyes dart over to me then, ticking down my body, and suddenly I'm the one those murder-eyes are being pointed at. He steps up to me, the sharp angles of his face more severe than I'm used to. "Let me see," he demands in a low, gruff voice. Instinctively, I tug down my waistband, showing him the star. But even though he touches it, eyes flicking downward as he counts the points, he guides my hand away, head shaking. "I meant the rest of your skin. Did they hurt you?"

But I know what he's really asking.

Did they mark you?

Instead of waiting for me to answer, he pulls up my shirt to reveal my stomach, and then my sleeves to reveal my arms. His inked fingers sweep back my hair to inspect my neck, shoulders. "Where?" he asks, an impatience growing in his features.

"My knees," I whisper, unsurprised when he falls to a crouch. Cool fingers graze against the red rash the asphalt had made, and then around to the backs of my knees, cradling them as he takes an inventory.

His jaw ticks. "Where else?"

I roll my eyes, pretending I don't feel the fire of Nick's stare on us. "I don't know, Remy. Maybe my back."

I go willingly when he spins me, shucking up my sweater to inspect my back. I never thought to check it, to see if the man pinning me down had left any damage, but the gritty burst of noise Remy makes is clue enough.

There's an unhappy tilt to his mouth when he turns me back, but it softens when our eyes meet. "You took care of him," he says, cradling my jaw. He doesn't need to tell me he's going to kiss me this time. It's perfectly telegraphed, from the pitch of his chin to the palm he tucks beneath my hair, resting heavy against the nape of my neck.

"Remy kisses me like he's a goddamn soldier going off to war."

The words I'd said to Sy come rushing back to me when Remy does just that, capturing my mouth in a deep, bruising kiss. He tastes bitter, like beer and days of distress, and I twist my fingers into his t-shirt and ride it out, because it's everything—*everything*— I'd wanted from Sy last night. It's mindless and slow, devouring in a way that would have lesser woman's legs buckling.

Across the room comes a sharp, startling burst of sound, and Remy and I flinch apart, looking toward it.

The plastic water bottle is crushed in Nick's tight fist, and if murder had been in Remy's eyes before, then I don't even know what to call Nick's expression.

He looks like he's one second from punching a wall.

"Sit," Sy growls from the couch, "the fuck," he points to the couch opposite, "*down*." When Nick and Remy just stand there, glaring at one another, Sy barks, "All of you! We need to talk."

"Me, too?" I ask, but the words are full of contempt. Do Dukes talk? I thought they settled everything with their fists. Or with drugs, alcohol, sex, and avoidance?

Remy grabs my hand and pulls me over to the armchair, dropping into it and pulling me into his lap. His fingers dip beneath my waistband, touching the star, and across the room, Nick balls his fists.

A tiny squeak comes from the kitchen, and the Archduke comes running across the open floor. Sy scowls as the kitten passes him and I wince as his little claws dig into my skin, finding purchase in my legs to climb into my lap.

Instantly, I tug him close, pressing a whisper into his fur. "Hey, Archie."

"He missed you," Remy says, running his finger down his nose. "Been crying and looking for you all over."

Archie kneads into my sweater, gazing plaintively up at me, and I say, "Thank you for watching him."

"Hey, he's a Duke. We take care of our own." He gives Nick a hard, pointed look. "You gonna take a seat, or just stand there contemplating all the ways you want to shank me?"

Nick steps out of the safety of his room and sits next to his brother, arms crossed over his inked chest, knees spread wide. Nick and Sy are wildly different in a lot of ways. Nick is pale, Sy is dark. Nick is loose, Sy is tightly controlled. But seeing them next to one another, both sporting busted lips and yellowing bruises under their eyes, really drives home how similar they look.

Sy opens his mouth to speak, but Remy gives a jerk of his chin, saying, "Nick. It's time."

"Time for what?" Sy asks, looking between them.

Nick angles his head toward his shoulder, twisting until his neck cracks. It highlights the tension of the tendons in his throat. "I owe everyone here an apology." He chews the words like they're gristle, fixing his stare at the table between us. "I fucked up."

Sy snaps, "You think?" but the loud, humorless bark of laughter comes from my own chest.

Nick's eyes flit to mine at the sound and he leans forward, resting his elbows on his knees. For the first time I notice that some of the bruising beneath his eyes is just exhaustion. "You had me so fucked up, Lavinia. You pushed me. You know you did."

Teeth clenching, I go to stand. "I'm not listening to this."

Remy yanks me back. "Let him say his piece," he demands, voice warning.

Once again, I'm reminded of the truth of things. Remy and Sy... they don't care about me. Not really. Remy only cares about answers. Sy only cares about *them*.

"Go on." I smile bitterly. "Tell me more about how I was asking for it."

Nick laces his fingers together and squeezes. It's such a perfect mirror of the way Sy looked when I was patching him up after the attack—sullen and defeated—that I almost laugh again.

Is this how Nick sees it?

A loss?

"It's not an excuse," he says. "It's an explanation. Things just got so..." Another flex of his fists, a twitch of his jaw.

"Maybe," Sy says, lip curling, "if you'd come to one of us, none of this would have happened."

To this, Nick nods. "Lionel was going to come for her. I shouldn't have kept that from you, and I shouldn't have made the decision to hand her over. Not alone." He looks up at his brother, then at Remy. "What happens between Kingdoms affects us all. I get that now." At Sy's narrowed stare, Nick insists, "I *do*."

It's difficult to remain silent as he offers more of an apology to them than to me, but I do. I never expected anything else.

Sy doesn't stay quiet, though. "I'm not talking about that, Nick. I'm talking about how you think with your dick instead of your brain. When it comes to pussy, you need a goddamn minder." He nods at Remy. "We risked our hides to get her back. We're not letting you put us in that position again."

Nick twists to glare at him. "What does that mean?"

"It means that we need to project a united front, but as far as everyone in this room is concerned, the Duchess only has two Dukes."

Nick shoots to his feet. "Fuck that!"

"No, fuck you!" Sy stands slower, but looks no less menacing. "Remy and I put in the work to get here. Three years we spent being Saul's bitch while you ran free in South Side on your little quest to avenge a murder that you can't even prove!" He jabs a finger into Nick's shoulder. "Now, you're going to earn it. You're going to show us you can be trusted with her—with *us*. And that starts with you looking her in the fucking eye and saying you're sorry, because I'm not going to order her to forgive you." Sy shakes his head, nostrils flared. "I'm sick of cleaning up your messes, Nick. This one's on you."

Remy speaks next, his voice vibrating next to my ear. "He's right, Nicky. You're not square with us until you're square with her."

"Never going to happen." All their eyes swing to the matter-of-fact tone of my voice. "He's not sorry," I point out, gesturing to him. "To be sorry, he'd have to acknowledge what he did. He'd have to face up to being a narcissistic, self-serving asshole who never thinks past his own needs and wants, and certainly never past his own dick. Not that it matters," I scoff. "Even if he made some sorry attempt at an apology, I wouldn't accept it."

Remy sighs. "Vinny..."

I fly off his lap, dumping Archie in my place. "Did he tell you what he did?" I wonder, looking between my two Dukes. "Did he tell you that I got on my fucking knees? Did he tell you that I *begged*?"

The emotion sinks from Nick's eyes, leaving them empty and hard. "Lavinia—"

I speak to Sy and Remy, but Nick's the one I look at as I go on, "Or that I cried? Did your precious Bruin tell you that he stood there and watched Perez backhand me—"

Nick looks away, muscles rippling. "Stop."

"Did he tell either of you that he liked hurting me so much, he *came inside me*?"

Nick finally explodes, roaring, "Stop!" I don't understand why the coffee table suddenly goes lopsided, tilting to one end in a sad slant. But then it hits me that Nick has kicked it, breaking the leg. Sy grabs his arm, dragging him back, but Nick wrenches free, and it's like whiplash. Now when he looks at me, he just seems tired. Defeated. "I went too far," he says, voice gruff. "I lost control and now you hate me. Is that what you want to hear, Little Bird?"

"Don't," I warn in a low, deadly hiss. "Don't you ever fucking call me that again."

I don't realize Remy's standing until his arms come around my shoulders. It's not a restraining move, his forearms loose against my collarbone, but the threat is there. "We're not going to order you to forgive him, Vinny. But we need a ceasefire on this. Sy is right, we need a united front."

"Nothing's changed," I say, ducking out of Remy's grasp to make sure Nick understands that I'm speaking to him. "You don't get to touch me without permission. You don't get to tell me what to do. And I'm sure as fuck not sleeping in your bed *ever* again."

With his jaw clenched tight he stares at me for a long moment, and I think maybe he'll refuse my demands. He could. We both know it. Even if Sy and Remy say no—even if I learn to be a self-defense master—I'm never overpowering Nick in a physical fight. He can take what he wants, when he wants it, how he wants it.

But then he pushes out this bitter ghost of a laugh. "Fine. I've got bigger shit to deal with anyway."

He turns and crosses the room, heading straight to his bedroom. The door slams behind him, and I look over at Sy and Remy, both seeming as unsure as I do about what is, at best, a shaky truce.

10

Nick

I PACE in my room for an indeterminable amount of time, so wound up that I almost consider bailing and heading to the gym. But if the whores in South Side have heard about what I did, then there's no chance Mama B and the cutsluts haven't. My reception at The Hideaway was bad enough, and they aren't even loyal to the Duchess. What the fuck will the bitches of West End have to say about it?

I'm not in any hurry to find out.

For a moment, I wonder if Lavinia even realizes how many people in this fucking place are on her side. Or, maybe more accurately, just not on mine.

This is why, when Remy walks into my room an hour later, I'm coiled so tight that I almost think of finally giving him that fight he'd been asking for. "I told you," I seethe. "I fucking told you it was pointless."

Remy closes the door, only to pull a marker from his pocket and uncap it. "Bro, you barely even made an effort. What did you expect?"

"I can tell you what I didn't expect; you molesting her the second she walked through the fucking door," I hiss, pacing in front of him. "What the fuck was that? Even before everything went down, she barely let me touch her. A few days with you and suddenly she's the model Duchess. Fuck!" I bury my fist into the nearest vertical surface, which unfortunately for me, turns out to be the exterior wall.

Solid fucking stone.

"Goddammit!" I growl, shaking the ache from my fist.

Remy clucks his tongue, turning to press the marker to the door. "You're such a baby sometimes, Nicky."

"Fuck you." He's right. I know he's right. It's just this fucking *thing* inside of me that makes my organs feel like lava. I can't push it down. I can't find a way to hide it. Turning to him, I put voice to the anger that's been burning inside of me since I saw his mouth descending on hers. "So when you came to see me at the Hideaway, you conveniently left out the part where you're fucking her."

"I'm not fucking her." He's drawing something on my door, the felt tip of the marker gliding over the surface. He's had a real bug up his ass about not drawing on the tower, but I guess the doors are too new for him to care. "Do you even know what condition she was in when Sy brought her back?" He glances at me over his shoulder, not giving me a chance to answer. "She didn't know what was real. She didn't even know her own body anymore."

I stare at him. "What does that even mean?"

Of course I remember the way she looked when Sy brought her back. The image of her on that couch, pale and lifeless has been seared into the backs of my eyes for the last week. It's easier now, since she just walked into the tower looking a million times better. She looks healthy. Rested. Alert and sexy and *vicious*.

There's never a day or a time when I don't think my little bird is the sexiest woman I know.

He makes a bold, sweeping curve with his marker. "It means she was only half a person. You and Sy... you don't know what that's like. But I do." He tilts his head, considering, and then begins roughing out the shape of a face. "We had her on an IV drip. She couldn't walk by herself, so every few hours, we'd have to help her to the bathroom. She'd sleep all day, but even that was a battle. She'd have all these nightmares. Sleep paralysis, Sy calls it." His mouth thins to a tense line. "I read to her a lot. I sat with her. I took care of the cat. I kept trying to get her to talk about her sister and Tate, but every time I brought it up, something in her eyes would just shut down, so Sy made me stop." He makes a wide arc on each side of the door. Hair. "But I didn't fuck her."

Some deep part of me unwinds.

Until he adds, "But I will. Probably soon, too. You're going to have to find a way to deal with that."

It's so much fucking harder that it's Remy. If any other guy put his hands on Lavinia like that, I wouldn't have to think twice about blowing his brains out. With him, the thought doesn't even pass the processing phase, because the infuriating thing is, I love him, too.

"Sy?" I ask, voice rough as sandpaper. "Him, too?"

Remy shrugs. "I don't think they're fucking, but they've gotten... close."

My teeth clench. "Close to fucking?"

He gives me a wry look. "To *each other*, you psycho. Man, Sy had you pegged. You really do need a minder when it comes to her. Look at you, so fucking one-track. The Nick I know should be examining this from every vantage, but all you care about is what's going into her pussy." He rolls his eyes, blocking in the shadows of the eyes. "Like I was saying, Vinny and I are going to fuck. My balls have been blue for her since day one. So if you're going to pull another nuclear fucking meltdown, tell me now."

I can only hope he doesn't hear the desperation in my voice when I ask, "Would it stop you?"

"Nah." He says it plainly, coloring in the hollows of the cheeks. "But it'd give me time to play it smart." When I turn to start pacing again, he lets out a sigh. "Look, it's not about you. I'm not trying to fuck you up here. I gave you first dibs, and then I gave you second dibs, but me and Vinny... we have some chemistry. I don't exactly know what it is yet, but I suspect it involves some of the best orgasms of our lives."

I whirl on him. "Could you shut the fuck up?"

The marker pauses below the nose of the drawing. "Too much? Yeah, sorry. I just want to make sure you're okay with—"

"I'm not," I snap, dropping onto the bed. I force myself to take a breath. To imagine it. To think of Remy and her in his bed, moving together. To wonder what she'd sound like. I take it in with my inhale, the blinding hot instinct to rush back out there and steal her away before he can.

And then I blow it out with my exhale.

"But I'll deal." Because Remy is right. I need to see this from every angle, and all the other options end in catastrophe. I always knew what the Duchess' role would be. I asked him to wait until I got mine, and he did. That's more than any other guy in this town would give me.

He stands back, and even though the design on my door is barely a face, nowhere near finished, he caps the marker and nods. "Just... give it time, man. Sy was right. You need to earn it."

I don't tell him that I already have. Sy might have broken into the mansion and gotten her back, but I was the first one to save her. I was the one who spent months setting up all the dominoes. I gave her everything I could. I gave her my brother. I gave her my best friend.

When he moves to leave, I look at my split knuckles and say, "Not here." Looking up at him, my voice feels too rusty to hide the plea. "Don't fuck her where I can see or hear. I can't—I won't be able to—" My muscles lock in protest of everything I want to say.

Remy hears it anyway, bringing a palm down on my shoulder. "I won't."

For a good couple of hours, I let myself hate him. It never sticks, though. That's just how we work. If it has to be someone, then I'm lucky it's him, because Remy knows how to appreciate the special things.

Doesn't make me feel good about it, though.

And then there's my brother.

I know she and Remy have a little bond going on, apparently deeper than I'd realized, considering all that shit about her talking him down from the belfry and being some sort of mania touchstone. But Sy? I sensed it the minute they walked in the tower. I know how to read people—it's what kept me alive for two years in South Side—and there's unmistakably a new *ease* about them. It's a familiarity I wasn't expecting, watching them move in sync without even having to look at one another. That's the result of some serious fucking proximity. He spent her first two weeks here hating her fucking guts, and now my sexually repressed, rage-fueled brother is protective of her all of a sudden?

Well, saving the fucked-up spawn of the rich and powerful *is* sort of his thing.

But even that wasn't as bad as what I've seen these past three days. I've been poking around, and it's become obvious that she's living out of Sy's room. Everything of hers is in there. Her clothes. Her shoes. Her books. Her cat. It's not just some emergency situation, either. Her fucking underwear is in Sy's top dresser drawer. His pillows smell like her goddamn shampoo.

I spend a long time seething at the unfairness of it all. I saved her first. She never moved into my room. She never touched my back like she touched his. She never slept in my bed long enough for her scent to seep into the pillows. The more I think about it, the more I need to know. It's stupid. All it'll do is rub salt into the wound, stinging at the rawness of losing her, but now that she's finally here, I need a piece of her.

Any piece.

I wait until the house settles, listening to the creaks and groans. Remy's music turns off around two. I know when Sy goes to bed because his door is uneven, growling against the floor every time it closes. I haven't heard anything from him or Lavinia in hours.

When I can't take it anymore, I drag my desk beneath the ancient ladder that stops halfway down my wall. I climb on top and pull myself up the rungs, ducking out into the rafters. Most people can't really tell, but this chamber in the tower is too tall to have finished walls to the ceiling. From up here, everything is open to me. It's why I chose my room to begin with. It's the same room my Pops had when he was a Duke. It was the same room the Bruins who came before us used.

And this is why.

It's not my first time kicking around in the rafters for fun. It's just my first time up here for necessity. Slowly, I make my way around the edge of the tower, passing Remy's room first. He's already in bed, stark-ass naked. He's got one hand behind his head, shoved beneath his pillow, while the other is laying across his cock. I'm easily thirty feet up, but I can still tell he's not completely asleep. Probably just got done jerking off, if the flush over his chest is any indication.

I continue past in a silent crouch, using a drainage pipe for stability as I crawl over the partition between Remy and Sy's rooms.

That's where I find her.

The room is almost completely dark, except for the screen of Sy's laptop, casting a faint glow. It's just bright enough to see the shape of her on the far side of the bed, though.

They aren't even touching.

Some of the stiffness in my spines melts away.

"... because you didn't do it, did you?" The words are spoken so quietly that I can barely make them out.

Sy's are more defined, gritted through a tense jaw. "I told you, it makes it worse."

She's turned toward him, her thigh exposed. "You have to do it every day. It's called conditioning, idiot."

My big brother's gaze is trained on the other side of the room.

There's an irritability to the crease in his forehead. "I don't want to. Drop it."

She lets out a sigh so soft, I see it more than I hear it. "What's the big deal? You come so fast, it'll only take a minute or two." He turns his head slowly, swinging a hard glare on her, and she pivots to her back. "I'm not picking on you. I guess I just don't see the inconvenience."

My hand tightens around the pipe and I crouch lower to make out his hissed reply.

"Because it's impossible to walk around all day with a hard-on the size of a fucking bus!"

Any hope I have that they're talking about something else goes right out of the window, and I feel it. The lava sensation. The urge to climb down there, rip those blankets off of them, and show my brother who she belongs to.

"But you're hard right now," she argues, and a growl builds in the back of my throat at all the possibilities to explain why she even knows this. "You'll sleep better. And after so long, it'll start to realize it has an outlet, so it won't be constantly—"

"You don't know that!" he snaps, lifting his neck to glare at her.

She props up on her elbows to glare back. "Yes, I do! And we're not going to be able to move forward if you don't get it under control, so—"

It doesn't matter that the blankets are covering him. I can perfectly see the line of her arm moving beneath them, right to his crotch. Sy emits a rough, shocked sound, but then he's so silent that I'm sure he's not even breathing.

She's touching his dick.

The fact rages around in my brain like a hurricane, flinging every other thought aside until there's nothing left but the way it feels to watch that blanket shift, up and down, up and down.

Sy releases a long, strained noise, and then Lavinia leans close to whisper something, and I can't hear it, and it makes me want to stab someone. Fuck, what is she saying? What is she doing under there? Is she getting wet? Is she going to—

I know instantly that I can't watch her fuck him.

It's just like I told Remy. I won't be able to stop myself. I'll go fucking crazy. This is bad enough, isn't it? Isn't it enough that she has his cock in her hand? Isn't it enough that I can hear her sweet voice asking, "Let it go, Sy?" Isn't it enough to watch my Little Bird rest her cheek on my brother's shoulder as she strokes him off?

But no. She can't fuck Sy. Even if he could get that monster of a dick into a girl, he'd never last long enough. I know I'm right when he digs his head back into the pillow and seizes, releasing a string of bitten off grunts as he comes. She barely got a dozen strokes in before he popped his top, and she instantly moves away, dipping down beside the bed to clean her hand on a towel.

Afterward, they're silent. They don't touch. They don't kiss. They don't whisper goodnight to one another. They turn in opposite directions and close their eyes, and that's the only reason I'm able to go back to my room.

I DON'T GET much sleep, but then I haven't since...

Nick...

Don't make me go with them...

I'll be good for you...

I'll give you what you want...

I'll let you love me...

I spend most of the night on my laptop, going over the notes I've been keeping. It came as no surprise to me that the box with all of Leticia's shit in it is gone. It wasn't hard for me to work that out—that it wasn't Lavinia's box, but instead, her sister's. Going from there, it was easy to see the photo inside was of Tate and some other girl—most likely Leticia herself, and judging by the foliage, the cast of the sunlight, and the terrain, probably taken at the cliffs sometime in the fall.

The box is gone, but I didn't spend two years under Daniel's mentorship and not learn a thing or two about backups. I have photos of everything.

It'd be a lie to say it isn't gnawing at me. I'd gone to South Side to find her killer when I should have been looking North. Dead girls just seemed more Daniel's speed than anyone else's. That doesn't mean my time on the Avenue was pointless, and I keep trying to remind myself of that. I might not have found Tate's killer, but I still found a lot. Intel can get a person pretty far in Forsyth.

I flip past the photo of the rock, the dried wildflower, and the photograph, stopping on the receipt. This one has been bugging me. There's something here. The box was full of shit that seemed random, but Leticia put it all in there for a reason. The photo, the dried wildflower, the rock, the ribbon with the bloodstain, the bullet; these are tokens of emotional significance.

So what's with the receipt?

It's from an ancient pharmacy—East End's oldest still-standing business. On the front is a purchase list for a twelve-dollar phone case, a charger, and a pack of sour candy, but the back has numbers scrawled on it.

4009.

Not a phone number. Too short to be a zip code. A combination? Entry code? I ruminate over this for a long time, doing searches online, but it's not enough to go on.

When morning comes, my eyes feel gritty and sore, and the sound of Sy's door opening shatters the peace in the tower, slamming me back to reality. I wait until I hear him leave, because if I know my brother, then being a little concussed and a lot injured isn't going to disrupt him from a morning jog. My brother is a creature of habit. I think it's how he keeps the monsters at bay. The slightest bit of chaos sends him into a tailspin.

Sure enough, ten minutes later, I hear the sound of the door to the stairwell opening and closing.

I shut the laptop and venture out, going straight to his room to peek in on her. At least when she's asleep, she isn't able to fix me with that fucking *look* in her eyes.

But she's not there.

I check the loft, the bathroom, the kitchen, but Lavinia is gone and so are the shiny new trainers Sy had bought for her weeks ago.

Motherfucker.

They're gone for over an hour.

I spend it pacing and huffing, checking my phone for any messages. That's how Remy finds me when he slumps out of his bedroom in nothing but a pair of loose, designer boxer shorts.

"Would you fucking stop?" he growls, scrubbing a palm over his face. "You're pacing way too loud for seven in the goddamn morning." I pointedly pace over another squeaky floorboard and he flips me off, disappearing into the bathroom.

Sy and Lavinia come waltzing in moments later.

Both of them are flushed and dressed in sweat-soaked athletic wear. She freezes at the sight of me, her eyes hardening over, but Sy only pauses for a moment, giving a jerk of his chin in greeting.

"You're up early," he mutters, sauntering to the kitchen. Lavinia quickly follows, sticking closely behind him, and I lean against the archway to watch him pass her a cold bottle of water. He seems to be continuing an earlier conversation when he tells her, "Verity's in there, too. If you can't reach any of us, she's your next best bet. She can contact Mama B or one of the senior DKS if—"

That's when I notice what Lavinia is holding in her hand.

I straighten. "You gave her a phone?" The line of Lavinia's back goes rigid and she clutches it closer, as if I'm going to take it away. "What if she—"

"Has a way to call when shit goes sideways?" Sy snaps, shooting me a glare. "The Duchess is a target. She needs a way to keep in contact."

Not if someone's always with her.

She could use it to get away. She could call Cash, the Counts, the Lords, *anyone*. She could call for help from *us*. But saying all of that would just make her swing that hateful, furious gaze on me, so instead I just shake my head. "That's risky."

Sy shrugs, twisting the cap on his bottle of water. "Your Duchess might have been a prisoner, but ours isn't." Remy chooses that moment to amble in, and he gives Sy a nod at the words. "We don't have the time or resources to keep anyone locked up. If she wants to run away and get snatched up by her dad or Perez, then she can be my guest."

Remy offers a less crazy rationalization. Imagine that. "Come on, Nicky. Sy was barely conscious in that motel room. She had his loaded gun, his phone, and his car keys, and she's still here." He punctuates this by sliding onto the counter and pulling her between his legs. She goes easily, and from the quick, sideways look she gives me, I'm guessing Sy's not the only one she feels protected by. He frames her face, forcing her gaze to his. "Not much of a bird if she can't fly a little."

"Speaking of..." Crossing his arms, Sy pins me with a glance that's probably supposed to look authoritative. I can see the cracks, though. The wariness. "Remy and I had a talk a few days ago. The Princess is kicking up dust about the Duchess not meeting Royal criteria."

"Royal *criteria*?" she asks, turning to settle her back into the cradle of Remy's legs. "I'm a blood legacy. What more criteria could they possibly need?"

Remy links his arms around her shoulders, humming. "Institutional."

Comprehension dawns. "You're enrolling her."

Sy nods.

"Wait." Lavinia whips a wide-eyed stare to me, and then Sy. "Seriously? I get to go to school?"

Remy's mouth ticks up. "*Get* to? You make it sound like a fun thing."

I pinch the bridge of my nose, teeth grinding. Here they are stressing how dangerous it is to be a Duchess, and they're just going to throw her into the fucking fray. "How would you even do that?"

"Pops," Sy answers, swiping his wrist over the sweat on his brow. "He called in a favor with admissions."

My smile is brittle. "He's pulling out his Bruin weight for our Duchess?"

"He's pulling out his Bruin weight for *me*," Sy corrects, eyes tight. "Even if he'd help me, and he won't, Saul already used his to get you in. Pops owed me one, so I called it in."

Lavinia looks like she's about to vibrate out of her skin. "When do I start? Today?"

Sy pauses, looking caught off guard. "Well... no. Sometime next week, maybe." She deflates a bit, and if he'd thought to fucking ask my opinion, I would have told him that Lavinia's been locked up for over two years. That any chance of freedom or normalcy would excite her. That he shouldn't offer her something that isn't in his power to give freely and immediately, because otherwise, she won't trust it. Sy explains, "We have to take you in to set everything up, but Mama B is pissed we went MIA for a week. We've got scheduling to do over at the gym—and brackets to set up for Friday Night Fury. She'll have my ass if I don't show."

Remy tugs her back into his body. "And my life drawing class is doing studio work off-campus this week."

"But," Sy offers, "on Monday, one of us can—"

I step in. "I can take her." The room is silent, Lavinia tensing, but I've never had a problem filling up space. "I have class, anyway."

Sy and Remy exchange a look and there's a long beat, the kind designed to make me feel like an outsider. It's been this way since we were kids—two against one—until Tate came along and finally gave me a fighting chance.

Lavinia doesn't even look like she's breathing.

The tension in the room grows to a crackle, and I reach up to rub my eyes. "Look, you said I had to earn it, so you have to give me a chance. No one would protect her on campus more than I would. You know it's true. Plus," I add, pretending I don't see her jaw go rigid, "if the goal is to project a united front, then the other houses should see that we're a unit again."

"It'd be an act," she grinds out, but I just shrug.

"They don't have to know that."

Sy lifts his chin at Lavinia. "This is up to you. If he makes you feel uncomfortable, then you can wait until Monday, or maybe one of the pledges can take—"

"Like fucking hell!" Over my dead body will a goddamn *pledge* escort the Duchess to campus. "The pledges don't even pack any heat!"

But something sparks in Lavinia's eyes and she steps forward, breaking out of Remy's loose hold. All of us watch her walk up to Sy and strain up to whisper something in his ear. His hand comes down her hip casually, holding her steady as he takes in whatever she's saying. Unbidden, I get a flash of the two of them from last night, the way she whispered to him, too low for me to hear, right before he came.

I stare daggers at them, teeth gnashing.

When she pulls back, it's to give him an expectant look.

His eyes narrow. "I seriously doubt that's a good idea."

"It'll make me feel safer." There's a stretch of silence where Sy just stares at her. And then she says, "You promised," and Remy and I share a quick look.

My brother never makes promises.

Whatever she's talking about, it makes him inhale, long and deep, nostrils flaring wide. We all watch him break, but only Lavinia knows what he's caving to. "You have to leave it in the car," he says, opening the cabinet behind him.

She nods. "Totally."

He points a finger at her. "And no murder!" I don't need his words to confirm my suspicion. We keep all our spare guns in the safe hidden behind the cabinet.

She sends me a fiery glare before batting her eyelashes at him. "Kneecaps aren't murder."

Remy raises his cup of coffee. "Atta girl."

Sy pauses from punching in the code to bark, "Do *not* kneecap my brother!"

"I won't." She links her hands behind her back, looking as innocent as a doe. "So long as he keeps his hands to himself."

"Great," I mutter, going to get my own gun. "Be ready in ten."

"Everything straight?" I ask when she finally emerges from the registrar's office. She's wearing this short little skirt that's been driving me wild all day. I suspect she's wearing it on purpose, just to get a rise out of me. Probably hoping I make a pass so she can use that gun Sy gave her. Well, good job, Little Bird. My cock's been a rock-hard throb in my pants all morning. Mission halfway accomplished.

Her eyes cut over to me and she grunts. We haven't been exactly on speaking terms during this little excursion to campus. The drive here had been nothing more than a complicated silence. She ignored me, but she was also so fucking stiff, that gun held tightly in her fist, that every twitch of my hand had her muscles locking up.

"Ready for the dog and pony show?" I ask, reaching out to brush a lock of her pale blue hair from her neck. The campus was nearly dead when we arrived, but she was in the office for two hours. Students are filling the campus now, their loud voices carrying under the eaves of the administration building.

She goes rigid, pointing a scowl at my hand, but she doesn't slap it away. She just grinds out, "Watch yourself," and spins on her heel, sashaying away.

Fuck, the way that skirt hits her thighs is doing things to me. For a moment, I stand there, struck stupid, wondering why I'd been dressing her up in all those tight pants. Lavinia in a pleated skirt and ass-kicking boots is practically a weapon of mass erection.

I catch up to her a couple of seconds later, deciding to take advantage of the fact she can't shoot me right now. Sliding my arm around her waist, my hand rests casually on her ass, feeling the shift of it as she walks toward the crowded courtyard. She stiffens, but I don't relent. This is the whole point of the outing—to show everyone she's still my Duchess. We may be falling apart behind closed doors, but the rest of Forsyth doesn't need to know that. If that means I finally get to touch her the way I want, then that's just a happy coincidence.

"If you put those fingers under my skirt," she hisses, voice dripping with venom, "I'm going to cut them off one by one." Her expression remains perfectly blank and I'm reluctantly impressed.

"Taking a page out of my book, eh?" It doesn't keep me from skimming the smooth skin of her upper thigh. I fight back a shudder at the softness there. "Relax, Little Bird. I'm not going to overstep. People would believe this more if you'd kiss me, though."

"Maybe they would," she agrees, "but like your fingers, if you want to keep your tongue, I'd reconsider that."

Quietly, I ask, "Are you going to be a bitch about this forever?"

Her shoulders tense, and I know it was the wrong thing to say, even though it's a valid question. We'd had something before I fucked it all up. An understanding. Give and take. It wasn't enough —I'm not sure anything could ever be enough—but it kept me moving forward.

Until it didn't.

My phone vibrates in my back pocket and I fish it out of my pocket with my left hand, unwilling to release my hold on her. Thumbing the screen, I see a new text from Killian: *We need to talk.*

That single sentence is followed by a link to an address that I know on sight is Daniel Payne's home. Or was. I guess now, like everything else of Daniel's, it belongs to Killian. It burns sour in my stomach, being summoned like this. Just like Daniel used to do. I get a flash of dark alleys, the sharp tang of blood, pleas and tears, and girls.

So many crying girls.

My skin feels itchy with it, like just one sentence is able to call back a sense memory of every fetid thing South Side has to offer. This is my fault. I should have known going to the Hideaway the other night would open that door. Once again, the Lords own a piece of me.

"We gotta go," I say, glancing up to see Lavinia bent over, adjusting her boot. I didn't even feel her slipping out of my hold. Suddenly, every rotten memory dissipates, leaving only the sight of her creamy skin. My eyes drag along her bare legs and I tilt my head, trying to catch sight of her panties.

"Fuck, that girl's got a tight ass."

"Right? I'd like to see her bent over the end of my bed."

I whip my head around and see two scrawny twerps ogling Lavinia.

"What did you say?" I bark, taking a step toward them. They both startle, jumping back when they see me, my size, and the tattoo on my face. It's obvious that neither of these pimply shits have had their dicks inside a woman before.

"Nothing," one says, voice barely a squeak.

The other one, clearly prepared to lose his life, adds, "Dude, chill."

My eyebrows rise at the same speed as the adrenaline coursing through my veins. "Did you just tell me to chill?"

His eyes dart down to my balled fist. "No... uh, sir?"

My hand shoots out and I grab him by the collar of his shirt. His buddy looks like he may have just pissed himself. "Do you know who that is?" I ask, twisting his head so he's facing Lavinia, who's frozen as she watches the scene go down. He shakes his head and I sneer into his face. "That's the Duchess, asswipe, and no one looks at, breathes on, or even fucking thinks about disrespecting her. Understand?" He nods even more furiously, a fat tear building in the corner of his eye. What a pussy. Must be an East Ender. "Apologize."

"I-I'm sorry." The other kid mumbles his apology, too.

I hate them more for being able to say the words so easily.

Lavinia rolls her eyes. "Let them go."

I really, really, really, want to smash his face in, but the expression on her face is hard and irritated. I release the kid and then shove a hand into his chest, propelling him into his friend. "Since this is your first day having testosterone, I'll give you a pass. Don't you ever look at the Duchess again. Got it?"

"Y-yes."

"Get the fuck out of here." They scurry off, and I take a deep breath, noticing that a crowd has been forming, watching the scene with bated breath. I straighten my shirt and stretch my arm around Lavinia's shoulders, pulling her into my side.

She doesn't fight me, all too aware that we're being watched. That was exactly the ruckus we needed to draw the right kind of attention to ourselves. I spot at least one Count near the fountain. He'll run back and let Lionel know his girl is back under our protection.

DKS notices, too.

"Duchess!" One of our pledges stops in his tracks, eyes wide as he takes us in. "You're back." He looks way too happy about seeing her, a dopey smile forming on his face, and I think about giving him the same treatment as the other kid. But then recognition sparks in Lavinia's eyes and the worst thing that could possibly happen does.

"Hey!" She smiles. For *him*. "Ballsack, right? How've you been?"

A few more DKS pledges hover behind him with stunned expressions. The Duchess doesn't talk to *pledges*. This kid looks like his soul just left his goddamn body. "Good! Great! Look." He reaches up to shuck up his sleeve, revealing his cub tattoo. "Pretty cool, yeah?"

Her eyes flash excitedly at the sight, and it kicks up the memory of her tattooing it there, cradled between Remy's legs as he gently coached her. "Yeah, it healed up nice!"

He beams back, opening his mouth to add something, but then his eyes land on me.

Ballsack straightens, dropping his gaze. "It's nice to see you on campus, Duchess." The deference to me doesn't last long, because he raises his eyes—*insolently*—to tell her, "We just want you to know, if you ever need anything, we've got your back." He jerks his head at the group behind him and they all give solemn nods. His eyes flick to me, lighting quick, and I almost break.

They know what I did.

They're offering to protect the Duchess from her own motherfucking Duke.

Lavinia is blushing.

My fists curl and I breathe, long and deep, to remind myself that gutting pledges isn't the Duke way. Obviously, we're going to have to make a different kind of show later.

We walk the rest of the way to the lot, linked but silent, my fingers grazing her shoulder. The only reason I don't chase after the DKS hopefuls to put them in their place is because I suspect the interaction has chilled her out a bit. It doesn't last long. The instant we reach the SUV, she ducks away from my touch, diving into the seat to reach for her gun.

I allow myself the walk to the driver's side to fume about it.

"Where are we going?" she asks as I slam my door.

"Dukes' business," I say, cranking the engine. "Killian texted."

"You mean Lords' business," she says, propping a foot up on the dash. My eyes go straight to her inner thigh. I doubt the move is on purpose. Lavinia is a lot of things, but seductress has never been one of them. She comes by it naturally, not even intending to make my dick spring instantly to life.

Darkly, I agree, "Lately, the two seem to be intertwined. Whatever this is, I'll make it quick. Get you back to the tower."

She looks away, eyes focusing out the window as she fists the gun, and I find myself unable to hold back the words that have been building in my chest since I saw her on the couch, battered and unconscious.

"I'm glad you're back."

I watch the side of her face, but I don't know why. She doesn't react at all, her face carefully void of any emotion. "Lavinia," I try, but she doesn't answer. It's strange, the push-pull that's been warring between us for two long years feels so out of reach. I almost wish she'd spit in my face.

It isn't until I reach out to hook my finger around a lock of hair, tucking it behind her ear, that she reacts at all.

Her thumb cocks the hammer on the pistol.

I only let my touch linger for a second, thinking that being shot wouldn't be so terrible if she were the one pulling the trigger.

Hatred is better than nothing.

"WHERE ARE WE?" she asks, looking up at the house.

It's located on a quiet street on the edge of South Side. It's not a mansion like the Lucia sisters grew up in, but it's not a modest bungalow like my parents' house, either. It's a large brick home, a McMansion, clean and tidy on the outside. The perfect cover for a crime lord. No one suspected he had a former hooker as a wife and a stepdaughter he was grooming for the sex trade tucked away inside.

"This is Daniel Payne's old house." I kill the engine and scan the street for anything out of place. I trust Killian, *sort of*, but after Sy got jumped, I can't be sure of any of these bastards. "I guess it's Killian and his Lady's now, with his dad dead and her mother in prison."

"Hm." Her mouth slants unhappily, taking it all in. It's probably surreal seeing how the other Royalty lives. "Smaller than I expected."

"Not every King has a castle, Little Bird." She shoots me a dark look. "I'd tell you to stay in the car, but I know that's a waste of breath," I say, pulling out my gun and checking the magazine. "Stick close. This should only take a second."

We get out of the SUV and start down the walk. The neighborhood is quiet, the lawn neat and trimmed. At the door, I raise my fist to knock, but find it already slightly ajar. I check our six, but see nothing. Pushing the door the rest of the way open with my elbow, I touch the butt of my gun and feel Lavinia do the same.

"Yo!" I call out. "Payne, you in here?"

The house is quiet, nothing but the sound of Lavinia's boots on the hardwoods as we enter. "Maybe you got the time wrong," she suggests.

My phone buzzes again, and I check it.

K: *In the garage. Door off the kitchen.*

"Goddamn it," I mutter. I'm a fucking Duke now, not one of the Lords' foot soldiers. Not anymore. I'm going to have to make that clear.

To Lavinia, who's only a few feet away, I order, "Wait in the kitchen." I don't want her to be part of this.

"Whatever," she says, leaning against the island.

I approach the door leading to the garage, a discomfort settling over my skin like static. Something isn't right. Part of it is the sharp whine of something electronic. Part of it is that the sound comes from behind me, not from the garage.

I spin, fingers already on my gun, but the shock comes fast and furious, zapping into the skin on my neck. I lurch back, but a second shock comes as fast as the first and I fall, collapsing on the tile floor. My body seizes uncontrollably, teeth clenching on my tongue, and I grind out a scream as the taste of blood fills my mouth.

"Run!" The words are forced through my teeth, spoken to the blurry visage of Lavinia's boots.

Instead, she saunters closer.

Go, I want to say, but I'm too busy struggling to make my limbs react, heart jumping wildly. When she bends, I think she's helping me up and I want to lay into her. This is stupid. Fucking *run*!

She doesn't help me up.

She pulls my gun from my waistband.

That's when I see movement to my left. Another person. Slim, dark-haired, undeniably feminine in her flowy sundress. I narrow my eyes, trying to see past the pain. In the woman's hand crackles another jolt of electricity.

Is that a fucking taser?

What the hell?

"Lavinia," I grunt, trying to get up, but I feel the weight of a body on top of me, see the sparks igniting the taser in her hand.

"Settle down, Pretty Nick," a voice says, calm and soothing as I feel the smooth barrel of the gun—*Lavinia's gun*—pressed against my temple. "It's time for you to get a taste of what it feels like to live in a cage."

11

Lavinia

"Jesus, he's heavy," Story grunts, dropping one of his feet. I grunt, too, because she's not wrong. Nick's a solid wall of muscle, and when he's limp like this, it's roughly like trying to haul a very tattooed elephant across the floor. I wasn't sure the taser would be enough to take him down, but Story assured me, through a haunted recollection, that her mother used it to knock out all three of her Lords last year. If the surge of electricity was enough to take down Killian Payne, she was sure it could take down anyone.

She was right.

"Just drag him," I wheeze, not giving a shit when his head bangs against my shoe. We only have a few minutes before Nick's conscious again, so we need to hurry up and get him in the cage.

Yeah, *cage*.

It sits in the center of Daniel Payne's former garage, the size of a large dog crate. Three of the walls are solid metal, except for the front, which has bars welded into it. It looks sturdy and inescapable, especially with the thick chain and padlock hanging from the open door.

"So your stepdad had a dog?" I ask, voice strained as I kick the door open with my foot.

She grunts, helping me hoist him inside. "Nope."

Pausing, I ask, "Do I want to know what he used this for?" I look around the room. Along one wall hangs well organized tools, most sharp, with metal teeth that look like they can cut through almost anything. They're shiny and clean, but Daniel Payne never struck me as the type for manual labor.

Story puffs a lock of dark hair from her flushed cheek. "In most cases, it's better not to ask. It's the only way I survived living in this place."

I can't argue with that, so I focus on shoving Nick inside, his pretty, unconscious face smushed into the hard floor of the cage. He moans softly, brow wrinkling, but he doesn't open his eyes. Not yet.

Story walks over to the workbench while I secure the padlock. A second lock clicks into place, this one electronic. I look over and see her holding a small black remote. She shows it to me. "The red button sets the locks. The green electrifies the bars." She presses the green button, and a soft hum emits from the cage.

I can't help but laugh, knowing full-well that it must sound completely fucking unhinged. "And I thought *my* dad was a psycho."

Story gives me a deadpan look. "Lavinia, they're all fucking psychos." She glances back at the cage where the only movement is the twitch of Nick's fingers. "Never forget that."

I dust my hands off. "Well, thanks for helping me out. There's no way I could have orchestrated this on my own. They've got eyes on me all the time." It's not quite the same as it was before, with Nick. Sy doesn't watch me because he wants to own me. He does it because I'm a part of his world now, and that means something.

Something I haven't quite figured out yet.

"They should," she says, still winded. "You're their Duchess and you guys have had a lot of targets on your back." She looks at the cage, eyes hardening. "But you're not the only one with a reason to get payback on this prick."

Nick's slurred curse cuts through the room. "Son of a—what the —Lavin—" Story and I watch as he tries to lever himself up, only to slump back to the floor of the cage. Have to hand it to her. That taser packed a hell of a punch. The more he struggles to gain coherence, the more my blood thrums with excitement. To see him there, locked in that box, hurting and confused...

It's time people remember who I am.

Some might say revenge is best served cold, but those people aren't Lucias. We're vipers. We strike fast and hard. Nick Bruin is about to find out firsthand that his 'Little Bird' has fangs.

"You're not squeamish, are you?" I ask, taking the remote from her. She shakes her head and I stride over to the cage, kicking it with the toe of my boot. The rubber sole keeps me from getting shocked, but Nick cracks an eye open at the sound, breaths coming faster. Underneath that slack, incapacitated glaze in his eyes is a flash of hot fury.

"Lavinia..." He takes a breath, releasing it in a growl. "What the fuck is this?" His hand reaches out for the bar, and I smirk.

Zaaaap!

"Motherfuck!" he screams, jerking away. Well, that woke him up. He gives a rapid series of blinks, eyes rising to mine. "What the fuck is happening?" He looks between me and Story, but instantly disregards her. "Lavinia, get me out of here."

"Let you out? Like you let me out of the elevator?" I pretend to think about it, finger tapping my chin. "Nah."

His hand reaches out, and it happens again.

Zaaap!

I throw my head back, barking a laugh. "God, you're dumb."

"Son of a bitch!" He tries to rise, but there isn't enough room, and I love it. I love the way his legs are crushed awkwardly against his body. I love the way his chest is curled over his thighs, packed in there like a nice little psycho sardine.

It's art.

Remy could probably appreciate it.

Tapping the remote against my hand, I explain. "I'm just giving you a taste of your own torture, Nick. Thought maybe you'd like to see what it's like to be trapped in a cage."

He stares at me, unblinking now, eerily still, and I see when it finally hits him—exactly what this is. "You can't be fucking serious," he breathes, fists balling against the floor. It's obviously taking everything out of him not to grab the bars again. "I apologized!"

My boot meets the bars with a dull sound that's dwarfed by my scream. "You fucking did *not* apologize!"

Some of the color is coming back to his face, turning the tips of his ears a bright magenta. But he doesn't flinch. "Fine," he grinds out, lips curling back to expose his teeth. "I apologize. I'm sorry I shoved your bitchy, ungrateful ass into the elevator and sent you home to daddy. But did you ever stop to think," he adds, shifting to glare at me full-on, "if you'd told me exactly how bad he is, I wouldn't have done it?"

I laugh—*genuinely* laugh. "Wow, you really are the biggest asshole that life has ever spat out, aren't you?"

His smile is so sharp, I bet I could cut myself by slapping it off his face. "You know I'm right. If you'd let me in, none of this would have ever happened. But you just couldn't do that." Now he's the one to laugh, low and bitter. "I had it wrong before. About why you stay. About why you keep finding yourself shuffled from hand to hand. You're just too fucking proud to let anyone save you." Something significant sparks in his eyes. "It's not how you're different from your father. It's how you're the same."

Zaaap!

"Jesus Christ!" He shakes out his hands, expression tightening. "Lavinia, this isn't funny!"

I glance over my shoulder, tossing Story a grin. "Well, it's *kind of* funny."

"You little bitch," he says, directing his venom at Story. "Do your

Lords know you're doing this? That you've got an ally held hostage?"

"No," she says, casually walking over. "And you're goddamn lucky they don't, because if they did, then I'd have to tell them why I agreed to this." Her wide, innocent eyes narrow. "Trust me, that's a little secret you don't want me to tell."

His eyes dart to mine, then back to her. "What did she tell you?"

Her arms cross over her chest, revealing the tattoo on her wrist. "The truth about what you did that night in the Hideaway's basement. I know it all, Nick." She walks over and crouches down, looking him right in the eye. "You're the one who broke into that room. You raped her, recorded it, and then showed up later, pretending to be a big, bad hero. So yeah, I could tell the Lords. But then they'd kill you." She looks up at me, face contemplative. "Doesn't seem fair, though, does it? No one deserves to kill you more than Lavinia."

"See?" I toss my hands in the air. "That's what I've been saying!"

Nick has always been the strategically silent type, but there are few times I've seen him at a loss for words. Now is one of them. He stares at Story, who has him by the balls, and from the slack set of his mouth, he knows it.

"How dare you," she says, eyes narrowed into slits. "My guys stood by you. They backed you up. They gave your sorry ass shelter when no one else in this town would have you, and this is how you repay them? By manipulating them to get what you want? By making them complicit in something you knew they wanted no part in?" Her face turns to stone, transforming her from the sweet Lady I've come to know into the fierce Queen this town will come to fear. "*My* Lords are not your fucking puppets."

It's obvious the Lords are protective of Story. That's how it goes in the Royalty. But it's my first time realizing that viciousness can go both ways, because the hardness in her eyes is unmistakable.

She'd kill for them.

Nick looks up at me, mouth twisted into a deranged smirk. "So that's the plan, Little Bird? You leave me here to rot until the

Lady calls her guard dogs and serves me up? How is this going to go?"

"I can't believe Daniel wanted me to lose my virginity to you." Story shakes her head, standing. My eyebrows hike up and she rolls her eyes. "Don't ask. My part is done. I just need you," she kicks the cage, getting Nick's attention, "to know why I did it, and what's going to happen if you decide to retaliate against me or the Lords."

If looks could kill, she'd be a corpse, considering the way Nick is glaring at her.

She turns to me and leans in, giving me a quick kiss on the cheek before whispering in my ear, "This is between you and him. Make his pretty ass pay. Whatever that looks like in the end," she pulls back to level me with a serious look, "I want you to know I'll be behind you."

"Thank you," I tell her, voice too full of emotion to say everything I'd like to. There hasn't been a lot of discussion on how this ends. Maybe Nick dies here. Maybe he doesn't. Maybe we both do.

Either way, this is the end of something.

She shrugs, bumping my fist. "It's about time Royal women started sticking together."

We both watch as she exits the garage and closes the door behind her. It's just us now. Me, Nick, and an electrified cage.

"Your girlfriend's gone," Nick begins, trying to shift around in the cramped space. "You've roughed me up and made your point. Now, you can let me go."

I cross my arms, looking my fill as the silence envelopes us. For a moment, I consider that he really is pretty. Even with his faded bruises and furious expression, Nick Bruin is ridiculously handsome. Strange to think I might have gone for someone like him in another life. "Do you remember the first time we met?"

Instantly, he answers, "You kicked me in the face."

"Do you remember why?" I ask, watching him struggle to find a comfortable position. I know from experience one doesn't exist. "You said Royal bitches were weak. Which I thought was pretty funny, because I've known a few Royal women, and all of them had to bear one kind of torment or another. I thought to myself… Royal men couldn't handle half the shit we have to put up with," I toss the remote in the air, grinning, "but it'd be really fun to watch them try."

He finally goes still, nostrils expanding with a huff. "So, what? We spend the night in here?"

I arch an eyebrow, bending to pick up my bag. "We?"

A pause. "You're leaving me here."

"Nothing gets past you, *Nicky*." I grab a bucket and a bottle of water, setting them both just outside the cage.

He swings an incredulous gaze to them. "That's all you're leaving me with?"

"It's more than I got," I reply, voice hard as nails.

The acceptance sets in slowly, all emotion seeping from his eyes. What's left is an unfathomable shade of blue. "So help me god, Lavinia, if you hurt them…"

"Who? Remy and Sy" I laugh, the sound a touch too crisp. "I don't want to hurt them. They're dicks, but they're easy dicks. This is about us, Nick. Or have I been gone so long that you've forgotten our deal?" I crouch down to say the words that have been swimming in my head for days. Weeks. Maybe even months. "You hurt me, I hurt you."

"You can't leave me here," he shouts as I walk to the kitchen door. "I'm still your fucking Duke! You have to obey me!"

"Obey this," I say, flipping him the middle finger.

I hear the crackle of electricity followed by another string of curses as I turn off the lights and shut the door, locking it behind me. My heart pounds, adrenaline pumping in my veins for doing something so drastic. But only Story knows I'm here. Nick's right. He is my Duke and technically, I'm supposed to obey him. But he's also supposed to protect me, and he didn't.

And now he has to learn what it's like to be someone's bitch.

Mine.

NICK: Saul sent me on a pick up. Might take a few days.

Sy: You need backup?

Nick: Stay home. Taking a few pledges with me. Dropping the bird at the door.

Remy: Watch out for the peridot.

Nick: You got it brother.

NO ONE GREETS me when I arrive home. No one locks me up. No one demands to know where I've been, what I've been doing. There's music coming from Remy's room, but it's some weird, muted, melodic electronica that's completely unlike the loud, frantic stuff he usually plays. Nothing is like it usually is.

But the strangest part of all is that I'm here.

I spent three hours driving around Forsyth in Nick's SUV, no destination in mind. I could have taken it all the way to Mexico, and none of them would have stopped me. Instead, I'm here, hiding Nick's keys in the cabinet above the refrigerator. I'd parked the SUV a few blocks down, deep inside an alley bisecting two rundown warehouses. My blood is still singing with the victory of it all; the knowledge that Nick is suffering, the awareness that I have access to a phone, a car, and two guns: Nick's and the one Sy gave me.

I turn the pistol—*mine*—over in my hand, thinking that it feels right in my palm. The weight of it is perfect, and it's fully loaded—Sy showed me himself. All of this, the weapons, the way out, is as close to freedom as I've ever had.

That's how Sy finds me a few minutes later: waiting patiently and dutifully with my pistol on the counter, clip already removed. I exhale, releasing the tension I've been holding since I sent that text message from Nick's phone. I spent an hour studying their exchanges, making sure I got the tone just right.

He pauses at the sight, giving me a slow nod. "I assume everything went okay."

I move so he can lock it back up in the gun safe, not even

peeking at the code. I don't need to. I still have Nick's gun, after all. "Yep, I'm all registered."

He slides me a wary look. "And Nick?"

My grimace is only half-faked. "Insufferable as always, but seemed in a hurry to offload me."

"He said he had a job." Sy frowns and it makes my stomach flip anxiously. I'm really banking on some level of ambivalence here. Just in case, I slide up on the counter behind him, legs parted just so. "I hope Saul isn't planning to—" His words die in his throat when he turns to me, eyes dropping to my thighs.

My feet sway casually. "He didn't seem nervous," I offer. "Just impatient."

There's a long beat where I can practically see Sy's eyes dilating, zeroed in on the skin below my skirt. He doesn't even try to play it off smoothly, looking away with a hard breath. "I need to run to campus for my afternoon lecture, but I need to have a fight with Remy first, so you should make yourself scarce for a bit."

My legs stop swaying. "You're going to fight with Remy? Why?"

Sy shoves a hand in his pocket, the tips of his ears glowing red as he not-so-discreetly adjusts his erection. "I've had a lot of trouble getting him to take his meds lately. Ever since we worked out that his doctor's a fucking hack, he's been..." Sy's jaw locks. "... *resistant*."

Now, I'm the one frowning. "Well, maybe he has a point." Remy had been the one to explain the situation to me. It was in those days after I came back, when everything was fuzzy and disorienting. Remy wasn't exactly cogent himself, pacing around Sy's bedroom as he fed me information in energetic, ranting bursts. It's just like that with Remy. Sometimes I'm less Duchess and more a captive audience.

But Sy shakes his head. "The doctor's been bought—that's pretty obvious. But I've done a lot of research, and the diagnosis and treatment is medically valid. He needs this shit to stay evened out. I can already tell he's starting to cycle again. This reminds me. There's something I want you to do."

My stomach sinks. "What?" Aside from attending the fight a few days ago, neither he nor Remy have pulled their Duke cards on me.

He leans against the opposite counter, finally meeting my gaze. "You know that guy we saw at Felix's place? Cash?" At my nod, he asks, "Is he the kind of guy you'd want to *not* see me kill?"

I freeze at the look in his eye. Nick's killed people—possibly a lot of people. I'm not sure about Remy, but he has the disposition. Live in Forsyth long enough, you tend to get a feel for that kind of thing. But Sy seems to prefer violence in a competitive atmosphere. He just wants to win—dominate. He's never struck me as the type to kill unless it was necessary.

Until now.

Holding his stare, I carefully explain, "I used to babysit him every now and then when he was a kid. He's an obnoxious little shit, but he's not like the Counts. In the increasingly long list of people I'd want to see dead in this town, Cash Money is one of the few who doesn't rank." It lingers bitterly in my throat that I'd have to ask him not to kill someone.

Luckily, he doesn't make me. "Then tell him Remy's off limits. I don't like him having a free-for-all contact to North Side's product. Remy isn't a junkie." Sy lowers his chin, pinning me with a dark look. "But under the right conditions, he could be. I'm not about to watch that happen. You get me?"

It all makes sense then.

Sy would kill to win. He'd kill to survive. And he'd kill to protect the people he cares about. It prickles at the back of my neck like something dangerous and inevitable.

Inwardly, I wonder if Nick is still conscious.

Outwardly, I give his brother a smile.

"I'll track him down. Cash will listen to me." Sliding off the counter, I add, "And don't worry about Remy. I'll get him to take his meds."

Sy scoffs. "He won't take them for me, but you think he'll take them for you?"

"Yes." I reach for the pill organizer that's always sitting right by the fridge. "I have something you don't." Before he can ask, I flounce past him, flipping up my skirt to reveal my sheer panties.

A quick glance over my shoulder reveals that his lips are parted, that hand in his pocket adjusting his boner once again.

Smirking, I stop in front of Remy's door, knocking twice. I hear Sy coming around to watch from a distance, feeling the heat of his stare on my back as I wait. When the door swings open, I take a quick inventory of what I'm working with. Remy's eyes are hooded as he does the same thing, his gaze sweeping up and down my body as I assess his mood. His hair looks more mussed on one side than the other, as if he's been in bed. He's wearing a threadbare Led Zeppelin t-shirt that's peppered with tiny holes around the collar, and a pair of jeans that probably cost eight-hundred-dollars.

His eyes pause on the pill organizer in my hand, a tendon in his throat tightening. "No."

"You didn't even let me speak." I pout, reaching out to tug at the hem of his shirt. "If you take them, I'll let you draw on me."

"Not today."

"Remy..." I flutter my eyelashes as my fingers dip beneath his shirt, toying with the hair below his belly button. "What if I wanted to get naked for you? Be good for you?"

I don't catch the shift in his eyes soon enough to follow it. Suddenly, his fingers are wrapped around my throat, grip so tight that the flash of pain makes me gasp. "Don't," he hisses, eyes full of daggers. "Don't you *ever* bring that fake shit to me. I might be crazy, but I'm not fucking stupid."

I stare up at him, heart fluttering like a stampede, and I try to find the anger, the steel, the hatred that's always gotten me through moments like these—moments with weak, bitter men who lash outward—but I can't find it. I can't see the heartless, empty Maniac who enjoys hurting and maiming. I can only see the Remy who stood on that Belfry, weeks ago, so fucking beautiful and broken.

I can only see myself.

The soft, hurt sound that emerges from my throat is more about that realization than the pain of his hold, but I watch it slam into Remy with all the force of a punch.

Instantly, he releases me.

There's a stretch where I rub the raw skin, and he just... stares at me. He looks at me as if he's just come out of a dream. He rests his forearm across his doorjamb and buries his face into it, groaning. "I'm not having a good day, Vinny."

I don't need to turn to know that Sy has, at some point, lurched forward from the kitchen entryway. I can feel the tension rolling off of him as he watches, waiting. To intervene? To rescue me again?

I give him a shake of my head. "You're right, Remy. That was fake." I watch Remy's fist flex at the roughness in my voice. "So here's something real. For every pill you take, from now until... whenever..." I lower my eyes to the pill organizer, a storm brewing in my gut. "I'll tell you something about my sister."

Remy jolts back, arm falling to his side. I know why he's been so hovery and attentive lately. He thinks I have intel about what happened to Tate. I'd given him the picture, but I could tell it just raised more questions.

He holds my gaze as he reaches for the pill organizer, and I'd be lying if I said it didn't sting, but it's not in the way he'd think. It's not because he hurt me. It's not even because I actually did want to undress for him, to feel his touch on me, to lose myself in an hour beneath his hunger for my skin.

It's because Leticia isn't even here, and somehow, she's still outshining me.

A minute later, Sy watches from Remy's open doorway as he takes all three pills, one after the other. "You good?" Sy could be asking Remy, or he could be asking me.

We both give him a nod, but I'm the one to clear my throat. "Go on, we've got this."

The way Sy looks at me then makes my chest go tight. There's this terrible, aching gratitude in his eyes, and it occurs to me why he and Remy are such good friends. Sy isn't a faker. He thinks I've done something important here.

I want to tell him that it's nothing. I'm used to bargaining with fucked up people. In some ways, it's all I've ever known. It's not a talent. It's what being a Lucia—being a Royal of Forsyth—has shaped me to be.

When Sy is gone, Remy looks at me from the corner of his eye. I'm expecting him to ask about Leticia pretty much right off the bat, so when he says, "Get on the table," I'm oddly relieved.

I hop up on his tattooing table, slowly unlacing my boots. We're solid here, beneath the light he flicks on, waiting as I lay back.

He jerks his chin, "Shirt." He doesn't wait for me to remove it, running his fingers under the hem and lifting it over my head. A second later, I'm on my back and he's got one marker between his teeth and another pressed into my skin. It lasts longer than I'm expecting, and I let myself get lost in it. The cool tip of the felt. The warmth of his fingertips. The way his forehead creases when he tips back, only to dive back in again.

On one of his passes over my collarbone, he mutters, "I didn't mean to hurt you."

My throat jumps with a swallow, and I know he sees it when his mouth tightens. "Why don't you want to take your meds? Sy says they're good. You know he wouldn't mess with you."

He shakes his head, a lock of platinum hair falling into his eyes. "It's not about Sy."

"Then what?"

Remy's fingers go to my throat, fingertips trailing over something. Had he left a mark? He dips down to press his lips to the flesh, lingering long enough that I can smell the faint whiff of weed clinging to his hair. But when he leans back, he's all business again. When we're like this, I'm just a canvas to him. Compliant. Clinical. Clean. "Every fiscal quarter, I have to meet with my father to go over his 'investment' in my future. It's tomorrow."

"Oh." I've noticed the strange vibe in this room ever since I got home. It's not the mania I'm used to. This is something slower, simmering beneath the surface, but no less consuming. "Is that why you seem stressed?"

"Stressed?" He makes a derisive noise. "I'm not stressed. I'm just... searching."

"For what?"

A jerk of his shoulder. "Rebellion. Futility. Anarchy."

I watch as he ducks down to draw a line beside my breast, his tattooed knuckles grazing my stiff nipple. "What does that have to do with taking your meds?"

"If I go there all medicated and quiet," he explains, tongue peeking out from behind his lips, "then he'll think he's winning."

I roll my eyes. "It's always about winning with you three, isn't it?"

The corner of his mouth twitches. "To the victor..."

"... go the spoils. Yeah, yeah, I've heard all about it."

"So about your sister..." he begins, sweeping a line down the inside of my arm.

"Don't ask me what she was doing on the cliffs that night," I warn, trying not to shiver. "I don't know."

Remy pauses and a faint flicker of surprise comes over his eyes. It's probably the first time anyone's accepted his memory at face value, without tossing out qualifiers like 'if'. He recovers just as quickly, asking, "She ever fuck other chicks?"

I've been asking myself this ever since I realized what the picture was. Tate and Leticia. It's been nagging at me for days. It's unlikely they'd cross the boundaries between west and north for a mere acquaintance. "Honestly, I have no idea. If she really is... gay, bi, pan, whatever... she would have hidden it. And she definitely wouldn't have told me. We fucking hate each other."

His eyes flick up to mine. "Why?"

"Same as always, isn't it?" I give him a bland smile. "To the victor..."

"... go the spoils." He smirks, finishing a whorl over my elbow. "Even in North Side, huh? Tate would have gone for that. She and Nick always went wild over problematic pussy." Smoothly, he adds, "Guess you know all about that. Tell me something else."

"About Leticia?" I sigh, thinking back. If she was hiding it, she had good reason. Our father wouldn't have accepted her being with another girl—not because he cared that she was attracted to women, and not even because the woman was a West Ender. But because it didn't fit into his plan. Attraction or not, she was destined to marry Perez and keep the line going. Maybe Leticia wanted something for herself. Something that was all her own. If that's the case, I can't say I'd blame her. It's just weird to think about, since Tate wasn't just hers. She belonged to the boys, too.

Men that are now mine.

"I might have seen her kissing girls at parties once or twice, but I always figured it was performative. She likes putting on a show. Tricking people. Hoarding their secrets. You can't really trust anything she shows you. Most of it's probably fake." Gradually, I realize, "You wouldn't be able to stand her."

"Maybe not."

"That's two," I warn him. The thought of lying here all afternoon and talking about my sister makes me feel vaguely sick to my stomach. "I'd say you get one more, but you're not asking the right questions, so I'll give you something a little more specific." He straightens for this one, capping the marker as he meets my gaze. "Mama B told me Leticia came into the gym before she went missing. Said she was looking for someone."

Remy blinks. "Tate?"

I shrug, sitting up to inspect the intricate design. Twin stars, mirroring one another, their sparkles and whorls descending my arms. It always goes back to that with Remy, doesn't it?

He combs his fingers tightly through his hair, tugging. "Fuck, that would be classic Tate. She and Nick, still causing trouble together, even after..." There's a wistfulness in his eyes that fascinates me. It doesn't last long. "That's why my dad is being such a dick this year. Sy, he can handle. Nick, though..."

"Not a fan?" I guess, feeling my neck prickle at the mention of him. I'd checked my phone for the forecast earlier. It's going to get pretty cold tonight.

Remy shakes his head, jaw tight. "He hated Tate, too. The first time they met, I thought he was going to disown me."

I slip my shirt back on, feeling strangely disappointed that it's over. "What was she like?"

"Tate?" He leans back against his workbench, spinning the marker between his dexterous fingers. "Well, she was West End down to her fucking marrow. A lot of people didn't get that about her, because she didn't like the gun running. But that's how it really is around here. We fight with our fists—our bodies. Tate was into that."

"Athletic?" I ask, thinking of Sy taking me for a run earlier that morning. Even injured and half-concussed, he was running circles around me.

Literally, he had to run circles around my struggling ass to keep up any hope of a workout.

He grins. "Big time. She could give Sy a run for his money when it came down to stamina. They used to train together back before we even called it 'training'. It was just fucking around back then."

Everyone talks about Tate like she was perfect in every way. Too good for Leticia, probably. "But your dad didn't like her? Why?"

"For one, she was chaos personified." His mouth tightens into a grim line. "I'm pretty sure my dad thought we were all fucking her. He chilled a bit once he found out she was a lesbian and there was no risk of me knocking her up or something, but he still didn't approve. Tate's family wasn't exactly upwardly mobile, if you know what I mean."

"If anyone knows what you mean, it's me." I slip back into my boots, tying the laces. "So he didn't want you shacking up with your lessers."

"No. Actually..." Remy gives me a long, considering look. "He'd want me to be with someone more like your sister."

I look up, skeptical. "Even though she's North Side?"

His head tilts. "Why do you talk about your sister like that?"

"Like what?"

There's a pause—a hesitation. He pushes past it to say, "You talk about her in present tense."

I don't like the coldness that settles over me. "My sister fucking tormented me throughout most of our childhood," I say, trying to explain it to myself as much as him. "But I don't want to think of her being dead. There's no body," I point out. "No proof she's *not* alive."

I don't understand the tension in his expression until he says, "I saw her fall from the cliff, Vinny."

He thinks I'm doubting him.

"And you fell with her," I say, hopping down from the table. "You lived. Maybe she did, too."

He scratches his head, that divot returning to his forehead. "Right." Shaking it off, he reaches for his sketchbook, smoothly picking up the discussion as he presses the marker to a page. "Anyway, my dad wouldn't care about her being North Side. He isn't loyal to any Kingdom. North, south, east, west. It's all development potential to him."

My head swims with it all. Tate's chaos. Leticia's social value. Across town, one of my Dukes is a prisoner, and I didn't tell him this, but the electrical shock wasn't Daniel's idea. It wasn't even my idea. It came from a textbook that Remy had read to me the day after I'd been rescued.

The more I think about it, the more I'm sure Story was right.

All dads are psychos.

The sound of paper ripping draws my gaze up, and Remy's closing the notebook, extending a torn page to me.

I blink, reaching for it reluctantly. It's saturated in black marker —still damp. "What's this?" I ask, even though Sys words from before stomp through my brain.

"Solid black means he's sorry about something."

"I freaked out. Put the wrong color on you." Remy glances at my neck, and then away again.

"Oh," I tell him, handling the page carefully. "I forgive you."

It should burn to give it so freely, but it doesn't. Maybe that's why Remy's so scary: because he's so fucking forgivable. We're alike in ways that people like Sy and Nick wouldn't understand, and times like these make me wish we weren't. Because I understand the anger simmering under his skin, the tight, suffocating knowledge that your existence is owed to someone who doesn't deserve any thanks for it.

"So... these meetings with your dad..." I start, feeling a malicious glint building in my eyes. "You ever bring a date before?"

Remy's gaze creeps to mine.

Slowly, he smirks.

SY SPENDS the whole evening pacing.

He's not really obvious about it because he paces between semi-legitimate tasks. He goes to wash a dish, and then crosses the living area to put up a sweater Remy had thrown over the chair days ago. He angrily shoos the kitten away from the spiral staircase only to follow him into the kitchen to shoo him away from the table. My awareness of him is just faint enough to notice these things as I lie on the couch, reading.

Sy picks up his shoes.

I turn a page.

He carries them to his room.

I turn a page.

He crosses in front of me to grab a beer bottle from the coffee table.

I turn a page.

"What," he finally says, stopping in front of me, "are you even reading?" Wordlessly, I lift the book in front of my face, letting him read the title. I can practically hear his eyes rolling. "Stop reading my textbooks."

I turn a page. "Nope."

"Can't you find anything better to read?"

"Probably." I turn a page. "But I'm starting classes on Monday, and you're basically pre-med like me, so maybe some of your psych bullshit will come in handy."

From my periphery, I see his knuckles tapping against his thigh. "We should make it an early night." I lower to book to see him, noting the tension in his shoulders. A touch too quickly, he adds, "We need to get up to run in the morning, for your conditioning. We should be well rested if we're going to push your endurance."

Pointedly, I let my eyes crawl down his body, unsurprised to find a bulge in his pants. "Right. *My* endurance." Since I'm still wearing the skirt, I lift a knee, belly fluttering when he instantly drops his stare to my bare thigh.

"Lavinia," he says, low and strained. There's a thread of warning beneath the desperation, and I close the book.

"Fine. Let's go to bed."

I've been sleeping in Sy's room for a while now, so I know all of his nightly routines. He usually goes around the tower turning off lights and locking up, spends for-fucking-ever brushing his teeth, takes twenty minutes to write in the journal he won't let me read, and then fights with Archie for another twenty minutes.

Tonight, I follow as he beelines for the bedroom, shucks off his shirt, grabs Archie by the scruff of the neck, and sets him just outside his door before slamming it shut. He all but dives into bed, which would be funny except for that fiery gleam of anger in his eyes. He glares at the ceiling as I slip out of my skirt, removing my top and replacing it with the shirt he just removed.

He turns off the lamp before I even get a knee on the bed.

I blink rapidly, adjusting to the darkness as I slide into bed beside him. "Gee, Sy. Is there something you want?"

"Don't," he growls, so rigid that he barely jostles as I settle in. "You're the one who made it do this. I was fine until the sun went down. Suddenly, I'm pitching tent in the middle of my fucking study hour."

"Good," I say, unapologetic. "You got through the day, right? That means it's working."

"What it means," he replies, voice clipped, "is that it's ruined my fucking night."

I knock my fist into the pillow, fluffing it up. "Oh, boo hoo. Your 'conditioning' ends in an epic orgasm. My conditioning ends in shin splints. Cry me a fucking river." Rolling my eyes, I add, "And also, stop talking about your dick like that."

A pause. "Like what?"

"Like it's a separate sentient being. It's just a dick. Most guys have one."

Shortly, he counters, "Most guys don't have people constantly horrified by it."

I hum. "You've obviously internalized everyone's reaction to your dick, creating an unhealthy relationship with your own body, not to mention—"

"Stop reading my textbooks," he snaps, and then his hand is on mine, yanking it over the distance between us.

Unceremoniously, he shoves my palm onto his hard cock.

"Hey!" I instantly snatch it back, reaching over to flick on the lamp. "If the point is to win at sex, then let me be crystal fucking clear! Only losers need to force someone to touch them."

Even though something in his eyes flinches at the word—loser—he still glares back at me. "Well, you're taking your sweet fucking time." Nostrils flared, he pushes down the blanket, exposing the bulge beneath his shorts. "Get rid of it!"

I gape at him. "The deal wasn't that I'd be your nightly handjob delivery system! If you want to be good at this, then you need to think of something other than your dick."

He looks murderous, teeth gnashing. "Like *what*?"

"Like..." I gesture to him, momentarily at a loss for words. The most baffling thing about Sy is that he's actually fucking hot. If he'd just play into it a little bit and not ruin it, he could have girls hand over fist. "First of all, bedroom eyes aren't glaring daggers at the girl half naked in your bed."

He glares harder. "What the fuck should I do, then?"

For a moment, I'm so caught up in the irony of the situation that

I almost have to laugh. His brother would have been balls deep in me five minutes ago. Sy might just be the only man I've come across in the past two years who has no interest in what's between my legs.

I know something he does like, though.

I grab the bottom of my shirt—*his* shirt—and pull it over my head, freeing my breasts. "Suck on my tits."

Every hard line of his face goes slack for a second, like his brain is doing a factory reset. "What?"

"My tits. Suck on them." I enunciate clearly. "At some point you're going to have to put effort into making a woman feel good."

He does this thing where he pushes his fingers into his eyes—oh yes, this is *such* a burden—but eventually levers himself up, fixing a dark-eyed gaze on my tits. His mouth parts as if he's about to say something, but all that emerges is the rosy point of his tongue, licking out to wet his lips.

He touches me first, lifting a hand, pausing only for a blink before cupping me in his broad palm. Sy's touched me before, of course. That day Remy ate me out, when Nick watched, Sy pressed me up against the wall and groped me. That one night in his bed, him rutting against my paralyzed form. The time in his parents' basement, frenzied and full of anger. But all of those were clumsy attempts, just the wrong side of aggressive, full of a resentment that I didn't fully understand at the time, and probably still don't.

Tonight, though, he touches me... gently.

He holds the weight of my breast in a palm and sweeps his thumb up over my nipple. He watches his skin press into my skin, and there's a curiosity in the movements, unsure but unhurried. Without thinking, I arch into the warmth, fingers tangling into my discarded shirt.

Sy's eyes jump up to mine, but dart back to my nipple when he thumbs it again, bringing it to a stiff peak. His forehead puckers. "Does that mean—uh, are you—do you—"

"Yeah," I breathe, feeling dangerously unfiltered. "It's good."

It's not just the touch of his rough fingertips. These are a fighter's hands. Hands that have been honed to hurt. Hands that know the grip of a gun, the hilt of a knife. They're skilled in a lot of things, but not in this.

Here, he's the undercard.

When he finally dips down to run his tongue around the circumference of my nipple, I shudder at the heat. It's a tease, but not finessed enough to be intentional. Unthinkingly, my fingers knit their way into his soft, curly hair, and he falters, briefly, before taking my nipple into his mouth.

"Oh," I gasp, pushing into it. "Shit. Yeah, just like that."

He gives a soft rumble that I can feel vibrate all the way down to my bones. Switching to the other breast, he gains a little confidence, closing his mouth around it while his hand massages the other. The needy heat between my legs has been an issue ever since that night in the motel room. Remy's been painstakingly stoking it, hotter and hotter, with every kiss, every tickle of his marker against my skin, every glimpse of him walking around here, shirtless, muscles shifting beneath ink. That has to be why these little sessions with Sy, which are artless and too rigid, have basically become the equivalent of putting my finger into a light socket.

The moan that bursts from my chests surprises me.

From the way he backs off to stare at me, mouth slack, it's possibly surprised Sy even more. I can't take the scrutiny, not when I'm like this, practically naked, vulnerable and ridiculously turned on.

"Don't," I warn, pushing him back with both hands. It's barely any work at all to whip my panties off, tossing them blindly aside, and Sy's face gets harder as he watches me do it.

"What are you—?"

"Just... just let me..." I straddle his hips and he remains frozen, silent as I hook my fingers into his boxer shorts, giving them a testing tug. "Like last time," I explain, recalling that night of the Baron's party.

His answer comes in the form of his silence as he allows me to free his cock, even though his chest expands with a hard inhale. I spend a long moment staring at it, trying to remember what makes this thing so unappealing. Right now, all I can see is a dick. A beautiful dick. A dick I can't wait to feel against me. The thought of having it inside me seems impossible, but the thought of riding up against it?

Yes, please.

When I glance up at him, his pupils are blown wide. "I won't be able to hold it." The words are spoken with a strain that's visible in his body, the tendons in his neck stark and rigid.

"Try," I command.

And then I slide up, lowering myself onto his hard, hot flesh.

The second my pussy makes contact with him, he's hissing, hands coming up to clamp around my hips. "Oh, *fuck*."

I wince at how hard and big he feels rammed against my core. His length stretches across my pussy, and I can feel him everywhere —tip to tail. For a moment, it's as if we're breathing each other's gasp, skin against skin, sweat building between us. We hang suspended as we absorb the sensation—the closeness.

When Sy looks up at me, his eyes are so half-lidded that he looks drunk, the space between his brows knitting together. "You're so wet," he whispers, the words filled with a strange awe. "Because of this?" He flexes his hips upward and I can't stop the soft, needy cry that escapes.

The grin he gives me, edged with a smug wickedness, is the worst part about it.

It's a winner's smile.

"You like that, don't you?" he says, taking over my movements. He glides me back and forth, my weight nothing in his strong arms. "You like riding my cock."

I'd tell him no, or to fuck off, or to shut his pretty mouth, but I'm too close to it—that elusive release—to give a shit. I just *want*, and who the hell ever thought this man would be the one to give it to me?

Annoyed, I begin to rock into him. *Hard.* Taking care not to let the tip slip inside, I press my palms flat against his muscular chest and ride him. Maybe I should be gentle. Maybe I should guide Sy into it, show him that sex can be slow and selfless and respectful and fair.

Instead, I ride him like a goddamn horseback.

It's greedy and impatient, and I don't fucking care. I use him more than I coach him, throwing my head back as my hips undulate. He makes these small little grunting noises, so soft that they never even leave his throat, and they drive me forward, faster. There's this ridge just under the head of his cock and every time my clit glides against it, fireworks erupt in my belly. I chase it doggedly, too horny to care what I must look like.

Sy's fingers tighten on my hips, clamping hard enough to bruise. "Wait, wait, wait," he says, the words a rushed jumble. I barely hear them, so close now that my thighs are trembling under the force of my bucks against him. "Dammit!" he shouts suddenly, his body seizing, hot cum exploding between us. "Fucking fuc—"

I place a hand over his mouth, not wanting him to ruin this for me. Sure, he came too soon, too fast, but his cock is still pulsing between my legs and his cum is perfectly sticky and warm. I ride him wet, rocking against him as he grows limp. I don't care. He's big enough that I don't *really* need him to be into it. So I chase it, the want and heat and the feel of his cum, and when my body explodes, a surge from my core, pulsing through my nerves, clenching my muscles, it feels like victory.

To the victor...

I clamp my thighs around him and shudder, biting down on a cry.

I'm still catching my breath when he lifts me off his body and rises from the bed, tossing me a shirt, which I'm assuming I'm supposed to use to clean up. I wipe the cooling cum from between my legs and even in the faint light I see the tension in his shoulders.

"So," I start, unsure of what's happening. "I think we made some—"

"That was your fault," he snaps. "The tits, climbing on me like that. You fucking wanted me to humiliate myself, didn't you?"

"What?" My head is still a little foggy, but I realize he's talking about ejaculating too soon. "No. Sy, that's just part of the proc—"

"Is that what gets you off?" He whips around, dark anger clouding his face. "Humiliating me?"

"You're being crazy."

"No, you're just a slut who gets off on demeaning men."

"Hey!" I bark, bolting up. "Don't you fucking dare call me a slut."

His face twists into a flushed snarl. "Fine. You're a whore who can't keep her legs closed. You should be the one who's embarrassed! Not me!" He reaches past me and grabs a pillow. "I'm sleeping on the couch."

He opens the door and Archie, who is waiting right outside, darts in before he slams it shut. The kitten hops up on the bed, purring when he reaches me.

"What the fuck was that?" I ask the kitten.

"*Mew.*"

"Exactly," I say, tossing the dirty shirt across the room. "He's a fucking lunatic."

12

Nick

DANIEL CAME TO ME FIRST.

A lot of people don't know that. They think I just put on my shoes one day, started walking, and didn't stop until I hit the Avenue. It's bullshit, though. Daniel had been trying to recruit from other Kingdoms for a while before he found me. Obviously, I told him to go fuck himself.

And then Tate was killed.

Getting close to a King, earning his favor, is an opportunity many don't get. Sure, I'm a Bruin, first in line for a Dukeship, but I was just out of high school. Getting close to Saul would have taken years. Doing Daniel's dirty work was the easiest, fastest way into the inner circle.

When I finally accepted his offer, I only told one person why: My dad. He's always understood me a little better than my pops. Tate used to find it fascinating, the whole biological aspect of our relationships being largely superficial. Pops gave me his DNA and his name, but my dad—Sy's biological father—was the one who really taught me how to fight with something other than fists. He taught me how to fight with my mind, how to look and see, how to play things to my advantage. Davis Bruin knows how to fight in the ring, but Manny Perilini knows how to fight in the streets. That's why it had to be him.

Naturally, he didn't like it. He spent hours trying to talk me out of it. It wasn't a good weekend. Tate had just been put in the ground. Remy was locked up in the hospital. Sy was roaming around bars and begging for as many fights as he could get. The fault lines between us were already growing too deep to cross, so I figured, what better time? Everyone would believe, and they'd need to, if Daniel was going to buy it.

Dad realized pretty quickly that I wasn't going to change my mind. *"Well, if you're going to do something stupid, you might as well do it smart."*

So we made a plan.

I had to get in touch every Sunday, no matter what. I'd slink away to whatever dark corner South Side allowed me and leave him with any intel I'd gained from the week. He'd protect it, keep a record, and then I'd crawl back into the gutter to collect more. The deal was that, if there ever came a time when Monday arrived without word from me, he'd come down to the Avenue and find me. I had some close calls, but it never actually came to that. Still, though. Useful.

Problem is, we put an end to that when I returned to West End.

I could rot here for a week and it wouldn't send up any flags.

The cage is hard and cold, and when I wake up from another brief doze, my neck is fucking killing me. I'm not sure how long I've been here, but the sun stopped shining through the tiny garage door windows hours ago. Probably early morning, if the October chill is any indication.

There's nothing to do here but think, and that's what I do. I try to fight with my mind. Look and see. Play something to my advantage. There's no way out of the cage. I spent my first few hours in here working that out. The bars on the front are electrified, and it's just enough voltage to put me off touching them.

I'd try yelling out, but some force inside my chest makes me turn away from the idea. Pride, I guess. At least there's water. Gotta hand it to her. It's sort of fucking brilliant. If I want to drink—and I've been putting it off as long as I can—then I need to reach through the bars and get zapped, which makes the bucket she left me to piss in a particularly nice touch.

Christ.

My girl is a fucking sadist.

Into the suffocating darkness of my cage, I grin.

It's in the small hours of the morning that I hear anything. The air has that feel to it, a touch of damp, a stillness that settles like a void, that tells me it's maybe three or four. I'm curled up tight, just as much to preserve my body heat as to endure the confinement, when I hear a disturbance from inside the house. My muscles coil anxiously as I listen, waiting.

If the Lady told her Lords, then I'm as good as dead. She wasn't wrong. I suckered them into this shit. If it'd been the Lords playing the Dukes, then we'd do the same. Even worse, it could be Sy or Remy. This would mean they found her out. That they'd need to punish her. That they're about to find me here, defeated and diminished, trapped, helpless. There's really no good way this ends.

I don't think I've ever heard anything as loud as the door to the garage opening. It cleaves through the silence, making me stiffen in anticipation.

But when the light comes on, it's just her.

The tension drops from my muscles like a boulder. "Morning, Little Bird."

She's standing in the doorway, her eyes blank as she takes me in. The sweater she's wearing is Sy's. It's so long on her that I can't tell whether or not she's wearing shorts beneath it, but the slight bulge near her hip is a tipoff. Her hair is pulled up into a sloppy bun, little locks of pale blue escaping every which way, and her eyes are bloodshot. Her boots are tightly laced, and it's the only thing about her that feels deliberate. She took time to lace them. My car keys are dangling from her right hand, and her left hand is holding a paper bag.

She walks into the garage, tucking my keys into her pocket.

"Is that a gun in your shorts," I ask, voice rusty with disuse, "or are you just unhappy to see me?"

Wordlessly, she drops the paper bag before reaching beneath the sweater to take out the gun. She folds herself down onto the garage floor, and she's only four feet away from me, which is why I suddenly know what's in that bag.

"Fuck," I mutter, knocking my head back into the metal wall of the box. "You're actually fucking diabolical."

She pulls out one of the foil wrapped tacos and slowly—torturously—unwraps it. "Have you ever read The Bet?" Holding my gaze, she takes a big, borderline pornographic bite of the taco. Her jaw works for a few seconds. "Short story. Published in the 1800s. Anton Chekhov?"

I stare.

"No?" She chews, watching me. "Essentially, it's about these two guys—a banker and a lawyer—debating the death penalty. The lawyer says it's more humane to confine a person for life than to kill them, because life is inherently valuable, even under the worst of circumstances. The banker says a life of confinement is the cruelest punishment of all, and that death would be a mercy. What's life without freedom?" She takes another bite.

My stomach rumbles.

"So they make a bet," she goes on, looking far too comfortable. "The banker tells the lawyer to spend five years confined to a room on his property. If he can endure it, then the banker will pay him a shitload of cash." Her smirk is dark and brittle. "This doesn't need a spoiler alert, does it? The lawyer forfeits."

Sighing, I wonder, "Is there a reason you're giving me a book report? Because I'm not the one who put you into that chest."

"You put me into the elevator."

"Yeah," I snap, getting annoyed. "Because you were being unreasonable. It wasn't a punishment." She stares at me for a long stretch. Angrily, I relent, "Fine! It was, but it wasn't the same."

"Of course it was the same." Her face hardens, but she continues eating. I wonder if she's even hungry. "And even if it wasn't, here's the thing about boxes and cages, Nick. They aren't always literal."

Tiredly, I ask, "What do you want from me?" I'm expecting her to think about it. To really dig in deep. To probably come out with something annoyingly demanding, like an insistence that I sit and reflect on my naughty behavior, or craft a sincere apology, or dedicate my life to saving kittens or whatever.

Instead, she answers instantly. "Oh, I just want you to suffer."

I know Remy and Sy think I'm a little crazy when it comes to her, and maybe they're right, because yeah, I'm completely fucked right now—locked up, no way out, completely at the mercy of someone who wants revenge.

And it's a physical battle to stop myself from smiling.

Clearly, I fail.

She freezes, lip curling. "Are you *smiling*?"

"You hate me." I shrug. "And you're going to let me out."

She shakes her head. "Wow. How do you even begin to reconcile those two thoughts? Either your last two brain cells are busy fighting for third place, or you literally don't know me at all."

"I don't know you?" Nodding, press my shoulders into the wall of the box. "You didn't tell the whole story. The banker was free, but it didn't do him much good."

She pauses, brow knitting together. "What?"

"The Bet," I remind her. "In the years the lawyer was locked away, using his time to study and enrich himself, the banker lost all his wealth. He fucked his life up."

Slowly, she puts the taco down. "So you have read it."

"Who do you think brought you books, Lavinia?" I tilt my head, smirking at the shock on her face. "That's right. I've read everything you've read, from Augustine's trashy romances to that tattered clock manual you fished out of our cabinets. I've read the textbooks. The magazines. The poems. I've read the fucking shampoo bottle you keep in the bathroom." I lean so close to the bars that I can feel the hum of the electricity. "Every piece of knowledge that's gone into your head these last two years has gone into mine. I know every fucking inch of you."

I watch her recover, tucking away all of her surprise and replacing it with scorn. "That doesn't mean anything. Except that maybe you're a psycho with far too much free time."

"No?" Looking away, I remember, "The whole point of the story is that freedom is a corrupting force in the hands of the wrong people. I mean, on the last day of the bet, the banker was going to kill the lawyer just to avoid paying him."

She gapes at me. "That's not—!"

"And it's not even like the lawyer decided captivity was too much. He just reached the end of his enlightenment and wanted to go to heaven to unlock his last achievement, so really, you're kind of misrepresenting the whole thing."

Her eyes flash so hot, I can almost feel them warming me. "You've been in that cage for eighteen hours, and you're seriously telling me… what? That freedom is overrated?"

"That's not what I'm saying at all." I shift as much as I can, pinning her with a look. "Those years you spent locked away, I was locked away with you. You didn't know it. You didn't even care. But you see, Little Bird, I'm the lawyer in this clumsy little metaphor you so arrogantly walked in here with. I could have left anytime, but I didn't. I stayed. I studied. I reached the limits of my enlightenment, and you know what I learned?" I rap my knuckles against the bars of the cage, making the voltage surge. "Hate is big, baby. Bigger than love. People move mountains for hate. They kill for it. They fuck because of it. They feed it, stoke it, nurture it."

When Sy brought her back, she kept giving me these looks, like I was nothing. It was fucking unbearable. I wasn't lying that day when I explained to Remy that I need things when I'm near her. Her attention. Her touch. Any of her.

All of her.

I let the smirk free. "Right now, I'm the most important person in your life."

The light fades from her eyes, leaving behind a girl—a woman—who looks too worn for her age. Suddenly, I regret saying it, because tears begin welling in her eyes.

"This is just a joke to you, isn't it?" Even through her tears, I see the hatred, but beneath it is the exact same hurt I'd been so terrified to see the night I ran away to South Side.

I turn away from it now, staring at my knuckles, and the letters tattooed across them. *D-U-K-E.* A fist of Forsyth, protector of West End.

A fucking joke.

She laughs, quiet and strained. "You want to know what's sad? For a while there, I actually wanted to believe you loved me. No one's ever said those words to me before. Just figures, doesn't it? Someone finally notices me long enough to feel something for me, and it's this... this fucking insanity." There's a ghost of a sniffle, but I'm too much of a chicken shit to face it.

Again, I ask, "What do you want from me?"

"I already told you!" she snaps. "I want you to fucking suffer!"

The explosion building in my chest abruptly breaks free. "You think you had to lock me up to do that?!" I hurl the words at her, and for the first time, I feel like this cage can't contain me. It's too small, pressing against the parts of me desperate to spread, expand. I clamp down the urge to thrash against the solidity of it. "You wouldn't let me save you, but you let Sy save you! You sleep in his bed." I ram my fists against the bars, feeling it zap into my knuckles. "You sleep in his fucking bed!"

Her expression twists. "Sy doesn't expect me to be his pet slave in repayment for it!"

"Is that what you think?" My laugh is edged with disbelief. "When's the last time you touched his dick, Lavinia? Open your fucking eyes."

"That's between him and me," she insists, eyes growing darker.

"This stupid fucking jealousy shtick of yours? You have no right to it. You had a million chances to really save me, and you didn't, because all you care about is yourself!"

"You were mine," I remind her, teeth gnashed. "I was honest with you. I gave you everything in my power to give. I protected you, and you spat in my fucking face!"

Her eyes grow wide and wild. "You protected me?!" The shrillness of her voice cuts through the room like a bullet, ricocheting. "You couldn't even protect me from yourself!"

"I did protect you from myself!" I roar, the words coming from a place so deep inside that it feels like an exorcism. "Why the fuck do you think I gave you back!"

She stares at me, her eyes growing impossibly wider. "You can't seriously be telling me you gave me back to my psychotic father for my own good." I know the admission was a mistake the second she reaches for the gun in her lap, because there's a violence in her eyes, and it's *screaming*. It promises pain, misery—death if it can give it.

But Lavinia's always had this anger problem. It's part of why I knew she'd work as Duchess, and it's part of why she's going to fail at it. Because every Duke eventually comes to learn that it can lead to a win or a loss, and anger doesn't really care which.

In her anger, she fumbles the gun.

It bounces against the smooth floor, knocking against the hard epoxy and skittering across the distance.

I react on instinct, lightning-fast, pushing my arm through the bars just as she dives for it. The electricity burns like a bitch, making my teeth clench as I grab the cool metal of the pistol. Her fingers barely get a graze on it before I'm yanking it through the bars, growling against the pain of the shock.

And then I have the gun.

Lavinia falls back, heels scrabbling against the floor as I raise the barrel. "Oops," I say, tapping it against the metal. "Sucks for you."

The color drains from her face and she freezes there, sitting on the cold floor, eyes fixed to the gun. "You'll have to kill me." Her face hardens as she says the words, as if she's just realizing the truth of them.

She'd rather be dead than let me free.

My brain flicks through all the paths that diverge from here, but mostly I think about the words still ringing in my ears.

... this fucking insanity...

I turn the gun over in my hands, knowing just from feel alone that it's mine. This pistol was with me all through my years in South Side. It's the same gun I've trained on her countless times—long before she became Duchess. If it were a person, it'd know her almost as well as I do.

"We could have been good together," I tell her, testing the weight of the gun in my palm. "If you would have given me one fucking chance, we could have—"

But it's useless.

Even I know there's just no coming back from some things.

The look on her face when I toss the gun back would almost be funny if I weren't on the verge of braining myself against the wall of the cage.

Clearing my throat, I explain, "If you're going to do something stupid, then you might as well do it smart." I hug my legs to my chest, thinking of late nights spent in her grimy, South Side motel room. If those are the best I'll ever have, then what's the point? "Don't let me out until you stop hating me," I decide, voice gruff. "It's all the same to me."

13

Lavinia

My feet beat hard against the pavement, ponytail whipping left to right as I stare sightlessly at Sy's broad, muscular shoulders. I've never exercised as much in my life as I have these past few days, and despite the fact I'm only running off three cumulative hours of sleep, something about it is strangely soothing. Sy leads us through East End again, just like that first day he'd taken me on a jog, and every puff of breath I release sends a cloud into the cold, misty air. My ankles hurt, my eyes feel gritty, and every time my soles connect to the asphalt, I'm jolted with another spike of anger.

Does Nick think I'm stupid?

Because I'm not.

I know this is a control thing. It's deliberate in that special way, but it's also a manipulation, as if I'm going to see it as some sort of gesture.

Fat fucking chance.

I left him there in the cold, in the dark. It's been four hours, but my hands still feel like they're shaking. The memory of fumbling that gun, giving him the upper hand, still makes my face feel hot, even as the chilled wind cuts across my cheeks. *So stupid*. Now I've given him freedom. Not in a literal way, of course. But if a cage can be a state of mind, then freedom can be, too.

He's free because he made the choice not to be.

Motherfucker.

My fists curl harder as I clear the distance between Sy and me. He speeds up instantly, as much to make sure he wins as to keep a pace with me, and I finally explode, thrusting my hands out to shove him.

He barely falters, stopping, it seems, only to pin me with an annoyed look. "What was that for?"

"You said you'd teach me how to fight!" The words are meant to be sharp, but emerge on several puffs of wheezed air. "I stepped up your training last night. Now it's your turn."

His mouth goes pinched at the mention of what happened last night. "That wasn't training," he says, eyes narrowed. "You just wanted to get off!"

I snap, "News flash, robot boy! That's the most important lesson I could possibly give you. People using your body to feel good is the only kind of sex I've ever fucking known, so be grateful that you could actually throw me off when you had enough. Some of us don't have that luxury!"

He looks me up and down, mouth twisting. "This is about Nick." I start to argue, but before a word even escapes my mouth, he shakes his head. "You can't beat Nick. He's easily got a hundred pounds on you."

It burns like lava in my throat, the knowledge that Sy is wrong. I've already beaten Nick. It's such a Duke mindset that I nearly laugh in his face. Power is about more than fists.

But fists can't hurt.

"I want you to teach me how to punch someone—the right way," I demand, knowing that my face must be flushed a deep scarlet. Crossing my arms, I add, "If you do, I'll teach you how to get a girl off using only your fingers."

His face screws up. "Why would I want to learn that?" The disgust in his voice is belied by the way his eyes instantly drop to my tits, all mashed together with the way my arms are crossed.

"Because," I answer, eyes rolling. "Girls won't care how fast you come if you get them off first. Isn't that why you asked me to do this? If you want to be good at sex, then it's not really that difficult, Sy. She just has to leave satisfied."

He stares at me, the hair at his temples dark with sweat, and it'd be easy to get a little lost in the way the morning sun shines off his bronze skin. Take away the hostility and stiffness, he looks exactly like someone I'd want to sink into, as if these sparse mornings of waking up curled into his body make more sense than anything ever has or ever will. If it weren't for the coldness of his eyes, Sy could trick someone into believing he's the epitome of warmth itself.

And then he opens his mouth. "Fine. Teach me how to appease the bitches of Forsyth, and I'll teach you how to act like one."

That's how I find myself, an hour later, standing in front of him in the tower, the large clock face above glowing with the morning rays. We stare at each other for a long moment, though I'm not sure why at first. Music is coming from Remy's open doorway, but it's muted, like an afterthought to the way he's shuffling around in there, getting dressed, collecting his things. Archie does one winding loop around my ankle, but must sense the strange tension in the air, because he ultimately totters off toward his bowl in the kitchen.

Sy and I are still engaged in this epic staredown when Remy finally emerges, looking both tired and flustered. Without breaking my gaze, Sy greets him with a dip of his chin. "Remy. Have a seat."

"I have things to do," he starts, not sparing us more than an electrified glance. "And I already took my pills, so don't give me your bullshit this morning. I have to feel the sky today or I'm going to start losing colors again." Remy seems particularly bothered by this, scrubbing his fingers through his hair, looking harried. "Everything is going to be cold soon. The sun isn't eternal, Sy."

Sy just nods at the rambling incoherence. "Fine." Then, to me, he says, "Go ahead and hit me."

Remy doubles back, dropping his bag on the sofa. "On second thought, I've got ten minutes."

Frowning, I shift my feet. "You haven't taught me anything yet."

"Maybe I'm teaching you how to take a fucking order," he says, eyes narrowed. "Or have you gotten so comfortable around here that you've forgotten who your Dukes are? *Hit me*, Duchess."

The temperature of my blood rises, but even as my hands curl into tight fists, I can already tell any hit I land will be infuriatingly insubstantial. Duchess or not, I'm still a Lucia. We don't fight with our bodies; we fight with our venom.

Remy climbs onto the couch, the soles of his shoes dirtying the cushions as he perches on the back. The flash of delight in his eyes is almost enough to dull the roar of anger pulsing through my head. "Get him good, Vinny. He might not look it, but he's got a bit of a glass jaw under all that ego."

When nothing happens, Sy sneers. "Look at you, wasting my time. Or was this all a ploy to get my fingers into your pussy? I bet it was. Should have known a whore like you would only care about what's between her legs."

It hurts.

The punch, I mean.

I throw it without a shred of thought as to function or form, my knuckles cracking against the sharp cut of his jaw. The pain shoots up my wrist, stabbing into my forearm, and the sound I make is half yelp and half growl.

Sy doesn't even flinch, even though the hardness falls from his features. "Yeah, that was pretty bad."

I cradle my hand, teeth clenched. "You didn't tell me how—"

"I'm not talking about the punch," he says, grabbing my hand. "I'm talking about the way you let me get to you so easily."

Remy points out, "The punch *was* embarrassing, though."

I shoot him a warning look. "Less commentary from the peanut gallery, Remy!"

"Do you always provoke that easily?" Sy asks, giving me a wry look. "I didn't even get to the good stuff."

My nostrils flare. "The *good stuff*?"

"I'm a psych major," he replies, checking my knuckles for damage, "and you're the poster girl for daddy issues. I have so much material to insult a girl like you with that it's actually funny."

"Know what I think is funny?" I ask, offering a cutting smile. "The fact that men fail at fatherhood on such a statistically massive scale that there's an actual term for it, but somehow it's used to insult *women*."

Remy's brows do something complicated and pensive. "She might have a point."

Sy rolls his eyes. "Whatever. Try again." He curls my fist for me this time, pressing down on my thumb. "This time, keep a straight line from your elbow, through your wrist, to your knuckles. Try to hold it through the punch." Before he lets my hand go, however, he pins me with a serious stare, voice low. "Anger is useful if you know how to harness it. But you should never, *never* strike out with it. Anger is as precise as dumping two tons of water into a bathtub from a cargo plane. You want it to fuel you, not drive you. You let anger take the wheel, you're going to crash."

When I have my fist back, I look at it, the straight line from my elbow to my knuckles. I think of how Sy looks in the morning sun, and then I think of how he looks in the depth of night, lazy-eyed and desperate as he fumbles for my skin. I think of how he owns me here and now, but when the clock strikes midnight, I'm the one holding the leash.

It isn't anger that drives my next punch.

It's certainty.

Not a certainty that I can win. That was never in the cards for me—not here, not when it comes to fighting with my body. But a certainty that winning doesn't matter. At the end of the day, a body can be a weakness just as much as a strength—even his.

This time, Sy's head rocks to the side with the force of my punch, and it still hurts—god, like a bitch—but the pain is a lot easier to take when I can see him wincing with some of his own. "*Fuck.*"

Remy whistles. "Not too bad of a hook."

"Yeah..." Sy rubs his jaw and I can see him visibly fighting back a spark of his own anger. "Of course, you telegraphed it from a mile away and your stance is all wrong, not to mention—"

"So you're saying I should try again?" I ask, flexing my fist.

Sy pauses.

"Actually..." Remy hops down from the couch, eyes full of life. "I changed my mind. You're coming with me this morning."

Any satisfaction I might have gotten out of Sy's obvious hesitation to be punched again melts away with my frown. "Where are we going?"

"Shopping." Remy slides his hand in his pocket and pulls out a black credit card. "The sun is out and the biggest daddy issue in Forsyth is about to bankroll the Duchess' new wardrobe. What do you say?" When I shoot Sy a wary look, Remy adds, "Come on, we'll get you a dress for tonight. Something sexy. Something rebellious."

Wryly, I guess, "Something skanky?"

"Not at all," he assures, slipping into a leather jacket. "Something expensive and classy, with *just a touch* of skank."

His moods are like whiplash, but that tracks with the diagnosis. Sy's books say that shopping can be a trigger and a person with bipolar disorder can easily overspend. The glance Sy gives me confirms this. There's no way he can let Remy loose without a monitor, and from the looks of it, that's going to me.

I arch an eyebrow at Sy. "I suppose I could use a few things that aren't a cutslut castoff."

He rolls his eyes, but waits until Remy is out of earshot to say, "I don't care if he spends every last cent of his dad's money, but once he blows through the limit, it'll be drugs, and then sex, and then god knows what fucking else."

Geez, that's reassuring. "I'll do my best." I give Sy a brittle smile. "Although I have recently been reminded what my place is as Duchess. Remy is my Duke, after all."

There's a red spot on Sy's jaw. Not bad enough to be swollen, but not insignificant enough to avoid a slight bruise. "I was just trying to rile you up," he says.

I shrug. "Doesn't make it any less true, does it?" It's fascinating how still Sy can get. The second I slide up against him, he's just like those gargoyles guarding the four corners of the tower. A bear-headed statue, stiff and unyielding, keeping watch as his eyes dart around in search of Remy.

"What are you doing?" he asks, jaw tight with clenched teeth.

I place my palm on his warm chest, gazing up into his wary blue eyes. "Let's get something perfectly clear. I've passed through a lot of hands on the way to yours, Simon Perilini. I've been locked in boxes, closets, rooms, and towers. I've spent days, weeks, months, not even knowing which way is up or down, and I'd forget my own fucking name before I forgot the most important thing of all." I brush my lips against the red welt on his jaw, pressing my words into the tenderness of it. "You never need to remind me who I belong to." I pull away, deliberately letting my knuckles graze the hardness bulging from his sweats.

"WHAT IS THIS?" I ask, turning it over in my hands. Remy had emerged from his room with it, not long after Sy had scurried away.

Remy glides smoothly down the last flight of stairs. "That's a helmet, baby. Nicky and Sy would gut me if I fucked up that pretty face." He's holding one of his own, and the moment we push through the door, I understand why.

Outside, he approaches a black motorcycle.

I've heard it rumbling outside a few times but never processed it as belonging to Remy. He slings his leg over the seat and pats the spot behind him. "Hop on, Vin."

Briefly, I falter. I've never been on a motorcycle, but it's not the machine that worries me. It's the driver. Remy is a wildcard, subject to sudden whims and impulses. Who's to say he's not going to drive the bike off a cliff? But, as I hesitate, staring at his long, lean body, the spread of his hips as they straddle the seat, the bigger part of my fear is being that close to him. Leaning on him. Figuratively and literally.

His eyebrow rises, tongue sweeping out to wet his bottom lip, and fuck. *Fine.* I approach the bike and he takes the helmet from me as I stop before him, shuffling my feet, uncertain. He rises from the seat to place the helmet over my head, but he doesn't secure it. Not immediately.

First, he touches my chin, tilting my face up to his. Remy searches my eyes, his own a plundering green. I'm not sure what he's looking for. Maybe he senses the wariness in them. Maybe he sees something deeper, evidence that I'm hiding something. Maybe he just likes the color. Either way, I remain perfectly still as he dips down to brush his lips over mine.

They're warm, despite the cold, and the slickness of his tongue prodding at the seam of my mouth is basically fire. Sparks explode down my limbs and I let myself feel it, just for a second. I wind my fingers into his chaotic hair, overwhelmed by the scent of his cologne and leather, and the thought I have isn't good.

I wish I were sleeping in his bed tonight.

"Just hold on to me," he says, pulling away. "I won't let anything happen to you." He secures his own helmet, giving me a slick grin as he kicks the bike to growling life. I mount the bike behind him, winding my arms around his stomach, feeling the hard muscles beneath the thin T-shirt he's wearing under his leather jacket. I feel the force of it all the way down to my marrow. The vibration against my sensitive places. The energy. The reckless, rumbling power.

The bike is sure something, too.

"That was…" I gasp, helmet only halfway off my head. "Oh my god!"

Remy grins. "I know."

I wish I did, but I don't know how to articulate it. Riding on the back of that bike is the opposite of being caged. It's wild and free, fast and thrilling. For the first time in—maybe ever—I felt like I could finally just breathe. And being pressed up against the man in front of me? *Jesus.* If working with Sy over the past few days hasn't made me horny as fuck, that ride sure did the trick.

"You like it smooth and fast," he says, seeming just as breathless as I am when he tips my chin and licks my lips apart. It's an oddly seamless continuation of the kiss he'd given me before I got on, as if he's picking up a thread of a conversation we'd been rudely interrupted from finishing. "I'll remember that."

He hooks the helmets on the back of the bike, and I look around, trying to figure out where we are. It's a narrow strip of road, with businesses on the bottom floor and apartments or offices above. I spot a tattoo and piercing parlor, a skateboard shop, two vintage-thrift stores, and a shop specializing in crystals and products that promise to 'enhance your vibration'. I should've known Remy wouldn't shop at the mall. Not with *that* wardrobe. His fingers thread through mine and he takes me to the nearest door. Loud, energetic punk music blasts us as we step inside.

A woman behind the counter nonchalantly glances up at us, and then does a double take. "Remington!" she gushes, coming around the counter to greet him. She's almost as tall as Remy, covered in tats, quarter-sized gauges hanging from her ears, shoulder-length blue-black hair. I can't even count the piercings. "It's been months, you fucker!"

"Jade," he says, fingers squeezing mine. "This is Vinny."

But her focus is already fixed on me, drinking me in with eyes that grow wider once they land on our joined hands. "Really…" she drawls, eyebrows climbing high.

"Erm—Hi." I glance around, uncomfortable with her attention. The shop is unique. The scent of new leather is mixed in with a curated collection of vintage clothing. The styles merge seamlessly, classy but aggro. "Nice shop."

"Thanks," she replies. "It's a labor of—well, not just love, but also obsession."

Remy explains, "Jade designs a lot of the clothes. We took some art classes together while we were, uh..." He scratches the back of his neck, looking at Jade for help.

"At the hospital," she says. "That's where we met. Saint Mary's." She pulls a face. "Total shithole. You should see the online review I left them."

"Oh." I glance between them, suddenly understanding the look they share. There's a comfort within it, one I haven't seen him have with anyone else—not even Sy. If I had any kind of real attachment to Remy, I might even feel threatened.

But I don't.

Definitely not.

"Jade showed me her vision," he continues, "and when she got out, she opened this place."

I offer her a smile. Not her fault that she and Remy shared some kind of institutional bond. "That's really cool."

She gives him a warm grin. "Well, I couldn't have done it without Remy's start-up money."

He shrugs. "What's the point of money if you can't invest in shit you like?"

"He's modest, but speaks the truth." She lifts her chin. "So what's up? You here for the boots? I just got them in."

He runs his fingers down a rack of shirts, the inked letters on his knuckles rippling. "Vinny needs some real clothes. Not this basic shit she got from the girls down at the gym."

Jade looks me over, worrying one of the piercings on her lip. "Full workup?"

"Whatever she wants." His hand slides from the small of my back down to my ass. He squeezes it while also pressing his lips to my temple. "I'll be over there looking at those boots."

He wanders off with a flippant wave, leaving me alone with

Jade, who seems to be mentally cataloging my body. The scrutiny is overwhelming, and I fight the urge to cross my arms protectively. Can she tell how skinny I am? Are there bruises still visible? Has Remy told her who I am, what my last two years have been like? My last two weeks?

As if noticing my discomfort, she says, "I just need to get a sense of your style, that's all."

"Style?"

"Like what colors you prefer." She reaches for an oxblood pleather dress, and then changes her mind, tucking it back in the rack. "How about fabrics? Vintage or new? A mixture?" My jaw opens, but no words come out. I look over to Remy, but he's lacing up a pair of boots, caught in his own world. "Vinny?" Jade asks, drawing my attention back to her. "What do you want?"

I blink and think back to 'before'.

Before West End, where I've been expected to dress like a cutslut.

Before South Side, where I was expected to wear what was given to me, and to take damn good care of it, because nothing else was coming.

But it's not so easy.

In North Side, I'd worn uniforms all through high school, never needing more than jeans and a few T-shirts or casual things at home. There must have been a time where I saw something—on a rack, on a person, in an advertisement—and thought about wanting it. But I can't remember it. Even if I could, maybe I'm not even the same person anymore. What twenty-year-old still covets the things she liked at fifteen?

I look into Jade's dark brown eyes, dread swirling in my stomach as I admit the truth. "I have no idea what I like. I… I'm not sure anyone's ever asked me before."

Something passes between us, and it's nothing as kindred as whatever she and Remy share, but it's something. A connection. She nods, eyes clearing, like she's seeing me for the first time.

"Then he's brought you to the right place. I understand that more than you know."

~

Two hours later, we've picked out three dresses, four pairs of jeans, countless tops in dark, bold tones, three pairs of shoes, two skirts, and a lacy selection of bras and panties.

Remy oversaw that personally.

During the clothing changes, size adjustments, and shoe try-ons, Jade doesn't ask about the yellowing bruise on my hip or why my ribs are so noticeable. She does regale me with stories about herself. How her father made her try out for wrestling when all she wanted was to take art. She freely goes into the reason she was in the hospital—a lifelong struggle with depression and years of gender dysphoria. It wasn't until she got help that she ultimately made the decision to transition, and things got better. "It's still a struggle," she admits, sending me a sunny grin. "But I finally feel free."

Free.

Yeah. Not me. Not yet.

"Actually, Remy was having a wicked manic episode at the time." She tucks a tag under the fabric, letting out a chuckle. "He threw me a birthday party, complete with one of those plastic-wrapped Swiss cake rolls, a toothpick stuck in the center. We couldn't set it on fire, of course, but it was still a really elaborate affair for a 2am shindig at Saint Mary's." Her smile softens. "And then he helped me pick my name."

"Yeah?" I ask, glancing over at him. He's picking through the clothes piled on the countertop.

"I'd spent years wanting to be a Mallory or an Ariel or something, but he suggested Jade. He said it matches my aura—that it would surround me with protection."

"That definitely sounds a lot like him."

We share a look and she snorts. “I know. He can be so pretentiously full of shit, can’t he?”

“Pretty much non-stop.” Still, I can’t help but relate. “But he has a way, I guess. Of making it sound and feel special.”

“That’s exactly what I mean.” She pauses, looking oddly sober. “You know, I’m glad he has someone who can appreciate that without falling headfirst into it. I always sort of worried about him. Remy’s an amazing guy, don’t get me wrong. He’s one of a kind—I suppose that’s why I had to collect him.” She gives me a crooked smile. “But I always knew it’d take a really special woman to handle his highs and lows. He’s lucky to have you.”

I lock up, fully intending to correct what’s clearly a huge misunderstanding, but suddenly he’s sauntering over, strips of black lace hanging over his finger as he politely tugs me away from her. “Wear these tonight.”

My heart and well, let’s face it, pussy, pulses at the implication. “Okay.”

“Go ahead,” he drops into the chair just inside the dressing room. “Try them on for me.”

He yanks the curtain closed, shutting out the rest of the boutique. Feeling the heat of his eyes on my skin, I lift my shirt and remove my bra, then push my jeans down, kicking them off along with my shoes. His eyes dart toward the star as I lower the cotton panties I’m currently wearing, then to my tits and below.

I don’t really give a second thought to being naked in front of him. Remy has seen every inch of my body beneath the hot shine of his tattoo table’s lamp, from the thin skin of my throat to my bony ankles.

He stands, handing me the bra, and then watches me with those intense green eyes as I put it on. His fingers blaze a trail of fire as they graze my skin, helping me with the clasp. The pads of his fingers are rough, running down my spine to the curve above my ass, and I watch, mesmerized, as his eyes follow.

“You have two little dimples here,” he whispers, fingers prodding. “Did you know that?”

My breath is caught in my throat. It'd be easy to blame it on my nights with Sy, but that wouldn't be honest. The truth is, Remy's had my eye since that first time he drew on me in the tower. His body and the way it moves. How his eyes feel, searing into me. The shifting ink over his muscles. Even his hair, the way it somehow matches his moods, unkempt one moment and swept back the next.

But mostly, it's the way he touches me.

Maybe it should matter that it's not real. That it's only because he thinks I hold some key to what happened to him and Tate that strange night two years ago. But in moments like this, it doesn't matter at all.

Because Remy touches me like I'm precious.

Important.

Special.

And it makes me fucking *burn* for him.

Our eyes meet in the mirror, and I see that same desire reflected back. It's just as corrupted as mine, twined with something dark and unspeakable, and when he spins me around, his palms hot on my shoulders, I think I see it pulse through him, jaw flexing as he drops to his knees.

Breaking my gaze, he sweeps a palm down my thigh, behind my knee, coming to rest on the unfinished viper tattooed on my calf. Briefly, I wonder if he can smell, see, *sense* how wet I am.

"Lift up your foot," he says, voice dropped and so raw that it reverberates to my core. When I do, he spreads the pair of panties apart, guiding one foot after another into the leg holes. He glides them up my legs slowly, eyes following the ascent, and I get lost in how reverent it feels, my lungs constricted around a needy whine.

He stops just short of sliding them over my hips and I give in to the instinct to bury my fingers into his hair, fisting the white, blond tresses. He looks up at me, a smirk on his mouth as he pitches forward to press a slow, hot kiss on the star tattooed beside my hip.

Without warning, he slips his fingers between my legs.

My knees nearly buckle as he slides into my folds, invading, claiming, *owning*. When he goes suddenly still, I know exactly why, but the look on his face when I pry my eyes open is enough to make me shudder.

His mouth is slack, bottom lip shiny, as if he'd been halfway through wetting it, and *his eyes*.

Fuck, his eyes are wide with shock and as hot as lava.

"Christ, Vinny." His brow crumples in want as he slides his finger back, only to plunge deeper into my slickness. Meanwhile, his other hand is busy fumbling for his fly, popping the button and lowering the zipper.

It's not a good feeling to know that I'd take it. I'd let him fuck me right here in some random dressing room, and it would almost certainly be the best sex I've ever had.

But then...

"I don't care how much money you invested in this place, Remy," Jade's voice carries over the music, "if you have sex in my changing room, I'll castrate you."

He freezes, hand shoved into his pants, cheeks splotching with redness, and I bite back a groan as I watch him carefully pull back from the dangerous edge of need in his eyes. He mutters, "Fucking cockblock," and angrily—roughly—pulls the panties the rest of the way up. The most I get is him squeezing my ass when he stands, but he's still panting these sharp little anticipatory breaths when he does it. "We're finishing this later."

He ducks through the changing room curtain, and the first thing I do is make sure there's no drool dripping down my chin. I get hastily dressed, calming my heart and libido as I get my shit together. My reflection in the mirror is flushed and dazed, sweat beading up on my skin. I've spent weeks dreading the moment one of these men would take me, and now I'm apparently fucking desperate for it.

When I step out from behind the curtain fully dressed, he's already paid, waiting for me with a bundle of packages under his arm, stacked neatly to insert into the tail bag at the back of the motorcycle. The moment may have been broken, but the look he gives me as I approach tells me it wouldn't need much to mend it.

We say goodbye to Jade, who gives me an uncomfortably knowing wink, and a moment later, we're out on the street.

Clearing my throat in an attempt to shake off the fireworks, I say, "Thank you.

Remy couldn't really understand the significance behind it. I'm not even sure I do—not yet. To anyone else, they're just clothes, but to me it's a little slice of freedom. His fingers push the hair off my cheek, and he says, "Those old things were dragging you down. You're not a cutslut. And you're made for more than hand-me-downs, anyway. You're Royalty. You're the Duchess." He tugs me close, leaning down to whisper, "My guiding star."

The kiss isn't deep and consuming like the ones earlier. This one is pure sweetness, his lips sealing against mine slowly, gently.

It isn't any less hypnotizing.

"Mr. Maddox isn't going to know what to do with you," he says, offering me his hand as I sling a leg over the motorcycle, "but don't you think for a minute that I don't."

14

Lavinia

For a brief moment, I think I might actually miss Nick.

He would never drag me to a country club for dinner, and if he did, he'd be glued to me like a shield, ripping out the eyelids of any of these assholes frowning at my blue hair.

Of course, he'd also walk me in like a dog attached to the leash he's holding, so... no. He's in the right place. Tucked snug in his cage, exactly where he belongs.

"Don't let me out until you stop hating me."

Enjoy eternity, I guess.

"Jesus, I hate these people," Remy says, tugging aggressively at his tie. I've seen this man in many forms. I've seen the Maniac, frantic and wild-eyed, threatening to jump. I've seen the Duke, cocky and confident, walking into the gym to watch a fight. I've seen him stripped down to just 'Remy', sexy and shirtless, lounging lazily on his bed.

But I wasn't prepared for Remington Maddox.

The black suit fits him like a glove, turning the rough-and-tumble man who owns me into the picture of contrast. Black pants, white dress shirt. Black blazer, white pocket square. He'd come out of his bedroom looking like this, clearly someone who's used to dressing for such occasions. I bet he could knot that necktie blindfolded, with one hand bound behind his back.

Sure, there are signs of the artistic genius visible beneath the finery. The tattoos on his knuckles. The ink peeking out from beneath his collar. The silver rings on his fingers. The marker tucked behind his ear. His hair, combed but still somehow chaotic, as if it's decided to rebel, too.

But the long lines of his body fill out his professionally tailored suit impeccably, and I finally understand that you can't take the breeding out of a man—not even Remy. Two halves of himself are fighting one another here. The essence of his spirit and the obligation to his name.

I feel the same about being a Lucia. Slipping into a dress that I don't even know the cost of yet, in order to avoid embarrassing a man who's more powerful than me?

I have experience with that.

Blood runs deep.

So does conditioning.

"Although, seeing you in that dress almost makes it worth it." His fingers graze my shoulder, dragging over the thin straps holding up the sheer dress. The fabric is thin—almost transparent—and only just barely a shade darker than the color of my skin. If it didn't have tiny, shimmering beads embedded into it, I'd probably look naked at first glance. It's provocative, yet strangely elegant, and Remy keeps sending me these *looks*.

Still, he moves just as fluidly in a suit and tie as he does when he's barely dressed in the tower, loping casually through the gallery as he guides me toward a set of stairs. Around us, people turn to look, doing double takes, although it's hard to say which of us stands out more.

Remy has a theory, apparently, bending down to press it into my ear with a drawled whisper. "Every bastard here wishes they could swap places with me tonight."

He directs me up a set of stairs, through the double doors and into a fancy room. The plaque by the door says 'The Alexander Room'. Remy nods to it and says, "When I was a kid, I used to call this the Santa Room."

I laugh. "Why?"

"Because they'd have this big Christmas party in here every year, and Santa would come and take pictures. There'd be games and cookies."

"And your parents brought you?"

"Sometimes," his eyes dart around the room, "or a nanny."

There's no Santa in sight tonight. Just a room full of rich men and women sitting at round tables. It's such a familiar sight that I half expect my father to be here, but that's just paranoia. He's not the country club type. Forsyth has all kinds of nooks and crannies for the wealthy elites, and he prefers dark, exclusive back rooms that people only dare whisper about.

Wait staff weave through the crowd with glasses of champagne. Remy seamlessly snags two and hands one to me. The other, he swallows in one gulp. After, he looks at the empty glass, mouth twisting. "Yeah, I'm going to need something stronger than that." He reaches into his pocket and pulls out a tiny packet of pills.

I'd notice North Side junk anywhere.

They're stamped with a viper logo.

"Where do you get that?" I hiss.

He shrugs. "That guy, Cash Money. Gave him a call this morning."

Sy's demand rings in my ears. I'd hoped to avoid it—talking to Cash. But I can see now that Sy's fears weren't unfounded. To someone like Cash, a lowly nothing trying to rise up North Side's ranks, a customer with pockets as deep as Remy's is too juicy to ignore, no matter the rivalries. I know how it goes. He starts him on stimulants. Nothing too extreme. Build a relationship. Offer him a sample of something new, something stronger, and wait for him to come back for more. Wash, rinse, and repeat, until Remy's so strung out on the most expensive shit—Viper Scratch, a dope so powerful, it'd end your life just as soon as ruin it—he might as well just sign his trust fund over. It's a funnel that's been tried and true since as far back as I can remember.

I rest my hand on his. "Don't you dare get high and leave me to deal with this on my own."

He gives me a long, annoyed look, but when all I do is glare back at him, he rolls his eyes. "Fine," he grinds out, tucking them back into his pocket. "But that means you'll be the one keeping me even all night." His eyes land on a table across the room. Even with a finely groomed beard and dark hair, there's no mistaking Remy's father. Green eyes, hair graying at his temples, expensive menswear. The genes are strong.

In front of him, laid out on the table, are four phones. They each look a little different, one in a red case, another in a white, one in silver, one in black.

Maddox men and their colors...

Remy follows my gaze, scoffing. "Yeah, you can guess where I got my compulsive behavior from, can't you? The man needs to be reachable twenty-four-seven, across multiple lines. God forbid he leaves a phone in his pocket—or worse, at home." He slides me a long-suffering look. "So don't expect more than half his attention."

I take this in, nodding. "Noted."

"Guess we need to get this over with." Sliding our palms together, he leads us to the table, where his father is already sipping a drink. There's only one other chair at the table.

"Dad," Remy says, fingers reflexively squeezing mine.

He's frozen stiff as we approach, and when we pause in front of him, I get a better look. His eyes are a darker green than Remy's. More hazel, really. They're also pointed right at my tits. "Remington," he replies, eyes flitting over his son to me and then down to his phones. I see it then. The compulsion. The way his eyes flick over each black screen before returning to us. "I didn't know you were bringing..." I can practically see him editing the words in his head. "... a *date*."

"Well," Remy caresses the small of my back, "you never said I couldn't."

Instantly, his father waves over a waiter, and after a tense moment of silence and standing, the man returns with another chair, squeezing it beside the one that was meant for Remy.

"This is Lavinia," Remy says, surprising me by pulling out my chair. I take it, easing down, fighting the urge to run. "She's the Duchess."

If his father's eyes weren't affixed to one of his phones—the one in a glossy, crimson red case—I think he would have rolled them at the title. "Of course. I should have known."

My muscles tighten at whatever implication that was meant to convey.

Remy sits next to me, draping that long arm over my shoulder. Again, his father gestures to the waiter. Like before, it only takes a few minutes for him to return with three drinks. I shouldn't be surprised at the lack of being given a choice, but I'm still on the heels of that shopping trip, and suddenly, I find myself unwilling to be told what to eat or drink. Not by another entitled man.

Remy, on the other hand, looks at that glass like it's water in a desert, immediately lifting it to his mouth. I pin him with a look. He grimaces but only takes a small, measured sip. Under the table, I squeeze his thigh.

His father begins, "Normally, I would have welcomed the thought of you bringing a date, but tonight, I'd planned to discuss your treatment." He leans back in his seat. "I'm not sure that's appropriate discussion in front of your... friend."

Maybe the champagne is already going to my head, because the words are out of my mouth before I even have a chance to grasp him. "His *Duchess*."

His father shoots me a nasty look. "I don't care if you want to call yourself the Queen of England. It's a private matter." Mr. Maddox is smaller in stature than his son, but you wouldn't know it by the way he holds himself. Aloof, assured, that special jut of his chin that all the powerful men in this city seem to favor.

"Whatever you say to me, you can say in front of Vinny." Remy grabs my hand from his thigh and lifts it up, kissing my knuckles. "Actually, she's the reason I've had a breakthrough."

"A breakthrough." Mr. Maddox laughs. "Is that what you call having an outburst in Dr. Weatherby's office?"

"You mean the doctor you've been conspiring with?" he asks, smiling crisply. "I know you've been paying her off to manipulate my therapy."

"Is this some new fixation, Remington?" His father looks unconcerned by the accusation, reaching out to adjust his row of phones before sitting forward to pin Remy with a stare that drips of condescension. "I'm paying her *fee*, a hefty one at that, because that's what it takes to get your head on straight."

Remy shakes his head. "Drop the bit, dad. I know what went down at Saint Mary's."

His eyebrows rise. "Do you, now? I'd certainly like to hear about it. No one would tell me a thing." At Remy's scoff, his dad leans back, frowning. "I don't know what kind of narrative you've spun, but my memories are perfectly clear. My son was troubled, and I wanted him to get the best care available. Is that such a crime?"

"Don't do that." Remy's fists clench so hard that I fight a wince, my fingers still entwined with his. "Don't twist everything around."

"What am I twisting?" He raises his palms, and there's an unavoidable exhaustion in his eyes. "You always do this, Remy. You latch onto some absurd suspicion and build it up in your mind until it makes you crazy. This is why you need to see Weatherby."

Remy's nose flares. "You told her not to let me talk about Tate."

"Why would I do that?" he asks, convincingly dumbfounded. Even though he glances at his phones again. "What would I possibly have to gain by paying someone to stop you from talking about a troubled, lonely street urchin who killed herself?"

"Don't talk about her like that!" Remy snaps.

His father tosses me a look, as if to make sure I'm watching the spectacle. "Now who's preventing whom from talking about the poor girl? Because if you want to talk about her, then we can at least be honest. Tatum's death was a tragedy. But she only hung around you and your friends because she was a leech, and deep down, you've always known it." His eyes flick over to me before narrowing on his son. "And she doesn't matter anymore, Remington. She's dead. What more is there to talk about?"

I wait for the explosion. For Remy to jump out of his seat and make a scene. I'm about to jump out of my seat and make one myself, but Remy leans forward and speaks in a low, even tone. "You're right. She is dead, but she sure as fuck didn't kill herself."

"Here we go," he says, reaching for his glass, "more delusions. That's what I'm paying Weatherby hand over to fist to put a stop to."

"It's not a fucking delusion. It's a goddamn memory," Remy hisses, and when his father looks down again, louder, "Would you stop looking at the goddamn phones! You know what I saw that night—what triggered my break—and that's why you had me locked up. You were afraid I'd be tied to it, and even worse, it'd create a scandal. That's all you care about. Image and prestige. Not giving a shit that one of my best friends was murdered—in front of me!"

That last line is loud, rising above the chattering voices. The room stills, eyes swinging our way.

Mr. Maddox's eyes flare hot. "Do not," he whispers, voice clipped, "make a scene!"

I take a deep breath and say, "Mr. Maddox, Remy's telling the truth."

"Is that so?" The man watches his son, disappointment hardening his features. "I knew it was a mistake to let you attend Forsyth. You're just getting worse, using the people around you to validate your psychosis. You do realize that's what he's doing," he asks me, specifically. Mr. Maddox gestures to Remy. "He's using you to give these figments life. It's what he's always done. Or," he adds, turning to Remy, "have you not told her exactly what Tate was to you? How she helped fuel your delusions? How she'd encourage you to throw away your meds? To give in to your sickness?"

I glance at Remy, surprised to hear this. The way everyone talks about Tate, she comes off like the second coming. But from the way Remy's eyes darken, I sense there's some truth to his father's words.

"She wanted me to be myself," Remy says, voice tight.

His father scoffs. "She wanted you to be unstable. To spend money, party, do drugs—"

Remy's hand comes down on the table—hard. "You didn't know her!"

"I know enough," he hisses back, barely keeping composure. "She wasn't good for you. If you'd rather remember her differently, I have no problem with that. But I will not have you spinning her suicide into some elaborate conspiracy to further—"

"Tate wasn't alone that night on the cliffs," I cut in, because maybe Mr. Maddox is right. Maybe I don't know the full story. But there's one thing I'm completely sure of. "My sister was with her."

"Your sister?" he asks, giving me a hard look.

"Leticia Lucia." There's not a soul in Forsyth that doesn't know that name. Not just because our father is powerful and well-known, but because when she went missing, a call went out in the community. If Leticia Lucia was seen, she was to be returned home. *Immediately.* "My father is—"

"Don't insult me. I know who your father is," he says, the disdain clear on his features. Being under the weight of his gaze is just as intense as being under his son's, and because of that, when he tilts his head, assessing me with a lazy, pompous scowl, I already know what's coming. "Last I heard, he'd sold you off to the flesh trade. I didn't realize the Velvet Hideaway rented out by the night. Is this something new Daniel's son is trying out? Because if I'm bankrolling your appearance here," he tips his glass to his lips, eyes crawling down my body, "we might as well head to the parking lot so I can get my money's worth."

Remy bolts up, rage clouding his eyes. His arms are halfway across the table when his father slowly shakes his head. "You touch me, son, and I'll have you sectioned in a heartbeat. You'll be locked up, away from your friends, your Dukes, and your precious little Duchess."

Remy shows his teeth, tendons straining. "Keep pushing me, old man."

"You know, my son doesn't like liars," Mr. Maddox tells me, looking far too casual. "Now might be a good time to drop the act."

I eye him. "What act?"

He gestures to the space between us—me and Mr. Maddox—and smirks. "This act where you pretend we've never met before. The introduction, the forced ignorance..." He mockingly grimaces. "It's all a bit flimsy."

Remy's green eyes swing to me, wide and angry.

My jaw drops at the implication. "I've never met you in my life!"

His father just stares at Remy. "This all makes sense now. My son, all cozied up with one of Lionel's daughters. The lesser one, granted. Has she told you why everyone suspects her of murdering her sister?" He looks at me, flashing a placid grin. "Oh, I suppose she hasn't. I've heard whispers, though. Sibling rivalry can get rather ugly, can't it, Miss Lucia?"

Remy cuts in, "She didn't kill her sister."

Mr. Maddox shrugs. "Maybe. But how do you know? If I remember correctly, this little delusion of yours has never featured any actual suspects." He dips his chin toward me. "Who's to say it wasn't her? She is a Lucia, after all. You know as well as I do what they're capable of. Or have you already forgotten what triggered your first episode?" He spins the stem of his wineglass, eyes full of a polite malice. "Truthfully, I think I preferred Tate."

I shoot upright, hand on Remy's back. "Come on, this piece of shit isn't worth it."

Moving my hand to his bicep, I get a feel for how tense and coiled he is, every muscle in his body ready to leap. Of all the versions of Remy I've seen, this is one I haven't experienced yet.

The fighter.

I lower my voice to a whisper, soft and coaxing. "Remy. I need you to look at me now. Can you do that?"

He obeys, eyes sliding to the side, meeting mine through a fog of rage. Immediately, it begins to fall away, leaving a man who's just a touch too raw—too lost. "Vinny..." I can practically see his throat closing around what he wants to say, but his eyes are screaming it.

"Let's go," I decide, pulling him away.

I feel every eye as we walk out of the room, but honestly, I don't give a fuck. I stand by him, shoulders pushed back, chin raised high. Let these entitled assholes think what they want. Maybe they see Lavinia Lucia, daughter of North Side. Maybe they see its cast off, South Side's gem-studded whore. But I make damn sure I leave as the Duchess to West End, hand-in-hand with my Duke.

Neither of us speaks until we're outside the nearest door, huddled under a curved awning. Remy presses his back against the wall and grabs for me, wrenching me so fast and hard that my shoulder gives a protest at the force. His fingers push frantically at the hem of my dress, shoving it up until it's bunched around my waist. I know what he's looking for and I won't deny him. Not when he has that look in his eye, wild and vicious.

His fingers count the points of the star, one after the other, over and over. His lips move as he counts, but there's no voice to it, soundless yet rushed. On his fifth pass, he finally gulps in a large lungful of air.

"Remy..." A tremor runs through me at his touch. For once, it soothes me as much as it does him. "You know I believe you. Sy and Nick believe you."

His eyes snap up to mine. "Have you fucked my dad?"

"What?" I shriek, fighting to lower my voice. "No!"

But I can see the doubt in Remy's eyes, the swirling suspicion. "He said you've met."

"He's lying," I insist, flinging my arms out. "Where would I have met him? When I was a kid? When I was at the motel, under constant supervision? Or at the Hideaway, where even Nick had to break in to—" But the word gets trapped in my throat—the reminder of what the three of them did. How they claimed me.

I can see it land on Remy's face though, eyes darkening. "You promise."

"Yes."

"You swear on your fucking life."

"Yes!"

His eyes fall closed when I cup his cheek, finally letting my dress flutter back down my legs. "He does this, Vinny. He twists everything around until I don't know up from down. *Fuck*, he makes me so fucking crazy!" He runs a hand through his hair, pulling too hard at the roots. "It's bad enough that my brain can't decide which way is up sometimes—that it thinks it's a rollercoaster—but he makes it worse. He does it on purpose. He knows I can't—" His teeth slam shut with whatever he wants to say, and I don't like it. Ever since we arrived here, Remy's shut himself up, pushed it all down. It's not like him.

My thumb rubs a soothing circuit against his cheekbone. "Fathers suck, Remy. Something in this town poisons them."

Still tense, he reaches into his pocket, pulling out his phone. He clutches it tight, and for a second, it looks like he's about to hurl it across the parking lot. And then I realize it isn't Remy's phone.

It's his father's.

The red case is distinctive, and Remy glares down at it. His rebellion. "It wasn't true," he demands, eyes flashing angrily. "Those things he said about Tate were a lie. She didn't know—she didn't understand my diagnosis. There was never a time she didn't want me to be okay."

"I know," I say, even though I don't. It's just that I can see the storm brewing in his eyes, and I don't think I can handle it alone. "Let's go home. To Sy."

But he breaks away, pacing a tight, frenetic path back and forth. "You can't lie to me, Vinny. Not ever. When you lie, it lets him in. You understand that, don't you? He'll use it." It's only then that I notice the parking lot, the rain pelting the pavement, the flashes of lightning in the distance. "You weren't there. I know you weren't there. I saw you, but I didn't see *you*. I know I didn't. I know it." But I see the seed of doubt in his eyes, and it doesn't matter that he's trying to fight it back, to keep hold on what he knows to be true.

"I can call him," I stutter out, digging into my tiny clutch purse for my phone. "Sy can come and get us, so you won't have to drive the bike in the rain, and then we'll—"

"No." His hand closes over my wrist, and when I look up, his eyes are black. "I've been patient, but you've been ducking my questions, Vinny. You need to tell me all of it—everything. About your sister, about that night, about what happened after." I don't even notice the sharp, resentful thing in his eyes until it suddenly morphs into a steel resolve. "And I know where I need to be when I hear it."

15

Remy

I DON'T EVEN HEAR the thunder until I cut the bike. It's dark out here, pitch black, but a flash of distant lightning reveals the cut through the trees. I don't need it. I could walk this trail with both eyes closed. It's better like this, anyway, with the wind and the rain, the sky battering the earth with her anger. It makes sense, fits together in a predictable way. I'm watching the universe stomp its feet, its howls being carried by the wind, its tears falling from the heavens.

I jump off the bike without a second thought, breaking the chain of her arms around my waist so forcefully that she teeters, crying out as she catches herself. I'm there first, though, steadying her only to rip the helmet from her head.

It's only when I get a good look at her, her gray eyes wide and wet, that I pause, considering the ride. The rain beating against my helmet, soaking through my suit, freezing the tips of my fingers.

But I need to know.

So I lift her from the seat and begin dragging her toward the trees,

"Wait!" she shouts over the screams of the sky, raindrops falling from her eyelashes like tears. "Are you going to tell me where we are?"

"Yes," is my answer, but it emerges in a conflicted tone that makes her face screw up against the wind. She looks fucking miserable. She's cold—shivering—and soaked down to the black, lacey underthings I'd picked out for her this morning. I don't like the black ember of guilt settling in my gut—never have, never will. Usually, I'd give it away. The black. The reprisal.

I need to fucking *know*, and I'd drag her kicking and screaming through this mud to make sure I do.

But I wouldn't feel good about it.

She's my Duchess.

Goddamn it.

Clumsily, I remove my jacket, and it's useless, waterlogged and too heavy, no warmth inside of it at all, but I drape it over her shoulders, anyway. "I'm not good at this," I tell her, swatting the wet hair from my eyes.

"At what?" she yells back.

I answer with a frustrated growl. It's never a problem when I drag Sy or Nick through the mud with me. They're warriors, blood and bone. Even Tate seemed carved from stone, to the point where I'd often forget she was a girl at all.

But Lavinia is a Royal woman. She's soft and delicate, and maybe Sy wants to harden her into the same stone Tate was made of, but I don't. I prefer her just like she is, standing before me so small and yet so big, the tip of her nose glowing a vivid pink. She doesn't know it yet, but there's just as much strength in her frailty as my muscles. In the knobs of her elbows as she punches into the sleeves of my jacket. In the furl of her brow as she hugs it around her slender middle. In the tilt of her head as she searches my eyes.

"It's a short hike."

Her crimson-red lips drop agape. "A short *what*? Remy, I'm in heels!"

I look down at her elegant feet, bright red toes peeking out of the leather. She's right. She'll break her fucking neck walking up the path in those. Annoyed, I begin rolling up my sleeves. "I'll just carry you."

"You want me to piggyback ride through the woods with you?" Thunder booms overhead, and the silence that stretches in its wake makes me certain she's going to reject me. "Remy, what are we doing here?" She's looking at me in the familiar way. It's the same expression everyone wears when they're wondering whether or not I'm off my meds. Except this time she knows I'm not.

"Do you trust me?" I yell over the storm. But since I'm pretty sure I don't want to hear the answer to that question, I amend, "Do you *want* to trust me? Because I want to trust you!" She bites her lip, watching me with big, worried eyes, and it's a physical battle to not just take her by the arm and tow her to the summit. "I can order you!" I remind her, beating my chest in emphasis. "I'm your Duke, and that means you're mine! The Duchess serves at my pleasure." I can already see her shutting down, becoming all that hardness Sy's been trying to mold her into. Shaking my head, I add, "But I won't order you to do this. This isn't a cage, Vinny. No box. No prison. There are things I'll make you do because I'm your Duke, and this isn't one of them. This has to be free or it's nothing at all."

She watches me closely—too closely—arms hugged around her middle. A few days ago, I told Nick that Vinny's had a fucked up life, and I see the vestiges of it swirling in her eyes. She's afraid of me. She's afraid of this place. She's afraid of giving in, seeming weak.

She's also brave. "You have twenty minutes," the resignation weighs her shoulders low, "and then I'm calling Sy."

"Alright." I twist, squatting. "Let's go."

She relents, hiking up her skirt, slinging one leg around my waist and then the other. I hook my arms around her legs, holding her tight, and stand. She's light—as weightless as the rain, or the wind, or the dead leaves whipping around us—but I carry her like she's a boulder, too substantial to drop. There's a shock of cold on my neck that I almost don't feel until a blaze of heat proceeds it. Her nose, her cheek. She buries her face into my neck and I shield her from a gust of wind, my mind fixed to a singular point.

I fight the urge to run up the hill, releasing all the rage and anger I didn't unleash on my bastard of a father. But I've got this girl on my back, my compass, and I don't want her to fall, to slip away as her sister had two years ago. It feels right that I finally bring her here, to the place we first met, without either of us really knowing, and I refuse to let her go. So I keep my grip tight and strong, and I can practically taste the marks I'm leaving in her thighs as I trod us further and further.

"The first time I came up here," I tell her, huffing as I hike, "was for a Boy Scout trip in the third grade. We camped at the top, under a sky full of stars. It was all hotdogs and s'mores until a thunderstorm rolled in during the middle of the night—two of them, both coming from different sides. It felt like we were under attack. Two gods battling it out in the sky."

"Were you scared?" she asks, breath hot on my ear.

I shake my head. "No. It was like I could feel the electricity under my skin." I look back, catching her profile in a flash of lightning. "The next time I came up here, I was thirteen and buying weed from a prick from North Side. Little did I know, he'd laced it with something. I hallucinated for three days before coming down."

There's a long pause before she breathes, "Three days?"

Nodding, I remember, "Yeah, I rode it out in Sy and Nicky's basement. It's what triggered my first episode."

"That's what your dad was talking about." I hear the guilt in her voice, through the chatter of her teeth. "Jesus, Remy. I'm... I'm sorry."

I shake my head. "Not your fault, Vinny."

Her grip tightens around my neck. "But my dad made those drugs, he—"

"Isn't you. I want you to know that I get that." I draw my head back, catching her eye, wanting her to know that I mean it. "After that, I came up here a few times with Tate. She liked the quiet. The peacefulness. Nicky was never much for it. You'd never know it to look at him, because he's always so composed, but he likes things to be loud and unpredictable. It makes him still somehow, getting lost within the havoc of things. It's why he always clicked with me." Thinking, I add, "And Sy... well, he likes the quiet, but not the peace. He always needs something to do. Restless son-of-a-bitch, isn't he?"

"Yeah," she answers slowly, as if she's putting the pieces together. "Remy, are you... are you taking me to the cliffs?"

But she asks just as we arrive at the crest of the hill.

I exit the tree line and onto the flat sheet of granite that makes up the highest part. Away from the thick branches, the flashes in the night sky give enough light to navigate closer to the edge. Across the river, dots of yellow lights push through the trees from nice houses overlooking the water.

"Widow's rock," I say over the rain.

Vinny is silent as I ease her to the ground, intensely aware of her warmth and then the loss of it. The second I turn to her, she's taking a step back, a shock of horror in her eyes. "I can't—" she stutters, shivering. "I don't think I can be here." She isn't looking at me when she says it. She's staring out over the edge, the color vanished from her cheeks.

"You've never been up here," I realize, something within me unwinding as I follow her gaze. The river is black. A fathomless abyss. A span of nothingness that could swallow us whole.

I lace my fingers behind my head and bask in the sky, letting out a laugh. "I knew he was full of shit. I knew it!"

When I look at her, she's bracing a gust of wind, so rigid that you'd think she was holding back a tide. "She didn't die." Vinny shakes her head, looking around. "She wouldn't have been taken down like that. Not here."

But I can see the doubt in her eyes. She's telling herself a lie that she has to believe. I get the sense it's something that keeps her going. Makes the cogs of her fate keep turning. Keep her from the yellow.

I get it.

I do.

Feeling heavier than I did ten minutes ago, I confess, "I never could figure out who would come after Tate. My father is right. She wasn't a threat to anyone. She was just this random girl from West End. She was fun, and she kicked ass, but she was broke. She stayed out of the business. She wasn't a problem." I look around, trying to see that night, to remember something other than the sky. "But I'm starting to think that maybe she wasn't the target."

Vinny stares at me, expression shifting. "Leticia."

The name, and all the baggage that comes with it, hangs in the air. Leticia Lucia could easily be a target and there are countless suspects. "A King's daughter is born with a bounty on her head." I gesture to her. Her dripping hair. Her tense frame. Her rosy cheeks and chattering lips. She looks like a doll who's been forgotten in the park, dirty and tattered. "No one knows that better than you."

"You were wrong before. I have been up here." She swallows, throat clicking so loudly that I can discern it from the beat of rain. "Just never from this side."

The silhouette of her profile pulls at the memories of that night. Leticia and I were on the edge. Ringing in my ears. Tate slumped over on the ground. Falling. The wind. Red lights. Stars. Always stars.

"We were there." I point to the spot, then up to the sky. "Jacks in your eyes."

Vinny studies the area, but her eyes are clouded and glazed, her cleavage hitching with these small, panicked breaths. "This is where she...?"

"Right here," I rush out, feeling an odd excitement mixed in with this squirming anguish in my chest. I go to the edge, right up against the drop-off, and look down. It should scare me, but it doesn't. I know what it means to take this leap. I understand the wind against my face, know where it lives, feel its age against my cheeks. I've felt the water below, cold and consuming. "Can you feel it? The dust in the air? This place is ancient, older than our ancestors." Some part of me needs her to feel it. To understand. "We must look so fucking small to the wind up here. Don't you think? Little specks, with our little problems, being exhaled by the lungs of the universe." I turn to her, seeing the torment in her eyes, and the only way I know to soothe it is to take her hand, tugging her closer to the edge. I peer down into the abyss with her, giving her my most precious secret. "That's the part I remember the clearest, Vinny. The thought that came to me when I jumped. That we're all just stars inside of a grave we haven't laid down in yet. That your sister and I were going to die." I touch her cheek, rubbing at something that could be a raindrop or could be a tear. "And it wasn't so bad."

She jerks away, eyes wide, grief lining her face. "Why would you tell me that?"

I blink the rain from my eyes as I take her in. She told me she thinks Leticia could still be alive, but I don't feel it. Not in my gut. "Because I wanted you to know how beautiful it was."

Her eyes swim with dread. "Death isn't beautiful. Death is *nothing*." It's all over her face. The worry. The tension. The fear. She's thinking that she needs to call Sy. That I'm doing something impulsive. That I'm at risk right now, on a cliff that could be the edge of my world, begging for a sweet slice of nothingness.

I raise my chin, staring down at this woman who's as scattered as the stars, but just as sharp as the lightning slicing through the chasm between north and west. "Then show me something," I say.

The gears in her eyes turn as she struggles to understand what I'm asking. Is this a challenge or a command?

In truth, it's neither.

I know when she surges up to kiss me that she's figured out it's a plea. That I'm begging for something bigger than myself. Something I can hold in my hands, palms fixed to her cheeks as I cradle her skull, forcing my tongue into the fiery heat of her mouth.

Something so solid that I can slip against her skin as I claw the straps of her dress off her shoulders. Something warm and soft, her tits giving to the pressure of my hands as I take and take and take.

She's the one to push my shirt off, her icy hands tearing the buttons as she pulls and tears, careless and frantic. I almost wish I hadn't asked, because now I wonder where the energy is coming from. Are her nails scratching into my back because she's afraid I'll jump? Or is she tugging me away from the cliff's edge because she needs to feel my skin on hers?

Do I even care?

A bolt of lightning zigzags over the water, followed immediately by bone-shaking thunder. I grab her hand and haul her away from the cliff's edge, dragging her, stumbling and breathless, toward the patch of meadow that meets the trees. She goes still when I stop, but there's a moment where she searches my face, licking out to catch a bead of rain on her lip.

I stare, transfixed, as it disappears behind her teeth. "Tell me," I demand, reaching out to trace the path of another droplet, cold and slick as it tracks down her temple.

"You can fuck me," she says, her voice sounding so much sturdier than she looks. "That's what you need, right? I can be that for you. You can—"

"Vinny..." I touch her throat, feel the pulse of her heartbeat against my palm like a snare drum. "I *am* going to fuck you. I'm your Duke. That means your body belongs to me. It's not going to be gentle. That's not how I do it. And I'm not sure how long I'll last, because I've been about to bust a nut since I saw you walk out in that dress, but I'll make it good for you." I feel her swallow against my hand and I follow it with my palm, sliding down to her sternum where her heartbeat transforms into a furious flutter. Wings banging against her breast. "That's not what I need, though. You know what I need to hear."

It's not about the words or what they mean. Not really. They matter less than they probably should.

It's about making her surrender.

Feeling her beside me as we jump.

Knowing that she's with me as we fall.

It arrives on the tremor of her shiver, her wet lashes fluttering. "I want it," she breathes, pressing her palm to my bare chest. "Please, just... fuck me. *Please.*"

There's something in her tone, the way she sounds a second from bursting into tears, that makes me reach for her, anchoring our bodies together. That's all it takes for her to latch onto me again, impatient, hands scrabbling at my chest. Sure, the fear is there. The sweet despair in her eyes. The tremor in her fingers as she grasps me closer. But there's heat here, and it's scorching; celestial bodies crashing to earth in a storm of cinder and ash. Her mouth, hot and frantic, tastes as sharp as the ozone from the storm, and when our skin hums, it's the same vibration as the electricity in the air.

Lightning skitters overhead, followed by another crack, this one so close that I can feel it bounce between us, echoing off the rock, rattling our brittle bones. I push down the soggy dress, tearing off the lace that clings to her tits. Squeezing them together, I mouth both nipples at once, tasting the rain and the current. They react, sharpening into hard points, and when she threads her fingers into my hair, pushing my face between them, I feel her gasp more than I hear it. My cock swells, hard and raging. The way she rocks against me confirms what I've known since I felt her pussy earlier, slick and swollen.

She's so horny, she'd beg for it if I made her.

We fall in a heap on top of the sticky leaves, bonded with the earth, the dirt and wet and dead things. I surge into her, pressing with my weight until she's flat beneath me, allowing her eyes to reflect the stormy heavens. She's so fucking beautiful here, soft and pale, hard and warm, fire and ice. There's no mistaking this girl, not tonight, not underneath me.

Vinny is here.

She's real.

She's *mine.*

I hook my fingers in her panties and pull them down her legs, impatient and unseeing, my eyes glued to hers as she watches, incandescent with anticipation. I know what she's been doing with Sy at night. Touching him, guiding him, conquering him. I also know it's a part of why my fingers find her slick and ready, her hips bucking into me, an instinct older than time.

I slip down her body to spread her thighs, pushing them apart until I feel the strain of her muscles. The sound she makes when I dip down, licking a hard stripe up her slit, could rival the roar of the storm. Her thighs battle my hands to close around my head, but I don't let her, forcing them wide as I tongue into her folds, making her feel what it means to have me like this.

"You do this to me," I say, rising up so that I'm hovering over her. I guide her hand to my straining cock. She fists it first, grabbing it through the fabric before fumbling for my buckle, eyes glazed and hungry. "Do you know that?"

"Yeah," she says, not looking away from me as she frees my cock, spreading her thighs for me. "I'm ready, just... just like this."

I shudder at her touch, and her eyes widen when I circle the base of my cock, stroking it for her, letting it bob against my hand, tip tightening, dripping. I wish I could paint this—the way she looks on the leaves, a star inside of a grave.

I press against her, seeking her heat. "Once we do this, there's no going back, Vinny." I gaze down at her as I hold myself steady, the tip of my cock slotted against her slick heat. "This will make you mine. Not just your body. Not just because you're my Duchess. You understand, don't you?"

I can't say the words, but I know she can hear them. I can see it in the furl of her brow, the lightning overhead making her eyes flash with terror.

Sy can take her body.

Nick can claim her mind.

I want her soul.

"I know," she says, chest heaving with these huge, gulping breaths. "Take it."

It spurs me on, and I barely register the hard press of the rock under my knees, eyes focused on her body, cock zeroed in on the warm, slick heat between her legs. I catch her breath into my waiting kiss when I punch in, knocking her very essence down my throat.

Her pussy is perfect.

For a long moment, that's all I can think about. The way I fit inside her, stretching her, her pussy holding me like a goddamn vice. The feeling doesn't fade, but it does expand big enough for my other senses to register. To hear the keen of her cry. To see the wrinkle of agony between her brows as she digs her head back into the ground. To feel her fingernails pressing their crescent moons into my shoulders.

I crash into her like the turbulent tide, tasting the immediacy of something definite in the back of my throat, bitter as blood and just as sweet. "Look at me," I growl, pulling away only to plunge back into her body, my cock buried so deep that I feel her wince, even if she doesn't show it.

Her eyes, screwed shut, open to me like petals in the spring, and I fuck her.

I fuck her hard, driving her into the wet ground, and I fuck her slow, the tip of my nose pressed to hers until I'm the only thing she sees.

16

Lavinia

My fingers keep slipping against Remy's skin. I claw my nails into his back for any sense of feeling tethered. With every punch of his hips, I hear my own voice crying out, but I don't recognize it. His wet hair sways above me, and every crash of his body into mine knocks droplets to my cheeks, cooling my overheated skin.

This must be what sex was meant to feel like. No awkward fumbling. No malice. No violation in the dead of night.

There's still pain—the ground hard against my back, his hips battering into me, his cock stretching me open for him. There's pain, but no hurt. Only the thunder above and his lips, so red as he grunts, plunging into me again and again.

He tips down to kiss me, but it's without precision or intent, as if he just wants to consume my exhales into his lungs, and I let him. Fuck, I'd let him take anything if it meant more of this. His palm on my jaw, holding me steady as he jolts my body into the mud, fucking me in a way that might seem full of anger to anyone else, but I know better. I can feel the desperation, see the plea in his eyes as he rumbles along to the rhythm of the clouds.

He wants a piece of me that doesn't exist. He wants intensity, substance, emotion, solidity, but inside, I just feel empty.

And I use him to fill the void.

It's so wonderfully dirty, and even if I had the power to control my destiny, to choose another person and place and time, I'm not sure I would. Remy looks like a beautiful ghoul above me, the ink on his skin shifting, making it seem alive, and I give in to the impulse to press my mouth to it, lips latching onto the soft skin of his neck.

"Fuck," he spits, fisting his hand into my hair as his hips pick up tempo, cock slamming into me. "Need it, Vinny. Give it to me, give it to me..."

The orgasm comes like the storm Remy described earlier. My body and his, warring against one another, fighting it out until the release comes in a torrent of bruising grips and bitten-off fricatives. For once, I embrace it, letting the sensation ripple through me, spreading outward like a bolt of lightning from my core to my fingertips, forking off into the sweetest petrichor.

"All blue, no yellow." When I open my eyes, he's staring down at me, head tipped against my own, hips punching in an erratic beat. "Indigo. Did you see them, baby? Did you see where we are?"

I cup his cheeks and pull his mouth to mine, wet from the rain, dirty from the ground, and I promise him, "I saw them."

His forehead presses into mine, and his breath is hot when he exhales a deep, rumbling groan. The final thrust is hard, distinctly painful, and so welcome that it almost feels like I'm coming with him. "Fuck, fuck, fuck, Vin," his jaw tightens. "Fucking hell."

He lands on top of me, cock still pulsing inside, and rolls us to the side in a mass of floppy limbs. His chest heaves and I rest my ear against it, listening to his thumping heartbeat. It's only then I realize the rain has stopped, the storm moving to somewhere in the distance. I look to the skies, but they're still cloudy, a blanket of nothingness covering us. Even so, what I said was true.

I didn't just see the stars.

I felt them.

THE ONLY SIGN of my late night arrival is a dog barking in the distance, an alert to the people in Daniel's tidy little community that something is amiss. Little do they know that prior to his death, this house was run by a kingpin and now it's the scene of an ongoing crime.

It must be nice to live with blinders on. To ignore the dog's warning bark. To sleep every night in your own bed, on your own volition.

I walk through the house with a limp, unhurried stride, my limbs still twinging from a mixture of exhaustion, desolation, and utter fucking satisfaction. I feel as though I must weigh a metric ton, and it tickles at my awareness, how strange it is to open the door to the garage without collapsing.

Wordlessly, I flick on the light.

There's a long moment where Nick covers his eyes, and I know that feeling. How blinding light can be when you've spent so long without it. The sting, the ache in your temples, the physical cringe.

Annoyingly, it doesn't take him very long to adjust. "Jesus *fuck*," Nick says from his spot in the cage, eyeing me in the buzzing fluorescent light over the workbench. "You look like you survived a tsunami." His voice is rusty and quiet, piercing through the stillness with an abruptness that even seems to make him flinch.

I think back to what happened just an hour or so ago, and yeah, that seems apt.

"What, did you have a fight with a tiger?" he asks, blue eyes dull with the same exhaustion I feel. His eyebrows hike. "Broke into the cutsluts' dressing room and started a brawl?" He's playing it off. The effects of being trapped here. Hungry. Tired. Alone.

I know when he fails that it must be bad.

Pretty Nick rarely lets his mask slip.

"Do you ever shut up?" I ask, well aware that I look more like a drowned rat than anything else. A well-fucked drowned rat, granted, but it makes sense he's wondering why I'm standing here, late at night, in a once-sparkly dress that's now covered in mud. My elbows are rubbed raw. My hair is a matted mess of dead leaves and grass. And Nick can't see it, but Remy's cum is still flaky on my inner thighs.

But since he's Nick, I see the moment it comes to him. No, not comes.

Slams.

"Which one?" he asks, hands balling into fists. Any attempt at artifice falls away, leaving a haggard, threadbare gaze. "Which one fucked you?"

"That's not why I came."

His lip pulls back in a sneer. "Oh, you didn't come to gloat? Sure. Why else are you gracing me with your wild, unfettered presence?"

Carefully, I tuck the keys into my cleavage. "Because we need to talk."

"About?"

I grab the metal stool from the workbench and drag it closer to the cage. *Closer*, not close. I hoist myself and the tattered skirt of my dress onto it. There's a moment of silence where I try to figure out how to say this. He spends it staring at my bare, dirty legs.

Shamelessly, he reaches down to adjust himself.

Jesus Christ.

Rolling my eyes, I begin, "I want to talk about why you really went to South Side for two years."

"So it was Remy, then," he says, mouth twisting into a bitter grin. "Should have known. You actually seem satisfied. Sy couldn't have—"

"Remy wasn't the one who told me." I confess this freely, without reservation. But I don't disagree about Remy being the one to fuck me, and the longer I don't, the more Nick slumps into his cage, eyes tightening. "It was you, actually. I don't always know what's going on in your thick skull," this is a lie, one I wish wasn't true, "but I've learned a lot about you these past few months, the biggest being that you're unequivocally loyal. Violently so. Only one thing would send you to Daniel Payne, and I'm pretty sure it's revenge." After a beat, I add, "Also, there are files about it all over your laptop."

He scowls at me. "That's password protected."

"Please," I scoff. "I cracked that in ten minutes." If I didn't know better, I'd say he looked embarrassed. But since he's Nick, he just stares back like the defiant bastard he is. "Lavinia Bruin? What are we, in middle school?"

"So, what?" The dark bruises beneath his eyes tighten when he glares back, and I get the sense he's holding onto something. A weakness. "Anything worth knowing is trapped up here." He taps his temple.

Nodding, I say, "Yeah. Figured as much."

I slide off the stool and walk over to the electrical box on the wall. Flipping the switch, the slight hum that was barely noticeable once you got used to it, vanishes, leaving the room in a placid silence. When I look back at Nick, he's staring at the bars. After a second, he thrusts his hand out, gripping the steel.

Nothing.

His chuckle is rough, serrated in a way that sends a chill up my spine. "Honestly, I already got used to the pain. So if this is some kind of threat to get me to talk, then—"

"Remy thinks Leticia is dead."

Nick looks up, and the days of being stuck in that cage shine back at me. That's what he's trying—badly now—to hide. Nick wants out, but he'd never ask, and he'd certainly never beg. "Maybe she is. Maybe she isn't."

The tears that well within my eyes surprise me just as much as him. "I hated her, you know." I walk around the garage, this big empty cavern in the middle of rows of happy homes. "She was my father's daughter, through and through. His precious Leticia, so perfectly cruel. Do you know what she used to say to me after father let me out of the chest? '*Clean yourself up*'." My laugh is a soft, wretched thing, and I watch as it pulls Nick's gaze to mine. "Remy wants me to tell him it's all true. That Leticia and Tate were lovers, and the whole thing was probably romantic and tragic and beautiful, but truthfully? I don't think she was capable of compassion or empathy, let alone something like love." Raising my chin, I recall, "She was bulletproof. Nothing got in and nothing came out. She never complained. She never said no. She cut people down with nothing but a flick of her smile, and it was... *stunning*. She was everything, *everything* that Forsyth wanted her to be. She was cold and elegant and pretty, and if Leticia couldn't survive this goddamn town, then, Nick..." I give him a bland, watery smile. "I'm fucked."

The vestiges of that fake bluster bleed away, and he trembles with a shiver. "If you'd let me protect you—"

"You can protect me," I cut in, voice sharp, "by telling me everything you know. What you found out from Daniel. What you learned from the Lords. Anything." There have been countless times I've found myself in a position to beg. The first time I ever grasped it and lowered myself to bother, it was to Nick.

Turns out, the second time is, too.

"Please," I breathe, the word sour with the taste of bile. "Dead or alive, Nick, I need to know what happened to my sister. I don't think I can move on until I do."

The shadows cut hollows of his eyes, but the blue of his irises blazes through them. He leans back, stretching against the bars for the first time in days. "I've always known Tate was murdered. There was no way she would have killed herself. I didn't know about your sister, but I knew something was happening with her. Something good. Before she died, she'd just put a down payment on an apartment, and she had that soft glow, you know? The one chicks get when they're getting consistently laid." His eyes rake over me, like he's seeking confirmation. "But mostly she was just kind of... happy. And in a place like this, that was noticeable enough."

Nodding, I ask, "So you didn't think she killed herself?"

"I knew she didn't. I knew it that night. I knew it when the cops wouldn't listen to me. I knew it when Remy lost his mind, and I knew it when I walked away from my family and legacy and to serve the enemy."

"But why the Lords?" I ask. "Did you think Daniel killed her?"

He tips his head back against the cage, rolling it back and forth. "I spent years chasing down every lead, every thread, and every dark and shit-filled rabbit's hole trying to find that out. Did Daniel kill Tate? I don't think so. She would've been a speck on his windshield. But he was into pussy and property, and back then I thought I might find a link. I didn't." He rubs his chin, the stubble thicker than I've ever seen it. It makes him look roguish and frayed, and frustratingly handsome. "But I can admit that I'm not sure now, Little Bird. There was another player on the board I didn't know about, and trust me, the Lords didn't either."

"Remy thinks Leticia was the real target."

"He may be right. The Royals have a real hard-on for the Lucia girls." His grin is wolfish but full of spite. "Which is about the only thing I do get."

"So that's it?" I wonder, hardly believing it. "You spent two years in South Side being Daniel's prized lackey, turning your back on your family, your friends, your Kingdom, doing god-knows-what in the name of justice, and you just... have nothing to show for it?"

The shutters fall over his eyes with such force that I nearly take a step back. "You don't know me. Maybe I found something, maybe I didn't. Maybe I have enough dirt on the Kings to burn this whole fucking place to the ground. Or maybe," he grinds out, "I had something to show for it and she spit in my fucking face."

The force of his words stuns me so hard that for a long moment, the only thing I can do is gape at him. "What was I, Nick? Some kind of surrogate mission? Did you see a sad, trapped girl, and think to yourself, 'well, maybe I can save this one'? Or was I just some sick reward you consoled yourself with for time spent in South Side? Is that what I am? Your participation trophy?"

"See, you think it's one or the other," he says, staring up at me coolly, "but you were all of those things. And since you're so hot for the truth tonight, I suppose I'll give you some more. I'm not sorry. Not for wanting you, taking you, saving you." He tips his head down to peer up at me, flicking the bar of the cage. "Every soldier needs something to keep him going."

"You're not a soldier anymore," I point out.

He looks around, gesturing to the door, the keys. "And you're not in a cage."

I wrap my arms around my middle, fighting a shiver. "So where does that leave us?" I wonder.

Nick lets out this harsh little laugh. "Oh, it never leaves us. Some things you just don't shake off, Little Bird." When he looks at me, I see something I've searched for but still don't expect. There's an ache in his eyes. It's a loss that's older than the cage he's sitting in, and when he speaks, it's in a voice that sounds rubbed raw. "I'm not sure I can go back to the person I was before I met you."

"Funny." I don't laugh. "I was just about to say the same thing." I walk over to the cage and Nick shifts. He watches me carefully, as if I'm a snake ready to strike, but that cunning look vanishes when I insert the key into the padlock and open the cage door.

He doesn't move. "I said not to let me out until you stopped hating me."

"You were right," I say, standing back. "You are the most important person in my life. But not because I hate you. You're the only person who can help me find out the truth about my sister. You're the closest hope I have to putting this to rest and moving on with whatever sad joke of a life awaits me on the other side."

He looks up at me, arching an eyebrow. "So you're saying you need me?"

"Goddamn, *seriously*?" My voice is shrill. I hate it. I hate everything about this moment. I hate that he gave me a moment of real sincerity and I hate that I saw it. "Fine! I need you. Get out of the fucking cage before I change my mind!"

"Alright," he says, shooting forward to start a slow, agonizing escape from the cage. It looks painful. Pathetic. He hisses when his muscles seize, and grimaces at the pain in his back. These are all feelings I know well. A string of curses echo in the garage as he hunches, stretching his feet.

I don't feel bad. I'm not sure I feel anything. Putting someone in a cage isn't a great moment. Freeing them isn't much better.

I STARE AT THE JOURNAL, which is sitting on the counter. Sy writes in it every morning and most evenings. I've only gotten a couple of glimpses of the pages, always snatched away before I can truly decipher it.

But the second I open my mouth, Sy drolls, "You're not reading my journal."

I finally break, "Just one page!"

"No."

"One sentence?"

"Okay."

I perk. "Really?"

He shoots me a glare. "No. I told you. It's required for my Human Behavior class. Everything in it is confidential."

My palms drag down my face. I don't think he realizes how impossible it is to live with a book I can't read.

"Is he still in there?" Sy asks, standing over the stove as he makes breakfast. Remy's phone is going off, and we both try to ignore it. There's a nice rhythm to my mornings now, and it's surprisingly a comfort. Sy knows that I like my eggs over easy, my toast slightly burnt, and my coffee black. '*Like your heart, Sy.*'

Maybe living here isn't so bad.

"Since he got home," Remy replies, popping a handful of pills in his mouth and then making an obnoxious show about swallowing them. It's dramatic and unnecessary, but I know it makes both me and Sy feel better witnessing him taking his meds. Last night was crazy enough. I don't even want to think about what that would have looked like with Remy unmedicated. "Well," Remy adds, face pensive, "he did take a piss around six, and then I heard him cuss out the Archduke on the way back to his room."

I pause, holding my coffee midair. "Do you know everything going on in the tower?"

"Hard to sleep with this thing going off every twenty minutes." Remy taps his cell phone before raising an eyebrow in Sy's direction. "But I do know a lot. Like someone needing to work on his foreplay, if that's what you're asking."

"Christ," Sy says, running his hand over his face. "Remy—"

"Look, I'm here for you if you need some tips. The Duchess just likes to be handled a certain way, that's all. I know for certain, one-hundred-percent guarantee, that she likes to have her pussy—"

"Stop!" My entire body has turned an unnatural shade of pink. "Just... stop."

Remy shrugs and neither Sy nor I can make eye contact for a full thirty seconds.

I didn't have the chance to give him his 'lesson' last night.

Here's hoping he taught himself.

For the millionth time since waking up, I hear Remy's phone go off. His own phone, not the one he stole from his father. But from the way a stony sort of delight crosses Remy's features when he glances at the screen, I'm betting it's his father calling about that very thing.

Sy must make the same calculation. "You can just block him."

"I could." Remy shrugs, putting the phone back on the counter. "But his misery is entertaining."

"Anyway," Sy finally says after clearing his throat and sliding the plate of breakfast in front of me, "Nick didn't say anything else about what Saul had him doing?"

He's asking me, because officially, I was awake and sitting in the living room when Nick returned home from his trip. Unofficially, Nick and I came to an agreement on the way home from the Payne house. This was after I stopped at the drive-thru and bought him six hamburgers and a milkshake, all of which he consumed in less than the ten-minute drive back to the tower. It was clear that neither of us had any desire to tell Remy or Sy what had been going on between us for the last few days. I explained the excuse I made up about him doing a job for Sy. He seemed impressed at how well I covered my tracks, but it's obvious he's not in a rush to let the guys know I got one over on him. So here we are again, tied up in secrets and lies. Reliant on one another.

Not my favorite position.

"Nope," I reply. "He just said he was beat from doing Saul's bidding and not to bother him. All he wanted was 'some fucking peace and quiet'." I add the finger quotes for legitimacy.

Remy, still shirtless, hair mussed from the shower he took the moment we got home last night, shrugs. "Well, at least he wasn't working for the Lords for once."

"Yeah, no," I say, choking on my coffee. "Not this time."

"Listen," Sy says, leaning over the counter. His shoulders tense, and it rustles his shirt up to reveal the hard muscles of his biceps. I fight the urge to tug it back down. "I've got a busy day on campus. My professor roped us into a research project and today is my shift in the lab. Can we meet at the gym tonight for our workout?"

"What about family dinner?" I ask. I missed the last two, and although facing everyone at the gym—the DKS, Mama B, and all her cutsluts—sounds as good as having my skin peeled off, I know I can't avoid it forever. These are my people now. Remy and Sy need me to support them, and I've accepted I need to at least pretend to have Nick's back in public. Plus, I need to give Ballsack and his boys my thanks for being the presumed pledges Nick took on his 'job'.

Sy lowers his voice. "Yeah, we can work out after it's over—when the gym is... quiet."

Even though the thought of working out on a full stomach is less than appealing, I shrug. "Sure, yeah. That works for me."

"Great. Nick's up for Friday Night Fury." He looks over at Remy. "You think he can hack it after that job Saul sent him on?"

I straighten, only now realizing Nick is up next for fighting.

Neither of them have seen him yet, but Nick isn't in fighting condition. He can't be. He just spent the last three days trapped in a cage.

Not that they can know that.

Fuck.

"You know him," Remy says, voice wry. "The devil works hard, but Nicky works harder." As he passes, Remy runs his hand down my back, sending a flare of electricity down my spine. It's been like this since we had sex. The ride home was basically spent on the edge of a needle, our bodies pressed together on the bike. It's like a bolt of that lightning shot through me and hasn't burned out. "I'm heading over after my drawing class. I've got ring time scheduled with Bruce later."

He walks off, vanishing into his room, but my shoulders tense at the name. Bruce is the one who got Sy so worked up in the locker room that he tried to choke me on his cock. If Sy notices my discomfort, then he doesn't react. What would he say, anyway? '*Sorry about that time I tried to sell your pussy for a watch*'?

Gross.

"You start classes on Monday, right?" he asks instead.

I straighten. "Yeah, just a few more days." Everything is hanging uncertainly in the air. Remy, Sy, my precarious truce with Nick, being a Duchess by choice instead of force. But I can't deny I'm excited for the little corner of normalcy that will be attending classes.

Sy watches me, eyes narrowing. "How do you plan on staying busy in the meantime?"

My eyes shift over to the clock face. I've been reading up again, getting my bearings on the tools and mechanics needed to try to make it work. "I have some projects."

Sy follows my gaze, looking doubtful. "You're okay with being alone here with him?"

"Yeah," I say, trying to firm up my voice into a confidence I don't feel. "I think we've come to an... understanding."

"Good. We don't have time to play mediator anymore." He drops the pan into the sink and heads into the bathroom.

Cranky.

Guess that answers my question about whether or not he's taken his lessons into his own hands.

I finish my breakfast just as Remy returns from his room, portfolio slung over his shoulder, jeans barely hanging on his narrow hips. I don't mean to give him a *look*, it's just that I'm remembering last night, halfway wondering if he's as sore as I am and halfway searching for that man who'd pushed me down into the dead leaves and told me I was about to become his.

I'm just wondering what that means.

The answer comes when, a moment later, he drops his portfolio and traps me, hemming in against the wall as his green eyes bear down on me. "You keep eyefucking me, and I'll never get out of here."

"I'm not—"

He swallows my disagreement by diving down and capturing my mouth with his. That crazy lightning-bolt feeling explodes in my belly, fraying a soft, plaintive sound from my chest. Remy meets it with a hungry sound of his own, reaching down to cup my ass. He yanks me up against him, the hard line of his dick grinding into my pelvis.

"Fuck." He pulls away just to mouth at my jaw, muttering, "Can't do it here. Promised Nicky."

"What?" I say, too dazed to untangle the words.

He just sighs into my neck. "Wear that black dress Jade gave you to family dinner. Duke's order." The leather thing is strappy but covers everything. Sexy but not slutty. It's probably perfect.

"Sure." Anything to make him not stop doing that thing with his teeth on my earlobe.

Of course, then he pulls away. I bite down on a frustrated sound just as I realize my fingers have made a tight fist into his hair. I quickly release him, only to catch the edge of his smirk as he grabs his bag and swaggers out the door.

Sy stands between the bathroom door and the kitchen, stiff and awkward, so I'm guessing he watched all of that go down. The expression on his face is all twisted up, like he's doing higher math equations. I can almost see them running through his head, like, should he kiss me goodbye? Is that part of our deal?

"Right. Tonight." He strides by. "Later."

Later?

The door shuts behind him, and I'm left pondering Remy's oozing sex appeal versus Sy's complete dysfunction, and whether or not I'm going to survive the whiplash. Oh, and let's not forget the unrepentant asshole sleeping off his three-day cage vacation.

It's hard to see how a normal Royal woman, even under normal circumstances, can handle it. I'm basically dealing with one-and-a-half Dukes at the moment and even that's too much for my brain to juggle. Remy's intense kisses, Sy's intense staredowns, sex on a cliff, late night fumbling.

How can a normal Duchess have the bandwidth for anything else?

I'm about to find out.

I take my plate to the kitchen and refresh my coffee, heading up to the loft. My toolbox is right where I left it, along with the manuals. After a long moment of panicking about the enclosed space, I dart up the narrow staircase into the part of the tower that houses the inner workings of the clock. Something tells me these men are stuck, just like the face of this clock, announcing the Dukes' chaos to all of Forsyth.

I may be the only one that can fix it.

~

THE CLOCK IS A MACHINE.

Machines rust. They fall out of alignment. One part breaks and another follows. They're troublesome and complicated, but entirely rational.

That's what I'm thinking as I tinker, following one problem to the next. The main gear shaft is all mucked up, which threw the chain off its axis, which sent the opposing rod off-kilter. They're all just silent pieces of a puzzle, which might strike me as a profound thought one day.

Time can be broken if your world is small enough.

I follow the links in an effort to find the beginning, the end. Gear shaft first. Rusted, immoveable, stubborn piece of shit.

Huffing, I whip out my phone, the time flashing as half past ten.

Duchess: *Anyone seen my lube?*

Duke Sy: Is this a prank?

Duchess: *No, I need my lube and it's not in my box.*

Duke Remy: I can be home with some all-natural lube in a jiff. Get naked on my bed and I'll get your box good and wet.

Duke Sy: JFC.

Duchess: *I'm talking about the lubricant—oil—that I need for the clock cogs.*

Duke Remy: Oh, I don't think cum would be good for that, but if you need someone to oil up your cogs, I'm here for you, baby.

Duke Sy: I haven't seen it-later.

Later. Seriously?

Duke Remy: Oh, the little canister of oil? I borrowed that. For my bike. It's in the bag hanging by the door.

Duchess: *Thanx*

Dreading another pass through that tiny stairwell, I hoist myself off the ground, brushing my knees. But before I can even start for the door, it opens.

Nick stands in the entry, blocking my way.

The first thing I note is that he hasn't shaved yet, the thick stubble a shade darker than the hair on his head. The second thing I notice is that the circles beneath his eyes have hardly faded. If anything, he looks actively worse than he did last night. That would probably surprise most people, but not me. I happen to know the most brutal part of escaping a box comes twelve hours later when your muscles are screaming. Sleep doesn't come as easily as you'd thought it would. You're hungry, but your appetite has turned its back on you.

Nick looks fucking miserable.

Excellent.

He's wearing an old band shirt and ratty jeans, the tattoos on his arm blotted by the shadows. Sunlight barely reaches this chamber of the tower and the few anemic bulbs hanging from the ceiling are probably old enough to be hung by Edison himself. I'm alone in a dark, crowded space, and Nick Bruin is blocking the only exit.

Not excellent.

His hand stretches out, and I suddenly realize he's holding the can of oil.

"I was coming down for that," I say, glaring.

His hand twitches the same way it had last night, tremors from being shocked for three days. "Now you don't have to."

Reluctantly, I reach for the can, straining over the distance. I get this vision in my head of him snatching it away at the last second, only to grab my wrist and—

But he lets me take it.

Our fingers brush as I retreat and I flinch back, curling the can close. Figuring the best thing to do is ignore him—and absolutely refusing to thank him—I return to the gear, folding myself down onto the floor.

I get about five minutes into scrubbing the metal with a wire brush before it hits me that he hasn't left. Glancing over my shoulder, I find him inspecting one of the fallen rods. "What?" I snap.

He nods up at the beams. "If you want to lift that thing up there, you're going to need someone with upper body strength." Nick's shoulders are still folded into a sad curve, as if it hurts just keeping his spine straight.

"You're atrophied."

His eyes narrow. "It was only three days. I can hold my own."

I give the gear an aggressive scrub. "Is this about the rod or Friday Night Fury?"

There's a long beat of silence before Nick scoffs. "I'm fighting some sophomore LDZ. I could win that with one arm."

"I hope so." I stare at his hands, still giving the sporadic tremor, fully aware of the worry in my eyes. “I don’t think anyone is going to take it well if we lose to the Lords.”

Nick just shoots me a sharp, vicious grin. “Leave the fighting to me, Little Bird. You have your own project.”

He’s talking about the clock. “Well, half the pieces are broken. There are spiders burrowed in every crevice, and the main cog is so rusty I doubt a gallon of this oil will make it move.” I dump some oil onto a rag and begin working it into the grooves.

Nick, annoyingly, sits down, settling against a beam about twenty feet away, socked feet crossed at the ankles. Casually, he asks, “So how was it?”

I don’t look up. “How was what?”

“Getting fucked by Remy.” I fumble the gear and it clatters between my legs. The air around us vibrates with Nick’s low chuckle. “Girls say he’s good at giving head. Definitely not better than me, but—”

“I’m not talking about this,” I say, shutting it down.

“Did he fuck you hard and fast, or was it all slow and sweet?” He muses, “Never can tell with Remy. Sometimes it’s like he wants to rip a girl’s skin off, but occasionally he likes to take his time, do it right.” Though his voice is casual, I can see the flame of jealousy in his eyes—something he has no right to. “It was in the rain, right? Makes sense. I can see him getting off to the drama of it.”

I bang the can of oil down, turning to him. “Fine, you want to know so bad? The heavens opened. Angels were singing. There were trumpets and cherubs. It was easily the best fuck I’ve ever had.”

Nick stares at me, slowly bringing his hands together in a clap. “You sure know how to drive a knife into a guy, don’t you?”

Rolling my eyes, I stand to fit the gear onto its axle. “I don’t see why you should care. You’re the one who made me his Duchess. You knew what was going to happen before I did.”

He doesn’t argue with me. I’m sure we both remember that first night, right after he won me, when he insisted to Sy and Remy that he was willing to share. Instead, he says, "Eventually they're going to wonder why we don't just kill your father."

"Because Saul wouldn't let them." I raise my hand, waving it. "Ripples," I say, repeating something he'd told me early on.

"Murdering a King is like throwing a rock into the water," Nick had said. *"It makes ripples. The closer you are, the more you feel them. You're way too close to that rock, Little Bird."*

He snorts. "If you think Saul is the ripple I was talking about, then you're definitely not as smart as I—"

My head whips toward him. "I know what the ripple is, idiot." I meet his eyes, catching the flash of surprise there. "I lived under his thumb for most of my life. I know what his real legacy is. It's not drugs, and it's sure as hell not his children. Give me some credit."

His face twists. "If you knew about his failsafe, then why'd you ask me to kill him?" But immediately, his expression clears. "Right. I guess Forsyth and the Royal system haven't been very good to you. Get far enough away, the ripples won't touch you." He gives me a creepy grin. "That's some dark shit, Little Bird."

"I never asked you to kill him," I remind Nick. "I just asked if you would."

"So, what? It was a test?" His head snaps back. "Did I pass or fail?"

"I haven't decided yet."

Truthfully, I wasn't entirely sure he knew until just a minute ago. There's a reason my father is so obsessed with who his Kingdom passes on to. It's meant to be someone loyal. Someone he can control, long after he's gone. Whoever that person is, they'll have this whole city under their heel.

And right now, that person is Perez.

"Your sister..." When I look up, Nick is staring at his hand. I follow his gaze and notice a twitch—a tic—just before he curls it into a fist. "I can't tell you if she's alive. But if she's dead and there's no body, then I know where to go to look."

I straighten, all thoughts of cogs and machinery cast aside. "Where?"

He tips his head, watching me through his lashes. "Where do bodies go to not be found?"

Blinking, I realize, "The Barons." There's just one problem with that plan and it makes me laugh. "You're crazy. The Barons would never narc about a job. Their whole operation hinges on a century of secrecy."

He gives a slow nod. "There'll be a price. You might not want to pay it, so think long and hard before I set this shit in motion, because once I do, there's no going back."

His words rustle up the memory from last night, Remy entering me, pressing me into the ground as he whispered so roughly that I'd become his. I look down at the cog in my lap, considering it carefully. "The Barons... they'll want to spill blood. It's the only currency they recognize."

"Probably." The crackle of tension between us rises to a crest when he insists, "The others can't know. Sy and Remy wouldn't let you—" He looks away, the muscle in the back of his jaw ticking, and I wonder what he's thinking.

Is Nick's willingness to let me walk into the House of Night and possibly never leave some kind of fucked up gesture?

A pensive silence settles over us, and I spend it watching him in my periphery. The hand twitches, the muscle spasms, means he's feeling the effects of the electricity, being shocked over and over again inside the cage.

I suppose everyone in Forsyth pays a price for something.

"Set it up," I decide, meeting his gaze.

Dread builds in my gut, but it's not alone. It's accompanied by an iron resolve, because I'm a Lucia—the Duchess of West End—and a little spilled blood isn't enough to scare me away.

17

Sy

DINNER TAKES FOREVER.

Don't get me wrong. I appreciate the community of it, the tradition. My first year at Forsyth, I'd missed that. Having grown up with Nick, three parents, six grandparents, Dad's tribal pals and Pops' old DKS buddies, I was accustomed to a full, boisterous dinner table, and a one-dollar value burger inside my empty dorm room was pretty fucking depressing. It was definitely one of the draws of pledging DKS, and fuck, I love the food, but tonight my patience is on a hair trigger.

"Take a breath, bro," Remy says, shoveling a forkful of banana pudding into his mouth. "And eat some of this. It'll take the edge off."

Easy for him to say.

He got laid last night.

I shake my head. Unlike Remy, who is attracted to every addictive substance in the world: sugar, pills, booze, pussy… only one thing will take the edge off for me.

"I didn't work out today," I snap. And I didn't get jerked off last night—his fault, by the way, for getting her home so late. She was probably too fucked out from him to bother caring about her obligation to me. Cracking my neck, I search for my inner calm, tucking away all my frustration and…

Fine, I'll admit it.

Jealousy.

"I just need to get in the ring," I mutter, curling over my plate. "Blow off some steam."

Remy rolls his eyes at me, because he has some kind of sixth-sense for my bullshit.

"Ignore him," Nick says from across the table, voice rough. Speaking of shit, he looks like it, sporting a ragged beard that makes him look way too much like Pops. It annoys me that tonight's Fury is for him. His hands have been weirdly unsteady all morning. Clearly, I'd be better suited. There's a touch of sallowness to his skin and something about it makes him look gaunt, haggard. The only good thing I can say is that he doesn't have any injuries. When I asked him about what kind of job made him look like he survived three days in a Mexican jail, he blew me off, just saying, "Bruin stuff."

I won't pretend that doesn't rankle.

Something tells me whatever he was doing is going to come back and kick us in the ass, but Nick's exploits, like Remy's pudding, are not my focus right now.

The object of my obsession is talking to Verity and cleaning up the leftovers, and my eyes are drawn to her like a magnet. She's wearing a black dress, the lacy neckline scooping to show a modest portion of cleavage while the bottom is soft and fluttery, swaying enticingly over her thighs every time she turns or takes a step. Ever since she became Duchess, I've begun noticing the feminine figure in a way I'm not used to, my gaze traversing their curves, my mind offering whispers of how it might feel to follow them with my hands. The dress she's wearing accentuates hers, showing off the way I've been feeding her since I got her back from her father. She's still too skinny, but her hips are a little fuller, her bones a little less pronounced. There's color to her skin again, and when she turns, I find my gaze wandering to her legs, which look smooth and inviting.

A lot of the DKS boys are staring at her, too.

When she bends down to grab a fallen napkin from beneath the buffet table, Remy mutters a low curse. "*Goddamn*. I don't know what you've been doing to our girl, Sy, but keep going. Her ass is looking nice and perky."

Rolling my eyes, I stab my fork into my salad. "She's probably been malnourished for the better part of two years. If she wants to have any hope of getting into shape, she's going to need to put some weight on. Not everything is about your dick."

She doesn't know it yet, but I've got her on a dieting plan to fill her out a little more, and I've been watching—a little too eagerly—for the results. It's strictly health-focused. The fact that her ass is growing rounder, almost sculpted into the perfect shape, is just a coincidence.

Mostly.

"At least there's no sniping," Nick rumbles, picking at his dessert. "Can't deal with bitches and their drama today."

Lavinia has handled her re-entry with DKS better than expected. Unlike last time, she's dressed appropriately, she's been helpful and friendly, and I even caught Mama B giving her a playful grin earlier. I don't know what caused the turnaround in attitude. Although four days of being held captive in a box at her father's house probably had something to do with it. In fact, ever since her return, she's been the model Duchess. Attentive to Remy. Civil to Nick. Obedient to me.

The problem is that she's a female.

A woman.

A *Royal* woman.

Making men soft and compliant is what they do to gain control.

I can still feel the weight of her on me from the other night, when she climbed on top of me to fulfill her own needs. That was nothing to do with me or our arrangement and everything with her being horny. Most guys would be more than happy to be used like that, but I was so pissed off about blowing my wad and feeling unmoored, lost, inexperienced, that I didn't really have a chance to consider what it meant.

She was horny.

Was she horny for me?

Like, specifically?

I look over at her, and she's looking this way. Not at me. Not at Nick. Her eyes meet Remy's as he sucks the pudding off his finger, tongue flicking the ring under the tattooed 'D.'

Jesus Christ.

"Can you be any more embarrassing?" I ask. This is what I hate about sex. The flashiness. The bragging. It's like no one can fuck a girl without broadcasting it to everyone. I mean, I have the biggest dick in this frat—possibly even in this whole fucking city—but do you see me pulling it out and slapping it on the table?

"Can't help it," Remy says, looking unapologetic as he leans back in his seat, adjusting the front of his pants. "I got a taste of what it's like to be buried balls deep in her, and I want another hit." He lifts his hand and gestures for her to come over, not even hearing himself. She probably has him right where she wants him, addicted to her cunt.

She hands a stack of plates to a passing cutslut and comes our way, hovering beside Remy. "Guys," she says, resting her hands on her hips. "Everything okay? You need some more dessert?"

I look at Nick, and then Remy. Are neither of them seeing this?

She's definitely too well-behaved.

I'd written it in my journal this morning.

L: Alert but noticeably sleep deprived. Subject is gaining weight. Suspiciously non-combative. Shaved her legs yesterday. Displays a new willingness to endure proximity to N. Vaginal intercourse between her and R last night at appx 11pm. Completed orgasm, followed by stillness. I assume sleep. No injuries.

"Just wanted to remind everyone in the room who you belong to," Remy replies, hand running up the back of her thigh. I watch as it vanishes under her dress, his tattooed forearm stark against her smooth thighs.

I know the second she stiffens, eyes widening as the tendons in his arms shift, exactly where his fingers have wandered to. "Remy," she begins, a warning in her voice, but he just tuts.

"I'm your Duke tonight, Vinny."

The wideness of her eyes relaxes, and I assume at first it's his words, that there's something about calling himself her Duke that puts her into weird Stepford mode. But then a glaze falls over her eyes, her lids growing heavy, body swaying to the rhythm of... whatever he's doing beneath that skirt—fuck, I wish I could see—and I realize she's just into it.

He's making her feel good.

Nick's eyes, just like every other guy in the room, track every movement. Remy isn't subtle, and neither is Lavinia, who puts one hand on his shoulder and grips hard enough that her fingers wrinkle the fabric of his designer shirt.

It's not a surprise when Nick suddenly lurches his chair back with an ear-splitting screech, storming away. All three of us watch as he ambles past the tables, throwing the doors open and disappearing behind them.

N: Withdrawn. Exhibiting signs of injury but predictably unwilling to speak about it. Low mood, irritable. Subject being a little bitch.

"And he says I'm the drama queen," Remy mutters, the muscles in his arm still steadily shifting.

R: Active. Alert. Head Check: 8. Taking medication without difficulty. Willing to take his meals socially. Well-rested following intercourse with L. Spent an inordinate amount of time in the shower this morning. Appears unconcerned with her behavior. Lack of inhibition. Subject being a little bitch.

"Do you have to do that to him?" I ask, already dreading going home tonight. No one throws a fit like Nick does—silently, tensely, turning the whole mood of a room sour without even making a sound. "You know he can't handle this shit."

And he's not the only one, I want to say. My cock is harder than a lead pipe.

Remy just fixes me with a look. "We've kept every end of our bargain, and now it's his turn. We can't keep coddling him. He needs to learn to deal with it."

I want to ask him how he can do that, sit here and talk all casually while his fingers are playing with her cunt. It'd be nice to know how to use my fingers, too, only my lesson got delayed on account of him fucking my tutor.

"I can't sit here all night," I snap, throwing down my napkin. "I'm going to get ready for my workout." I nod at her. "And you, too. Go change. You have more than one Duke to attend to."

At least she doesn't look disappointed. I've noticed that despite the bitching and moaning she puts up at any mention of exercise, there's always a light in her eyes right before we get started. I see it now, even as Remy unhappily removes his hand from her skirt.

He sighs, long and beleaguered, only to tug her down, bringing her mouth to his. Right before their lips meet, however, he slips two fingertips into her mouth.

The same fingers he'd been touching her with, I realize.

She pauses as she tastes herself and I watch, hypnotized, as she accepts it, her pink tongue peeking out to slither between them. But then Remy is there, his tongue meeting hers as they lick around his fingers, slow and uncomfortably sensual.

I stand, clearing my throat. "Now, Lavinia." Remy lets her go, smirking when she springs upright, her cheeks blazing red as the DKS boys look on in varying degrees of interest. I keep my hips twisted away from the table, hiding the unhidable.

My dick bulges inside my pants, unmistakable.

Lavinia's eyes glance at it, and then dart quickly away. "Just give me a second in the dressing room," she says, skittering away.

Remy arches an eyebrow. "I highly recommend the dessert."

THE THREE OF us dispersing seems to do the trick for clearing out the dinner. When I exit the locker room, the place is empty other than Verity and a few other cutsluts in the kitchen. I take a few laps around the gym and hit the weights in the corner, getting myself warmed up. When Lavinia walks out dressed in tights and a sports bra, her blue hair secured back in a high ponytail, my blood is already pumping. I quickly hop into the ring while she hesitates on the edge.

"What?" I ask, annoyed.

"I've never been in the ring before," she says, worrying her lip. "I mean, as a Duchess and a ring girl, but never as a... fighter?" She says the word dubiously, as if she's unsure I'd let her use that word in reference to herself.

I shrug, swiping sweat from my brow. "It's not a big deal."

"It is a big deal," she says, wrapping her hands around the rope. "To the Dukes, at least. Fighting is your... well, everything."

"Then you should do fine. You fight back more than any opponent I've ever been up against." My eyes travel down her body. "You just use different weapons." Choosing to remain silent about that, she works her way through the ropes, already breathing heavily when she gets on the mat. "You're seriously that out of shape?" I eye her heaving chest, the tight Lycra squeezing her tits together. "How is that possible?"

She shoots me a hot glare. "Did you miss the part about me living in captivity for the last two years?" I'm pretty sure she mutters a sharp '*dumbass*' at the end of her sentence, but I decide to let it slide. "Okay, so, what's tonight's lesson?"

Snagging a sip from my water bottle, I begin, "Now that you've learned not to break your hand when you throw a punch, I just want to go back to a few of the basics." I gesture for her to meet me in the middle of the ring. She stares up at me, so open and trusting that my eyes are drawn to her lips. The fervent shade of them. The plush give when she rakes one through her teeth. The faint shine of her saliva.

Briefly, I wonder if she still tastes like her pussy.

"If you're in a situation you need to get out of, the best thing to do is KISS." She frowns, eyes dropping to my mouth. My hands curl into fists and I get this split second of clarity that I could do it. Kiss her. Push my tongue between her teeth and *take*. Refusing to fall into her gravity, I snap back, elaborating, "'*Keep it simple, stupid*'. K-I-S-S."

Her eyes narrow. "Simple."

I approach her, hands hovering over her body heat as I go through a series of motions. "Throat, eyes, knee, stomp and," I lift my knee, "groin. Obviously."

She throws me a dark smirk. "Obviously."

We practice the moves, going over each one. The first time I touch her—my hand cupping her elbow to correct her form—she flinches. It's a small thing, and if her hair weren't right below my nose, I might have even missed it.

"Keep your shoulders square," I say, resenting how low and breathy my voice sounds.

She does as instructed, which just shimmies her back against me, her ass a hairsbreadth from brushing my cock.

"If it's a random guy on the street, any of these should take them by surprise, but if it's someone more physical—more savvy—"

"More like your brother...." She twists to glance at me over her shoulder.

I refrain from telling her Nick could shake any of these off. "Yeah, or another Royal—I want you to learn how to get away."

Her mouth purses unhappily. "That's incredibly lame and not what we agreed to."

My thumb skates down her lower arm as I let her elbow go. "I agreed to teach you how to protect yourself. This is part of it."

Across the gym, Verity turns off the kitchen light and waves to us before exiting the back door. It's just the two of us now. Alone. I inhale, taking in the mixture of shampoo and sweat.

"Fine," she sighs, shoulders losing some of her tension. "Teach me how to be lame."

"Give me your hand." That's how it starts, with holds, clamping my large hand around her skinny wrists and teaching her how to manipulate her body, how to leverage her strength against mine. The further we go, the more I have to touch her. Hands on her waist, crotch against her backside, forearm curled over her breasts. I make sure the touches are precise and purposeful, but they keep... lingering. I walk her through a clinch hold and there's nothing sexy about having her head wedged under my armpit as she struggles against me, and yet...

My dick might die.

It probably looks comical from the outside, my six-foot-four frame combined with two hundred pounds of muscle, getting the slip from this tiny wisp of a girl, but that's what she needs to learn. Lavinia is never going to out-fight Nick or even Perez. But I can help her get a head start, and sometimes that's enough.

"Got it?" I ask, when she gets away from me for the tenth time.

"Yeah, I think so." She nods, her face fully flushed. There's these spots on her arms where I've restrained her that have been rubbed to redness, and I find myself staring at them as I gulp down a quick drink of water. They're all splotchy and irritated with the shapes of my fingers and I wonder if her hips look the same. "What's next?" she asks, drinking from her own bottle.

I watch the bob of her throat as she swallows. "Chokeholds."

Capping her bottle, she tosses it aside, swaggering to the center of the ring with a wicked grin on her face. Then she moves into a squatting wrestler pose, hips swaying back and forth. "Bring it on, big bear."

Fuck.

There's no way she's not goading me.

Abruptly, I lunge for her, catching her body and dragging her tight, painfully, against my chest. I flatten my arm around her neck, bicep flexed, and I can feel the flutter of her pulse against my overheated skin. Recovering quickly, she fights against me, and I still her, speaking low in her ear. "Pull my hand off of my neck and bend it backwards." I let her run through the motions, while not giving too much slack.

"You're holding me too tight!" she whines, giving a spirited thrash.

Lazily, I reply, "I don't think an attacker is going to take it easy on you just because you bitched a little bit. Try harder." Grunting, she bucks against me, the scent of her hair trapped in my nose as her ass bumps against my crotch. It's taking everything in me not to throw her to this mat and rip the Lycra from her body. Focusing, I command, "Try to get your arm under mine, pushing it aside long enough to get leverage."

She struggles against me, hips wiggling against my cock. "Your arm is too fucking big." She grunts. "Just like your goddamn cock."

Everything goes still for a moment and then I'm pushing her—shoving her—away. She takes it in stride, hopping a few steps ahead as I turn, hands propped on my hips. I take a short, slow walk around the ring, trying to tuck away the tight, angry, *horny* feeling that's constricting my abdomen. Deep breaths. Calm. Ocean waves. Tranquility.

My balls are killing me.

Breathlessly, so quiet that I barely hear it, Lavinia says, "Sorry, I was just—"

I give a curt shake of my head, pulling my discarded shirt from the floor to wipe my forehead, wicking off the sweat. "Again?"

When I turn back to her, she's chewing on her lip—not helping—and giving me this look. If she weren't a Lucia, I'd assume she felt guilty. "I let it get to me," she explains. "I shouldn't have said that."

"Yeah, you should've." Shrugging, I return to the center of the ring. "Piss off your opponent. Go for the jugular. Be a viper." She winces at the word, but for the first time, it's not an insult. "Use the weapons you've honed, Lavinia. Just because you don't like where they've come from doesn't mean they aren't useful. Now." I pin her with a look. "Again."

From there, it gets complicated—for me.

Every move, every action forces her body closer to mine. I want it, but I hate it. I fucking loathe the way I'm one step, one touch, one moment of weakness from losing control. I try to focus on the work, on the hand movements and teaching her to use her brains, but this is a test for me just as much as for her.

"Ah ha!" she yelps, finally slipping out of my grip. "Gotcha! I win!"

It'd take my breath away, actually—the way her face goes alight, arms raised in victory, mouth spread into a jubilant grin—if it weren't for the impulse.

The competitor, the *winner* in me strikes out, reaching out and grabbing her. It's easy to toss her to the cushioned mat. She goes down like a feather, landing on her back with this stunned, confused expression that might be funny if not for the storm raging within me.

I jump on her, knees straddling her tight little body, and then I reach out, hands clenching around the delicate column of her throat. "What about this, Lavinia? Think you can get away?"

Eyes shuttering, she grapples at my hands, nails digging into the skin. There's no way she doesn't feel the hard press of my cock between us, and it gets harder the more I have her under my control. I grind against her, finally giving in to the craving for a warm spark of friction. I'm so much bigger than she is. I could just take her if I wanted, rip her pants down, whip my cock out, and force it inside her hot, wet, tight—

She grabs my cock.

The grip is much like the one I'm using to hold her neck, except her motion isn't rough. It's tight. Firm. My hands loosen and my hips jerk, a hiss escaping my clenched teeth.

She pants up at me, her mouth pursed into a hard, disapproving line. "If you want a handjob, Perilini, you don't have to rough house me to get my attention. I already agreed."

I fight the urge to wring her neck, instead tightening my thighs and rolling us so that she's on top. I don't ask. I don't beat around the bush. I don't even give her the chance to have an opinion about it.

I reach up and shove at her sports bra, wrenching it over her full, round tits. Her whole body jostles as I fight to get it over her head, off her arms, throwing it to the side.

"Ride me," I tell her, flexing my hips up. There's an eagerness in my voice that I fail to mask, but I try to distract her from it, reaching up to palm her tits just like she showed me. I feel a rush when the nipple pebbles in my hand. "Ride me like you did the other night." Her hips rock in a slow, deliberate roll, dragging down my length. "Ride me like you're fucking me." I reach out and hold her chin, forcing her to look at me. "But this time it's about me. Not you."

That's what I want. I can't have it. I can't get 'balls deep' like Remy or rip my way into her like Nick. But I can lie in the winner's ring and let her pleasure me like a Duchess should.

"Way to sweet talk a girl," she mutters, but grinds against me, tits bouncing lazily with each thrust. Even through the layer of clothes, it feels like delicious torture, her pussy sliding against me as she braces her palms on my chest. I feel like we're in an oven, my skin so hot that I can feel the sweat springing up.

But when I look up at Lavinia's face, her expression is weak. Passive.

Jesus.

She's bored.

I clamp my hands on her hips, stopping her.

"What the fuck is going on?"

"Huh?" she asks, giving me a little nudge with her pussy. "Harder? Faster?" When I just stare up at her, she deflates, looking tired. "I don't know with you anymore, Sy. Tell me what won't piss you off when I make you come."

Then it hits me. The force of it is just like the right hook Pops got me with when I was fifteen and thought I could take him down in the ring. *Slam!* Right in the jaw.

I push her off, dropping her on the mat with a thud. She grabs for her top, using it to cover her breasts. "What the hell, Perilini?"

I bend my knees and rest my elbows on them, my cock furious at me for stopping. "Something tells me you didn't look like that with Remy." I lace my fingers together, squeezing my fists so hard they tremble. "I fucking suck at this."

"I know." The look she gives me is a huge *duh*. "That's the whole point of this little lesson thing, right? You suck at sex. I suck at defending myself."

I snort. "Yeah, well, at least you're making progress. I'm just..." I wince, unable to say it.

"You're not a loser, Sy," she says, slouching next to me, and I shoot her a look. What the fuck. That was *not* what I was going to say. "You're a repressed, sexually stunted, monster-cocked misogynist. None of those go great together." She rests her hand on my arm. "I feel like... somewhere along the way, you and your brother thought the way to get an orgasm was through beating your partner into submission. I mean, some girls get off on that. Sometimes I've even..." If she wasn't flushed before, then she is now, her cheeks turning a deep scarlet. "What I'm saying is that you need to give a shit about the other person. I'm not talking about love, or even... like. You just need to want them to feel as good as you do. And if you don't? If you can't feel that for me, or for any other girl, then you're never going to be good at sex."

I know what she's saying is true. I felt it that night she rode me, unconcerned with what I was feeling or doing. But it still chafes at something deep inside. A sense of pride? Some long-nurtured wound? Either way, my jaw clenches at the thought. "I don't know what you like."

She ducks her head, trying to meet my eyes. "Yes, you do. I've been telling you—showing you. All this time, I've been telling you."

Sighing, I look at her. We're close on the mat, her arm pressed into mine. I reach out and gently tug the top out of her hands, making her drop the bra. She doesn't fight me. What's the point? Once it's gone, I flatten my palm over her tit because I know she likes it. Remy said she also likes it when she has something done to her pussy, but knowing him, it involves eating her out and that shit isn't happening. Not a fucking chance.

So, focus back on her tits, tugging at her nipple until her back arches, and a soft exhale comes from her parted lips. I spend a long moment staring at them, thinking back to that first night in the motel when she asked me to kiss her.

Kissing isn't something I normally like to do. It's all spit and teeth, and there's a good possibility I'm just bad at it. But for some reason, I've been thinking about it all night, and I finally give in to the impulse, bending to brush her mouth with mine.

The second our lips touch, there's a low, humming buzz of heat.

She leans into it, opening her mouth to my tongue as her hand runs down my bare chest. Her fingers toy with the hair on my lower belly, making a slow, deliberate descent as I lick into her, a groan building in my chest.

She hesitates when she reaches my cock, her fingertip tracing the length of my shaft over the fabric of my sweats to the painful, swollen head of it, jutting against my waistband. Gently, she squeezes.

I hiss into her mouth. "You know I'll come if you do that."

"Take a deep breath, big bear," she says, nudging my lips with hers. "This isn't a fight. Work with me, not against me."

I plunge my tongue into her mouth, mostly to get her to shut up, but partly because focusing on something else, someone else, gives me the slightest bit of distraction. "What do you want me to do?" I ask between deep, plunging kisses.

"You can kiss my neck," she says, dropping her head to the side. "Or my tits."

I close my lips around the soft skin of her neck, just below her jaw, and feel her heartbeat against my tongue as I suck. At the sound of her soft sigh, I suck harder, knowing full well I'm leaving a mark that everyone will see later.

This makes her breaths deepen, and when she tangles her fingers into my hair, I lick down her collarbones, pushing her back as my mouth finds her tit.

The thing about Lavinia is that she has a fucking fantastic body. I cup her breasts in my hand as I lick and suck, considering that she's the perfect womanly form. Nick and I have always shared a type. It used to annoy me when we were younger, because I'd never really let myself look at a girl like that until Nick brought her around and put her under my nose. Remy would call it sibling rivalry, as if I only wanted something when Nick had it. But that wasn't strictly true.

Nick just has great taste.

She leans back on one elbow, sprawled across the mat, her muscles loosening as I lave her nipples with the flat of my tongue. I'm so dedicated to the task, so absorbed in her little hitches of breath, that I almost miss her reaching into my pants.

My stomach does a violent flip at the first brush of her fingers against my skin. She doesn't handle me like she used to. There's no more pinching my cock distastefully between forefinger and thumb to avoid making any meaningful contact. There's no grimacing or shudders.

She just grasps me, pulling me from my pants with a long, full-palmed stroke. "That feels good," she whispers.

She could be talking about my cock.

She could be talking about my mouth on her chest.

She could be talking about the square root of pi for all I care.

Slowly, she works from the base to the head, thumb toying the tip. The urge charges through me, the uncontrollable need to thrust, to come.

I slap my hand over hers on my cock, already panting like a dog. "I can't."

"Deep breaths," she repeats, voice smooth as satin as she guides my hand to her waist. "Just keep taking deep breaths."

I inhale and then kiss the round curve of her shoulder. I inhale and kiss the center of her sternum. I inhale and bury my nose between her breasts, willing my cock to hold on for just a minute longer.

"You said you'd teach me," I rumble, muscles seizing with the way she's stroking me. "My fingers..." Running my hand down her stomach, I pause at her waistband before pushing my fingers underneath the tight leggings.

Wordlessly, she spreads her thighs, and some part of me is stunned stupid at her easy willingness to let me into this soft, warm, private place. I touch her pubic mound first, finding it smooth, hairless. I need to put that in my journal, but right now, I'm just lost. I poke and prod until she grabs my wrist, leading me into the soft warmth.

"Right here." She presses my finger into the slippery folds.

"Fuck." I feel like I've just been gutted somehow, and when I pull back to stare into her heavy eyes, I'm embarrassed at the wonderment in my voice. "You're wet."

Her mouth parts with a long breath, and she nods. "That's... kind of the point, isn't it?"

I *made you wet*, I think as I glide my fingertips up and down her slit, watching her body slacken more and more. Her thighs fall wider, but when I venture lower, she guides my wrist back up.

"No where else," she insists, pressing my fingertips through the fabric of her pants. "Right. Here."

"Yeah," I agree, feeling the little nub. *Her clit.*

The understanding that I make her wet keeps sending a jolt of want to my balls. There's something excitingly primal about the concept of her body getting ready for me, wanting me, preparing for me, without even knowing who or what I am. I breathe in and out, realizing that she's doing the same. Her gasps are different, though, the rhythm synced to the way I touch her, short little movements that beat in time with the rock of her hips. Her hand fists my cock, and even though the angles are all awkward and stilted, she keeps pace, jerking my cock to the same rhythm I'm rubbing her clit. Our bodies have this conversation, a connection, and I finally allow myself to sink into the feeling. The feel of her womanhood, her skin, her wetness, her breath. I watch her so intensely that I don't even think about where we're doing this. How could I when she's planting her heels on the mat, bucking up into my fingers?

Her face glows redder, and she makes a sound, soft and needy, that sends my nerves into a victorious fury. She's close. I can feel it in the growing slickness on my fingers, see it in her expression. There's this desperate little divot between her eyebrows and I'm wondering if she's faking it, faking this whole thing, but then she gasps, followed by a deep inhale, her hand clenching around my cock as she shudders against my side.

I'd never admit it, but it's the satisfaction of making her look like that, *sound* like that, that makes me come, hard and fast—too fast—spilling all over her hand. It should feel disappointing, watching her build up to this deep, body-wracking, all-consuming climax as my cock just lamely surges with absurd amounts of cum, but it doesn't.

It feels like victory, and nothing feels better than that.

"Fuck," I mutter, not sure if it's about the orgasm, the mess, or having my mind blown.

She looks up at me, the overhead lights at the gym shining down on me, and I'm not sure it matters.

18

Lavinia

It's been approximately twenty-four hours since I was in the gym for Family Dinner—or as I may refer to it from now on, the night Sy figured out how to get a girl off. I can tell he's thinking about it when we walk in for Friday Night Fury, because I watch surreptitiously as his eyes dart straight to the ring. His back stiffens, and he gets that weird, shifty walk that means his dick is getting hard.

I fight back a grin because the sight of this handsome, hulking beast of a man blushing himself into a fluster over anything even remotely sexual hasn't stopped being funny. The darker truth is that the minute my father handed me over to Daniel Payne, I knew a big portion of my life's purpose would be to pleasure men. Over the years, I've had a lot of free time to ponder what that might entail. Every knock on the motel door, every footfall down the basement steps, I braced myself for it, sure the time was arriving for me to make good on my 'value'. I've imagined the worst scenarios possible. Old, rich, monstrous men forcing me to my knees. Pain. Degradation. Violation. Humiliation.

I did not expect what would transpire between me and the Dukes. Well, two of them, at least, because Nick certainly has lived up to the hype. But Remy and even, Sy?

It's not so bad.

A new little niggling worry in the back of my mind flares to life that perhaps Sy was right about me all along. I've been taken and owned, and I've found pleasure at the same hands that bruised me, so maybe I really am just a whore.

Because I've been horny as fuck for days now.

"I'm going to go check with Mama B and make sure everything's lined up for the undercard," Sy says, fussing with the hem of his shirt. Sy is normally a very tidy type of asshole, so I've intuited that when he wears his shirts untucked, it's an attempt to cover the monster in his pants. Before he slips into the growing crowd, his eyes meet Remy's and they lift chins—a silent conversation passing between them. I can read it, and it says, "*Watch her.*"

I can't tell if they're worried *for* me or *about* me.

What they don't realize is that, for the first time in my life, I'm not feeling the urge to bolt. I haven't decided what that makes me yet. Weak, for laying back and accepting the shitty hand fate has dealt me? Or is this strength, rooting around to find the bits of being their Duchess that can work to my advantage?

I don't know.

When I got home from my lesson last night, I retired to Remy's room and watched him paint. It was a smaller canvas, but you wouldn't have known it to look at him, frenzied and covered in black and red pigment, eyes barely tracking me as I climbed between his sheets and laid my head on his pillow. I watched him move and let his energy feed me, build me, shape me.

Mostly, I just feel ready.

Remy glances at me, doing a double take as his eyebrows knit together. "You turned dark purple." His fingers ghost the side of my face. "What's with all the amethyst, pretty girl?" There's an energy to him these last couple nights that I don't like. Pupils big and black, he's too jittery, more easily distracted than usual. Even now he's got that marker between his teeth, gnawing away at the cap absentmindedly, jaw flexing and straining.

He's high.

"I'm not purple," I tell him, not knowing exactly what that means, but hating how he's become so in-tune to my shifting emotions. There are a lot of things I need to hide and the more Remy focuses on me, the harder it gets. Smoothly, I lie, "It's just loud in there and I'm not used to all the chaos." I tug at the ruffles on my shirt. "Or all the attention."

"Sy would call that classic second-child syndrome or something," he says, eyebrow quirking. Besides a pair of ripped up jeans that hang perfectly on every part of his lower body, he's wearing a black button down with the sleeves rolled up and the boots he got from Jade.

"Nothing about my home life was 'classic'," I argue, but he's probably not wrong. I was taught to be invisible, quiet, unseen and unheard to give Leticia space to shine. It's not something that prepared me for the role of Duchess.

He presses his hand just above the V of my neckline, palm flat against my skin. "You're nervous."

"I'm not nervous."

I totally am.

I should be back with Nick right now, prepping him for his fight, playing the attentive ring girl. We haven't been alone since we worked on the clock together and he offered to go to the Barons with me. He and I share another secret and it makes me feel squirmy—amethyst purple, apparently—like something is wrong. It's a little bit like the tickle you feel in your throat before you get sick. It's just the kind of thing that will make him think more than he should.

Remy's palm is still flat on my chest, but he takes the marker out from between his teeth and traces my collarbones with the capped top.

"A tattoo would look sexy here," he says, tilting his head like he can already see it. "I'm just waiting for the right whispers. You'll let me, won't you? When the time comes?" His green eyes bear down on me like a wide, dark chasm, and I almost think of telling him the truth. That I wish we could be in his room right now. I'd let him draw on me, ink me, fuck me. Whatever he wants.

"You're my Duke," is my answer, eyelashes fluttering as his hand slides up my chest, around my throat. "My body is yours." The words don't taste as bitter as they should, and while part of the reason is that I've come to accept this as a means to an end, the rest is far more complicated.

When it comes to Remy, my body is in capable hands.

Cradling the back of my neck, he pulls my face to his, pressing his forehead to mine to quietly say, "Go be a good Duchess and prep Nicky for the match. He's not gonna bite."

Sometimes I think Remy is a mind reader.

"I'm not sure he wants me there."

His lips curve. "You and I both know that isn't true."

Dammit. He's right. Again. "Fine. But if I'm not back out in fifteen minutes, come find me."

I sense his eyes on my back as I weave through the drunken frat boys and tipsy sorority girls toward the locker room, disappearing into the fray. But I pause when I catch a flash of a familiar face. At first, I'm sure I must be imagining it. There's no way he'd come to West End to sling his junk.

But sure enough, standing between the bathrooms, leaning against the wall, is Cash Mallis.

He's passing off a baggy to a fresh-faced LDZ member, not even trying to be discreet about it. It's a part of the job, knowing when to signal who you are and what you've got. Advertising at its sleaziest.

Remembering Sy's words from a few days ago, I change course, storming over to grab him by the arm. "Are you fucking insane!" I hiss, dragging him to the side.

Cash's mouth spreads into a grin. "Lavinia! I thought you'd be here. Damn, your ass is looking tight."

"First of all, *ew*. Second of all," I slap him upside the head, "are you trying to get yourself killed?"

He rubs his head, jaw dropped in outrage. "What?! I'm just hustling!"

"Not here, you aren't." I thrust a finger at the door. "You're going to walk out of here and never come back, do you hear me?"

He scowls back. "Friday Night Fury is open to all houses."

"You're not in a house!"

He argues, "Think again. I pledged to Kappa a couple of months ago."

"Great," I mutter, teeth clenching. "Cash, you have to get out of here. If Sy sees you selling North Side dope in his territory, he's going to kill you. And there's a very good chance I'm being literal."

Cash frowns, still rubbing his head. Moron. "Come on, Lavvy. We had a whole moment back there with that Felix guy. It was beautiful. A real moment of inter-house cooperation. I'm building bridges here."

"And you're going to get pushed off of it." I shove him toward the doors. "I mean it, Cash. Stay away from the West End, and—I cannot stress this enough—Remy."

Cash's eyes light up. "Dude, *Lav*, that Remy guy is a Maddox. Did you know that? He's fucking loaded!"

Oh no.

The stars in his eyes are unmistakable, all the sparkle and delight of a drug dealer who just lassoed himself a fat cash cow.

I slap him again, and then again, and when he brings his arm up to shield his head, I slap them, too. "You," *slap*, "are," *slap*, "not," *slap*, "listening!"

He slaps my hands away, "Because you're making my fucking ears bleed, woman!"

"I'm trying to save your life," I hiss, and there must be something frightened in my eyes, because he finally goes still, watching me. "Sy is sparing you as a favor to me, *if* I can keep you away from Remy. So you're going to head back to the Avenue and hustle there like a good little pill pusher. You understand me?"

He stares at me like he's trying to see me, the real me, the one who is no longer a part of the Count's world but a Duchess—and that's who I work for—who I protect.

"Whatever," he says, shoulders going loose, but I see the lie in his eye as he walks toward the back exit. Cash may not have Royal blood, but he's a viper through and through, and he'll just settle down and lie in wait.

A bell chimes back in the gym, the first fight is starting. Shit. I hurry down the hall, distracted, and that's when I run straight into her: Verity.

"Hey," I say, looking over my shoulder, making sure Cash really left. When I turn back, her eyes roam over my outfit. The last time I was here, I needed her help with looking like a real Duchess, but I'd chosen this one myself, under the watchful assistance of Jade.

"Not bad, Lavinia," she says approvingly, looking pretty dolled up herself in ripped up denim shorts and a sparkly halter.

"Remy's friend helped me out," I say, glancing surreptitiously over my shoulder to make sure Cash has left.

She laughs. "Ah, Maddox money. Well, wherever he took you, they nailed your vibe."

"Thanks." For some reason, her approval means something to me. I jerk my head to the locker room. "Is Nick in there?"

"Yeah." She scowls, subtly adjusting her boobs. "Alone, by the way. We heard what he did to you. It violates every principle of the Dukes' system. They're supposed to protect us, not—" She swallows, maybe noticing the hot tears pricking at my eyes. "Sorry. I'm sorry. I just want you to know that we all talked about it—even Haley—and agreed that none of the cutsluts are stepping in tonight to be his ring girl. We wouldn't blame you for blowing it off."

It's not that I'm upset about Nick because that score has been as settled as it can be. I'm stunned by the girl in front of me. First Story, and now Verity? Camaraderie from the women in the Royal system isn't how it's done in North Side. It's opposed to my entire combative relationship with Leticia and what I observed from the many Countesses over the years, who have always been catty and cutthroat, bitchy and paranoid. But kind? Supportive?

I didn't see that coming.

Taking a deep breath, I say, "Even though I'd like to bail on him, I'm not. I'm a Duchess now and I'm taking those responsibilities seriously. I don't want the Dukes to look anything but unified in front of the outside world. Inside, we may be a huge fucking mess, but as far as everyone else is concerned, we're solid."

She gives me a long look, something decisive crossing over her face. "You're really good at this, Lavinia."

My cheeks heat. "Eh, I'm working on it."

"No, seriously," she insists, giving me a soft grin. "I wasn't sure at first, because you're from North Side and the daughter of a King. And okay, fine, I was jealous—maybe even a little hurt—that I wasn't chosen." She watches me, pensive. "But the more I get to know you, the more I'm sure they picked the right woman for the job."

I'm not sure 'picked' is the right word. More and more, it just seems like some kind of shitty cosmic fate has hurtled us toward one another, stars colliding.

God, I've been around Remy too much.

I rest my hand on the locker room door. "Thanks, Verity. And tell the other girls I appreciate their support."

She gives me a small smile and heads out to the gym. I push the door open and wind through the rows, hearing him before I catch sight of him. I see his open locker first, the last on a middle row. He's just to the side, around the corner, but the name *Bruin* is painted in marker on the inside of the locker behind him. Before making myself known, I let myself inspect the photos taped inside.

One is old—vintage. A man bearing a striking resemblance to Nick stands with his fists up, sweaty and wild-eyed. This must be his father, Davis Bruin, the man who gave up his Kingdom to Saul.

Another photo is of three boys and a girl on what appears to be a basketball court. They're spindly in that awkward way kids are when they're still growing into their long limbs, the boys posing shirtless in the sun. They're standing close but not touching, chins thrust up, eyes hard. There are no tattoos, no guns, no scars, but I can still place the boys instantly.

Remy, Sy, and Nick.

Remy is the skinniest of the three and despite the small, vague smirk he's wearing, there's a distinct bleakness in his eyes. His hair is short, practically buzzed, and it takes me aback to see him like this, pink-cheeked and soft, and so... clean. Unblemished by ink, spared the chaos of his unruly platinum hair. He looks all wrong, like a boy who hasn't been given the providence of freedom yet. *An empty canvas*, my mind supplies, and that's exactly what his eyes show back at me. A hollowness, and an impatience to fill it.

Meanwhile, Sy is the opposite. It takes me the longest to match him up, his black hair being worn long, swaying just past his shoulders with less curl than he has these days. I study him for a long moment, fascinated by how much he's changed since boyhood, but also how much he hasn't. Even back then, he looked like a fighter, that special gleam of pride touching his eyes. His skin is a warm brown, darker than I'm used to. Evidence of a summer spent in the sun, perhaps? Weirdly, I get the feeling that I would have really liked to have known him back then. He looks looser here, beautifully carefree and—he'd probably kill me if I ever said it aloud—absolutely fucking adorable.

Nick is still somehow the most different. Sure, there are no tattoos and it feels odd to see his skin like this, blank and smooth, but that's not the reason. His hair is a lot like it is now. The bit of ego in the way he holds himself, arms crossed over his chest, isn't much of a change, either.

It's just that he looks so...

I struggle for a moment to describe it, because I've seen it a lot, but never on Nick.

Happy.

That's it.

His blue eyes are bright and full of life. He's smirking a lot like Remy is, but he wears it better. His tongue is peeking out, pushing at the edge of his smile, and there's zero doubt in my mind. If I'd met this version of Nick when I was a kid, I would have fallen head over heels. Even with just a still image, he oozes this... charisma, limbs long and loose, a basketball clutched between his palms. He looks fun and wily, nothing like the arrogant, steel-faced soldier I'm used to.

This, I'm guessing, is a Nick who hadn't learned about the dark corners of Forsyth yet. A Nick who hadn't found himself behind a trigger yet. A Nick who hadn't lost the people closest to him, a boy whose biggest concerns were probably schoolyard scuffles and flirtatious girls.

What might have he become if the girl next to him had never died?

Because I know right off this is Tate.

She's as tall as Remy, as carefree-looking as Sy, and as magnetic as Nick. Her hair is a warm auburn, so long that it grazes her hips. Almond-shaped eyes over a broad nose and thin lips against a round face. Her skin is almost as dark as Sy's. She's nothing like I expected her to look, and somehow exactly right. She has her hip popped out, lips pursed as she obviously fights a smile.

So this is the girl Leticia was... involved with.

I feel a sadness at the sight of her, the knowledge that the light in her eyes has been snuffed out. What must she have been like, to roll with boys like these? Tough, certainly. Unwilling to take their bullshit. Hard enough to bring them down a notch, but soft enough to be a safe haven if they could lower themselves to ask for it.

That's not Tate, my mind whispers. *That's you.*

The thought is wiped away by the sudden shock I feel at the sight of the last photo in his locker.

It's of two blonde girls in school uniforms. One is radiant, smiling prettily at the camera while the other wears a sharp frown, looking just off to the left of the frame. The radiant girl has her hair curled flawlessly, hands clasped behind her back, shoulders squared. The other is slumping, body slightly curled as if she could hide herself. But she can't. No one knows that better than me.

The photo is of me and Leticia.

I reach out and snatch it away, rounding the corner to ask, "Where did you get this?"

He's sitting on the bench, tape dangling from his teeth. The sound of my voice doesn't startle him, nor does the sight of the photo I wave in his face. "Your bedroom," he answers, unapologetic.

Although he lost weight during his time in the cage, it just makes his muscles appear more defined and veiny, any excess flesh withered away. The tattoo on his shoulder tenses when I stuff the picture into my pocket, but he doesn't look up, just continues wrapping his knuckles. Or trying to, at least. The piece he's working with sticks to itself and he balls it up, tossing it onto a pile of others on the ground.

Huffing, I fold my arms. "You want some help?"

He grunts, ripping off a new strip of tape. "I've got it."

I let him struggle, watching his jaw lock tight, forehead pinching as he ruins another piece. "God-fucking-dammit!"

He stands, but before I can warn him, he's slamming his head into the corner of the open locker door above him—Remy's from the looks of it. He swallows another curse and decides to close the locker door with his fist, crashing a hard punch into it. It closes noisily, a dent in the metal, but apparently that wasn't enough, because he punches it again, and then once more.

I stare at him, unblinking. "You done?"

He slams both palms against the metal doors and pauses there, dropping his head between his shoulders. This isn't the bright, happy boy from the photo in his locker, and it's not the stoic South Side soldier I've some to know. This is a man on the ragged edge, scarred and inked, battle worn and exuding exhaustion.

The tendon in his throat is sharp, and even though his eyes fall closed, his body is vibrating with tension. When he speaks, it's low and terrifying. "I swear to god, Lavinia, you do not want to be in here right now."

I lean against the bank of lockers, unmoving. "Call the fight."

He cuts those wicked eyes at me over his lean bicep. "Fuck that."

Rolling my eyes, and having expected as much, I point to the bench. "Then sit down and let me help you with your wraps."

His shoulders sink, a long, resigned sigh falling from his nose before he straddles the bench, landing heavily. I grab the tape and straddle the bench in front of him, ripping off a long strip. His knuckles were already red and scraped from being in the cage, but now there's a fresh cut from the locker vent.

"Idiot," I mutter, taking his hand in mine. His fingertips twitch against my palm, calloused and thick and heavy. Ever since I put him in the cage, I've been seeing Nick in a new light. I spent years thinking of him as this imposing figure, unbeatable, unshakable. But Nick's not unbeatable. He's flesh and bone, miles of veins, a network of tendons, and a tight pile of muscle. I've beat him once, and I could do it again.

So what could a LDZ do?

"Do you need more support in your thumb?" I ask, focused on the task. "Sy always makes me double up, but he has that old fracture he's always complaining about."

"Why are you helping me?" When I glance up, Nick is giving me this look, a crease in his brow. His eyes rove my face slowly, taking in every morsel of my features, inch-by-inch. "You don't even like me."

It isn't about being a proper little ring girl. It's not about the fact I fucked Remy and have been attentive to Sy, and I'd be a bad Duchess to ignore my third Duke. It's not even that I look at Nick, so frayed and worn thin, and feel a silent, secret mourning for the shining, expressive boy in the photo.

I tell the truth. "It's about doing what's best for our house." Looking down at his fist, I test the joints before grabbing his other hand. "I like this place. I like learning how to fight. I like the cutsluts. I like the pledges and the way they treat me like a person, even if the three of you tell them not to. I'd rather be a Duchess of the West End than a daughter of North Side, and if your house falls apart because of something I did to you…" Glancing up, I finish, "You might not deserve better, but they do."

He stares at me, his blue eyes boring into mine with something akin to awe. "You really are the perfect Duchess."

My jaw tightens, and I yank the tape to break it, jarring his arm. "It helps when you get to actually have a choice in the matter."

We walk out minutes later as a pair—a fighter and his ring girl—and it might be fake, but it's convincing. I'm feeling pretty proud of that fact, up until he's standing at the corner of the ring, about to enter.

An odd bit of hush falls over the Dukes' side of the gym, and it takes me too long to realize why. The kiss. They're waiting to see if I'll give it—if the rumors they've heard of Nick betraying me are true.

I don't think much about it beyond the necessity.

Straining up on my toes, I press a quick, firm kiss into the pulse point of his neck, struggling not to fling myself away once it's done. My lipstick print stands out starkly against his skin and I fight the urge to wipe it away, turning to find Remy and Sy.

Everything I said to Nick about why I'm helping him is true, except one omission. If this house falls apart, then I have nothing left: no home, no friends, no protection, and as much as it hurts to admit it, no family.

~

REMY'S on me the second I take my seat. "Was that Cash?"

"Who?" I look around, pretending I don't know what he's talking about, which is when I catch Sy's eye. He doesn't look pleased.

"The guy you were talking to before." Remy grabs my chin, forcing my gaze to his. "Was it Cash Money?"

"Oh, him." I make a casual, dismissive sound, taking Remy's hand in mine. "No, that was just some pledge asking where the bathroom is."

Remy watches me closely—too closely. I'm a Lucia. The ability to tell a lie is pretty much embedded into my DNA. But somehow, I get around Remy and forget all my cues, his green eyes piercing straight through me. I know I'm fucked when his hand slips away. His expression closes up, shutting me out, and even when he turns to watch Nick square up with the LDZ guy, there's a coldness to his eyes that makes me look worryingly at Sy.

That's why I miss the first hit.

I see it in Sy's face, though, the way his brows crouch low when he winces. I hear it through the roar of the crowd, half of them excited, half of them enraged. When I turn to look, Nick is staggering, but clearly doing his best to shake it off. The first time I saw Nick fight in here, it was like watching an artist. The hits, the taunts, the arrogance. Nick commanded the fight, leading Perez always where he wanted him. He planned, he calculated, he strategized.

Tonight, Nick barely even gets past watching the LDZ's foot movements.

He takes a hit to the jaw, one to the ribs, another to his chin. He always backs away and regroups, and I can see the annoyance simmering behind his blue eyes, but the fire... the first isn't there.

His heart only looks half in it.

Remy leans forward, elbows on his bouncing knees as he watches, and he sees it, too. "Where the fuck is Nick tonight?" he growls, scowling as Nick takes a mean right hook. I can hear the smack of skin all the way up the bleachers.

"Son of a—shake it off, Nicky!" Sy calls next to me. "You've got thi—"

Nick takes another hit, this one a foot right in the hip. He sways and doesn't fall, but it's close, and watching him struggle to keep his bearings puts my teeth on edge.

This is going to be a bloodbath.

"Fuck this, I'm going down there," Sy says, pushing past us. He moves like a freight train, one second on the bleachers, the next up on the ring, shouting, "Time! I need a fucking time-out!"

The ref approves, and the LDZ sophomore Nick thought he could take so easily, struts over to his corner.

Nick limps to his.

"This is bad?" I ask, but I already know. It's really bad. Nick is losing and I'm the reason why. He's worn out, exhausted, his body a wreck from the days in the cage.

His hands are still twitching.

Remy shakes his head, not even looking at me. "Bruins don't lose. Not on our turf."

The rustle of the crowd changes during the timeout, less cheering, more chatter, and that's when I start to hear the shit-talk.

"I knew letting that no-good traitor in DKS was a mistake. Legacy or not, he's more loyal to the Lords than us." I turn, shoulder brushing against Remy's to see who said it, but there are a dozen frat boys surrounding us, all with the same disgusted, annoyed expression on their face.

"You think he's throwing it?" I hear.

"I heard he spent a week at the Hideaway. He probably made a deal for free pussy," someone else says. "I'd probably throw a fight for less."

Remy tenses beside me. He hears the gossip, too.

"Plus," another adds, "he chose a Lucia as his Duchess. You just know that bitch is scheming. I bet he's laying pipe to all the other houses."

"Man, this is bullshit," a deep voice mutters, this one closer. "Waited all this time to become part of DKS and who do we get as Duke? A fucking turncoat."

I face Remy. "You don't believe that do you?"

"Nicky's no turncoat," he replies, eyes flashing over the scene. Sy has Nick's face in his hands, giving him a stern talk. Blood runs down Nick's temple and I should be out there, giving him water, doing my job, but instead I'm here marinating in the certainty that there's not going to be a victory party tonight. "I need to—"

Remy shoots to his feet. "You need to follow me," he commands, taking my hand. He pulls me off the bleachers, down the crowded path between the ring and the seats. He drags me right past where Nick is talking to Sy, those cold blue eyes watching as we pass.

"Where—" I ask, but he's pushed through a door and down a hallway. It's vaguely familiar but in a hazy, distant sort of way. It's not until we get to the steps that I abruptly stop. "This is where I was kept the night Nick fought for me."

"To the balcony," he says, not stopping. "Hurry up. Once that time-out is over, Nicky will be too, unless we fucking do something."

"Do something?" I ask, but he's already up the stairs, fingers curled too tightly around mine to do anything but be dragged along. It's a different feeling this time when we emerge at the top, the whole gym spread out beneath us. Across the way, I see the box seat, with the bookies and Mama B, Saul up against the rail looking absolutely irate.

Directly below them are the Lords.

They're in the same seats they were in that first night, watching their boy take on Nick Bruin. Story is perched on Killian's lap, her arm looped over his shoulder, and they all look happy.

"Okay, what are we doing here?" I ask, trying to get a hold on Remy's mental state.

His jaw is working, teeth clenching and unclenching as he looks out below. "Nicky's got no color. No reds, no blues, no yellows." He shoots me a sidelong glance. "He's got nothing to fight for."

Instantly, I'm reminded of what Nick said to me the other night.

"Every soldier needs something to keep him going."

"There's only one thing that'll bring out the beast in Nick Bruin tonight." He spins me around and shoves me against the railing, his chest solid against my back. "Remember that night, when I found you up here all alone?"

I swallow and nod. "Yes."

He touches my hip, ducking his thumb beneath my shirt. "I wanted to fuck you so bad, Vinny. Claim you right above everyone, show them that we'd already marked you as ours. But back then I couldn't. You still belonged to the Kings. Lords, Counts... whoever."

He yanks up my skirt, rough and fast, and I fall forward from the force. He bends to speak against my neck, voice ragged. "But tonight, you're ours, and I can show anyone I want."

Energy, in its purest form, vibrates through Remy. It's like along with whatever drug he's on, he's caught the mood of the crowd, the frustration of his best friend, the desire to fuck and fight. The way it mingles with his sharp, curt jostles of my hips, hands tearing my panties down my thighs, sends a shock of worry through me—one I haven't felt in a while.

"Remy," I begin, grabbing hard at the metal bars as I hear his belt buckle being undone. "Remy, wait."

He kicks out, spreading my ankles. "Why? None of what those guys said is true, is it? You're not loyal to North Side."

I shoot up, jaw dropping. "Of course not!"

He fists my hair, tugging my head back. "Then what's the problem?" His voice is too hard—still angry over the Cash situation—and I'm not sure how to mend it. "Don't you want to help your house, *Duchess*?"

The bell rings below, signaling the fight is back on. Nick's distracted, though, eyes searching. He's looking for me and it clicks. Remy wants him to find us. "You think he'll Hulk out or something if he sees us." I look over my shoulder, but Remy's too busy pulling his cock out of his pants. Stiff, hard and red. "But I don't think—"

"You don't need to think," he says, reaching down to jab two fingers through my slit. "You just need to be loud and look good. Think you can do that?"

The words sting just as much as his fingers when he pushes them inside, rough and invasive. The awareness chimes through me that this hold is breakable. Sy's taught me how. I can get away from him.

I don't.

"I can do that," I decide, watching the ring. Down below, Nick's opponent circles him, but Nick is only half focused on the other guy, still scanning the crowd.

"What if we're just distracting him?" I worry, but my belly

bottoms out when Remy begins rubbing the hard tip of his cock through my folds. I suspect this is going to be very little about my pleasure and more about Remy making a point, but my body doesn't seem to get the memo that this is to serve a greater purpose.

"That's it. Be my good girl." Remy makes a low, rumbling sound at my growing wetness. "Don't worry about Nicky. I know how my boy ticks."

My hands grip the railing as the head of his cock bumps against my clit. "Oh, fuck."

"Have you ever had it like this?" he asks, spreading my cheeks with his palm. I think for a minute he's going to go for my ass, but his fingers dip lower, spreading the warm heat around. "Out in the open, where anyone can see us?"

"No." I don't know if Remy understands how limited my sexual experience is. I'm thankful for his though, because he knows how to make it feel so good that my knees buckle when the head of his cock nudges inside, stretching me from a different, new angle.

"Come on, Nicky," he breathes. "Look at me and our girl."

I don't know if it's their psychic connection, or if somehow he heard him call his name, but Nick's eyes dart up to us at the same moment Remy decides to slam inside. My cry is anything but quiet, escaping my mouth in a shocked yelp. I'm grateful for the bars in front of me, keeping me upright, holding my weight as Remy forces his way inside. It's too fast, too soon, and my body is torn between squirming away and bowing myself closer.

"Stop pushing me out," he grunts, kicking my ankles wider. The stance lets him thread his way deeper and the hard, bruising grip of his fingers on my hips yanks me back into him, spearing me wholly on his cock.

"Oh, god—oh, *fuck*!" I don't mean to be looking right into Nick's stare as I say the words. It's just that my body is so overwhelmed that I can hardly pay attention to anything that isn't the liquid hot fire between my legs.

I see the tic in Nick's jaw as Remy curls over me, around me, clamping his teeth into the side of my neck as he bucks, shoving me into the bars.

"There we go," Remy pants, and I know when Nick's eyes move just a little to my right that their gazes are meeting. "Watch this, brother." Remy pulls his hips back and punches them forward, violently, his forearm like a steel bar across my chest.

Nick gets punched in the face, knocked back so hard that he lands flat on his back.

"Oh, shit!" I hiss, half because of the blow, half because of the way Remy is fucking me, these short, painful, brutal slams of his hips against my ass.

"Don't worry about him," he says, and it's hard to think with Remy fucking so frantically in and out, his feet keeping me spread apart, but I keep my eyes on the ring, on the beatdown and defeated man who tried his best to ruin me.

This could be *his* ruin.

I watch as Nick rises, spitting blood on the mat. He looks at it for a moment, a splatter of bright crimson, and then slowly raises his gaze to the LDZ lordling.

"There it is," Remy grunts, crushing me closer.

The fire grows in Nick's eyes, his hands balling into tight fists. What is unleashed isn't a man's fury; it's a Bruin's force. Wild, animalistic, feral.

The first blow is a kick, solid in the ribs. The next is a punch, hard across the jaw. The hits land hard, just like Remy's thrusts, and if that isn't enough, the entire gym explodes from his comeback, the screams ricocheting off the metal ceiling, drowning out the sound of mine and Remy's panted grunts.

"Come for me, Vinny," he says, but I'm too caught up in the match, in the utter force of Nick Bruin, to be anything more than what he asked of me. A good girl. A good Duchess. A warm, willing hole.

Down below, Nick finishes the LDZ with a quick, decisive TKO. I watch as he stands over his defeated opponent, chest heaving, glistening with sweat. He looks like the soldier again, blank-faced, chin raised arrogantly. But his eyes aren't on the man he just destroyed in the comeback of a decade.

They're locked on mine.

It's only then that the shudder starts at my core, spreading outward when Remy surges into my clenching muscles, holding me so tightly that I have nowhere to go except into the solid expanse of his chest. My mouth opens in a silent scream as I come, barely registering the warm flood of Remy's release being battered into me by his driving hips.

By the time I come down, Nick is gone, disappearing through the locker room doors.

Remy collapses against me, breathing warm, damp exhalations into the juncture of my jaw. He raises a palm to smooth my hair away, lips soft against my cheek as he speaks, low and dangerous.

"Never fucking lie to me again."

THE PARTY that night is wild.

Everyone is drunk. *Everyone*, including me.

Over the music and the partying, I can hear the deep vibrating hum of the tattoo gun. Across the room, Nick sits in Remy's chair, head tilted to the side, getting his victory tattoo.

To the victor, I raise my plastic cup before throwing it back, finding only lukewarm dregs.

Remy hasn't looked at me once, not since he stormed down the balcony stairs, angrily fastening his fly. Neither has Nick, but that's more of a relief than anything. The knowledge of how much head-space I occupy with him is unsettling. I know how Nick feels about me. He's proven it over and over again, but it still comes as a shock when the intensity of it is put on full display.

"Here," Sy says, swapping my empty cup out for another. The liquid inside is fruity, specifically designed to get women shit-faced and loose.

I eye him, wondering if that's his goal. "What are you doing?"

"Being a good host," he replies, leaning his elbow back on the bar. "Is that so impossible?"

"Yes." But it is a party, and a victory party, at that. Sy does love to win, even if it's living vicariously through his brother's. Every Duke accomplishment is one of his own, I guess. Remy's loud voice carries across the room, distracting me from my thoughts. I frown as he changes the needle in his gun, grinning over at Haley as she hands him his tools. "So he's pissed at me."

"Well, yeah." He watches his best friend and brother, a wayward curl falling into his eyes in the way his hair tends to do when he's like this—easy and relaxed. "You lied right to his face, and Remy doesn't tolerate liars."

"I didn't—"

Sy's stare is hard, his dark eyebrows hiked to his hairline.

"I was doing what you told me to do!" I explode. "Keeping Cash away from him. What did you want me to do? Tell him the truth? Because then he'd be pissed at you instead." Maybe I can talk Remy into taking his pills sometimes, but I'm not stupid. Sy is far more important when it comes to keeping him balanced and well-behaved.

First, there's a long sigh, and then he looks at his friend. "This is a tricky situation, Lavinia. Remy spends his whole life chasing one dragon to the next. Going after that high means that sometimes I have to bullshit him just to keep him safe. Problem is, he's been lied to by his family for years now, and we're talking big lies. The kinds of lies that make you question your own reality, and when you have a diagnosis like his? He's been jerked around a lot." He shifts and I feel his hip rub against mine. "You like him. I can tell. Everyone does. But the thing that keeps him from chasing every female who's nice to him is a finely-honed sense of distrust. The difference with you is that he *wants* to trust you."

"But you want me to lie to him." Jesus, my head hurts.

"If you have to." He nods, like this logic makes sense. "But you need to get better at it. A lot better. Remy has a high level of emotional intelligence. Sometimes it's not that you're telling a lie so much as *how* you lie." He tips the mouth of his bottle toward me. "You looked him in the eye and told him a load of not-even-believable bullshit. That's not acceptable."

The irony here is that I've been lying to these guys for days—weeks. I lied about my father coming for me. I lied about keeping Nick in the cage. I'm lying about our plan to go to the Barons for information.

But somehow I'm in Remy's crosshairs for lying about Cash Mallis?

"Whatever," I tell him, ready to leave the bar. Honestly, I'm ready to leave the whole-ass party. But Sy snatches my wrist as I pass, pulling me back. I look him up and down. "What?"

He sucks on the inside of his mouth, eyes dropping to my chest. Finally, he says, "Maybe we can go upstairs while it's quiet."

My eyes dart from his face to his cock, hard and pressed against my thigh. "You want a lesson? Right now?"

He falters for a moment, eyes tracking mine, before he firms his expression back up. "That's what we do, isn't it?"

"Sy," I begin, batting down the flare of disbelief. "Look at me." I point to my face, knowing it's blotchy, eyes probably puffy. I'd had a bit of a cry on the ride home, Remy stiff and silent next to me. "Do I look like someone who's in the mood to touch your dick?"

His eyes narrow and he drops my wrist—well, more like he throws it down. "Don't be one of those bitches who expect a guy to read her mind. If you have something to say, then say it."

I laugh, the sound humorless and too quiet. "Wow, for a guy who can read someone else's emotional intelligence, you should try gaining some." At the flash of rage in his eyes, I spread my arms. "I went out of my way to do something to help someone I like, and they ended up punishing me for it. I'm fucking miserable!"

He crosses his arms over his chest, mouth tensed into a tight purse. "You let Remy fuck you on the balcony to make my brother jealous, but suddenly you're too good to get me off like you promised?"

The words shouldn't hurt, but it feels like a slap, anyway. A reminder that my presence is tolerated for what I can be used for: protecting Remy from Cash, helping Nick win his fight, jacking off a horny, desperate, frat-boy…

In the end I'm a Duchess, at their whim.

I raise my chin, biting back, "I'm just not in the mood, so you can either force me to get you off like your brother would, or you can take your five-fingered best friend and go inflict all this romance onto it!"

His eyes shutter, expression turning cold. "Well, here's the real viper, the poisonous little slut who doesn't give a shit about her obligations, so long as she's getting her own needs met."

I barely process it when he grabs the plastic cup from me and slams it across the room, punch spraying all over, because right then Nick saunters over to the bar, shirtless, beaten halfway to a pulp. He leans over the counter and demands a beer, and I finally see his victory tattoo.

It takes me a second to realize that's what it is—inked into his skin for eternity—because I've been staring at it all night.

The perfect shape of my red lipstick print, tattooed into his neck.

He slides his gaze to me through a swollen eye, taking the drink from the DKS manning the bar. He raises it lazily. "To the victor…"

I don't hear the rest of it, don't want to, and don't care. I'm done with the Dukes for the night, and leave them and the rest of the idiots in the tower to celebrate without me.

19

Nick

I'VE SEEN myself as a lot of things. Son, brother, friend, traitor, spy, soldier, fighter and Duke. The one identity that doesn't hang right on my shoulders is student. It's particularly noticeable sitting at a table in the student center with dozens of other Forsyth students.

Part of it is because I used to roam the campus under false pretenses, pretending to be a part of the community to gain access for Daniel. I'd spy on his son, negotiate with the other frats, trade in sex, drugs, weapons, or whatever product I was commanded to push. But carrying a backpack, sitting in class, copying notes and cramming for tests...

I feel like an imposter.

Not because I can't do the work. I can, and do. Academics aren't really a problem for me. They're just boring, so fucking tedious that it's a psychic pain to sit still. I'd rather spend my time using my hands. Punching, stabbing, finger on the trigger of a gun, spreading my Little Bird's thighs and smelling her sweet, hot, heat.

Jesus, I think, watching Lavinia stand in line to get a coffee across the open space, *I really miss getting pussy.*

"Bro."

It'd feel so good to just get in there, feel the tight clench of her cunt, and show her that Remy's got nothing on how I can make her fee—

"Nick!"

I snap my eyes away from her, over to Sy, who barely contains his eye roll.

Our gaze meets over the pile of food on the table. "Stop obsessing."

"I'm not obsessing," I say, going back to my burrito. "And that's pretty rich, by the way, coming from the dude who's spent the last two days sulking about losing his handjob partner."

"I'm not sulking," he says, back going rigid. His eyes dart over to where she's moved up in line, leaning toward the barista as she gives her order. Sy slouches in his chair. "And she's not my 'handjob partner'." He scowls and pushes his salad away, fiddling with the wrapped cookie that came with it. "She *is* pretty pissed at me, though."

"When did you start caring if people are pissed at you?" I ask, mostly because I'm fishing for information about why Lavinia is mad at him.

Sy raises his glower to me. "It's just a comment. I didn't say I gave a fuck if anyone is—"

Remy snorts, his fork stabbing into some deconstructed wrap he got at the sushi place. "He started caring when she stopped going into his room at night and wrangling that monster in his pants."

I know she's been going into his room at night, and I know she's been giving him handjobs on the regular. I know there's some kind of arrangement I can't quite put my finger on. I see it all from my spot in the rafters. But I also am aware she slept up in the loft the last two nights—alone.

She's definitely mad at him.

"I'm not the one icing her out for trying to keep you safe," Sy bites back.

"She lied." He frowns down at a piece of raw meat, and then brings it to his nose to smell it. "Brassy orange, no shame. I don't do that shit."

Sy slides him an impatient look. "For Christ's sake, Rem, that's the problem. You think someone trying to help you is being shady, but it's normal. Normal people do whatever it takes to protect the person they care about. You make it so the people who give a shit about you have to lie to you."

"*It was for your own good, son,*" Remy mocks, scoffing. "Heard that bullshit before. No thanks."

Sy huffs. "You can't let your trauma stand in the way of forming meaningful connections."

Remy's cheek lifts with a grimace. "Did you get that from a psych book or one of your culty self-help podcasts?"

Sy's face screws up, and he slams his fist on the table. "Those podcasts are not culty—"

"Both of you, shut the fuck up!" My snap is loud enough to get the attention of the tables around us. I glare at the kid next to me until he grabs his food and scurries off. That's the other annoying thing about being a student here. There's no real hiding what I am. Even if I wanted to blend in, I couldn't—not with all my tattoos. I refocus on my brothers. "Sy, all you do is piss people off. Everyone at this table knows you put all this energy into lecturing us on our issues to avoid facing up to your own. You're into Lavinia and you can't handle it, so you're sabotaging it like a fucking headcase, buy a clue."

I flick my eyes over to where the barista hands her something that looks less like a coffee and more like a milkshake. "And Remy, seriously? You think you're the only one allowed to have trust issues? She grew up with a father whose mental manipulations rival Thanos, and he's a goddamn supervillain. If her biggest flaw is trying to keep some low-level junkie from selling you viper crap, then boo-fucking-hoo." I glare at them, raising the burrito. "I've put her in your hands, so stop fucking her up. I mean, goddamn. At least she doesn't want to flay either of you alive, because I know for a fact that's what she's dreaming of at night when it comes to me."

I bite down hard on my burrito.

"She'll come around, Nicky," Remy says, looking too flippant. "She hasn't pointed a gun at you in days."

I mutter, "Doubt it," and Sy points his fork at me.

"I think he's right. She pulled that stunt with Remy the other night, when you were losing. She let him do that."

"Yeah, sure, she 'let' him." I'm not mad at Remy for fucking her up on that balcony. He knew what I needed to get my head back in the ring and take out that LDZ punk. But I saw Remy drag her up there and bend her over that railing—saw the pinch of her brow, the panic in her eyes—and I know for certain that wasn't her idea. She may not have fought him off, but he had her out-sized.

"No, seriously," Sy replies, voice lowered since she's on the way over. "I've been working with her on some self-defense moves. She could have slipped him if she wanted."

I'm not mad about it, and okay, maybe I've jacked off one or six times remembering the way they looked, but that doesn't mean I liked watching Remy pound into her as she gasped and took it. I give him a hard look. "If that's true, it just means she *wanted* his dick."

"Probably," Remy says, kicking the extra chair out with his foot as Lavinia walks up, "but she wanted you to win more."

I want to tell them what she told me in the locker room before the fight. That my winning wasn't about her or me, it was about our house. Our territory. Our people. I want to tell them how good of a Duchess she's becoming—better than I ever expected of her—but I don't.

Greedily, I keep it all for myself.

All of our eyes shift to Lavinia as she walks up, looking the perfect co-ed in her ripped up jeans and cropped shirt. It reveals a hint of her belly and under the table, my dick twitches, wanting a taste of that smooth, soft flesh. She's looking particularly pretty today. I've already seen the pledges eying her around campus and it's a legit fucking inner battle to not claim her here, to show everyone this sharp-eyed, forked-tongued girl is *mine*.

"What?" she says, eyeing each of us, like she knows we were talking about her.

See? This is why this whole scene is weird. The student center, the eating around other people, the backpacks and homework. The normalcy. Not one of the four of us is normal—not individually, and definitely not together.

No one else makes a move to say anything, so I clear my throat. "How, um, was your first class?"

She stares at me for a long beat and then sits in the chair across from mine. "Fine, I guess. I've already read all the textbooks, so even though I feel pretty behind everyone else, I think I have a better grasp. Plus, the professor gave me some resources to use so I can catch up." Despite the fact she probably *is* behind—horrifically, and I would know—there's a light in her eyes that I haven't really seen before. She tucks her hair behind her hair, shooting Remy a quick, hopeful glance. He's been getting those all morning, but he's been a brick fucking wall. "Maybe Remy can take me to the Art History building later? My advisor said I should take it next semester for my Humanities requirement."

She's excited.

For school.

I throw Remy a look.

Make it right, fuckface.

He pointedly takes his marker from behind his ear, silent as he kicks back, fanning open a sketchbook to a half-inked drawing of a naked girl. Although the face isn't defined enough to make out, the tits are clearly too small to be Lavinia, who's pretty good about hiding her disappointment behind annoyance, pursing her lips as she scans the room.

I pipe in, "I can take you. Maybe I'll take it next semester, too."

She shrugs, fucking her straw in and out of her drink. "Whatever."

Geez, darling, don't do backflips or anything.

Over her shoulder, I see the dark shadow of my Baron contact, Will Reynaud, walk through the room. Barons always seem to have this fucked up vibe, like they suck in the light around them, disappearing into the crowd. I watched them for a time, back when I was working for Daniel, trying to figure out how to make myself as still as them—as invisible.

Will doesn't look at me once as he approaches, seeming like just another student on his way to get a shitty burger, and it really is impressive that I don't even feel the slip of paper he throws into my lap as he strides on by.

I sweep a burrito crumb from my lap, smoothly grasping the paper in my hand.

One flick of my eyes reveals a name.

Carter Hodge.

Message received.

Sy stands then, his chair creaking against the floor as he snatches up the gory remains of his salad. "I need to turn in a paper before one," he explains, a scowl still etched on his face. I worry at first he's seen the exchange between me and the Baron, only then he slides an ornery look in Lavinia's direction, and I realize she's giving him the Remy treatment.

So help me, all of these bitches need a culty self-help podcast.

He picks up his bag and wordlessly—so fast and subtle that he could be a Baron—slides the cookie in front of Lavinia before stomping away.

She stares at it for a long moment, eyes narrowed. I almost expect her to offer it to Remy, turning this into the endless circle of pitiful cookie-giving, only she puts her palm over it and swipes it toward her torso protectively.

I'm the next to stand. "I've gotta be somewhere. You good?"

Both of them nod without looking at each other.

It tugs at my gut like a stab wound that Lavinia likes Remy more than me. That she wants him to fuck her. That if things were just a little different, she'd probably crawl into his bed tonight and give him all the things I've tried so fucking hard to get from her. But if I could, I'd stay and try to help them smooth it over. It's a fucked up place to be, watching the girl I love fall for the men I love, the conflict of wanting them to have what they want warring with my own instinct to take her away and keep her for myself.

But maybe this is how it has to be. Maybe I can't have her. Not alone. Not without Remy making her into her art, or Sy making her into a fighter.

Maybe not at all.

The point is, I'd stay to do something if I had the time.

But I have a job.

~

I GET the text at ten.

Sy is just starting to make his neurotic 'going to bed' noises, and just like every night lately, that routine includes walking by Lavinia every ten minutes. She's lazed out on the couch, engrossed in some book her professor wrote a decade ago. She reads like a goddamn computer, eyes scanning the pages fast enough that it makes me wonder if she's even absorbing it. But I know she is.

A lot of people assume because she's a Royal woman—and a King's daughter, at that—she isn't smart, but they'd be wrong. Even with two years in captivity, she found ways to keep her mind limber, inhaling anything with words. But even though she'd ask for food, sweets, beverages, she never asked for books. It took me a long time to figure out why, considering she obviously wanted them.

It was the show of weakness. Letting us get a glimpse into her brain, even something as small as the knowledge that she's intellectually voracious, was never on the table for her.

I watch as Sy does another pass to the bathroom, and sometimes I wonder how we're related. He's annoyingly obvious, shooting her these little glances as he walks by.

Lavinia turns another page.

Not tonight, brother.

"I have a craving," is what I say, stuffing my phone into my pocket. I'm on the other couch, facing her, slumped down into the cushions as I stare at her. Sometimes, I've found, if I'm quiet and subtle about it, she'll let me watch her. Since speaking has bulldozed over that unspoken rule, Lavinia's eyes flick up, flashing in annoyance. "For a brownie sundae."

Her eye twitches.

Jackpot.

Standing up, I stretch, not missing the way her eyes slide to the inch of exposed abs I grace her with. *That's right, baby.* Hate me or not, I'm still pretty. I go to the kitchen first to gather what I need from the safe, and then I walk back out to ask, "Wanna ride with?"

She looks like she's about to say no, which means I'm going to need to find a way to signal that shit is going down. Only then my hapless, horny brother walks by and she's shooting up from the couch, putting her book away.

"Let's go."

Sy pauses, his thick eyebrows scrunching. "You're going somewhere?"

"Ice cream," I explain, lacing up my boots. "You want something?"

It's after ten. Sy would sooner lop his own ear off than consume a carb after ten. As expected, his nostrils flare wide. "It's after ten!"

I shrug. "Your loss."

"But," he argues, getting that hardness in his eyes that signals he's holding back a fit, "it's *after ten*. We all have class tomorrow. You can't just—"

Well, this shit needs to be shut down. "I slept when I got home. I'll be up all night, anyway. Just go to bed. We'll be quiet when we come in."

Lavinia returns with her shoes, stomping into them as she shoots Sy a low-key murderous look. "Is that okay with you, *Duke*?"

Sy has this thing where his muscles ripple whenever he wants to hit something. It's an awful tell, which is something I've tried to get him to stop a hundred times, but here he is, rippling all menacingly at her. "Do what you fucking want," he hisses, storming away.

The sound of his door slamming makes her jump, and even though she glares in his direction, I can see the anxiety lining the corners of her mouth.

"You shouldn't do that," I tell her, shrugging into my jacket. "If you keep pushing him, he's just going to keep pushing back. Sy doesn't lose."

She strangles her feet with her shoelaces as she ties them. "He can be such a prick sometimes."

"Yeah, sometimes. Most of the time. But sometimes he can be..." 'Nice' isn't exactly the word I'm looking for, only maybe it is. He saved her. He nursed her back to health. Sure, his lizard brain wants to fuck the spark of life from her eyes, but he does better at holding it back than most men would.

Better than I did.

"I know," she says, mouth scrunching pensively. "I just wish..." She trails off, but I know what she's thinking.

"You wish, for once, the guy who's into you wasn't a little bit psycho?" At her pointed look, I smirk. "Newsflash, Little Bird. We're all a little bit psycho. The difference between us and the rest of the world is we don't hide it from you."

She broods silently over this as we descend the staircase to the bottom of the tower. Lavinia obviously only said yes to this little outing as a way to put some space between her and Sy at bedtime, but now that we're alone, I turn, stopping her.

"Don't freak out, but there are two Barons waiting at my car."

She freezes halfway down a step, eyes flying to mine. "Does that mean...?"

I nod, pulling a gun from my waistband—the one Sy had given to her. "We're going to see their King."

She takes the gun with wide eyes. "Their King?!" She finally drops to the next step, face lined with worry. "Nick, an audience with the Barons' King isn't something you do at ten-o-clock all willy-fucking-nilly!"

"I know." I turn and keep descending. "I've had it planned all day."

We get down two more flights before her fist slams into my back. "Thanks for telling me!"

"You're welcome." At her aggressive silence behind me, I cave. "This way, you wouldn't have had to lie about where we're going. Remy and Sy will forgive me. They're used to my stunts. But if they knew you'd been bullshitting them all day to do this..."

They'd forgive me, but her?

I'm not so sure.

She seems to consider this as we get to the bottom of the tower, and by the time I turn to her, she's chewing on her lip, sliding me these slow, confused glances. "Oh," is all she says.

Again, I say, "You're welcome," and shove the door open.

The West End is the best at night. It has all these empty little nooks and crannies for hiding. Alleys. Empty warehouses. Abandoned buildings. I think other people look at this place and see a derelict shadow of its former self, but I see refuge, every corner a foxhole.

And two Barons are waiting within one.

They're hidden in the shadows, but I can feel them before the black toes of their boots step out of the darkness. Girls around here want to belong to the Princes more than any other house—the dumb illusion of them worshipping their Princess driving that particular rep—but they get wettest for the Barons.

They're both in black from head-to-toe, something Daniel would have beat out of his soldiers. Too obvious, too campy. But the Barons wear it naturally, their hair dark, their tattoos all well-hidden behind sleeves, bangs, and douchey turtlenecks. Always one sort of mask or another with these ones.

"Bruin," greets one of them.

I nod, making sure Lavinia is close enough to touch. "Will."

"Your phones," he says, holding out a palm.

Lavinia shoots me a dark look, and after a moment of consideration, I nod. We pull out our phones and place them in his hands. He passes them off to the other Baron—Liam—before holding out his hand again. "Guns."

Saw that coming.

I reach behind me to pull my pistol from my waistband, removing the clip before placing it in his outstretched palm. If we'd come unarmed, it would have looked fishy. Before Lavinia can act, I smoothly snatch the gun from against the small of her back, doing the same. "Want my jock next?"

"Maybe." Will doesn't smile. "Check the car," he says to Liam, who uses his phone camera to begin checking the undercarriage.

Throughout all of this, Lavinia and I stand side-by-side, waiting patiently. I'm not stupid enough to try sneaking a weapon or GPS tag in the car, so it doesn't bother me when Liam begins searching the interior, but I can see the anxiety building in my Little Bird, her hands wringing against her midriff.

"What now?" she asks when Liam gives Will a nod, the car coming up clean.

Will gestures to the SUV. "Now you put your hands on that window there so we can frisk you."

Stiffening, I immediately reach out to grab her wrist, pulling her behind me. "Either of you put your hands on her, I won't need a gun to take you out."

His eyes darken. "I'm taking you to see my King, Bruin," Will reminds me. "You think we're just going to trust that you're not packing another piece on you?"

I extend my arms. "Frisk me all you want. No one's laying a fucking finger on her."

Will shrugs. "Then the deal is off."

"Wait!" Lavinia ducks around me, flinching when I wrench her back. "Your Baroness—Regina, right? She can search me." She peers up at me, eyebrows raised. "That's fair to everyone."

Will and Liam exchange a look before the latter begins tapping at his phone. A moment later, it dings. "She's going to meet us there," Liam tells Will.

They swing their gazes on me.

Flexing my fists, I relent, turning to press my palms to the glass. Will is the one to search me, patting his hands down my sides, my hips, my thighs, my—

I arch an eyebrow. "So you do want my jock. Gonna buy me dinner first, champ?"

Will doesn't laugh. "Stand still," he says, crouching to check my ankles, stuffing two fingers into each side of my boots. "You have what we asked for?"

I stare into the glass, staring back at the reflection of my blank face. "It's in the passenger seat. Ask Liam."

Liam jerks his chin in answer and Will backs off. "Bring it, and follow us," he says, tossing me the keys he'd pulled from my pocket.

I put Lavinia into the car first, placing the box on her lap. "Hold on to that."

"What is it?" she asks when I get in beside her, cranking the engine. "Guns or something?"

My mouth flattens as I pull out behind the Baron's sleek, black Lexus. "Or something."

Leaving West End never feels quite right, but it's even worse when we begin heading north, following the sinister red glow of their taillights. The car is quiet, no music, no air or heat, just Lavinia, silent and still at my side.

"Just follow my cues," I say, glancing at her. "I know you like firing off at the mouth, but—"

"I know what it means to insult a King," she cuts in, an edge of bitterness to the way she looks at me. "I can play it cool when I need to."

But it's not long before she begins cracking.

"Where are we going?" she asks for the third time. She's gnawing away at a fingernail beside me in the passenger seat, her gray eyes scanning every bit of road. "Are we even in Forsyth anymore?"

"Maybe," I answer. "They aren't really the territorial types." The Dukes have the west, the Lords have the south, the Princes have the east, and the Counts have the north.

But the Barons are everywhere and nowhere.

It's a forty-minute drive before the dark car in front of us slows, turning onto a back road that's so darkly lit, you'd think the fucker vanished into thin air. I take the turn carefully, slightly annoyed. I wasn't prepared to be so far from home.

"This is crazy, right?" Lavinia has this thing where she babbles when she's nervous. "I mean, they take you and me out, that's a victory over three houses. The Dukes, the Counts, the Lords..."

I glance at her, slightly impressed. "You're thinking like a real Duchess now, Little Bird."

She ignores me, going on, "No one knows where we are, and this is really far from West End, so even if we needed help, we couldn't call for it, because we don't have our phone and we wouldn't know where to tell them to go."

"Chill," I snap, trying to see through the dark path in the trees. "If the guys need to find you, they can."

"How?"

I give her a long look, my eyes flicking down to her neck. "Same way they found you when Lionel took you."

She freezes, hand coming up to touch the small scar on her neck. "The tracker," she breathes, eyes widening. "I forgot that was even there." She looks disturbed by the realization that she could so easily forget I'd put the tracker under her skin.

I look back toward the road. "Aside from that night, I doubt Remy and Sy have even tried to use it," I say, conversationally. "You're lucky."

"They could have tracked me," she realizes, the color leaving her face. "When I had you in the cage at Daniel's, if they'd taken one look..."

"Like I said," I swing the SUV into a clearing, jerking to a stop behind the sedan, "*lucky*."

There's another car waiting—the third Baron and their girl, I'm guessing. Still, I wait for all four of them to climb out of their cars before killing the engine, opening my door. Lavinia follows my cues, sticking close as we approach.

Their Baroness is even more reserved than Lavinia, carefully avoiding looking my way as she gestures to her. "Duchess. If I may?"

My skin feels stretched too tight as I take the box from her hands, watching the Baroness in her long, black gown, lead Lavinia to the hood of the Lexus, waiting patiently as she gets into position. *Jesus*, what a fucking position it is, too. Hands on the hood, legs spread, bent at the waist, perfect for grabbing those hips and slamming my hard, twitching cock into—

I glance at the Barons and notice they're all staring, heavy-eyed as they look on appreciatively.

I snap my fingers to get their attention. "Hey! Forsyth's Halloween enthusiasts can keep their eyes forward or lose them." All three turn to me, unimpressed, but apparently willing to humor the basic fucking tenants of Royal decorum.

"She's clean," the Baroness says, giving Lavinia a soft smile.

The third Baron, Billy, waits with the Baroness as Liam and Will lead us to an ancient, moss-covered building. The marble mausoleum probably looked shiny and bright at some point, but now it's faded and dirty, covered in vines that drag against our heads as we duck into the door.

Inside, it smells like earth and pine. Pitch black, Lavinia grabs my arm as the door closes behind us. With the flick of a lighter, a flame appears, dimly illuminating the space to reveal another door —heavy, wrought iron, creaking loudly as Will drags it open.

We enter into a stone-lined corridor that leads underground. The stairwell is cold and damp, but this part of the tomb is warmly lit, candles lining the walls that lead to a passageway that looks well-worn. Beside me, Lavinia gives a little shiver, and I look over to see her arms crossed tightly over her chest, jaw clenched.

Wordlessly, I sling my arm around her shoulders, folding her into my side.

She lets me because she's cold, her stomach still partially bare with the cropped top she'd chosen for her first day of school. She's small but solid against me, and every time she shivers, I give her arm a little rub.

The chamber we empty out into is the height of hilarity.

The ceiling is tall, adorned with an intricate, gilded chandelier. There are no real modern conveniences here, the room bare with dark corners, stone floors bearing ornate rugs that are worn thin and probably mildewed.

This isn't where the Barons live.

Which means we're in their crypt.

In the middle of the room is a large, round table. It's a heavy-looking antique that was probably here before they vaulted this hole up into the mausoleum it is today. The chandelier lights the center of the table more than anything else, and there are only two chairs.

One of them is occupied by a masked figure.

The King.

I expected the mask—a thick bronze design of a mouthless devil's face that's been passed down for generations—but I'm not expecting to see him at the table, extending a hand in invitation. My hackles raise, because Lavinia was right. This is big. Too big, I'm realizing. This isn't a short and sweet chat. It's the King of the Barons on his throne, one gloved hand resting on a skull beside him as casually as a gear shift, as he invites me to make a deal.

Goddamnit.

I step forward, but the King tuts, raising a finger to Lavinia. "Don't insult me, boy. I know who really wanted this meeting," he says, voice aged and deep.

Will and Liam walk around us to flank their King, one on either side, and I relent unhappily, following Lavinia to what's meant to be her seat. I loom behind her, hands on the back of the chair, hovering close enough to pull her back, if necessary.

Noticing her nervous look at the skull, the King speaks. "This is Roland. The very first Baron. And you are?"

She swallows. "I'm Lavinia. Lavinia Lucia."

"And Nicholas Bruin. The fist of Forsyth." The King gives the skull a small caress. "But that's not true, is it? You're not our fist, you're our bullet." His head tilts, ever so slightly. "How is the gun trade in West End?"

Blandly, I answer, "It's fine," and lean over Lavinia to place the box on the table, sliding it over the distance.

The King gives it a thoughtful look before opening it; long, spindly, gloved fingers twitching before he reaches in to pull out the contents.

Lavinia jerks back, back hitting the chair. "Oh my fucking—" she twists to peer up at me, hissing, "I've had that in my lap for the last fucking hour?!"

I palm the top of her head, turning her back around. "You can find the rest of him at the coordinates I'll give you once we leave here safely."

The King inspects the severed hand, which I'd chosen on account of the small diamond tattoo gracing its middle finger. "How did you kill him?" he asks.

"He's dead. Does it matter?" When the King just looks up, waiting, I bite back a sigh. "Bullet. Execution style."

The King makes a small humming sound, placing the hand back into the box. "Well, I suppose it'll do." He curls a finger at Liam, beckoning him over. "Take this to the Baroness. Show your sinister sister what happens when she lets another man's hands wander into her wicked garden."

I guess I should have known it'd be a punishment for the Baroness. A statement. It makes sense. Still, I watch with Lavinia as Liam walks the hand away, and I feel a knowledge, an awareness, stir to life inside of me.

This won't win the Baroness' love.

It'll only win her fear.

Lavinia twists to look at me. "Who...?"

I shrug. "I don't ask questions."

The King leans back in his seat, watching our exchange. "That's what I like about you, Nicholas. Good or bad, death is all the same to you. That's hard to find in a killer these days."

I cut to the chase. "I'm here for information."

The King shakes his head. "No, you aren't. She is."

There's a stretch of silence where Lavinia realizes this is her shot. I watch as she sits up straight, hands wringing in her lap. "My sister, Leticia..." she begins. "Sir, did your Barons ever collect her body?"

I tighten my fingers around the back of her chair, annoyed that I can't see his expression. The place where the mouth should be is smooth and sunken, covering anything identifiable, only two dark holes where his eyes bore back at us. "Whether we did or didn't, you think that's something we'd tell you freely?" He touches the skull beside him, thumb sweepingly lovingly against it. "Our whole house is built upon the altar of secrecy. If we start telling people what's buried in our crypts, then it's not much of a secret, is it?"

Lavinia tries, "I was hoping—"

"That you'd be an exception to a century-long rule." The King scoffs, looking obnoxiously regal in his throne. "You really are your father's daughter, aren't you?"

"We paid your price," I remind him.

"The price for an audience with me," he responds, shrugging back. "If all it took was a dead body to plunder our drawers, Forsyth would turn into a river of corpses"

"So what do you want?" Her voice is hard and curt, patience wearing thin. "If there's another price, I'll pay it."

The candlelight flickers, reflections dancing in the aged bronze of his mask. I'm not sure what I'm expecting when he reaches into the pocket of his fine black blazer, but I know before I see it that it's nothing good.

He extends his hand to reveal a silver revolver.

I have Lavinia behind me with one strong yank; the chair stuttering against the stone floor.

But the King raises a hand, popping the cylinder open to showcase its lack of bullets. He slants to the side to meet Lavinia's gaze behind me, voice wry. "Bit dramatic, this one."

"You have no idea." The words are light, but her voice is just as tight as my muscles feel. The chair is right behind me now, my legs pressed against her knees, and when I feel her hands on my hips, moving me to her side, I go against every instinct to follow.

"What the hell is that for?" I ask.

"This gun once belonged to a Duke. He tried to sell us on their benefits. Easier, he said. Faster." The King inspects it, turning it so that the candlelight catches its angles. "But the Barons have never liked guns. Shooting someone is so impersonal, don't you think? Just raise the barrel and pull the trigger, and that's the end. Assuming you're a good shot." He raises his gaze to me. "I assume you are."

My teeth grind. "I am."

Sounding bored, the King declares, "It's just that there's no romance to killing someone with a gun."

I spread my arms. "What can I say? Necrophilia just isn't my thing."

Using a gloved finger, he gives the cylinder of the revolver a spin. "See, it's my philosophy that you should have to get your hands dirty to take a life. You should have to feel their last breath. You should be forced to appreciate the weight of their soul leaving. If you can't look death in the eye and shake her hand, then you don't deserve the honor. It's about understanding the gravity of a kill. It's about respect." The King dips his chin, peering at me through the shadow of his mask. "I don't think the Dukes respect death, Nick Bruin."

Lavinia speaks before I can. "Maybe the Dukes respect life."

"Do they respect yours?" he asks.

She pauses. "Honestly, it depends which one you ask."

The King lets out a quiet, malevolent chuckle. "I was there the night this one won you. It was poetry, the way he moved. You could tell how badly he wanted you in that belfry. It was a real Bruin fight." He swings his unsettling gaze back to me, raising a finger. "Now, fighting—that's getting your hands dirty. Did you know the Barons and Dukes used to associate? Kind of like you do with the Lords now." His voice takes on the wistfulness of an old man reliving his glory days. "We were the only two houses with a gratitude for *real* violence. Not the tough guy acts we all put on today, of course. I'm talking about the artistry of death. It's been lost now, but I like to hear the old Kings talk about it from time to time. Do you want to know what they say?" The King leans down to the skull, as if it's whispering to him. After a beat, he hums, lifting his gaze to us. "They say 'to kill someone with your bare hands is an act of love.'"

I sigh, raising my chin. "Yeah, cool. Murder gets your dick hard. We get it. Tell us what you want."

"It's not about what I want." He reaches into his blazer again, and I know when I hear the clink of metal exactly what he's about to do. I stand rigidly as he pulls out three bullets, but the second he gently places one into the cylinder, I'm dragging Lavinia out of the chair.

Will catches me around the throat before I make it halfway over the table.

Fuck.

I'd almost forgotten he was still here.

"Oh, calm yourself, boy," the King says, placing the other two rounds in the cylinder—three bullets, alternating chambers. "Only death can give up her secrets. You need to ask her what you want to know."

Lavinia swallows, loud in the dark silence of the crypt. "I don't suppose death has a toll-free number I can call."

"Of a sort." King places the gun in the middle of the table, palms up as he backs away. "Come now, William. That's no way to treat our guests." I shove Will off easily enough. The Barons might be sneaky, quick little fuckers, but they can't match me for size. Will slinks off back to the shadows, and the King fixes Lavinia with a stare. "This is your choice to make. You can take it or leave unharmed."

"Take what?" she asks, and there's fear in her voice. The instinct to drag her out of here, protect her, save her, is so engrained in me, so fucking embedded into my muscles and psyche, that it takes me longer than it should to figure out the score.

"Fuck that," I snap when it finally hits me—what he wants her to do. "No fucking way. Out of the question."

The King taps fingertips across the forehead of the skull. "I can see your Duke already knows the gist, so understand this. My Barons might not be armed with guns, but they can kill just as fast." He spares me only a short glance before refocusing on Lavinia. "I'm giving you the benefit of using your preferred weapon. This is a courtesy I don't have to give, but if death shines her favor upon you, then I'll answer your question."

She looks at me, and then him, and then the gun. "You want me to... shoot someone?"

"You get one shot." I see her shiver in my periphery, and then the King finally makes his demand. "Put the gun to your temple and pull the trigger."

Her eyes fly wide. "*What?*"

I can't see the smile beneath the mask, but I can hear it. The ominous joy in his voice. The way he props an elbow on the table, fingers twitching excitedly. "Do you know what they'd call a Duchess back in the old days? The fury of Forsyth." He gestures to us—me and Lavinia. "Yes, the fists and their fury. That's how they got the name, you know. Friday Night Fury." His voice lowers to an eerie timber. "I see such a beautiful fury in you, Lavinia Lucia. I don't have a dog in this race, but I wonder if death will see it, too. Will she find your fury better served at her side, or here, with *him*?"

For the first time since the gun came out, I look away from him to see her face. To tell her that this is bullshit. There's another way. The Barons were never going to do anything but jerk us around, make us beg and scrape for a morsel of nothing.

Except she's staring at the gun, chewing on her lip.

She's thinking about it.

She's *considering* it.

I haven't put a lot of thought into what happened to her sister. She was probably a bitch who would have ended up being another burden of Forsyth, and from the way Lavinia talks about her, it sure as fuck doesn't seem like there's any love lost between them.

But in some deep, fundamental way, I understand.

I'm a brother.

Suddenly, I know for certain that I can't handle hearing her answer. "All right." I grab at my jacket, shrugging it off. "I'll do it."

20

Lavinia

It's hard to believe there was a time I told Nick his front in South Side was all for nothing, because I'm standing in the middle of something enormous. I've never been inside the Baron's crypt before. I don't think I've ever known anyone who's been here before. A lot of people assume its very existence is a myth, but here we are, because Nick has access to this. He has access to the Avenue and the Lord's brothels. He's been inside the home of the Counts' King and come out unscathed.

Nick Bruin has crouched himself into more of Forsyth's hidden corners than possibly anyone alive.

And I'm about to watch him die.

The light is low, candles flickering against the shadows of his sharp face as he slips out of his leather jacket. He doesn't look at me. He doesn't flinch. He holds the gaze of the Baron King, faceless behind his bronze mask, and wordlessly holds out the jacket.

For some reason, my attention is fixed to his neck as I mechanically reach out to take it. The tattoo of my kiss print is raised, still healing, and I remember with such clarity the moment when I put it there. The intense hush of the crowd, the heat of his chest against my palm, and most clearly, the rap of his pulse knocking against my lips as I pressed my mouth to it.

I can't stop shivering.

The King doesn't look bothered by Nick's offer to replace me. If anything, he adjusts in his throne, more intent. This is all just theater to him. Dinner and a show, something 'romantic' to orchestrate. Ridding himself of a potential King is a bigger score than taking out the disgraced daughter of another Royal. Nick's just done him, and every other King, a favor.

My stomach does a violent flip.

The King tells Nick, "Have a seat."

"Nick," I whisper, but I'm not sure what to follow it with.

We don't have to do this? I'd rather it be me? Your life is worth more than the truth?

I'm not sure I could make it sound sincere, and the slow, knowing look he slides my way tells me he's aware of this. He jerks his chin at the King. "Can I have a second with my Duchess?"

He settles back in his seat, waving a gloved hand. "Make your arrangements, say your goodbyes." I bet if that mask weren't covering his face, we'd see him licking his lips excitedly.

"This is insane," I hiss, pulling Nick aside. "That man is insane."

Nick's hair has grown since leaving South Side and a thick strand slumps in front of his eye. He never shaved after I released him from the cage, his beard thickening over his jaw. The two combined make him look less pretty, but still devastatingly handsome.

He looks down, reaching into his pocket. "We always knew there'd be a price." I stand, paralyzed, as he presses his keys into my hand. He keeps his voice a low, intense whisper. "Tell Sy there's a storage building on Krembly Street. It's between East End and

Killer's boundary line, a territorial dead zone. Building 44. Have him take what's inside and burn it."

"Nick."

He pushes the strand of hair away, eyes blank and hard. "Give my laptop to Remy. Tell him the password, show him the files."

"*Nick.*"

Flames flickering in his blue eyes, he rushes on. "The coordinates for the guy I killed can get you out of here, so listen carefully." He pushes the words into my ears—some warehouse in West End.

"Nick, I can't—"

"Yes, you can," he insists, his voice snapping me back to reality. "Listen to me, Little Bird. My dad knows everything I know. If you ever need to find another weak spot inside the Royalty, he'll help you."

It's not that.

A couple of weeks ago, I would have been happy to kill him. Maybe I'm not enough of a Lucia to have felt jubilant about it, but there would have been relief, a sense of justice to his suffering, a rightness to knowing that he's flickered out of existence the same way he came into it. I try to find it now, to remember the cold way he looked that night as I got on my knees and begged him to save me. I call up the image of him above me, forcing himself into my body, the searing intensity of his anger as he took a piece of me for himself, clawing his way inside. I remember the night he hit me, the sting of his palm against my face, and the years—Jesus, *years*—of him coming to my motel room, the basement, always locking the door behind him on the way out, one more captor.

The anger is there, maybe even the hatred, but I can't feel it as easily or as acutely.

For some reason, I just keep seeing the happy, charming boy I'd seen in the photo he has taped to his gym locker. I see what Nick could have been and I see what he could still be, because the man standing before me, willing to give his life to offer mine some kind of closure, isn't the monster I've come to know.

This is a selfless act.

That means somewhere, buried deep under layers of Daniel Payne and the stench of death, Nick Bruin actually cares about something more than himself.

Nick must see something in my expression because his own stone mask flickers. It's barely a blink, the way his eyes flash with something soft and sorry. "Fifty-fifty shot, Little Bird. I'm not dead yet." He covers it with a cocky grin that's too sharp to be convincing. "Just need a little luck."

"Yeah, we have a lot of that." It's meant to sound sarcastic, but my eyes are fixed to that tattoo on his neck and it's driving me so fucking crazy that the words come out empty, dull. Why would he do that? Why does he take everything I give him and turn them into these immortalized miseries?

I know the answer.

I just don't like it.

The next time I raise my gaze, he's staring at my mouth. I remain still as his hand snakes around my neck, cold fingertips prickling my nape as he tips my head up. I'm expecting the request as distinctly as I'm expecting him to not bother asking. A kiss for luck, one for the road, truly his finest manipulation yet—a cruel coda. Wouldn't deny a dying man a kiss, would I? I watch the impulse tighten his features, and then I watch it bleed away, something in his face collapsing in defeat.

I stare at him in confusion. *I would have let you take it.*

He stares back with a sad grin. *I know.* "Remy and Sy will keep you. They'll take care of you. If you let them, they'll—" A word catches in his throat, and for a moment, I think I might be watching Nick give up on something.

Life?

Being a Duke?

Me?

When he tips down to press his forehead to mine, his scent covers me just as tangibly as the leather jacket he pulls around my shoulders. I give myself a moment to memorize the smell, the cool of mint gum, the warmth of the spicy deodorant he uses mingling with something harder to place. He smells like West End; leather, stone, and the sharp edge of metal.

"I know my love isn't worth anything to you, Lavinia." His other hand brushes mine where it hangs, limp at my side. "But maybe theirs will be."

My voice is caught in my chest, caged within my lungs, fluttering as wildly as the little bird he's always accused me of being. I set it free to tell him the truth. "I'm not worth it. I'm not worth any of this."

His fingers grasp, squeeze, eyes piercing through mine. "You're worth more."

Nick loves me.

I can see it in his eyes when the mask wavers, but mostly, I just... know. There's a good possibility he has for a long time, and the trouble is, I couldn't take it. I understand that now. It settles over me, the knowledge that I'd rejected it because it didn't make sense to me. I wasn't made to be loved. Worshiped. I was made to be hidden—shoved into dark, hidden holes and left there. I was made to be alone. I was made to be *lonely*.

What he feels for me is twisted and selfish, but maybe I could have shaped it into something that didn't hurt so fucking much instead of starving it to shrink into this angry, bitter *want*. I simply don't know how.

I don't know how to be loved.

He gives my neck a little squeeze, fingers lingering in a slow drag as he pulls away. But the second the connection breaks, he's turning, marching to the chair. He snatches the back and drags it closer to the table, dropping into it with a hard expression.

Just like that, he's the soldier again, chin up, eyes dark and piercing. I press my fists into my diaphragm as if it could hold in the storm building in my gut.

Nick reaches over the table to take the gun.

The King's voice shatters the air around us like glass. "William," he says, flicking a hand. "It's time." Will emerges from the shadows with something blue wedged under his arm. He shakes it out like a bedsheet, bending to arrange it around Nick's chair.

A tarp.

"Oh, my god," I breathe, pressing my palm to my forehead. "Oh, my god..." This is all going too fast. I need to think, I need to—

Nick opens the cylinder, holding the King's eyes as he gives it a spin. With a jerk of his wrist, he closes it, thumb cocking the hammer, and suddenly I know that I can't do this.

I can't watch Nick die.

It soothes something inside I wasn't aware of until now, a fear so secret that I've been pushing it down. Locking Nick in the cage, playing with my victim until his brains are splattered willingly on the floor...

That's the part of me that belongs to my father.

And I'm better than a viper.

"Stop." My voice rings out sharp and sure, the stone floor solid beneath me as I cross the distance between us. "Forget it. Let's go."

I never make it.

One of the Barons slipping out of the darkness gets to me first, grabbing me with hard hands, one covering my mouth. I fight against him but, in the second before I reach Nick, his hand darts up, pressing the gun to his temple.

The room stills to just the sound of my heart pounding in my ears.

And then he pulls the trigger.

21

Lavinia

My gasp feels pulled from somewhere so deep inside of me that I double over at the waist, breaking away from the Baron. My body overcorrects for the force, an instinct to pull me away from the sight and shape of him until I topple to the floor, landing hard on my backside.

My ears ring, and for a moment, everything feels bizarrely slow. The flames on the candles wave instead of flicker, and it's just like that night at Felix's when Nick shot him in the head. That's how I know he's dead. The garble in my ears, the way my heart stutters, the slowness of it all.

My eyes are wide on the blue tarp beneath me, waiting for the warmth, the rush of blood.

It never comes.

First there's a sound, metal on wood, and then Nick's aloof

voice. "I win." My senses come rushing back so fast that I feel dizzy, raising my gaze to find him loose-limbed and whole. His profile is horrifically casual as he stares at the King, waiting. "You know how it goes. To the victor and all that."

"Well, this is disappointing," he says, sitting more stiffly than he had before. "You would have been such a good addition to my collection." The King turns to stare into the shadows, hand heavy as he flicks his fingers. "William. You know what to do."

Will steps forward, face scrunched in outrage. "But we can't just—"

"An agreement was made in blood," the King snaps. Lower, he adds, "We have more than one reputation to uphold." The dissatisfaction is clear in his voice. "Give them what they came for."

Will storms off and I struggle to get my feet beneath me, lightheaded and so cold that my extremities feel numb. Nick doesn't look at me. He just pops open the cylinder and pours the bullets out. They hit the table—one, two, three—clinking noisily as they scatter, and then Nick slings the revolver across the length of it.

It comes to a stop at the King's hands. "Keep it." His gloved hand hurls it back, pushing it so hard that it'd hit Nick square in the chest if he didn't reach out to snatch it first. The King leans back, adding, "It was your father's."

If this is a surprise to Nick, then he doesn't show it, smoothly pocketing it. "What exactly is Will doing?"

"You'll see," is all the King says.

Nick taps his fingers on the table, looking bored, and I hover at his side, trying to gather the parts of myself I'd lost on the floor, waiting to be covered in his blood.

I'm still shaking.

Will returns minutes later, carrying a bundle in his arms. As he approaches, Nick stands from the chair, and even now—even after almost splattering his brains in this sick pit of darkness—he still angles himself to protect me.

Will holds out the bundle.

To me.

We stare at it until Nick lets out a soft, "Shit." Confused, my eyes ping between him and the wad of old cloth, but he doesn't react when I reach out to take it. "Lavinia…" he starts, an odd warning to the tone of it.

Gently, I lift the cloth, uncovering what's beneath it.

Leticia.

It should horrify me to realize I'm holding a skull, but it doesn't. I stare at it, trying to place this as her—my sister, Leticia Lucia, the gem of North Side with her shiny hair and razor-sharp smile. The skull is brighter, tidier than the one at the Baron King's side, but it doesn't take me long to know it's real. Possibly, some part of me has always known. The world has felt much too small since she left, as if her absence had carved some permanent void.

Leticia's smile sparkled when she laughed, a back molar bearing a golden crown.

The skull has the same one.

I'd know it anywhere.

"It's her." The words emerge shaky with the chatter of my teeth. I can't tear my eyes away from it. This is a girl who will never laugh mockingly in my face again. She'll never dance across my father's marble floors to watch me be locked away. She'll never become someone who holds Forsyth under her twitchy trigger finger. If she'd at one point fallen for a tough, charismatic fighter from the West End, then Leticia will never know what it's like to feel Tate's love change her into something less ugly.

My sister is dead.

I look up, straight into the King's shadow-eyes. "Who called on you to collect her?"

The King stares back, head tilting. "Do you really want to ask another favor of death?"

Instantly, I'm certain I can't handle another roll of their dice. Not with my life and not with Nick's. Forsyth has enough bodies hiding in this crypt, and I refuse to add another. This is all we'll get from the Barons.

"No," I decide, covering the skull. I'm not sure if I'm the one that has started moving toward the door or if I begin just blindly following Nick, but before we exit the crypt, the King's voice rings out.

"Girl," he calls.

I stop and turn.

He raises his head, the tips of his horns gleaming in the candlelight. "I showed you this so that you'll recognize you're fighting above your weight class. Both of you. You may be the spawn of Royals but you know little about how our world works. Accept the knowledge I've given you and don't come back."

"Is that a warning?" I ask, but he waves his hand, dismissing us for good, Will and Liam emerging from the shadows to escort us into the darkness.

I CAME to the Baron's crypt with a severed hand in my lap, and I leave with a skull in its place.

Nick is quiet beside me in the driver's seat, a hand slung over the steering wheel as he drives us toward home. There's an ache in my chest. It's as heavy as a boulder and just as big, and I try my best to keep it trapped there, lost within the debris of whatever had broken inside me while we were in that crypt. It's dark in the cabin of the SUV, but occasionally we'll pass another car, the headlights sweeping across the sharp angles of Nick's pretty face. When that happens, my eyes are drawn to the tattoo on his temple. *237*. I only get a flash before it's gone.

I'm the first to speak, my voice ragged and shaky. "You didn't have to do that." He tosses me a quick glance, shrugging. "I didn't want you to do that," I add, scanning his stoic expression.

That hard soldier mask hasn't fallen away, and he wears it comfortably, relaxed in that special, artificial sort of way I've grown used to. The words I want to say feel hollow and ineffectual.

Thank you.

So I root around all the broken things in my chest to find something else to fill this thick, suffocating silence with. "Leticia wasn't a good sister." He doesn't look away from the road as he reaches out, kicking on the heat. It's only then that I realize that I'm still shivering, my body tight with the tension of holding in the tremors.

"I got that impression," he says.

"She wasn't a good sister," I repeat, tightening my grip on her skull. "But she was a good Lucia. I guess, in some way she's a part of me. Whether I like it or not, she's... she *was*..." The boulder bangs against my ribs and I clear my throat, trying to shove it back into place, tight and tidy with my shivers.

In my periphery, Nick turns to give me a look. "Are you going to cry?"

The brusque sentence gives me pause. "No," I say. And then, "Does that make me a bad person?"

His eyebrows tug toward the center of his forehead. "What would I know about being a good person? I just executed some poor fuck for fingering the Addams family's girlfriend."

Slowly, I turn my gaze to the road; the trees whizzing past us in a blur of shadows that could be hiding anything. "Right."

The rest of the drive is silent and surreal, and I can't get warm. My bones feel as though they've been transformed into ice. I keep thinking about the fact I have Leticia's head in my lap. Some sick part of me is cavalier about it and for a while, that's the part I embrace. She'd do the same for me, I'm sure of it. We were made to be rivals, created by a man who loved nothing more than pitting us against one another, and Leticia always beat me. She glowed in the light of my defeat, but she's not glowing tonight. She's dead. I'm alive.

Tonight, I win.

"You know how it goes. To the victor and all that."

We get home at midnight. We exit the car and I spend a moment looking upward, the sky vividly alive. It strikes me somewhere in my sternum, seeing the same stars she and Remy had that night when they jumped from the cliff.

Nick doesn't wait for me.

He closes his door and stalks through the shadows toward the tower. I push my feet hard to catch up to him, to walk through the doors as a pair of victors, the fist and his fury.

The tower's staircase has never felt colder. I'm still wearing Nick's jacket, but I'm not imbuing it with anything resembling warmth. Shock, maybe. The climb to the top is spent watching him, the way his back shifts beneath his plain white shirt. He's not acting like himself, too quiet and still, but I'm not sure how to break it, how to pull him back.

I keep Leticia clutched close as we enter through the party room, but the second we step through, Nick veers to the right, meandering to the bar. I watch as he stretches over the bar top, snagging a half-empty bottle of something amber from beneath it. He unscrews it and tips it to his mouth, his throat swelling and contracting with long, hard swallows, eyes fixed to the ceiling.

"Nick?"

Swallow.

"Nick."

Swallow.

Gently, I place the skull on the bar, and then I turn to him, reaching out to curl my fingers around the neck of the bottle.

He gasps when I take it from him, swiping a wrist over his mouth. "Jesus fucking Christ." He coughs, his eyes growing wet, and I understand why when I take a swig from the bottle. It stings the whole way down my esophagus, making my organs cringe and squirm.

When he meets my gaze again, he looks frayed and tired and pale, and something in my gut finally unwinds.

The soldier is gone.

I cap the bottle and set it next to Leticia. "Are you okay?"

"Well," he swipes the bottle back before I can stop him, my reflexes shot, "my brains aren't splattered on the Barons' discount hardware tarp, so I'd say I'm fucking fantastic. Wouldn't you?"

It seems like anger at first, and I'd understand. It's my fault. In no universe was Nick going to let me do that. So yeah, I'd understand the anger. But then his free hand reaches out to touch my own—a nudging caress—and I realize it's not anger at all.

This is relief.

"We can't tell them," he says, voice wrecked as he slumps onto a stool. "Not about meeting with the Barons. Sy will flip his goddamn shit, and Remy..." Nick gives me a long, significant look. "Remy will want to ask. Do you understand?"

But I'm already nodding. "He'd pay the price." He was willing to take a swan dive off this tower if it meant having Tate back. To find her killer? He'd pull the trigger.

Nick lowers his gaze to the bottle, his shoulders looking suddenly too heavy. "You're still shaking."

I wrap my arms around myself, trying to stop the tremors. "I almost watched you kill yourself."

"Don't want to see me dead, Little Bird?" He tips me an impish grin. It's said jokingly, giving me an out.

"No, I don't."

The smile flickers and then fades away. He holds my stare as he sets the bottle aside. "You don't hate me anymore?"

I answer honestly. "I don't know." I also step up close to him, our heights equalized by his slump on the bar stool, and reach out to cradle his jaw, the thick stubble soft against my palm.

Nick goes eerily still, frozen as I pitch forward, our noses grazing.

His eyelashes flutter, but don't close as I brush my lips against his. Maybe that's what I'll remember most about it—the intensity in the way he looks at me as he reaches up to touch my throat, mouth parting to take me inside.

I kiss him the way he's always wanted, licking against his rough tongue to taste him, thumb digging into the hinge of his jaw as I deepen it. He makes a low, rough sound into my mouth, but even though I feel his hand on my hip, he doesn't use it for anything but a sweep of his thumb against my skin. It'd be a lie to say it doesn't stir the ember in my belly to life. Nick kisses like it's something he wants to savor, slick and unhurried and sexual in some unavoidably primal way. These hands have hurt me. They've locked me away. They've tossed me to the vipers. They've pulled and clawed and bruised.

But tonight, they're as gentle as his kiss.

When I pull away, he doesn't chase it.

"Thank you," I say, sucking the taste of him from my lips.

His eyes are heavy and glazed—from the liquor or the kiss, I'm not quite sure. Either way, the hand on my hip falls away, and he sighs, the rest of the tension falling from his frame. "You're going to fucking kill me, girl." Despite the words, the grin he sends me is incandescent.

For a split second, he looks a lot like that charming boy in the photo.

It makes me take a step back, clearing my throat. "I'll need a place to hide her."

Some of the mirth sinks away, but not all of it. He looks at the skull, nodding. "There's some loose stones just outside, in the stairwell. I'll hide it. Keep it safe."

I nod back. "I know you will."

He doesn't follow me to the stairs. Halfway up, I take a glance over my shoulder and see him on the stool, nursing the bottle of bourbon as he stares unseeingly at the bar. I wonder if he's as cold as I am, if the liquor burns but doesn't soothe.

It's dark and still upstairs.

Sy and Remy are already in bed, ignorant of the fact their best friend almost died tonight. The boulder in my chest bangs again, persistent and unwilling to be ignored, but I try my best to swat it away as I wander in search of a place to release it. Somewhere that can thaw these rattling bones.

I go to the greatest source of warmth I know.

He's resting on the left side of the bed when I push through his cracked door. He keeps it open for me now, ever since the first time he pulled me out of the darkness. I stand before his bed with chattering teeth and shivering lungs, my arms wrapped around my middle as if I'm still cradling Leticia's skull, unwilling to give up the weight of her. A slice of light from the window reveals that Archie is asleep in my usual spot, curled into a tight ball of white fuzz against my pillow.

"It's after midnight," comes Sy's deep, rumbling voice. When I say nothing, he sits up, hand shooting out to flick on his lamp. "Where the fuck have you—" The words get bitten off when his eyes land on me, arm suspended halfway in its return to his body. Urgently, he asks, "What happened?"

But I'm too busy staring at his bare chest to answer—not that I could—the warmth of his bronze skin beckoning me closer. I press my knees into the bed and crawl up its length. It's selfish, I know it is, to seek his heat, to climb into his lap, straddling his thighs and clutching his neck in a pitiful, greedy embrace.

He feels like a bright, roaring fire, the heat a welcome shock to the frigid cringe of my skin. Even though he's stiff against me, arms held out to his sides in alarm, his body is so soft that I sink into him. The boulder bangs and crashes, and even if I wanted to hold it back, I couldn't.

I bury my sob into his warm neck, shoulders heaving with the force of it. My cries surface like a wave crashing through a gate, guttural, body-wracking.

Sy's voice rings out, sharp and dangerous. "Did Nick do something?"

I shake my head, a wretched sound yanked from my throat as I sob, clawing him closer. The truth would just confuse him, because I don't even know who I'm crying for. Leticia, for being dead? Nick, for being alive? Me, for holding the grief of them when I'm not even entitled to it?

I feel Sy's exhale against my temple, slow and measured, and then his arms slowly close around me. First against Nick's jacket, and then more tentatively, dipping beneath it to engulf my waist.

His words come fiercely, in a voice that's still thick with sleep.

"Jesus, Lavinia. You're fucking freezing." His fingers tug at the jacket to remove it, but that would mean letting go of him, abandoning all this heat and softness, so I refuse.

Naturally, he doesn't let me.

He pries my arms from around his neck, unmoved by the miserable sound of protest I make. "Come on. Just get this off…"

I gave myself to him once, that night in my old bedroom. I let him move and hold me, offered him a faith I didn't feel, and he made me better, if not whole. I do it again, allowing him to strip the jacket from my shoulders, his palms rubbing warmth into my upper arms. I try to avoid his gaze, shielding my cries with the veil of my hair.

He brushes it back and ducks into my line of vision, giving me a glimpse of his furrowed brow. "Tell me what happened."

I shake my head, but the moment I try to tell him something—anything, nothing—another wretched sound breaks free. Sy's face collapses and he tugs me back into him, letting me wind my arms back around his neck.

He whispers, "I don't know what to do." But he tries, knitting his fingers into my hair. Sy cradles my head against his neck, letting me cry and clutch, and I don't know how long it lasts, but it's long enough that he must realize this is bigger than an awkward, rigid embrace in the middle of his rumpled blankets.

"Come on," he says, voice firm and decisive as he lifts me from the bed. I follow because I couldn't possibly not, sticking close to his heat as he draws me to his door. I hang onto his arm like it's my only tether, and even though the sobs abate, my eyes still swim with the remnants. We walk through the living room, and then push through another door, and I neither realize nor care where he's taking me until he reaches out to flick the light.

Remy makes a low, displeased sound into his pillow, and then rolls over to fix us with a disgruntled squint. "It's not loud!" he snaps. Only then do I realize his music is playing, a quiet, desolate melody that tugs at the wound in my chest.

The annoyance instantly falls from his face when he sees us. There's a pause as he watches us, the gears turning. "Nicky?"

Sy shrugs, saying, "No." Quieter, with an edge of nervousness I'm not used to hearing from him, he tells Remy, "I don't know what to do."

Remy drinks me in, from the crown of my head to the soles of my shoes, and then rises to a sitting position. The sheets fall away to reveal he's naked. He rakes his fingers through his tousled hair and lifts a hand to beckon us closer. Wordlessly, Sy leads me to him.

Inked fingers reach out to touch my waist, my ribs, my thighs, prodding the surface of my flesh with a pinched brow. Searching, it occurs to me. "She's not hurt?"

"No," Sy answers, shifting uncomfortably.

But then Remy looks up into my eyes, holding them just as tangibly as his hands hold my hips, and his forehead smoothes. "Yes, she is."

"What?" Sy's eyes scan me. "Where?"

"She's fucking screaming with yellow." Remy's mouth flattens to a grim line. "It's not the kind of hurt you can see, Sy. I'm going to take this off." He says the last part to me, as soft as a feather, lifting my shirt over my head. I'm not surprised when his inked fingers dip into the waistbands of my jeans next, popping the fly. If anything, I'm glad to be rid of them when he shucks them down, as if some part of the crypt may have clung to my clothing like a foul odor, following me home. Remy leaves my bra and underwear, peering up into my eyes as he pitches forward to kiss the tattoo beside my hip. "Come here."

He leads me into his bed. Remy has a good mattress, surely paid for with his father's money, and when I settle into the middle of it, it's still warm from his body heat. Propped on an elbow, he drags the blanket over me, his fingers touching my jaw, turning me to look into his green eyes. It's uncomfortable, the knowledge that I'm too bare to hide from him, that I've brought all this rot into a place that's become safe for me, that I would tell him everything that's rending my insides to ribbons if my vocal cords would just work.

Instead, I turn into him, seeking his warmth.

"She wants me," he says, thumb brushing the wet skin beneath my eye, "But she needs you." He swings his gaze to Sy, jerking his head in invitation.

It's a relief to feel the room bathed in darkness again, to feel Sy's weight behind me, sliding beneath the blankets, skin hot against my back. It's better to be pressed between them as they settle, Remy's hand never leaving my cheek, catching my tears like raindrops before they can dampen his designer pillow.

Sy hovers behind me, close enough to feel his flesh, but far enough to be dissatisfying. The whisper he pitches to Remy is almost too quiet for me to hear over the rushing in my ears. "Like this?"

Remy's hand leaves my cheek to reach behind me. He grabs Sy's wrist and drapes it over my waist. "Like that."

Sy's fingers twitch before dipping around, pulling me up tight to his chest.

Yes.

Just like this.

For the first time since stepping into the crypt, my muscles give, crashing into a relaxed state with all the grace of an elephant on rollerblades. In the midst of it, I find myself able to offer two words.

"I'm sorry."

I feel Remy's lips against mine without seeing, the dark too thick, too obstructive. "I forgive you."

He thinks I'm apologizing for the lie. I never would. Given the chance, I'd do it all the same, with so few options available to me. The lie is nothing compared to what I'm apologizing for now. There was a time when they were four, and someone took Tate away from them, just as someone had taken Leticia away from me, and just as someone had nearly taken Remy.

Nick could have died tonight.

That's what I think about as I let sleep drag me under. I've lived so long without any choices that I've forgotten the havoc they bring. To choose is a freedom.

The freedom to win.

The freedom to lose.

Despite the fact we walked out of the crypt with the information we wanted, hearts beating, lungs pumping, it doesn't feel like there are any victors.

Not tonight.

22

Remy

WHILE ADMIRING HER SKIN, I linger on the bruises. They're yellowing now, old enough that I can't make out the shape of my own fingertips. I still know where they came from, my fingers digging into flesh and bone as I slammed into her from behind. I know they shouldn't get me hard, but they do. It's the purple of it, the sense of tenderness. I put marks on peoples' skin all the time, but it's different when the mark is beneath it.

Her stomach ripples, caving as my fingertips glide from hip to hip. Sy's been feeding her well and a part of me wants to tell her, *See?* She used to be scared of him, but he'll take care of her, make her strong, transform her into the Duchess she was always meant to be. Nick will keep her safe and spry, because he's never what he seems and always what we need.

But me...

What will I be?

That's not something I usually consider, preferring the here and now, because tomorrow… I can't predict that. I think about it for a long time as she sleeps beside me, Sy having already peeled himself from her bare skin to have his morning jog. My class starts in an hour, but for now, I let myself indulge in the sight of her in my bed, so soft and warm.

When her eyes flutter open, I'm still fixated on the bruises, thinking. Always thinking. That's what she and Sy don't get about the drugs. They let me consume it all. The thoughts become more of a library and less of a tornado when I'm on them. I can let every idea come and pass, tucking it carefully away just as the next arrives. I know it's not good or healthy, but goddamn. How is it fair that they feed me three pills every day but tell me I can't have the one I want?

"What time is it?" she croaks, head turning to search out a clock.

"I don't have a clock in here," I tell her. "Time is just a countdown to things I don't want to do." Everything fun happens spontaneously, without the need for measurement or devices. Temple propped on my fist, I press my thumb into the yellowing skin. "Did it hurt?" Her eyes are still swollen and red from the crying jag last night, and she gives me a bleary stare, blinking in confusion. "Did I hurt you?" I elaborate, shifting my gaze to the bruise on her hip. It's almost directly over the tattoo I'd put there, seven points and their galaxy of decaying blood.

Her eyes follow mine, and she swallows. "Not like that."

I don't say I'm sorry because I'm not sure I am.

Instead, I bend down to press my lips to the yellowing spots, explaining, "You lied to me. I had to show you that you're too close for that now. I warned you that night on the cliffs that it'd make you mine." When I glance up, she's staring at me, eyes wide and wary. "Not just my Duchess or my steady fuck. I let you in. You get that, don't you? I opened my soul to you, Vinny. I know it's ugly—maybe it doesn't even mean anything to you, but—"

"It does," she argues, frowning. Her fingers thread tentatively through my hair, my eyes fluttering closed at the sensation. "I'm just trying to take care of it," she whispers, voice rough as gravel.

I push into her hand, luxuriating in the feel of her fingers against my scalp. "I want to tattoo you this week." That's what I've been thinking about all morning, even before Sy had woken up. I've been looking at all this skin and positively fucking itching to cover every inch of it. I haven't felt something like this since Nicky got his first piece, and never in my life have I felt it with a girl. Not even Tate.

"Oh." Her fingers pause in their lazy scritching, but only for a second. She knows I'm not asking permission, but she still gives it. "Okay."

The swelling in my chest is almost too much to bear. It's too complicated to call excitement, although it's close. This itching, restless, impatient urge to get started is so strong that I can't help but fidget, fingering the elastic of her underwear. Black lace. "What do you want?"

Her eyebrows knit together. "What do you mean?"

"For your tattoo." My dick has been hard since she slid beneath my blankets, and I don't think twice about rolling over her. "What do you want?"

Her thighs spread for me, letting me grind myself against her lacy panties. "I don't know," she says, frowning. "I never know."

There's a yellow ochre in her eyes that makes my hips still, a hollow depth of frost I saw in her last night that hasn't departed quite yet. I try to chase it away with my lips, dipping down to kiss her. Her hands skate up my ribs, so soft that it tickles, but even though she opens her body to me—spreading her thighs for my hips, parting her lips for my tongue—it's not enough.

"What happened last night, Vinny?"

The spark of lust in her eyes dims. I sweep her hair from her cheek and watch as she makes a choice. Tell me or not? "You were right," she says, her whisper warm and damp against my lips. "Leticia's dead."

I push up to look at her. It's strange. I've wanted so badly for

Vinny to accept this, but now that I see it, I just want to erase the hopelessness in her eyes. "We don't know for sure. She could still—"

She pushes me off.

Seriously.

She clenches her thighs and does this little bucking twist with her hips, and then jarringly, I'm flat on my back, watching her climb out of the bed.

The fuck?

"Can I show you something?" she asks, jamming her feet into the leg of her jeans.

I gape at her as she pulls my shirt over head, still thrown off balance. I might not be as big as Sy or anything, but goddamn. She totally just fucking manhandled me. My dick gives a confused little twitch. "Uh, okay."

She waits, watching as I step into a pair of boxers, giving my dick a sad little squeeze before caging it up inside a pair of jeans. I'm not sure what I'm expecting when she drags me out of my room and to the door, down the flight of steps that leads to the party room, but watching her feel around the stone wall just inside the main stairwell isn't it.

"What are you looking for?" I ask, shivering, wishing I'd thrown on a shirt, too.

Her gaze is distant but focused, fingertips searching all along the wall. "He said it'd be here," she mutters, turning to the opposite wall and trying that. It's not long before her fingers catch on something, her body kicking into motion as she pulls a stone free, and then the one beside it. This has to be some cranny Nick has found, probably relayed to him over beers in his parents' basement, his dad or his pops telling stories of their glory days.

She pulls out a wad of frayed fabric and turns to me. "This is her," she says, pulling back the fabric to reveal a skull.

Last year, my anatomy drawing class had a deal with the science department where we got to study their incoming shipment of specimens. It was my favorite class—the only one I had perfect attendance for. Skulls, yes, but also femurs and scapulas, metacarpals that hadn't been assembled into the shape of a hand yet, organs in formaldehyde, animal fetuses and malformations. One of those drawings became the inspiration for a tattoo on my forearm; a two-headed bear cub. Sy and Nick. My perfect little fucking malformations.

I crouch down to get a better look, mouth parted in fascination. "How do you know?"

Lavinia just says, "I know," and I get it. Strip away the skin and flesh, muscle and veins, and I bet I could place Nicky and Sy.

I reach out, hand hovering over a cheekbone, but don't make contact. "She's beautiful," I breathe, eyes tracing the curves and dips, the angles and lines. I want to draw her, to match her up to the vision I've had in my head all this time. A beautiful dead girl.

When I look up into Vinny's cold, gray eyes, I see a hurt there.

"It's not the kind of hurt you can see..."

So I touch her instead, palm gliding up the back of her thigh. "Almost as beautiful as you," I add, because it's true.

I don't want to draw Vinny. I want to draw *on* her—in her. I want to shape her into a piece of myself. Her expression falters, something falling away. I'm not sure what it is exactly, but it leaves her without that steel armor, a vulnerability to her gaze. I wonder if Nick realizes.

Pick Vinny over someone else, and you have her in the palm of your hand.

"Where did you find her?" I ask. If Leticia's body was found, maybe there's evidence, a way to track whoever was with us on the cliffs that night.

But Vinny's face falls. "Remy..." She shakes her head, lips forming around words that never come. "Please don't make me lie to you again."

I feel my own face fall. "You can't tell me."

She reaches up to place the skull back inside the wall. "It's not that I don't want to, or that I don't trust you. I just..." Sighing, she leans against the wall, arms crossed, shoulders curled to protect herself from a hurt she's expecting me to give her. She looks so much smaller than she had mere seconds ago. "I just can't."

Intuitively, I know why. Whatever this information is, it's dangerous. She's protecting me. I stand, fixing her with a hard stare. "Does Nick know?"

She nods, biting her lip. "Yes."

"And he's got your back? He's keeping you safe?"

The words make her flinch in a way I don't understand, but she answers, "Yes," with an intensity I'm not expecting. "Nick would do anything to keep me safe." Lower, she repeats, "*Anything*."

"Okay, then," I decide, hemming her in against the wall, cradling her jaw. "I trust you."

The kiss is slow and sweet, and even though the tower is roughly the temperature of a morgue freezer, it heats me from within, stirring my blood to life as I plunge my tongue into her mouth. Sy will be running up here soon, telling us to get ready, that we'll be late for class, but I take my time, and Vinny…

She unfurls against me, uncrossing her arms to wind them around my waist, bringing me close. "The tattoo…" she whispers, brushing her mouth against mine. "I know what I want."

"Anything," I say, that gnarled excitement spurring to life.

Her eyes flutter open to meet mine. Once again, I see that flash of vulnerability, her whisper sounding far meeker than it deserves to. "Give me wings?"

I think about this, watching her hazy eyes. Nick calls her his Little Bird, but it doesn't quite fit. Vinny isn't made of feathers and small, breakable bones. She's something more ephemeral than that. A shadow that expands and contracts.

I touch her lip. "Only if you promise not to fly away."

She smiles against my finger, so open and sweet that I ache with it. "Cross my heart."

THE WEEK GETS SO busy and bogged down with responsibilities that there isn't room for much more than routine.

Sy always wakes first. Vinny goes jogging with him, and I don't know what they talk about—if they even do at all—but after that night she came to us, bleeding her soul all over her cold cheeks, she and Sy have been back to normal. Bickering in the mornings. Ignoring one another in the afternoons. And at night...

At night she disappears into his room with him.

Whatever they're doing, it can't be too elaborate. She's always flustered and impatient in the mornings, and Nicky and I always share a tragic look. Sy apparently knows how to get a girl horny, but he's not making much headway with doing something about it.

On Friday morning, we watch this same song and dance—Vinny emerging from his bedroom short-tempered and irritable, while Sy strides out looking perfectly satisfied—and Nicky mutters, "What a fucking waste." Solemnly, I nod back in agreement. The only one of the three of us with unfettered nightly access to her wet pussy is the guy who doesn't even know what to do with it.

Whatever they're doing, Sy is a fucking beast at Friday Night Fury, absolutely creaming this poor Psi Nu sucker in the ring. Nicky, Vinny, and I all watch from the side as he bobs and weaves, kicking the guy's legs out from beneath him. They grapple a little, but Sy lands a sick uppercut in the third round that takes the Psi Nu right off his feet, a clean TKO.

Later, at the party, after Sy has gotten his victory tattoo, I watch from the couch as he and Vinny cross paths at the bar. It's pretty packed tonight, so they shift past one another full-bodied, him reaching out to steady her by the hip. I'm not sure anyone is expecting it when he dips down to press a quick but no less sensual kiss to her lips, licking out to meet her tongue before smoothly gliding away. Vinny blushes and twists to watch his retreat, licking the taste of him from her mouth.

Yeah, she's horny as hell.

Proud of my boy, though.

People whisper about it, and after that, both the DKS boys and the cutsluts watch them—Sy and Vinny—and I know what they're all wondering. Has he fucked her with that firehose in his shorts, yet?

Nick and I share a long, knowing look, because we're both aware they haven't.

I don't really get a chance to pay respect to my idea until Sunday.

It never comes perfectly formed. It starts more like a puzzle. Dozens of pieces scattered across the table, a hodgepodge of shapes and colors. I know whatever the chaos is will create a design, but it's not until I have them all flipped over and sorted into little piles that it starts to make sense.

I pace outside the bathroom, listening to the sound of her inside. The faucet turning on and off. The rustle of the shower curtain. I spin the marker in my fingers, round, and round until this thing swelling in my chest bursts to life, propelling my fist to the wood.

Bang bang bang.

"Are you almost done?" I shout, voice too loud and clipped. I try the handle and the door actually gives. Vinny has on dark purple boy shorts, one arm threaded through the strap of her bra.

"Remy, what the hell?" She covers her chest, jaw dropped in outrage. "Shut the door!"

I barge into the steamy bathroom and grab her hips, driving her against the wall. Then I pluck the lacy bra from the crook of her arm and toss it aside, uncaring of the glare she shoots me. Her hands are still clamped over her tits, making them full and round, but no—not now. Using the marker—washable instead of my usual permanent—I start drawing the design on the flat plane of her chest.

"Is this some kind of break?" she asks, tone completely serious. "High? Low? What are we dealing with here?"

"Not a break," I say, raising my eyes to hers. "A *breakthrough*."

I push her out of the bathroom, through the living room, and into my bedroom. "Get on the table," I demand, knowing my tone is too curt. This isn't anger. It's passion. Inspiration. An artist needs his muse.

She tries to look down at the design on her chest, but it's out of her line of sight. "Not until you tell me what's going on!"

"Your tattoo," I explain, turning to the table. "I can finally see it. Crystal clear, like stars during an eclipse." Shifting through the sheets of paper, sketches, drawings, a few colored, others black and white, I find a half-baked concept I'd started a few days ago. It's been nagging at me ever since, but I had a real bitch of a paper due, and if I'm going to prove my dad wrong and remain a Duke, then I need to pay more mind to actually passing.

Eventually, I stand in front of her and run my hands down her arms, traveling past the bend of her elbow to where she cups her tits. Gently, I pry her fingers off, one by one, and rub my thumbs over her nipples, gently working them into hard peaks. It's not necessary for the art or anything. I just like seeing her horny. "It's been coming to me in pieces. Little flashes. Sometimes it's like that. Marathon, not a sprint, that sort of thing." I pause, eyes darting up to hers. "You'll let me, right? You'll let me give you your wings now?"

Her pupils expand, and she swallows, nodding her approval. "I'm ready."

She lies back and I get my supplies together, pulling the sterile needles from the autoclave in the corner, picking through the bottles of ink. "This will take a few sessions," I warn her. "And the location, it's gonna hurt like a mother. Just let me know if it gets to be too much."

She tilts her head to the side, watching me. "I have a pretty high pain threshold."

I flash her a smirk. "You're the Duchess. Of course you do."

Once everything is together, I sit on my stool, snap on a pair of latex gloves, and roll over to her. It feels good to be back in the seat. Aside from Sy and Nicky's victory tats, I haven't had a good, solid session in a while. We're eye to eye, and I grip her chin. Brushing my lips across hers, I taste the mint of toothpaste and smell her soapy skin, and I wish I would have fucked her first, hard and slow, loosening her up. But the image is burned into my head like a goddamn cattle prod. It won't let me rest until I get it down.

I run my hand down her neck and start the prep, cleaning off the marker and disinfecting her skin. She shivers from the cool liquid, goosebumps rising, nipples tightening, but she stays still. It was the first thing I loved about her, how willing she was to lay on my table and let me have her skin. The template comes next, and I rub it on, getting it exactly where I want it.

Once it's right, exactly right, the lines aligning with the vision in my head; I grab the gun, giving it a couple testing zaps. "Ready?" I ask, resting one hand on her belly.

"Yes." Her eyes are wide and trusting.

The vibration fills the room, runs through my veins and thrums in my ears, and I push aside everything else and begin the slow, tedious cycle of inking and then wiping away the excess ink and blood. I can tell it hurts when her body tenses up, fingers curling, her breath caught.

"Too much?" I ask, pausing.

Her jaw is tense, but she grinds out, "No. It's weird right? It hurts, but it also feels... enthralling?"

"Yeah, it's the good kind of pain, right? Makes you feel alive." I allow my eyes to slide down her body. "You wet?"

Her cheeks blush pink. "Um. A little?"

Not that I tell her, but my dick's been hard since I put her on the table.

Slinging my hair back with a jerk of my neck, I bend back to the outline, ignoring the prickle of sweat on my neck. "Focus on how I'm gonna take care of that for you once I'm finished. Okay?"

She nods, mouth twitching as she stares up at the ceiling. "Okay."

I lose track of time when I'm caught up in my art. It's why I don't usually do big pieces on anyone but Nicky, who can tolerate hours and hours in my chair without complaint. Others... I get so absorbed that I forget they need breaks, rest, a chance to feel something other than the nagging sting of it. It's annoying, a shock to my brain to be yanked out of the act so suddenly. But Vinny's design has carved itself into different phases in my mind, so I work slower than normal. Every part of it has to be perfect.

I'm not sure how long it takes, but I know that by the time I look up, reorienting myself to something that isn't her skin, the light in the window has shifted.

"There," I say, snapping off the gun. I eye the outline, the skin raised and raw. "I think that's enough for now."

I put down the tools and slide my hands under her body, lifting her off the table. Without question, I take her right to my bed, sitting on the foot of it. Grabbing the tube of ointment, I carefully spread a layer of the thick, shiny cream over the angry lines. She tips her head back, relief clear on her face as she winds down, and I spend a long moment staring at the long, soft column of her throat.

Before I've even finished capping the ointment, I'm pressing my tongue to it, licking a slow path to her chin. Her eyes fan open in the millisecond before I capture her mouth, kissing her like I've been thinking about for hours. "It's sexier than I even thought."

"The tattoo?" She makes another futile attempt to look at her own chest.

"Seeing you marked." I run my hand down her body, over her tits and down her belly. *Fuck*. This is all mine. Mine to mark. Mine to play with. Mine to dive inside.

Her chest rises and falls, every expansion and contraction seeming to make the tattoo's wings move. "It's not the first tattoo you've given me."

"True, but it's the only one you've wanted." I think maybe that's it. I didn't give it to Vinny to prove that I own her. I gave it to her because she's mine. There's a difference, and it hit me full force that night on the cliff when I buried myself inside of her for the first time. I did warn her. There's a reason I don't tattoo other girls. Being that close to someone is dangerous. Wanting them for more than their body, wanting to see myself inked into them, is an invitation for misery, because Nicky, Sy, and I have this in common.

We don't do things by halves.

We fuck like we fight, and we love like we die.

Vinny is a danger. A potential misery. Normal women leave or cheat or lie or just fucking *die*, but Royal women? They do all of that with an intensity that rivals the sun. I might not agree with his methods, but I understand Sy's reservations with having a Duchess.

But something inside of me has latched on to something inside of her, and I've accepted it.

So I slide my hand under the tight shorts and feel the sticky heat of her arousal. My cock swells in reaction, and I climb over her, hooking my fingers into the edge of her panties and tugging them over her hips.

I know exactly what I want.

I toss the panties on the floor and spread her thighs apart, dropping my nose against her wet heat. "You smell so good, baby."

"Remy, *gross*." She squirms, but I clamp my hands down on her thighs to still her.

I argue, "No, it smells different," and dart my tongue out to taste her. "Sharp like steel. Like adrenaline. You've been sitting on the edge of a knife for hours, just letting your body percolate and build." I flatten my tongue against her pussy, tasting and taking and feeling her body shudder with it.

"Oh," she breathes, falling back on the bed. "Oh, fuck."

Humming, I slide my hand down to my cock, giving my balls a squeeze.

And then a heavy fist lands on my door, knocking.

"Come in," I call, winking at Vinny before diving back in.

The door opens, and I hear, "Hey, man, do you have any of that ta—" Sy goes abruptly silent in the doorway. And then, "Fuck. Uh, sorry." I look up and see his nose wrinkled in distaste.

I give Vinny's clit a lingering kiss before giving Sy my full attention. "Why don't you take over?"

Sy frowns. "Take over what?"

"Eating our Duchess' pussy."

Her knees clamp shut. "Remy!"

"That's a hard pass," Sy says, jaw tensing. He looks down at Vinny and adds, "No offense, I'm just not doing *that*, ever."

I push her legs back open and inhale her scent. It's changed a little. Cooled. *Asshole.* I kiss down her inner thighs, working her back into it. Between kisses, I say, "You're missing out, bro." I reach her pussy and kiss her clit. She squirms and her hand reaches out, fingers clawing into my hair. "She's so good like this. Putty in my hands." I smirk up at her from between her legs. "I wonder if that's why he can't do it. Not enough fighting?" I brush my knuckle over her opening. "Or maybe it's because, in his fucked up mind, you'd be the winner."

"It's none of those things, asshole," he says, hand reaching down to not-so-discreetly adjust his boner. "I'm just not putting my face down there. Or my mouth."

While he talks, I give my girl what she needs, and her deep, airy moan fills the room. She yanks at my hair, pulling tight while I grind against her foot, dying for friction. But I can't help but notice the lack of a door closing. Sy doesn't leave, and a slow slide of my eyes reveals he's still in the doorway. For a dude not into eating pussy, he sure seems to like watching me do it.

Which is pretty fucking bogus, if you ask me.

I look up at him. "If you want a show, go turn on some porn. Participants only, dude.

He hesitates, but then asks, "What does it taste like?"

I give him a look. There's no way he hasn't sucked the taste of her off his fingers before. "Trying to put that into words is like trying to explain string theory. Pussy tastes fucking amazing, and it's never the same twice." I gesture for him to come closer. Vinny sighs, eyes staring at the ceiling in frustration, and I give her clit a little caress with the pad of my thumb. "Be patient, Vin. My boy needs to learn how to properly eat a woman out. You'll get your orgasm. Promise."

I'm doing this for you more than me.

"Take my spot," I tell him, moving up the bed, sliding behind Vinny and cradling her against my chest. "Spread for him," I order, cupping her tits and massaging them—taking care to stay clear of the fresh tattoo. Sy walks forward with the air of a man who's inching into battle. Shoulders squared, face hard, a little flicker of uncertainty in his eyes. He eyes her cunt like it's a demon, but finally kneels before her.

Lavinia's eyes are wide and wary, and right before Sy moves to dive into her pussy, I realize what's going to happen. Anything I can do, he has to do better. He looks like he's about to eat our girl alive.

I stop him. "Hey, go slow. Easy. There's a lot of nerves down there, and they are *not* into going eight rounds with your tongue. I've got her warmed up for you, just... spar. Playfully."

Since she's progressively eked her knees together, I run my hands down her body and use my long arms to grab for her thighs, spreading them wide for him. I hold her open, and he stares at her pussy.

His face is still screwed up.

"Christ, you're going to give her a complex. Vinny's pussy is amazing. The sooner you realize that, the better you'll be at mastering it." With one hand, I reach between her legs and roll my fingers on her hot little nub. She exhales and tries to close her legs, but Sy's hand snaps out and holds them wide. "That's the spot," I tell him. "*Gentle.*"

There's another long moment before he sticks his tongue out, flat and awkward. Vinny tenses against me, but I kiss her side of her neck, lathing my tongue, distracting her until he makes contact.

He licks her pussy.

A shudder rolls up her spine. "Ah!" she gasps, back arching.

He looks up, eyebrows hiked to his hairline. "Was that right?"

Vinny nods, hips rising, and grunts out a, "Unnnnhunn."

He grins.

"Suck on her clit," I tell Sy. "She likes that. Don't you, Vinny?" She nods, fingers curled in the bedspread and Sy, for once in his goddamn life, follows directions. "Fuck her with your tongue. She's so good and wet, yeah? You do that to her, you know. You've been doing it all fucking week—making her strung tighter than a goddamn piano wire."

Sy gets really excited when he hears about this, mouth opening wide to tongue her, which isn't a surprise. For some reason, he's always been on this kick that girls don't want him. Sure, his dick is scary, but if he ever gave someone a chance to get used to the idea, he'd be a fucking sex god. Instead, he storms away at the smallest sign of hesitation. Insecure fuck.

He's not storming away now, though. His eyebrows are a little furrowed, but the crevice between them isn't disgust. He's feeling his way around here, testing as his tongue makes a tight, sweeping arc around her clit.

The woman under me writhes from the attention, body twisting in pleasure as we both dote on her. Finally, she thrusts a hand in Sy's hair, the other clutching my forearm so tight that her fingernails sting. My cock is ramrod straight, drilling into her back. Every move she makes gets it harder.

I turn to whisper into her temple, "You think you can come for him, beautiful? You feeling it?" She nods, face twisted into my arm. Her quick panting breaths heat my skin. I can see her toes just starting to curl as Sy knees up closer, tongue working her harder now, determined, pointed. Her hips rise and fall, legs trembling, and I fist a hand into her hair to keep her close, rumbling to Sy, "Let her come on your tongue, man."

Sy's tongue firms to a point over her clit, and I don't even know what this fucker was worried about, because he flicks her into a complete mess of fricatives and bucking hips, her mouth opened wide around a keening cry.

The room fills with color, blindingly hot, as she comes hard against his mouth, her whole body lurching with the force of it. Sy makes a sound, deep and guttural, and plants both palms onto the mattress for leverage, forcing her to take it. Her hands are thrust in his hair, thighs clamped around his ears, and *Christ*. She's basically fucking his face, her hips chasing the point of his tongue.

She settles into these little panted cries, her muscles seizing with every pass of his tongue.

I thumb her mouth and say, "Keep that open for your Duke, Vinny."

I ease her back on the pillow, body limp and fluid. There's a strand of hair plastered against her face and I gently brush it back as I tell Sy, "Come on, brother. It's her turn to taste you."

He shoots up, fingers clawing at his fly, and I'm not sure I like the look in his eye. It's feral and barely controlled, polluted with an edge of menace. Exactly the kind of thing Vinny will fight against.

"Chill," I whisper, hoping she doesn't hear over the rush of her pulse in her ears. "She's a sure thing. Just give it to her."

He knows what I mean—I can tell by the way he takes a deep, measuring breath. For him—for this moment—giving is better than taking. When I slide out from beneath her, it's because I know Sy will be good to her. Giving in to his impulses is easy, and he never takes the easy way out of anything. We trade places, passing at the corner of my bed, and I have my shirt off and my dick out before I even kneel on the mattress between her knees. Sy is just as worked up, so it's no shock when he has his monster out just as quickly, standing near the edge by her head.

She already looks wiped out, which is just how I want her when I spread her thighs, slot the head of my dick up against her slick entrance, and slide inside. It's a slow thing, nothing like the last two times we fucked. This one is for Sy's benefit just as much as ours, and I can feel his wide eyes on the point where we meet, my dick disappearing into her wet hole.

Vinny arches her back, hand shooting out to grab a hold of something, anything, and finding Sy's hand. "Remy," she pants, head digging back into the pillow. "Oh, fuck—oh, *god*—"

Sy grasps her hand and watches in fascination, mouth parted. "Is she... tight?"

"Fuck yes," I grunt, my balls already drawn high. I've been dying to be inside her all week, and I barely allow my hips to retreat before driving my dick back into her.

Sy's eyes are heavy, dropped into slits as he leans forward and palms her thigh, spreading her for a better look. "She's fucking soaked."

"You did that." It probably stings a little to know my dick is enjoying the fruits of his labor, but Sy doesn't show it.

He just grips his cock and tugs at the head, straightening to loom over her. "Look at me," he says, voice wrecked as he jerks his cock.

Vinny's eyes flutter open, but she sees his cock before anything else, his hand gliding up and down the shaft. Before she can protest, I lever myself down, grinding myself into her clit, balls deep. The glazed ecstasy returns to her eyes and she strains up, just a hair, to flick her tongue out, licking at what I know from experience is the most sensitive part of a man's cock.

Sy doesn't come.

My thrusts stutter, but I keep at it, surging into her as Sy holds fast, staring intently at her plush lips. Without even a second of hesitation, he dips down to rub the head of his cock against the crease of her mouth, and it's so fucking hot.

She instantly closes her mouth around it.

"That's it," I grunt, punching my hips into her. "You're gonna make us come, Vinny. Think you can take us both, baby?"

She's so drunk off her orgasm, she'd probably agree to anything, but the way her cheeks hollow with a hard, deliberate suck, make me think she's doing it because she just wants to.

Sy growls, a ragged, raw sound ripping from his chest, and I know when his thighs tense, muscles flexing, that he's about to spill on her tongue. So I grab her hips, tilt them up, and slam into her one last time, allowing the ripple of liquid hot pleasure to course through me.

Sy's gasp is preceded by his hand wedging beneath her head, holding her still with a fistful of hair as his cock begins to pulsate, jerking wildly between her lips. My own cock twitches along as if we're synchronized, my cock emptying into her with long, violent jerks that make stars explode behind my eyelids.

Her throat bobs with a hard swallow, taking every drop Sy had to give her, and I hear a rumble come from Sy's chest as he backs away, the head of his dick flopping from her mouth.

"Such a good, patient, willing girl," I tell her, bending over her to press a kiss to her red cheek. When I pull out to collapse beside her, I leave enough room for Sy in the bed. To my surprise he takes it, flopping onto his back, forearm thrown over his eyes. Her eyes flutter shut, and soon she's asleep between us.

After a few minutes, Sy finally recovers, eyes dropping to her body. His fingers reach out for the tattoo, ghosting over the outline. "A butterfly?" he asks quietly.

"Not exactly," I answer, although Vinny could own a butterfly. Metamorphosis, change, rebirth and all that shit. But this one was inspired by the sight of her holding Leticia's skull. Vinny wants wings, but she's not a bird. She's nocturnal, celestial, an omen of death, for some. I explain, "It's a death's-head moth," and even though he raises a questioning eyebrow, I leave it at that.

No one knows better than Sy that victory tattoos are personal, a depiction of who we are at different phases in our lives. Lavinia may think she's ready for wings, ready for rebirth, but before she can fully transform, she'll have to go through something else first. Grief.

23

Lavinia

NICK WALKS past me while I'm sitting at the kitchen counter, reading an essay on body dysmorphia. It's not homework—or at least not the kind I'll get any academic credit for. I've always been aware that a big part of being Duchess is patching up wounds, stitching the Dukes back together. It's the way it's always been, someone pre-med in the tower to clean up the injuries from the fights. A woman who'll nurture and heal.

As it happens, my Dukes' biggest wounds aren't the kind I can stitch.

I'm absorbed in the material until I see Nick's bare chest crossing my periphery.

I turn just in time to see him enter the bathroom.

It's bizarre living with Nick these days. I was used to being the prisoner he babysat, and then the prisoner he owned. I was just beginning to get comfortable with the thought of living with someone I hate, always aware of his movements, listening, watching.

Ever since that night in the crypt, things are different.

I know it's not just me. He's stopped glaring at the others when they mention taking me somewhere. He doesn't follow me to classes. He watches me while we're home, but it's not with that suffocating, dogged intensity that always vaguely made me feel like I'd never left the Crane Motel. We orbit around each other, and if talking needs to be done, then we do it. Without resentment. Without anger. Without bitterness.

Something is missing, and I'm pretty sure we left it on the Barons' mausoleum steps. He was willing to die for me. I was willing to save him. Whether I like it or not, that means something.

An agreement was made in blood.

I can't stop watching him, tracking his movements, spying on him through the tiny sliver of bathroom door he's left ajar. Leaning back, I see that he's at the sink, a shirtless swath of inked back muscles, peering into the mirror. There's this feeling I get in my chest when he's around. It's complicated and twisty, but it's edged with an odd thrill, as if I've met someone new.

And I don't hate him.

None of that changes the fact that Nick is an insufferable asshole. A *hot* asshole, but still... an asshole. I haven't forgotten who he's been, but I can't deny who he's become.

Closing the textbook, I suddenly hear water running. Not the shower. Definitely the sink. Slowly, I slide off the stool and walk over to the bathroom door. He's studying his face in the mirror, twisting and turning his neck, checking out his beard.

"What are you doing?" I blurt.

He checks his reflection again and tugs at the thick hair. "Shaving this off."

"Oh," I say. "Why?"

"Well," his eyes flick to mine. "I didn't grow it intentionally."

Right. He grew it because he was locked in the cage.

"So it doesn't really feel like me," he continues, running his fingers under the water. The sink is almost full. "It's just a by-product of a situation that I let get out of control." Again, our eyes meet in the mirror. "Obviously it got out of control before the situation at Daniel's house, but… you know what I mean."

I do, except…

"Huh."

He turns. "What?"

Shrugging, I answer, "I don't know. It sounds like maybe, along with the hair on your face, you've had a little emotional growth."

He groans, and it startles me. "You really need to lay off Sy's psych books."

I gawk at him, but don't leave. I don't think I've ever heard Nick groan like that before. Outside of sex. Just because he's annoyed at something. It's so… human. I settle against the door frame. "I figured you were keeping it."

"Why do you care?" he strokes his chin. It's grown to the point where it's soft. I clearly remember from that night in the party room when I kissed him. Suddenly, his eyes dart to mine. "You like it?"

I roll my eyes. "It's a pretty well known fact that beards make a man exponentially more attractive."

His responding smirk is almost enough to make *me* groan. "Then I definitely should shave it. Nick Bruin can't get prettier. Men and women would just start orgasming on sight."

I snort.

He lifts his shoulders. "Just stating the facts, Little Bird. I didn't give myself that nickname."

"No, I'm sure you would have gone for something way more modest."

I watch as he fills his palm with a thick layer of shaving cream, and then dips his razor in the water. His eyebrow raises and our gazes meet in the mirror. "Wait." He pauses, lather inches from his face. "*Do* you like it?"

Like a deer caught in headlights, I freeze, completely unable to answer. I wasn't lying before. Beards on men are universally hot, and it's doing him a lot of favors. Like this, he looks gruff and manly, a touch haggard, like he's someone who's been through a lot. There's an honesty and authenticity to it that Remy's taught me to appreciate in people.

And I sort of hate it.

Part of it is the reminder of how it came to be. I don't regret locking Nick in that cage, but that doesn't mean I'm proud of it. I was shown a part of myself—the viper part—that I'm learning to be careful about embracing. It was a means to an end. An eye for an eye.

The other part of me just misses his face.

It's not like I spent two years around this man and never noticed how attractive he is. Some nights, it was the only bright thing in my life. Looking at him, appreciating the lines of his face and how it'd shift with his smirks. In a world as ugly as ours, it's nice to see something pretty. Nick Bruin is, without a doubt, a piece of art. He's already covered it up with Remy's ink and all that South Side stoicism. The beard is just another layer for him to hide behind.

My cheeks heat as I look away, unable to bear his reaction. "It's better without."

There's a long moment of stillness, and then the rustle of water. "Alright."

When I look back up, Nick is lathering his face. His eyes are fixed attentively to the task in the mirror, but I can see a satisfied glint in his eyes that makes my insides wither in embarrassment. I don't know why I stay, my feet glued to the floor as I look on, but it's possibly because I'm interested in seeing it stripped away, revealing the real Nick Bruin beneath.

When he lifts the razor, there's a twitch in his wrist. He shakes it out, but it makes me straighten, mouth pressing into a grim line. "Is that still… from the shocks?"

"It's nothing," he says, flexing his fist. "It hardly ever happens anymore."

Suddenly I realize why he's kept the beard all this time.

I give a full-bodied sigh, stepping up to snatch the razor. "Turn around and keep your mouth shut."

I'm already regretting it when he obeys, leaning back against the sink, his torso a long, muscled, inked curve as he stares down at me. "You gonna clean me up, Little Bird?"

I scowl, grabbing his chin to wrench it sideways. "Stop calling me that." I make the first sweep with the razor down his cheek, leaning around him to dunk it into the water.

"Little Moth doesn't have the same ring to it," he answers, gaze dropping to my chest. "Although, I think I get it. Papery wings. Drawn to bright flames. Nocturnal." His eyes spark and he smiles with the half of his mouth that won't pull at the cheek I'm shaving. "Remember when you used to stay up all night? Back at the motel?" I hum noncommittally, dragging the razor over his jaw. "I had a hell of a time finding places to get you food from. Everything that was worth half a shit closed at eleven, so I used to drive farther and farther out to find you something new."

I frown, half in concentration, half in memory. Some of the first things they took out of my room were the microwave and fridge. "How thoughtful of you. *Stop* looking at my tits." I give his chin a flick and he finally raises it.

"Candy and soda were easy," he murmurs, throat shifting beneath the razor. "Lots of twenty-four-hour gas stations."

Pausing, I dip the razor and say, "I know what you're doing, Nick." I was probably the first person he ever had to really take care of. The first person he had to feed. The first woman he ever had to buy tampons for. The first victim he ever had to make sure stayed alive. "You did your best for me back then. *Mostly*." I give him a significant look, remembering last Christmas. "I get it. That doesn't make you a hero."

He blinks, blue eyes dark in the anemic light of the bathroom. "I know that."

"But," I add, dipping down to get beneath his chin, "thank you."

I'm getting better at that.

Thanking him.

I shake it off of me like something sad and nettled, dipping the razor to start on his other side. When his hand settles on my hip, I don't even flinch, the motion feeling so casual and contained that it lacks urgency.

And then he says, "What would you say if I told you I wanted to kiss you?"

I drag the razor down, feeling the texture of the hair as I sever it. "I'd say I have a razor blade to your throat," I mutter, focused on the task. "So tread carefully."

"I'd let you cut me," Nick says. In a moment of whiplash, he adds. "You shouldn't have shown Remy the skull."

I raise my eyes to his, trying to find the connection there. There was a moment with Remy where I considered deflecting, but it didn't last particularly long. "I need to be honest with him. As honest as I can be. He understands."

Nick hums, moving so I can get his other cheek. "He didn't have anything to say about it? A memory?"

"Nothing." Bitterly, I remember the words that spilled from his mouth when he saw Leticia's skull. "He said she was beautiful."

Nick watches me, those blue eyes searching, plundering, calculating. Eventually, he snorts. "You're jealous? Of a skull."

"Am not."

"You can't bullshit me, Little Bird. I'm a younger sibling, too." His thumb moves on my hip, a gentle, soothing gesture, and when he speaks, it's in a quiet timbre. "She could never have held a fucking candle to you."

The razor stops and I try—I really do—not to look into his eyes. But I fail. It doesn't mean so much. Nick never knew in her life and isn't the kind of guy who'd appreciate her in death. Nevertheless, it settles something inside of me to hear it. Never before has anyone preferred me over Leticia Lucia.

Clearing my throat, I get back to business, trying to shake it off. "A candle was never the kind of fire I was worried about."

Nick's thumb keeps moving, a slow circuit against my hip. "So you knew, then? About Lionel's stockpile."

"Of course I knew." I dunk the razor once more, returning to his sideburn. "Leticia knew." Suddenly, I wonder, "How do *you* know? I doubt even the Counts do. Maybe Perez."

He hums deep in his throat. "I have my ways. It does make me wonder if she—"

I know when the words cut off, Nick's thumb going still, that he's holding something back for my sake. Annoyed, I tell him, "You can say it."

I already know, anyway.

"Leticia probably was the target," he says, eyes sliding away as I turn his head. "Tate was too clean, too inconsequential, and if what the Baron King told us was right—if we're fighting outside of our weight class..."

"Then this is King shit." I nod, having already worked that out. "And Tate and Remy were probably just collateral damage."

"Exactly."

I can tell his mind is working in overdrive when he doesn't try to sneak a glimpse of my tits as I dip the razor again. "You want to know who her enemies were, don't you?"

His thumb begins moving against me again. "None are as obvious as you."

"I didn't—"

Nick rolls his eyes. "I know. I'm just saying. Who could hate Leticia as much as you did?"

"No one." I scoff, moving toward his mouth. "Not possible."

In a careful murmur, lips tucked in for me, he asks, "Could your dad have done it?"

Leticia's been gone for more than two years. Of course I'd considered this. "The thing you have to understand about my father is that he treasures an investment. Leticia was his biggest. He molded her, shaped her into what he needed her to be." Sighing, I lean closer, careful around his philtrum. "It's why Perez is still in line for his Kingship. It's not that he's the best, or the smartest, or the strongest. It's that my dad's already invested in him."

"And Perez needed her," he gives me a significant look, "or *you*, to cement his position, so it probably wasn't him."

I agree. "Perez isn't smart enough to hide all this. He's good at taking people. Abducting them. Hiding them. But covering up a double murder?" Shaking my head, I give the corner of his mouth a slow swipe of the blade.

"Remy ran," he says, eyes going distant. "He wouldn't have run from some peon like Perez."

"Especially after watching his friend get murdered," I wager.

Nick grows quiet as I finish up, scanning every inch of his face for anything I've missed. When I grab the towel, using it to clean away the shaving cream and revealing the skin beneath, I step back, gesturing to the mirror.

"Well?"

He seems to snap out of some deep, dark hole in his mind, twisting to look at his reflection. Raising a hand, he rubs over the angle of his jaw. "You tell me," he says, meeting my gaze through the mirror. "You like it like this?"

I shift uncomfortably. "I don't see why my opinion should matter."

He dips his chin, fixing me with a dark look. "Little Bird, your opinion is the only one that matters."

I feel the blood rush to my face, not comprehending how he can just say things like that. I know he wants me. Nick is the least subtle man I know when it comes to wanting my attention. It's just the bluntness of it. The lack of fear. The complete absence of shame.

"My opinion?" I toss the towel at him, trying to play off the tension. "Your face is the only good thing about you."

He catches the towel, eyes flashing in delight. Bouncing a finger at me, he says, "See, I know you're telling yourself that's an insult, but we both know it's a compliment."

Turning on my heel, I stride out of the bathroom with fiery cheeks.

With enough lube, I've learned that getting them off is easy. Sometimes it's hard work and my hands are killing me by the time it's finished, but I won't deny there's a strange satisfaction when it finally breaks free, loose, and slippery.

"Gotcha," I say, grinning down at the collection of clock pieces. It took me a few days, but I finally got the whole section apart. I just need to sand, clean and oil it, then put it back together.

I gather the brass pieces in my hands and carry them back down to the loft, where I left my cleaning supplies.

"Take that, fuckface." Nick's voice carries up from the living room. "Twenty. Beat that."

"The only thing you're beating is your dick," Remy says, "at night, in your room, *alone*."

Sy's soft laugh carries up to me. "Burn. Good one, Rem."

The sound of palms slapping echoes off the high ceilings. I roll my eyes, determined to ignore it.

"What are you laughing at?" Nick asks, voice breathless. "You only got to seventeen."

"I have twenty pounds of muscle mass on you, little brother," Sy replies. "Which just means I'm lifting that much more weight than you."

I finish sorting the hardware, and as a reward, allow myself a peek downstairs. They're standing around the pull-up bar installed between two beams, which I've been using off and on as a makeshift clothesline. The three of them are in various stages of undress. Nick and Remy are shirtless—as always. Sy has on a T-shirt with the sleeves ripped off and the neck cut out. I've learned pull-up contests, along with push-ups, sit-ups, and how fast one can run a mile, are a common occurrence between the guys. I knew they were competitive, it's their whole thing, but now that they're all getting along better it's reached a new level. I never know when a spontaneous contest is going to happen, but so far, it's been at the gym, passing an empty playground, and once in the parking lot on campus.

This morning, they competed over who finished breakfast first.

Boys.

"He's got you there. Sy is one swole motherfucker." Remy has his hair pulled back out of his face with one of my elastic ties, and I think I might like it—the unobstructed sight of his green eyes as his grin spreads. "Although if I was working off that much sexual tension, I'd probably be ripped, too."

Sy's easy grin snaps away, leaving a scowl. "Shut up."

"Nah," Nick says, frowning at his brother's obscene muscles, "I'm man enough to admit that the only extra weight you have on me is your cock."

"I said shut up," Sy repeats, slamming his fist into Nick's bicep. If it hurts, Nick doesn't show it, just giving his brother a mocking smirk.

"Huh." Remy's forehead creases pensively. "Do you think a cock weighs more when it's hard, or is it the same amount when it's soft?"

"What the fuck are you talking about?" Nick asks, taking a swing at Sy but missing when he darts out of the way.

"Cocks," Remy stresses, eyebrows lifting. "Isn't that what we were just talking about?"

"My dick weighs the same all the time," Sy says, arms crossing over his chest.

"How do you know?" Nick asks, dropping his fighting stance. "Have ycu weighed it?"

Sy's head jerks back. "What? No."

"Oh my god," Remy adds, laughing. "You have. Hey, no judgment here. You would all fucking shudder to think the experiments I'd do on my cock if it looked like yours."

The tips of Sy's ear turn a sudden glowing red. "No, I haven't fucking weighed it! I just know."

"There's a way to solve this, you know," Remy offers, gesturing toward the kitchen. "We have a food scale."

"Fuck, no!" Sy insists. "We are *not* weighing dicks."

"Why? Afraid you won't live up to the hype?" God, Nick is amazing at trash talk, but he's even better at goading his brother.

"Or maybe you're just too afraid of comparing and realizing that your dick isn't as big of a fucking deal as you think it is."

"Jesus Christ, I'm not doing—"

Something clicks in my head.

"Wait!" I shout, hopping up. This is the opportunity I've been waiting for. "I think Nick's right."

Three pairs of eyes swing to me.

"Of course you do, Little Bird. I'm always right." Nick grins smugly as I walk down the stairs, Archie at my feet. "But what am I right about this time? Exactly."

"That Sy's dick isn't that big of a deal." I walk over to them and get hit by their warm, sweaty scent. "And he shouldn't be ashamed of being different, because everyone is different."

Sy spins and levels me with a hard look. "Are you seriously suggesting I pull out my cock and weigh it on a kitchen scale to prove some feel-good, body image bullshit?"

"God, no." I hold up my hands. "Please do not put your dicks on the kitchen scale. I use that to weigh out my smoothie powder." Carefully, I suggest, "But maybe it's time we destigmatized Sy's difference."

"Have you been reading my psych books again?" he asks, advancing on me with curled fists. "I told you to fucking stop!"

This is dangerous territory. For one, I'm not actually a psych major, and even if I were, it's not like I'd be qualified to diagnose anything. But every night I go to bed with Sy. Every night I slide between his sheets. Every night I touch him, hand shifting under his blankets as he digs his head back into the pillow. He's gotten better at kissing me before and during, even if they usually do come upon me abruptly, like he's remembering something he's forgotten. And the kisses... they're electric, energized, charged with the same tension I feel beneath my palm when I stroke him into a shuddering mess.

But we've just hit this wall.

He'll almost never let me look at it, during.

Slowly, I start, "Penile dysmorphic disorder is—"

Laughter bursts from Remy and Nick's mouths, try as they might to push it down, and Sy erupts with a loud, "No!"

Annoyed, I cross my arms. "You have a fucking issue, Sy!"

"And it won't stop reading my goddamn textbooks!" Sy turns on his heel and storms toward his room.

I hold my hand up to Remy and Nick, indicating I want them to wait for a second and follow him. When I get to his room, he's tearing off his shirt, muscles rippling beneath his warm, tawny skin.

I keep my voice low, soft. "Sy."

"I'm not doing this." He rummages through his drawer, looking for a clean shirt. His back muscles ripple, making the tribal tattoo move in sync. "I'm not going to be put on display in front of those asshats just so they can make fun of me."

"No one is making fun of you." He gives me a hard look. "Okay, well, they're always going to mess with you, that's just how you are together, but I really think they'd want to help if they knew how."

"Talking about my freak of a dick isn't going to help." He slams the dresser drawer shut. "Where do you think this came from, Lavinia? You think it just sprung up out of thin air? I'm sick of people talking about it!"

"They've already seen it."

"Not like—" He lowers his voice, hissing, "Not like *that*."

Exhaling a measured breath, I say, "Your hangups with this are holding you back, and you know it as well as I do. I'm not saying you should be swinging it around all the time. I'm just saying you shouldn't hate it, and this could be a way to make you see that it's not so bad." When all he does is plant his palms on the dresser, fuming, I decide to try a different tack. "Please?" I step behind him and rest a hand on his hip, watching the touch crest through his muscles. "I'll make it worth your while," I add, breathing against his tattoo. Dirty tactics, for sure. "And you won't look stupid. I'll make sure of it."

He turns, eyebrow raised. "Really."

The skepticism in his voice borders on derision, but I still say, "I promise."

Sy has this thing about image that's annoying but pretty normal. He wants everyone to know he's the best. At school, at fighting.

At sex.

I know he relents when he huffs, this big exhalation that makes his shoulders contract. "Goddamn it."

I grab his hand, pulling a very reluctant Duke back to the common room. Nick sits on one end of the couch, while Remy leans against the other, teasing Archie with a string.

"Sit," I tell Sy, pointing to the middle seat. He squeezes in between them, and I face them from the opposite side of the coffee table.

"What's the plan, Little Bird?" Nick cups his crotch. "Need me to show Sy how a confident man regards his cock?"

Fucking obnoxious asshole.

But... "Honestly, that's exactly what I want you to do—"

Before I get the entire sentence out, Nick stands, pushing his shorts and then boxers over his hips. "Like this?"

I spend way too long gaping at it, staring at the trail of hair, the flaccid cock, the tattooed knuckles covering his balls when he cups them in a palm. "Yes." I swallow, dragging my eyes away from his body. "Just like that."

I've been living with three guys for a while now, and I've been at the gym enough to have some pretty serious dick-flashing under my belt. Sometimes I wonder if this is just what living with guys is like, or if it's a West End thing.

Nick kicks off his shorts and Remy, apparently not ready to be outdone, rises. "Vinny, your boy is an artist. A few classes on the human form, and you get used to dicks being in your face for hours."

"What about tits?" Nick asks, voice completely serious. "And pussy?"

Remy sniffs. "Nah. I mean, we all pretend we're cool with it, but I had a half-chub the whole time." He gives me a cocky grin and thumbs at the button on his jeans. "Thank god you're not the model in my class, Vin. I wouldn't have been able to make it."

"Thanks?" I say, staring at the golden hair and tattoos that travel under his belly button to the darker thatch above his cock. It swings casually between his legs as he steps out of his pant legs.

They're both standing, their dicks at Sy's eye level. He looks like he's about to explode, but I catch his eye and give him a small nod. "Your turn."

"I know."

He doesn't move.

"Don't be ashamed."

"I'm not!"

Yet still, no movement. Not an inch. I raise an eyebrow, and finally he grunts, quickly standing and yanking down his joggers. His cock springs out, and yeah, okay. Seeing it like this, next to the others, the difference is noticeable. Even unaroused he's got a few inches on the others and some girth, to boot.

"Stop looking," he hisses to the room and sits back down. Remy and Nick do the same.

"So, I think the best way to handle this," I start, walking around the table. Archie darts between my feet and I look down, trying not to trip. When I glance up again, the three of them are watching me closely. My eyes dart down and I freeze. "What the fuck?" I look away for five seconds and all three of them have grown at least twice the size as before. I eye the cocks pointed at me like three missiles locked and loaded.

"Stop acting surprised that you get us hard," Nick says, threading his fingers behind his head, putting everything on display. "And if we're going to compare, Sy may be the biggest, but I think I'm the hardest."

"I've got this wicked curve," Remy says, running his narrow fingers down his length. "Hits all the right spots, doesn't it, Vinny?"

"I, uh..." Fuck. This may be harder—*more difficult* than I thought. "The whole point is that we're *not* comparing." My face feels as hot as Sy's ears look. "You should say something nice about Sy's dick."

Remy takes this easily in stride. "Well, it's fucking enormous."

Sy covers his eyes with his hands. "Jesus Christ."

"Okay." I gesture to Remy. "But that's not really a compliment. It's an observation."

Remy frowns. "To a guy, that's a compliment."

Sighing, I ask, "Anything else?"

Remy seems to really give this thought, glancing down into Sy's lap. "I mean... look, it's a magnificent dick. I don't know why he's so wound up about it. If I had a dick like that, I'd be naked twenty-four-seven showing that thing off."

Nick snorts. "You already do that."

Remy's still staring, head tilted in consideration. "Is your dad hung like that? Because goddamn, your mom must—"

"*Actually*," Nick cuts in, scowling, "he gets it from my mom's side. Which is kind of unfair, if you ask me." To me, he adds, "Not that my dick isn't 'magnificent', too."

I ignore his wink. "There, see? That's a compliment. I bet all kinds of guys wish they had your dick. You should be proud of it."

Sy grinds out, "Yeah, I'll be marching in a parade any day now."

"Nick," I prompt, giving him a look. "Tell him. It's not *bad*, right?"

Nick leans back into the couch, knees spread, balls heavy between his thighs. "You're wasting your breath. Our mom is literally a fucking pro at making men feel great about their dicks, and this one is like a brick wall."

Leveling me with a look, Remy puts his hand on his cock, adding, "You know, if anything, you should be making Nick and I feel better about our pork swords. You're touching Sy's on a nightly basis. Nick and I settle for scraps."

Nick looks away and very pointedly doesn't say anything. He shouldn't. I've never touched his cock outside of coercion, bribery, extortion, or outright force.

Squeezing his shaft, Remy goes on, "Sy keeps bitching about

girls not being down to get impaled on that thing, but here's the truth. He's the only one out of the three of us who's never had his masculinity called into question on the basis of dick size. That's, like, kinda privilege if you think about—*ow*, you shitheel! Don't slap me when I have my dick out!"

Sy, who looks one sideways comment from slapping Remy upside the head a second time, says to me, "Are we done yet?"

But Nick barrels over him. "Everyone knows it's not the size that dictates your manliness, anyway." I know the second I see that sharp glint in his eye that the following words are going to annoy the shit out of me. I'm not wrong. "It's how long you can last. And I can definitely last longer than you two."

"You wish," Remy bursts, clearly outraged. "Foreplay is my thing. Bring it."

I look at Sy, and he's staring down at his hands. The hands that are covering his dick—or some of it. His hands are huge, but... well, his dick is bigger.

Now that I think about it, Nick might be a genius. Sy's gotten really good at holding his orgasm back—not that they'd know—and this might be just the thing to inspire some confidence. Outlasting them.

Winning.

"You in, man?" Nick asks Sy. "Or are you afraid..."

"I'm not afraid," he snaps back. "That's just the dumbest fucking challenge since that time Remy dared us to hang under the railroad trestle while the train was passing."

"Wait—you *what*?" I hold up my hands. "On second thought, I don't even want to know." Exhaling, I drop to the couch opposite them, tilting my head as I watch Sy. "I think you should."

His lip pulls up in bafflement. "You want us to jack off together?"

"'Want' is a really strong word," I say, and it's difficult to make eye contact with them instead of staring at their crotches, but I think I do a passable job. "Just... consider it a lesson. Or a test."

"A test." Sy's eyes perk up. A test, of course, is another version of a challenge. God. These Dukes.

"A test where, regardless of how well you do, you get an orgasm at the end." Since they all look willing, but not exactly enthused, I add, "And in the spirit of competition, why don't I sweeten the pot?" At once, their eyes all fly to mine, interest piqued. "I'll go to bed every night this week with whoever lasts longest."

The muscle at the back of Sy's jaw pulses, and I'm afraid this is pushing him too far. Sy is going to fucking kill himself trying to outlast the other two, but this is what he needs. Something to *win*. I just know it.

"So..." Sy's eyes narrow. "How does this work? Are you going to... use your hand, or—"

"No!" I burst, eyes narrowed. "You're going to use your own hands!"

"The rules need to be very clear," Nick says, his cock already giving an excited twitch. "Things tend to go sideways when they aren't established up front."

Remy nods. "No one wants jizz going sideways, Vinny."

"The rules are that you jerk off," I say, settling in. Since these are bears and I'm the viper, I very clearly see all the ways in which this can be manipulated. "And you have to jerk off. No stalling. Your hands have to move faster than you blink. If your free hand isn't on your dick, it needs to be at your side. No pinching to distract yourself."

"Fine." Nick manspreads, fisting his cock nice and slow, wrist twisting at the tip. Remy follows him, looking just as relaxed as he leans his head back, staring at me through his blond fan of eyelashes. Sy, however, is sandwiched between them with a surly expression, giving his dick a slow, short stroke.

The problem here isn't balancing my premature ejaculator with the other two.

It's Nick.

In no universe am I ready to sleep in his bed, let alone do

anything else in it. Maybe we've reached a point in our relationship where I don't want him dead, but that's hardly naked cuddling territory, and from the dark, heavy-lidded way he watches me as he lazily fists his cock, that's exactly the kind of thing he'd be looking for.

So I guess I'll need to work things in Sy's favor.

I did promise, didn't I?

I unzip my hoodie, revealing the tight, thin tank I wore to bed last night. The cool air hits my skin, eliciting a shiver. I ignore it, tossing the hoodie aside to cross my arms, pushing my tits together.

Nick's eyes jump right to my chest, fist going still. "You're not wearing a bra."

"No."

"That's not fair."

I shrug. "You're blinking. Better get that hand moving."

Remy leans into the corner of the couch and lifts his chin. "Let's see that tattoo."

Slowly, I drag my fingertips over the moth, just above my breasts. We had a second session last night, and it's still tender, so I tug the collar of the tank down carefully, far enough to expose the tattoo, and coincidentally, the top swell of my tits.

Remy grins and picks up his pace, sliding his hand down his length. I watch him expand, thickening in his palm, and feel heat burn between my legs. Remy wasn't kidding before. His cock does hit all the right places, and it's impossible to look at him, miles and miles of tattooed, wiry flesh, and not imagine the way he'd feel beneath me if I went to straddle him right now.

"She's playing you," Nick says, seemingly unaffected by my cleavage.

Except the fact his cock gives a sudden surge of pre-cum.

I tug my top a little lower, and Nick visibly bites down on a shudder, his blue eyes locked to the skin. Beside him, his brother is doing the same. Staring. Tongue sweeping a wet circuit over his bottom lip. Cock weeping with thin, sticky fluid.

"Play me all you want, Vin. I don't give a shit." Remy, on the other hand, doesn't even try to hide his excitement. "Play with yourself, too. I don't know about these two, but I can take it."

Nick shoots him a sudden, hot glare. "Shut the fuck up!"

Remy grins, wide and loose. "That's my girl."

The tank top comes off easily, sliding over my heavy breasts, and I watch, enraptured, as Nick's chest caves with an exhale that doesn't seem to end.

He rakes his lip through his teeth, groaning. "Fuck, that's so dirty, Little Bird."

It'd be a lie to say some of the tingling between my legs wasn't due to the power of it. The way Remy begins sweating, thighs flexing up into his fist as I skate my fingertips over the swell of my breast. How Nick is so tense that the tendons in his arm barely shift as his hands work his cock, eyes watching me pinch a nipple. That Sy—this bulging bear of a fighter—can look so lost and desperate as my thighs slowly part.

Their gazes on me, a vast vista of green and blue, are so tangible that I swear I can feel them caress me with their minds.

I lean my head back, mouth parted as I massage my breasts. "Come on, Nick..."

His jaw clenches, the apples of his cheek blotched with red. "Don't—don't—don't fucking talk to me." The ember in my belly flares into an instant inferno, because he never said please, but this?

This is begging.

I wet my lips, spread my thighs, and raise my hips. "Don't you want to come for me, Nick? Right here?" I run a fingernail down the valley between my breasts, writhing, and Nick's face flashes with something akin to rapture. "Don't you want to cover me? Don't you want to make me taste—"

"Goddamnit!" he growls, shooting upright just as his cock begins pulsing, thick ribbons of cum spilling over his fist. "Fuck!"

Remy snorts a laugh. "Shit, dude, you never had a chance. You've been backed up for weeks. Don't even try to lie."

Nick falls back onto the couch, breathless as he scowls at me.

"Whatever. One day, you're going to come to bed with me, and it's not going to be because I beat these two fucknuggets in some stupid-ass game."

I give him a bland, humorless smile. "Keep dreaming." Then I turn my gaze on Remy, who's still looking all loose and smoldering. This is going to be a problem. I doubt Remy's ever had a quick jerk in his life. He's the sort of guy who'd indulge in it. Take his time. Draw it out.

Leaning back, I push my fingers into my mouth, swirling my tongue around them and pull them back out, slick and wet.

"What are you doing with those, Vin?" Remy asks, licking his lips.

"You're the one that said I should play with myself," I tell him, spreading my legs and shifting aside my panties. "Just giving you what you asked for."

My first touch hits like a flame being lit. I got pretty good at taking care of my own needs in those tiny hotel rooms, and unlike these boys, I thought I had a certain level of control over my body. Until I see the three of them... Nick's chest heaving, his hands sticky with his own cum. Remy's eyes laser focused, darting between my tits and pussy, and Sy... well, for once he doesn't look tense and pissed off, but I do recognize the expression. It's the same one he has before any competition. He's here to win.

That's my Duke.

Always a victor.

Rubbing my fingers over my folds, I raise my gaze to Remy's. "You remember the first time you used me as a canvas?"

His eyes wander over my skin. "I'll never forget."

"You got me off, too."

"You did *what*?" Nick shouts. "When did this happen?"

Remy's lips twitch, and I push one finger inside, then another. My fingers are small, nothing like their cocks, and for a second I almost cave, considering telling Remy to flatten me on the table and get this over with.

"I fucked her with my marker. The thick one." He shrugs. "I just needed to see what our girl could take."

Nick leans forward, elbows on his knees. "She liked it, didn't she?"

"He made it good for me," I confess. Remy always makes it good for me. Like right now, our eyes hold, and I watch his Adam's apple bob in his throat. I can tell by the way his forearm tenses and the tremor in his abs that he's a lot closer than he's giving away.

He turns his head to Sy and studies him for a moment, then says, "You gonna cave?"

"Nope," Sy replies with a tense shake of the head.

"Okay." He lifts his chin at me. "Gimme a taste of those pretty fingers, and I'll get this over with."

I look over at Sy to see what he thinks. It's not exactly a violation of any of the rules. He gives the slightest nod, and I pull my fingers out of my throbbing pussy and lean forward. Remy meets me halfway, his hand furiously jerking his cock, tip blistering red. He grabs my outstretched hand and shoves my fingers in his mouth, groaning around them as he sucks away the taste of me. It only lasts a few seconds before he jolts back, sinking into the couch with a deep, gritted whine. His brows crush together as his cock pulses with the first wave of cum, dribbling down his knuckles.

"Fuck, Vinny." Breathlessly, he wrings the last of his orgasm from his shaft, squeezing. "Nectar of the fucking gods—"

A growl rips through the room, followed by Sy's release. His thighs flex, pushing his hips into his fist as he erupts, eyes locked onto the head of his cock as it surges cum onto his fist, his thighs, his belly. "Son of a bitch," he mutters, assessing the mess. He looks between his friends. "I won, right?" He made it, barely, but the small, vicious grin on his mouth tells me that's enough.

Nick rolls his eyes. "I guess so."

"Good job, bro," Remy says, holding up his hand for a high-five.

Sy ducks away, glaring at the cum dripping from Remy's hand.

"Oh, right," Remy says, giving his palm a frown. "Not to be picky or anything, but is there a prize for second place?"

"You sucked her fingers!" Nick shouts, throwing his hands wide. "That's your consolation prize."

"*That* was a negotiation."

I feel the argument ramping up, which hardly seems fair. All three of them got orgasms, and I'm sitting here fucking *burning* with need, clit throbbing. "Stop!" I bark, and the words are out of my mouth before I really have a chance to consider them. "Everyone gets a prize."

They do?

I do.

"For being good sports," I elaborate, my eyes glued to their cocks. I'm not sure when the sight of a dick became appealing to me. Last month, I was thinking about how weird they are, and now I'm practically vibrating with the urge to feel one.

"Yeah?" Remy asks. "Like what?"

"Like this."

Sy's the first one I go to, rounding the coffee table to drop to my knees between his legs. I look up into stunned blue eyes, his mouth parted in surprise when I reach for him. He's still thick and hot, not quite flaccid, cum running down the shaft.

I should probably look him in the eye when I guide him to my mouth. Guys like that. Sexy. Sultry. Instead, I get lost in the curiosity of it, sliding my lips over the swollen head and tasting the slickness. It's not the first or even second time I've had him in my mouth, but it's the first time I savor it, thighs pressing together as I work my tongue against his head. Sy hisses, his hand coming to rest on my scalp—not pushing, just touching—and when his hips jerk upward, I get the sense it's involuntary.

"Christ, Vinny," Remy breathes, his voice dropping an octave. "You look so good when you have that thing in your mouth."

It's not a blow job, though. It's just a taste, and when I ease away, Sy is gaping at me openly. "Good job, big bear," I say, feeling my cheeks flame as I turn to the man at his side.

Remy's sprawled back in the corner of the couch, cock resting in a pool of cum against his inner thigh. When I move between his legs, he spreads them, head leaned back on the cushions as his eyes flash excitedly. He's the one to grab his cock—impatient, greedy—sweeping it over the pool of cum on his thigh before guiding my mouth to it, palm warm against my neck.

"That's our good girl," he rumbles as I sink down, taking it into my mouth. He twitches in my mouth, his dick making an attempt at surging back to life. I'm almost tempted to draw him out, build him up again to feel the hardness of it.

Almost, but that's not what this is about.

I lick Remy clean, lingering on the tip, and he shudders, legs seizing like he's being electrocuted. Oversensitive, probably.

Reluctantly, I release him.

One prize left.

The one I'm dreading.

Nick watches me intensely as I pass his brother to approach him, my stomach doing flips. I could deny him, turn away and let the three of them bicker about the way things are—two of them being my Dukes while the other is just a glorified guard dog.

But I don't.

I settle on my knees before him, wary but resolved as I look into his blazing blue eyes. His cock, flaccid a moment ago, is already thick and ready. He wants this. He wants *me*. That's never been put into question. Maybe that's part of the problem. It's both the most and least attractive thing about him, and I'm completely at a loss to reconcile it. It's thrilling to be wanted so completely, but dangerous, just like that day in the crypt. Nick is the human equivalent of a partially loaded revolver pointed at my temple, and every rejection is a pull of the trigger. If I wasn't made to be loved, then I definitely wasn't made to give it back.

He loves me so much—how can I ever return that kind of affection?

One kiss at a time, maybe.

"It won't bite, Little Bird," he says quietly, and I realize I've been staring at his cock while lost in my thoughts.

His words are light, joking, but there's a tight coil of tension running through his muscles. Everything is hard. His abs, his biceps, his shoulders, his jaw...

Everything except his eyes.

There's a softness there I'm not used to seeing, something cautious and already defeated, as if he's expecting me to turn away.

I hold his gaze when I reach for him, so I see the way his expression collapses when I wrap my fingers around his cock. His forehead pinches in rapture, jaw going slack as he tracks the way I pitch forward, bringing him to my mouth.

I kiss it.

It's wet and slow, my lips pressed to the soft flesh like it's another mouth, tongue swirling out to catch the slickness of his release, finding it salty and still warm.

"Fucking hell, Little Bird," he breathes, voice full of awe as he reaches out, sweeping the pad of his thumb against the corner of my mouth. His eyes are zeroed in on the place where we meet, the head of his cock snug between my lips, and I think I see something in him break to have this: me, touching his cock, through no machinations, no manipulations.

Just because I want to.

A strong surge of precum meets my tongue, and I kiss it away, taking it into myself. It's gentle, sincere, and I can tell he understands that it's the best I can give him. At least for now.

I pull away, and his fingertips drag across my face, skating over the stickiness of him on my lips. His eyes hold something steady and assured, and when he lets me go without the demand for more, I see it for what it is.

A promise.

24

Lavinia

THERE'S nothing college students hate more than the person who has a million questions and makes the professor run over time.

Turns out, I'm that person.

"Ms. Lucia," the professor says as he packs up his belongings. "Unfortunately, I have a meeting in ten minutes across campus, but if you need more assistance, you should consider joining a study group."

"Right. I'm not struggling or anything." I hesitate and avoid the glares of my classmates as they exit the room. "I just find the subject interesting, and I was wondering if you have any suggestions for additional reading?"

He pauses, sliding me a surprised look. "Well, I wish the rest of the class had your enthusiasm," he says, before shooting out a list of books and essays. I've already read most of them, but some of them are new and sound intriguing, so I thank him again, hike my bag over my shoulder, and head into the hallway. It's hard to articulate what I'm looking for. I doubt anyone can understand what it's like to be alone for all those years with limited mental stimulation.

Now that I can talk to people, read anything I want, or search for information on the internet?

It's awesome.

And sometimes overwhelming.

Not the content. That's great. It's the people. There are so many of them. Loud sorority girls and physically erratic boys. They jostle and joke and bang around, and there was a time that kind of thing wouldn't bother me, but I can barely remember it. It's taken me a few weeks to pinpoint it—what makes me feel so uneasy being out in the open like this. I'm always dogged by this low-level, nagging anxiety that I'm not where I should be. That I should be running away from something. That I'm not meant to be here, in a physical sense. I'm just not used to the freedom.

The thought causes me to run my finger down the back of my ear, where I know the tracker is embedded. Okay, maybe *freedom* isn't the right word.

But the guys trust me now. Probably too much, considering what I did to Nick—not that they know—but they let me walk around campus like this. Alone. Which is more than I can say for the current Princess, who may as well have a leash around her neck.

I gawk at the Princes as I pass. Somehow, they each have a hand on her, one with an arm around her shoulder, another with a hand tucked into her back pocket, and another in front of her, pulling her by the wrist. She must be pregnant already. There's no one more possessive and needy than a Prince who's expecting a little fuckling.

"Shit!" The guy in front of me drops his backpack. Pens and pencils fall out of the pocket and scatter noisily across the floor. I step aside, trying not to run into them, but eyes have turned to the ruckus, people glancing over their shoulders to see what's happened. It would probably be a good look, as Duchess, if I just—

"Let me help," I sigh. From what I've seen, the general populace of Forsyth University doesn't have a very high opinion of the Royalty. Sure, they're afraid of us. They fall in line rather than fight back. They covet our positions. But ruling through fear has its limits, and no one knows that better than me. If I'm going to be Duchess, then I want people to know the West End isn't like the North.

So I kneel to pick up a pen that's rolled behind a pillar, flashing the guy a tight grin. I reach for it, bent over and straining, which is when a pair of shoes comes into view.

Snakeskin boots.

My heart sinks.

I'm still on my knees, but I lurch back, scurrying to get back into the main hall. The closest I get is a messy collision into a hard body, hands clenching painfully around my upper arms.

"Hey!" A palm is clamped over my mouth midway through my scream, trapping it inside my throat. That doesn't mean I don't fight, legs kicking out on instinct. It's embarrassing, really, how everything Sy has taught me flies right out the window in favor of old habits. Kick, scream, thrash, bite, scratch. These are the wild flails of panic. Of *anger*.

Sy's words ring in my head.

"You let anger take the wheel, you're going to crash."

I force my flailing limbs to go still just as a door opens, the man behind me hauling me inside. It's a storage closet, light dim, the scent of disinfectant almost knocking me over. Four walls, closing in, a confined space.

But I try to push down the panic. The feeling of suffocation. The rapid pounding of my heart. The instinct to kick and scream and throw myself at the nearest immovable object.

I breathe.

Just like Sy taught me.

The man holding me shoves me off, sending me smacking straight into another body.

Perez's body.

"Oh, hell no." I spin, trying to get past the Count blocking me in—Lars—but I already know it's pointless. Perez is a bit of a soft little shit, but his other Counts are athletes, ripped and brutal.

Still, I'm about to find the sweet spot between his legs like Sy showed me when Perez yanks me back and sneers, "Chill the fuck out. We need to have a little talk, *Duchess*."

"Are you fucking kidding me?" I ask, gaze pinging between them, hyper-aware of their every twitch, my joints aching with the restraint not to fight.

Perez nods at Lars to leave the closet. "Guard the door."

The second Lars is gone, I whirl on Perez, snarling, "If you wanted to meet, you should have just sent me a text like a normal person. We could get coffee and have a chat." My snark probably isn't as convincing as it could be, considering it's spoken in a breathless voice, wide eyes scanning the walls.

Perez, who's bouncing a padlock—up and down, up and down—smirks. "Oh, they let you have a phone now?"

I inch toward the door, muscles coiled. "Yes, but I'm sure it has a GPS tracker in it, so the clock is ticking." I cross my arms over my chest, trying to look tough instead of terrified, because I won't give Perez the satisfaction of assuming it's for him. "Are you delivering a message from my father? If so, you can tell him to fuck off."

"Your father didn't send me," he says, eyeing me with those dark, beady snake eyes. "Pretty sure he's written you off as a lost cause altogether. About damn time, if you ask me. I was getting sick of pretending you were worth the effort. You see..." He snaps his wrist, tossing the padlock from one hand to another. It takes me a moment in all the panic to notice it for what it is.

The padlock from the cedar chest at my father's house.

Perez smirks when my eyes home in on it. "Your sister is a prize. Sexy, smart, powerful. I used to lay some of my junksluts out and pretend they were Leticia as I fucked them. But you?" His eyes crawl down my body, lip curling. "You've got the body, but let's face it. You're second best, and Bruno Perez doesn't settle."

"Well, good luck getting your prize," I grind out, annoyed that his words have found purchase, stinging at a wound deep inside. "Since she's dead and all."

He snatches the padlock out of the air, pausing with narrowed eyes. "So you're finally admitting it. You killed her."

I shake my head. "Not me."

"I bet you did," he sneers, fisting the padlock. "You always were jealous of her, pissed off that she got all the attention."

I scoff, inching back. "You want to be my father's son so bad that you've deluded yourself into thinking you know about our family. You've seen exactly what he wants you to see and nothing more."

Unbothered by this, Perez shrugs. "I'll tell you what I do know about. His business. *Our* business."

My shoulder brushes a shelf and I bite down a gasp, the walls feeling too close. "Christ, would you just cut to the chase?"

"Word got back to me that you're interfering with transactions between my dealers and their customers." He looks down at his hand—the one missing the finger Nick cut off—and his face hardens. "I can put up with a lot of shit, Lavinia, but not that."

"What are you talking—" But then it hits me. Cash. I told him to leave Remy alone, twice.

Perez's eyes flash with barely controlled anger. "See... it was one thing when you told him to stop selling to Maddox, but a whole other when you kicked him out of that fucking fight. You want to run away from North Side and be Duchess of the West End trash heap? Fine. But you will *not* be cutting into our bottom line, Lavinia."

I raise my chin, pinning him with a glare. "I was following orders from *my* Dukes about *their* territory. West End doesn't want the shit you're slinging."

"West, East, South..." He hurls the padlock aside, causing a bottle of solvent to crash to the floor. "Forsyth has been buying our shit since before Viper Scratch was a twinkle in your daddy's eye, and you're not about to stand in the way of the empire I plan to inherit!"

I flinch at the outburst, but try to hide it. It's so hard to think when I'm in here, sweat springing up on the back of my neck, heart thrumming like a hummingbird. "You and I both know Viper Scratch isn't just normal dope. That stuff is shoddy garbage. Get the dosage wrong, and you can take down an elephant with one pill."

"I don't fucking care!" He lurches forward, shoving a finger in my face. "This wasn't some goddamn negotiation between Kings, which means you have no authority over my dealers! You need to remember your fucking place!"

My phone buzzes, the sound loud in the small, cramped space. I don't answer it but we both know who it is. One of my Dukes, looking for me. I was already late before this kidnapping snake cornered me.

Perez nods down at the phone in my pocket, still visibly fuming. "Got your pussy on a leash, huh? Learning the Bruins are no different than the Vipers? They may be all soft and cuddly, but we both have fangs." He gets closer, uncaring, when I flatten myself against the wall. "How do they like it, Lavinia? Do they fuck you like animals? Do they get you down on all fours and ride you like the mangy bitch you are?"

I remain rigid so he doesn't see the tremors. They're not for him. The only scary things here are these four walls closing in on me. "It must just kill you." Raising my chin, I meet his glare with a slow, sharp grin. "No matter how hard you try, you'll never be a real child of North Side. I might be a mangy bitch, but I've got the name. The blood. The pedigree. Do you know the real reason my father keeps your no-name, nine-fingered ass around?" I pitch my voice to a whisper, as if I'm telling him a secret. "You're expendable."

It comes faster than I'm expecting.

"Piss off your opponent. Go for the jugular. Be a viper."

He strikes quick, the hit slamming into my temple before I see him even move. My neck snaps to the side, head hitting the door. Thank God, because otherwise I would have dropped to the floor. Instead, I'm able to get the space necessary to jab up with my knee, slamming it hard into Perez's groin.

He sucks in a gasp, doubling over, one hand grabbing for me as I wrench the door open. Lars is on the other side, but he's not expecting me, his reaction slow enough that I'm almost able to dart out of reach. His fingers catch the bottom of my shirt, but with a burst of power, I break away, my shirt ripping up the side.

It's enough to do what Sy taught me.

I run.

The crowd in the hallway has thinned, the next set of classes having already started. I run toward the door, feet beating hard against the floor. My legs push and push, and there was a time this would have completely gassed me out, but mornings spent jogging with Sy have given me the gift of endurance—enough to reach the exit before either of them can catch up to me.

Nick is already there, though.

I see him before he sees me, the hard set of his frown as he stares down at his phone, probably waiting for my reply. He always looks so contrasted against the backdrop of campus. It's not just his tattoos, although that's a big part of it. It's the way he holds himself, loose in a way that's almost too deliberate, as if he's trying to fool someone into thinking he belongs. It's a physical battle to slow my steps, to not run into his chest and fist my hands into his t-shirt. He still catches the sound of me scampering closer, blue eyes rising to meet mine.

First, his expression smoothes. "Where the hell—" And then he sees my face. His hand freezes halfway to sliding his phone into his pocket, every part of his body going eerily still. "You're hurt."

I try to cover it up, shooting a worried glance behind me and hoping my hair shields the mark. "I-I was clumsy and I—"

His voice comes in a deadly, quiet timbre. "If you're going to lie, you're going to have to do better than that. Tell me. *Now*."

"It's nothing," I insist, sniffling. "I took care of it myself. I can occasionally do that, you know."

My play at aloof anger doesn't even faze him. "I know what knuckles look like on skin," he says in that low, lethal voice. But when he lunges forward to grab for me, I flinch—pure instinct.

He slams to a standstill, pupils darkening. "*Who* the fuck hit you?"

The reason I don't answer isn't to protect Perez. It's to protect Nick. After the crypt, I'm fully, horrifyingly aware of what he's willing to do. How far he'll go for me.

I can't risk losing him.

His nostrils flare. "Lavinia!"

"I can't!" My body deflates, and I do something I swore to myself I'd never do in his presence again. "Please, Nick." It tastes sour in my throat. But things have just begun to even out with the four of us. I know it's pathetic to think about it, but this last week might just be the best my life has ever been. So I do it. I beg. "Please, just let this go?"

Nick's blue eyes bore into mine, and in my periphery, I see his fists flex. He wants to touch me, but he won't. "Kiss me," he says, expression blanking out. "Kiss me and I'll let it go."

My face falls before I can hide it. Nick hasn't forced me to kiss him since that awful night he threw me back to my father. He's had plenty of opportunities, situations I might have given in, but he hasn't taken them. Not one.

Not until right now.

The bitterness is still there as I approach him, eyes fixed to his mouth as he waits. It's not even just the circumstance of it. It's the look on his face—hard and sharp and shuttered. Here, as I strain up on my toes to press my mouth to his, I'm not kissing Nick Bruin, Duke of West End. I'm kissing the soldier of South Side, cold and unreadable as his tongue licks out to taste mine.

If I thought I could kiss that coldness away, then I'm wrong, because he hovers there for a moment, nostrils flaring wide, and then snaps back, pulling out his phone. "I actually came to tell you I couldn't take you home," he says, fingers tapping over the screen. "I have a makeup exam I missed during the four days I was out. I need a passing grade by tomorrow, so I'm spending the afternoon in the Science building."

I try to look at his phone screen, but all I see are three numbers: 237.

My eyes flick to the tattoo. "Who did you send that too?"

He grabs my hand and pulls me outside. Before we reach the bottom step, I have my answer. Two pledges run down the sidewalk.

"Got your message," one of them says, and I instantly recognize him.

"Ballsack, I need you to get the Duchess home safe." He hands Ballsack the keys to the SUV. "No stops. No bullshit."

"Yes, sir," he says.

Nick looks at the other kid—well, *kid* seems like the wrong word. He's massive, with bulging arms and a thick chest. "Weasel, you're with me."

"Weasel?" I ask, trying to figure out the nickname, although clearly it's not important. "Nick, this isn't necessary. I can drive myself home. It's a straight shot to the—"

Nick pulls me against his side but continues to talk Ballsack. "If anything happens to her, and I mean *anything*—if she loses a fucking eyelash on the way home—I will hold you personally responsible. Got it?"

"Got it." I have to give him credit. He manages not to pee in his pants when Nick gives the order.

BALLSACK INSISTS on coming into the tower with me.

"This really isn't necessary," I say at the door, trying to stall. "I'll tell Nick you got me back safe."

"Sorry, Duchess," he says, eyes narrowing at the bruise on my cheek. I'd seen it in the mirror on the way home, an angry red that's already blooming into a brutal violet. "His directions were very specific."

"Whatever," I mutter, heading for the stairs. "For what it's worth, I don't use the elevator, so be prepared to walk."

He spreads his hand out, gesturing toward the staircase. "After you."

The climb is spent in silence, even though I can tell from his small, aborted breaths that Ballsack is constantly a second from saying something. It isn't until we reach the party room that he finally finds the...

Well.

Ballsack.

"Did someone hit you?" he blurts, looking uncomfortable when I turn to him. Uncomfortable, but also kind of adorably upset. "Because you know the pledges and I—and the DKS guys, too—we'd make them pay. Whoever it is." He stops, cheeks blushing a charming shade of pink.

It makes me smile. "Thanks, Ballsy. But I'm all good."

His eyes dart up to mine, brightening at the new nickname, and it's a reminder that I have to be careful. Nick isn't the only guard bear around these parts who'd get himself into trouble for the sake of protecting me.

At the top, I jab in the key code for the living quarters, and the first thing that hits me when I open the door is the scent of lemon and butter. Sy stands by the kitchen counter pushing a bowl toward Archie, who is standing *on* the Formica.

Ballsack and I share a look, and I sniff the air. "Are you feeding my cat homemade salmon?"

Sy stiffens, not even turning to deny it, and then nudges Archie off the countertop. "I had extra." He slides the bowl on the floor. "It's not like I made it for him." He wipes his hands on a rag, eyes darting to Ballsack. "What are you doing here?"

Ballsack starts to answer, but I cut in. "He was just giving me a ride home. Nick had a makeup exam." I've gotten lucky, with Sy not turning fully enough to notice my cheek, and Ballsack sends me a nervous look at the lack of honesty currently going down. I give him a tight smile. "You can go now. Thanks for the ride!"

He doesn't look convinced, but shuffles his feet uncertainly before moving to the door. "Remember what I said," he adds before leaving.

Sy is easy to dodge, too caught up in being embarrassed about pampering his arch-nemesis to bother putting me under a microscope.

Remy?

Not so much.

He waltzes out of his room, wiping paint-stained hands on a towel. "Did I hear someone say Nicky's still on campus? He was supposed to—"

It's not that I don't try to hide it, because I do, fanning my hair over my cheek. And it's not like I don't know it's useless. I live with these two. I can't exactly hide until it heals. In any case, Remy barely gets five steps away from me before he notices something's wrong.

The tear in my shirt.

Fuck.

He must notice the way I'm keeping myself turned away from him, because suddenly he demands, "Look at me."

Sighing, I drop my bag, preparing myself.

And then I look at him.

Remy's on me in an instant, ignoring my flinch when his hand grabs my chin, angling my face towards him. His green eyes flash with a dark, lethal rage. "Nicky did this?" he asks, voice hard.

"No!" I'm quick to say, hand coming up to wrap around his wrist. "Nick wouldn't—" Only that's not entirely true. Nick's knocked me around before. Still... "I promise you, Nick isn't the problem here," I insist.

Behind Remy, Sy appears, freezing at the sight of my face, getting a better look at the mark Perez left.

He stares.

Silently.

Remy doesn't relax at all, knowing it wasn't Nick. "Then who?"

I fidget anxiously, shooting Sy a desperate look. Nick and Remy...

they're volatile. They don't control their impulses like Sy does. If Sy had been the one to ask, I would have told him—no question. Remy needs to be handled a little more carefully. "I'll tell you—I will. But just... give me a few to decompress? I'm okay. It's not a big—"

"Don't fucking tell me it's not a big deal," Remy snaps, thumb digging into my chin, "Tell me *who*!" The tears come unbidden, pricking at my eyes like lava. The wetness turns Remy into a big, muddled blob of black and white, but somehow, I still see his eyes soften. "Goddamn it," he mutters, suddenly hauling me into his chest.

It rankles to cry in front of them again. To let myself be weak. To fall into Remy's arms and let him, once again, soothe away the hurt. I've been yelled at a million times by dozens of different people. I've built up a skin, hard like armor, something the words would bounce off of, emotional Kevlar.

Somehow, with him, it just doesn't exist.

His wide palm cradles the back of my head, whispering, "Someone put their fucking mark on you, Vinny. We can't let that slide." And then, more hesitantly, "Does this have something to do with your dad?"

I pry myself away from him and Remy lets me, looming over me with furrowed brows and an unhappy tilt to his mouth. "Just give me a few," I ask, wiping under my eyes. "I've kind of had a shitty day, you know?"

Remy watches me walk to the freezer and grab an ice pack from inside. Bonus of living with fighters—there's always ice packs. By the time I return, the hard, angry, *worried* crease hasn't left his forehead. Watching me press the ice pack to my throbbing cheek, he huffs a sharp sigh, tossing aside his paint-stained towel. "Fuck it. Come with me."

A couple minutes later, we're standing up in the belfry, Sy having followed us wordlessly. Remy pulls a crumpled Ziploc bag from his pocket, revealing three perfectly rolled joints. "It's not Count product," he mutters, taking one out and extending it to me. "Light it up."

Reluctantly, I take the joint, still sniffling. Sy stands behind me, flicking the lighter until a bright flame appears. I put the joint in my mouth and hold the other end over Sy's flame, puffing an ember to life.

I can still remember with perfect clarity the last time I got high. Cash Money, in my father's backyard, at our annual Christmas party, passing a blunt over the fence. Guys like Cash—the low level dealers—weren't actually allowed to be seen on the premises, so they hovered by the back gate, watching over the property for my dad. It was just business as usual to find myself in their ranks, always cast off to the side and hidden, just like the strays begging for scraps.

I exhale a plume of smoke into the sky above Forsyth, letting it calm my nerves. I never realized being protected—cared for—would be so much responsibility. I lean over the open archway—the same spot Remy stood when he sliced his arm. If I look closely enough, I can still see the dots of blood staining the stone beneath our feet.

"Whoever did this," Remy begins, taking the joint from my fingers. "Did you make them pay?"

"Oh, yeah." The smile that quirks my lips doesn't even feel forced. "I had a good teacher. I got away with one of your moves."

But when I look over my shoulder at Sy, he's just standing there, staring off into the distance. I don't like the darkness in his blue eyes, the way his jaw is clenched tight, the flex of his forearm as he flicks the lighter, over and over, restlessly.

Gruffly, Sy asks, "Does Nick know?" and I remember the kiss.

"Not who," I answer, looking down as Remy passes the joint back to me. "That's why he had Ballsack drive me home."

It's quiet for a long while after that, and I'm hit with the realization that the sun's about to set, floating somewhere behind West End's horizon. It's a special sight, one many don't get to see, and I let myself get distracted with the colors—orange, pink, purple. Beside me, Remy passes the joint back and forth, and if it weren't for how it all began, it'd probably strike me as romantic.

Sy's the one to break the silence. "We should kill him."

I peer up at him through the dying rays of light, confused. "Who?"

He scowls over the horizon, chin jerking toward North Side. "Your father."

I follow his gaze, stomach sinking. "It wasn't my dad. And even if it was, we can't kill him."

Sy's hot gaze swings to me. "What, so you're loyal to that scumbag all of a sudden?"

"No," I insist, completely forgetting the joint. "There are things about him you don't understand. He has protections—failsafes—that will level this whole fucking town." Shaking my head, I look to the north. It's weird to see it from here, so small, so far away. I lean to the side, propping my sore temple against Remy's shoulder. "I won't let him be the death of Forsyth. He doesn't deserve a legacy that big."

The door creaks a floor below, followed by heavy footsteps, drawing our attention to the hatch. Nick's head appears first and we all look back to the horizon, waiting for him to join us. It only seems right that he should be here when I finally tell the truth. I feel him come up behind me, quiet as we all watch the light get dimmer and dimmer, the faint image of a crescent moon hanging over East End.

"It was Perez." My mouth purses as I inspect the skyline. Houses and buildings and trees and life. "He's pissed because I sent Cash away at Friday Night Fury. But it's fine."

"It is now," comes Nick's voice. I turn because there's something about the tenor of it that makes a gnawing unease flip in my gut. The first thing I see is his bag—the same one he had at school. Then I see his hands, covered in blood.

Whirling around in alarm, I begin, "What—?"

Suddenly, Nick upends the bag, the contents landing on the stone with a heavy, wet smack.

It's almost a relief that I scream—that the reflex still exists within me to be faced with something as gruesome as this and react like any normal, sane person would.

Remy and Sy don't scream.

They stare at the severed head currently laying at our feet, Perez's blank face staring up at us, and then at Nick, who I'm only now realizing is wearing a significant part of him.

Perez.

There's blood fucking *everywhere*.

And Nick is here, head held high, offering this to me like some sort of terrible *gift*.

I can't tell if it's the weed that makes the world tilt a little or the fact I'm looking at Nick's murder victim. This wasn't a bullet, one-and-done execution like Felix. This was messy brutality. I grab out for Sy to hold myself steady, stomach turning violently. "Oh, my god."

"I thought you smelled weird." Nick's voice sounds detached as his blue eyes pierce through me. That's what it was. Mechanical. The soldier. "So I made you kiss me. Industrial strength disinfectant. Storage closet was the obvious guess." Nick pulls something from his pocket, and I'm not sure what I'm expecting. Perez's dick, maybe. Instead, it's a gleam of dull metal clanking noisily.

The padlock to my chest.

Nick holds it out to me, arm extended, and I take it automatically, my brain too frazzled to parse what I'm feeling in my hand.

"Christ, Nicky," Remy groans, thrusting his fingers into his hair. "The fuck did you do?"

But I'm the one Nick speaks to. "It was a mistake," he says, "letting him get away with hitting you the first time." In a rush, I remember that night in the warehouse when Nick passed me off to my father. The sting of Perez's palm when he slapped me.

My mouth opens and closes, but it takes a long moment for me to find the words. "You—and me, by extension—just plunged West End into a war."

"Good."

I whip around to gape at Sy, who's staring at Perez's head with a grimly satisfied expression. "What?"

"Fuck him." Sy kicks out, the toes of his shoe cracking hard against Perez's skull. "I'm sick of the Counts and their bullshit. Killian should have done something about him when he kidnapped the Lady, but they're too afraid of rocking the system." He looks up at us, eyes moving from Duke to Duke, and then me. "That shit ends today. I don't give a fuck what the consequences are. Forsyth is about to learn that West End doesn't belong to Saul. It belongs to *us*." He reaches out, and I'm not expecting it—the tenderness in his touch when he curls a finger, brushing a knuckle over the bruise on my cheek. "Just like you."

25

Nick

Lavinia lifts my hand in hers, her fingers soft against my palm as she inspects my knuckles. The light in the bathroom isn't very bright, but I can still count every single one of her eyelashes when she blinks, turning my hand to look at my palm. The guys are out there, in the living room, their voices a familiar murmur behind the bathroom door, and I watch her. Fuck, I watch her all the time now.

I get this flutter of a memory. The other day when she shaved my face for me, standing right in this same spot, her fingers gentle against my jaw. If there was ever any question, that experience with her would have sealed it. I need Lavinia to be mine like I need to breathe, and I'll do whatever it takes to have more of those soft, sweet moments.

Even if it means losing a piece of myself.

Winning her from the Lords, forcing her onto her back... those were shortcuts. The easy way. Cowardly tactics that would have never earned me anything real. I understand that now. Gaining the real things—the loyalty, the smiles, the tenderness, the respect—these take the kind of work that can't be rushed or gained through hurt.

Now, she does the same thing, tilting my face, searching for an injury. I know they're there. He got a hook in on my jaw, and he scratched my forearm up like a little bitch. Nothing serious, though. I can't even feel a sting.

In fact, I can't feel anything.

"He fought back," she says, mouth slanted into a displeased line.

I give her a look. Of course he did. Perez was a Royal. We always fight back. Nothing wrong with that. I wouldn't have felt as good about it if he didn't. It had to be like this. A fight to the death.

She looks startled when I reach up, skating my fingers over the curve of her cheekbone. Perez's blood, still sticky and damp on my hands, leaves a trail over her skin, and I stare at it for too long, his blood on top of her blood.

Wrong.

I try to use my thumb to wipe the bloodstain off her cheek, but it just smears more and more, and it's not right. He shouldn't be on her like this. The thought of her covered in the stench of his death makes my chest feel suddenly tight, and I scrabble to erase it, to free her from it. Grabbing her shoulder, I yank the collar of her shirt up, barely hearing the confused sound she makes as I scrub the fabric over it, desperate to see it gone.

"Hey," she says, hand wrapping around my wrist. "Hey, it's okay, let's just—"

I freeze at the way she sounds, quiet and coaxing, as if she's talking to a rabid animal.

I suppose that's what I am.

Mechanically, I drop the shirt, letting her go, but it doesn't make it better. She's still staring up at me with wide, worried eyes, showing me the rag she's been using to clean my knuckles. Wordlessly, she lifts it to her cheek, swiping the smear of blood away, easy peasy.

Something inside me unwinds when the blood disappears.

She looks down at the sponge, and then my arms. They're still crimson and brown, the blood drying on my skin now. I want to tell her how it felt to wrestle Perez down to the ground. How his neck went from rigid to loose all in a single heartbeat. I want to tell her that it wasn't easy, but it was the first kill I ever had that felt like an actual victory. I want to tell her the Baron King was right all along.

But I can't seem to get it to surface. Everything feels strangely cold and numb, and I'm not sure why. I've killed dozens of people. Bullets in skulls, sawing through bone, blood and muscle—none of these are new to me.

So why can't I relax my fucking muscles?

That must be it—the tension in my body, strung like a wire that's ready to pop. It came upon me as I was hitting him, pinning Perez to the ground out behind the athletic department. It was sloppy to do it there, to not have a plan, but I couldn't stop and I didn't want to. Over and over, I slammed my knuckles into his face. I thought of Lavinia's cheek, the mark he left, and then I got this flash of memory. Lavinia crashing to the floor of my bedroom, palm covering her face as wet eyes glared up at me. Suddenly, Perez wasn't just Perez.

He was me.

I broke his neck a second later, a clean, sharp snap.

"Okay," she says, exhaling a measured breath. "Let's get this off."

She pulls my shirt over my head and I try to cooperate, lifting my rusty, rigid arms over my head. She goes for my pants next, her fingers dipping into my waistband and popping the fly. Her throat shifts with a swallow before she bends to push them down, boxers and all. My cock greets her eagerly, bobbing as it's released. I'm not sure who's more shocked at the hardness of it. It doesn't feel like anything to me. Throbs but doesn't yearn. An urge without a man attached to it.

Lavinia shoots up, keeping her gaze averted. "I'll be right back."

I stand, naked and erect, as she throws open the bathroom door, calling Sy over. "Get rid of these," she says, voice low but still audible. "Burn them or something?"

He answers, "Your shirt," and I glance over, seeing a muddy brown mark in the shape of my handprint smeared over her shoulder.

She looks at it and then grabs the hem—torn and stretched from whatever altercation she'd had in that supply closet—and yanks it over her head. "This, too."

It flusters me to know they're probably getting rid of the head. Don't they realize that I brought it here for her? It doesn't matter, I guess. The whole meaning of it was lost the second she opened her jaws and shrieked in horror at the sight of it. But I'd spent the extra time to saw it away, and I'd been so excited to drive it over here to show her, although now that I really consider it, I don't know why.

Grand gestures have never been my thing.

Sy must take them from her, because a moment later, she closes the door. I watch wordlessly as she pulls back the shower curtain, leaning over to turn the faucet. Her hand reaches out to test the temperature, and then she adjusts the knob.

I think I want to kill someone else.

The thought settles over me abruptly, my fingers twitching with something so deep and instinctual that I don't even think to question it. Perez wasn't enough, the gaping maw inside of me demanding more. Her father will be next. Maybe, after that, the other Counts. How many men have touched her without having the right? Can I kill them all?

Yes.

"Get in the shower, okay?" She stands before me, shifting from foot to foot, her gray eyes searching mine. "Okay, Nick?" I shift my eyes to the spray of water, but when I make no move to step inside, she folds her arms around herself. "You're really freaking me out."

My eyes fly to hers, and I see it. The spark of uncertainty. I note, "You're scared." And now that I think about it, "You're always scared of me." I'd say I'm sorry, but I'm not sure what I'd be sorry for. Existing, I guess.

This is just who I am.

Some of the doubt vanishes, leaving shrewd eyes and her arched brow. "Please. You wish you were scary." I stare at her chest, the swell of breast over her bra, the half-finished moth with its wings spread as wide as two willing thighs. "How—how did you kill him?"

"He's dead. Does it matter?"

Not always.

But for her, it does.

I answer by raising my hands, showing her my empty, blood-stained palms.

She stares at them, and whatever armor she's had pulled around her all day suddenly falls away. "Jesus, Nick, you didn't have to—"

"Yes, I did." Whatever's in my voice makes her look at me, her eyes softening as we remember the same words.

"...to kill someone with your bare hands is an act of love."

Just like that, it was worth it.

After a second, she reaches behind her, unclasping her bra. But she clutches it to her chest before it falls away. "I-I'll go in with you, okay? We need to get all that blood off." She worries at her lip, asking, "Will you get in with me?"

Blankly, I nod.

"I wish you'd say something."

When I don't, her face falls, twisting the numbness in my chest into more of a hollowness. She undresses, baring herself to me. Seeing her body is the first thing that almost cracks the ice that's grown around my lungs.

Almost.

Taking my hand, she leads me into the shower, lifting a leg over the tub, then the next, watching me intently as I mimic her. I think I'd probably bash my own head against the wall if she asked me to right now, but that's always been the way with me, hasn't it? I wasn't made to steer myself. I was made to take commands. To be an instrument of mayhem. A soldier. A sharp-edged tool.

Gently, she commands, "Tip your head back for me?"

I obey.

If I'm going to be anyone's weapon, then I'm going to be hers.

The water pounds against my scalp, tickling down my neck, shoulders, back. It doesn't feel good, and it doesn't feel bad, and I'm still not sure where all the feeling's gone. Since I've memorized this set of motions, I wet my hair, letting the rivulets of nothing run down my face.

"Good, that's good," she says, and something inside me cracks free at the praise, shuddering in pleasure. I watch as she pauses, scrutinizing me. "Can you wash your hair while I get all this off you?" at my nod, she reaches around me to wet a new, clean sponge, whispering, "Good."

My stomach clenches.

I barely get beyond dumping a glob of shampoo into my hand before I'm rendered motionless, frozen at the feel of her hands, scrubbing the sudsy cloth over my muscles. She takes it in stride, using my distraction to work the blood off the skin covering my forearm, still half-suspended with a palmful of shampoo.

"I don't know what happened or how it feels to do that to someone." She looks right into my eyes as she says it, her mouth pursed tightly. "But I need you to come back to us now, okay?"

I grunt as she moves the rag lower, hand brushing my cock.

Her eyes flick down to it, and then to my chest, lathered with soap that's turned pink. "Is that what you need?" she asks, pausing to catch my reaction when she brushes against it again.

My eyes slide closed, mouth parting as a sigh pushes through.

Slowly, her fingers close around the shaft, her palm hot and soft as she gives it a slick, gliding tug. I hear her get closer more than I feel her, the softness of her whisper grazing my ear as she commands, "Come back to me, Nick."

One of my hands shoots out, slamming hard against the shower wall, while the other snatches a fistful of her hair. Somehow, through the blinding need of turning my face to hers, I find the presence of mind not to *hurt*. Not pulling her hair. Not forcing her to give me another kiss. I just hold her there, close enough to feel her breath against my chin. If she fought, I'd let her go, but she doesn't.

And that's when it tumbles out, as messy as an open wound. "I'm sorry." She pauses and I shake my head. "Not for Perez. The only thing I regret about that is taking so long to do it." The water beats down on us, her hand still on my cock. "I'm sorry for sending you back, and for everything that happened before that. I couldn't see it until it was too late, and this is probably fucking worthless, but in case you need to hear it, I'll tell you." Our foreheads press together. "I'm sorry."

She tilts her face up to me, hand squeezing my cock as her lips brush against mine.

I part my lips, so still that when she licks at the rim of my mouth, I don't even tip into her. I just extend my own tongue, meeting hers with a deep, desperate rumble ripping from my chest. Lavinia kisses me carefully, like I'm a stick of dynamite about to blow.

She might know me better than anyone, living or dead.

All the while, her hand slides up and down, sending a cascade of sparks throughout my nerves. I surface so gradually that I don't even realize I'm rocking my hips into her fist until she begins swaying with me, her eyelashes wet against her bruised cheek.

"Is that good?" she asks against my mouth, her palm twisting at the tip. It's a practiced, deliberate motion that punches a grunt from my throat, and she swallows it with another kiss, pulling this sickness out of me. I understand what this is now. A thorn that's stuck under my skin, festering into sepsis.

And she draws it out, looking so fucking beautiful as she strokes me, heavy eyes blinking open to watch me panting for it, chasing her cherry-red mouth like it's a beacon in the dark. I get my arms back next. Hands. Shoulders. I use them to touch her, fingertips grazing the supple sides of her tits. She flinches, but she moves into me, neither an invitation nor a protest. Just an awareness.

My balls draw up tight before I'm ready to let it go. Not just the sense of orgasm, but the lingering numbness that keeps it bay. I'm not ready to feel it all—the anger, the bitterness, the stab of hurt I'll feel when she walks out of here to return to my brother's bed. In here—in the quiet, secret, dark places—Lavinia is mine.

Out there in the light, she belongs to them.

It surges inside of me like a tempestuous wave, pulling the thread thin until it snaps, and *fuck*. Fuck, I hope she can forgive me. I grab her by the hips and drive her back, too hard, too fast, her back colliding with the wall. There's a flash of panic in her eyes that I don't want to see, so I bury my face into her neck as I begin thrusting—sharp, forceful punches of my hips into the circle of her hand, the tip of my cock jabbing into her hip. I reach down to grab her ass, as if crushing her closer isn't just ruining my own goddamn friction. I fuck her hand like it could ever be enough, grunting her neck with every bang of my body against hers.

Her free hand finds its way into my hair, stroking more gently than the moment calls for. "That's it," she whispers, the words jagged with the assault of my hips crashing into her. Even though I'm all strained tendon and wild thrusts, she's nothing but sweet and soft. "You've done so good, Nick. Come for me now, okay?"

I couldn't hold it back even if I wanted to.

I slam forward, fingers clutched around her neck hard enough to bruise as the orgasm rips through me. It spills against her hips in frantic surges, and I don't even recognize the sound I'm pressing into her shoulder, quiet but frantic.

Her arms wrap around my waist and she pulls us together, our bodies wet and naked, fused into one. I don't just feel the release, but the rise and fall of my breath, the thudding of my heart and all her skin, alive against mine.

Darkness beckons me. I sense it just inches away, but this girl—

this woman—has drawn me back and I'll cling to her like a lifeline for as long as she'll let me.

What I don't know is what will come from my act of vengeance, but the people of Forsyth need to understand one thing: no one lays a hand on the Duchess except her Dukes and survives.

Even if that means starting a war.

26

Remy

One of the most annoying things about being Sy and Nick's best friend is that they're fierce individuals, but sometimes so alike that I can't help but feel like a stray. Like right now, for instance, the way they're both still and composed and looking perfectly chill as all five Kings enter the room.

Meanwhile, I want to gnaw my fucking fingers off.

Growing up, I always had problems with authority, so it's not like finding myself in front of powerful men who wanted to slap the everloving shit out of me is something new. The stakes sure as hell have grown, though.

I wouldn't know it, looking first at Nicky, and then Sy. Both of them have the perfect poker faces, chins raised, ready to face this head on. Nick has that cocky tilt to his mouth that always makes people flustered with the impulse to put him in his place, and Sy...

Sy looks like a Bruin.

Fuck the biological bloodline bullshit. I never really thought much of it myself. Sy's a Bruin just as much as he is Perilini; just sometimes one dad's influence shows more than the other. Here he's all Davis Bruin, arms crossed to show off his bulging, sculpted muscles. *Don't fuck with me*. He exudes it.

Doing my best to copy him, I slouch further in my chair.

Fuck, I wish I were high right now.

All three of us are silent as the Kings filter in. First, Ashby, King of the Princes, in his finely tailored white suit, and then the Baron King, in his black suit and ornate bronze mask. They're an interesting contrast; light and dark, day and night, sterile, bright and ominous shadow.

Next, our own King, Saul Cartwright strides in, his stony face not even bothering to grace us with a look. After him comes Killian Payne, King of the Lords, and although he's got a bit of that blank-faced Nick-action going on, I can still see annoyance clear in his features. I bet he's got better places to be, and I suspect all of them are between his Lady's supple thighs.

Man.

I know the feeling.

Lionel enters last and I try hard not to roll my eyes. Bit theatrical, if you ask me. We're meeting in one of the only neutral places in Forsyth, too close to the campus for any substantial squabbles. It's a building I've only been to once, the day after Sy and I got our titles as Dukes. Even then, we only stayed for ten minutes, nodding along to Saul's directives like we weren't bored out of our minds and ready to get to the real business—the massive celebration waiting back at the tower.

This place was the original Forsyth courthouse, built sometime in the 1900s. It fell out of use about the time the Royalty came to power. Not nearly enough pomp for the Forsyth elite, with its peeling walls and squat hallways. But in truth, I really like it, my eyes drawn to the intricate plaster molding, imagining the thought, care, creativity some old, dead fucker put into making it look... regal. It kind of reminds me of the clock tower, rich with history, the air thick with the scent of dust and old, crimson conflict.

If these walls could scream...

It's on the historical register, so it's kept up alright, but it's only ever used for shit like this: cross-Kingdom meetings, initiations, and what we're here for today, punitive tribunals.

This is just like being in Catholic school all over again, staring up at solemn men in their ridiculous garb as I get my dressing down.

One by one, they all take a seat behind the bench, nothing but the sound of an ancient boiler chugging to fill the space.

Until Ashby speaks. "Well, you all know why you're here."

Lionel Lucia, never one to miss an opening, instantly springs up, face flushed with fury as he jabs a finger in our direction. "You fucking mongrel bastards!"

Killian shoves him back to his seat, shooting the man a glare. "They get to prove their innocence, Lionel. Save it."

"Yeah, I'm not gonna do that," Nick says, voice perfectly clear. "I killed Bruno Perez." Lionel looks at the others, gesturing to Nicky as if to say, *See?* Ashby's face is hard with displeasure. Killian sighs, and the difference between him and Nick suddenly seems perfectly clear. Saul, on the other hand, looks like he could jump over that bench and strangle Nick himself.

Sounding bored, Nick goes on, "These two had nothing to do with it, though. I acted on my own, independent of the system." And here's the smirk, sharp and cutting. "It was fun."

Lionel leaps from his seat again, reaching into his jacket for the gun he's not even bothering to conceal. Sy stiffens when he sees the piece. None of us are packing—tribunal rules. Apparently Lionel is above those, too.

The Baron King gets there first, slapping Lionel's hand away. "Oh, sit down, Lucia. You're not the only judge here. Let the boy speak." The Baron pushes Lionel into his seat, and then turns his masked nose back to Nick.

"He attacked our Duchess," Nick explains.

Ashby looks around the room, as if he's confused, searching for the punchline. "And?"

"And he paid for it." Nick announces this while studying his fingernails. Jesus. To be that calm and collected instead of a mass of frantic energy.

"This is ridiculous," Sy jumps in, unwilling to let Nicky go down alone. "Let's just be honest here. Lionel and his Counts have been bucking Royal rules since as far back as I can remember. I might not have snapped his neck, but I stand behind my brother for doing it. Hell, I wish I'd been there to do it myself. It's about time someone struck back at your slimy, slithering bullshit."

"This isn't how things are done," Ashby insists.

The Baron King finally speaks, agreeing, "There's a reason our Royals have cross-Kingdom impunity. It is, if I'm not mistaken, the only thing standing between the three of you and a multi-house mobbing." He gestures vaguely to both Lionel and Ashby. More apathetically, he adds, "And Lucia girls are such troublesome creatures. Ask yourselves if she's really worth the trouble, Nicholas. The last time I saw you, she seemed so willing to trade your life for trivialities, didn't she?"

I look at Nick, confused, but Nick just stares coolly back at him. "That's between me and her."

Ashby interrupts, "Royal women have always been a vulnerability to their men, but no one made you choose an heir to a rival house as yours!"

"I didn't want one at all." Sy sits forward, fixing them with a hard look. "In fact, I remember being explicitly told in this very room that having a Duchess was non-negotiable. And why? What was it Saul told me?" He looks as if he's calling up a memory that I know for a fact is already at the forefront. "Oh, right. Because they give us something to fight for. And yet, when we fight for her, you drag us into your farce of a courtroom to get a dressing down. How does that make sense?"

"Watch," Saul growls, "your tone."

"He's right." All eyes turn to Killian, who's nodding at Sy. "I don't know how it was in your time, Ashby, but speaking from a more… *recent* experience," the barb at the man's age is pointed, making Ashby's eyes flare, "you force us to form attachments and then punish us for protecting them. It's fucking stupid." Ignoring the heat of the other Kings' eyes, Killian casually continues, "The fact is, we give North Side too much leeway with the system. What's the word you used? Impunity. We always have. And we all know why."

"Keep pushing me, Payne." Lionel grits out, tense and taut. "You'll find out exactly why."

Killian raises a palm, laughing humorlessly. "See? How the fuck do we let that stand?"

Ashby whirls to tell Killian, "Nothing is stopping you from arming your own house."

Killian sits up straighter, his eyes as hot as lasers. "Let's make one thing perfectly clear. My house is armed to the fucking teeth. Lucia defies territorial agreements by arming his. He should be the one sitting before us."

Lionel snorts. "I'm not the one ambushing Royalty."

"Your Counts ambushed my Queen. They kidnapped her and tried to rape her. I only allowed Perez to survive then because I was under my father's command." Killian out sizes every man on that panel by five inches and fifty pounds. He's also at least twenty-five years younger. The Kings may be glib, but there's deference to the Lord because of his sheer size. "Don't play the victim, Lionel. None of us are buying it."

Nick's eyes flick from Killian to the rest of the men. "Hey, I didn't ambush Perez. He attacked my Duchess on school property, and I ran him down. Our fight was clean. I just bested him. Again."

"And now he's dead," Ashby says. "That's not how we do it."

"West End has taken three of my heirs," Lionel says, voice low with controlled rage. "I have no one left to precede me, in blood or title. This is an act of war!"

Nick shrugs. "Not my fault you hitched your wagon to a baby back bitch."

But Saul jumps in, face contorted in disbelief. "That's rich, Lionel, coming from the man that wired this town to blow to hell and back if he doesn't get his way. You couldn't even keep your own daughters under control." He gives Lionel a pointed look. "The women in your house seem to find trouble under your rule, don't they? Is that the Duke's fault as well?"

"Stop!" Ashby shouts, palms flat on the table. He peers down at Nick. "We know for a fact you were ordered to leave the Counts alone, because it was decided in this room, weeks ago, after you stole his daughter from his own home." He regains composure, looking pompous in his crisp white suit. "At the time, we considered this to be an inter-house conflict. A contract dispute, if you will, over the ownership of Lavinia Lucia. That was a confined situation. None of us care which bed the northern whore finds herself in. But the Duke's messiness continues to infect the rest of the houses. On top of a dead Count, my nephew, Felix, has gone missing. Considering his last appointment was a weapons drop with the three of you," he gives each of us a significant look, "I'll put two and two together and say that we have a rogue house on our hands. Your own King can't control you. You're rabid."

Saul slams down his fist, his eyes murderous. "Are you calling my abilities into question?"

"That's exactly what I'm doing!" Ashby glares back, and suddenly, the scene unfolds. It's not just old men fighting. It's decades of squabbles like this. Royals bickering over territory. Over soldiers. Over women. It spreads in front of me like an inevitable landscape. "Which is worrying, because you don't even have a legitimate claim to that fucking seat!" Saul shoots up, and Killian places himself between them. Ashby goes on, gesturing to Nick, "If this is the Bruin that takes your Kingdom, this institution is doomed."

Nick pipes in matter-of-factly, "I don't want to be King."

"Of course you don't. You're too busy sowing chaos with your disloyalties to head a house!" Lionel sneers. "Your word is worth less than the dirt on the bottom of my shoe, boy."

That statement settles across the room in only the way the truth can. Lionel's right. Partially. Nick's loyalties are his own: to Sy, his parents, me and the Duchess. He's too wild to be contained to one role for the rest of his life. Unfortunately for him, when he stepped back into the ring and took the win, he shackled himself to this fate.

Ashby eyes slide over to me. "And what do you have to say, Remington? How does it feel to know your fellow Duke has murdered a Royal, dragging you into a war?"

"Honestly?" I shrug, not bothering to lie. "I think it's fucking hilarious. That punk bitch had it coming."

Killian says in a warning voice, "Remy, watch it."

"Don't give him orders," Sy says, glaring at Killian. "If you'd settled the score a year ago when Perez attacked your Lady, none of this would have happened. Since none of you would man the fuck up, it fell on us. We're not going to apologize for it. And seeing as how you're all here, you should hear this. The Dukes are done hanging off the ropes. If someone comes at us, *any* of us, we're hitting back."

Saul snaps, "You're not King of this goddamn house! You're not even a Bruin. You don't get to make those calls, Perilini!"

Sy, fuming, clamps down on a remark he clearly wants to make and smartly remains silent.

"That's enough," Ashby says, looking annoyed. "We can argue about this all day. It wouldn't be the first time, but there's no escaping the consequences for your actions." He looks down the panel. "Does anyone have a motion?"

"Strip these mongrels of their titles!" Lionel bursts, fist coming down on the bench. "And enforce the return of my daughter to her home."

I jolt out of my seat. "Abso-fucking-lutely not!" Lionel's mouth parts—to argue, no doubt. I speak over him, voice low and deadly. "You'll never get her back. You're lucky I wasn't with Sy that night when he found her. I would have slit your fucking throat in your own goddamn bed."

Lionel looks at the others, disbelief clear on his face. "You're going to let one of our *lessers* threaten me like that?"

"Technically," Nick offers, "that wasn't a threat. It was a hypothetical."

Ashby isn't amused. "Mr. Maddox, another outburst like that and you'll be removed from the rest of the tribunal." Sy grabs me by the forearm and pulls me back down in my seat.

When the Baron King stands to speak, I doubt anyone's expecting it. "I propose no punishment. Lionel's viper had it coming. The Bruin boy earned his death. If not the Dukes, then another house would have taken him. To stand and face a foe—to fight for your life, instead of seeing it snuffed out with a pellet of lead? The viper's death was an honor." The masked Baron turns his focus to Lionel, ignoring everyone's exasperation. "You speak a big game about the Dukes being out of control, but Perez was..." He pauses, gloved palms out. "Well, calling him a blood-thirsty lunatic would be an insult to my house, so let's just say he wasn't fit for the Royalty. If he acted on his own, then he deserved death. And if he acted on your orders—" Lionel opens his mouth to speak but the Baron lifts his gloved finger in warning. "I'd consider your next words carefully, Lucia, because if you were behind any of these acts then you'll be the one we shine the spotlight on today."

"I agree with the Baron," Killian says, arms crossed over his chest. "No punishment."

Ashby opens his mouth to vote but Saul cuts him off. "I have an alternative." Nick watches our King carefully, eyebrow slightly raised. "Royal probation. One month. Friday Night Fury can commence, because all of us have investments in those fights, but they lose one week, and access to the gym for training is off the table."

Sy bursts, "What?!" and Saul shoots him a glare. "How do you expect us to win if we can't train?"

"No frat activities," he goes on in a gritted voice, ignoring him. "No other appearances. No trouble at all, period." Saul lifts his chin. "And the boys will do one run for you each. Whatever you need, they're at your service."

Saul shifts forward and back in his chair, and it makes me itchy. I haven't seen him this worked up since Vinny moved into the tower. Leave it to Saul to find a way to make losing a fight a distinct possibility.

"This is bullshit," Nick mutters under his breath, but then gets louder. "I did this. Not Sy or Remy. This is on me, I should take the heat."

Ashby chuckles. "That's part of the problem, boy. You don't realize that every move you make affects the rest of your fraternity. Every single one of them is at risk from your behavior. You need to take some time to really understand what it means to be a leader." He looks down the line. "Can everyone agree on the terms of probation?"

"No," Lionel says like a petulant child.

"Yes," says Killian.

"Yes," votes the Baron.

And then Saul. "Yes."

"I'm also a yes," Ashby says, banging a gavel on the wooden podium. "But it's the last amount of leeway I'm inclined to give."

~

THINGS in the tower that night are tense.

There's a couple hours where Nicky and Sy hunch over in the little nook below the loft, staring out the observatory windows as they talk in quiet, intense tones. I watch them from the doorway to my bedroom, feeling these unbearably orange niggles of suspicion that they know more than me.

Vinny, too.

She floats around the space like the moth on her chest, throbbing too hard to ignore, but too ephemeral to get a hold of. She worries, though. That much is obvious. When Sy goes to bed, shutting the door behind him, she lingers around the spiral staircase to her loft, waiting to be called inside. She's got this mahogany-tinted aura about her. Anxious, maybe. Pissed off.

"He's not mad," I tell her when she wanders into my room, her gray eyes drinking in my newest series of canvases. "Not at you, at least."

She reaches out to run her fingertips over a smudge of orange sky, feeling the raised, messy texture of dried acrylic. "I know. Sy isn't like you and Nick. When he's mad at me, he'll tell me. In detail. Aggressively." She slides me a look and I grin, small and devious.

"He's not a subtle guy," I agree, tapping my marker against the workbench as I watch her.

Every time she's in here lately, she's looking around, poking through my canvases. I can tell she favors the darker ones. The pieces slashed with red and black. She always looks at them longer, going still as her brain soaks in the pathos. Right now, she's fixated on a demon, her onyx skin singed with fire, jaw open wide. I don't care for it. It looks like something you'd find at a head shop—commercial and mass produced.

"Earlier," I say, tapping my marker faster, harder against the worktop, "at the tribunal, the Baron King said something."

She reaches out to touch the demon's face. That's another thing she does. She always feels the texture of the paint. If she were anyone else, my eyes would twitch in annoyance, but I always let her, feeling a fissure run through me at the sensuality of her touch. "Yeah?" she asks.

My marker keeps tapping. "Something about the last time he saw Nick. That you were willing to trade his life for something trivial." Impatiently, I ask, "What was that about?"

She shrugs, tossing me a confused glance. "Well, he was there that night, wasn't he? When Nick fought Perez for me?"

Frowning, I watch the marker, tapping. That could be it, but, "He acted like—"

"Can I have this?" She turns, holding up a charcoal sketch of Sy I did it right after we moved into the tower. It was part of a study on skin color, so he's dark, the charcoal smudged out from the shadows. His eyes are unfinished, making him appear wraith-like, but I was so happy about the way I captured his hair—a dark, curly mass of energy following a fight—that I never bothered to complete it. "It's really good," she says, eyes wide and hopeful.

Wordlessly, I take it from her, going to my shelf and grabbing a can of fixative. Vinny follows, watching eagerly, hands clasped in front of her. She observes closely as I lay the paper flat, spraying a fine layer over the smudges and whorls.

"Might need a few coats," I explain, laying it next to a series of sketches I finished for my life drawing class.

"Thanks," she says, pushing up on her toes to kiss me.

I have more questions, but her tongue is hot and distracting, and when she drops her hand to cup my dick, the fuses in my brain spark to life. Instinct kicks in, because fuck yes. Wherever this is leading is more interesting and fun than going over the words of Kings.

I reach for her shirt, pulling it up, breaking away only to rip it over her head. The skull in the center of the moth stares back at me, so close to being completed, its wing spread wide. I touch it just like she'd touched my canvases, slow and reverent.

Everything falls apart after that. Lips and teeth, nails digging into flesh, wet and warmth and starshine. It's so saturated with purple that I'm inside her before I even get my pants all the way off.

I've never fucked a girl like I fuck her just then, laid out on my bed, my eyes drinking in the sight of my ink covering her chest. I fuck her sweet and brutal, shoving her thighs wide, hips hammering into her as my lips make love to the piece on her chest. She cries out, fingers clutching and bruising, and it's the best kind of music.

Afterwards, she sleeps in my bed.

But I don't.

In the stretch of stillness between her breathless afterglow-sighs and the steadiness of her sleeping breaths, I think of snakes and horns. When I roll away from her and pull up my pants, I watch her from the corner of my eye. She tosses and turns, the silky expanse of a thigh hitched over my rumpled blanket like she's seeking something to press against. But she doesn't wake up.

A moment later, I'm pushing the blade of a knife into a small, viper-stamped pill, crushing it into a fine powder. White pigment, clean and new, and the black barrel from an old pen help it go up the chute.

Black means sorry.

It's bitter in the back of my throat, but I'm used to it, cleaning up the evidence quickly before gathering my markers. I give her sleeping form, serpentine and curled, one last look before slipping out the door.

Across the tower, Nick's room is dark.

I don't mind it. It's almost better this way, squinting into the fog of shadow to make out the outline I'd left on the inside of his door days ago.

Vinny's face.

I spend the next five hours in front of it, frantically giving life to the vision that's throbbing in the back of my mind. If Nick stirs, waking to the sight of me in front of his door, then I don't notice it, too absorbed in the desperate need to exorcize it from my brain.

~

WHEN I GET to campus the next morning, my head is still firmly located in Nick's room, ruminating over the image I've painted there, so I'm already annoyed. The worst part about studio time is that the teachers expect you to show variety. Spending too long on one piece—one style, one color, one subject—is an academic death sentence, but that's just how the machine inside me runs. My brain can't merely glance off an inspiration. It needs to hold it down, stare it in the eye, learn the substance and purpose of it. It takes weeks, months, sometimes even years.

It doesn't help that my father is waiting at the entrance of the fine arts building.

He has a cup in each hand, a long wool coat pulled around him as he waits. His beard is well groomed, like always, and his hazel eyes pierce me like lasers. When I freeze, hand fisting the handle to my portfolio too hard, he gestures to me with a coffee. "I come in peace."

I push past him, swiping my student ID against the card reader. "Fuck off. It's too early for this shit." The surprise is reckless of me. He stopped incessantly calling my phone three days ago. That was a sure sign of an incoming ambush. Sy would be embarrassed at my lack of situational awareness.

"For you, maybe," he says, following me into the building. "Or should I say late? You look like you haven't gotten a lick of sleep. Predictably. You never were very good about taking care of yourself."

Ignoring him, I climb the stairs to the second floor. I share studio space with three other people, but none of them are in yet, so I flick the lights on, dump my shit into my corner, and shuck off my jacket. "If you're here for the phone, you can forget it. I already chucked it off the clock tower."

I sense his pause more than I see it, busying myself with the fresh, new canvas in front of me. "Well, that's too bad," he says, setting the coffee on the table beside me. "But easy come, easy go." After a beat, "It's been destroyed?"

I shoot him a glare. "That's what I just said, isn't it?"

Sighing, he lifts his own coffee to his lips. "I don't know why you're so pissy with me, Remy. All I've ever done is—"

"Manipulate, control—"

He fixes me with a hard look. "What's *best* for you."

"Yeah," I say, scoffing, "you're a real giver."

"That's enough." His mouth tenses as he sets down his cup. "I don't like this. You're not taking care of yourself. Simon is no longer updating me on your day-to-day condition. And to top it off, now there are all these rumors about you being involved in a murder."

"It's none of your business," I insist, feeling antsy and amped up. I'd snorted another pill before leaving the tower, and now it's battering against my chest.

"My own son's reputation is absolutely my business," he argues, voice rising. "You're growing too visible here, Remy. Allowing you to become a Duke was obviously a mistake."

I whirl to him, incensed by the casual displeasure in his tone. "You didn't 'allow me' a goddamn thing. I fought for it. I worked for it. I took it. None of it is because of you!" It's why he hates my major. There's nothing in it that he can point to and say, '*That's because of me*'. It's not big enough—not flashy enough. "That's the real reason you hate me being here, isn't it? You can't own a part of it, and it drives you fucking crazy."

"Oh, Remy. You can't really be so blind, can you?" Father tilts his head, a sad smile softening his features. "I own so much more than you think. Your tuition, your degree, your transportation, your dues to Saul." Shrugging, he notes, "The only reason they want you at all is because of my money."

I bark a humorless laugh. "Is that what you tell yourself?"

"I'm only saying this so that you'll see these people for what they really are." His face grows firm, eyes hardening. "They don't care about you. Not like family does. Not like I do."

I'm shaking my head before he even finishes. "That's a lie. You don't know them."

Gently, he responds, "It's the truth, and somewhere deep down, you know it."

"Sy—"

"Thinks you're his lab rat. You're his dissertation, son. Your diagnosis, your behavior—it's his midterm project." He lifts a hand, gesturing wildly. "And Nick? He wants your connections to the law. It's the only way he could possibly get out of all this trouble he's been in."

"Where are you even getting this?" I ask, gawking at him. "Nick's never asked, not once—"

"But you have." Father raises his chin, daring me to deny it. "How many calls have you made to your uncle this year alone? How many times have you used your connections to the police force to get Nick above water? A little cover up here, a little extortion there."

He gives me a sad look, full of dread. "You do it because you're a good man. I know that. You want to take care of the people you love. But sometimes, all people see is what you can do for them."

"Stop." I push my fingers into my gritty eyes, temples throbbing. "You're twisting things around."

But he barges on. "They'll stab you in the back. They'll use you. They'll go along with your delusions to make you feel accepted."

"No." I shake my head, fingers twitching with an impulse I can't even give in to. Vinny isn't here to show me her star, but I still try to count them, vivid in my memory, envisioning the points.

One, two, three, four, five—

"And don't get me started on the Lucia girl," my father goes on, voice flippant. "It's a bit convenient that a King's daughter ends up in your bed, isn't it?"

Losing count, I snap, "You don't know anything about her."

His grin holds, knowing and cold. "I've had more women in my bed like her than you can imagine. She's *using* you, Remington. For your money, your connections, and your power. Put your marks on her—your bears and silly stars—but don't think for a second she's loyal to you."

My head snaps up, the words stabbing through my thoughts like daggers.

...your bears and silly stars...

How *the fuck* does my dad know about her tattoos?

"No," I tell him, slamming my hands over my ears. "You're lying! Shut the fuck up!"

I turn and face my worktable, taking a deep breath. Several, filling my lungs with air, trying to still my mind. This is what he does, I remind myself. He needles and pokes and prods until I'm twisted up and can't find my way back again.

Not anymore. Not with Vinny.

My hands drop, slamming on the metal table. "I'm not letting you get in my head and mess with my mind. People may fake their way into your life and into your bed, but that's not my life. I have real friends, a family, and a girl I can trust."

I say this aloud, facing the paints and pens and paintbrushes sorted into the shelf in front of me. It's less to him, than to me. A mantra. But I have to face him. I know that. Curling my hands into tight fists, and I spin, ready to show him real power.

But he's gone. No longer in the doorway. No longer sucking in my air. No longer existing. I rush to the hallway and find it empty.

I blink, filled with a blinding, blood-rushing anxiety that he was never here to begin with. Panic builds, mixing with the lingering bitterness of the Viper shit in the back of my nostrils. Jesus Christ. Here or not, I let him get to me, but there's one thing I won't let him do.

Get to her.

27

Sy

"Did you take my book on human sexuality?" I ask, impatiently picking through the stack of texts on the tabletop.

"I don't think so," she says. But since she rests a hand protectively on top of the backpack next to her on the floor, I know she's full of shit. "You probably just left it at home." She likes to do this thing where she bites her lip, eyelashes giving a small flutter whenever she wants to distract one of us. Remy would never suffer something so obvious, and Nick is too good at forming his own mask to ever buy someone else's.

It works on me, though.

Every time.

"I'm not going to get mad." I hold out my hand. "I just need it. I have to annotate this godforsaken paper."

Lavinia and I are sharing a study table in the library, sitting across from one another. Beneath the table, her shoes have been shucked off, her feet resting on my lap. It's one of her little challenges, desensitizing my constant and unfortunate boner, but it might also be another kind of test.

I didn't invite her into my bed last night. It was a clear anomaly. Usually, I'm the one impatient to get in there and feel her hands on me. I've even gotten pretty good at it—I think.

My journal is growing progressively more erotic. I curl my forearm around it protectively as I glance down at a page I wrote in a few days ago.

L: Likes her nipples touched. Not pinched, not plucked, just touched. Enjoys kissing, especially neck and chest. Doesn't like having her clit stimulated following an orgasm. Have not tried to insert my fingers vaginally, but the subject doesn't appear as unwilling as she has in the past and I'm curious to see how she'd respond. Chest turns vibrant red when aroused. Notable lack of pubic hair, but it is unclear if this choice is hygienic or sexual in nature.

Some nights, when I'm feeling ambitious, I even know to return the favor, tucking my fingers into her panties and rubbing her clit as she spreads her thighs to give me access. I know the soft drag of her teeth against her lip as she bucks into it, fingers squeezing my cock harder. But I don't always get her off. Sometimes I come first and we clean our hands before rolling over and falling asleep.

Sometimes, I pretend I'm sleeping as she finishes it herself.

But last night, none of that happened. I laid in bed and stared at the ceiling, silently seething. Not at her, though. At Saul, mostly, for knowing how to punish me so goddamn effectively. If I don't train —if I can't hit and win—then I'm going to lose the threads that keep me tethered.

So these little touches are her testing the waters just as much as my control. And I'm used to her taking my books. It's a compulsion with her, but I hate that she's using them to psychoanalyze me with them. Like how she read up on body dysmorphia and used that information to manipulate me into that competition with Nick and Remy. A competition I *won*—but still. I grew up with a mother who analyzed everything, from my wet dreams to my lack of a serious girl or boyfriend, and I'm not really into the Duchess plundering my damn psyche.

I take another glance at my journal, pausing.

I'm okay with being a hypocrite.

Her eyes narrow, like she doesn't quite believe I won't get mad, but ultimately relents. She opens her backpack and bends over, giving me a gaping view down her shirt, and pulls out the book in question. She sighs. "Is this it?"

She knows goddamn good and well it is. I take it and grunt out, "Thank you."

See? I can be a ray of fucking sunshine.

It's just that I'm not feeling it. I'm not feeling much of anything other than this festering irritation about our probation status. The weight of the decision is dragging me down. Should I have kept a tighter rein on my brother? Would that have made a difference? Or is this because I've been distracted? Consumed with this blue-haired vixen that sleeps in my bed and puts her hands on me every night, coaxing me into a mass of hormonal desperation?

Fuck. Everything is just a fucking mess.

It's been twenty-four hours since the tribunal, and I'm trying my best to process the outcome. Probation. No fights. Playing bitch for the other Royals. I'm not stupid. I know I'm the level head of this whole operation. If Nick or Remy knew just how badly I wanted to strike out, they might encourage me.

So I hide it.

Saul's the one that proposed the punishment—most likely because he knows how to make it hurt. Getting kicked out of the Dukes? That would have made us legends. No, this is petty bullshit to keep us in our places. Already, I can feel my inner ocean growing turbulent, muscles restless, jittery and on-edge. Remy's up next for Friday Night Fury, and now even that's been pushed back a week, someone else billed in his place. It's going to be fucking forever before I get in the ring.

It'd be so much easier to think clearly if I could just get some good hits in. If I could spend a couple hours pummeling the bag, sparring with Bruce, lifting weights until this buzzing energy under my skin dissipated.

Most of all, it'd be so much easier if I could think of something other than Lavinia's pussy.

I should have let her jack me off last night, but the truth is, it's not enough anymore. It barely even takes the edge off. It's like the more I get of her, the more I want. Suddenly, the thought of her hand on me seems lackluster. I need more. Ever since I watched Remy sink his dick into her, it's all I can think about. I almost regret watching so closely, my eyes fixed to the head of his swollen cock as he notched it up against her entrance, thrusting inside. I know that's what he was doing, too—showing me. Putting it on display. Letting me see what it was like to watch her cunt expand around a hard cock. How wet she got for it. The way her back arched when he fucked it in and out of her.

He wasn't trying to rub my face in it or anything.

But he kind of fucking did.

If anything, I think it's getting worse. This morning she walked past me, sweaty from our too-short run, and the scent of her body odor, ripe and raw, drove me to take a long, cold shower. And now, with the weight of her feet in my lap, so casual and loose, I look at her and imagine it for the millionth time: her beneath me, thighs spread wide. I think of the sound she'd make when I rub the head of my cock through her slit. I think of the resistance I'd feel as I pushed inside. She'd gasp. She'd probably tell me it's too much, but she'd take it. She'd be good for me. She'd stare up into my eyes as I slid inside.

That's one scenario. I have about a dozen. In some of them, it's quiet and soft, and I kiss her as I coax her through taking all of me. In others, she fights, and her angry, tear-filled eyes shine up at me as I fuck her, brutal and fast. In some, she's the one who does it, straddling my hips and sinking down, so sweet, not even a whimper.

I honestly can't tell which one gets me harder. But they all have one thing in common: I come inside of her, filling her up, spurting every fucking drop into her slick, tight cunt.

It's all I think about anymore.

I take a deep breath and do what works the best. Distraction. From the punishment, from the loss, from my goddamn blue-balls. There's something that's been bothering me. Something Lavinia mentioned in the belfry before Nick showed up with his demented version of a grand gesture and it came up again at the tribunal.

"So," I look around, making sure we're alone. "Care to share any more about what the deal is with your dad being 'armed to the teeth?'" Those are Killian's words from the tribunal. In the belfry, she mentioned a failsafe. It was clear at the tribunal that Nick knew all about it, which isn't a surprise. I've known for a while that Nick's cross-territory knowledge about Forsyth was extensive, but increasingly, I feel more and more left in the dark. Especially if he's going to keep making moves without us. "Because I'd really like to know exactly what that means."

Her eyebrow rises over the book she's reading, highlighter tucked between her teeth. "Now?"

"When I hear constant threats about him having something that can 'level' a whole town, I'd rather not wait."

Her expression shifts, voice lowering. "I know it's hard to imagine, but besides being an absolutely shitty parent, my dad isn't just power-hungry. He's also paranoid as fuck."

Sighing, I think of Remy. "A bad combination."

"Yep." She leans forward, pushing her heels into my balls. I grimace and shift away, only making it worse. "For the longest time, I thought it was just some kind of North Side fairy tale—you know, not the sanitized Disney kind, but the horrific original ones. The Grimm brothers, where daughters are sold off, or people cut off their hands and feet to appease dark forces and gain gold or a thousand bales of hay." She rolls her eyes, like she knows she's getting off topic. "I kind of always assumed my father built these myths to keep the soldiers in line, but when he really started grooming Leticia to marry Perez, she was privy to more Count business."

Lavinia has her hair up in a messy ponytail, but there are these loose tendrils of hair framing her face. She blows one away from her nose. "And since Leticia couldn't possibly find out something that massive and not rub it in my face, we both found out it was true."

I stare at her, blinking. "So... what's the truth, exactly?"

She looks left, and then right, pitching her voice lower. "My father spent years—decades, maybe—wiring Forsyth with explosives. If he's compromised, anything of value will go down with him."

My head snaps back. "Anything?"

"*Everything.*" Her eyebrow arches. "The University, the Hideaway, the Baron's Crypt, and the Prince's Palace—"

"Everything tied to the Royalty." Startled, I guess, "The Tower."

Nodding, she adds, "And probably the gym, too."

"Fucking hell." I shake my head at the enormity of it. "Are you sure? How is that even possible?"

She leans back, face exasperated. "I don't know, Sy. How is any of this possible? Buying and trading women, killing innocent girls, selling bullshit drugs on the street. This place is the hellmouth—only the demons here are human."

I run both of my hands through my hair, trying to wrap my head around it. "I guess this explains why the Lords didn't destroy the Counts after they kidnapped their Lady."

"And why my father gets so much leeway from the Kings." She presses her toes against my inner thigh. "Everyone has always played by the rules around here. I mean, except your brother." I catch the small, twisted smile on her mouth. The way her eyes slide down. The slight flush of her cheeks.

Christ.

Our Duchess grew up with a psychopath, and now that they're not fighting, Nick's deranged behavior may tick one of her boxes after all. I fucking knew she had daddy issues.

Shaking her head, she meets my gaze, head tilting. "Any idea what to do about it?"

Surprised I'm even being asked, it takes me a second to answer. "Not a fucking clue. But Lionel isn't the only power player in town. I have to wonder what kind of competing failsafes the other Kings have set up."

"Mutually Assured Destruction," she says, mouth twisting unhappily. "That seems on brand for these assholes."

The idea of the Royals having enough firepower to take one another out should be disturbing enough to kill my boner, but Lavinia stretches out, her toes brushing against the length of my cock, making my thighs clench. I place my hand over her foot to block her touch, ignoring her teasing glance.

"Would you just," I growl, snatching up her foot, "fucking *stop*?"

She raises an eyebrow, giving her toes a pointed wriggle. "Look, if we're all going to die in some Royal pissing match then I'm going to play footsie under the table."

I try to move her foot away, but not before she rubs her heel into my balls, sending another surge of blood to my cock.

"Lavinia..." My voice is low with a warning as I hold her foot still. "I've got a ton of work to do and I'm not in the mood."

She stares at me. "Not in the mood? You?"

Not for that, I want to say. Not for footsie. Not for quick, perfunctory handjobs in the dark. "No," I say instead, sounding laughably unconvincing.

Our eyes meet and there's a glint of something obnoxious lingering in hers. No, not obnoxious. Arrogance? Cockiness? She knows I'm lying. The hardness beneath her foot is enough to tell her that.

She grinds her heel down my length. "Why are you holding out, Perilini?"

"I said not now." I shove her foot to the floor, the thrust hard enough that she jolts at the force. Guilty, but stubborn enough to not show it, I sneer, "Jesus Christ, what happened to no meaning no?"

Her face falls, and I'm not expecting it. The disappointment.

The hurt? Like maybe she'd been hoping for something to go down.

No.

That can't be it. She gets a sense of pleasure out of this little game—teasing and taunting me. If she has any idea how tenuously I'm hanging by a thread, she'd be running the other way. Already I can feel the urges surfacing from my inner ocean of calm. There was a time that just made me at risk for starting a fight. Right now, the thing I want most is to see my dick buried inside her cunt, pulsating with my release.

"Lame," she says, but pulls her foot into her own lap. "I bet Nick and Remy would be ecstatic to have me rub them off in the library."

The look she gives me is nonchalant, dismissive. *Intentional,* knowing one little jab is enough to draw me into her game. But not today.

Lionel may not be the only one with a bomb lying under the surface.

Mine is just more personally destructive.

~

I PUSH past Lavinia and jog up the stairs to the tower. The mere thought of it rankles like a betrayal, but maybe this weekend, I can see about a membership at another gym. For now, jogging is the only exercise I'm going to get, so I take advantage, treating the stairs to the top like it's a competition.

Naturally, I win.

The resulting endorphins are weak though, no thrill to the victory of beating Lavinia, who's still gaining muscle mass and endurance, lost behind me before we even reached the halfway mark. I've already tossed my bag on my bed, heading for the kitchen when she reaches the door, chest heaving from exertion.

"I think I'm having a heart attack," she says, hand covering her rising tits. "I know we can't go to the gym, but making me chase you up the stairs is unnecessarily cruel."

"I didn't make you chase me," I say, opening the refrigerator for a bottle of water. On cue, the cat comes racing from wherever he was hiding, pushing his way around my ankles. "Not now." He persists, jumping up my leg and clinging to my pants. "Fucking—"

I shake him off—not hard—but he slides across the hardwood.

"Jesus, Sy," Lavinia cries, scooping him up in her arms. "I know you're pissed at me, but don't take it out on the Archduke."

I raise a hand to him, gaping. "That cat has shed more drops of my blood than I can count."

The kitten squirms in her arms, jumping out and dashing into Nick's room.

"Look. If you need the exercise so bad, can't we just train here?" Flustered, she looks toward the living room. "There's plenty of floor space. Plus, you told me you'd show me how to do that takedown move."

I swallow half the bottle before answering. "There's a list of cardio on the closet door if you need something to do." I start toward my room, but she cuts me off, sliding in front of me with a stony expression.

"Okay, what's your problem? Are you mad at me for Perez? Because I didn't ask to be—"

"I'm not mad," I say, which would be really convincing, except my hands are balled into tight fists.

She gives them a pointed look, shoulders curling inward as she crosses her arms. "Uh uh. Is this about the library, then? Because I was under the impression you liked me touching your dick, but all of a sudden, you're blowing me off."

"Maybe," I grit out, "I'm not in the mood to tip-toe around your weaknesses today. Pretending like you're making progress is fucking exhausting."

I try to make the insult land, but she's a Lucia. Vipers just strike back when you provoke them. Chin jutting out, she steps close to snap, "You think I can't handle myself? Because I can take you, and you know it."

I snort. There's that misguided cockiness. I wonder if she realizes how alike she and Nick can be. Crossing my arms over my chest, I jerk my chin. "You didn't handle yourself so well with Perez, and look how that ended. One messy corpse and three Royal probations."

Something in her eyes shutters, and I know I've found a chink in her armor. She blames herself. Just a little. "I got away."

"Okay. So you ran. Bravo, Lavinia." I slow clap, the sound echoing off the rafters. "You've always known how to run away like a little bitch. Don't expect a gold star from me."

A hot belligerence builds in her eyes, making her mouth purse tight. "You think I can't defend myself? Try me," she dares, planting her palms on my chest and pushing. "Come at me. You're such a big man. What are you afraid of? Losing? To a *girl*?"

My patience snaps like a twig, and I lunge for her.

She reacts faster than I'm expecting, jumping out of my reach, and it throws me off. I'm used to training with other men. Big guys. *Slow* guys. Lavinia is compact and agile, though. To add injury to insult, she gets in two solid hits to my ribs, fists smacking into my muscles. I turn to her, fuming. We don't usually spar like this, with bare fists and pulsing anger, and there's a reason. I can break bad on some motherfucker like Bruce, burying my knuckles into him over and over again.

I would break this fucking girl in half.

"Go on, Lucia," I taunt, holding my arms out. The name makes her eyes turn fiery and I like it. I like the way she squares up to me, the hard set of her mouth. I like when I tell her, "If you're going to hit me, then make it count," and she reacts instantly.

She punches me in the jaw.

I don't even flinch. "You're holding back," I note, scoffing. "How are you going to train with me if you don't even have the balls to hurt anyone?"

"I've hurt plenty of people." She readjusts her ponytail before lining her shoulders back up. "Just how hard do you want it?"

I raise my chin, demanding, "As hard as you can give it." On the inside, there's a rogue wave barreling toward me, but externally, I'm still as stone, waiting. "You wanna prove you can take me? Stop hitting like a girl, and just hit!"

Lavinia puts up a big front. I get it. The life she's led has probably been sixty-forty posturing and hubris. She's good at it. Convincing, probably, to someone who doesn't know her like I do.

I see the wince in her eyes a second before her knuckles make contact.

"Again," I growl, barely even feeling jostled. I need more. I don't know why, but I know the pain, however small, dulls the roar of the wave. "Fucking clock me!" She doesn't even set up for it this time, striking out. "Again!" The next hit barely knocks my cheek—a bad aim. She's losing it. It's all over her face, the flush of red, the angry brow. "Again!"

After the fifth hit, her eyes begin to get shiny in that specific sort of way. A lot of people don't understand this about the fight—that you pull from a part of yourself that's wild and unfettered, and it doesn't care if you only want certain parts of it, it'll all break through.

"Don't you fucking cry!" I snap before the tears can fall. "You need it. You need to hurt. It's something I see in most of DKS, in one way or another. I see it in Nick and Remy. Me, most of all. But you..." I watch her trying so hard to gather all that emotion back up, shoving it down. "Yours is different, Lavinia. You don't need it because it's fun. It's not even that you want to win. In fact, I'm betting you'd be fine with losing so long as you got one good shot in. So fucking do it!"

It's only half disingenuous. She does need it. Nick took her kill. I can see it in her every day, the need to push back at the world. It's the only thing about her I can understand—the only thing I can really get a grip on.

Mostly, though, *I'm* the one who needs it.

I need the pain to ground me. I need the hit to remind me I'm still on my feet. I need the adrenaline, the touch, the proof that I'm more than a ticking machine. The fight is the only place I make sense.

Gradually, she gains control of herself, blinking back the flood of her own inner ocean. I've felt the pull of this tide—I know the unending force of it—so when she squares up to try again, our gazes meet over the distance and I feel proud. Proud, and for a split second, fucking terrified. In a blink, she swings out with just the right amount of anger—not too much—arm straight as it flies toward me.

I think I might love her.

The notion bludgeons my head from the inside while Lavinia's knuckles take care of the outside.

It's a beautiful hit. Artistry. Truly enough to rattle my teeth. I can barely hear her feral grunt over my ears, fucking screaming. It's possible that I stagger—just a little—but it's lost in the rush to grab a fistful of her hair and crush our mouths together.

Now she's the one caught off guard, mouth parting in surprise as my tongue dives between her lips. I pull her hair too hard and she hisses, her fingers digging painfully into my sides as we crash to the floor in a sweaty, breathless heap.

It's not the same as a fight. I wrestle her arms down, pinning her wrists to the floor as I kiss her, and it's a horrible proxy. There's no blood or sting, no sense of stakes, no one watching to see when I win.

But fuck if it isn't close enough.

She makes a grunting sound, struggling against my hold. "God, getting hit makes your dick hard, doesn't it? Of course it does." Despite the snarl to the words, her face is flushed a vivid pink, eyes heavy with lust.

I stare down at her, grinding my cock into her hip. "Thought you could take me?"

"Not when you're sitting on me, asshole." She works one of her hands free and pinches my nipple, twisting it.

"Son of a—" I fly into action, straddling her torso. I tuck one of her hands between my leg and her side, then get a hold of the other one and do the same, effectively restraining her. I enjoy it a little too much, watching her buck and squirm. "You want to fight me? Do it. Get free."

She's completely immobile, other than the wriggling of her lower body, which keeps knocking into my balls.

She wets her lips, peering up at me with dark eyes. "If you get any harder," her eyes blink heavily, gaze coming to rest on my crotch, "that thing is going to smother me."

Unconsciously, I follow her gaze to the bulge in my pants. It's pure instinct to rock against her, and I get this vision—this absolute fucking crazy-making image—of what we'd look like if we were naked, my cock between her tits.

I'm pretty sure I used to have a stronger will than this. There was a time I'd see her ass in a tight pair of pants and just turn the other way, shoving the feelings down. Now, I find myself yanking her top up, jostling both of us with the force of it. I stretch it over her tits, revealing her bra. Lacy. Black. Some expensive front-closure contraption Remy bought for her.

With one twist of my fingers, it unhooks, falling to the side.

"What are you doing?" she asks, her voice quiet.

I stare at her tits. So perfect. Round and supple. "Do you know how much I hold back all the time?" I ask, voice ragged as I palm each breast. "When we fight? When we mess around in my bed at night? All I do is hold back, Lavinia." I cup them in my hands, squeezing them together. Her nipples pebble under my thumbs and I bend to take one into my mouth before licking my way to the other. She tastes good. Like both sweat and soap, like sweetness and conflict—like everything I can't have.

I rise up, licking a hot path between her breasts and sit back, panting. I've been watching a lot of porn these past few weeks. If I wanted to lie to myself, I'd say it's just part of being a guy. But the truth is, it's her. Being with her. Anticipating her coming to my bed at night and wanting to not embarrass myself. It's the thought of bringing her something she doesn't need to walk me through. Surprising her. Pleasing her.

I dip my hand into my shorts and pull out my cock, stroking the length.

"What are you going to do?" she eyes it warily, taking in the familiar length.

"Whatever I want."

I spit on my hand, slathering it on the length of my cock, then press her tits together again and slot the head into the crevice between them. The first plunge feels like a revelation, thrusting my dick between her tits, watching her head tip up to watch.

Her lips part like she's hypnotized. "Does that... feel good?"

Not answering, I pull my hips back, dragging my cock against her flesh before pushing back. "You ever had anyone fuck your tits before?" I ask, bearing down on her.

Her head drops back, eyes unblinking as she stares at me. "No."

It shudders through me like a bolt of electricity. I'll never be the first cock she takes in her cunt, her mouth, her ass. The knowledge that I'm the first to fuck her like this is more potent than I'm expecting. I like to think I'm above it—the need to conquer a woman like this.

Maybe I'm not.

I bite the inside of my cheek, willing myself not to come. Not yet. *God-fucking-dammit*, not yet.

Mentally, I follow our lessons, finding a rhythm, taking my time, and the longer I move against her, the more her body moves with me. Hips writhing in time to the pumps of my hips. Breaths heaving her chest up and down with each push. My cock is leaking like a motherfucker, sticky fluid slicking the way for me as my fingers dig into her, thumbs scraping over her nipples every now and then.

It's the feel of her around me, the firm flesh of her tits, the punchy little cries that make me go to the hilt. Her tits are big enough to take the girth of me, but the tip presses out to the hollow of her throat, jabbing into the soft skin beneath her chin. My balls drag against her ribs, and her nails press into the outside of my thighs.

It's slick and hot, the two of us staring at one another as I fuck her chest. It's fast and hard, and even though I'm probably hurting her, she doesn't seem to mind, her tongue swiping out to wet her lips, like this is doing something for her, too. It's as close to fucking a girl as I've ever gotten and I can feel the tingle, my balls tightening as my release rushes up.

And it's still not enough.

The frustration builds within me, hot and angry, and I rear back, dick slipping away.

"Sy," she says as I hook my fingers into the waist of her pants, wrenching them down. Her thighs snap closed as I tear them from her legs, over her ankles, tossing them away. "Sy," she repeats, alarm clear in her voice when I grab her knees, prying them apart. "Hey, wait!" She pushes up to her elbows, trying feebly to back away, but I yank her back, forcing my way between her legs. I smell her heat before I get there. Remy was right before. Her pussy smells fucking amazing, and I know that she's wet even before I touch her.

"Stay still," I snap, fisting my cock with one hand and pushing her thigh apart with another. When I lean forward, rubbing the tip of my cock through her folds, her body locks up, tense and rigid, and I know it's fear.

One quick glance proves it, her eyes wide and pleading. "Sy, don't—"

I could.

I look down. Her pussy is so pink and open, and I feel her on my dick, hot and slick. It takes me second to find my bearings, it's all folds and secrets and sensitive parts. She's fucking soaked for me—from *me*, nothing but a quick and stilted titty fuck—and I use the wetness to glide the tip of my dick to her entrance, slotting right up against it, careful not to push through.

"Stay still," I say again, giving the shaft a few fast tugs. Truthfully, I don't need it. The sight alone of my dick against her hole is enough to make my balls go tight, the proof that we fit together the way a man and a woman should. All it would take is one thrust.

The orgasm slams against me with all the force of a flood that's been held back too long. I grunt as the first surge arrives, my dick jerking as it feeds it into her. "Oh, fuck," I gasp, fingers digging into her soft thigh as I empty into her hole.

Or as close as I can get, anyway.

The cum spreads into her folds, messy and imprecise, and in a fit of annoyance, I pull my dick away to replace it with my fingers, fucking the cum into her angrily, resentfully.

"Oh," she breathes, raising her hips into my hand, fucking herself on my fingers. "Don't stop, don't—" Her head is thrown back, fingers scrabbling against the hard floors. The tendons in her neck stand out in sharp relief, her tits red and irritated from my hands and cock.

Without thinking about it, I duck down to prod my tongue into her clit, almost getting hard again at the sound she makes, loud and startled as her fingers wind into my hair.

I always thought I'd be grossed out by eating pussy, but I see now what Remy meant. The power of it is heady and acute. I feel it now as I peer up her body, my fingers burying my cum into her as my tongue teases her into a trembling mess. She's not tense anymore, the fear replaced with an urgency that's clear in the buck of her hips, the grip of her fingers around my hair, the soft, desperate cries spilling from her red lips. It's sloppy, the sharp taste of my own release mingling with the sweetness of her arousal, but she clutches me close, guiding and greedy, using my face just as much as I'd used her tits.

She might not want my dick.

But she wants me to have her pussy.

She comes on a strained cry, her heels grinding into the floor as she arches into my mouth. I make a sound of my own, low and rumbling and victorious as I lick her through it. My fingers, still buried inside of her, feel the clench of her muscles as she seizes and my brain picks that thought up and saves it for later. God, to feel that around my cock, just once...

I crawl next to her and lie on my back, the two of us staring at the ceiling as we catch our breath. I feel sticky and wrung out, my dick spent against my thigh but still willing to stir at the sight of her bare body, the occasional quake skittering through her muscles as I watch.

She closes her knees, thighs rubbing together, and there's this sheen to her eyes that I don't often get to see. Like she's drunk. Blissed out. *Satisfied*. "That was—"

"Are you my girlfriend?"

She turns to stare at me. Her face is slack, but her eyes are distinctly startled. "Uh. What?"

I turn away, swinging my gaze back to the rafters. "We fool around. We live together. We kiss sometimes, even when we're not having orgasms. We fight, and then we make up. Isn't that what having a girlfriend is like?"

There's a long moment of silence where I wonder why I even asked. This is why I can't do this shit during the day. At night, I have an orgasm, roll over, and pass out. Now I'm all fucking filter-less and off-kilter.

Eventually, she answers, "I guess... well, I belong to you. And Remy." In a lower, slightly disgruntled voice, "And sometimes Nick."

"But are you our girlfriend?" I press, pushing my hand through my hair.

"Do you want me to be?" she asks, sounding strangely belligerent.

Instantly, I say, "Yes." And then, "No." And then, "Fuck, I don't know. I've never had a girlfriend." Maybe when Remy and Nick call her their Duchess, that wraps a bow around it for them, but I never planned on having one in the sexual sense. Now there's this girl in my bed, my pants, my mind, and I just know she's *something*, and 'Duchess' doesn't cover it. I struggle—badly—to put it into words. "I need some fucking parameters here."

"I'm not sure how to be a girlfriend, Sy." She rests her cheek against my shoulder. "I've been a daughter, a piece of property that's traded, and then this... the Duchess. I've barely figured that one out."

I try not to take it as a rejection. I don't think it is. Because she's so strong, so bossy and determined, I forget that Lavinia must feel lost sometimes—just like the rest of us. I swallow. "Whatever. I was just wondering."

She turns to face me, eyes holding mine. "There would be worse things than being Simon Perilini's girl."

"Yeah?"

She nods and kisses me, light and soft on the lips. A contrast to the violence before. It's not until later that I realize that although she didn't say yes about being my girlfriend, she also didn't say no.

28

Lavinia

If I ever thought the Dukes were unbearable after a victory, then I had no real understanding of what they were like after a loss.

It's not a real loss or anything. There wasn't ever a moment in the ring where someone else's glove was raised. The other side didn't throw a party to celebrate. There was no trophy or belt or girls stolen out from under their noses.

This is the kind of loss that drags on in the ears of strangers.

Royal probation.

The energy that buzzes between them is somewhere between pissed off and vengeful, followed by a heavy dose of depression. I know them all well enough to understand how they'd all usually react to something like this. Sy would train until he's too exhausted to feel anything else. Nick would hustle and engineer things back to their favor. Remy would either stop taking his drugs or begin taking the wrong ones at a worrying volume.

But all of that has been taken away.

The gossip around campus makes it worse, the spotlight shining on every member of DKS as they walk across the quad or sit in the student center. Each and every move is like one big walk of shame. The only relief is when my Dukes get back to the tower, but even then, it's like three rats circling in a cage.

They need something to do.

Sy has taken to compulsively working out in the living room. Remy is lost in his artwork, headphones firmly attached over his ears as he works on this piece he's doing of the Baron King. We've had two more sessions on my moth, but it needs to heal before he can add more. And Nick?

Well, Nick follows me around, room to room, usually quiet, thinking about something he's not quite ready to share.

"You know what I keep thinking about?"

Until now, apparently.

Nick leans against the cold bricks, legs sprawled in front of him. We're up in the area of the clock tower that holds the mechanics. I've almost rebuilt the clock parts, which has been intricate, tedious work that I'm not even sure is anywhere approaching 'right'. He's got his ring in his hand—the one with the brass Bruin on it—and he keeps flipping it up in the air and then snatching it into his palm, fidgeting with it.

Tink.

"What?" I ask, straining to tighten one of the bolts.

The ring spins and falls, his hand coming out to grab it. "We need some leverage on your old man."

I spare him a dry look, wondering, "Are you saying you don't have any? You've been the one in the trenches for the last two years."

His eyes tighten as they follow the ring. "Nothing big enough. I mean, not unless you count... well, *you*."

I give the wrench a hard pull. "I doubt he does."

He holds the ring out, brows furrowing as he inspects it. "He wanted us to send you back. At the tribunal, that was one of his requests. But you're right." He closes his palm around the ring, his head falling back against the wall. "He doesn't really care about getting you back. He hasn't made a play in weeks. He just wants to—"

"Take away your shiny new toy," I grumble, wincing as I struggle with the wrench.

Nick's silent as he watches, a shadow filling his eyes. "We need to do something about your dad's failsafe."

I bark a humorless laugh. "Oh, you mean the four-square miles of bombs running under our feet right now?"

"Yes." He flips the ring again.

Tink.

"Don't you think that if someone could have done something about it by now, they would have? The other four Kings don't seem happy about it, and they're not exactly powerless."

Tink.

"I get the feeling those old geezers are so set in their ways, they don't even realize how fucked up they've become," he says, catching the ring and jamming it onto his finger. He leans over and holds out his hand, making the universal signal for 'gimme'. Defeated, I place the wrench in his palm and watch as he rises to his feet to get to the bolt. He tightens it easily, the long muscle in his forearm tensing as he ratchets it up and down. "But we're not old, and I don't like the idea of living on a live-wire."

I sit back as he tests the rest of the bolts, tightening them where he feels a weakness. Something like this would have annoyed the shit out of me a few weeks ago: someone going in behind me and testing my work, finding it lacking, doing it their way.

Now, I just sit back, arms around my knees as I watch his muscles and sinew. The Bruin brawn sure is something, Nick's back flexing with every revolution of the wrench. If it were summer, I bet he'd have to take his shirt off.

Clearing my throat, I shake out of that insidious, creeping daydream. "You're on probation. You can't do anything right now without risking your title."

"My title." He scoffs. "I wasn't lying when I told them I don't want it, Little Bird." He glances at me under his arm, the tendons shifting above his wrist. "I don't give a shit about any titles. I came back into the fold for one reason." He points the wrench at me. "To win you."

He could have told me that a million times before and I would've called bullshit. But not anymore. I understand him better. I believe him. Nick sacrifices for the people he loves and I don't doubt that he loves me more than most.

It's still an uncomfortable realization that I try not to think so much about. Accepting that I've somehow gained a guardian attack-Bruin is one thing. Facing the other aspects of it is hard enough when he's *not* in front of me, all flexing and rippling and... pretty.

Ugh.

He finishes tightening the last bolt and drops the wrench into the toolbox.

"My sister loved secrets," I say, trying to get my brain back on the rails. "I think Tate was her biggest one yet—maybe one she would have fought for, tooth and nail."

He sits opposite me, making a winding motion with his hand. "Elaborate."

"To leave with Tate," I explain, eyebrow arching, "to truly escape my father? She had to do more than run. She'd need something else."

"Leverage." His expression smoothes. "Just like the kind we need."

I nod. "Leticia had access, knowledge, and resources that I was never privy to. On top of that, she was good at it. Conniving, you know?" *Like you*, my mind whispers, thinking of Nick. My stomach twists at the thought of him and my sister having something in common and I scramble to my feet, holding out my hand, offering it to him. "So maybe she already put in the work."

Nick gives my hand a short look before grasping it, rising to meet me. "You think she found something," he guesses. "Something useful."

I stare up into his blue eyes, my voice firm and sure. "Oh, I'm certain of it." Leticia wouldn't have left for anything less.

Nick searches my face. "How would we find out what it was?" And then he groans, hand rubbing through his hair. "Are you going to make me break into that house again? That dog really doesn't like me."

"No," I tell him, feeling the buzz of energy in my chest. I take his hand. "Because you may have already stolen what we're looking for."

He stares at me for a moment, comprehension dawning over his features. "The box."

I grin and drag him downstairs.

~

NICK PULLS the SUV behind a nondescript beige office building. There's nothing but the street numbers affixed to the side, and I don't like it. The street is dark and too normal-looking. Silent. Still. East End is always so neat and tidy; it reminds me of North Side. Money and pretense.

My skin crawls with unease.

Nick cuts the engine and rests his wrist on the wheel, casual in a precise way that tells me he's on edge, too—just better at hiding it. "We still have about ten minutes." When I nod, his thumb taps the wheel, eyes scanning the street in front of us. "We could make out."

I peer out my window, eyes rolling. "Seems like a nice way to get ambushed."

Nick knows I'm right, which is why the offer is hard to take seriously. His next question isn't a joke, though. "Are you fucking Sy?"

I turn to look at him, not sure what surprises me more; the question or the mildness it's asked with. The familiar snap is on the tip of my tongue. *It's none of your business*. Only, he's watching me back with such an aloof expression that the defensive feeling never arrives. "No," I answer, nervously rubbing my knees. "We just... you know. Fool around. Sometimes."

Despite the words, I think of Sy's question from yesterday and have to fight back a grin.

"Are you my girlfriend?"

Sy is this massive guy, so strong and commanding, but sometimes I get these glimpses of the boy within—the man who doesn't have any experience with girls—the ear-blushing, stilted, fumbling lover that is Simon Perilini.

Every day, I find myself hoping to catch another glimpse of it.

"Hm." Nick rests an elbow on his door, inspecting his nails. "He's just been really wound up lately."

I groan, head falling back. "God, tell me about it. I mean, he's intense even on a good day, but ever since the tribunal..."

Nick meets my gaze, his mouth set into a grim line. "Just be careful with him, alright?"

I blink. "What does that mean?"

"Sy can be..." Nick shrugs, looking away. "Explosive. Like a faulty fuse. I'm not saying he'd break bad on you or anything, just... sometimes I think his urges to fight and fuck fork off from the same root."

Slowly, I say, "Okay."

After a moment, Nick sighs. "He got in a fight this morning." I turn to decipher whatever it is I hear in his voice. Disappointment? Dread? He glances at me, explaining, "He used to do that a lot back in the day, before he found DKS. Pick fights, find someone to beat the shit out of, get into all kinds of heat. He hasn't gotten into a fight outside of the ring in years."

"Oh," I say, trying to figure out what this means. "Is he... in trouble?"

Nick shakes his head. "It was some random LDZ in the parking lot outside of campus. Killer's letting it slide. For now." The last two words are ominous, signaling a weight that I didn't realize Nick felt. I get the impression that, however Sy used to be, Nick possibly got familiar with smoothing things over for him.

It's a weird flip of the tables.

Nick must sense my awe because he glances at me, snorting. "I know it's hard to believe, but there was a time when Sy was the problem child and I was the good one."

"You're right," I say. "That *is* hard to believe."

When the ten minutes are up, he shifts. "Hand me that case," he says, pulling his gun out from under the front seat. Smoothly, he reaches behind himself to tuck it into his waistband before handing me a second pistol.

I trade it for the metal case lying in the floorboard below my feet. Nick swears up and down there's not a severed body part inside, but I still grimace as I hand it over. "You really think they'll have what we need?"

All we have to go on is the old receipt we found in Leticia's box. I figured it was worthless—nothing there but four random numbers scribbled onto the back, and no way to figure out what they go to—but Nick told me he's been mulling it over for a while now, making calls, doing recon on the pharmacy.

Now we're here, at some weird, back-alley company.

Nick explains, "Bastion Security is owned by Ashby. He knows everything going on with the businesses in his territory. Word on the street is they keep tight records on all of their clients." He slides me a look. "Extortion, robbery, blackmail... easy things to do when you know everything about how a place runs." With a jerk of his chin, he gestures to the building. "I confirmed through one of my old South Side contacts that Kilpatrick Pharmacy is one of their oldest clients. We can at least see if we can find a video of the day she bought that stuff."

Okay, so it's still a long shot. The only thing keeping me going is the fact she kept that receipt. She wouldn't have kept a random piece of trash in that box. My sister was a lot of things, but sloppy was never one of them. She had to have known there was only one person who'd find this trove of clues: me.

We step out of the car, but as soon as I round the front, Nick stops me. "There's one more thing."

I look at the hand he has on my arm—not gripping, just holding—and then his eyes. "What?"

He opens his mouth and then closes it. The low light of the alley punctuates the deep set of his eyes, carving them into hollows. "The thing is... this guy we're meeting..." he stalls, scowling for some reason that I can't suss out.

"Yeah?" The unease in my gut grows. "Spit it out."

Nick takes a breath. "This guy—he thinks me and you are together, like a legit couple." Nick looks toward the building, jaw tight. "And I need him to go on thinking that."

My nose screws up. "What? Why?"

He whirls back to me, hissing, "Because, it's just one of those things we have to do to get the intel. Don't ask questions!" My head snaps back in outrage, but before I can bitch him out, he gently jabs a finger into my shoulder. "You know, I ran South Side for two years pretending to be loyal to Daniel Payne. You can handle a few hours as my girlfriend."

"Fine!" I snap, keeping my voice low. "But you should have told me before we got here!"

He links our hands together and drags me across the alley, ignoring the daggers I'm glaring into the back of his head. On the way to the door, I hold up the receipt, searching for something, anything that makes sense. There's a date and time on the slip of paper, and underneath, I can barely make out the three items she purchased. A phone case, a portable charger, and a package of sour gummies.

It's the last one that keeps tripping me up.

"Tisha hated sour candy." I think about how, when we were kids, she'd toss it out if she ever got any: trick-or-treating, church functions, goody bags from friends' birthday parties, holiday baskets.

"Yeah," Nick says, pressing the button by the glass door, "well, Tate loved them."

I watch him from the corner of my eye, feeling nervous and out of sorts. As soon as Nick mentioned checking the video, I had to wonder if he just wanted to see if Tate was with her. It seems far-fetched that we'll find anything useful on a video that's over two years old. If it even exists.

Through the glass, I see movement at the end of the hall. A skinny guy appears, walking toward us. His brown hair is shaggy, long enough to brush his shoulders, and he's got a thin, pitiful-looking mustache that must have taken him years to grow. His bright Hawaiian-print shirt is the loudest thing about the moment, and he approaches us without any sense of alarm, his feet bare.

I raise my eyebrows at Nick. "This is the big scary guy we have to convince we're dating?"

Bullshit.

I try to tug my hand away, but Nick tightens his grip, too focused on the door opening to notice my furious stare.

"Pretty Nick," the guy greets, licking his lips. "Pretty on time and pretty fuckin' fine." He smirks, eyes crawling down Nick's body. I know an eyefuck when I see it, and this guy is already balls deep. He lifts his chin. "Ready to pay up for the put up?"

"Charlie." Nick hauls me up against his side. "This is my girl."

Charlie's mouth turns down as he looks at me. "Ah, I don't know, Nick." He scratches the back of his head, pulling a face. "I don't do threesomes. Not with chicks. I mean, no offense. She's got a great rack, but it's lost on me. I'm more about vibing on this." He makes a long, serpentine gesture to mimic Nick's body.

"Oh," I whisper, "my *god*." I twist to gape at Nick. "Are you whoring yourself out for this?"

"Hell yeah, he is," Charlie gushes.

Nick shoots Charlie a sharp look. "*No*. I brought the alternative payment. The one we discussed. At *length*." From the long-suffering look on Nick's face, this isn't a conversation he wants to revisit.

Charlie's face falls when he sees the case in Nick's hand. "Oh." Clearly disappointed, Charlie lets us in, locking the door behind us and punching in a code. "Can I just..." Turning to Nick, he brings his forefinger and thumb together in a pinching motion. "Just a little?"

"No," Nick answers, unequivocally. He hands the case to Charlie, who takes it with a beleaguered expression.

"I hate this fucking town. Hot guys everywhere and none of them will sell their ass to you," he grumbles, waving us toward the back. "Third door on the right."

We head down the hall, and a small glance over my shoulder reveals that Charlie's eyes follow Nick's ass the whole way. The room we enter is filled with computer equipment, the air humming with the vibration of fans. There's a giant cup of soda and a pile of discarded snack wrappers on the desktop. The room has an odor. It's not good.

"Oh," Charlie says when he enters, like he's noticing his little depression nest for the first time. Scurrying around us, he pushes the garbage into the bin on the floor, clearing his throat. He sits in a chair and gestures for us to grab two others. I move to take one, but Nick grabs my hips suddenly, pulling me down into the other with him, settling me on his lap.

I try my best not to lock up as he winds his arms around me, breath rustling my hair.

Charlie begins, "Since you gave me a general date—and that pic of your abs—I already pulled up the file." He opens a tab, and the screen is split into four black and white sections. It takes a moment to process it, but there are four different security cameras: the front checkout, the parking lot, the pharmacy counter, and the drive through.

I twist to give Nick a look, mouthing, *your abs?*

Nick pointedly doesn't notice this. "Is this the best resolution?"

"It's shrunk to fit the frame," Charlie says, glancing over his shoulder. His eyes fall to Nick's arms around my waist. "Did you have a time?"

"Yeah," I say, pulling out the receipt again. "Ten-forty-seven. AM."

Charlie narrows his eyes and turns back to his screen, pressing a few keys. "Keep an eye out on what you're looking for and tell me when to stop."

The videos start moving at high speed, all four at once, and I scoot forward to track it. My eyes and brain try to keep up with the images, people coming in and out, the clerk and pharmacist talking to customers, stocking inventory, answering the phone.

Nick curls close behind me, his hand moving to my hip as he ducks in. "Since she was a paying customer, but not buying meds, we should focus on the front," he tells me, his eyes obviously as strained as my own. "I'll watch the parking lot."

"Go back," I say, knowing we've gone too far.

Charlie rewinds and slows the footage. Someone walks in the front door in a sweatshirt with the hood pulled up and I jump, pointing. "There," I say.

"That's a dude," Nick replies, his thumb rubbing a soothing circuit into my hip.

Frustrated, I argue, "No. See the flash of light on the hand? It's a reflection. Those are rings. Leticia always wore three on that hand."

Nick pauses to ask Charlie, "Can you make that bigger?"

"Yeah, sure." Charlie clicks around, expanding the frame to fit the whole screen.

It's still grainy, and it's hard to see her face, but I recognize the shape of her, slender and elegant, and the way she walks, smooth and graceful, floating like a dancer. "That's her."

"You're sure?" Nick asks.

"Completely."

He deflates. I can feel it in his body beneath me—against me. "Right. Okay." The disappointment is even clear in his voice. No Tate.

"So… she goes in," I say, watching my sister's moves. It's strange seeing her like this, in an unguarded, unknown moment, especially now that I know I'll never see her again. "She grabs the case and charger."

She heads to the counter, puts the items onto it, looks down, glances toward the door, and then…

Leticia grabs the sour candy, placing it beside the case and charger.

Nick and I share a look.

"Expand the parking lot," he says, leaning so far over, he'd dump me out of his lap if it weren't for the way he's clutching me close. Charlie presses two keys and the screen shifts. There are several cars in the lot, but one is idling by the curb, exactly where Leticia had been glancing. It's not a car, though. It's a Jeep. The top is on, of course, making it hard to see inside, but once Leticia pays, she walks out and goes directly to it, hopping inside. On the video, it's easy to see her toss something into the backseat to a shadowy figure.

"Tate," I whisper, touching the forearm Nick has clamped around me. "She's in the back."

"Who's driving?" Nick says, squinting. "Do you recognize this Jeep?"

I shake my head. "No."

But then the driver takes off, turning the car in a tight U-turn, giving us a full view of his blond hair and sharp profile.

Nick slams back into the seat. "Son of a—"

We look at one another. I pull out my phone. "Guess it's my turn to make some calls."

WE SIT in the car for a long time, staring out the windshield at the building in front of us. There's something heavy rising in my throat, a fist clutching my lungs, and for a second, I think I might be sick. It might have been different if we'd planned this. *Maybe*. But we just left Bastion Security fifteen minutes ago. It's all happening too fast.

"I don't know if I can go in there." The words emerge in a thin rasp, as if I'm just testing them out, determining the truth of them.

Nick rests his Bruin ring against his curled forefinger, thumb flicking it into the air again.

Tink.

"Okay."

"I went into the motel," I say, feeling weirdly defensive about it. "I slept there with Sy for three nights."

Tink.

"I know."

I go on, "I'm not a coward. It's just different here." And then, "You wouldn't get it."

Tink.

Nick finally looks at me, blue eyes hardening. "I wouldn't get it?" Shifting to slide the ring onto his middle finger, he asks, "Do you know why I asked you to pretend we were together back there?"

I scoff. "Because Charlie wants your dick, and you needed a way to let him down gently?" Curtly, I add, "And because you wanted to make me sit on your cock."

Nick snaps, "That wasn't it at all." The sharpness of the words makes me flinch. "I don't let people down gently, Little Bird. And I didn't ask you because I don't trust Charlie. I asked you because I don't trust myself."

I pull a face. "With... Charlie?"

"No, I mean—" Flustered, he looks forward, out the windshield, pointing to the building. The Velvet Hideaway. "You know what's back there? Behind the building? The Pit. You've heard of it, right?"

I fight down a shiver, hugging my middle. "Of course I've heard of it. It was my sword of Damocles for months."

Nick jerks his chin in its direction. "Then ask yourself what kind of guy Daniel would want in there, on camera, fucking his best girls." Turning to me, he raises an eyebrow. "Someone good-looking, right? Someone with a nice cock. Someone who could look scary."

I freeze, eyes growing wide. "You mean, you... did that for him? With the Hideaway girls?"

His eyebrows crouch low, making him look menacing. "I'm not stupid, Lavinia. I know what I look like, and I know when it's useful. I can put people at ease with a smile, or I can make them nervous. My face—my *body* is a weapon." He shakes his head, reclining back in his seat. "Do you have any idea how easy it could have been for me back there, with Charlie? I could have had Bastion's whole operation laid before me with nothing more than —" His words bite off, face hardening as he looks at me. "But I'm done being that kind of weapon. Do you understand?"

I'm not sure I do. "You didn't trust yourself?"

He sucks his teeth, tapping the steering wheel. "Sometimes, when I'm out here on the streets, doing shit like this... I lose perspective. Sometimes, the mission is all I can see." He lifts a hand, reaching out to tuck a strand of hair behind my ear. His eyes follow it, burning a trail across my cheek, my temple. "The mission, and you."

The cabin is quiet and dark, and Nick is close—close enough that I inhale the scent of him, spicy and industrial. I think of walking back into that place, the Hideaway, and remembering what we are. A prisoner and her guard. A victim and her attacker. A Duke and his pawn.

Swallowing, I ask, "Can we pretend for just a little longer?"

Nick's blue eyes blaze into mine, and I worry for a moment that he'll get the wrong idea. But he just takes my hand, lifting it to brush his lips across my knuckles. "As long as you want."

I didn't plan on ever going back to the Hideaway but here I am, walking hand in hand with Pretty Nick Bruin as we cross the parking lot. Story meets us at the side door—a private entrance to the office—and only gives our hands a brief look before waving us in.

"Hey," she says, "Get in here before anyone sees you."

We're not here to see Story, though. Or Killian. The Lord we're looking for is sitting behind his desk, forehead creased as we walk in. Tristian Mercer watches me and Nick closely as the door shuts behind us.

He looks disgruntled. "Anyone want to explain why you dragged me down here on a Thursday night? Because Killer already told you Sy was off the hook for that scuffle with Tucker today. What more do you want?"

I hadn't told Story what we needed Tristian for—just that it was important.

"It's not about that." Nick pulls out a tablet and queues up the video, sliding it across the desktop. Tristian picks it up and watches the video play through twice, chin propped on his palm, clearly bored.

"What am I looking at?"

"You," Nick answers. "Isn't that you driving the Jeep?"

Tristian looks down again, recognition taking hold. "Uh, sure... maybe?" He plays it again and slowly nods. "Rath crashed that Jeep into a dumpster behind the liquor store our freshman year during LDZ initiation." He points at something on the screen. "You can see the bent fender here. So yeah, sure, that's me." He looks up at us. "Why?"

Nick rolls his eyes. "Watch it again—do you remember who you were with that day?"

Tristan clucks his tongue. "Man, that was like two or three years ago. How am I supposed to remember that?"

Story looks between me and Nick. "What's this about?"

"That's my sister," I finally tell them. "The one in the passenger seat, wearing the hoodie. There was someone else in the backseat."

He narrows his eyes. "Seriously?" Comprehension crashes onto his face and he rears back. "Whoa, I did *not* kill your sister, if that's what this is about. I didn't even know it was her!"

"Cut the shit, Mercer," Nick says. "You knew."

Tristian holds up his palms. "I didn't. Back then, people just referred me for things that met my specific skill set."

From the way his lip curls, it's clear Nick doesn't believe him.

But I press forward. "What did you do for her, exactly?"

"I think..." Tristan studies the video again. "Yeah, if this is the one I'm remembering, she needed help with a remote detonator. Not my favorite way to light shit on fire. Personally, I like the smell of gasoline on my skin for a few days, but, hey. To each their own."

"So you met up with Leticia Lucia and helped her with a detonator?" Nick asks, looming above the desk. "A detonator for what? Where? Be specific."

Tristian sighs, sliding the tablet back to Nick. "Yeah, I programmed a phone for her, but it was just the raw mechanics. She never said what the explosives went to. It's not something I do often, and it was pretty elaborate, so it took me some time." Looking impishly pleased with himself, he turns to his Lady, explaining, "I left a group of contacts on it. All she had to do was call the contact of her choice, and the fuse would blow."

Nick's jaw tenses. "And you didn't think to ask what she was planning to blow up?"

Tristian swings a glare to Nick. "No, I didn't. I don't ask questions." He raises his chin defiantly. "Do you?"

Nick doesn't even blink.

I hold up the receipt, pointing to the numbers scribbled on the back. "Do you know what this is? She would have written it down while she was in the Jeep with you."

"Well, yeah." He leans back in the chair, hand snaked out to pull Story closer. "That's probably the passcode to unlock the phone."

"The phone." Nick says slowly. "The one you gave to Lionel's heir. To remotely detonate explosives."

I see it come together on Tristian's face when the pieces click. Surely, Killian gave his men a rundown of the tribunal meeting and the discussion about my father's cache of explosives. He touches his lip. "Ah, fuck."

"Yeah, fuck," Nick says, turning to raise his eyebrows at me.

"Look, dude, I had no idea," Tristian insists. "I'd never met the chick before. I didn't know who her dad was or any of that shit. I just knew that the two of them..." He gives Nick a significant look. "They were hot, bro—like, seriously, all over each other. We're talking making out, groping, teasing. I was hoping they'd let me in on it, if you know what I—*ow*!" Story scowls at him, looking unapologetic for the slap she just landed to the back of his head.

He rolls his eyes. "Sorry, sweetheart, but it's true. I was just a stupid frat boy looking for pussy and shit to light on fire."

I believe him, and from the scowl on Nick's face, he does, too. "Thanks for your help, Mercer. Make sure no one knows we were here, and we'll make sure no one finds out you created the key to Forsyth's complete annihilation."

So my sister not only had the means to destroy my father if he came after her. She had the means to destroy anyone. Which means one thing. Leticia wasn't killed for running away.

She died because she didn't run far enough.

~

THE STREET outside the Tower is quiet, typical for a late Thursday night. Sy and Remy are probably upstairs and I'm wondering how we tell them everything we just found out.

Nick parks the car and exhales, leaning back in the seat. I feel like I've spent all night watching him like this: tracing the lines of his face in the shadows, waiting for his blue eyes to find mine within them.

Slowly, they do. "So what was your sister's backup plan? To blow up Daddy if he tried to stop her from running off with Tate? Or to blow up all of us?"

I answer honestly. "I don't know." Leticia was cold and calculated, but a plan of destruction and death on so wide a scale would be a thing of utter fucking madness. "I doubt it was either of those," I admit, remembering my sister, thinking of her skull, still tucked away in stone, up in the tower. "Tisha was good at what she did, Nick. She wouldn't hold something like this in the palm of her hand for the sake of it. If I had to guess, I'd say it was just... insurance. A way to make a credible threat."

"You realize what this means," he says, searching my eyes.

Nodding, I agree, "Whoever killed her and Tate... this was their motive."

"And anyone could have had it," he finishes, not looking happy at the realization.

Two steps forward, one step back.

Nick's eyes never leave my face, descending to my cheeks, my nose, my mouth. His hand is still gripping the steering wheel, and I can hear a faint creek when his fingers tighten. "I guess we don't need to pretend now," he says, eyes dark.

"We don't," I answer, finding my gaze narrowed onto his lips.

Later, I'll swear and up and down that Nick was the one to surge forward first. It'd be a lie, though. I'm the one to push my mouth against his, setting off a cascade of pyrotechnics I feel deep in the pit of my belly.

Nick meets me instantly, a hand coming up to tangle in my hair, crushing me close as he grunts into my open mouth. Our tongues meet like magnets, and he tastes sharp, like desperation and heat and *want*. It's the first time I let myself acknowledge that I've been squirming for this all fucking day, watching his shifting muscles and stoic eyes. To be the one who makes him groan, low and strained, as he roughly wedges a hand between my knees. To fist my hand into his shirt and wrench him over the center console, so frenzied that I slip in my haste to meet him. I don't give myself time to think, to feel anything except this ember in my belly flaring to life, hungry and demanding.

It's a power I never knew I wanted, the knowledge that someone could be mine, any time, any way. Nick would kill for me—die for me—and I feel his hunger for me like a wild, angry thing. For the first time, I let myself indulge in the crush of his brow as he kisses me, sloppy and too hard, too fast, as if he knows it's a hairsbreadth from being snatched away.

Kissing Nick is like trying to harness lightning.

It isn't until he pushes his palm up my skirt, rough against my inner thigh, thumb grazing my center, that I freeze, sense flooding back to me like a sledgehammer. I gasp as I rip myself away, chest heaving, mouth so hot that I swear it could be glowing in the dark.

Nick snaps back to his side of the car like a rubber band.

We both sit back in our seats, the cabin noisy with our labored breaths.

Awkwardly, I straighten my skirt, whispering, "I think we should stop pretending now."

That's the problem with Nick. He'd die and kill for me, but his love is too savage and twisted to endure without hurt. Tonight, the prospect of it is sexy—painfully enticing. But what will it be like tomorrow, when he wants to hold me down again?

What will Nick's love look like when I'm unable or unwilling to return it?

He clears his throat, reaching down to not-so-subtly adjust himself. "Yeah, alright."

We open our doors at the same time, and I gulp in the chilled air as I tumble out, eager to reorient myself. That's when I hear the sound of music—the same fast-paced chords I often hear coming from Remy's room late at night. It's echoing down the street, distant, yet close, and when I bend my neck to peer up the tower, I see the windows of the party room's floor illuminated.

Nick and I share a dark look before entering the tower.

The climb is slow and quiet, and even though he doesn't look back at me, I can still feel his awareness like static across my skin. Maybe the hardest part of tonight is that we haven't been pretending at all. Nick wants me, and in some deep, primal way, I want him back.

At the top, Nick yanks the door open and Ballsack must be on door duty, because he grins when he sees us. "Hey!" he cries, eyes foggy with intoxication. "Duke! Duchess! Welcome home!"

"Isn't this specifically *not* supposed to happen?" I ask, pointing to the crowd of people behind him. "Or did the probation get lifted?"

Ballsack snorts. "Oh, hell no. This is what we call an unofficial event," he explains, waving to another kid who rushes over with two drinks. "Those bastards canceled Family Dinner, but even though the Dukes aren't on the bill tomorrow, gathering before a fight is tradition. We're not gonna let those shriveled old fucks interfere with crucial DKS rituals." Sniffing, he squares his shoulders. "We all talked about it and decided the underclassmen are willing to take the fall. Plus," he adds, twisting to gesture to a group by the stereo, "We invited some LDZ guys to smooth over that little spat before. Mutually assured destruction."

It's a surprisingly sweet sentiment, but I don't think I can relax enough to have fun. I look back at Nick, assuming he feels the same way, but he grabs one of the red cups and tips it back, swallowing it in one gulp.

"Good call, Ballsack." Nick hands over the empty cup, face blank. "Hit me again."

"Seriously?" I ask him, lowering my voice. "After everything we learned tonight, you're going to just... get fucked up and party?"

Nick stares at me. "What else am I going to do? If I worried all the time about the rope that's constantly tightening around my neck, I'd never do anything else." I gape at him and the tattoo on his temple shifts when his eyes pinch. "Maybe this last week has confused you, but I'm not a hero, Little Bird. I'm the piece of shit heroes call when they need dirty work done. You find one of those, give me a call. In the meantime..." He pushes the drink toward me. "Take it while you can."

Relenting, I take a reluctant sip. The drink is fruity, spiked with something hard that burns down the back of my throat, and I realize Nick's right. Wallowing over this new information isn't going to change anything. Not tonight, at least. We've all been living on top of my father's intricate deathtrap for years. One night of debauchery isn't going to set it off.

And if it does?

Then I guess we went out having fun.

I take another sip, feeling warmth instead of the burn. The place is packed, from every fresh-faced recruit, to the more mature faces of upperclassmen. It looks like every DKS member showed up, along with all the cutsluts. Verity's talking to a few people back by the dartboard, and Haley's sitting with a few girls I don't recognize, watching Remy give a brother a tattoo.

"Hey, Nick." I look over and see white-blonde curls and a lot of cleavage.

"Brittany," Nick says back, and then nods at me. "You've met the Duchess."

"Yeah, hi," she says, eyes flicking down my not-so-party-ready outfit of a skirt and an oversized hoodie. Her hand rests on Nick's forearm. "Can I get you anything? A drink? A blunt? Or...?" The unspoken offer that hangs in the air is obvious enough without the way she bites her lip.

That, plus the way the other girls no longer seem to be giving him cold glares, tells me the cutsluts have dropped their moratorium on entertaining Nick. I'm not mad about it. I'm surprised they gave me the courtesy at all, and I *have* been looking decidedly non-murderous around him. They probably think we've buried the hatchet.

Maybe they wouldn't be wrong.

Problem is, Nick's gaze drops to the hand she's still resting on his forearm, and for a second I feel this white-hot jab of spite. The moment makes my chest constrict, a dull ache that forces me to think about taking a breath. Nick would be well within his rights to take any woman in this room. Plus, I just got him all worked up in the car. Why shouldn't he? It's not like I'm putting out for him.

I raise the cup to my mouth and start to turn away, oddly unwilling to watch him take her up on the offer.

It's the most Lucia-like I felt in a long while.

But then he gently removes her hand, saying, "Nah, I'm good." He lifts his chin. "You should go check on Weasel, though. He looks like he could use some company."

Something in her eye falters, but she still grins back. "Sure, okay."

She's barely two steps away when he leans over and runs his thumb down my cheek, drawing my eyes to his. "Jealous, Little Bird?"

I immediately scoff. "Hardly."

He doesn't look convinced, eyes dropping to my mouth. "I see how it is. I can't have you, but I can't have anyone else, either. Is that right?"

It *is* right. I can't rationalize it and I don't try. It's greedy and senseless, and I won't let Nick have me, but the thought of him choosing someone else makes me want to fucking *scream*.

Leaning away, I say, "Have whoever you want," and feel my stomach churn with the words. "I'm not stopping you."

Nick watches me, those blue eyes studying mine too closely. "You're right. I *can* have any pussy in this place. But in case I haven't made it clear," he ducks down to speak into my ear, "it's you or nothing. Never doubt that."

In a blink, his heat is gone. I watch, hypnotized, as he grabs another drink and weaves through the crowd, all cocky smiles and knuckle-to-knuckle fist bumps. The weirdest thing of this whole day is that I know he's telling the truth. After all we've been through—after all the hurt we've inflicted on one another—Nick still wants me more than anyone else.

The tension in my chest dissipates, and I leave the crush of the bar. Nick has made his way to the dartboard, his smack talk loud enough to carry over the music. My eyes seek out Remy, who must sense me watching him because he pauses what he's doing to reach down, grasping the neck of his beer bottle. The long, greedy look he gives me while taking a pull settles in my bones like lava. His pupils are wide and black and it makes me shiver, being under the phantom weight of his attention.

Before I take another breath, he's back to work, the hum of the tattoo gun sending a chill down my spine. I've gotten addicted to the feel of the needle in my skin, and the way his hands and mouth touch me when he's finished?

That's not so bad, either.

Since he's clearly too busy to take care of the pressing situation between my legs, I retreat, searching for something—anything—to cool me down. I duck between two couples making out and take a step right into a solid wall of muscle.

Big hands steady me, and I look up into lazy blue eyes. "Oh," I say, relieved to find Sy. And then, "Jesus, Sy, your face!"

There's a nasty scrape just below his eye, already scabbing, the skin around it red and raised. He responds by dipping down to kiss me, hard and slow, the nearby whistle of a DKS member spurring him to gather me close. "Hi," he says, breathless and deep, and from the bulge digging into my hip, already hard. "I've been looking for you. Where have you two been all night?"

"Long story." I put my hand on his chest, indulging in the feel of him, always so warm and solid. I suppose I've found the advantage of having three Dukes. If I won't let myself have Nick, and Remy is too busy to see to me, then there's always Sy. "Can we talk about it tomorrow?"

"Yeah. Sure." He's hot. I can tell by the way he pushes back his mop of curls, eyes fixed to my mouth. He's also something else...

I narrow my eyes, noting how his muscles are loose, even though his eyes are quick and cutting. Oh, and his thumb keeps making small circles on the skin just below the low rise of my skirt. "Are you drunk?"

He gives an easy shrug. "If I'm going to be forced to spend the next month as a loser, I'm going to need to self-medicate."

"You're not a loser," I tell him, pushing up on my toes to soothe him with a kiss.

His hand winds around my back, crushing me to him, deepening the kiss. I'm well aware this is more PDA than Sy would usually be comfortable with. We only just worked up to brief kisses in front of the frat, and now his hands are all over me, clutching, rubbing.

If he were sober, he'd never kiss me like this in front of all these people—deep and frantic, just like he is in the dark, late at night, when we're tangled in his bed. Shamefully, I meet his intensity with my own, unable to hold back the surge of want that's been building within me all day.

Sometimes, when Sy looks at me, I see the parts of him that match Nick.

And right now, I want them.

29

Sy

The fight with the LDZ pissant barely lasted three minutes.

It's not like he didn't have it coming, shoulder checking me on the way to my car with a sharp, muttered comment.

"...aren't bowing to a house that's run by some virgin fuck."

"The fuck did you just say to me?" I asked, whirling on my heel to push him. I know what Nick and Remy think: that I'm just on edge, falling back into old habits, losing a grip on my control. But that's not the truth of it. I could be on the top of the goddamn word and I wouldn't have let something like that fly. Neither of them would have, either. But Nick and Remy aren't carrying around this annoying fucking reputation. They're allowed to get into skirmishes in the back parking lot, knuckles crashing against the LDZ's jaw like a hammer. They're allowed to let loose, to back up their threats with violence.

Why the hell can't I?

The guy I scrummed with—Tucker—is standing over by the stereo equipment with his three LDZ buddies, laughing as he drinks our booze. That's half of the reason I feel so buzzed tonight. It's like the warrior equivalent to blue balls, only landing four hits before Nick and Remy hauled me off the guy.

But Lavinia...

She tastes sweet and bitter, like the cocktails the boys have been passing around to the girls, hoping to get them loose and willing. And it's working. All night, all around me, people have been making out. In the corner by the staircase, barely cloaked in shadow, a senior DKS member has a cutslut by the hair as he fucks her face. There was a time I would have shut something like that down, but tonight, I let it fly, and people have noticed, taking advantage. Every flat surface is occupied by a couple, and if I let myself look long enough, I'm betting some of them are full-on fucking, struggling to be subtle about it as the guys push their dicks into the girls, hidden beneath skirts that look a lot like the one Lavinia is wearing.

I finally understand it.

The need for flesh, the heat of her tongue against mine, the frantic pulse of blood and life, the instinct to dig myself into her cunt...

Tonight, I'm not a victor.

I'm not leading a house.

I'm just a man.

Lavinia makes a small, startled sound as I reach down to palm her ass, lifting her skirt for maximum contact. But when I drag her toward the couch in the back, she follows, her lips never leaving mine, so she doesn't mind. I've been searching for her all night, restless with the urge to feel her against me, just like I had yesterday, and I'm not disappointed. She stumbles along with me, her hands fisted into my shirt, and it just makes me more frenzied, fingers digging low into her ass cheeks.

Three recruits are lined up on the cushions, taking hits off a bong in the shape of a bear's head. I pull away from Lavinia to jerk my head at them. "Beat it." They scramble out of the way, one dropping a lighter. It bounces off the floor, and he moves to pick it up, but the look I give him is enough to make him forget it and back away slowly.

Sitting, I go to pull Lavinia into my lap, but she beats me to it, straddling me with an urgency that's unexpected, but not unwelcome. I grab her hips and yank her up close, flexing my groin up into her.

"Hey," she breathes, raking her teeth over her bottom lip. "What happened here?" Her fingertips are gentle against the scrape on my cheek.

I fist my hand in the back of her hair and say, "Don't worry about it," before dragging her mouth back to mine.

This.

This is what I've needed all damn day.

Her weight on my lap, the little sigh she makes into my mouth, the way she surges closer, her pussy grinding onto my dick. My blood feels so fucking full of it, like it's been replaced by something atomic and rabid, and I throb with the need to do something. My inner ocean of calm is little more than a dried pond bed at this point, and I don't fucking care anymore.

All the practice and handjobs and titty fucks in the world can't keep me in check tonight. Especially not when she leans into me, pressing her tits against my chest to whisper, "Want to go upstairs?"

I flick my gaze to the corner as she sucks the skin below my ear, watching the LDZ guys. "I can't wait that long." Shoving my hand between us, I roughly push her panties aside and plunge my fingers into the damp heat. The second I feel how wet she is, slick and hot, a harsh rumble rises from my chest. "Neither can you."

She gasps, rising up to give me room, but I also catch the way she looks over her shoulder at the room full of recruits, brothers, LDZ, and cutsluts. When she looks back, I see the hesitation tugging at her mouth. "Hey, just... take a deep breath," she says, grinning with her cherry red lips, "then we'll go upstairs, and I'll take care of you."

I press my forehead against hers and hold her eye. "You're my girl, right?" I ask softly. She nods. "Then this is part of it. Being seen. Being... together."

Her eyes drop to my mouth and it's hardly even a pause. "Okay." She exhales, hips moving against mine. "You want it like—"

"Ride me, just like you did at the Baron's party," I demand, brushing back her hair so I can see her face. "I want to feel you."

The look she gives me, heavy-lidded but simmering hot, tells me she's feeling the same thing I am. Dark, awkward fumbling isn't what either of us wants. We're beyond that now. I knew it yesterday when I came into her folds, when she quivered against my tongue.

The hot, energized part of me wants nothing more than to take her upstairs, get us both naked, and find out what that even means. But the agitated, drunk part of me looks at that Tucker douchebag —at everyone in this fucking room—and just wants them to see what I see.

That Lavinia Lucia wants my dick.

It's easy to let the music and shadowy corner swallow us. Lavinia shifts back, breathing just as eagerly as I am, and kisses me while reaching for my fly. Her face flushes with vivid splotches of pink that I follow to her jaw with my mouth, down to her neck. I shudder when she finally reaches into my pants to pull my cock free, her soft, cool skin against my hard, blistering flesh. I shouldn't even be able to get harder, but the sensation of her palm wrapping around me makes it happen. The small tickle in the base of my cock, the pump of blood making me longer and harder.

We both look down at the same time, our foreheads pushed together as we watch a clear drop of precum bead on the tip of my dick. Reaching out, she rubs it with her thumb and then brings it to her lips.

She holds my gaze as she tastes it.

My jaw goes slack.

Smirking, she rises up and guides me under her panties,

sighing when the tip brushes across her pussy. She likes how long I am, that I cover the length of her, tip to root, nudging at her ass crack, pressing against her clit. Mostly, I try to hold it together as I feel her slickness against me, my hands digging into her hips to steady her.

I wonder who got her wetter.

Me or Nick?

"You like that?" I ask, guiding her hips, making her pussy slide against me. When her eyes fall closed on a soft moan, I look over her shoulder, making note of everyone who's watching. The bong-smoking recruits from before, all three of them, have their eyes glued to her ass, still covered by her skirt. I'd expected that much. Haley, the cutslut, is all the way across the room, but she's watching.

One of the LDZ guys is, too.

Not Tucker, the one who called me a virgin, but his buddy, beer suspended halfway to his mouth, is openly gawking at us.

It feels good to know they're all seeing me like this—claiming my girl.

Good, but not enough.

I slide my hands up her thighs, beneath her skirt, around to her ass, and we move. The rhythm we fall into is natural, her eyes so dark as she rides me, soft, blue hair falling around our faces like a veil. It'd be easy to get lost in it, to shoot off right here, right now, and I'm hot—so fucking hot—from the booze or the urges or *her*, but I hold it back to sweep her hair away, getting a peek at the eyes on us. A man and his woman.

Her hips roll against me as we trade frantic, obscene kisses. She knows to stay on her knees, giving me room, and I massage her ass, keeping her wide open for me. Thighs tensing, I brush my fingertip along her asshole, feeling the puckered ridge. She lets out this little hitched cry that makes me pant like a dog under the fever of knowing she likes something so dirty.

"Don't stop." Her nails dig into my biceps and her hips rock with purpose. "Don't stop." She slots us together, an attempt to build that final round of friction. She's close, her mouth opened against mine as she gulps in my air, which is why she probably doesn't hear when Ballsack yells out.

"Fuck yeah, Perilini, get it!"

There's a round of shocked laughter, and then a chorus of cheers, but when I look up, the first pair of eyes I make contact with across the room are Nick's.

He watches us for a moment, and then turns pointedly away, the knot in the back of his jaw tense.

The LDZ prick is watching us, though. Eyes narrowed, Tucker jabs his elbow into his friend's side, saying something to him that I know must be as snide as the curl of his upper lip.

Teeth gnashing, I grab Lavinia by the hips and wrench her up—just a little, just enough to grab my dick and notch the head of it against her entrance.

She freezes, chest heaving as she licks her lips. "What are you...?"

I give her ass a hard squeeze. "Just the tip, okay?"

Her eyes widen, darting side to side. "Here? Now?" She tries to wriggle away and I indulge in the feel of it. "Sy, I already told you I can't—"

I yank her back, hissing, "I've never once asked you for anything, Lavinia. Never."

She pauses, an unease falling over her features. It's because she knows I'm telling the truth. All those nights of her hands on me, I never told her to. I never ordered her into my bed. How many days have I spent in class, daydreaming about her mouth on me? And I've never asked for it.

In a futile effort to hide the part of me that's desperate to tear her apart, I cup the back of her neck, holding her close until our mouths are a whisper apart. "You can take just a little bit, right?" I move my hand, rubbing the head of my cock against her. "Just let me in that much. Please?"

The plea burns sour in my throat, but I give it freely, watching as she blushes even redder, whispering, "Just the tip?" Warring emotions cross her face. Fear, want, guilt. I tug at them all until she relents. "Fine, but—"

I grasp my cock. "Ready?"

Before she can answer, I'm already bearing up, wrapping my arm around her neck to press her down.

She gasps, loud and shocked, as the head of my cock breaks through, entering her.

Her lips move, but I don't hear what she says, my ears so full with the rush of her around my cock. It's so much hotter than I imagined, and *tight*. Fuck, she's like a vice around me, and for the first time, I understand it. The Velvet Hideaway. That's what her pussy is, smooth as velvet as I rock up into her.

I feel the resistance as she tenses up. "Th-that's all I can take."

My hips flex and release in a rhythm that's older than me—primal, instinctual. I couldn't stop it if I wanted to. It's as necessary as breathing, fucking the head of my cock into her tightness thoughtlessly, gaining another slow inch. "You can take a little more," I whisper, barely recognizing the sound of my own voice. "Come on, baby. You're so fucking wet, I can just..."

Her brows crush together and she winces, head shaking. "It's too much—*ah*!" Her yelp is as sharp as the stab of my cock, forcing another inch into her.

She tries to ease herself upward, away from my cock, but my arm is as immovable as steel against her shoulders. It just gives me the room I need to glide out and push back inside, and even through the almost unbearable tightness, her cunt strangling the tip of my dick, it hits me. I look at her, breathless and awed as my hips move. "I'm fucking you."

Her hand claws into my shirt, teeth clenched. "It hurts."

"You're taking it," I argue, fucking in and out of her mindlessly, recklessly. It's not even halfway in, but it's sex. It's wet and hot and so much slower than I want, but I'm fucking her, and that fact alone running through my head is almost enough to make me erupt.

Her head shakes, cheeks having lost their color. "I can't, please, I'll— I'll use my hand."

I'd know a fight anywhere, and right now Lavinia's thighs are levering her up as my arm forces her down. I don't even think about it. I fight back, and it's just like the sex we're having. Instinctual, fundamental, a force as vital as the blood buzzing through my veins. I grip her hard and shove up, jamming my way inside.

A cry rips from her throat, and she falls against me. I don't know what the sting is at first, her teeth digging into my shoulder, but I know the pain, driving me harder and deeper, just like it always does. Maybe later, I'll think of myself weak for giving in to the call to fight—the urge to fuck—but right now, I clutch her close and let it take me, too intent on getting inside, feeling her around me, making her mine.

"Sy," she grinds out, trying to pull away. I hold her in place.

"I'm close—just," I growl, pushing her down, "fucking chill."

She's so busy enduring it that she probably doesn't even notice the air against her ass as I ruck her skirt up, spreading her wide.

"Holy fucking shit," someone exclaims. "Dude, he's nailing her!"

I don't need to see the eyes on us when I feel the weight of them, only enhanced by the sting of her teeth sinking into my shoulder, hard and punishing, the same way I'm hurting her. I'm not sure which of these lights my body on fire, but I grunt and crush her close, feeling it spread through my limbs like an explosion.

My body seizes, and she tenses over me, bracing herself. I come so hard that my vision goes white. Somewhere in the back of my mind, I know everyone is seeing it, my cock pulsating as it pumps her full of my cum. In the valley between mindfulness and the complete fucking chaos that is finishing inside of a girl, I forgive them. *Everyone*. Nick, for chasing pussy so hard. Remy for falling in love with the art of it. The guys in the frat for rarely thinking of anything else.

It all makes sense to me now.

Pussy is fucking *transcendent*.

I'm not as deep as I want to be, only halfway in, and it's still so tight that it's a miracle I have any circulation at all, but it's a religious experience. My thighs quiver with the force of it, jaw clenched on a hiss as my cock surges itself to exhaustion.

"Fuck," I breathe, landing against the back of the couch, muscles going limp.

I win.

"I told you to stop," she spits. It's not a surprise when she shoves off of me, my spent cock slipping out of her as she backs away on wobbly legs.

"Wait," I say, voice lazy and slurred, but she punches out when I reach for her, knocking my hand away.

The escape isn't a surprise.

The look on her face is.

"You want to be a normal guy so badly?" Her eyes are wide and wet, bottom lip quivering. "Well, congratulations. You're just like the rest of them, Simon."

Even in the shadows, I see the shimmer of cum as it drips down her inner thigh.

I refuse to look at her, instead tucking myself back into my jeans.

My hand comes away with a smear of blood.

Staring numbly at it, I argue, "You're always saying you can take me," but it's pointless.

She's already slipping into the crowd of people, most having the good sense to turn away, as if they didn't just watch her getting fucked.

Most have that sense.

Tucker doesn't.

He lifts a shoulder in a shrug, and then his drink, the gesture clear and readable.

My mistake.

It's supposed to inflate this feeling in my chest—a feeling I'm not embarrassed to admit that I love: Victory. It's not that it isn't there, because it is.

The pride is just lost inside this strange hollowness.

I know more than anyone that sometimes you walk away from a win broken down and battered. Bleeding or with a limp. The best victory comes after a hard fight, and Lavinia and I have been going the rounds for weeks now. There was no way she wasn't going to feel a little pain, but she's tough. That's why it had to be her. She's proven that to me, time and time again. No, she *challenged* me. She knew what she was getting when she agreed—and she *did* agree.

I have nothing to feel bad about.

Nothing.

Standing, I zip up, not caring when a few cutsluts glance my way, eyes curious. Enough people saw me fucking my girl—actually fucking her—that the gossip will start to filter through the crowd and all the rumors and whispers about my ability to satisfy a woman, about being a *man*, will be put to rest for good.

I've just gestured to a recruit to go get me a beer when my brother parts the people like Moses cutting through the Red Sea. I plaster a drunk—*hollow*—grin on my face, knowing if anyone understands how momentous the occasion is, it's him. Nick lost his virginity when he was fifteen, in the backseat of some skank's car. He spoke about it for hours that night, laying back in his bed, bouncing a baseball up and down, both our dicks getting hard as he relayed it, beat by beat. The whole time, I kept thinking that it wasn't right. I'm a year older. I should have been the one teaching *him.*

Burning with jealousy, I still gave him a high-five.

There are no high-fives tonight.

He storms up to me and slams his hands into my chest, knocking me back violently.

"What the fuck did you do?" he shouts, loud enough to draw more attention our way.

"Can you be a little more specific?" I ask, not willing to let him take away the buzz I'm supposed to be feeling. "It's been a long week."

The recruit shows up with my beer, and I reach for it. Nick snatches the bottle, liquid sloshing on the floor. "The Duchess just ran upstairs." His voice lowers, dripping with venom. "With blood running down her legs. I repeat: What the fuck did you do?"

I see the dark glint in his eye. He knows exactly what I did, and instead of coming over here with the celebratory drink I'm owed, he's being a petty, jealous ass. Like always.

"Nothing you haven't," I reply, pushing past him, "but at least I got permission first."

He grabs me by the shoulder and spins me back to face him. The muscle in the back of his jaw tics and mine does the same. We're brothers here, through and through, each of us measuring the other up, and I understand exactly what this is. We're one second from a Nick Bruin meltdown because I got my dick in his precious pussy before he could get his back in.

I wait for him to throw the first swing, the anticipation sparking over my skin like static, but even Nick knows we can't hash this out in front of guests.

"Get non-members out of here," he barks at the recruit, who hasn't moved. The command snaps him into action and three DKS round them up, Tucker included, and guide them toward the door. The LDZ brothers don't fight or argue. They understand just as well as we do that family business—*house* business—is private.

After they're gone, Nick bends down to tighten his shoelaces, muscles tight and coiled, and I laugh, the sound just as empty as this pit in my chest.

"Okay then," I say, making a show of rolling up my sleeves. I guess I'm ending this night with two victories. One for losing my virginity, and one for beating the shit out of my brother.

Nick prepares by scanning the crowd gathering around us, gaze locking onto someone by the bar. "Verity," he says, voice clipped as he jerks his chin. "Go upstairs and check on Lavinia." Her eyes skip from him to me, but she doesn't ask questions, just nods and vanishes up the stairs.

The hum of Remy's gun goes still and a second later, he ambles over and looks between us, brows pulled tightly together. "Come on; don't be bringing this red shit around here. Not tonight. I don't have the energy for it." But then he glances around. "Where's Vinny?"

"Upstairs," Nick answers, eyes never leaving mine.

His eyes look toward the ceiling. "The fuck is going on?"

I raise my chin, giving a cold smirk. "You see, Nicky here thinks he's going to beat my ass for being a little too rough with the Duchess. Apparently, he's the only one who gets to do that."

"Too rough?" Remy looks at me, dread filling his eyes. "What did you do?"

"I fucked her," I say, but even though I still feel that whisper of pride, I feel the hollowness of it more. "She asked for it—I didn't force her." Even as I say it, I know I'm skirting a line, but they wouldn't get it. It was hot, and she was wet, and she *let me in*, and my body took over. Flustered, I add, "It's nothing a little Advil and an ice pack won't—"

Crack!

Nick's fist slams into my jaw. The crowd behind him pinches tighter, shocked voices merged with the music. I taste blood and spit it on the floor, turning to fix him with a slow, lethal glare. "Little brother," I warn, "think about what you're doing."

Perilini vs. Bruin is a matchup of the century. The kind of fight people would pay big money to watch—not because of the sportsmanship, but because for once, the true victor would be declared. The rightful leader of this group of misfits.

"I told her this would happen," he seethes, fists still balled at his sides. Louder, he barks, "I fucking knew you'd do this! I gave her to you—both of you—and you sat up there and fed me some bullshit about how you'd be better at taking care of her." He shakes his head, laughing darkly. "Almost twenty-two years old, and you still don't know how to untangle your hard-on from your fists."

"That's one mighty glass house you're living in," I say, the wave building. "We wouldn't be here if you hadn't spent the last two years running wild, selling your soul and skills to South Side. If you hadn't stolen a King's daughter out from under his nose and killed, maimed, and decapitated your way under her skin." I take a step closer, feeling all the emotions of the last few days—maybe longer—bubbling to the surface. "If it weren't for you and your own goddamn impulse control issues, we wouldn't be on probation—much less at risk of losing the whole goddamn frat!"

"Don't try to turn that shit around on me," he says, eyes flashing. "I did what no one else had the balls to do."

Wildly, I gesture to the crowd. "You admitted it yourself! You don't give a shit about DKS. *All* you want is her pussy, and now you're throwing a tantrum because she gave it to me instead." The tide in me feels like it's been rocked by an earthquake, the ocean floor shifting under my feet. All these months of holding us together—the club, the Dukes, Lavinia—have dragged me in deeper by the undertow. "Without me, you wouldn't have a home, a family, protection... and you sure as fuck wouldn't have her. Don't forget," I hiss, jabbing a finger into his chest, "*I'm* the one who saved her."

Nick's fiery gaze follows my finger, and I know what he's thinking. If I were someone else, he'd cut it off and give it to her as a present. Instead, he sends me a dark, empty grin. "So you think you're the hero here? After what you just did?" Head shaking, he looks me up and down, lip curling. "Yeah, I fucked her, but at least I saw it for what it was. Look at you flexing, like cramming that thing into someone who can't even fight you off is worth being proud of. You're no hero, big brother." He looks me in the eye, showing his teeth. "You're a fucking loser."

The tidal wave unleashes, wild and out of control. I lunge for him, but a wall of wiry, ink covered muscle wedges between us, shoving me back.

"No!" Remy shouts, and behind the white-hot rage, I feel the hands of my frat brothers cinched around my arms and shoulders. "We're not fucking doing this. This is exactly what he wants—you know that, right?" Bodily, Remy pushes me away from Nick, jabbing two fingers into his temple. "He gets in your head and fucks with everything! Yellow and red make bronze. Open your goddamn eyes!"

Shoving him off, I stare at my friend, his eyes dilated and crazed. "Oh, this is rich. You're two walking fucking disasters. Remy won't stop snorting Viper junk long enough to understand what's even happening, and you," I say to Nick, still hungry to feel his bones beneath my knuckles, "you're still sneaking around behind our backs—don't deny it. You think we haven't noticed all of these excursions you've been taking her on? Face it," I snap, "Neither of you can function without a minder!"

"Oh, and that's you, right?" Nick asks, eyes belligerent. "Maybe you can get down from your cross long enough to realize no one wants you minding them!"

I can feel where the punch would go—right here. I'd lay into him. Remy would mix in with it, maybe some of the frat brothers, maybe even some of the cutsluts. It'd be ugly and bloody and beautiful, and I can't even feel the urge to get it started. I look at them, these men who are supposed to be my brothers, my family, in blood and spirit, and I don't feel it. The threads that used to hold us together aren't there anymore.

And I'm sick of pretending they are.

"Well, I quit," I say, turning to the stairs. "I'm done."

Fuck this.

No, fuck *them*.

I shrug off the recruits and push past Remy and my brother, leaving them both behind. I get to the stairwell and jog up to the third floor, pushing through the door and into the dark silence. Remy and I got the party started before the sun even set, so none of the lights are on up here, casting the cavernous space in nothing but the eerie glow of the skyline seeping through the clock face.

I give myself a second to breathe—to think.

And then I hear the voices.

Looking toward the bathroom, I see a slice of light. The door is cracked barely an inch. The whisper is quiet and faint, and the closer I get to the door, I realize it's Verity.

Turning my ear to the crack, I hear her saying, "...won't need stitches, but we should clean it." The voice is soft and hesitant and so careful that it makes my fists clench.

There's a long sniffle, and then Lavinia's garbled reply, "I'll do it."

Without thinking, I push the door open. Lavinia's on the toilet, knees open, and Verity is wiping the blood away from the soft skin of her inner thighs. I watch, frozen, as Lavinia takes the rag, face stained with tears. Wordlessly, she gathers up her blue hair and twists it, holding it with one hand as she ducks her head, pushing the rag beneath her skirt.

When she pulls it back, it's red.

My mouth parts with my punched exhale, and Verity whirls around, spotting me.

Her face transforms into something I've never seen on her before—twisted and fierce—the face of a woman who could have been a Duchess but wasn't.

"Get out," she barks, barreling toward the door. "Get the fuck *out*!"

She shoves the heel of her palm into the door, slamming it in my face.

It's quiet after that. No voices. I can't even hear the party happening downstairs. Maybe they all cleared out. Maybe I've just gone deaf and I can't hear anything besides the sound of my own brain, whirring through a slideshow of Lavinia's thighs.

I wander to my bedroom, that wisp of pride I'd felt before evaporated into something sharp and acrid. When I flip on the light, the bundle of fluff on my bed squirms into a stretch, Archie's eyes opening to peer at me in the doorway. Dragging a palm down my face, I'm hit with this red-hot yearning to turn back the clock. To start the night over again. To put myself in a place where I know she's going to crawl into this bed with me tonight. To know that when I wake up, I'll find her curled against me, skin to skin.

But none of that will happen.

It only takes me a few minutes to dump all my clothes into the same duffle I'd brought them in. My laptop, my phone, my shoes, my books.

Before I leave, I reach down to touch Archie, his head bumping up into my palm with a purr. And then I place the journal on the pillow, *her* pillow, and I walk out the door, leaving my wake of destruction behind.

30

Lavinia

Not to sound like a martyr, but getting hurt is part of being a Lucia. Physical, emotional, spiritual... nothing was off-limits. We were tested, broken down, built back up, and taken apart again.

I survived my father.

I survived Nick Bruin.

I will survive the pain inflicted on me by Simon Perilini, but that doesn't mean it doesn't hurt. Part of it was my fault, anyway. There's a word for it, buried deep in Sy's textbooks. Transference: attaching romantic feelings to a person in a protector role.

Sy saved me from the box. Protected me from my father. It's natural I'd develop some kind of feelings for him even if it is illogical. *Transference.* It's the only thing I can think of that would have caused the reaction I had after he hurt me. The way I'd cried, torn up and bloody, in the bathroom while Verity helped me. While I *allowed* her to help me. That's how bad it was.

Nick's waiting outside when Verity pulls her car to the curb.

The clock on her dash tells me it's just after three in the morning, and I clutch the bag in my hand before turning to thank her.

Before I can, she shakes her head. "Don't mention it." Her gaze dips to the bag. "Are you going to be okay?"

"Yeah." The twenty-four-hour clinic she took me to is a no-questions asked kind of place, but I told them the truth: that my partner is well endowed and too much for me to handle. The doctor sent me away with a packet of Epsom salt and instructions for warm baths, ice packs, and a sample bottle of lube. "*It's your friend*," she said, pushing it into my hand. "*Use liberally.*"

"No, I mean—that's good, but what about...?" Verity tilts her chin toward where Nick is approaching the car. I texted him ten minutes ago, letting him know we were on our way.

I give her a smile that feels tired and worn. "Nick's fine. We've sort of... hashed things out."

She looks relieved, but he's at my door then, swinging it open for me. Ducking down, he looks between us, asking, "All good?"

Verity and I share a quick look at the stilted, awkward way the question emerges. "Call if you need anything," she says as I step out.

Nick reaches the tower doors, holding them open for me. Ignoring the look I send him, he asks, "Are you going to be able to... take the stairs?"

I roll my eyes. "My pussy might be a little broken, but my legs work fine."

He even has the good grace not to say *I told you so* when I end up taking the climb slowly, wincing at the rub between my legs. By the time we get to the top, I begin wondering if it wouldn't have been better to just take the elevator. Sure, I would have had a panic attack, probably passed out, but still.

Ouch.

In the bathroom, I toss the bag in the bathroom drawer under my tampons and curling iron, and go through the motions of getting ready for bed. When I look in the mirror, I put on a brave face like I'm not embarrassed, hurt, humiliated. The suspicion still lingers, though.

What if Sy isn't the freak? What if it's me? Could a girl like Haley take him? Or one of the other cutsluts? Would they cry in the bathroom afterwards, like big fucking babies about it?

When I emerge from the bathroom, Nick is waiting, having already kicked off his shoes and shucked off his shirt. "Sy left," he says, one hand propped on the doorjamb, blocking the doorway. "You could come to bed with me."

The bare expanse of his chest looms in front of me, muscular and covered in ink. I stare at it, mesmerized. "To... sleep?" I clarify.

He leans back, eyebrows knitting together. "Christ, it's not like I'm going to try anything." Shoving his fists into his pockets, he turns away. "Forget it. Just don't go to Remy. He's all hopped up on that shit tonight."

I could sleep in Sy's bed. It's not like I'm afraid of him, I'm just...

Disappointed, maybe.

Disappointed and lost, because I've fallen into this habit. When we get hurt, Sy and I go to each other. He doesn't always make it better. Sometimes he doesn't even care. But that's how I know it's okay. At some point, I came to accept that me and Sy are each other's medics, and I can't shake the phantom urge to go to him, because I'm used to hurting. I am. But being with Sy taught me that hurting is better—just a little—when you're not alone.

Before Nick gets too far, I break. "Wait." He stops, the muscles in his back flexing as he twists, raising an eyebrow at me. "Okay," I decide, turning off the bathroom light before following him into his bedroom.

I step over the threshold slowly, not having been in here since the day I took back Leticia's old cigar box. It's messier than I've ever seen it, clothes and books scattered around, but not dirty. Just lived-in. Nick's smell is concentrated in the air and I breathe it in, wondering what feeling it will elicit.

Dread? Fear? Comfort?

The answer is an odd, simmering eagerness that doesn't lessen any when he unzips his fly, pushing his jeans down his hips. I look away, belly fluttering as I enter. "Do you have a sh—"

Wordlessly, Nick reaches to his bed and plucks up a shirt, extending it to me.

I recognize it as the one he was wearing earlier.

I change with my back turned, leaving my bra on as I pull his shirt over his head. It's large and soft, imbued with the same scent of his room, but cleaner, more soothing. Stepping out of my skirt next, I turn, hands wringing, as I watch Nick close the door.

"Leave it cracked?" I ask, pulling the hem of the shirt lower. "For Archie?" But then I get a glance at the door—the back of it—and shuffle forward to see. "What the fuck?"

Painted on the back of Nick's door is a girl. Blue hair. Black eyes. There are snakes in her hair, like Medusa, but they're curled on each side of her head like demon horns.

She's holding a skull.

No.

I'm holding a skull.

Nick scoffs, scrubbing his fingers through his hair. "I don't know. He's been working on this shit for days. Don't freak out if you wake up at five in the morning and see him standing there."

It's disconcerting, but I can't really pinpoint why. Remy has drawn me before, and some of them were gory, disturbing, but for some reason, this one makes me shiver. I get this impulse to ask Nick if this is what I look like, even though that'd be stupid. It's stylized, not exactly super realistic.

It just bothers me.

When I turn back, Nick's climbing into bed, leaving a vacant space for me at his side. Giving the demon-snake girl one last look, I turn off the light and join him, easing myself onto the mattress, inching between the sheets.

We lie there on our back for a long stretch, silent. It's hard not to remember the last time I was in this bed, tied down, crying my soul all over the sheets. It makes me feel tense and too alert, the smallest rustle from the other side of the bed resulting in a flinch.

Nick finally sighs. "You don't have to sleep here."

"I know."

There's another rustle, and then he stills, voice low and defeated. "You're never going to forgive me, are you?"

Turning, I struggle to make out his expression in the darkness. The arm closest to me is wedged behind his head and he's staring up into the darkness, unmoving. I've only slept with Nick a few times—enough to know this stiffness isn't usual.

I answer honestly. "I don't know." Half of me feels like it could, but the other half is still terrified to trust him. Will this new attitude of his hold forever? Or is the person who hurt me so callously, so selfishly, still in there? "I know that you're trying," I offer, needing him to know this much.

Nick and I have always had this balance between us, and it turns much like the cogs in the clock upstairs, always revolving.

You hurt me, I hurt you.

But maybe that can extend to more than the miseries we pass back and forth like currency—debts and payments.

Maybe I can try a little, too.

Nick's the one to flinch this time, his body jolting in surprise when I press against him, resting my cheek on his chest. He's warm and hard and solid—sturdy like his brother. My knees bump up against his leg, and reluctantly, I thread my leg through his, the rough hair covering his shins scratching against my calf.

The muscles under my cheek shift when he repositions his arm, pulling it from beneath his head to curl around my shoulders. It's a slow, testing touch, as if he's expecting me to react badly. When I don't, burrowing in against his side, he curls his fingers around my upper arm, palm dragging against the skin with a light caress.

I don't see him turn, pressing his lips to my forehead, but I feel it—the pressure, the warmth, the expansion of his chest when he lingers, inhaling the scent of my hair.

When he sighs, his body goes lax against me, muscles dropping their tension.

Sleep comes more easily than I'm expecting.

I DON'T FIND the journal until after we return from our classes, strung out on a lack of sleep. Nick tells me his Dad called to say Sy's moved back home for a bit, to 'get his head on straight.' I don't know exactly what it means, but I'm fine with a little space. I'm not sure how I feel about Sy right now or how I'll feel when he returns. I'm too busy trying to heal my body from feeling like I got rammed by a freight train.

But when I enter his room to collect some clothes for a shower, I find it there, sitting on my pillow.

The forbidden fruit.

I stare at it for a long time, gnawing my thumbnail as I consider it. I've watched Sy write in it for weeks now, desperate for any little peek, and now it's just... there.

An offering.

Sitting on the edge of the bed, I pull it into my lap, rubbing my thumb over the worn leather. It feels wrong, like a violation, to open the cover.

Simon Perilini, it reads. *A study in human behavior.*

Turning the page, I'm greeted with a crudely drawn color wheel. Green, red, blue, orange, yellow, black. In each slice of the wheel are words. Red is *violence, energy, chaos, overwhelming*. Yellow is *grief, sadness, pain (emotional), death*. Blue is *calm, comfort, trust, goodness*. Orange is *betrayal, lies, deception*. Purple is *lust*, but there's a note beside it: *Pain (physical)?* Green is *sickness*, white is *healthy, renewal, clarity*. And black...

Regret, reprisal.

Black means sorry.

This is Remy—his code, his colors. Straightening, I turn to the next page, titled 'Head Check', which features the one-to-ten scale Remy told me about my first night back. Flipping through them, I realize this is *all* about Remy. Toward the back, on a page dated three months ago is this entry:

R: Cycling since Wednesday. Refuses medications. Extreme aversion to yellow today. Sensory issue? Subject isn't forthcoming.

All of them are like that.

Or at least they were.

Until September 27th.

L: Dehydrated following prolonged confinement. Exhibits dissociation. Subject is only sporadically alert. Injuries include—

I flip the page, seeing the one dated two days later.

L: Subject is more alert today. Sleep is improving. I've been rolling her to her side at night, as the supine position appears to make her most susceptible to sleep paralysis. Doesn't voice an appetite, but eats when prompted. Expresses a deep concern for her stupid fucking asshole cat, who I did feed.

The laugh escapes unexpectedly and I fold my legs beneath me, ravenous to absorb it all—every word. It's thick, dated all the way back to two years ago, but it'd only take me one night to get through it, flying through the pages, soaking every pen stroke into my mind.

Closing the journal, I tuck it under the pillow.

This isn't something I want to inhale in one breath. I want to savor it, give each page the thought it deserves. Still, it's hard to grab my clothes and leave it there, a treasure trove of insight into not just Remy, but Sy himself.

Tomorrow.

Tomorrow, I'll read another page.

PROBATION KEEPS us home for Friday Night Fury, but from the way Verity tells it over the phone, that's for the best.

Bruce lost to Lars, one of the only two Counts left. The frat is probably fucking losing it. There'll be no victory party tonight. No celebration. No victor. No spoils. It's the first fight of the academic year in which DKS hasn't won the main match of the night, and if I had to guess, my father is insanely pleased.

Annoyed at the thought, I spend a couple hours up in the clock tower, trying to figure out what I'm missing, why I can't get this fucking prehistoric beast to work. I've worked and reworked it, but I can't get the mechanism to catch, and it's not helping my mood.

The only thing that does is reading another page.

This one is from a year ago.

R: Low appetite. Not well-rested. Subject is quick to temper today, but I disagree with the diagnosis of a mood disorder. Painting with a lot of orange following a session with his doctor. I suspect someone has lied to him, but he's not speaking about it. Probably his dad. R has always displayed a deep resentment for dishonesty. He frames this as a disloyalty, but from my own observation, it's more of a phobia toward abductive reasoning. R is prone to catastrophization and delusion. Without all the facts, his mind reaches to fill in the details, which will often be negative and grandiose. Keeping an eye on him today.

THE ENTRY I read on Saturday, curled up on Sy's bed following a jog alone through West End, is from nine months ago:

R: Sleep deprived. Absent of appetite, but active. Subject is seeking stimulants again. Intercourse with multiple women over the week and an increased desire to train with me. I suspect he's chasing endorphins, which would explain the tattoo piece he's started on his ribs. The chosen design (clown smoking a blunt) has no emotional or creative significance.

There's a sentence scribbled out, and then:

Subject would fuck anything on legs. Note to buy him more rubbers.

MONDAY'S ENTRY, from a month after the last one, is somehow even bleaker:

R: Subject is in a depressive state and not attending class. Ignoring my texts and has locked his door, resulting in a visit to his RA around noon. R is beginning to smell and hasn't showered in days. No fresh canvases in his studio. If following his usual pattern, I expect him to worsen over the next few days. Will observe him for more overt displays of self-harm.

Solemnly, I put the journal away and give in to the impulse to seek him out.

We sit together up in the belfry that evening, just as the sun is slumping toward the horizon.

He's animated as he points out each section of Forsyth, unable to sit still. "I know Sy's over there." He points to a spot that would be close to his parents' neighborhood.

"How?"

"It's shrouded in black."

I stare out over the city, wondering if it can ever be that easy.

~

TUESDAY'S ENTRY is a little more positive, and I read it up in my loft after spending the day turning it into a more comfortable reading nook:

R: Subject is in good spirits following a new medication. Well-rested. Appears to be eating well. Active. We lifted weights at the gym together. He doesn't seem to be chasing. Competitive but not aggressive (any more than usual). We had a discussion about his dad, who's been attempting increased involvement in his medical and academic care. Always happens around this time of the year.

~

WEDNESDAY, I flip to the back of the journal, hoping for something a little more recent, and pause on this:

R: Subject on a roller coaster of emotions, but for once it's not connected to his chemical imbalance. N returned home. Surprised both of us. Not just for a visit. He wants to come back for good, reclaim his title and join R and I in the tower next year. I was already apprehensive about the long-term effects of this change for R. It's going to involve a move, an elevated position of power, and attention—all of which could trigger delusions of grandeur. The addition of N, who has erratic, deceptive, and aggressive behaviors, could cause even more extreme conflict. But N also understands R. He allowed the subject to tattoo his forearm—solid black—a sign of trust and apology. Will keep a close eye on the dynamics.

I read that one twice, aware that the following pages will inevitably involve me. Finding out what Sy thinks is something I've wanted for a while, but the thought of really knowing makes my heart pound anxiously. I shove the notebook under the mattress Ballsack and his boys hauled up the elevator for my loft.

I HOLD off as long as I can, but Thursday, I'm sprinting up to my loft, digging the journal from beneath the mattress, and flipping the page, breath caught in my throat.

This one has three entries.

R: As predicted, N's arrival has thrown the house into complete upheaval, and along with it, the subject's stability. Color talk. Erratic mood swings. Hyper sexuality. Chasing. Obsessive drawing—all centered around one image: the girl. After last night, I don't see this ending positively. For any of us.

N: Already conflicting with authority. Doesn't like Saul's attitude. Inexplicably eager for his initiation fight. Moved into his room with nothing but a trash bag half-full of clothes. Secretive.

L: She stayed so still at the end. Uncertain why.

REMY HAS BEEN WITHDRAWN and aimless all week, starting and stopping projects. He keeps playing what I now think of as his erratic music, and I'm starting to appreciate how well Sy handled his mood swings because I'm at a loss. Do I give him space, or do I nag him into okayness?

On Thursday, I plan to ask Nick his opinion, but pause when I find him arranging weapons on the kitchen table.

"Did I miss something?" I ask, eyeing the guns and knives, all sorted into neat rows. "You didn't kill someone else, did you?"

I'm only half-joking.

"Just taking inventory," he says, grabbing a rag and wiping down some pieces. He's wearing a plain white undershirt that's tight in the shoulders, muscles shifting under the fabric as his hand scrubs the metal. "Cleaning what needs it. Seeing what Sy took with him." It's the first time Nick's mentioned Sy since his brother walked out, and I watch him closely, trying to decipher the blankness in his expression. But all I get is his turning to call out, "Remy, bring me your heat!"

At first, I'm pretty sure Remy's going to ignore the request—he didn't answer when I knocked this afternoon—but sure enough, he emerges, carrying a sheathed knife and two pistols. Carefully, he rests them next to the others, reaching up to rub his nose.

"This everything?"

I gawk at him.

He looks like he hasn't slept in days. There are these tiny capillaries around his irises which are blown out, and it makes him look like he's been crying.

But I know better.

Nick hums, jerking his chin at me. "Bring me yours—the knife, too." Before I get more than three steps away, he adds, "And bring me that revolver. You know where it is."

My stomach churns as I think about it, and even worse when I actually retrieve it from the top drawer of Nick's dresser. I hold the weight of it in my hand, only now noticing the intricately etched letter 'B' on the barrel.

I return with my pistol, the revolver, and the knife I'd stolen from under Nick's pillow weeks ago, setting them on the table with the others. "I know you're the Dukes and all, and it's kind of your *thing*." I say, sliding up to perch on the tabletop. "But this feels like a bit much."

There are eleven guns and five knives, of varying caliber and length, but one stands out among the sleek, modern Glocks.

"What's this?" Remy reaches for the revolver and Nick and I share a look. We've been inching around the tornado that is Remington Maddox for days now, and I'm not sure how much longer we can avoid the wind.

I know he plans to lie before Nick's mouth even opens. "It's something I got from—"

I cut in, "He got it from the Baron King." Nick swings a hard, sharp gaze on me, but I just shake my head. After reading those journal entries on Remy, I think I'm beginning to understand a little better. "It's how we got Leticia's skull. We didn't tell you because we knew we couldn't get any more information out of them without putting one or all of us at risk."

Remy stares at me, his pupils blown and dark as he holds the revolver. "You went to see the Barons?" Rubbing his nose again, he turns to Nick. "Alone? Just the two of you?"

Nick sighs, straddling a chair and picking up a pistol. "We just needed to know for sure if Leticia was dead or not. The Barons were the obvious place to look."

"How?" he asks, wild eyes moving between us. "The Barons don't give up information like that. Not for you. Not for anyone. Remember three years ago? The Prince who went missing? Even Ashby couldn't get anything out of them, and he's a King."

"Remy," I sigh, reaching out to grab his shirt. I pull him between my legs, framing his face with my hands. Even like this—even close enough to look me in the eye—his gaze is still jumping around: my nose, my hair, my cheek, my mouth. "It's not important."

He jolts back, face contorting. "Don't tell me what is and isn't important. We've got enough shit going down here without some fucking debt to the Barons hanging over our heads."

"There's no debt," Nick says, standing to fix Remy with a hard stare. "The Dukes and the Barons are square, but we won't be if you go poking around, asking more questions. That's why we're keeping this under wraps. It's nothing bad."

I know the last three words are a lie, but Nick believes it, so it comes out sincere—a touch irritated.

After a moment of watching us, Remy looks down to run his fingers along the engraving on the barrel. On a good day, it's impossible to know what's going through Remy's head.

Today is not a good day.

The silence stretches on, his green eyes fixed to the 'B'. "It's a nice piece. What? Twenty? Thirty years old? You can tell from the grip design." He studies it carefully, getting that bothered, faraway look I've seen too much of in the last week. "Why would he give you something like this?"

I know I shouldn't, but I look at Nick. His expression gives nothing away—as usual—but he raises an eyebrow and says, "The simple answer is that the Baron is batshit crazy, and no one knows why the fuck he does anything, but the real one is that apparently that gun belonged to the Dukes. My dad specifically. I guess he was feeling generous."

Remy takes a deep breath, nostrils flared wide as he raises his gaze to us. "Let me get this straight. You got this gun," he lifts it, pulling the hammer with his thumb, "and Leticia's skull from the *King* of the Barons, for an undisclosed price?"

"Don't get your fucking jock in a twist over this," Nick snaps, shoulders tensing. "You've been bouncing around here like a meth-addled kangaroo. If you could stay sober for a few weeks, then maybe we'd be a little more fucking forthcoming."

Before the simmering anger in his eyes can burn hot enough to get physical, I pull him back to me, pressing a kiss to the corner of his mouth. "Remy, please. Trust us, okay? It was nothing." Lower, I stress, "*Nothing.*"

Slowly, he places the revolver back on the table, his jaw suddenly tight. There's a coldness to his eyes that I never like to see, and when Nick asks, "Dude, *what*?" he just shrugs.

"Nothing."

As he's storming away, Nick gives my shoulder a hard shove, hissing, "Good fucking going!"

I shove him back twice as hard. "He's all over the place! Do you really want to risk messing with his head more?"

Unaffected, Nick stares through the sight of the revolver, eye lined up with the empty barrel. "Tomorrow is his Friday Night Fury, and he'll finally fight some of this fucking energy off. He's just anxious with Sy gone this long."

Deflating, I wonder, "Are you?"

Nick spins the chamber, snapping it shut, and shifts his gaze to mine. "I think my brother belongs in the tower, if that's what you're asking." He wipes his hands on the cloth. "But I also think he needed some time to cool off. He'll be back when he's ready to face his shit."

"How do you know?"

He walks around the table until he's in front of me, fixing me with a long, burning stare. When his hand slides around the back of my neck, pulling my face to his, I don't resist, spreading my thighs to let him in close. "Because he's hooked on you as much as the rest of us, Little Bird. He fucked up, and this may be hard to believe, but sometimes it takes the Perilini-Bruin men a hot minute to realize it." Nick's eyes drop to my mouth. He tilts his head before tipping forward, pausing just before our lips meet to hold my eye. It's a new thing with him, ever since that night we slept in his bed together. If he wants to kiss me, he'll shoot his shot, but he always gives me the chance to back away or lean in.

Right now, I lean in, eyes sliding closed.

I don't regret it.

The kiss is slick and slow, his tongue licking my lips apart as I grasp his sides, feeling the warmth and strength of him.

Since three nights of sleeping beside him was enough to test my resolve, I haven't been to his bed since Saturday, nervous of how something like that might work once I'm... healed. Will he demand more? Will the bulge I wake up to being poked in the back with become my responsibility?

He releases me, slow and easy, reaching up to touch my bottom lip. I know logically things are a fucking mess, but looking at Nick right now, I wouldn't know it. He's got this lazy, indulgent grin on his face, so close to looking like the younger version of himself I'd seen in that photo that it makes something in my gut melt into liquid heat.

"Go check on Remy while I get all these pieces cleaned," he says, sighing. "It's best if he doesn't start to ruminate."

I find him twenty minutes later.

He's sitting with his back against the stone, one leg kicked out toward the ledge while the other is bent, the leg of his jeans pulled up to reveal his pale knee. It takes me a long moment to figure out what he's doing, his spine a curve as he looks down at his knee, hand moving in a strange rhythm.

Then I see the needle.

"What are you doing?"

His rhythm never falters, the long, straight needle going into his flesh, over and over. "Spider web."

Gawking, I clarify, "What is that?"

He pauses to dip it into a tiny bottle of ink near his hip. "Needle."

"I know it's a—" Regrouping, I try a different question. "Why are you using that instead of your gun?"

It looks gruesome and crude, and from the stories he's told me, a lot like what I imagined his tattoo operation looked like in high school. Slow. Painful.

His voice is raspier than usual as he flicks his hair from his face, returning to the web. "This is a finer point."

I wonder if he really believes that, or if it's a lie. Either way, I'm pretty sure I know the truth. Chasing, Sy called it. Endorphins.

Carefully, I sit down beside him, wincing at the sight of the needle going into his skin. "Hey, look at me. Please?" When he does, chuffing out an annoyed breath and raising his eyes, I ask, "Head check?"

"You're not Sy." He scoffs, swinging his attention back to the web. "I only give Sy my numbers."

I frown. "I told you mine. Before. When I was—"

His head snaps up. "I told you not to let him get in your head."

"Sy?" It's not unusual to have a conversation with Remy where I'm not following all the steps, but this seems more specific than usual.

"Not *Sy*." His eyes flash. "My father."

I frown. "I haven't seen your father." I think back. "I mean, not since we went to dinner with him. That's the only time I've ever seen the guy."

He looks down, visibly fuming. "Yeah, well, that's not what he says." The next poke of the needs goes deeper than I'm expecting, making me flinch in surprise.

Without thinking, I snatch it away, acting lightning fast as I hurl it over the edge of the belfry. "Stop fucking stabbing yourself!"

Remy reacts instantly, eyes flaring wide when his palm comes up to press against my throat. But he doesn't squeeze—not this time. He gives me a long, boiling stare and then growls, ripping his hand away. "How the fuck do people like you sort these?" Shoving his hand into his hair, tugging at the roots, he rants, "Colors and numbers and letters—they just slither in and jerk me around, but you... you just fucking bat them away. Red, yellow, twos and threes and sevens. He puts them in here!" Remy jabs the tip of his forefinger into his temple. "And then he just walks away!"

Breathing deep, I wonder, "Are you talking about your dad?"

Frustration explodes his features, but it's replaced with exhaustion just as quickly. "Goddamn it, this is what he does, you know?" He drags his palms down his face, and when he pulls them away, I see the dark conflict in his eyes—muddled confusion, along with dark smudges underneath. Too little sleep. Too many stimulants. The more I read, the more I realize his dopamine is fucked, and his lack of routine and sunlight is only increasing his erratic behavior. I feel his paranoia inching up and without Sy here, I'm afraid it'll get worse.

Scared, I ask, "I don't know, Remy, tell me. What does he do?"

He looks out over Forsyth, the sky reflected in his eyes. "He lies, Vinny. All the time, every day. Even when he's telling the truth, he's only telling the parts of it that help him hide something worse." Intensely, he whispers, "His skin isn't real. He puts it on every day, but it's always orange and red. Sometimes I wonder if he even exists at all. Sometimes I wonder if *I* even exist at all. Maybe he made me like this." His eyebrows knit tightly, face twisting. "Or maybe I died that night on the cliff and this is all just neurons firing off in a skull whose brain is rotting."

"Hey," I say, stomach plummeting as I rise up on my knees in front of him, forcing my way into his lap. "Don't—don't talk like that. This is real. Remember?" I tug down the waist of my leggings, showing him the star.

He touches it without reservation or thought, like it's automatic to press his fingertip into the points, counting. Brows crouching low, he tugs at my shirt, and I don't protest when he pulls it over my head. I know what he's looking for. His touch is feather light as it grazes the line of the moth.

He blinks at me, slow and heavy, eyes so bloodshot that it makes my own sting to stare into them. "You can't let him in, Vinny. He thinks you're bad for me, and he'll do whatever it takes to poison us."

"I'm not going anywhere," I assure him, winding my arms around his neck. "I'm your Duchess."

His eyes flutter closed, hands sliding around my waist to my backside, down the curve of my ass. "Even though Sy hurt you?"

I lean down to press a kiss to his jaw. "I've survived worse than Simon Perilini."

He runs his nose along my ear, breath hot and loud. And then he pulls me closer with one arm while his other hand abruptly begins fumbling for his belt. "Let's fuck."

I freeze, wanting to but afraid. Every part of my body craves him just as much as it throbs for Nick and misses Sy. But the ache between my legs is still there, and as much as I trust Remy—and I do—he's too erratic right now. I'm afraid he may get lost in the feel of it.

Placing my hand over his, I admit, "I need more time."

He goes rigid, lips stilling against my cheek. "More time?"

"To heal." I shift nervously. "You know, from... uh, the other night."

"Your pretty pussy." A shudder runs through him. I'm expecting the kiss, but I'm not expecting the frisson of energy behind it. His fingers clawing painfully into my ass as he grinds into me. "I bet it looked just like the first time, didn't it? Blood and blue. *Cyanine* blue."

I did some research after reading Sy's color chart. Blue means trustworthy, calm. Cyanine is a specific type of color pigment used in painting. His thumb rubs against my star, and I take it for good sign. Remy wants to be grounded, to have faith in me, to trust me, and I can be his calm if he'll let me. If he can't count on his father or even Sy right now, he can count on me.

Remy needs endorphins.

Those, I can give.

I reach down to wedge a hand between us, squeezing his length. "I can still make you feel good. I can still be... blue?"

He peers at me through dark, glazed eyes, breathing, "Yeah. I've been thinking about your mouth, Vinny." When he presses two fingers to my lips, he barely gives me the chance to let him in before sliding them past my teeth, pressing into my tongue. "You sucked my cock so good before. So sweet and purple."

Before I even have a chance to parse that, he's lifting me up, shooting to his feet. Eager fingers fumble for his belt again, but I press against him and ease his shirt up first. I push up the hem until my hands meet his and he yanks it over his head. My lips press against the hard muscle of his chest, along the tattoos and smooth skin. I suck his nipple, then blow air across the tip to watch it pebble.

His hands blaze a frantic trail over my skin, running up and down my arms, my back, under my shirt. I kiss down his lean belly as I descend, running my fingers through the soft hair that vanishes beneath his waistband. I taste his skin, the inked flesh, sensitive and warm. His belly dips, and I make quick work of his belt, the metal hitting the stone wall before I unbutton his fly.

It's no surprise Remy's not wearing shorts, his cock springing out the instant I lower his pants. I reach for him, running my hand down his length, feeling along the curve that's sent pangs of pleasure through my core. His hand moves to the back of my head, shifts, his long fingers threading through my hair. His grip is tight, sure, and I let him pull my mouth closer, face tipped up to watch him.

"Suck it, Vin," he says, thumbing my bottom lip while guiding the tip of his cock inside.

The first taste is sharp and salty, the warmth surprising against the heat of my mouth. I take my time licking the shaft. It's not a tease. It's just like the kiss I'd given Nick earlier. Slow. Sensual. Imbued with things I'm not prepared to say.

Groaning in frustration, Remy yanks me by the hair and directs me to the head of his cock before pushing between my lips, thrusting so deep that I nearly choke. Noticing my reaction, he tightens his grip. "Can't you take it? You took Sy and now he's inside you. He did, right? He came inside your pussy?"

I struggle to nod and he makes a sound—low and hungry in the back of his throat. His pace shifts, as does my own, Remy's hips bucking—fucking—into my face. It's only briefly I can catch sight of his expression, but every time I do it's stony and tight, lined with some unspeakable agony.

His hands grab my head like a basketball, fingers tangled in my hair as he drives his cock in and out. I'd like to say it's not a good feeling, this sense that I'm being mindlessly used, but it'd be a lie.

Heat builds between my legs, and I squirm.

"You won't let me fuck the red back into you," he pants, pulling me off his cock just far enough that I can look into his eyes. "But you can touch yourself. I know you can."

I shake my head, mouth full of cock. This is about him, not me, but he strokes his thumbs over my cheek, gentle and soft, saying, "Do it, Vin. Don't make me fall without you, baby."

Face searing hot, I slide my hand down the front of my leggings, to the wet heat building between my legs. I tentatively brush over my clit for the first time in a week and exhale sharply when I feel the spark of arousal, relieved that it feels good.

That I'm not completely broken.

"That's right," he says when I find my rhythm, fingers gentle but sure. He lets me take the lead, leaning back and watching, eyes heavy, jaw slack. With the evening sun catching on his white hair, sending it ablaze in the dusk, he looks like a beautiful ghoul, pale and covered in ink that might as well be tendrils of smoke creeping up his chest.

My heart twists when I see him like this, the torment carved into the lines of his face as if he's the tragic marble statue of some crumbling civilization.

It doesn't take long, but I never expected it to.

My orgasm comes in a rush and he pulls me closer, nudging the back of my tongue as I shudder and cry, chasing the pleasure just as much as he is. I feel his cock thicken, and then hear his hitched inhale, his hands cupping my cheeks to still me. Our eyes lock together as he holds me in place to accept his release, his cock giving a strong pulse.

Warm, salty cum floods my tongue and I knee myself closer, ravenous to take it all—every drop—as if I could pull the sickness out of him and neutralize it with my blue.

He eases me off his spent cock, but doesn't let my face go—not until I swallow, throat bobbing as he watches. When two of his fingers jab at my mouth, I open for him, and it's just like mornings when I watch him take his pills.

"That's my girl," he says, eyes distant and dazed as he pushes his fingers against his tongue. "My good girl..."

I'd love to say that it soothed the edge off of him, but the frenetic vibe still hums beneath the surface. If there's one thing I've learned from reading Sy's journals is that it won't last. The question is what will the fallout be when it finally happens.

I know how to find out.

31

Remy

It's just like I remember it.

Nothing ever changes about this place. Even at three in the morning as I tromp through the foyer and through the formal dining room, it's as if nothing's moved. That's the table I used to do homework on—or pretend to do homework on. These are the floors I'd skate on with socks when the energy felt too big for me to possibly expend. The French doors I'd slam shut after arguments with my dad, the panes rattling like teeth. The desk drawer I'd swipe credit cards from, the armchair I fucked Tate's cousin in, the powder room where I snorted my first line, the wainscoting I covered in maniacal doodles.

The last one's been painted over, of course.

The only room in this house that was ever changing was my own. I don't even know how old I was—too young to remember, maybe six—when my dad finally gave up on his attempts to make me stop drawing on the walls.

"Here," he'd say, pointing at my bedroom walls. "Nowhere else in the house. Just *here*."

A bargain.

Everywhere else in the house was pristine. If I left a sweater on the sofa, it'd be put away by morning. If Sy were here—and he's not —he'd probably have something really profound to say about it, like...

Being starved of your ability to leave a mark on the world fostered a strong compulsion to deface anything in sight.

He probably wouldn't be wrong. It's a big part of why I love tattooing, forcing the universe to remember my presence, pieces of my thoughts living on in people who scatter outward like confetti.

The house is dark, but I traverse it from memory like a pro. When I pass the liquor cabinet, I reach out, smoothly snagging a crystal decanter. A sniff reveals it as gin and I tip it back as I turn toward the stairs, not bothering to be quiet when I stomp up to the second floor.

One after another, I tap the photos on the wall leading to the office—awful, stiff, posed things. I don't look at them because I already know what I'll see. Seven, nine, eleven, fifteen, all dressed up in a tie, empty eyes and a tense smile. The only thing here that isn't horribly orange is a plaque congratulating Remington W. Maddox III on creative excellence in Sacred Heart Preparatory's twenty-fifth annual student showcase.

I raise the decanter to it in cheers.

The door I'm looking for is at the end of the hall, unlocked, and I push through without hesitation, flicking on the light.

When I was a kid, I used to love my father's office, though I can't really remember why. It's not particularly warm or cozy, although, as I survey the shelves and cabinets, I have to admit that it's the only room, beside my own, that looks lived in.

"What the hell are you doing?"

I don't flinch in surprise. I heard the footsteps. "Just came for a visit," I say, distracted as I peruse his shelves. "I love what you haven't done with the place."

My father, tapping at his phone, sounds distinctly unimpressed. "You realize you set off the alarm, alerting security, the police, the fire department..."

"Yep." My eyes land on a crude antique dagger, set in a glass case. I point to it. "That's new."

Scowling, he presses the phone to his ear. "False alarm," he tells whatever sad schmuck is on the other end. "Yes, sorry for the inconvenience. You're not allowed here." He says the last part to me, but I'm too busy staring at the dagger.

"That didn't used to be there." I would have noticed it. It's ugly as sin, but interesting.

My father huffs. "It was a birthday present from your Aunt. What do you want?"

I turn to him, placing the gin on his desk. My dad is about three inches shorter than me. He stays in shape, but he's not imposing—not physically. Raising my chin, I ask, "Want to fight?"

He rolls his eyes. "For Pete's sake, Remy. It's three in the goddamn morning, and you came over here to... what? Relive graduation night?"

The night I graduated high school, we got into it, quick and dirty. He likes to act as though it was some big, elaborate showdown, but the reality is a lot simpler. I beat his ass. In and out. One and done. Knocked out his right canine.

"I came over here to tell you to stay away," I clarify, swiping a fountain pen from his desk. I tap it against my palm, head tilting. "But I figured laying you out cold would be a nice feature."

My father looks tired—exhausted in a way that isn't just about a lack of sleep. "I'm not afraid of you, Remy. And I'll stay away when you prove to me you're not surrounding yourself with the human equivalents of whatever it is you must have snorted an hour ago." My reflexes are lightning-quick, so when he strikes out to snatch the pen from me in one clean swipe, I'm shocked at his speed, left standing there, fingers still frozen around a phantom pen. "So if that's what you came to say..." He gestures to the door.

My teeth grind. "There's something else."

He lifts his shoulders. "Well?"

I came here for a reason, to prove to myself, one way or the other, what's real and what isn't. But now that I'm looking at the wall, the dagger, the alignment, everything fits—right in place.

I'm the only thing that doesn't fit in my father's house.

I could ask him outright. Maybe that's what all this leads up to, breadcrumbs leading me back here, back to him. Maybe he wants me to ask, to connect dots that don't really exist?

"You know what? Never mind," I say, waving him off. "It's not like you'd tell me the truth anyway."

My eyes track him carefully as he reaches down, a finger dragging a notepad to the edge of his desk. "She's good at bargaining, that Duchess of yours." He presses the tip of the pen to the small square of paper, wrist flying back and forth. "So pretty when she's scared. Those big eyes of hers, staring up at you in the dark. I wanted you to know I see the appeal." He lifts the pen, ripping the paper away from the pad, and then he holds it out to me.

It's one big scribble of black ink.

He raises his eyebrows. "Black means sorry. Isn't that right? It's been a long while since I've had anything to apologize to you about, but I suppose playing with your little toy applies."

I'd like to say it's a nice feeling, having it all figured out, the pieces clicking together seamlessly. The clarity is there, but it cuts through me like a serrated edge, my stomach dropping.

I look into my father's eyes and think about killing him. I could use that ugly dagger up there, sinking it into his throat. I could stab him with the very pen he's making a sorry attempt at apology with. Hell, I could use the gun that's resting against the small of my back, putting a bullet in his brain.

He doesn't deserve the beauty of it, though.

Instead, I leave, knowing only one thing for sure.

There used to be something else where that dagger was sitting.

"CAN YOU SMELL IT?" I inhale deep, eyes closed, feeling the vibration of the people around me. Friday Night Fury. Gym packed to the gills with DKS, Beta Nu, gamblers, hustlers, and regular, run-of-the-mill students. It's the only thing that's quieted the screams in my head. My lungs fill with the scent of two hundred people: sweat, perfume, adrenaline, horniness. It charges me like a battery, making my fists curl and flex. It's the exact opposite of where I went last night. No clean lines. No sterility. No orange. It's fucking anarchy. I'd eat this feeling up with a spoon if I could, fueling myself for the fight.

"Um, smell what exactly?"

I look down at Haley, her eyes bright and happy. She just about tripped over herself when I waved her over from the group of cutsluts welcoming guests. "The promise of a victory."

She nods along, and that's why I always liked her. Despite the yellow about her, she's here for the ride. The fun. The excitement. There's no introspection or hovering, no constant 'check-ins' or secrets. There's no depth with this girl, and that's fine by me. It doesn't hurt that she's always available, ready for the smallest scrap of attention. It makes it easy, non-committal—which is exactly what I'm looking for before a fight.

"Maddox!" I look over and see Cash Money pushing past the beer line. He approaches, his smile all teeth. "Mad dog, my man!"

I like Cash because even when he's fake, it's authentic. He wants money—wants to climb the North Side ranks—and I'm a juicy catch. He's never tried to hide it. The others think I don't know his hustle, but I do.

I just don't care.

His palm collides with mine in greeting, and I ask, "Didn't you get kicked out of these things?"

"Yeah." He laughs. "But that was before the Kings rounded all your asses up for that spanking. Lionel talked to Saul, and they came to an agreement. I've got an official green-light to hustle out here. Shit's wild, bro."

I shrug, scanning the seats by the ring, but the two Kings haven't arrived yet. "Good luck then, plenty of boys and girls looking for a hook-up tonight."

"Hey, listen," he says, grabbing my shoulder to turn me away from Haley. "I know you've gotten some heat about using, but you've been a loyal customer." His hand shifts and he slides something into my palm. The kid grins. "For after the fight, yeah? To celebrate your win. And you *are* going to win. Barons are bitch-made."

I look down at the snake-stamped packet and the three pills inside.

They're blue.

Not one to pass up a free gift, I close my fingers around it, saying, "Thanks."

Internally, I'm wondering how long until I can take them.

The bell rings, signaling the first fight is about to start. I need to get ready. Cash Money dips back into the crowd, and I pocket the drugs, gesturing for Haley to follow me to the locker room.

Sy has a whole pre-fight ritual that involves a lot of silence and brooding and visualizing. Nick's never been one for ritual, but even he has his little habits. Personally, I try to make every fight different, refusing to settle into a groove, to let it have power over me. The more spontaneous a fight *feels*, the better I do. Nothing beats my ass worse than having a *plan*.

I'm unbuttoning my shirt when the door swings open, which is nice.

That didn't happen last time.

"There you are," Vinny says, barging in the room. Her hair is up tonight, the blue all tucked away, and she's got this pinch in her forehead as she surveys the scene. Normally I'd be focused on the low cut of her shirt, but the cloak of orangish-gold following her distracts me. Her eyes cut to Haley, sitting on the bench, and then back to me. "You were gone when we woke up this morning.

We've been worried. I thought we were going to all ride here together."

I shrug off the shirt and hang it on a hook in the locker. "I had shit to do. I figured you and Nicky would manage without me."

She stares at me—one of those long looks where I know she's trying to figure me out, calculate where I am on Sy's chart.

Spoiler alert: I'm a fucking one.

Nobody's gonna stop me. Not my dad, not Nicky or Vinny, and especially not the Baron bitch I'm fighting.

Tonight, I'm showing them all what's up.

"It's not about managing," she says, lowering her voice, "it's about the fact you've been... unsteady, and plus, we agreed to present as a united front. Especially after the last few weeks."

"United front?" My smile feels sharp. I can practically see it slice through the concern in her eyes. "I thought that ship sailed when Sy ran away."

She narrows her eyes. "Are you blaming me for that?"

"No." Although I could. She encouraged Sy. I heard them every night in his room, getting him closer and closer. Anyone with eyes could tell he was about to pop. "This isn't about you, Duchess, It's about me." I glance at Haley and she gives me a small grin back. "I'm the one fighting tonight, and I don't need the distraction of DKS bullshit following me around."

"Hey," she says, grabbing me by the arm. Her eyes dart to Haley. "Can you give us a minute?"

"Sure," she says, standing slowly. Haley has this way about her—she's very in tune with her body. Her nipples are completely visible through her white tube top, and her skirt is so short that it's effortless to catch a peek of her hot pink thong underneath. Vinny watches the back of her skirt swish back and forth as she turns the corner to go deeper into the locker room. See? Easy.

"Are you mad or something?" Her eyes search mine.

I finally turn my full attention to her, shoulder propped against my locker. "What would I have to be mad about?"

She's wearing a tank top, and she's cold, gooseflesh springing up her arms. "I don't know. That's why I'm asking." Idly, she curls her arms around herself, giving her arms a brisk rub. "Are you... high?"

"No."

She frowns. "Is this about Sy? Because I never asked him to leave."

My jaw tightens. "Never said you did."

"Then what?" she bursts, eyes sparking in frustration. "Would you just talk to me?"

"You want to talk?" I ask, the anger rushing to the surface so suddenly that my body jolts with the force of it. "Let's talk about how you've been talking to my father, even though I explicitly fucking told you not to ever let him in!" My fists meet the locker and she flinches back, jaw dropping.

"You're still on about this? I already told you, Remy. I'm not speaking to your father." Annoyance sharpening the lines of her face, she lists off, "I didn't speak to him before we had dinner; I didn't speak to him after we had dinner, and I barely said more than a dozen words to him *at* dinner!" When I do nothing but stare at her, she deflates, asking, "What's this about? Because I wouldn't lie to you. Not after last time."

She could be lying right now, in too deep to possibly come clean.

But she's looking at me with those eyes—

"Those big eyes of hers, staring up at you in the dark..."

—and there's orange, but there's also blue, and for a moment, the confidence that's been tugging at my gut like a rusty fish hook twists.

Is it her, or is it him?

Is it both of them?

"Stop!" I claw my fingers through my hair, head throbbing. "I can't fucking think when you're looking at me like that."

"Hey." Her touch is as soft as her voice, fingers wrapping around my wrist, tugging my hand from my hair. "This helps, right?" She pulls my hand to her hip, tugging down the waist of her shorts to show me the star.

Silly stars.

I stare at it for a long time, wondering if he saw it like this. Soft skin, the black stark against her complexion. The thought of it makes my insides curdle, but then she's there, kissing my jaw.

"We can stop the fight if you need—"

"No."

She watches me, concern still etched deep in her features. "Are you sure?" At my stiff nod, she says, "It's our first fight together. What can I do to help you get ready?"

There's this voice inside of me that tells me to chill the fuck out. Let my girl help me and go out there and kick some ass, but it's overruled by something loud and demanding. The roar of the man threatening to come unleashed. I'm ready for it, for him, and I say, "I'm fine. Haley's got it."

"Haley."

I drop my joggers, revealing the shorts I'm wearing in the fight. "Nick's out there all alone. Like you said, united front. Haley was my ring girl before you came along. No reason she can't do it tonight."

Unlike my brothers, I've never struck the Duchess, but from the look on her face, you'd think I slapped her. "You're serious," she says, cheeks turning pink.

Needing to turn away from her blank, shuttered expression, I twist to call out for Haley. Confirming she's listening around the corner, she appears from around the corner and asks, "Did you need me?"

I hold up a roll of tape, facing her. "Can you wrap my knuckles? You know I never get it tight enough."

"You really do suck at it." She laughs, straddling the bench. Her eye flicks over my shoulder to Lavinia and back to mine. "Don't worry; I'll take care of him. We have a system."

I hear Vinny leave more than I see her, the sound of her slow, dragging footsteps receding, and the slam of the door behind her.

Haley wraps my knuckles, taking care to get it exactly how I want it. I don't pay much mind to it, curling my free hand into a fist and banging it over my head. Haley isn't alarmed. It's like she said. We have a system.

"Next," she commands, taking my other hand as I bash my head with the newly wrapped knuckles.

After, as I'm testing the tension of the tape, she rests her hands on my hips, gazing up at me with eyes lined in too much makeup. She's yellow, but it's always the happy shades with her, loud and miserable.

"Do you need *anything* else?" she asks, biting down on her bottom lip.

Right.

The system.

Haley's used to getting off with me before a match, but I didn't want it last time, and I don't want it now. She'd do whatever I wanted her to, though. I could bend her over the counter, doggy style on the bench, let her suck me off…

But those aren't the eyes I want on me. I don't need it. What I need is to show the Barons who runs this shit.

"Thanks," I tell her, brushing her hair off her face, "but all I need is five minutes alone."

Her smile falters. "Oh, okay. I'll just be waiting outside."

I wait for the door to close to pull out the baggy of pills, sitting down on the bench as I empty them into my palm.

Something borrowed, something blue.

Up the hatch it goes.

The next few minutes are a blur as I go from the locker room to ringside, the noise of the crowd getting louder every second. If I *were* a stickler for routine, then I'd be fucked, because Sy isn't here. I've never had a fight in this gym without Sy in my corner, yelling at me to watch my footing, and it doesn't feel right to do it tonight.

The undercard fight must have been brutal—there's blood smeared on the mat, and the refs are rushing around to clean it all up. With Haley by my side, it gives me a minute before I climb in the ring to scan the crowd. Nicky and Vinny are up front, his arm thrown over her shoulder. They're close enough that I can see his thumb moving in a slow, sweeping circuit beneath the strap of her tank top as he leans in to say something into her ear. She looks straight at me as she listens, sending me a tight, brittle smile that falls away the moment her eyes move to Haley.

Behind them are the DKS boys, and behind them are the pledges, but the seats to the left are reserved for Royalty.

Saul isn't a surprise. He had to come survey his Kingdom, watch as we're put in our place by the probation he recommended. Doesn't make a difference to me, though. I never train before a fight. Training is just another word for planning.

I'm marginally surprised to see the Lords: Payne, Rathbone, and Mercer, along with their Lady. They're laughing and drinking, having a good time, all smiles and touches, even though Saul keeps shooting them these resentful glares. No doubt Tristian has some money on the fight.

But the chair beside Saul is empty.

The King of the Barons must be sitting this one out.

It's not unusual. If anything, everyone would be shocked to see him show up at all. The initiation fight was an outlier, a spectacle. To watch a rival King's daughter be won by another house? No way was any King missing that action.

I guess I don't rank.

By the time I get in the ring, I'm buzzing so hard that my jaw aches from clenching it so much. The crowd is like a living, breathing, single entity. Their blanket of energy billows out to cover me, and I accept it with open arms, leaning out over the rope to help Haley up with me.

She glows up here, so yellow that it stings to watch her, and for a second I regret it all. It should be Vinny lifting my fist in the air, showing me off to Forsyth, escorting me to my corner, kissing me on the cheek.

The Baron is a stocky fucker—Liam, I think is his name. You wouldn't know it to look at them in the daylight, but the Barons' bodies are well-honed, adorned with ink that isn't anywhere near as good as mine.

I rile up the crowd the way I usually do, standing on the bottom rope and commanding them to be louder, wilder. Someone throws a drink at me, and I catch it, downing the dregs that haven't been sloshed onto the floor before chucking the can back in the direction it came. It makes DKS roar, and I raise my middle finger to them—to everyone—just to hear the approval in their cheers.

Jumping down, I meet the Baron in the middle of the ring, sending him a vicious grin.

By the time the fight begins, the pills Cash gave me are pumping hard through my veins, driving every swipe of my fist, every lunge of my legs, every taunt as I beckon him closer.

He gets one hit in.

One.

It rattles my teeth, and I taste blood, but I don't even feel it. Everything feels like it's going both incredibly slow and absurdly fast. Before the round ends, I catch the Baron with a sickening headbutt, right into the bridge of his nose. The act is fast, but the aftermath crawls, the Baron covering his face with both palms.

The Barons call a timeout.

When I get to my corner, Nicky is waiting, eyes sharp and alive. I look at him and it's bittersweet. I'd wanted for so long to have Nick here beside me. Years. It never felt right without him in here, and now that I finally have him, I'm missing Sy. It's as if the universe is sure of some unutterable destiny that says no one can have both brothers at once.

"Don't let him get you on the mat!" he yells over the din of the crowd, head poking through the ropes. "His grapple game is better than his fists."

I spit a mouthful of blood onto the mat, taking water from Haley. "I've got this shit, Nicky. Don't even fucking—" Glancing over to where Vinny is sitting, my words die in my throat.

The King of the Barons is sitting beside her, in Nick's vacant seat.

He's in full garb: tailored black suit, gloves, and mask. She's not looking at him, but her face is ashen and tense, and it's not obvious

—the mask doesn't have a mouth—but I know he's talking to her. He pivots toward her and lifts his hand, bronze horns catching the light, and slowly, *gently*, touches her chest, his gloved fingertips tracing the edge of the death head moth.

The ref passes by, blocking my line of vision, and when I can finally see her again, he's gone, Nick's seat empty once again.

It's like it never happened, Vinny clapping her hands when the announcer signals the end of the timeout. Beside me Nicky is saying, "...and his left ankle is weak, so draw him out. Got it?"

I hear nothing but the rush of blood in my ears; the pills coursing through my veins, the awareness that this is *my* house. *My* rules. *My* win.

I step forward and claim it.

HEAD CHECKS WERE Sy's idea, and no one really knows this, but he started collecting them long before we made it to Forsyth U. I went along with it mostly because it amused me, but a part of me—a small, secret part—hoped he could crack the code.

The problem is, it's not a code.

Numbers are too precise for what happens in my head. Colors are better; a hue, tint, tone, and shade for each feeling. Sometimes things are darker or lighter, redder or greener, grayer or brighter, duller or bolder. It's not a science; it's an art.

Right now, my mind is Jackson Pollock on steroids.

I lean my head back against the wall, nostrils flaring as I try to push it out of my brain, trying to enjoy my victory. It's useless, even with the adrenaline running through my system. I see it again, replaying on a fucked up, mind-bending loop. It's not always the same. Sometimes she's sitting in the King's lap, her arm around his neck as she grins. Others, he's holding her down, making her cry out for me—*us*.

But the color is always the same.

Bronze.

Bronze.

Bronze.

When the door to the locker room opens, giving a distant *thud*, I'm both expecting it and not. I'm tucked away in a shower stall in the back, the light dim as I take another draw of my beer. It smells like damp feet and soap, but it's private.

Mostly.

Her footsteps approach like a doppler as she searches for me, but I don't call out to her. I let her wander slowly toward the back, voice cautious as she calls my name.

My fingers tighten like a vise, my jaw clenching. I grunt low, sagging back. At the same moment, I see her gray eyes peeking around the stall. I think that's what I like best about them—the gray. They take on the color of whatever's around her. The blue of her hair, the green of my eyes, the pink of the sunset, the brown of the tower.

The bronze of a devil's mask.

"Remy? There you—" She freezes, and I think I see it, the shift of her chameleon soul drawing in the rich burgundy of the moment.

There's a second of confusion as her eyes descend, and the lightning in my nerves chooses that moment to erupt. It's so sharp that it's more ache than pleasure, my teeth gnashed around a grunt as it charges through me. I'd never admit it, but it's her skin that does it for me, the sight of the moth inked into her chest, the knowledge that I've made a mark on the universe, scattering, permanent.

Earlier, Vinny looked like she'd been slapped.

Now, she looks like she's been punched.

She physically recoils, a soft, choked sound escaping her throat as she pins me under her wide, shocked gaze.

I pull my spent cock from Haley's mouth, giving her head a pat. "Thanks, babe."

She thumbs at the corner of her mouth, but she doesn't look happy. If anything, she looks embarrassed as she shoots to her feet, sending Vinny a nervous glance. At my nod, Haley brushes past her Duchess, fleeing the building static and blazing bronze.

Smart.

I raise the neck of my beer bottle at Vinny, coldly offering, "To the victor go the spoils."

There's a long moment where she just stares at the tiled wall, arms folding around her middle. "Wow." Her voice is weak and small, but she shakes her head, repeating, "Wow," and I'll hand it to her.

She does a passable job at looking hurt.

Her eyes are shining in that liminal way, a few steps from brimming, but when she swings them onto me, they're full of fire. "I guess loyalty only works one way for you."

We're in the showers and the sound of her chewed words echoes, pinging back to my ears like a rubber ball.

It'd be easy to tell her what the relationship between a Duke and a Duchess is and isn't. Cutsluts are here for a reason. Any Duchess worth her salt knows better than to expect something as pedestrian as *fidelity*.

But that doesn't belong here.

I know just what I'm doing.

"Loyalty?" I ask. The lulling rush of my orgasm is already dissipating, leaving me itchy and full of red. "Like you, speaking to a rival King on my own fucking turf? Letting him fucking *touch* you?" When her mouth opens, I warn, "Don't deny it."

"I wasn't going to!" She flares up, hiding away the tender, broken thing I see in her eyes. "He was just being a creepy son of a bitch. What am I going to do, Remy? Kick a King in the nuts?" She spreads her arms, hapless and desperate in a way I'm not used to seeing on her. "Don't you get it? He was probably hoping you'd see. Both of you!"

"Oh, he was counting on it." My breath puffs out in these hard, rapid bursts that don't satisfy my lungs, but the strange thing is, I feel completely calm. "It was the gun, you know. Sloppy. I bet you thought I wouldn't remember." My brain whirrs in time to my pulse and I embrace it, darting forward to slam my palm on the tile beside her. "People like you and him, you think because my brain is broken that I'm a fucking idiot. But I figured it out, Vinny."

Her gaze is like a physical frisking, jumping around from eye to eye as she struggles to take me in. "Figured out *what*?"

"That the Baron King," I press my finger to the skull in the center of her moth tattoo, "is my father."

32

Lavinia

I WATCH HIM, so beautiful and wild and convicted, and a part of me breaks to see it. A bigger part is paralyzed in disbelief. “You've lost your goddamn mind.”

I'd like to think something more eloquent would come out in a moment like this, but no, apparently not. I welcome the anger, the shock, the swell of utter incredulity, because it's better than the hurt. That doesn't mean the hurt isn't there. It tears at a wound so old that it became a part of me long ago, and now I'm grasping at it, frantically trying to keep my insides from spilling out.

The rage is easier.

Because I'm pretty fucking sure Remy just announced his father is the Baron King to justify having his cock sucked by a cutslut.

“That's what you all want me to think,” he says, poking me with that finger again—hard, stabbing. “But you made a deal with my father, and that's a fucking fact.”

I react on instinct, slapping his finger away and lifting my knee, ramming into his soft, exposed balls. The bottle flies out of his hand, shattering against the hard tile, and he doubles over instantly, sucking in a hard, shocked gasp.

There's a stretch of silence, and then his choked, "Son of a fucking *bitch*!"

"Clive Kayes is the Baron King. Everyone knows it!" I don't wither at the sight of his fiery eyes when he raises them. There was a time this lethal fury would have scared me. Not anymore. I bear down on him, snarling, "If you want to fuck other girls, then at least have the balls to own it, you goddamn coward!"

"I'm a coward?" he hisses, cupping his groin. "I'm not the one trying to hide what I've done! "

Pressing my fingers to my temple, I yell, "You're not thinking straight, Remy!" But the eyes looking back at me are completely blown, more pupil than iris, and it makes a tight ball of alarm build in my gut. "You're fucking blitzed. What the hell are you on?"

His face is pinched and contorted as he tucks himself away, zipping his fly. "You're not turning this around me. I'm not the one who made a deal."

My stomach drops, because suddenly the answer is right in front of me, delivered to me by Sy.

"R is prone to catastrophization and delusion. Without all the facts, his mind reaches to fill in the details, which will often be negative and grandiose."

He never actually showered after his fight. His hair is weighed down with sweat, giving Remy an odd, gaunt-like appearance, the hollows of his cheeks seeming deeper in the dim light.

Defeated, the tears begin welling up. I blink them back furiously, unwilling to give him the satisfaction of seeing me cry over it all. When I'm steady enough to speak without my voice wobbling, I ask, "You want to know what the Baron King asked for? You want to know what Nick and I did to get that skull? The gun?"

"I already know," he hisses, the muscles in his jaw grinding just as hard as the glass under the sole of his boot. "You let him fill you up with his rot. He's been taunting me with it for weeks!"

It takes me a moment to understand what that even means, but the word triggers a memory. The night Nick won me in that fight against Perez, when Remy had me cornered up in the balcony.

"Nice pussy like yours getting all used up on geriatric King dick? Such a waste. They'll fill you up with five flavors of rot."

My head jolts back in disgust. "You think I sold my pussy to a King for intel?" My heart pounds and all I want is to scream in his face, claw off the handsome face that sucked me in, reveal the demon underneath. "I would never," I say, voice low, "*ever* fuck someone for information about my sister." He's still favoring his side, palm cradling his crotch. Like Sy taught me, I take advantage of his weakness and push his chest with both hands. "How dare you accuse me of something like that!"

He stumbles but springs right back, eyes crazed. "It's what they made you to be, Vinny. I see that now." Looking up and down my body, he sneers, "I know that revolver, Vinny. The first time I saw it was when I was eight, mounted on the wall behind my father's desk. I saw the etching, the 'B' on the barrel. I spent weeks obsessed with it, all fucking shiny and sleek. It's the first thing that made me want to be a Duke!" Head shaking, he looks as disgusted as I feel, lips pulled back into a livid grimace. "The Barons would never give up a body for nothing, and my father? He's a collector, and he doesn't give up his prizes without intention. And yet, he gave both to you!"

"Would you listen to yourself?" I inhale, no longer caring if I hurt him. "Imagine it, Remy. Think of me and Nick going there, visualize me offering my cunt for information, and ask yourself this:" I hold my arms out, shrugging. "In what fucking universe would Nick—our Nick, *my* Nick—let that happen?"

Remy stares at me, chest heaving, but doesn't speak.

Across the shower, a faucet drips onto the tile.

"The last two men who touched me without Nick's permission," I say, voice low and full of venom, "are fucking dead."

Remy starts, "That doesn't mean—" but his teeth click, jaw grinding away. "He could have let—"

"He wanted me to play Russian roulette with that revolver," I confess, arms going limp at my sides. My voice emerges dull and lifeless as I explain, "The King. That was his request. A fifty-fifty shot. It was some sick, twisted game to him."

A thick crevice digs its way between Remy's eyebrows. "What?"

Nodding, I go on, "Nick wouldn't let me, of course. He took my place and pulled the trigger on himself before I could find the will to stop him." I gesture heavily to Remy, who's standing stock-still, eyes dropping to my chest. "When I came to you and Sy—when I trusted you to see me at my fucking lowest—I didn't tell you because I was ashamed that I let it get that far. Ashamed that I almost killed your best friend for my precious sense of closure. But mostly," I add, giving a hollow, bitter laugh, "Nick and I didn't tell you because you're batshit fucking crazy enough to go back and play his mind games—because we didn't want to see you die—because we—" My voice cracks and I clamp down on the swell of tears. "Because we love you." Shrugging, I turn away from the sight of his face paling. "I guess that makes me the idiot."

~

THE VICTORY PARTY downstairs is the opposite of the clock face I'm staring at.

It runs without maintenance or supervision, people having already arrived to stock the bar with booze. I can hear them all down there celebrating, and it strikes me as odd. The Dukes aren't very good leaders, and god knows I'm shit at being their Duchess. For a long moment, there in the dark of the tower's main living area, I wonder why we're here at all. To fight? To mend? To sow enough chaos that the cycle starts again?

I climb the spiral staircase to my loft. It's nothing like it used to look, empty and flat and cold. There's the twin mattress, pressed up against the face of the clock, covered in blankets and pillows, most brought by Verity. Story sent some fairy lights and a fluffy rug that Archie enjoys dozing on in the morning rays. Nick dragged a bookcase up from the living area, claiming most of the books on it were mine now, anyway.

It's more of a reading nook now than the sad little nest it began as, but I'm not sure why I'm so drawn to it at first. To look through the cloudy glass of the clock face, survey West End and whatever's beyond? To turn and seek out the visage of this inner tower—the closest thing I've ever had to a home?

To reach beneath the mattress and pull out Sy's journal?

I settle against the pillows, flipping through, settling on some more recent entries—wanting to see myself through his lens.

Journal Note: *Made an agreement to work on our mutual weaknesses together. Her lack of physical ability. My lack of sexual competence. It's a strange arrangement, tense. Humiliating. Enlightening. I'll continue to document our successes and failures as we proceed.*

Then...

L: Subject gaining stamina. Able to go on longer runs and has mastered simple defense techniques. Can't say the same for myself. Pre-ejaculating seems to be the norm. At least L can get in a few strokes before I blow. Progress, I guess. L seems frustrated during lessons. Increasingly agitated and pushy. Her impatience makes me impatient and everything falls apart.

I pull my knee to my chest and skip to the next one.

L: Snapped is the only word to describe it. Pressured me to pleasure her. She directed me to touch her chest, demanding and pushing me to orally stimulate her nipples. Her skin turned a shade of pink and as a result a damp heat spread in her vaginal area. Her reaction caused my own, unprecedented urge. Pro: Brought L to orgasm. Con: Another early ejaculation.

Until I reach the last page Sy wrote before leaving.

I stare at it for a long time, the ink dark in the grooves of the paper, as if they'd been pressed with certainty and conviction—tattooed. I stare at it for so long, and so intensely, that I don't even hear the footsteps up the staircase. I feel him though, his weight dipping the mattress as he drops down beside me. I feel his eyes, too, as he tips to the side to catch a peek of what I'm reading.

Nick hangs there, back pressed into the pillows behind us, elbows resting on his bent knees, until he finally says, "Sy?"

Nodding, I run my fingers over the ink.

The page only has two words.

I'm sorry.

"Do you..." When Nick pauses, I turn to catch the careful, pensive expression he's wearing. He meets my gaze. "You miss him."

I move my gaze back to the words. *I'm sorry.* Sy has this very particular way he writes his 'S's and I always find myself fixated with them. "Yeah." It's easy to admit. To Nick. To myself. The harder part is the smile I plaster on—some twisted purse of my lips that feels oddly broken. "Weird, isn't it? We're such jerks to each other. But..."

But he's Sy.

He's the only person who ever looked me in the eye and told me to be better, and then taught me how. I find myself missing the most unexpected things, like the way he fixes my plates in the mornings, as if he's feeding a linebacker instead of a petite Duchess. I miss the way he'd pace around here at night, anxious to go to bed. I miss the way he'd feel next to me as I slept. The warmth of his skin when I woke in the mornings curled against his side. The softness in his eyes before he got too awake to realize he was holding me back.

I'm not sure what my face is doing, but it prompts Nick to reach over, grabbing the journal and closing it up. Placing it on the bed, he says, "Hey," and touches my chin, turning me to the still, dark intensity of his stare. "He didn't really want to hurt you."

I look into his eyes, the same blue as his brothers, and wonder which man we're talking about.

My answer is the same for both.

"I know."

Nick searches my eyes, and for a second I see it—that same unbearable softness that's been missing in my mornings. "Are you going to forgive him?"

It pulls me like the wake of a wave, the way Nick looks at me. There's always the same longing. Sometimes it's aggressive and too intense, but other times...

Other times, it's like a physical ache to turn away from it.

"I'm the Duchess." My eyes take in the shadows carved into his face. The tattoo on his temple. The smoothness of the jaw he's been diligent about shaving daily. His lips—the same lips that once kissed me in this very loft, traded for the luxury of a book. "Starting to seem like the main part of the job."

"And fighting," he says, thumb sweeping against my chin. "You're good at that."

I look up into his eyes, drowning in the softness of the blue. "What if I don't want to fight anymore?"

His mouth flattens into a grim line, but it doesn't last long.

I twist to press my mouth to his, but I pause—just like he does for me—to look into his eyes, to give him the chance to—

Nick clears the distance instantly, capturing my lips in a slow, cautious kiss. His fingertips tickle the skin below my ear as he cradles my cheek, and it spurs me forward, turning to climb into his lap, straddling his hips.

The look on his face when I tip back is some mixture of shock and dread. "Don't tease me, Little Bird," he whispers, voice hard as gravel.

Captivated by the reflection of the string lights in his eyes, I touch his jaw, my words emerging on a trembled breath. "Tell me again."

His hands find my hips. If I thought for one second I'd need to explain what I want, then I'd be wrong, because he stares at me, unblinking, unflinching, as aggressively as a man staring down the sights of a gun.

"I love you."

It's not the first time I've heard it, but it's the first time I've let myself feel the weight of it. The first time I've taken it into myself. The first time I've looked back into Nick's eyes and seen a man with a heart.

When I dive forward to capture his mouth, he meets me with a fervor that makes me gasp, his hands wrenching my hips into the curve of his body. I understand precisely what I'm dealing with here. A loaded weapon, a lit fuse, an accelerator with no brake.

I rock my hips into his hardness, shuddering at the harsh rumble against my tongue.

Nick abandons my mouth to push hard, wet, sucking kisses down my jaw. Every nerve in my body glows alight at the sensation, head tilting to give him access, and I thread my fingers into his hair just to clutch him close, but it's futile.

He's everywhere.

Hands on my hips, then my ass, then under my shirt, palming my back.

Lips on my neck, then my chest, then my jaw.

Fingers on my skin, then my lips, then tangled into my hair.

"What do you want?" he asks, voice rough with an undercurrent of desperation.

I go paralyzed at the thought of putting it into words.

Some of it's a new selfishness, but some of it's been there since the day I first saw him in that parking lot, two years ago.

I want to peel away this mask he wears and see the man beneath the armor. I want to experience Nick, just like this, soft and hopeful and eager. I want to spend a single genuine moment of passion with someone who wants me back. I want to keep these last two weeks of aching *want* for Nick Bruin and discard the shame of them. I want to be shown that the way he's looking at me right now dwarfs the memory of the hurt he's caused. I want to kiss someone and know, all the way to my marrow, that he'd never want to kiss anyone more.

But most of all, I want this:

"Show me," I plead into the crease of his mouth, reaching between us to shuck up his shirt. "Make love to me."

Nick takes this big, steeling breath, grabbing my shoulders to peel me away from his mouth. "Remember what I told you that night you let me out of the cage?" His eyes are heavy and glazed as they bore into mine, and despite having been the one to end the kiss, he's also the one leaning back in. "I said I wasn't sure I could go back to the person I was before I met you." At my nod, he watches me closely, words deep and full of weight. "If we do this, I won't be able to go back to the person I am right now."

Not very long ago, I would have interpreted those words as a threat. A warning. A promise. But I see it now for what it is. He's already mine. He's always been mine. I've just been so wrapped up in the trauma and pain of my past, the never ending fight to survive, that I couldn't grasp the gravity of it.

"I'm ready." I stroke his hair, pushing it off his forehead, and my hand trembles with the nervousness of giving this to him. "I'm ready to be yours."

Nick has always been exceptional at maintaining his frame, holding his mask, hiding an expression. But right now, a million emotions flicker through his eyes, too fast for me to parse as he hooks an arm around my back, bucks, and spins, dropping me against the mattress.

"Fuck," he whispers, hovering above me as his eyes take me in. His brows drop low, carving shadows in the hollows of his eyes. To someone else, he might look angry, but I know better. I feel the reverence in his touch as he palms the outside of my thigh, bending down to kiss me.

It's bruising, searing, the weight of him between my legs solid and sure. This time when I shuck up his shirt, he backs far enough away to let me pull it over his head. I've looked at Nick a lot these past years, and in the last couple of months, I've had more than one opportunity to feel his skin.

This is the first time I do it like this—slow, indulgent, appreciative—feeling the ladder of his abs beneath my fingertips. Nick watches me with a slackness in his jaw that I'm not used to seeing, but I'm too busy admiring his body to question it. I linger over a scar on his side, thin and pale, and remember the night it was put there—last Christmas. He'd come to my motel room to hide out for a few hours, stone-faced and injured—superficially.

"Remember that night?" He's almost as stony now, placing his hand over mine, pushing my palm into his side.

Swallowing, I nod, widening my thighs for his hips. "You killed someone."

He thrusts against my center, and even through our layers of clothes, it's like an electric shock. "Every time I'd leave you in that motel room, I'd wait outside in my car," he says, ducking down to press a soft, sucking kiss to my neck. "I'd jack off, thinking of this. Dreaming of what you'd taste like." His hand slides beneath the hem of my tank top, rucking it up. "Sometimes when Daniel was busy, I'd watch you on his monitor." He pulls the top over the swell of my breasts, my arms rising as he tugs it off. Then he slides down to kiss the skin, his tongue licking out to meet my peaked nipple.

I arch into his mouth, confessing what just may be my darkest secret. "Sometimes, I'd think of you, too."

Nick stills, lip catching against my breast as he meets my gaze. "Yeah?" I know the question is in mind. Why, then? Why did I fight him so hard? If I wanted him, why not just have him? But I can tell from the way he breathes, deep and bracing, the tip of his nose dragging against the valley between my breasts as he palms them up into peaks, that he already has the answer.

Back then, he wasn't *Nick*. He was an extension of Daniel. Of my father. Of Forsyth. He was another man with the keys, locking me away. He was sexy and gorgeous and brutal, and—maybe this is actually my darkest secret, "You were fucking *terrifying*." A shudder rolls down my spine at the darkness in his eyes, because that hasn't changed.

I can feel the restraint when he squeezes my tits, but it's still devouring, his mouth sucking hot kisses all over them. "I don't have to be like that, Little Bird." His blue eyes *blaze* as he unbuttons my shorts. "I know it's our thing. The push and the shove. We both like a good fight—it's why we belong here." I'm lifting my hips before he even has me unzipped, letting him push them, panties and all, over my hips. His voice rumbles as he descends, palms burning a path down my thighs. "But I can make you feel good." He pauses right between my legs, hands shoving my thighs open as he gazes up my body. "I could fucking worship you."

He licks a hot, aggressive path up my slit.

I'm not sure what's more electrifying: the slick pressure of his tongue or the fact he never breaks my gaze, blue eyes piercing right through me as I keen, toes curling. His hands are forcing my thighs apart, but it's laughably unnecessary. I spread them wide, sinking my fingers into his hair as I buck up against his mouth.

He closes his lips over my clit, and despite all the talk about worship, the look in his eyes borders on threatening, as if forcing me to feel the full breadth of his tongue is something he's expecting a fight about.

Nick licks my pussy like he's wielding a gun: my clit the trigger, his tongue the bullet, my eyes the pleading victim.

And his marksmanship is impeccable.

I struggle not to writhe beneath him, the flame in my center roaring into an inferno under the force of his tongue. Even if I wanted to break his gaze, I couldn't. He holds me there, pinned like an insect, thighs spread as he mounts his assault.

But when I get the telltale tug in my gut that approaches a coming tide, I gasp, "Stop, stop, stop." He jolts back, eyes heavy and hard, and I rush to explain, "I want you inside when I—"

That blank, angry look crumbles from his face in an instant, and then he's tearing at the buckle of his belt, muscles shifting artfully beneath his inked flesh. His voice is husky and breathless as his fingers find me, wet and waiting. "Has it been long enough? Are you..." he pauses, eyes darting down to my pussy, "better?"

"Yeah," I assure, trying not to laugh at the awkwardness in the words. For a second, he seems so much like his brother that my stomach twists.

But then Nick's pushing down his jeans, buckle rattling noisily as his cock springs free, and all I can think about as he stands is his body, so cut and defined into this savage piece of art. In the soft glow of the fairy lights, the tattoos Remy's inked into his flesh look intricate and sinister, and I'm struck with this notion that all three of them are as entwined as ivy, with their tangled roots and crawling vines.

No one could love just one of them.

It comes to me like a parting of clouds as he kicks off his jeans. Wordlessly, I get to my knees, watching him freeze, the tension in his muscles obvious as I rise to press a kiss to the center of his chest.

Maybe it's not that I was so terrified of Nick before. Maybe it's not even because I didn't know how to be loved, although both of those are categorically true. Maybe I couldn't accept Nick because I could only see the wilted leaves, so untangled from the other pieces of himself that some part of me recognized he wasn't whole.

Just like me.

I kiss his stomach, the ridges of his hard abs, and then lower to that tight cut of the 'V' beside his hips. But when my mouth follows the fine, blond trail of hair that arrows down to his cock, his hands find my head, stilling me.

"Lavinia." When I look up, Nick's eyes are glazed and wild, a lot like Remy's had been earlier. He gently thumbs my cheeks, saying, "You don't have to."

And I give him the most precious thing I have to offer. "I know."

33

Nick

I STARE DOWN in awe as her lips part, the head of my cock a breath away, swollen and already leaking. On some level, I'd already written all this off. The thought of Lavinia letting me touch her like this. Looking up at me, on her knees, so soft and open and inviting. It's all I've ever wanted. I'd dreamed of it—fuck, obsessively—for years, but I'd already started down the path of accepting that all I could get were the hard, violent moments where I took it, and those weren't worth it. I know that now. I've tried this every way I knew how. By negotiation, deep in the bowels of the Hideaway or over the breakfast table. By force, tied to the bed fighting me every inch of the way. I saved her. Used her. Abused her. Abandoned her.

God, it feels better this way.

Still, it's a physical battle not to thrust forward, to watch as she holds my eye, licking out to wet her plush bottom lip.

The first touch of her tongue punches every bit of air from my lungs. It's not just the sensation, slick and gentle, her tongue spreading the precum around. It's the way her eyelids slump, like she's drunk on it.

"Holy," I growl as she pitches forward, "fucking," sinking down, lips tight around my shaft, "shit."

Goddamn.

Her mouth is hot and wet, but it's the sight most of all, her lips around me as she reaches up to grab the base, humming. Sucking. Stroking. Bobbing. My lungs struggle to perform basic operations, and it's not right. My Little Bird on her knees like this. I'm supposed to be worshiping her.

It hurts to tug her off, and the surprised, dazed expression on her face when I do isn't helping. I soothe it away by bending to kiss her and it's unbearably fucking erotic, the fact that we're tasting ourselves on each other's tongues.

She goes down easily when I push her back on the mattress, and it's strange. I should be nervous as I lay her out, her naked body on offer before me, because those words...

Make love to me.

I want to. I want to be that man for her, the kind who treats her better than a duchess—a queen.

But the words, the implication of them, is like being interviewed for a position as someone's soulmate.

It's just a lot of fucking pressure.

Literally.

I've never made love to a woman before. I've fucked plenty, but it's always been hard and fast, even when it was Lavinia—but that's the last thing I want to think about. If I could, I'd erase the memory altogether, cover it with the sight of her gazing up at me right now, chest flushed as she rakes her lip through her teeth.

But I'm not nervous.

I know exactly what to do.

I brush the hair from her cheek, holding myself up on a forearm as I kiss the overheated skin. Her thighs are warm against my hips, and I don't think I'll ever get over it—the fact she's spreading them for me, letting me in. I accept it greedily because it's where I belong—I've always known it—rocking my cock against her folds as I kiss down to her neck. I suck a bruise into the skin there, dick surging at the sound of her low moan. It's as essential as the star on her hip, proof for tomorrow that this was real, that it happened. Maybe I'll even find myself counting the broken capillaries like a goddamn headcase.

She tilts her head, her fingertips finding my shoulders, and when she swallows hard enough that I can hear the click of her throat, I get the sense this whole love making thing is just as foreign to her as it is to me.

Lifting my mouth from her neck, I grab her chin to guide her eyes to mine. "Too much?"

Her eyebrows pinch in confusion, but smooth just as quick. I'm not stupid. I know the way I feel about her makes her all shifty and evasive. But she shakes her head, insisting, "It's what I want."

I watch her for a long moment, searching. There's a hurt in her eyes, but I know I'm not the one who's put it there. Sy? Remy?

I don't ask.

Instead, I tighten my grip on her face and push our mouths together, only letting her go to skate my fingertips over her tit, palming it up to feel her back arch. The noise from downstairs is rowdy and somewhere in the kitchen, the Archduke is rattling his food bowl, but Lavinia and I are distilled down to the point where I reach between us, grabbing the base of my dick and rubbing it through her folds.

The head of my dick slides through her wetness as it descends, slotting up against her entrance, and I break from the kiss to watch her fluttering eyes as I slowly—fucking agonizingly—push inside.

Her mouth parts on a gasp, the fingernails against my back digging divots into the skin. "Oh god," she breathes, eyes wide.

I freeze, teeth clenched against the instinct to fuck inside. "Hurts?"

But she shakes her head, the sole of her foot rubbing against the back of my knee. "Just... go slow?"

Fixated on the crevice between her eyebrows, I sink another desperate inch into her, grunting at the tight, wet warmth of it. I spit a low, "*Fuck*," my balls aching with the urge to slam forward. But I'm not my brother. I hold it back, enthralled by the way her body takes me, her chest heaving as she watches me back.

When she lifts her hips, working up against me, I tangle the fingers I have above her head into the hair at her crown, holding her steady as I sink to the hilt.

She hisses, and I think she means to say, "Fuck," but all she manages is the 'f'-sound, her teeth buried into her lip as she grinds her head back. I take the opportunity to dip down, licking a hot path from her throat to her chin as I begin rocking my hips.

Here's something about Lavinia I never knew.

When I'm fucking her and she actually wants it, she'll tuck her hand behind my neck and wrench me down for a long, obscene, searing kiss. I get lost in it, nearly forgetting the scope of the job as I pull my hips back and plunge forward, deep and hard. The sound she makes is rough and raw, her teeth sinking into my lip, but I can tell she likes it.

She raises her knees, wrapping her legs around my hips.

It sends a fissure of liquid-hot bliss down my spine to be clutched between her thighs, the heels of her feet pushing against my ass, spurring me on. When I break away from her kiss, she stares down between our bodies, face both slack and tense as she watches me fuck her. "Do you see it, Little Bird?" I tighten my fingers in her hair, nudging her back to meet my gaze. "We fit together."

She nods, but her eyes are dark and lost, fingernails pushing into my skin. So I tell her in every language, bending to suck her tit, hand reaching to clamp around her thigh. I hold her close as my hips roll, cock dragging and prodding as I search for it, tilting for a new angle, until—

"Nick," she gasps, hands jabbing down to claw into my ass.

"That's right." I grunt the words against her lips, staring into her eyes as they widen and then scrunch. "No one knows you like I do,"

I whisper, voice so wrecked I barely recognize it as my own. "No one can make you feel as good as I do." My hips rock, cock pushing right into her G-spot. "No one can love you like I do. You know that, don't you?" She nods, body coiling with a series of soft, punched whines, and I nod back, hips rocking. "Come for me, baby. Show me."

Her face screws up, cheeks such a lovely, violent shade of red as she digs her fingers into the hard muscles of my ass, setting my pace, forcing me faster, deeper. I kiss her as it builds—her mouth, her chin, her hot cheeks, the little patch of skin beneath her ear, the mark I'd made earlier.

Right as she seizes, her eyes fly open, locking with mine. "Nick..."

I feel her come around me, pussy clenching as she shudders. The long column of her neck stretches as she cries out, spine arching into me. I keep hammering away at that spot, dragging my cock against it stubbornly, relentlessly. It's a good thing I'm willing to worship her because watching her come undone on my dick is a fucking religious experience.

It isn't until after the tension in her thighs has snapped, muscles going lax, that I think of my dick as something other than *hers*; a tool to make those sharp little cries, a weapon to cause that aching twist of her face.

When I finally can, I rise up to give her a full thrust, watching as her pussy swallows me to the root, grasping me when I drag my hips back to do it again.

It's the sight of her beneath me that makes my balls ache, though.

She's spent, staring up at me with this glazed, bliss-out expression. When she releases my ass, it's only to run a hand up my chest, hooking around my neck.

"Tell me," I demand, so fucking eager to fill her up that I don't even think to draw it out.

I can see it cycling in her head, the question of what I want to hear. I don't want to have to tell her. I want her to look in my eyes, all fucked out and ready for me, and say the words I've waited two years to hear.

And she does. "I'm yours."

I bury my face into her neck when I come, slamming into the cradle of her hips as if I could dig my way further inside of her. I make some fucked-up combination of a grunt and a growl as it rips through me, my cock pulsing into her heat. It feels like it goes on forever, her fingers carding through my hair as my cock surges, filling her up.

She hums, cradling the back of my head, and it's so fucking sweet and perfect that, for a second, I'm convinced it can't be real. That's why I stay inside her so long, allowing her to milk every last drop. It's why, when I finally roll to my back, I tuck my arms around her waist and drag her with me, not allowing my dick to slip free. I hold her there, against my chest, dick softening within her warmth, unwilling to let it go.

When she tries to lift herself, I tighten my arms around her, shoving her back down. "Stay," I demand, voice ragged and hard.

She responds by stiffening against my hold, pushing against it, and I remember who I've fallen in love with here.

A fighter.

I loosen my hold, brushing my lips against her forehead. "Please?"

There's a moment where I'm sure she's going to be her usual defiant self, and it'd frustrate the ever-loving shit out of me, but I'd get it. I'd let her go.

Instead, she sags, sighing into the hollow of my throat as she stills. "Sticky," she murmurs, wiggling her hips.

My cock gives a feeble twitch, because she's right. I can feel my cum inside her, but it's amplifying this warmth in the pit of my chest to know she's so full of me. So I stubbornly—fucking tenaciously—move with her to make sure it doesn't slip free.

As long as she's with me right here, right now, this is real.

She's mine.

I'm hers.

And nothing else matters.

~

THE TOWER IS dark other than the sliver of light coming from the clock face. Our naked bodies are only halfway covered by a thin novelty blanket, and this close to the glass, the cold radiates, tickling at every piece of exposed skin. But she's hot against me, still straddling my hips—my cock is still inside her—and her weight against my chest is the only blanket I need. I still cover her, though, my hands moving over her back beneath the blanket as she burrows into my chest to steal my own warmth.

We've been dozing off and on for a while, but every slam from the party downstairs jolts me back awake. Lavinia's head is tucked under my chin, her hair wafting a sweet scent, and every time I dive back into awareness, I'm shocked fucking stupid all over again that she's still here. I hold her close, constantly pressing my nose to her hair, breathing in the scent of honey and sex, and Lavinia...

Lavinia explores me.

Her fingers find the ridges of muscles, lingering there, and not for the first time tonight, I'm hit with the heady realization that she digs my body. I'm not generally a humble person, so it makes me want to push into her touch—show her all the things about it that make my body powerful and strong. It's just like the day she said she preferred me without the beard, this little ember of satisfaction flaring to life.

When she touches my ring, I fidget with it—something that's become an unbearable habit. It's heavy and awkward and ugly as sin, but it's mine. When I reach around her back to pull it off, I turn it over in my palm, over and over, feeling the worn smoothness of the Bruin's head.

Her fingers trace every tattoo she can reach, as if it's her first time ever seeing them. Her back is soft and warm, and every so often, I'll let my fingertips wander down her spine, tracing the vertebrae as she breathes against my skin, moving to another section of ink on my chest, my neck, my arm. Sometimes she'll inhale, mouth parting, like she wants to ask about the pocket watch on my arm, or the angel weeping blood, or the eyes on the back of my hand, or the rosary around my wrist.

When she finally does find one to ask about, voice slicing through the silence, my dick is surging to life inside of her—thickening, lengthening, locking us together.

If she notices, she doesn't say anything. "What's with this?" she asks, pulling at my hand. Her fingers press into the skin above my wrist, tattooed a solid black, and I spin my ring with my thumb, watching the tendons shift.

"An apology," I rumble, so lost in the feel of her handling me, touching me, that I might as well be shitfaced drunk. She stills when I take her wrist, smoothly sliding the ring onto her little thumb. I worry at first she'll tell me no, take it off and throw it back in my face. Instead, she frowns as she inspects it, worrying it on her thumb a lot like I do. I flare out my fingers for her own to fit between them. "It used to be an LDZ skull. Remember?"

Her mouth turns down as she inspects it, trying to find the design hidden beneath. "Hm, maybe."

I'm not surprised she doesn't. Ducking my chin to press a kiss to her hair, I explain, "When I came back to West End, Remy was really upset with some of my ink. Sometimes I had to get pieces that were more... South Side-esque."

Her fingers wander to the upper and lowercase S's over my collarbone. Remy understood why I couldn't let that one go. Good or bad, useful or not, South Side is a big part of who I've become. It's taken me a while to come to terms with that, but he managed it pretty much immediately.

"So," I go on, giving my hips a careful, testing nudge, "I let him tattoo over the skull. It's solid black because—"

"Black means sorry," she whispers, eyelashes fanning out as her eyes slip closed.

She doesn't exactly seem opposed, so I hold her in place, rolling my hips to thrust. "Yeah. It was my way of saying sorry. In Remy's language."

I've never fucked someone like this before, going hard when I'm already inside of her, and it's insanely erotic to feel her wetness rushing to meet me. It's also unhurried and lazy, my palms moving over her back as I fuck into her just as casually as I'm stroking her skin.

"I told him about the Russian Roulette tonight," she says, tilting her pelvis to give me a better angle. It drives me so crazy that I almost miss what she's saying, too obsessed with the friction of pushing into her to pay attention.

When it finally hits me, I keep going. "Oh. Alright." She could tell me she set fire to the tower right now, and I'd probably nod along stupidly. I do ask, "Why?" but it's spoken in a breath between gentle thrusts, my hands finding the swell of her ass. "I thought we agreed that he'd—"

She makes this tiny little mewling noise, rocking into me, and all coherence goes right out the window.

Until she explains, "He accused me of trading my body to the Barons for Leticia's skull."

It's a testament to the power of the moment that my hips barely stutter, even though I push her up to look her in the eye. Tightly, I demand, "Want to fucking say that again?"

She shakes her head and plants her hands on my chest, blue hair grazing her tits. "It's bullshit, obviously, but he needed justification for..." her breath catches and she rolls her hips, eyes glazing over. "Fuck," she breathes, rocking into my thrust.

"For what?" I ask, reaching up to drag my fingertips down her tit, catching her pebbled nipple as I descend. Her clit is already swollen when I push my hand between us, rubbing my thumb into it. "What did he do?"

Remy has patterns.

I've seen him bouncing around here like a coke-addled goblin for the past week, but even though I did my best to make him take his meds, go to class, keep him out of harm's way, I knew a crash was coming.

Lavinia's jaw drops, eyes slamming closed as I rub her clit, thrusting into her wet heat. I don't think either of us expects it when I come first, thighs flexing as I buck my hips, emptying inside her for the second time tonight.

She reacts by grinding back—hard—and clenching around me with her own release. It's less intense than the one before, her dropping back down to my heaving chest.

It's almost like it never happened.

The chill seeps through the glass of the clock face and she sighs, burrowing close as I stroke up the bare expanse of her back.

I almost forget the conversation altogether, distracted by how wet she feels around my dick.

"I walked in on them," she says, voice rough as gravel. "Him and... Haley. She was sucking him off after the fight." I freeze, ducking down to try to meet her gaze. There's a wobble in her voice, and I know she's trying to hold back, but I wrap my arms around her and hold her close.

"Son of a bitch." A few pieces of the night click into place. The hurt I could see in her eyes, her need for comfort for reasons other than Sy and her healing pussy.

Before I can speak, she continues. "He was being such an asshole to me before the match, and it was like... I could feel him trying his hardest to push me away. You know?"

I knit my fingers into her hair, rubbing against her scalp. "Yeah. I know."

She touches that tattoo on my wrist—the apology. "He was rambling on about me having some kind of relationship with his dad—even though I'd repeatedly told him I hadn't seen him since the night he introduced us."

My lips press into a grim line. "He didn't believe you."

She nods, tonelessly adding, "He was high as a fucking kite."

"Lavinia..." Nothing gets Remy as crazy as his dad. It's one of the reasons I can't fucking stand the guy. Ever since we were kids,

Timothy Maddox has played Remy's problems against him. "Sometimes, Remy does this. I'm not saying there's an excuse for it, but sex? It's this big mania trigger for him. I don't think he can think straight."

She lifts up to look me in the eye, her bare tits pressing into my chest. I run my hand up and down her back. "It's not just the sex. He was *mean.* Like, completely delusional, making all these crazy accusations. Not only was I selling my body to the Baron." Even though she rolls her eyes, I can still see the wetness in them—the hurt. "Apparently, he's come to the insane conclusion that his father *is* the King of the Barons."

I stare at her, my hand coming to an abrupt rest on her hip. "What?"

Despite the question, I barely hear her response, so tied up in the thought that my brain can't spare the energy for anything else.

"His big 'proof'," she makes finger quotes, "is that he swears his father owned the revolver the Baron King gave us. Ergo, his father *is* the Baron King, and since he knows we made a deal with him, but not *what* the deal was, he made this ridiculous fucking leap that—because I'm a whore now, evidently—I traded my ass for it." She smiles, but it's brittle and bitter. "Can you fucking believe that?"

"Yes," I say, without pause or reservation. At the way her eyes go shuttered, I lift up to meet her, insisting, "Not that stupid shit about you trading your ass. I mean, about his dad being the King. *Fuck.*" I look out over the living area below, it all clicking into place. "How the hell did I not see this before? Timothy Maddox has sway—power—but he isn't loyal to any of the four corners of Forsyth."

She gasps when I roll us and stand, my dick slipping from her heat, and the look she gives me could melt steel. "You can't possibly be buying this complete load of horseshit, Nick."

"Hey," I say, kneeling to touch her cheek. "Listen to me. Remy is a fucking shit for doing that to you, and I'm going to beat his ass the next time I see him. And don't think I can't appreciate the fact that you just turned to me, asking to be made love to, because I'm just... some sure thing."

Her neck snaps back, forehead creasing. "Nick, it wasn't like that."

Softly, I argue, "On some level, it was. And I'm glad, because it means you get it. I'm yours, and now you're mine, so I don't fucking care. But Remy..." Shaking my head, I struggle to put it into words. "He isn't crazy. He sees more than people think, and that means there's something to this thing about his dad." I take her face in my hands, leaning in to pluck a gentle kiss from her lips. "And that means I have to check it out."

It's not easy though.

She watches me from the mattress as I pull on my jeans and it's fucking agony to look at her, all soft and naked and *mine* for the first time. There's only one thing I want more than to get back under that blanket and feel her against me.

The truth.

34

Sy

The thud of my fist banging into the heavy punching bag is the only thing I've found that takes off the edge. It's old. My dad bought it for us when we were twelve, the leather sides worn and smooth from thousands of hits.

Our parents didn't want us to be fighters. They tried everything else: baseball, football, martial arts and even wrestling. But the fights happened anyway, wild and feral after school with other kids that dared look at us the wrong way, or bare-chested against one another in the basement, seeing who could hit the hardest, leave the darkest bruise. Nothing stopped us. Not punishments or lectures.

Finally, Dad and Pops agreed to train us properly.

It's in our blood, no one can change that.

When I arrived a week ago, my parents didn't seem too surprised. They'd heard about the tribunal and probation. Not the specifics, though—at least, not Mom. Even if Nick keeps Dad updated on everything, my mom chooses to stay out of the nitty-gritty of Royal life. She left that behind, or that's what she says, although I know she's the one that brought that dress to Lavinia for the Baron's Equinox celebration. I can't blame her. With two sons caught up in the thick of it, a little willful ignorance probably goes a long way.

"Stay as long as you need," Pops said that night, squeezing my shoulder. "The tower is a pressure cooker. You wouldn't be the first Duke that needed to take a breather."

The shared look between Dad and Pops landed in my chest. They'd expected something like this when we made a run for Duke. Nicky and I in the same house? Guaranteed conflict. As I stood in their kitchen, ego bruised, it was easier to let them think that it was something as superficial as a dumb sibling squabble than to tell them the truth. I didn't think I could handle their looks of disappointment.

But my mom knew the real reason I was home. *Of course.* Her therapist spidey-senses homed in on me the minute I came in the door.

"What does Lavinia think about you leaving the tower?" she'd asked that night when she carried in a stack of clean towels to my room. The small space looks the same as when I left. MMA posters lining the walls. A couple of trophies and non-fiction on the book-shelves.

"I'm pretty sure the Duchess is perfectly happy to have some space from me right about now." I dropped my duffel on the end of the bed, avoiding eye contact, but I saw her reflection in the mirror over the dresser.

She tried her hardest to keep a straight face, but I caught the disapproving quirk of a frown. "Did something happen between you two?"

"Nothing I care to share."

She hovered around for a few more minutes, bringing me a fresh pillowcase and reminding me where to find the soap and extra toilet paper as if I didn't live in this house for eighteen years. "She's a strong woman," mom said, lingering by the door. "From what I hear, she's pretty impressive."

"Maybe not as strong as I thought." I rolled my eyes. "And stop gossiping about us with Mama B."

She tried to corner me again after that, but I don't need my mother's professional opinion to understand how and why I screwed up. I hurt Lavinia. *Hurt.* I caused her physical pain, and that wasn't part of the deal. I'd made it clear I would protect her—teach her to protect herself—and I ripped through that in one desperate, fucked-up thrust.

I hit the bag in a fury of angry punches, hoping one of them will finally make me feel better. It does nothing but make my knuckles and biceps ache, and it's not up to me anyway. I left her the journal. Lavinia hasn't left a book unread in her life—which means *when* she does read it, not *if*, she'll know. I fucked up, and I know it.

What happens from there is up to her.

"Keep that up and you'll either break the bag or break your hands." Wiping the sweat off my forehead, I turn and see Dad holding my phone in his hand. "Someone seems pretty intent on reaching you."

Shrugging, I turn away. "I'm sure it's just to let me know who won the fight."

It's the first Fury I've missed since freshman year—the first time I haven't been there to back up Remy.

"Remy won," he says.

"Of course he did." I pause, twisting to narrow my eyes at him. "How do you know?"

"Because you got six texts last night, hours before the calls started."

I grunt and turn back to the bag, lining up my fists. "I'm sure it's nothing that can't wait."

I rear back to start back up, but Dad's hand stretches out, blocking my shot. I raise my eyebrows.

"You may have walked out of that tower, but you left your brother, best friend, and a Duchess over there to pick up the pieces of whatever spat you're having." He gives me a serious look, handing me the phone. "You have obligations, son. Fulfill them."

The phone buzzes again and a name flashes across the front. It's Ballsack.

Teeth grinding, I answer the one. "Hey," I say, catching my breath. "What's up?"

"Jesus Christ, I've been trying to get a hold of one of you all day." His voice has that hollow sound, implying he's in the gym. "Something's come up," he says. "There's this rumor."

"You called me about a rumor?" I knew the shit from the party was going to spread. I'd intended for it to, but once things went sideways... *fuck*. I fight with the wraps on my knuckles, pulling at them with my teeth. "That's not an emergency, Sack."

"It is when it's about a hit coming down on your brother."

My heart stutters and I rip the wraps free. "What the fuck are you talking about?" I glance up at Dad and I see his forehead crease. "What do you mean there's a hit on Nick?"

Dad straightens, a dark look coming over his face.

"It's a rumor," Ballsack explains. "A few of the boys caught wind of it while doing a delivery to the Lords. Some shit about the Counts gunning for the heir in the tower. Word is that it's retaliation for Perez."

Lionel. It tracks. There's no way our probation is punishment enough for him.

"Thanks, man," I say, hanging up. I look at my dad. "Did you know about this? Pops?"

But I can tell from the glint of dread in his eyes that he didn't. "I knew that when Nick took out Lionel's number one Count he started a war." His face goes tight. "But no, Lionel would make sure that we didn't know about it. That tip had to have come from a friend."

We don't have many these days, not at the rate we've been

creating messes, but there has been someone decidedly in our corner for months now.

"Killian," I say, hating that I have to admit that, more and more, he's worked more as an ally than an enemy. Right now, we need as many as we can get. At the skeptical tilt of my dad's mouth, I explain, "No, he's changed. Not softer, by any means, just... more focused. Different from his father." I pick up the phone to call Nick, but it rings again, and this time the name on the screen feels like a kick in the gut. I spit a low curse before answering, "...hey."

"Sy?" Hearing her voice calms the war raging in my chest.

I glance at my dad, knowing my ears are probably glowing red. "Yeah, it's me."

"We need to talk," she says.

She's right. We do. About that night. About how I hurt her. About the man I want to be. But first... I have to warn my brother.

"I'll be there in twenty minutes."

THE STREETS outside the tower are never quieter than they are just after dawn breaks. A slant of sunrise reflects off the clock face, casting an orangey glow, and it almost feels magic. I jam my fists into the pocket of my jacket and stare up at it. Sometimes I look at the tower and almost understand why Remy respects it so much. The ancient mortar. The dusty bricks. The graying wood. It's seen generations of conflict, withstood the winds of Forsyth's chaos, weathered its storms and bitter cold. The skyline might change, but never this part of it, standing tall and imperious.

It's a fighter.

Like us.

The scent of stale beer limps up from the gutter, a sure sign of the victory party last night. The pledges are tasked with keeping the streets clean as part of their initiation. I did my shifts back when I was a lowly recruit, just like every other punk that comes through the ranks. It's tradition.

I guess I've been the only one whipping them into shape.

Inside, I take the steps to the main chamber two at a time, feeling a sense of relief no one changed the locks on me while I was gone. I wouldn't blame her if she did.

The feeling is fleeting, because once I'm inside, I find the tower empty. The lights are off. Nick and Remy's bedroom doors are open, revealing just how vacant they are, and I spend a long few minutes panicking.

Fuck fuck fuck.

Maybe she changed her mind. Maybe she never wants to speak to me again. Maybe Remy and Nick are backing her up, and they all cleared out before I could—

A hard slam comes from up in the loft and I glance up just in time to see Archie attempting to climb atop a shelf. He teeters and lands on the edge of a book, sending both it and the kitten crashing to the ground.

My eyes shift to the door leading to the belfry.

I climb the stairs, and the cat comes running, meowing relentlessly, weaving through my feet. That's what I get for feeding him people food. He always wants more. "Not now," I tell him, casting a gaze over to the mattress on the floor. It's rumpled—messy in a way that looks like it's been used for a wrestling match, not sleeping. My stomach churns as I stare at it, wondering which one got to sleep with her, but the sour taste in the back of my throat isn't jealousy. It's something a lot more bitter than that.

Shame.

It takes me a second to get past it, to swallow it down and step into the narrow stairwell leading up.

I find her, elbows propped against the ledge, staring out at the city.

She heard me come up the hatch—I know she did—but she lets me be the one to break the silence. It's a long moment before I do, my eyes drinking her in. The gentle wave of her hair. The curve of her back. The bend of one knee as she stands there in shorts, like it's not fucking freezing.

I finally work up the nerve to say, "Hey."

She dips her chin, not turning to look at me. "Hi."

"Did you get the journal?" It just spills out of me, and it's stupid. That's the least of our worries right now. But somehow, I don't think I can breathe until I know for sure.

She's twisting something on her thumb, large and metallic. "Yeah."

I recognize it as Nick's ring, the brass Bruin standing out as she spins it around and around. The closer I look, the more of him I see.

There's a big, dark hickey on her neck.

"Oh." Cramming my fists into my pockets, I ask, "You and Nick, huh?"

Her spine stiffens in response. "Don't you dare judge me, Simon."

"I'm not," I rush to say, and it's the truth. "I mean, I saw it coming. Nick can be a reckless, selfish, destructive asshole, but he can also be protective and... weirdly gallant." Rolling my eyes, I add, "That is, if he can get out of his own way long enough to show it to someone." I guess he finally has. "I think he'll do you right this time." *And if he doesn't, then he'll still have me to answer to.*

I don't say the last part, but I feel it. Some part of me might always feel this thing inside my chest, the responsibility to keep her safe. I'd like to say I don't know where it came from, but it'd be a lie. The night I rescued her from the cedar chest, she became mine.

When she doesn't answer, I think about the journal, knowing it was cowardly. I knew it then, and I know it now. Nick probably found the balls to actually say the words, and since I'm not one to be outdone, I tell her, "I'm sorry."

She turns to me, a gust of wind flinging her hair across her face. "When we made our deal, you trusted me with your body. I know I didn't always do a really good job, because..." Her eyes are shining with wetness, and she looks away, the embarrassment clear in the purse of her mouth. "Well, I don't actually have a lot of experience that isn't some asshole forcing himself on me."

She'd have hurt me less if she kicked me in the fucking balls.

"I'm sorry," I try again, my chest feeling like it's twisted.

She shakes her head, swinging those big, shining eyes onto me. "But you trusted me, and I tried, Sy. I tried to honor that. And when I trusted *you* with my body, you just..." Her voice cracks, and she wraps her arms around herself, as if the cold is finally making itself known to her.

Gruffly, I say, "I know," but it's not enough. It doesn't quiet this storm of guilt churning in my stomach, and it doesn't ease the pressure in my chest. "I just—I just wanted it to be over."

She blinks at me, forehead creasing. "Us?"

"No," I say, startled. "The rumors. The speculation. The urges." I turn my gaze away, scowling as my fists ball inside my pockets. "My stupid fucking virginity."

"If you'd asked me," she responds, a hardness in her voice, "if you'd given me time to work up to it, I would have done it."

I look at her, hit with such a wave of misery that I'm stunned. "Really?"

Sharply, she adds, "Not in front of the whole frat," and then she looks down, her cheeks reddening. "But probably."

"Lavinia..." I watch her, not knowing what to say—how to erase what's done. I try with the lamest gesture imaginable, shrugging out of my jacket and extending it to her. That's the rub, I guess. There's no wiping a slate clean, and even if there were, I don't have time to try. "There's a hit out on Nick," I finally say, slamming up all the stupid, useless emotions.

She straightens, arms dropping at her sides as she stares at the jacket. "What?"

"The tip came down from the Lords, I'm guessing." I nod my chin toward South Side in the distance, finally just walking up and draping the jacket around her shoulders. "Something about a contract for the heir in the tower."

She stares at me, unblinking. "My father?"

I shrug, not wanting to add to that soft, frustrated look in her eyes. "Where is he?" I ask. "Nick?" For the first time, I can see past my own bullshit to realize the strangeness of his not being here. The blankets on the mattress in the loft, the tangles in her hair, that hickey on her neck…

They obviously had sex.

He gave her his Bruin ring, for fuck's sake.

Why isn't he here to enjoy it?

Her shoulders curl inward, hands coming up to tug the jacket tight, and I get this little niggling feeling that his departure wasn't altogether welcome. "He left to—" Her gaze jolts up to mine. "Wait. The heir in the tower? Which one?"

I blink at her, thinking. "Well, I guess that could mean you too, but would your dad really call you—"

"Or Remy." She steps closer, eyes wide in alarm. "Sy, he thinks the Baron King might be his father, and Nick thinks he's right. That's where he went. He's checking his sources or whatever."

My head snaps back. "What?"

"Apparently," she says, looking away, "there was some compelling evidence."

I take a while to turn that over in my mind, just as Lavinia is doing with Nick's ring. It doesn't make sense—only, it actually makes perfect sense. The more I think about it, the more the pieces fit into place. I always did think it was odd that someone with as much influence as Timothy Maddox hadn't made any territorial allegiances.

"Shit." I rake my fingers through my hair, thoughts running a mile per minute. That means it could be Nick, Lavinia, or Remy.

It could be any of them.

Everyone I love is in danger.

I turn to her with wild eyes. "I don't know when it's going to happen."

Her eyes are just as frantic. "Sy, we need to find them."

I reach for my phone, pulling up my contacts. "I'll call my Pops; try to get some ideas on where Nick might be." To her, I ask, "Remy?"

But she shakes her head, eyes going tight. "We got into it last night. He wasn't acting like himself." Deflating, she peers up at me, face drawn. "Sy, I think… he might not know what's real."

My jaw tenses at the dread in her eyes. "I shouldn't have left him. Fuck!" I restrain the urge to throw my phone off the tower just for the catharsis of it. "He could be fucking anywhere. When he's having an episode… shopping, sex, drugs, adrenaline…" Shaking my head, I look out over Forsyth, waving a hand over the landscape. "Needle in a fucking haystack."

But my words make her eyes ping to mine and they light up. "I think I know a couple places where he might go." She instantly heads for the hatch.

"Wait!" I grab her wrist, whirling her back to me. "You can't just go alone! You might be the target." It's unlikely. Her father thinks of her as a lot of things, but his 'heir'…

Unlikely isn't impossible, though.

"It has to be me," she insists, backing away. "I know you don't understand, but whatever he's doing right now, he's either doing it to hurt me or himself."

She's right. I don't understand.

"I can get through to him," she says, eyes hard as steel.

I agonize over it for a few seconds, but maybe she's right. That day, up here in the belfry, she talked him off the ledge. That doesn't mean I don't feel a clench of worry in my gut. "Take your gun." Reaching out, I catch a lock of her hair that's flying in the wind, tucking it gently behind her ear. "Bring him back to me."

She holds my gaze, nodding. "I will."

But before she can open the hatch, I stop her again, and I can't really explain why. It's like I can't possibly leave this belfry until I know what I am and where we stand. "Are you still my girl?"

There's a visible stutter in her movements as she turns those gray eyes onto me. I know it's a selfish question. I don't even have the right to ask, let alone know. But she still releases a breath, asking, "Are you going to come back?"

"Yes," I answer, firm and sure.

She shrugs, turning away. "If you're a Duke, then I'll be your Duchess."

It's not the answer I want, but I hear the message, loud and clear.

If I want her, I'll have to win her.

Luckily, winning is what I do.

35

Lavinia

THERE'S REALLY ONLY one place he'd go.

It's probably why he took me there in the first place, so I'd know how to find him one day. I get turned around twice, the rural roads all looking the same, but when I get to the trailhead, his motorcycle isn't there. *Fuck.*

If he's not here, where is he?

Taking a deep breath, I push past the panic and pull for logic, starting with the last place I saw him: the gym.

Unfortunately, he's not there. Just a few guys punishing themselves with morning workouts. I force myself to check the locker room, bile rising to the back of my throat when I round the corner to the shower stall. There's a niggling fear that he may still be there, pale and unconscious, either the drugs finally getting the best of him or his own psyche.

I brace myself on the tile wall when I see that it's empty, nothing but the shards of glass where Remy shattered the beer bottle remain.

Maybe I shouldn't do this alone.

But I know if I call Sy, he'll come running, and protecting Nick is just as important. I exit the locker room and suck in a gulp of air when I'm back in the hall. Giving the cutsults' lounge a passing glance, I don't go in because if I see Haley, I may throttle her. Not just because she sucked him off, but because she had to have known he was falling apart. She did nothing but push him further over the edge.

My phone vibrates.

Duke Sy: Any luck?

Duchess: Not at the cliffs or gym. You?

Duke Sy: Yeah. Caught up with him. He's good. Wants to make a few more stops. U okay? Need us?

Duchess: Let me check 1 more place. Then we can regroup.

Duke Sy: Be careful.

Unfortunately, I strike out again. I thought maybe he went to Jade's, but when I go in, she's alone.

"Shit," she says, looking up from the register. "He seemed like he was really doing better."

Frazzled, I explain, "Yeah, well, he's spiraling. Stuff with his dad triggered him and he's just... I don't know." I look up at her, letting the worry hit me for the first time. "I'm kind of scared."

She walks around the counter and wraps me in her long arms. "I know you are. But he's out there somewhere. You have to keep looking."

I sniff and pull back. "Thank you. I will."

Her kind eyes bore into mine. "I'll see if he's reached out to anyone I know."

But I'm out of places to search.

Duchess: No Remy.

Duke Sy: Meet us at the storage building. Nick says you know the one.

Duchess: I'm on my way

I program the address into the GPS, but halfway there something nags at me. The sun is going down. I spent the whole day searching for him. He has to be somewhere. I look up and see the white circle of the moon already in the sky even though it's not dark.

Then it hits me.

I jerk the wheel, driving over two curbs and narrowly missing a mailbox. Remy wouldn't go to the cliffs during the day. He'd go at night—to see the stars.

His motorcycle is parked in the same spot as last time.

I hop out of the SUV and start running.

I hope I'm not too late.

I hope *Sy* isn't too late.

I hope my father burns in an inferno of fire.

I say a prayer of thanks to Sy when I reach the top, my lungs stable and my legs strong. If he hadn't pushed me so hard, so far, I never would have known my limits. For the first time in my life, I feel my own strength. Not just in my new muscles or expanded lungs. I'm not a little girl trapped in a box anymore. I'm the Duchess, and I only have one priority: my Dukes.

I jog out on the granite surface, heart thundering as my eyes scan the rock, but it's not hard to find Remy. He's pacing by the edge, hair wild, as if he's been clawing his fingers through it the way he does. He's shirtless, wearing nothing but a pair of jeans. Even his feet are bare, and from twenty feet away, I can hear him mumbling to himself, but the words are indistinct.

I freeze, glad to see him alive, but terrified to watch him in such a state.

I don't call out for him—not at first. I walk closer and keep my gaze fixed on him, at the back of his head and the way the wind makes his hair flutter, and when I get close enough, the side of his face, the shell of his ear and the slight curve his cheek makes.

"Remy." Softly, so as not to startle him.

Ironic, since it's Remy who ends up startling *me*.

He whips around to peer at me, wide-eyed. "No." His eyes, ringed with red, narrow into slits. "No. That's not real. Vinny isn't coming, asshole. You fucked that up. You fucked it up!"

Flinching, I try hard to recognize that he's not screaming at me. Inhaling, I call out, "Remy, it's me."

Shaking his head, he glares and points at me with the marker clenched in his fist. "Vinny wouldn't come out here. Not after what I did."

My feet shift nervously. "You mean Haley?" There's a morsel of satisfaction in knowing that he understands just how much it hurt me.

It's short-lived.

He buries his head into his palms, a gnarled, feral scream ripping from his chest. "The colors are a lie!"

Watching him drop to a hunched crouch, I make a move, slowly crossing the granite. The closer I get, the more I see. A scratch near his hairline, thick and jagged, made with a fingernail. Bruises from the fight—one on his jaw, another on his ribs. Dirt smudged on his cheek. His eyes are still dark and wild, but there's not quite so much of that rapid, drugged-energy from before. He should be cold, though. It's fucking freezing, and yet he looks as though he barely notices it.

"Remy," I repeat, shuddering against the cold. "It's me. For real. Your Vinny. Your canvas." I unzip my hoodie and tug away the collar of my shirt to show him the death head moth. "It took us six sessions. Remember? It should have only been five, but you ran out of ink and we had to stop."

"That's my brain talking," he mutters, mouth twisting bitterly. "Not Vinny. She hates me."

"I don't hate you," I say, taking a step closer. "Yeah, seeing you with Haley hurt like a bitch, but not as much as you pushing me away." I advance, and it's strange—the instinct. This is a man I've only known for a few months, but somehow I know that coddling him will only make him more suspicious. So I don't. "And not nearly as much as you basically calling me a whore and making me feel like Royal trash."

He blinks, eyes reflecting the glow of the moon as they wander to the sky, pensive, searching. "He just fucks with my head." I'm startled to see a fat tear running down his cheek. Swiftly, he brushes it away with the back of his fist. "Gets in there and scrambles it all around. Now everyone thinks I'm fucking crazy, and you know what?" He meets my gaze, his green eyes full of torment. "I think they might be right. I think this?" He points at his temple. "It's broken, Vinny, and there's no putting it back together. The pieces are gone."

"Hey," I say, now only a few feet away. I can see over the edge of the cliff, down to the water below. The distance is terrifying, and I can't help but think of Remy and Leticia falling—what it would feel like to hit that water, hard and cold. "You're right about your father. We believe you."

I'm not a hundred percent, but what I do believe is that Remy believes it—and that's all that matters.

"He's the one who broke it," Remy says, shooting suddenly to his feet. "He made me like this! And now I can't know anything." Suddenly, he's the one coming at *me*, jabbing a forefinger to his temple. "I can think, but I can't fucking *know*."

If I'd seen Remy coming at me like this a couple of months ago, I would have run for the hills. Now, I just reach out, catching his wrist in my hand. "Remy, stop," I plead, grabbing his face. "If you can't trust yourself, then you can trust me."

His eyes flick back forth between mine, face contorted with some unspeakably deep thought. "Can I?"

I answer fiercely. "Always. I don't want to hurt you. You broke my fucking heart last night, and I still—" My own eyes well with tears and I will him to hear me. "I've talked you down from every ledge I've seen you on, and I'll keep doing it. Because you're right. You're not crazy. You're just confused and tired."

He watches me closely, intensely, head tilting. "You weren't the one who let him in, were you?" His face sags with anguish. "It was me. He gave me the orange, and I smudged it all over." Another tear falls, but this time, I'm the one to wipe it away.

"It's—" *Okay*, I want to say, but it wouldn't be honest. "It's going to be alright."

"No, it's not." He takes my hand, voice thick with emotion. "I wanted to give you the black, Vinny. You know what it means, don't you?"

My heart twists at the misery in his eyes. "It means sorry."

"No." His face pinches. "I mean, yes, but—black. It's the best of all the colors. The definition, the range, the depth. You can't make other colors without it. It's fucking essential, you know? And the best part is that it covers anything." His face crumbles and he lifts my hand, flattening my palm to his chest. "I didn't have enough black to cover this."

His skin is chilled beneath my hand, and I frantically try to rub some warmth into it. "Remy, you're freezing."

Ignoring this, his gaze shifts just behind us, eyes zeroing in on the little meadow where we first had sex. "We were there, and I think..." He places both hands over mine on his chest, pressing hard, as if he could fuse our skin. "We gave each other something, and I ruined it."

"Remy."

He points up, head tilting back. The muted glow of moonlight settles in the hollows of his face, making him look like a ghost. "I waited here because I've never seen more black." He stares up at it in awe, and I follow his gaze, lulled by the solemness in his voice. "Sometimes it follows me around. The freckled darkness, always on my heels. It's endless out here, like the universe knows it has something to apologize for. It's for you," he says, eyes locking with mine. Reaching out, he tucks a hand behind my neck, pulling my forehead to his. "I think maybe it's always been for you."

"It's beautiful." A hot tear tracks down my face, and he follows it with the pad of his fingertip.

Slowly, the light dims from his eyes. "It's not enough."

As much as I want to stay up on this cliff and ground him, I know we can't. There are bigger threats out there than Remy is to himself.

"Listen," I say, trying to get him back to the moment, "we need to get out of here. We got a tip. My father put a hit out on one of us —the heir in the tower. Sy assumed it was Nick, but if you're right about your dad, then it could be you."

He looks down at me, forehead creased. "Lionel wants payback for Perez."

"Among other things," I imagine, lacing our fingers together tightly, "which is why it's probably Nick, but Sy wants us all together until we can come up with a plan, okay?"

His gaze darts over my shoulder, forehead creasing. "Sy's back?"

I squeeze his hand. "He's waiting for us."

The crease smoothes and his fingers tighten around mine. I sense a shift, a clarity in his green eyes. They drop to my neck, his thumb pressing into the tender skin, and I know instantly what he's seeing. The hickey. "Sy?" he asks.

"Nick."

"You and Nick?" He scrutinizes me closely. "So everything is white?"

It takes me a moment to remember the color from Sy's journal.

"...white is healthy, renewal, clarity."

I lift my hand to brush his hair from his eyes. The platinum hair —the *white* hair—which I now realize hasn't been bleached to death for the sake of a fashion statement. He's covering his head in white, as if it could fix him, as if it could make him—

Healthy.

Renewed.

Clear.

Swallowing back tears at the realization, I cup his cheek, assuring, "Just waiting on you."

His muscles loosen, and I tug him away from the edge, our fingers knitting together. The tension in my chest eases with every step we get away. He needs sleep, food, warmth, medication, and I'm already patting my pocket for my phone when I hear it.

I'm not sure if it's the startled bird that draws my attention to the woods, or the snap of a branch, but my eyes are already trained on the cleared path when a figure appears. He doesn't walk, he's just... there. Seeping out of the shadows. It startles me and I lurch in surprise, nearly stumbling.

"I knew you'd be here." He's wearing a suit, black and finely tailored, but I barely see past the gleaming point of his mask's horns.

The Baron King.

Remy's hand tightens around mine, jerking me into the cradle of his body. "Vinny, get back."

The King raises his hands, thumbs hooking into the bottom of the mask. Nick believed it. Maybe on some level, Sy did, too. But somehow I'm still shocked when the King raises his mask, revealing hazel eyes and a finely-groomed beard.

"It *is* you," I breathe, stunned.

Remy's father, Timothy Maddox, King of the Barons, stands between us and freedom.

"Vinny." Remy leans down, lips close to my ear. "Is this real?"

"Yes." I pull his hand to my hip, pressing his fingers against the spot where the star lies underneath my clothes. I don't give Maddox the chance to wrap his mindfuckery around Remy's fragile brain. "If this was going to be a dramatic reveal, then it's too late. We already know your little secret."

"It took him long enough." Maddox tucks the mask under his arm, taking a step forward. As much as I want to stand my ground, I don't think Remy needs to be close to him. I push him back. "I've been passing along little clues for years, but my son has been so focused on becoming a Duke that he can't own his legacy, even when it's right in front of him." The cut of his smirk is cold and casual. "Isn't that right, Remington *William* Maddox."

I'm not sure I follow, but making sense of this asshole is the least of my worries. "You need to let us pass. My father has a hit out on one of the heirs and since that includes your son, he needs to get somewhere safe."

If this news concerns him, he doesn't show it, but I guess that shouldn't be a surprise from a psychopath like the Baron King. I know firsthand how ready he is to watch blood spill. I guess that applies to his son, too.

"Remington," he says, ignoring me, his voice sending a shudder down my spine. "It's over."

"What's over?" I ask, looking frantically between them.

"This little foray into independence," he answers me, but stares at his son. Without the mask, I see the two faces become one. The eyes that watched with glee as Nick spared me the game. The sharp jaw, mouth set in a mocking slant just like it had over our dinner at the club. Slowly the features click together, like pieces of a puzzle. He goes on, "You're spiraling: manic, missing appointments with Dr. Weatherby, and I can't imagine what kind of garbage would show up on a drug test." His eyes sweep over Remy's bare upper body as if he can see underneath the tattoos to the scars and mutilations. "You've continued to self-harm, and on top of all of that, you're a liability. That contract, which I know all about, is the last straw."

"Don't listen to him, Vinny," Remy says, muscles coiling as he shifts his focus to his dad. "You're a fucking liar."

Maddox shakes his head, gazing at his son with such tenderness that I finally understand just how convincing he can be. "I've never once lied to you, your whole life. If you really think back, I think you'll find—"

Remy explodes. "You've been twisting shit around!" The vein in his temple pops as he surges forward, but I tug him back. He snarls, "Poisoning me about Vinny. Giving Nick that gun. All the little shit to fuck me up!"

"Clues," he says, eyebrows rising. Just as quickly, his face falls. "I had such hope for you. A brother in blood. A son of shadows. My black heir. Instead..." He gestures lamely, sighing, "A Duke." I get the feeling he's speaking to an audience, but it's just the three of us.

Or so I think, until I hear the low chuckles.

I startle as the outlines of three Barons become more defined. They're robed, wearing masks of their own, but I know them. I've seen their faces.

Will, Liam, and Billy.

All the air gets sucked from my lungs. "You're all named William."

Just like Remy's middle name.

"As I said," Maddox lifts his gloved hands. "I had such high hopes. But you keep stretching toward the light, son. Why is that?"

Anxiety tickles the back of my neck, but I speak anyway, "Because he's not a crypt-dwelling, bone-hoarding, secret-keeping psychopath, that's why."

The look he gives me is sympathetic, like I'm a fucking idiot. "It's attention, dear. He thrives on it—always has. Which is very frustrating when one is trying to maintain secrecy. You see now why he has to go. Sitting in that tower, putting himself on display when he should be in the darkness, with us. Do you understand," he asks Remy, "that you don't belong there?"

"It was you, wasn't it?" Remy looks at his father with such a demented amount of disgust that I tighten my grip on his arm, fearing that he'll charge him. "You killed Tate. You were here that night when I—"

His father gives a long, exasperated sigh. "Once again, you fail to decipher the clues in front of you. That's been your only saving grace. If you actually knew who killed her, this whole system would crumble." He fixes his son with a hard stare. "But it wasn't me." Tipping his head toward the Baron just behind him, he mutters, "Wish I had. It's made such an impression. You see what I mean."

The masked Baron nods once, voice solemn. "He doesn't understand death."

"Nor our relationship with it," Maddox adds curtly. "Don't insult us. We don't kill for vengeance or petty disagreements, Remington. We kill for the art of it—the respect for it. And sometimes, the Royals of Forsyth," he waves a hand elaborately, "give us the opportunity to worship it."

I blame the lack of sleep and the sheer trauma of the last week that it took me so long to see it.

When I do, my stomach drops. "My father hired the Barons to do the hit. He hired *you*."

He gives me a saccharine, condescending grin. "Smart girl. A father would be proud." He dips his chin. "Not yours, of course."

"You can't kill your son."

Maddox looks insulted. "Of course I can't. He might have fallen a little far from the tree, but he's still my apple. Remy belongs with me. With *us*. This little game with West End has come to an end." He tilts his head, staring me down. "You're right that your father contracted us. But it wasn't for him. It's your Bruin." Shaking his head, he adds, "Disappointing, though. When I saw what he'd done to the Perez boy..." His eyes sparkle excitedly. "Oh, it was truly a treat to collect him. We don't often get bodies like that, you know. He was murdered so viciously—with such love for you." Fisting his hands behind his back, he asks, "Did you keep his head?"

When I do nothing but gape at him, disgusted, he flicks a hand.

"In any case, I know how expansive Lionel's thirst for revenge can be. First, it's the Bruin boy, and then Perilini, for rescuing you from Lionel's home, and lastly..." His eyes jump to Remy's, darkening. "It will be you. But I won't let him order your death, son. If that means locking you away into my shadows, then so be it."

"No," Remy says, beginning to shiver. "I—I won't go back."

"You will. You've given me no choice. There's a spot for you at the hospital." When Remy sucks in a long, wet breath, his father softly assures, "Not Saint Mary's. A different one, with a higher quality of care, far away from Forsyth."

"No, no, no, no, no..." Remy drops my hand, our connection broken, and claws his fingers back into his hair. "I'm not crazy. You *are* the Baron King! I was right! I'm not fucking crazy!"

"It's a private set up," his father continues, unconcerned at the outburst. "Beautiful view of the Alps. You'll be safe and out of harm's way. I don't know why you make such a fuss. You know I'll take care of you." His voice drops into a softness that I know is only meant to be between them. "You'll be in the room next to your mother's."

My heart lunges into my throat, and I feel the cold creep down my spine. The thought of this man locking Remy away, hiding him in the darkness...

It might be a hospital, but all I can see in my mind is Remy, being stuffed into a cage.

A box.

A wooden chest.

I do everything Sy taught me. I breathe, pushing past the paralysis inching across my muscles, and declare, "You'll have to kill me first."

Politely, his father says, "Oh, I will." Swinging his gaze to Remy, he explains, "You'll come with me, or the next body in my crypt will be hers."

I reach out to touch Remy's stiff back, which is how I know his lungs rattle with his long, agonized groan. Scoffing, I say, "So much for not killing people over your own petty disputes."

"There's nothing petty about this," he snaps. "Remember what the old Kings told you the night you came to see me? To kill someone with your own hands..."

I shudder. "...is an act of love."

My own father has never loved me. There's never been any tenderness or care. For the first time, I'm grateful, because if this is what fatherly love looks like?

Give me contempt.

Maddox sighs. "I love you, Remington. Your blood is my blood. I tried to give you the light, to make you happy and keep you safe, but it wants to consume you. Can't you see that? And you." His eyes skim over me. "That night you came to me, it was like seeing a ghost. You look very much alike, you know, and your sister's body was so pristine when we found her. I wonder if yours will be the same. Skin like a pearl." He grins, the moonlight cutting his eyes into blots of darkness. "I sliced through her like butter."

I fight the rise of bile in my throat. "You're sick."

He shrugs, not arguing. "It's for the best. In truth, I'd always dreamed of my son's black wedding. She'd be the wickedest Baroness this town has ever seen. A sinister sister. A *queen*. He deserves no less. But this? You? The Count's scrawny little castaway?" He grimaces. "Unacceptable."

I reach around to the small of my back, and in a blink, I have the barrel of my pistol pointed at his forehead. "How about his fury?"

There's a moment of stillness, even the trees seeming to pause in their sway.

And then Maddox *laughs*.

He twists to grin at the Barons over his shoulder. "There's that West End finesse we all know and tolerate." His smile falls like a lead balloon, eyes turning ice cold. "Or used to. You see, I'm not your father, little girl. I don't head a house of sporadically disloyal cockroaches." He raises his mask, sliding it over his head, and the Barons behind him—all three—lift their hands.

The shadows *bleed*.

That's what it looks like when the Beta Nus begin stepping out of the trees, all at once. Robed figures, masked just like Barons, but with simpler designs, crawl out of the shadows. I freeze as they descend, more than I can count in the panic of the moment. Thirty? Forty? Fifty?

More men than I have bullets for.

"My darklings don't fear me. They follow me," he says. As they approach, their phone flashlights flicker to life and the whole cliffside is cast in an eerie yellow glow. William, Bill, and Liam position themselves at the forefront and Maddox adds, "Your death will be their act of love for me."

"You're not taking him!" I bark, even though my voice cracks. I step back, wrenching Remy with me.

He stumbles but backs away with me, saying, "This isn't real, this isn't real."

Keeping the gun aimed at Maddox, I can't see a way out. Even if I shoot the King and his three Barons, the other men will come for us. We could run, but we wouldn't get far.

There are just so fucking *many*.

"This isn't real," Remy keeps saying, eyes darting from masked figure to masked figure. He's back in his spiral, caught between panic and denial. He has to be so goddamn exhausted, and when I look in his eyes, that's what I see.

He's burnt out.

I jerk him closer to me, begging in a whisper, "Come on, baby, I need you with me so we can get out of here."

The Barons start to close in, and I pull him the only direction I can go: toward the edge of the cliff. It's fully dark now, the void below the rocky face swallowed in black. I only give it a quick glance before looking back toward Maddox and his ghastly bronze face.

When Remy turns to me, his eyes are wide and full of a grief that's big enough to fill the sky he's gifted me. "I'd rather die than let him take me." Reaching for my face, he cups my cheek in a cold palm, green eyes pinning me under their stare. "I'd rather die than let him take you."

I reach up slowly, covering his hand with mine. "I know." Taking a breath, I slide my eyes toward the black, and if I squint, I can see it: the reflection of stars freckling the surface of the water below. I think of the sky, of apologies and the beauty of birds, of flying away, but always soaring back when the wind commands it.

I know what we have to do.

Another tear races down my cheek. "Remy..."

He nudges my face, turning my gaze to his. "Hey." His lips curl into a sad smile. "We're all just stars inside of a grave we haven't laid down in yet." He brushes the tear from my cheek. "Remember, Vinny?"

The night he told me that, we were drenched in the sky, so

painfully alive that we could have powered the heavens itself. He tried so hard to tell me that jumping from this rock, knowing he was about to die, was beautiful. I couldn't see it then, but I see it now—so clearly that it steals the breath from my lungs.

The beauty isn't in the acceptance of death.

It's in the open defiance of it.

What could be more beautiful than the fight to survive?

"Fifty-fifty shot," I say, smiling tearfully as I parrot the words Nick said to me in that dank, dark crypt. "Just need a little luck."

We meet over the distance, our lips locking together in a kiss so soft that it hurts. I cling to it. To him. To the knowledge that somewhere out there, our family—our real family, however mangled and messed-up it may be—is waiting to gather us close.

His green eyes hold mine and his head moves, just a fraction, sort of wistful. "I love you, Vinny."

The truth is that, here in Forsyth, it's cold. Always has been. It's disappointment and death and misery and pain and unfair, and if love can exist for someone as beaten down as Remington Maddox, then maybe we're already lucky.

This flame, hot and sure in my chest, is more than people like our fathers will ever get.

It's how I know we're ready to jump. It's why I curl into his embrace, his arms winding around my shoulders and tucking me close. It's why I turn my head to peer into the chasm of nothing with him.

We step off the edge together, tangled like two vibrant vines.

Behind us, the sound of Maddox's scream echoes in our wake, but Remy and I don't make a sound.

We fall into the stars.

Just like he always knew we would.

AFTERWORD

The final installment of the Dukes story, Dukes of Peril, will release fall of 2022. Don't forget to pre-order!

~

Many of you ask, what do I read while I wait for the next book! Well, we always suggest you go back to the Preston Prep series (m/f, HS Dark Romance) first.

After that, you can always try one of Angel's dark romance books. The following books are all reverse harem. Mostly high school age, but steamy romance. None are as dark as the Royals but all contain elements of trauma and angst because that's how we roll. Each series, other than The Order, is complete.

The Allendale Four
Thistle Cove
Sparrowood Academy
The Order: The Cult of Serendee

ACKNOWLEDGMENTS

Royal Readers,

Literal cliffhanger, right? Everyone take a deep breath and know that like our Royals, we only give you what we know you can handle. You've totally got this! And we promise not to let it go too long without a resolution. Dukes of Peril is coming! Promise.

But really, thanks for following us through this insane book series. We had no idea how deep this would go when we started Lords of Pain 18 months ago. This universe, it just exploded, and we can't wait to continue to share it with you.

Special thanks to Lisa, Nikki and Crystal for being the best beta readers, ever. Anna & Nikki for being amazing PAs. The readers in Angel's Antics that keep us going! The Bookstagramers, Booktokers, Podcasters, bloggers and reviewers that have spread the love for the Royals all over romancelandia, we genuinely would not have the motivation to get these massive books out without your support.

If you're not in our group: Angel's Antics or following me on TikTok: Angellawsonauthor or IG: @lawsonwrites then make sure you do. We love to send out extras, share our favorites, and keep up with our readers between books!

Yer the best,
Angel

I'm writing this looking like Uma Thurmond in that scene from Pulp Fiction after John Travolta saves her from an overdose and they're in the car, riding home. Angel is absolutely John in this caffeine-fueled metaphor. Thanks for stabbing me with all those syringes. Can you believe we've been writing these jerks for two years now?

A huge thanks to Crystal, Lisa, and Nikki for their impeccable beta skills, and also for talking me down from a few (ahem) cliffs. I would have jumped while embracing you traumatically. Kinda mad that I now know the difference between lay and lie, though.

Shoutout to mine and Angel's cats for Archie inspo.

Most of all, thanks to everyone who's sticking around for this wild and twisty ride! We promise we only make you suffer so that when we stop emotionally hurting you, it'll be that much sweeter.

WHY IS THIS BOOK SO LONG?

Babes, if you only knew how much we cut...

Sam

P.S- I fully embrace the role of John Travolta in Pulp Fiction. I worry, we may be more like the scene with Marvin. "You shot Marvin!" with blood spray all over the car and someone needs to call The Wolf on everyone to get shit under control.—Angel

Printed in Poland
by Amazon Fulfillment
Poland Sp. z o.o., Wrocław

37021214R00321